CADE

THE SECOND NOVEL IN
THE MORTHENSTAR TRILOGY

B. K. CAIN

Library of Congress Control Number: 2025913402

Hardcover: 979-8-9993353-3-3
Paperback: 979-8-9993353-2-6
Ebook: 979-8-9993353-4-0

Second paperback edition September 2025

Portland, Oregon

Cover and book design by Rosie Struve and Bailey Cain
Illustrations by Katrina Zarate
Map created with Inkarnate

www.morthenstartrilogy.com

FOR PIPER
AGAIN

&

FOR ELLI, WHO MADE IT ALL WORTH IT

Table of Contents

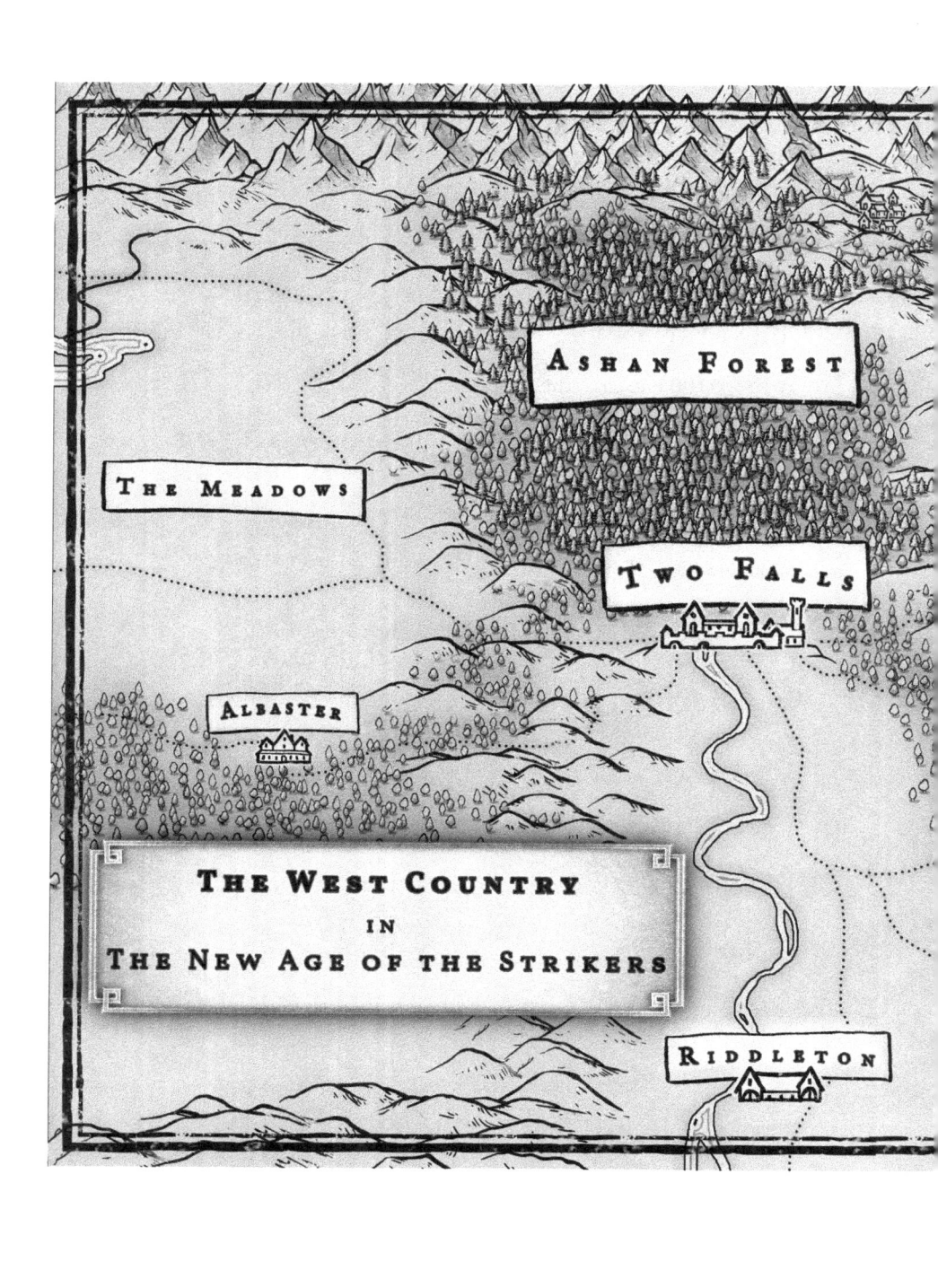

ASHAN FOREST

THE MEADOWS

TWO FALLS

ALBASTER

THE WEST COUNTRY
IN
THE NEW AGE OF THE STRIKERS

RIDDLETON

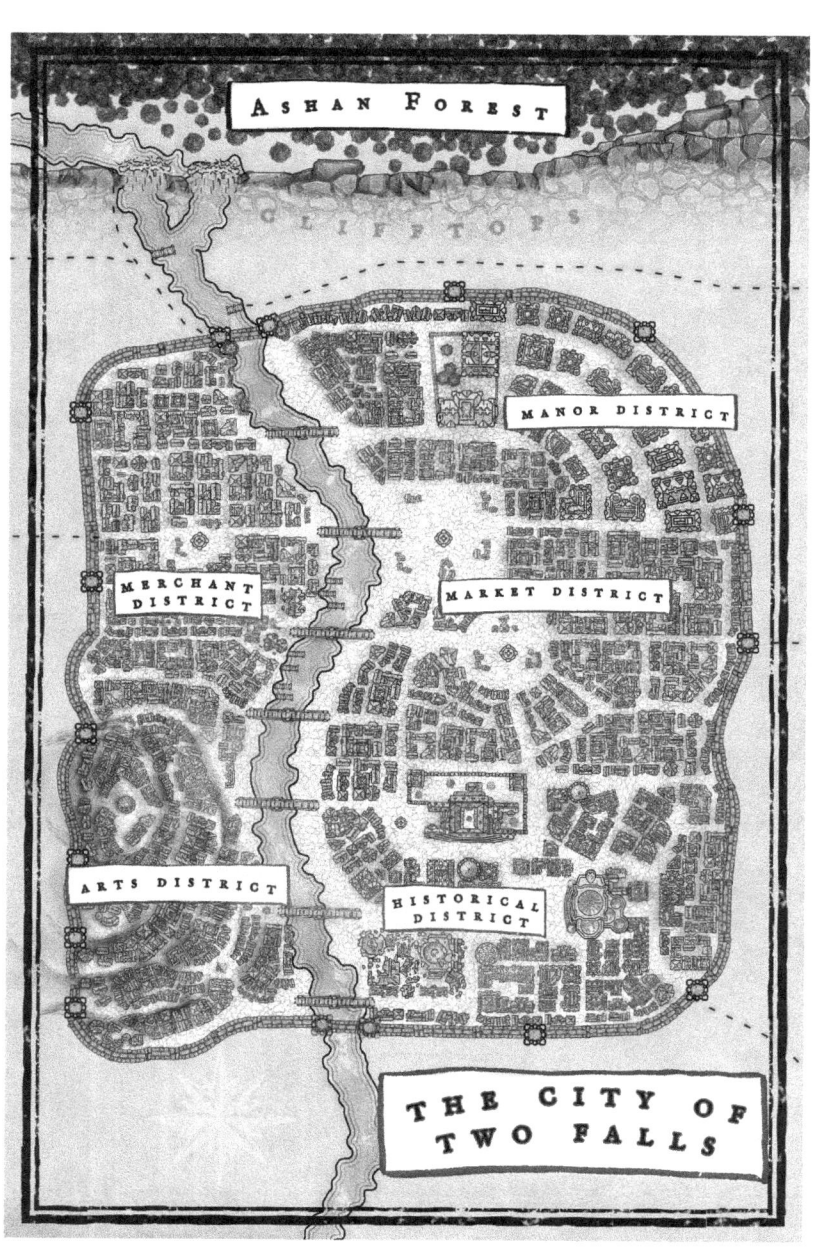

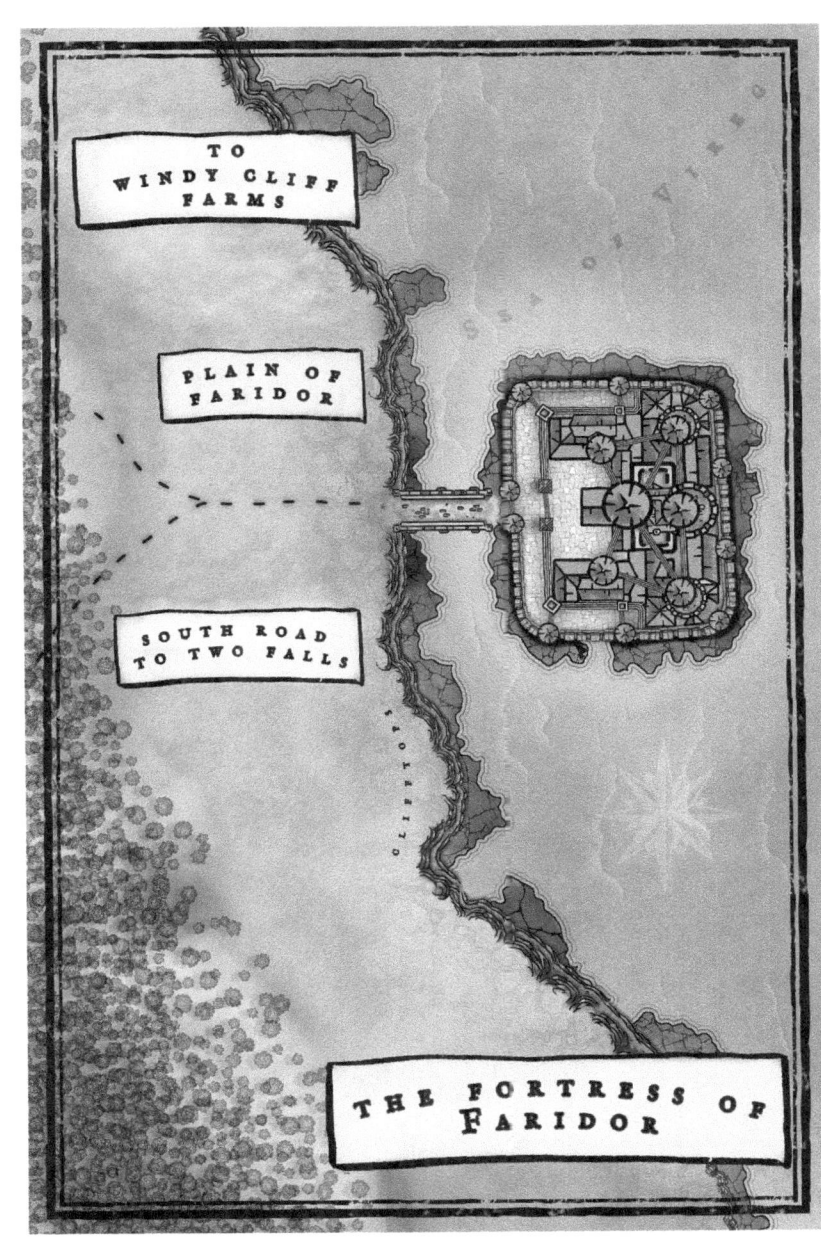

TO
WINDY CLIFF
FARMS

PLAIN OF
FARIDOR

SOUTH ROAD
TO TWO FALLS

THE FORTRESS OF
FARIDOR

PROLOGUE

THREE AND A HALF YEARS AGO

The sun glinted across the surface of the lake beneath the Jelani palace of Joymaril. The rays caught the tops of the small ripples like sparks flying from the crack of flint and tinder, flashing gold and red and yellow. The trees stretched their clawing boughs upwards to the sky. All was silent. Even the birds were quiet. No laughter or talking echoed down from the halls of the palace above. A chill of death hung on the air; the wind halted in its usual course.

A lone buckskin horse stood at the edge of the lake, ears pricked, looking out over the lapping water, watching and waiting. An ornate riderless saddle, well worn in the seat and with twisting engravings on the sides, was laid across the horse's back and girthed around its belly. A spare sword, unused, still in its scabbard, was tied to the rear section of the saddle. The horse raised his head and whickered a few times. There was no response. The horse pawed at the bank, jostling the silver and leather breastband it bore. The horse darted to one side and then the other, tearing down the thin stretch of beach, digging in its striped black forelegs, and powering off with its hindquarters until it froze again, head raised alertly for any sign of life. None came.

All at once, the stillness exploded into a flurry of violent motion. The horse at the edge of the water started and spun, darting back a few feet before swinging back around, head and ears pricked, watching cautiously, breath *whuffing* out of its flared nostrils. From the middle of the lake came a torrent of thrashing and gasping as Lord Cade V burst into the glare of the sun, mouth gaping open as his lungs screamed for air. For a moment, Cade lost his handhold on the partially submerged bridge that ran through the middle of the lake, and he fell back beneath the water, hands desperately clutching towards the sky above him as if he were being pulled under. But it only lasted a few seconds, and within moments Cade had broken the surface again, digging his fingers into the hard-packed stone and mud that made up the bridge. His white-blond hair was plastered wet and gray to his head, and he doubled over so that his open mouth was nearly resting on the surface of the lake as he squinted his eyes and shook his head. Droplets pooled at the tip of his nose and on his chin, dripping in a steady stream back into the water. After a few moments, he gritted his teeth with fresh resolve and bent his elbow, trying to scoot himself up onto the surface of the bridge. His legs kicked, searching for support. One of his arms was still below the water, as if something in his other hand was trying to drag him below.

With a mighty burst of strength, Cade managed to propel himself up onto the top of the bridge, where the shallow water lapped around his waist. He twisted around so that he was sitting on the edge of the bridge and reached down back beneath the water with his now free hand. He pulled slightly, and, with a great effort, Ilaina, the wife of his brother Laith, gently broke the surface in front of him. Her head was tilted, facing up to the sun, eyes peacefully closed. He pulled her up higher so that he could unfasten her belt, heavy and ornate with a sword attached, weighing her down so that it was nearly impossible for him to pull her up. His fingers groped at her waist, feeling for the clasp until finally it caught and went loose. He pulled the belt off and tied it around himself. The leather on the belt was creased and wrinkled next to the hole where Ilaina had worn it. Cade looked away.

He had watched from his bedroom window as his older brother and the others made their dash for freedom after springing Athela, the

Ashan, and the little boy from the dungeons. Although he would have never admitted it aloud, he inwardly wished that he could have gone with them. But they had not even thought to ask. He had seen Ilaina with them and then watched with growing incredulity as she stopped and easily fought off a few lower-ranking house guards who had been sent to stop them.

And then, as he saw two riders come out after them at the head of a phalanx of elite Joymarillian cavalry, his blood had run cold. He had seen their faces. His cousin Cira was one of them.

The other was a man named Lord Seth, who had been condemned to the Joymarillian prison for the rest of his life. *Cira had set him free.*

Wildly grabbing a sword, thinking that he would do something, *anything* to help Ilaina, he ran through all of the secret passages he knew to get to her. But when he came out it was just in time to see Lord Seth throw her body under the water as Cira watched, blue hood pulled over her head. For a few seconds, he thought that Ilaina would reappear at the surface, sword out, leaping at Cira, cutting her down. But she hadn't come back, and Cira had walked away, free, a spring in her step and a smile on her face as she talked to the tall spectre of a man standing beside her. Lord Seth said nothing, but Cade got a glimpse of his eyes, black as pits, with no life, no expression inside them. More terrified than he'd ever been in his life, he had hunkered down lower as they went straight past Cade's hiding place. The rest of the cavalry set off across the lake and into the woods in pursuit of Athela and Laith. Minutes passed, and the woods grew silent, and the thought began to occur to Cade that somehow, almost unimaginably, Ilaina was really dead. The thought was too much for him. He knew only that he could not leave her there. So he went into the water, intent on bringing her back.

Dripping, halfway atop the submerged bridge, Cade glanced around, realizing in a frantic moment that he was in plain view of anyone who cared to look out across the water from one of the palace balconies. He quietly slid back into the water, looping his arm carefully around Ilaina's waist, pulling her close to him so that she wouldn't float away, then dug his fingers into the bridge and began to pull himself back to the shore, keeping as low to the water as he could. He realized that he'd subconsciously been keeping Ilaina's face tilted up so that she could breathe. It hadn't occurred to him that she didn't need to anymore.

Finally, Cade's tired legs hit the pliant bottom of the shallows, and he stumbled onto the shore, pulling Ilaina up beside him, her legs floating out horizontally behind her. Cade twisted around and took her beneath the arms and pulled her up until she was on the bank, up to her waist in water, resting between his knees. Her horse approached cautiously from behind, startling Cade when it brushed the back of his neck with its dark muzzle. Cade whipped around and the horse snorted nervously, but he made entreating sounds to it in a soothing voice and rubbed its nose a few times. The horse stood quietly as Cade exerted his strength to hoist Ilaina up and over its back, her arms hanging down limply on one side. Cade led the horse to the hidden entrance in the bottom of the cave, slid Ilaina down, and from there on it was an ordeal of carrying her up hidden flights of stairs, through secret passageways and every back staircase he'd ever come across, until at last he sat in one of the secluded areas of his room, panting, eyeing the track of water that followed him across the marble floor.

He laid Ilaina out before him on a low wooden table. Cade gently reached forward and undid the tiny silver clasp that held her sodden cloak and pulled it away. The wound in her middle was deceptively small, just a small slash in her tunic, hardly even noticeable. Cade averted his eyes and forced himself to look at her face. The sight made him catch his breath and rock back heavily onto the floor. He clasped his hands together in a fist and held it tight against his mouth, biting his thumb as he studied her quiet features. He was glad that they showed no sign of any lasting pain; it was almost as if she had just fallen asleep. He half-expected her eyes to slowly open at any time, for the familiar smile to edge into place, for her to tease him for looking so worried. "Be careful, Cade, or word of the existence of your emotions might leak out, and *then* where would you be?"

He had loved her like a sister, a *real* sister. His brother had been absent for most of his life, and when he'd returned he was always cool and distant and perfect and untouchable. But Ilaina was different. The two of them had often been shunted to the side at formal occasions while Laith and the elder, more important members of the royal family were in the limelight. As a result, they had grown close. Ilaina, for all her seeming poise and elegance, had a distinct mischievous streak. During fancy receptions, the two of them would throw small pieces of food at as many dignitaries as they could reach, masking their guilt with a pair of perfectly innocent faces when met with a suspicious glare from one of their victims. To avoid bursting into laughter, she would force herself not to blink and would walk around like a semi-frozen owl anytime they were close to getting caught. It was all Cade could do not to dissolve into a fit of giggles at the sight of her.

Cade swallowed slowly. He should get her out of her wet clothing, but he couldn't do it himself; undressing her would be far too strange. So, instead, he walked from the dark back room into the front of his apartments, where one of his servants was waiting for instruction.

"My Lord," the servant said, bowing as Cade entered the room. If he thought Cade's wet clothes and hair were odd, it did not show in his face.

"Fetch Nadia for me, would you?" Cade said, carefully keeping his voice at its usual level of bored detachment. The servant withdrew with a bow, and Cade began to pace back and forth, thinking hard. *Cira's going to make her move now*, he thought to himself. *Now that she's freed Lord Seth. Now that Laith, Athela, Marc, and Rane are gone, there's no one here to oppose her. Except me, but I'm not a threat. If I were, she'd have seen to it that I'd been arrested or driven out with the others.* He stopped, noticing that he was still dripping quite a bit of water on the marble floor of his bedroom, and he retreated quickly into his wardrobe, throwing on a loose shirt and a pair of baggy drawstring pants, ones he usually wore for sparring.

When he reentered the main room of his apartments, he found Ilaina's maid, Nadia, waiting patiently for him, eyebrows raised quizzically, a polite, expectant smile on her face. Cade hurriedly ran his hands a few times through his pale hair, fluffing it out so that it stuck out in a number of gravitationally defiant directions.

"My Lord," Nadia said with a small curtsy.

"That will be all, thank you," Cade said to his manservant, who bowed and backed out of the room, closing the door behind him. Cade turned to Nadia. "Follow me, and you must please prepare yourself for a shock," Cade said, motioning with one of his arms towards the back room. Nadia's pleasant expression wavered, and she moved forward hesitantly, as if she had a sudden sense of foreboding. Cade followed closely on her heels.

Nadia slowly pushed open the door to the back room and caught sight of the body on the table. At her sharp intake of breath, Cade darted a hand around her head, covering her mouth so that her scream of horror was muffled. With a show of strength that belied her small stature, Nadia wrenched herself out of Cade's arms and flew to the table, clasping Ilaina's cold hand, burying her face in her side. Ilaina's body rocked slightly with the sudden disturbance; then she fell still.

"Ilaina," Nadia sobbed. Cade glanced around, swiftly closing the door behind him so that her cries would not be heard and arouse suspicion. Nadia, her tearstained eyes wide with shock, turned around to Cade, who hung back, his own gaze lingering on Ilaina's peaceful face. "Who could do such a thing?" she choked. "Who would dare to hurt her?" She stopped suddenly, her sobs hiccuping deep into her throat, and her eyes grew wide. "When Lord Argolaith finds out about this," she said, voice suddenly hushed, "he'll kill whoever did this with his bare hands."

"Cira did it," Cade said flatly. He didn't want to frighten her further with the information about Lord Seth. "And my brother is riding westward at a great speed at the moment, and I doubt he has any idea what has happened."

"I can't believe it," Nadia turned back around.

He let Nadia sit there for a few more minutes until most of her tears had subsided. "Nadia," he said finally. "We have to bury her, have to give her the proper funeral rites. You have to help me."

Nadia turned and looked at him, then nodded firmly. "I'll help you with whatever you need, my Lord," she said. "It's all I can do. Would you like me to get her Ladyship's other maids in here?"

"No, no," Cade said quickly. "We must keep this as small as possible. I have a feeling certain things are about to start happening in this palace, and if we are found to be aiding enemies of the throne it could have very serious repercussions at that time. Right now, though, all I'm worried about is getting her out of those wet clothes and into something...appropriate."

Nadia nodded, eyes swimming with tears. She was younger than she had looked at first, Cade realized, as she wiped her nose on a small handkerchief pulled from within her broad sash. He had never really noticed her before. Ilaina had a way of eclipsing anyone around her. But Nadia's devotion was truly touching, and Cade was fervently glad he'd made the correct choice of accomplice. Nadia rose to her feet, tucking the handkerchief back into her sash, and walked to the door.

"Nadia," Cade said suddenly, turning around. Nadia paused, looking back at him. "Make it something she liked. Her favorite."

Nadia studied him for a moment, then nodded and vanished without a word.

About an hour later, Cade was sitting back in his favorite chair, thin legs thrust in front of him, contemplatively tapping his lips with his fist. The door to the back room opened, and Nadia walked out. Her eyes were still red, but it seemed that most of her tears had been shed. Cade lowered his arm and raised his eyebrows in the form of a question.

"She's ready," Nadia said in a small voice.

Cade slowly rubbed his palms along the length of his thighs, then stood up and walked into the adjacent chamber and stood in front of Ilaina's body. Nadia had dried her hair and arranged it so that the red-golden curls fell over her shoulder and brushed her elbows. The dress was simple, white, with pale blue flowers embroidered around the sleeves and the neckline. Her face was quiet and as lovely as ever, if a little paler than usual and tinged with blue. Cade's breath caught in his throat, and he rested his hands on his hips for a moment and regained his composure. Nadia noticed this and lowered her eyes to the ground, not wishing to embarrass him.

"That will do," Cade said finally. It was the highest praise she could have received from the taciturn prince.

"My Lord, how and when will we be able to bury her? The family tomb is guarded, is it not?" Nadia asked hesitantly. "Lady Cira would probably do something to prevent it."

"We'll go tonight," Cade murmured, his eyes not leaving the face below him. "The guards won't question another member of the royal family. But she needs to have a proper burial tonight, or else her spirit will never find peace and she will not be able to look down on her loved ones." He swung around. "You understand that I will not, under any circumstances, allow that to happen."

"I do, my Lord," Nadia agreed.

"You may go," Cade turned back around. "Join me back here at sunset."

"Yes, my Lord," Nadia bowed and began to leave, then hesitated. "Should we not send some sort of word to Lord Argolaith so that he knows what happened?" Her voice grew hopeful. "He would surely return and take his revenge upon Lady Cira?"

"He would if he ever got the letter, and I can assure you that that will most likely not be the case if my cousin Cira has anything to say about it." Cade countered. "Go."

Nadia bowed and exited. Cade sat down beside Ilaina's body and stayed there for a long time before moving back into the main room of his apartments and staring down at the lake beneath him. He often retreated to his chambers to watch the sunset, marveling at the way the red light played upon the water, shooting its rays up to dance on the walls of the cliffs and the palace. Cade wished again that he could have gone with Laith and the others. He longed to escape the palace, to explore, to have adventures, to prove to the others that he was worth having around. Cade shook his head. He wasn't one to dwell. He knew full well that the upcoming weeks would be a trial for all involved, most of all him. And if he made it through, well, he had a few plans of his own.

At sunset, Nadia returned. Together, they bore Ilaina's body to the family mausoleum and buried her in one of the vacant spaces in the family crypt. Cade read her the last rites, feeling all the while as though he were simply putting on a show for an audience of ghosts.

The morning after the burial, and after considerable internal debate, Cade wrote a letter addressed to General Calchas, who had been Laith's commanding officer during his training in the Meadows. By reputation, Cade knew him to be honorable and trustworthy, and (most importantly) not in thrall to Cira. Cade had no idea whether the letter would reach him; it was a bit like throwing a pebble in the middle of a lake and hoping it would land in a certain spot. The Meadow patrols ranged far and wide on their missions, and contact with them was sparse at best. But the General was the only person Cade could think of outside the city who could potentially offer them any aid.

"Take this as fast as you can and get it out of the city immediately," Cade told Nadia, turning from his desk, folding the letter, and handing it to her. "Only a courier you'd trust with your life. Unless I'm much mistaken, we're going to be locked down very shortly, and we'll lose our chance."

Nadia, her eyes wide with alarm, had silently taken the letter and obeyed. Cade watched her go with little hope that the letter would yield any helpful results. Still, it felt better than doing nothing.

The letter dispatched, Cade resolved to remain calm and appear as boring as possible. For the next three days, he mostly remained in his room, reading. This activity was not unusual, and his family, as they usually did, ignored him. He went back over the scrolls and teachings of ancient Queens and Kings, the philosophers, those who had seized the throne, those who were imprisoned before ascending to power. Every now and again, one of his servants or one of the kitchen staff he paid for information would pop in to disclose some major development in the household. Cade instructed them to keep a close watch on Cira's activities. After a day or so, a servant came back with the report that a story (likely originating from Cira) was circulating that Ilaina had accompanied Athela and Laith on their flight from Joymaril, even though there were plenty of guards who had witnessed the murder. Cade half-expected one of the guards to come forward with the truth, but none did. It was almost as if a blanket of fear had descended over the city, terrifying the people into a petrified silence. No announcement had been made about Lord Seth's release (Cade suspected that Cira had done it without the knowledge or permission of her mother, the Queen, who had been the one to imprison Seth in the first place.) And so, with all of the indications falling into place, Cade prepared himself for what was about to happen and what no one else seemed to realize was coming. Then, on the morning of the fourth day, it arrived.

Before Cade had properly woken up and gotten dressed, a troop of royal guards threw open the door and marched into his room. "Lord Cade," one of them said. "You are officially under arrest by the order of the Queen and shall be detained for questioning by the tribunal."

"Tribunal?" Cade asked mildly, slipping out of his bed and pulling a shirt on, as if being arrested before breakfast was merely part of his morning routine.

"The Queen, the King, and the Princess Cira," the guard announced solemnly. "They are seeking to stamp out all pockets of disloyalty since the departure of Lord Argolaith and Lady Athela."

"Mm," Cade murmured nonchalantly and walked forward. "Well, get on with it, then."

The lead guard looked taken aback for a split second at Cade's unruffled response, then motioned with his head. Two of the other guards moved forward and grabbed Cade by his arms, flinging him into the middle of the armed escort.

They marched him out of his room and into the main hallway, where Cade was none too surprised to find the rest of the palace pitched into a state of pandemonium. Guards were as thick as flies as they moved through the palace, some of them dragging resisting members of the royal court. Many of these courtiers Cade recognized, some marching along without resistance, faces stony and silent. One of them, Cade recognized with a jolt, was Lord Oren, Marc's boyfriend. He was being escorted with a grim, intentional momentum by the guards on either side of him. Lord Oren was slender, soft-spoken, and gentle, and Cade was shocked to see a trickle of blood at the corner of his mouth—the thought of anyone possessing enough malice to strike someone like Lord Oren was inconceivable. Oren's countenance was set with a grim determination Cade had never before seen; he assumed that the young lord had just returned from the questioning of the tribunal, and there was little doubt as to the side Oren had taken. As he was whisked briskly past Cade, their eyes met for a split second and then he was gone.

In contrast to the uproar in the outer palace, the halls nearest the throne room were eerily deserted, far from the usual hustle and bustle of courtly life. The guards took him to the audience chamber, where a chair had been placed facing the thrones. Chains dangled from the arms and coiled on the floor by the chair's legs. Cade's stride halted as he took in the ominous sight of the restraints, but he continued towards it without resistance. There was a small bench against the back wall where a dozen noblemen and courtiers sat. Cade recognized them all as Cira's cronies and those individuals fanatically loyal to the Queen and the crown. Seated in the thrones were his aunt and cousin, with the King slightly off to the side, as if he weren't entirely part of the proceedings. The Queen's face was severe; Cira's was something different. Cade watched her as he seated himself and allowed the chains to buckle around his ankles and wrists. Cira had a deep look of gloating, of barely contained pleasure. She was enjoying this. She had wanted to cleanse the palace in this way for quite some time, Cade could tell. He took a deep breath. He had the sensation of stepping out onto the edge of a knife's blade; oblivion gaped open on either side.

"Lord Prince Cade the Fifth," the Queen began, holding up a piece of paper and reading off of it. "You are hereby accused of treason to the crown, allying yourself with the former Lord Prince Argolaith, your brother, and the former Lady Princess Athela. How do you plead?"

Cade didn't bat an eye. "Not guilty."

The Queen's scribe made a great show of writing this down, and Cade studied Cira's face. She was the one he would have to look out for. She was watching him narrowly, sizing him up. He refused to break his gaze. Beside them, the King was looking off into the distance in his usual benign, detached manner; Cade was fairly certain that the King had no idea where he was or what his wife and daughter were up to.

"That is most patriotic," the Queen sneered. "However, there is evidence to the contrary. Years ago, you were involved with the theft of certain letters under Lady Cira's possession, and you have also consorted and were friendly with the aforementioned traitors to the crown."

"Do you mean to say that you will execute me because of my blood relation to Lord Argolaith?" Cade asked. "If that is the case, I might ask you, my Lord and Lady—as well as Lady Cira—to examine her own ties to Lady Athela, who is *as* guilty as Lord Argolaith, if not more."

The King and Queen visibly shifted with discomfort, but Lady Cira remained still. "That is not what we asked you, Cade," Cira said silkily, speaking up for the first time. "Did you consort with them?"

"I did not."

"Did you aid them in their escape from the palace?"

"I did not."

"Did you bury the body of Lady Ilaina three nights ago?"

Cade was glad he had prepared himself. "I wasn't aware that she was dead," he said swiftly, not missing a beat. Cira eyed him for a few moments, narrowly. "Lady Ilaina escaped with Argolaith and Athela, did she not?" Cade asked innocently.

"Yes," she said slowly, darting her eyes over to the courtiers, realizing that he had maneuvered her into her own lie.

Cade let out a low breath and twisted his head, trying to move against the iron shackles that bound him to the heavy chair.

"What have you to say about the accusation that you were involved in the theft of letters that were directly addressed to Lady Cira and later used for the treasonous purposes of Lord Argolaith and Lady Athela?"

"What letters can you be referring to?" Cade asked innocently.

"*My* letters," Cira snapped.

"What were the sensitive contents of these letters?" Cade inquired. "Perhaps you can help me by jogging my memory."

The Queen opened and closed her mouth a few times, momentarily stumped by the innocence of Cade's inquiry. There was no way for her to respond.

Since Cira had returned from her sojourn abroad, mostly for his own amusement, Cade had set up a few spies to begin intercepting Cira's correspondence, figuring that it couldn't hurt to have some leverage over her in the future. A few of the most recent ones he'd had the pleasure of reading had contained veiled references to rebuilding the castle at Faridor, which Cade had dismissed as sheer folly, at least until a few days ago.

To pry further into the damning contents of those letters in the presence of the guards and gossip-prone nobles—even the loyal ones—would do nothing but spread the seeds of discord in the community and light the possible fires of rebellion among the people. For many, Kagai and Faridor were still evil names. The Queen, Cade could see, knew the contents of the letters but was more concerned with protecting her daughter's image than addressing the potential threat they conveyed. In the context of a public tribunal with a record being taken, she could say nothing about the papers without denouncing Cira as having a connection to Kagai and Faridor. The Queen regarded Cade, sitting motionless, face blank. Neither she, nor her daughter, nor her husband knew Cade well enough to know whether or not he was bluffing or telling the truth. Either way, they were caught.

"You know perfectly well which letters," Cira snapped, momentarily losing her calm.

"I'm sure I don't," Cade said evenly. "But you are welcome to search my rooms for them."

"We already have," Cira growled.

"And?" Cade inquired.

Cira made no reply. She had the uncomfortable feeling that Cade knew as well as she did that they had found nothing. Had he destroyed them? But he could not have known that the purging of the palace was going to occur. Or had he? Was he much smarter than she had given him credit for?

"Release him," Cira ordered with a reluctant glance at her mother, and the guards stepped forward. "I will have a word with my cousin alone," she announced. Cade felt the cold iron pulled away from his wrists, and he rolled his hands around to loosen the cramped muscles. Once he regained the freedom of his arms and legs he stood, bowing stiffly to his aunt and uncle, then followed Cira out of the room into a side hallway. She turned, looking at him eye to eye, studying him. They could have been twins, between their height, coloring, and the delicate proportions of their faces. Finally, Cira folded her arms and flipped her hair back over her shoulder.

"I have decided not to execute you," she said slowly.

"Thank you very much," Cade said mildly, with not a small amount of sarcasm.

"I do not think for a second that you are innocent," she went on. "but I think that you are intelligent enough to realize that loyalty to my sister and your brother is a loyalty which will result in a swift, painful end should you choose to pursue it. I think you will see that allying yourself with the crown will, in the end, reap endless benefits for you should you prove yourself worthy."

"I'm sure it will," Cade smiled.

Cira studied him for another moment, then extended her hand. Cade instantly took it and pressed his lips against it, then released it and stood easily in front of her, controlling the urge to spit the taste of her perfume onto the marble floor.

"You're smarter than Argolaith, do you know that?" she asked.

"I've often thought so."

Cira smiled. "Do you have a bodyguard?"

Cade clasped his hands behind his back and rocked back and forth on his toes. "No. No one has ever seen the need." *I'm not important enough*, he thought bitterly.

"Well, then, we must do something to rectify that oversight. I shall have one sent to your rooms later today. You will be watched, Cade, make no mistake," Cira told him and turned to re-enter the tribunal hearing. "You can stay in your rooms for the rest of the day."

"Thank you, my Lady," Cade bowed slightly as Cira disappeared into the adjacent chamber. Something inside him writhed at the snap of her orders. Then, after a moment, he reminded himself, *you are doing what you have to do to survive.*

"My name is Luther," the stranger announced. He had a smattering of gray hair and scars on his weathered face, dressed in the royal robes of a bodyguard, a hood and circlet placed over his head. Cade disliked him immediately. "I will protect you from now on. I shall advise you on whatever subjects you require, and I shall be at your disposal, day or night. I am a loyal subject of the King and Queen, and I shall in no way begrudge your blood relation to the traitor Lord Argolaith."

Dear of you, Cade thought wryly, but he nodded courteously.

"Behind me is my pupil, Weryn," Luther continued. "I'm sure you will find him a satisfactory servant as well."

"I'm sure." Cade sighed, bored and annoyed with his new bodyguard already. Loyal to the crown, a blind dislike of Laith and Athela; Cira just might have accomplished her goal of putting him on an infuriatingly short leash. Bodyguards were, by definition, meant to follow him closely at all times in spaces both public and private, and it was plainly obvious which master Luther really served.

Cade craned his neck slightly to catch a glimpse of Weryn, who was standing farther back. *Hmm*, Cade thought to himself, *here's something interesting.* Weryn, the apprentice, had shortish tawny hair flecked with gray and amber so that it almost looked like the pelt of an animal. He was broad across the shoulders but not very tall, and had the air of someone who could handle himself in a fight and knew it. Cade was intrigued. "Luther," Cade said, "It seems to me that for my own personal comfort, I might make do with having your pupil flanking me in person, as he is more to my own age. I think that you would do well looking after the overall security of my well-being within the palace."

"I will make decisions as to your personal security," Luther narrowed his eyes. His tone was like that of a chiding parent.

Cade spread his hands easily. "Please. I insist."

Cade could tell that Luther didn't particularly like this state of affairs, but the prince honestly didn't care. Weryn shifted behind Luther, keeping his face inscrutable. Finally, after a short standoff, Luther stiffly inclined his head. "Then I shall take my leave of you, my Lord, and begin making my initial checks around the perimeter of your apartments. Weryn, remain here so that you and Lord Cade can become better acquainted." With that, Luther rose and walked out of the room. He limped slightly in his left leg. *Thanks, Cira, for sending me a young and spry bodyguard.* Cade looked over, and Weryn, the younger bodyguard, approached and sat down. He studied Cade levelly with intelligent, clear blue eyes.

"You'll have to watch out for the old bat," he said finally. "He's got ears like a hawk."

"What?" Cade inquired, trying not to show his surprise.

"Luther," Weryn said. "We've been assigned to keep an eye on you rather than protect you. But I'm pretty sure you were already aware of that. Cira's promised him a whole lot of promotions and pleasant retirement opportunities if we manage to bust you for doing something completely treacherous. She went out and hired the most fanatically loyal bodyguard in the city."

"I gathered as much," Cade murmured.

"Good," Weryn again regarded him. "And my name's not Weryn. It's Wolf. That's what everyone calls me, except for Luther, and I think he only does it to irritate me."

"Wolf," Cade repeated, and indeed, the mottled mane atop the young man's head did remind him of fur. "I take it that you, yourself, are not an avid supporter of my cousin Cira?"

"She's a nutter," Wolf said bluntly. "Minute she started talking out against Lord Argolaith, I knew it. He used to teach some classes out in the city, him and Athela. I liked him. Athela was a bit cold, but he was always friendly, always helpful. Always liked him far more than Cira." Wolf glanced to one side. "I heard a rumor, besides," he said in a low voice, "that Cira released Lord Seth. In secret."

A chill shuddered through Cade's body. For a moment, his memory snapped back to the spectral figure standing beside Cira, looking down at Ilaina's slain body with empty, dark eyes.

"They say she has him under her control," Wolf continued.

"No one has Lord Seth under control," Cade muttered.

Seth's reputation had grown into something of a terrifying legend among the Jelani. He was said to be a full-fledged psychopath, immoral, unfeeling, with no shred of empathy running through his body. Though he was only Laith's age, he'd been locked away in the dungeons of Joymaril for many years by that point, while stories of the horrors he'd inflicted during his freedom grew and spread like a black mold. Marc, Laith's bodyguard and best friend, even bore a scar across his face, the relic of an "accident" that Seth had engineered.

Cade leaned in, keeping his voice low. "What exactly are you telling me all this for?"

Wolf smiled, conspiratorially arching an eyebrow and leaning in. "I'm well aware that you're not going to trust me right away, or even for some time yet. But if you're telling me that you, the brother of Lord Argolaith and the cousin of Lady Athela, someone who, if I have done my research correctly, has the smartest head on his shoulders of anyone in this place, if you're telling me that you're going to sit back while Cira takes over everything and twiddle your thumbs, well, then I'll just march right out of this room and help Luther do a perimeter check and never say a single thing out of line ever again. But," here he grinned, "if you're going to do something about it, I can and am willing to help you in any way I can."

Cade studied him. There was a glint in Wolf's eye that told Cade he was in earnest. He was right; it would be a while before he built up trust, but that would come in time. "How did you avoid detection?

I'm sure Cira's already interrogated many of the students at the city training school."

"I got through it the same way you did," Wolf looped his fingers together. "Lied through my teeth."

Cade let a slow smile creep along one side of his mouth. He liked Wolf. He wanted to trust him. "I'll need a pair of eyes and ears," he said finally. "For a while, at least, I won't be able to go where I need to go or see what I need to see. You can do that for me. And keep Luther off my back as best you can. Tell him you'll flank me. But the minute you're sure it's safe, I want you to go everywhere and learn all you can. It'll be vital."

Wolf nodded slowly, the glint in his blue eyes growing brighter. "So," he said slowly. "I suppose that means you're planning something?"

Cade smiled evasively and leaned far back in his chair, sliding a hand along the length of the arm, gray eyes betraying nothing, neither yes nor no. But Wolf narrowed his eyes sharply.

"I better go see what Luther's doing," he announced, then stood, bowed solemnly, and walked out of the room. Cade reclined in his chair, his thoughts churning over and over.

Over the next few weeks, life gradually returned to normal in the city, though the arrests of a number of the royal courtiers and their families passed by in silence, without a word of explanation or acknowledgment from the Queen. Those who had been imprisoned were dragged out and run through a barrage of questioning, then a few weeks later, they either disappeared altogether or were released without a further word. Those who lost their fathers, mothers, or children felt the bitterness burning within them, but there was no way to let it out without risking their own lives or the remaining lives around them. And beneath it all, whispers of the name *Kagai* began to course round and round like a whirling sea.

The Queen ruled as she had always done, with casual detachment and an air of haughty superiority. She rewarded the followers who had shown her unquestionable loyalty and shunned those who had escaped by the skin of their teeth. Guards marched through the palace and the surrounding city, and the subject of court gossip shifted from which royal was sleeping with whom to which royal was guilty of treason. Sometimes, these whispers would reach the ears of the King or Queen, and the accused would be seen shortly thereafter being marched along to the dungeons for questioning.

At this point, there was no doubt in anyone's mind that the power behind the throne was, in fact, Lady Cira. At every interrogation she was sitting at her mother's side, supplying damning questions that often resulted in the conviction of the accused. She worded her inquiries in such a way that escape was impossible. She surrounded herself with guards whenever she swept through the palace. No one was allowed to even look at her crossly, or they would find themselves being carted off to the dungeons before they knew what was going on. She locked herself in her chambers, writing letters, sending her own personal servants to deliver them to ensure that they did not fall into the wrong hands. She grew increasingly paranoid, and her malevolence had never known greater heights. Without her sister around to act as a target for her manipulative schemes, she began to cast a broader net, focusing instead on the people of the court and the surrounding city.

All the while, Cade kept to the back, avoiding being seen. He rarely, if ever, attended the royal gatherings and frequent banquets, and if he did, it was only if he was ordered to by his aunt and uncle. He made himself so incredibly boring that there was no possible way Cira would notice him. If he was out of his room, he was accompanied by a book; within, he read more and more. If Cira happened to pass him, he bowed as he was supposed to and made all of the subservient gestures that were expected of his station. Every now and then, Cade could almost feel the cold beam of her suspicion turning to focus its light back on him. More footsteps would haunt him through the halls, more of his correspondence would be hastily stuck back together to appear unread. But then Cira would become distracted; someone else would command her attention, and she would forget him once more. And it was in this way that, week after week, Cade survived.

But as detached as Cade appeared to everyone else, he was in reality deeply attuned to the pulsing heart of the court of the Jelani. Wolf proved himself invaluable. When he cloaked himself, everyone took him as a royal guard and stayed away so that he could flit through the palace faceless yet feared. If he dressed himself in garments other than those of a royal bodyguard, he was instantly welcomed into all of the circles of gossip, but as soon as he was gone, he was forgotten. He dressed as a citizen and walked the streets of the city, hearing the woes of the common people, their beliefs, their fears. He was a nonentity, circling and hovering around the people of the palace, absorbing their secrets and their suspicions. Everything he learned he told to Cade, who cataloged each name, each threat, each happening in his mind with razor-sharp accuracy better than any book. If he was told a name once, he would remember it forever.

As time went on and summer began to emerge in its full radiant heat, Cade and Wolf established an effective method of speaking to one another without being understood. When Wolf would enter Cade's apartments with his sword buckled across his back, Cade knew that Luther was lurking somewhere, listening for any hint of treachery to report to Cira. If the sword was at his hip, all was clear. When Luther was in their presence, they communicated with small hand gestures that Wolf made behind Luther's back and Cade read with his peripheral vision, never taking his eyes off Luther or betraying their communication. It got to the point where Cade merely had to read Wolf's expression to know what was going on: whether there was danger or whether he had to keep away for a few days to avoid suspicion. And, though Cade had long ago perfected the art of the enigmatic expression, Wolf found that he could read the young prince's body and know his thoughts. When his hands were at his mouth, he was especially pensive and wouldn't appreciate being disturbed. If they rested the arms of his chair, he was concerned about something, and Wolf would make a note to return later in the day so they could confer undisturbed.

One deep cobalt night, after a large banquet held in honor of the coming of the summer solstice, Cade and Wolf were out at the prince's balcony, looking at the silhouette of the trees and the city against the moon. The two were silent for some time, their extended exposure to one another over the months having made them comfortable in mutual stillness.

"What do you think?" Wolf asked finally.

Cade stretched out his arms, gripping the side of the balustrade and rolling his head about on his neck to work out a few kinks. "I think tonight is when they'll have it out. Remember, if you are seen..."

"You don't have to tell me," Wolf cut him off, then turned around and squinted up at the overhang at the rear of the balcony. He flipped his hood over his head, shielding his eyes. He tucked a veil around the lower part of his face so that his skin wouldn't show in the dim light. "I'll report to you right after," he said, his voice muffled beneath the veil. Cade nodded. A moment later, Wolf leaped onto the edge of the balcony and sprang up onto the slippery roof, scuttling along towards the center of the palace where the King and Queen's royal chambers were located.

A few minutes later, Wolf was perched precariously on the teetering edge of the rooftop above the Queen's inner sanctum. He slid down the curving dome until he was nestled in the crotch of the joining of two roofs, then he slowly crept along the gutter until he was seated at the opening of the roof, a circular space where the Queen could get some sun without having to leave her apartments. He slid down one of the pillars beneath the edge of the roof and sank down until he was nestled deep in a thicket of shadows. A fountain in the center of the open area burbled away, but Wolf trained his ears to the inner area of the room, where Cira and her mother had just walked in. Cade, even more acutely tuned to the behavior of others than Wolf, had noticed a slight tension between Cira and the Queen at the festivities that evening. Cade had surmised that something was going on and had sent Wolf to investigate.

"What is so important that you had to talk to me at this dreadful hour, Cira?" the Queen's irate voice snapped through the quietude of the surrounding night. "Can't it wait until morning?"

"You've been putting me off for long enough," Cira returned, in a tone dripping with malice. "I need to talk to you *now.*"

"Fine, then," the Queen dropped herself into a chair and folded her arms, looking up at Cira with distaste. "What is it?"

"I'm going to make the announcement soon," Cira told her, drawing up another chair, her register dropping into one more soothing and democratic. "All the signs are in order, my place is secure, and there's no doubt about it."

"Ridiculous," the Queen snorted. "Your father and I have never held with that prophecy nonsense, not when your cousin and your sister brought it up, not ever. It's preposterous. And you, believing the words of some wild soothsayer ten years ago. All your folly with rebuilding Faridor must be dropped immediately. *You*, the heir of Kagai. What nonsense."

Wolf's breath skipped, and his chest tightened over his heart so that it felt as if it were throbbing horribly. *The heir of Kagai? What on earth is she talking about? She can't really believe that she's...it's impossible.*

"Mother, I have seen the signs," Cira said impatiently. "Messages sent to me during my time in the Meadows. I have read every account of Kagai's prophecy. And the soothsayer *said...*"

"Listen to yourself, Cira," the Queen snapped. "You sound like a fool."

There was a pause. "They can't all be wrong. I'm the one."

"It's idiocy to go on speaking this way."

"Mother, just listen to what I have to say." There was a moment of stillness here, and Wolf surmised that the Queen had gone into a bout of surly, icy silence in retaliation. He heard Cira take in a deep, audible breath before continuing. "I am going to announce my ascension within a few days. After that, I will move to Faridor, taking with me most of the house guard to begin building up my army." Here, there was a very loud sound of one of the chairs scooting backward, and Wolf heard the Queen begin to pace back and forth angrily, her shadow passing back and forth on the floor below, while Cira remained seated, her tone growing louder and louder as she continued to speak. "Then you shall declare that all of Joymaril is to pay homage to me and to see me as their only rightful ruler. You and Father will, of course, continue to actually rule here, but it's all spectacle, do you understand? I have to create a sense of unity amongst all the people when I begin to rule this country, and I can't have division begin in my own home."

"Go back to your room," the Queen ordered tightly.

Wolf could hear Cira bristle at the tone. "I'm not a child anymore, mother, that you can order about. If it came to blows, I could defeat you without a problem," Cira hissed. "Now, listen. After you declare me supreme ruler, you will, of course, be compensated for your loyalty. As a token of fealty, you will send me all of the fighters graduating from the old Academy to make up my own personal Kagaian troops."

This time, when Cira paused the Queen made no immediate argument. *She can't have won her over like that*, Wolf thought incredulously. *The Queen isn't the type to capitulate that quickly.*

"What do you have to say?" Cira asked.

"I have a good mind to throw you in the dungeons for speaking in that way to me. You forget that I am still a Queen, and you are merely a subject," the Queen intoned haughtily.

"A *subject?*" Cira growled. "*Subject?* What subject was it that saw to it that the biggest threats to the throne are now hunted in the farthest reaches of this country? Who was it that influenced the purging of this city so that only those loyal would remain? Tell me, mother, I'd like to know."

"You may leave now, Cira. For your sake, I shall pretend as though this conversation never took place."

Cira was quiet for a second. "Then you refuse?"

The Queen laughed. "Go to bed. The heat has clearly addled your senses."

Wolf had heard all he needed. Before there was the sound of chairs scooting along the floor, he was back up on the roof and on his way to report to Cade.

"It'll happen soon then," was Cade's only reply after Wolf had finished his retelling. If the bodyguard had expected a more heated response, he didn't show it. He stood, as he always did, while Cade reclined in his chair, his hands to his lips.

"Should we make our move now?" Wolf asked when Cade had been silent for a few minutes. He moved across the room and slung himself over the arm of a settee, raising his eyebrows expectantly. Cade looked up as if he were surprised that someone else had spoken. He shook his head a few times to clear it.

"No," he said. "Cira's too strong. It'd be suicide."

"So when?" Wolf asked, pulling a knife from his boot and toying around with it in his hand. Cade eyed him sidelong as the blade spun around on the tip of his finger. Wolf glanced over.

"Patience not a virtue they taught you during school?" Cade asked sarcastically, arching a dark eyebrow.

"Did my best to resist all instruction," Wolf grinned. "So tell me what's up."

Cade leaned back, steepling his fingers beneath his nose. Wolf often noticed that although Cade was still only a teenager, he had adopted many of the habits and mannerisms of the older members of the royal court. While on any other young man Cade's age the actions would seem self-consciously theatrical, Cade did them so subconsciously and with such inner gravitas that somehow it seemed natural. He waited before he began speaking. Wolf was not impatient this time. He knew when to take his time with Cade and when he could press him.

"Cira, if I'm not much mistaken, will move against her parents within a few days, no more than a week," Cade began. "After they're out of the way, she won't stay here. If what you said is correct, she'll move off to Faridor and leave someone else here in charge, someone who is competent but easily manipulated. After Cira, the throne passes to the eldest and most favored of my female cousins, but she may bypass that entirely for someone she *knows* she can control."

"Hang on," Wolf flipped his knife around in his fingers. "How do you know right off that Cira is going to get the better of the Queen?"

"Cira will win," Cade said levelly and in measured tones, "because her mother underestimates her. The Queen is aware that Cira is intelligent, power-hungry, and ruthless, but I think that she is still blinded to the fact that Cira will do *anything* to *anyone* who gets in her way. Even the Queen herself."

"And then, after Cira's gone, we make our move?" Wolf asked.

"That would be correct," Cade smiled serenely. "Then we make our move."

"Sounds good. I'll be off to get some sleep," Wolf yawned, showing off a row of white, sharp teeth. "Night." He flipped the knife up with one finger, and Cade caught it with a quick sweep of his wrist. The door shut behind Wolf. Cade lowered the weapon and laid it down atop the table beside his chair. Then he reached out and, with his thumb and forefinger, extinguished the candle beside him. The smoke curled around his head in a blue wreath in the darkness. Cade let out a long breath and watched it puff away from him, swaying with him in the dim light of the purple sky spilling in from the balcony windows.

"It is with a heavy heart that I announce that my mother and father have both been taken ill this morning," Cira announced in a voice dripping with brave serenity. "They have been moved to a rear room of the palace where they are being tended by the best of the royal physicians. I am confident that their situations will improve in only a small amount of time."

Cira looked perfectly turned out that morning, her eyes glinting with a newfound light. Her light hair was swept up off her neck, and her dress had a high collar that gave her more height and framed her delicate face. Cade watched from the far back of the hall as the courtiers slowly began to talk amongst themselves in low voices, filling the room with the sound of speculative whispers. Cade kept his arms folded, watching Cira as she surveyed her subjects. A small smile came upon her face until she swept her eyes across Cade, then her mouth tightened and a look of hardness settled upon her features. Cade met her gaze, but his expression was without challenge. He didn't want to start a fight at this point. It wasn't the time.

Cira turned away then, flipping her long sleeves over her arms so they were less cumbersome. She had to reintroduce herself to her people as a Queen, and unfortunately, looking like a Queen also meant having to wear bulkier, more elaborate gowns. She was joined by the captain of the house guard, who had been promoted to her personal bodyguard. It was she who followed Cira silently as she walked along a back corridor to the infirmary.

Her parents were being kept in the far back area of the medical facilities, with curtains drawn around four-poster beds that were just as lavish as the beds in their normal living chambers. The walls were painted red, and the curtains were a deep purple covered with black and gold embroidery. The torchlight was kept low, at a comfortable level. Medicated incense was burned to keep the room smelling fresh, and the people inside it calm. A number of golden-robed physicians were chatting in one corner. When one caught sight of Cira, they separated and bowed. From her short height, Cira stared at them imperiously until they grew uncomfortable and scuttled for the nearest way out of the room. Cira drew back the curtains around her mother's bed. The Queen was being kept beneath three light sheets and a heavy embroidered comforter drawn up atop the summer heat. Powerful healing symbols were engraved on the headboard of the bed to encourage recovery, but Cira was quite confident that they wouldn't work this time. She sat upon the bed by her mother's legs and looked down. The Queen, normally so intimidating in her rich robes and her icy stare, looked weak, pale, and so frail that Cira fancied that she could break her in half with her bare hands.

"Feeling better, Mother?" Cira asked quietly, a smile of comfort on her face. The Queen slowly rolled her head over and looked at Cira, her eyes vague and unfocused, physically incapable of speech. *I rather like it this way*, Cira mused. *Our conversations now are so much more interesting than they have been.* She reached over and took her mother's clammy hand in her own and patted it a few times. "Don't worry, I'm sure you'll be better in only a few days. Now, it's time for your medicine, and I've arranged it so that I should be the one to give it to you." Cira stood, parting the curtains and walking over to the medicine chest, where a thick paste was made ready. Cira took the small bowl and walked back to her mother's bed. The first dose had been quite easy to administer, almost *too* easy, in fact. Cira had been looking forward to some amount of excitement, but it had all been dreadfully dull, and she had been careful to calculate an amount that would completely incapacitate her mother while not killing her. From then on, it would be tedious but simple enough. Cira tipped her mother's head back and painted the paste on her tongue, forcing her to swallow it down.

"That's good," Cira patted her mother's arm. "Father's already taken care of." She leaned over and kissed her mother's cheek and stood, parting the curtains again and laying the bowl back down on the top of the medicine cabinet. "Clean it out," she ordered shortly. "Have it ready for the next dose tonight."

The guard bowed and did as he was bidden.

Cira was in her chambers three days later, writing a letter to Faridor. Her pale hair spilled over her shoulder and onto her desk, rippling off the corner of the table when she leaned over far enough. She paused for a moment, biting the end of her pen, brow furrowed, green eyes scanning back over what she had written:

I am most pleased with your progress on my personal living quarters. From what you have reported to me, I am quite sure that they will suit my needs. I would, however, like a more extensive report on the amount of force that I will have at my disposal when I arrive. The trainees from the Royal Academy should be dispatched soon after I depart, and after Two Falls has been taken, I expect a new wave of recruits from the city. I am prepared to move all the contracts my family has with our overseas partners to ensure that trade continues as usual, with the major hub of activity, of course, being Faridor. I should be arriving soon after I have completed my business here.

Cira leaned back, satisfied, brushing her hair out of the way. She folded the paper into thirds and dropped a red dab of wax over the fold, flipping up the top of her ring and pressing her seal onto the wax. She stood and blew on it a few times and flapped it up and down in the air. There was a short knock on the door.

"Come in," she said shortly. The door creaked open and three men walked in, whom Cira recognized as the high priest and advisor to the royal family, a retired captain of the guard who served as a military advisor, and a woman who was her mother's personal bodyguard. The bodyguard's eyes were lowered. Cira took in their arrival wordlessly, but felt her heart start to thud within her chest. She slowly lowered the letter to the table and pressed her fingertips on it. The priest approached, wearing his best robes of state, his gray hair pulled neatly back. He had something in his hand. Cira gulped. This was what she had been waiting for entire life. It was here. She closed her eyes to savor the moment. It tasted like wine.

The three of them knelt in front of her, and the priest looked up. "The Queen is dead," he announced. "Let Cira of the house of Joymaril now be proclaimed Queen throughout the city. Let her name be taken down in the books of the house. Let the people worship her as they would a goddess. Let her take this burden and be with it for as long as she shall live."

With that, he opened his hand, revealing the ring symbolizing the Queen's power. Cira reached out a trembling hand and took it in her own, slipping the ring over her finger, pulling back the two delicate gold chains that tied the ring to a thin inlaid bracelet that she clasped around her wrist. It fit perfectly, the symbol of the Queen's destiny tying her to her people. Cira thought faintly of all the hands that had borne the ring and bracelet before her. Cira looked from her hand to the kneeling figures before her. The Queen's bodyguard's neck was stiff as a board, and there was something in the way she looked at the ground. *You're the first to die now that I'm Queen*, Cira thought to herself cheerily. *Can't have any upstart loyalists trying to assassinate me in my sleep, now, can I? Now that I'm Queen...Queen Cira.*

"You may go," Cira said to them. "Spread the word to the city and declare a period of mourning. I shall address my people tomorrow. I have much to think about, so leave me in peace. See to it that all preparations for the burial of the King and Queen are made."

"Yes, your Majesty," the priest said, and the three left the room.

Majesty, Cira repeated gleefully in her head. *Majesty, Majesty, Majesty.*

"It's done," Wolf said shortly, striding into Cade's room. "She's done it. Cira's Queen. She's going to make her royal address first thing in the morning, so we're going to need to hike our rear ends over to the city square so that it doesn't appear suspicious."

"She's moving a lot quicker than I thought she would," Cade said mildly, turning around from the balcony and stretching. His white hair was tousled, and he looked as if he hadn't been getting much sleep lately; fatigue was showing in his dark-rimmed gray eyes. Wolf took note, but kept his concerns to himself, knowing that bringing them up would only annoy the prince.

"Will you need me any more today?" Wolf inquired.

"No, I'll see you in the morning," Cade nodded to him and walked over to the couch, where he lay down and picked up an open book from the top of a stack already piled on the floor. Wolf bowed shortly and strode out of the room.

The next morning, Cade was awoken by the sound of horns being blown from the four corners of the city, summoning the people to the city square to hear Cira's announcement and witness the coronation. Black banners were draped in all of the hallways and streets of the city, and candles were lit outside every door to show mourning for the dead monarchs. The townspeople were buzzing with the news of the sudden change in power; there were few illusions about who was behind the expedited demise of the King and Queen. A few wondered hopefully whether another faction would quickly bump Cira off in the uncertainty of the transition, but there was little hope for such an occurrence. She was too strong; she had all the house guards under her control and influence.

It was more a product of curiosity and fear than loyalty that the townspeople poured into and around the square that morning. Purple Jelani guards stood together in thick knots, their eyes peeled for any signs of trouble or danger. The royal court had its own place on one side of the square, with chairs provided for some of them to sit, and the members of the direct royal family sat on another side. In the very center of the square was a marble platform underneath an ancient archway, with wide steps leading up to the top. An ebony chair waited, vacant and ready. As the square filled, there was not a sound in the air except for the gentle fluttering of the banners and flags of the royal houses and of the quiet shifting and shuffling of the citizens as they waited, wide-eyed and anxious, for Cira's first appearance as their Queen.

Cade was seated towards the front of the royal family's section, but wasn't as close as his rank would normally have dictated; it seemed Cira was still doing her best to make it clear that Cade and his immediate family were firmly outcast from Jelani society. Cade didn't mind, though it was a bother having to get dressed up for such an occasion. The members of the family were decked out in all their funereal finery, muted dark colors to befit the time of mourning. Cade could feel people's eyes on him as they looked across the crowd of royal family members, and knew that they were all pointing him out as the brother of Lord Argolaith, the traitor. He stared forward in silence, his gray eyes the same color as the sky above him.

All at once, there was a ripple starting at the back of the crowd, and Cade could dimly see the people parting to let someone through. Then he saw advancing rows of royal spears with banners tied to the ends, approaching like fins splitting the water. Cira had arrived.

She was absolutely resplendent in a dark purple and black mourning dress with a long train that fanned out behind her as she walked, contrasting her milky white skin. She wore the expression of someone who knew she was being watched and inwardly enjoyed the attention, even if her outward demeanor was solemn and mournful. Her head tilted ever so slightly, and all eyes followed as the guards parted and allowed her to walk through them and up the long flight of steps to the platform. She lifted her long dress out of the way of her feet, and she did not trip. She did not look down as she climbed the steps. The dark purple and black satin of the train of her gown rippled up the stairs as it was pulled. Finally, she finished her ascension and turned to face the crowd, staring slightly over their heads so that her expression was one of calculated omniscience. Her hands hung loosely at her side, not awkward. She was completely poised, perfectly relaxed. Cade imagined that she must have practiced this appearance.

The high priest approached from one side and climbed halfway up the flight of steps, then turned around to face the people. He raised his arms, the thick fabric of his robes falling stiffly to his waist.

"Let it be proclaimed from all corners of the city," he announced, "let it be proclaimed from all corners of the heavens, and let it be proclaimed to the farthest reaches of the earth that Lady Cira of the house of Joymaril is hereby crowned Queen." Here, he lowered his arms and walked slowly to the captain of the guard, who held a purple length of silk in her arms, at the top of which was a small bundle. The priest slowly undid the corners of the bundle, and the fabric fell away to reveal a plain gold circlet, the traditional crown of the Queens of Joymaril. The priest moved away, raising the crown to the sky, then turned and walked up the steps so that he was standing in front of Cira. He slowly lowered the crown onto her head. She stared straight through him, not letting the slightest flicker of an expression cross her face. If there was triumph there, it was only because Cade could feel it radiating from every inch of her body.

The high priest turned away again and took a small, jeweled cup filled nearly to the top with a deep purple paint. He faced Cira once more and painted three tiny marks between her eyebrows and three at the base of the part of her hair, symbols representing the sunset of her mother's rule and the rising sun of her own. With that, he stepped away, and Cira blinked slowly, the first time Cade had seen her do so. She slowly lowered herself onto the ebony throne. It was at this time that Cade imagined the crowd would usually break into cheers and applause in celebration of the new Queen, but the square was absolutely silent, no whispering, no jeering, nothing—just the quiet sound of wind blowing softly through the buildings surrounding the square. It was as if a great gloom had settled upon the hearts of the city dwellers as they looked at Cira, finally in the position of power that she had been fighting for all her life. Cade wondered what it would have been like if Athela had been the one to take the throne. Though her reputation was far from stellar, he couldn't possibly imagine her coronation being met with a more icy silence than this.

Cira did not seem to be put off by the cold reception. Indeed, she barely batted an eye, though Cade noted with satisfaction that her hands weren't loosely slung over the sides of her chair, but she was gripping the arms so tightly her knuckles were showing gray through the pale pink of her skin. Her back was perfectly straight, and the transparent dark stole she wore wrapped around one of her arms cascaded down into a small pile on top of the marble platform. The jewels in the brooch on her dress glinted in the dull gray sunlight, along with the ring and bracelet of power and the royal crown. She scanned the crowd with her wide-set green cat's eyes, looking at the faces for any traces of anger or outrage, but found nothing except the sweetest tinge of fear. Fear was something she could work with.

"I am Queen at last," Cira announced suddenly, barely needing to raise her voice, so deathly quiet was her audience. "As I sit here before you, I do not see the love of people for their ruler. I do not see joy; I do not see thankfulness. But I also do not ask for such things. I do not need them. This city has been growing soft and rich on the goods we have been blessed with through our holdings and our trade agreements. We have grown complacent. But I promise you such things will change now that I am Queen. There is more to be done. More we can do. Much more." Cira let this hang in the air for a few moments. She would have to proceed carefully.

"I shall not stay in Joymaril," she announced slowly and was pleased to hear the first buzz of mutterings and ejaculations emanate from the crowd. She let the noise die down before she continued. "At the end of this week, I shall take what guards I see fit, as well as the trainees from the Royal Academy, and move to my new residence at the fortress of Faridor off the coast of the city of Two Falls." More buzzing, even louder this time, like a swarm of bees. Cira enjoyed the sound for a few more moments, then held up her hand. At the gesture, the crowd immediately fell silent. She reveled in her power, lowering her hand slowly down to the arm of the chair. "I have found, through my extensive studies, that I am, in fact, the heir of Lord Kagai, and it is my destiny to continue the noble work which he began a millennia ago: the work of uniting this country under one banner. I have accepted this honor, much as I have the crown today."

Now the people were silent, watching her with wide eyes. Cade could see the disbelief written across their faces. *Cira, the heir of Kagai? Surely not.* And then, as Cade continued watching, he saw the expressions change as the enormity of the announcement fell.

"I cannot remain here to rule Joymaril as is my privilege and my innermost wish. But I assure you that I shall never be far away, not in words, in my heart, or in my deeds. I have decided, after much deliberation, to appoint a regent who will rule the city under my supervision and instruction. All decisions regarding public policy and issues will be sent to me, and I shall make proclamations as if I were still living here. I assure you that you will approve of my choice. Lady Vera, step forward."

There was a rush in the crowd as all heads swiveled around to look at the royal family's section. Cade wasn't at all surprised by Cira's choice, as Lady Vera was her second oldest female cousin and was known for being greedy but dim: the perfect combination of traits to suit Cira's purposes. Lady Vera was seated three rows behind Cade, and he was the only one who didn't bother to look around as she stood and made her way up to the platform where Cira was seated, looking benevolently down at her from the height of the throne. Vera wasn't terribly pretty, and since beauty was one of the chief methods by which the royal family rated their goods, she had mostly been kept shunted off to one side out of the way of her more attractive siblings. She had curly strawberry blonde hair and pale eyelashes, with a nondescript mouth and smallish eyes. When she smiled, her teeth were still slightly crooked, like a child's. She had the notable achievement of being one of the most premiere gossips in an already scandal-hungry court. Oftentimes, Wolf listened to her whisperings to get the first hint of any important news from the royal family.

As she made her way clumsily up the steps, trying to pull her long gown out of the way, Cade felt an inward twinge of pity for her. *This is probably going to be the highlight of her life, poor thing*, he sighed. *Little does she know that the only reason she was chosen is because she'll be easily manipulated. Cira will promise her power, prestige, and everlasting glory, and what she'll be is a puppet.*

Lady Vera finally made it awkwardly to the platform, where her ungainly approach roasted under Cira's disapproving gaze for a few moments. She knelt slowly, her head bowed so that she wouldn't have to meet Cira's eyes.

"Lady Vera," Cira purred, holding out one of her white hands, the one with the ring and bracelet on it. "Do you swear fidelity to me, and will you rule nobly and truly in my absence?"

"Yes, your Majesty," Vera mumbled, her face still pointed down towards the ground.

"What was that?" Cira asked, a mocking tone frosting the edges of her words.

"Yes, your Majesty," Vera squeaked slightly louder. "I will."

"Good." Cira leaned back. Vera reached up and kissed Cira's ring, then at a motion from Cira's hand, rose jerkily to her feet and went to stand beside Cira's throne. "Lady Vera will be appointed Queen regent and coronated at the new year," Cira said, louder, addressing the crowd once more. "I expect you all to show the same loyalty and love to Lady Vera as you would me. This will be a new time, an exciting time in this city. We stand upon the precipice of a new era. Changes are already underway. In a few months, Joymaril may even become the capital of the entire country!" Cira paused as the crowd digested this statement. "We shall become the greatest people in the world," she said slowly. "And this shall forever be remembered as a new golden age."

At least she seems optimistic, Cade thought to himself.

There was a finality in Cira's tone that clearly signaled that she was done with her speech. Beside her, Lady Vera looked around at the faces in front of her, uncomfortable and slightly confused: *Why weren't they clapping? Shouldn't they be clapping?* Cade could see that Cira still wasn't the least bit concerned with the fact that the people were watching her with mute disbelief rather than adoration. He smiled to himself and shook his head slightly. Lady Vera wouldn't be a problem to overthrow. She had no cunning; she lacked finesse. She had been born a bovine into a world of dangerous, lethal cats.

The crowd dissolved, and Cade found himself walking mechanically back to his apartments, acutely aware of the lack of buzzing whispers surrounding him that usually signaled the end of any of the royal gatherings. Everyone seemed to be stunned into a dreadful mute silence.

Once he reached his rooms and shut the door closed behind him, he walked over to his desk and sat down. On the desk was a letter he hadn't remembered seeing that morning when he had walked through his room on the way to the coronation. Had someone left it there for him while he was away? He gently moved the lips of the paper open. Inside was a hastily scrawled note from a hand he didn't recognize.

My Lord Cade—Your brother Laith was here last night looking for Ilaina.

I may be able to give him a message from you if he returns.

Cade's heart leapt at the words, but immediately his brow furrowed. The seal on the letter had been broken. Had someone read it? He assumed that it had been Nadia who had sent it to him, as only she and Wolf knew of his hidden loyalties, but it was unlike her to leave messages out in the open.

He picked up the slender piece of paper and held it over a candle until the very edge of it caught fire. He rotated it around, watching the flame lick up the side. He toyed with it, turning it, then his hand stopped still and his eyes focused on the very edge of the paper. There was a smudge—only a smudge, but it was a visible fingerprint. Cade looked swiftly down to the top of the desk. There was a small dab of ink that had slipped free of his pen and had partially dried. Nadia couldn't have written him the letter from his own room, had she? Who else could have come in? But everyone had been at the coronation, there had been no chance, no chance at all.

The flame gobbled up the last sliver of visible paper. Cade dropped the paper to the ground and stomped on it a few times to beat out the final vestiges of fire, then leaned back, deeply concerned. *Cira could have planted it*, he realized. *Tried to plant evidence against me.* He paced back and forth along the length of the room, trying to see both sides of the situation. *But what if Laith really* has *come back? Maybe I can get word to him.* Though this thought cheered him momentarily, he couldn't help but feel that he'd walked into some sort of trap.

Two days went by without much ado, though Cade was still deeply on edge. Nadia, when he asked her, had no idea where the letter about Laith had come from. Wolf hadn't been to see him in private since before the coronation, and while it could merely mean that he hadn't been able to slip away from Luther, the combination of his absence and the incident with the letter did nothing to settle Cade's spirits. He was sleeping less and less, spending more time awake reading deep into the night. But on the morning of the third day, there was something different in the air. For the first time in a week, he rose feeling more or less refreshed, threw on a clean robe, went to his washroom, and carefully shaved off the bits of fuzz that had been growing white on his lips and chin for the past few days. He eyed himself critically in the mirror. His face was still young; it showed no real wear for all the stress he had been under, perhaps some darkening under his eyes, nothing terribly important. Perhaps he should take it easier, get out of his room for a while, go riding. Cira would soon be gone to Faridor. He would have to wait a little while before he could put his plan into action, so there would be some time for him to relax and take a deep breath before the plunge. He had been treading water since Laith had gone.

Cade glanced down at his hands. His brother shouldn't have left him. He shook his head and rubbed more water into his eyes.

He changed into some comfortable clothing and walked out onto the balcony, gaze dropping down to the water below. It was a beautiful day. It had been too long since he had seen the sun; he had shut himself away. It would change. A new time was coming, and he wasn't afraid of it. He turned around and headed out of the door of his room.

He hadn't gone ten steps before there was a commotion from one side of his apartments. He whipped around, and Wolf pounced on him, fairly hauling him off his feet and dragging him back to his room, throwing shut the door and whipping around, his fangs bared.

"What is it?" Cade demanded, immediate alarm rising as he took in Wolf's shocking appearance. The left side of his face was mottled over in varying shades of purple, blue, and green, with dark red gashes intersecting them. Some of the cuts even went down his throat and disappeared below the neck of his ripped shirt. Wolf was panting like a winded animal.

"It's over, that's what," Wolf growled.

"What do you mean? What on earth happened to you?" Cade asked in a hushed tone, dread flooding into his chest, swilling around and making him almost sick to his stomach.

"Day of the coronation, I go back to our room and Luther's waiting for me there. Hits me over the head with a great big plank, knocks me clean out. Next thing I know he's asking me about our plot, about some letter."

"Did you tell him anything?" Cade asked swiftly, mind racing.

"Yes, I'm fine, Cade, thanks for asking," Wolf said sarcastically. There was dried blood in his hair, Cade noticed suddenly, but he brushed the surging guilt away. He had to focus; he had to survive. There would be time for guilt later. "But no, he didn't get a thing out of me. Don't worry about that. He asks me about some letter, and I say I don't know what letter. It went on and on, and then today he got fed up with trying to beat it out of me. He's going now to go tell Cira before she leaves. Minute he was out of the room, I got loose and came here to warn you."

"Has he managed to see Cira yet?" Cade asked, his voice rising.

"Not as I know," Wolf looked up weakly. He was leaning against the door for support, his spine slightly curved.

"Wolf, you have to stop him; he can't get to her," Cade turned on his heel and went to the wall, snatching down one of the ornamental swords he had been given for his birthday but never used. He threw it to Wolf, who caught it in one hand, the sudden weight of it bringing him down a few inches. It devastated Cade to see how tired his friend was, how broken. "I can't do it, Wolf; I'm not as fast as you, I'm not as good of a fighter, he'd kill me in a second and it would all be over. Do you understand?"

Wolf looked up, using all of his might to straighten his back. "Yes, my Lord." His hand tightened resolutely around the hilt of the sword. He tried to stifle his heavy breathing, but Cade could see the way his nostrils were flaring, the way his chest was still heaving.

"Wolf," Cade said, and then stopped, not able to think of anything else to say. Wolf smiled slowly, then was gone.

Cade retreated back to his desk and sat down, quickly losing himself in thought. He debated whether to run for it, to try and make an escape. For a few minutes, he nearly decided to do just that. *No,* he thought finally. *Stay calm. Keep your head. You've gotten yourself out of tight situations before. Wolf will handle it.*

Cade waited.

Wolf took a deep breath, gathering as much strength as he could muster, and leaped forward into a long loping run. He tore through the hallways, heading straight to the royal apartments where he was sure that Luther would have gone. Once there, he slipped inside the main door, crouching low. He could be too late; he knew that well. But something wouldn't let him just give up. Not only was his own life on the line, but he shuddered to think of the things Cira would do to Cade if she ever found out what he had been up to.

There was a tiny shuffle behind him. Wolf whipped around but saw nothing. He advanced forward cautiously. The rooms were dark and quiet and mostly empty, as Cira's things had already been sent on their way to her new home at Faridor. The room was decorated mostly in shades of royal purple, a spreading plume of carved white stone egrets winging their way along the walls and up across the vault of the ceiling. The remaining wall hangings had a disconcerting way of rustling in the wind blowing in from the open windows. Every time they did, Wolf felt a huge surge of adrenaline flush through his system, thinking that Luther was lurking behind one of them. He moved forward as fast as he dared. He harbored only one small piece of hope: the royal apartments were vast, spanning two floors and one entire wing of the palace. It would take Luther a good while to go through them and get to Cira. There could still be time.

Wolf advanced through a small corridor, peering into the rooms as he went by. His feet were gradually going numb, and his legs felt like lead. It was hard for him to keep his head from rolling forward on his neck. He wanted to sleep so badly.

A new noise, louder, ahead of him. Footsteps. Wolf's eyes dilated, and he honed all his senses forward, his shoulders loosening as he brought his sword up in front of his eyes. A figure entered the hallway, silhouetted against the open windows at the other end.

"My Lady?" it said hesitantly. It was a familiar voice. The shadow stopped still as Wolf crept closer.

"Not exactly," Wolf snarled, his teeth bared. His system was surging and pulsating with a new energy, a desperate desire to rip and to kill. Luther paused only a moment longer, then his sword was in his hand and he was running forward to meet Wolf's charge in the middle of the hallway. They clashed together with a brash, clanging sound of metal, the force of which sent a spray of sparks from the blades. Wolf was thrown back against the opposite wall with another surge from Luther, his arms turning weakly to jelly before he gritted his teeth and brought his sword up just in time to block another attack. He kicked as high as he could and caught Luther on the head, sending him to one side, buying Wolf enough time to take in a desperately needed gasp of air. Luther recovered himself and swung forward, Wolf parrying. They settled themselves into a vicious pattern of blocks and swings, accompanied by a hailing storm of punches and kicks over or around the blades. This was no time for flashy swordsmanship, and both of them knew it. It was a death match.

At first neither could gain the upper hand, for Wolf had studied under Luther for a long time and was well acquainted with his fighting techniques; he had even absorbed some of them into his own style. So when Luther swung at him, Wolf was already waiting with a block for it. Luther grew more and more frustrated, for he knew full well how exhausted Wolf must have been, but Wolf refused to retreat. His pupil pushed him forward farther and farther, out of the main room into the hallway. Here, they were given more space to fully swing at one another, which they did with a fresh frenzy. Wolf lunged forward, frantically stabbing at Luther, who blocked him and, with a show of immense speed, whipped around and bashed Wolf across the head with the back of his sword. Wolf let out a low grunt and fell backwards, hand flying immediately to his head, feeling a fresh torrent of warm blood flow from between his fingers. Luther was on him, his sword sweeping down, the air hissing as it was cut by the blade's razor-sharp edge. Wolf rolled from beneath him, his eye completely useless due to the blood pooling over it, sticking his eyelashes shut. With the fresh loss of depth perception, he could no longer spring forward and attack. He had to keep on the defensive, waiting for his opportunity to strike.

Luther swept a blow at him and Wolf dodged to one side, but Luther was waiting for this and kicked him square in the chest, knocking his wind out and throwing him against the back wall. Wolf was panting with his mouth open, but he blocked two more blows and realized he wasn't going to be alive much longer. Luther sensed his apprentice's imminent defeat and nearly let a smile escape his lips, sweat pouring down the sides of his forehead. One more blow sent Wolf's sword spinning out of his hand and clattering onto the floor. Wolf closed his eyes.

Luther reached back and swung, intending to take Wolf's head. At the last minute, Wolf tilted his head to one side, and the sword shaved through a few of Wolf's gray and blond hairs. He darted forward while Luther's arm was still completing the arc and lashed out, grabbing Luther's wrist and pulling it towards him. He thrust his arm up, and his other elbow went up hard and fast on the underside of Luther's arm, throwing it out of its socket. Still holding his teacher's wrist, he moved his hand up at the joint, breaking the arm at its elbow. Luther let out a cry of sudden and unexpected anguish, but before he could move any farther, Wolf had reached down, scooped up the sword, and sunk it into Luther's chest. He wrenched it to one side, and Luther crumbled off the end of the blade and sank to the ground, motionless.

Wolf collapsed beside him, uncertain of whether or not he was actually dead, too. His mouth was hanging open, and his muscles were spasming slightly as he tried desperately to slow his breathing down to a normal level. His eye was stuck completely shut, and his fingers had seized closed around the hilt of the sword. He stared at his hand and willed it to open, which it did, shaking, and he let it drop down beside him. Something told him that he had to keep moving, had to get out of Cira's rooms, had to get back to Cade to tell him that it was all right, that everything had been taken care of, that he didn't have to worry any longer about Cira, she would never find out.

"Well, well," a silky voice came from behind him. "What have you naughty fellows been up to?"

Wolf didn't even try to turn around and look up. There was a waft of fresh perfume through the bleary haze of blood and metal, and he dimly saw the edge of a soft silk gown swishing on the other side of Luther's motionless body. *Cira!* He screamed inwardly. *She's here, go, you've got to run! Warn Cade!* Wolf struggled to lean up on his elbows, but there was a laugh, and Cira's foot came forward, pushing him gently on the shoulder. Wolf went down like she had hit him with a sledgehammer.

"Excellent," she purred. "Guards, why don't two of you stay here? The rest of you, go and arrest my baby cousin Cade, will you?" There was the sound of footsteps, hollow through the floor to Wolf's throbbing ears, then the gentle touch of someone taking his shoulder and pulling him over so he was lying on his back. Through the mist, he saw Cira's hateful face, smiling gently at him as though she were actually an angel of love and mercy. Wolf wanted to spit at her but couldn't muster the energy. She reached forward and caressed the side of his face.

"Weryn...or Wolf, is it? I'll call you Wolf; it'll make everything far less formal. Wolf, I'm sorry it had to come to this, I really am. You and Cade both showed so much promise early on. If it wasn't for his nasty habit of constantly trying to work against me, I'm sure you and I would have gotten along quite well. All this, and for what? An impish brat who's too much of a coward to fight his battles for himself? No, it's you who's got to go out and do all of this while he sits in his room reading his damned books."

Wolf coughed, salty, felt it dribble down the side of his mouth. Cira made a *tsking* sound in the back of her throat and smiled cheerily. "Now, now, Wolf, don't die on me. I'm not quite finished with you yet. And I think I want you to stay alive for quite some time." There was a beat as Cira allowed him to digest the implications of her words. Then she continued: "I have a question for you. What is it about my cousins that makes you poor, weak-minded individuals so fanatically loyal to them?" She shook her head. "I just can't fathom it."

She was foggy in Wolf's field of vision, fading in and out, and even if he had understood most of what she said, he didn't have enough energy left to respond. She tilted her head to one side, feigning concern. She laid him back down so that he was left staring at the ceiling. Wolf faded out for a while then, giving in to the pull of the darkness surrounding him. But he was brought back when Cira said loudly, "Ah, you have brought him?"

Not Cade, they can't take him, Wolf thought, his eye opening, trying to refocus. *He's the only one who can break Cira. The only one who can get us out of this.*

"Good," Cira said, satisfied. "Take Wolf, drag him if you have to. Take them both to the dungeons."

Wolf was barely conscious of arms lifting him up off of the ground and pulling him out into the hallway.

Cade was already there, flanked by a massive amount of guards. At the sight of his bodyguard, Cade's head snapped up. "Wolf!" he yelled, and Cira strode towards him, a satisfied smirk on her face. "Is he alive?" Cade demanded.

"Doesn't look it, does he? Thanks to you," Cira smiled pleasantly. "He's alive. I can't tell you for how long after this, however. Life in the dungeons is rather difficult, and what I think he needs now is some serious medical attention. Too bad." She frowned prettily.

"I can easily understand why you hate me," Cade returned as calmly as he could while Cira waited for his reply, her back turned to his bleeding, slumped friend. *I shouldn't have sent him*, he thought angrily. *I should have just given up and accepted defeat. This wasn't worth it.* His spine stiffened in anger. He met her eyes squarely. "I'll sit on the throne long after you're dead, Cira."

Cira slapped him so hard across the face that he reeled back and fell to the ground. A moment later, he was pulled off the floor and hauled through the hallway towards the dungeons. People standing on either side parted for them, staring and whispering as they recognized Cade and his half-dead bodyguard. Dazed and disoriented, Cade thought for an instant that he glimpsed Nadia, her face ashen, peeking out at him from a crowded corner—but then she was gone, and Cade was sure he had imagined her. Cira strode resolutely at the head of the grim parade, her gown flipping back as she walked, hair glinting in the sun, face set in a firm, menacing expression.

At the entrance to the dungeons, she halted as Cade and Wolf were dragged up to face her. Cade kept stealing sidelong glances at his friend. *Wake up, please*, he pleaded inwardly. *Please, I beg you, Wolf, don't go.*

"Before I bid you my farewell, Cade, I feel I owe you a bit of an explanation," Cira smiled at him, tipping his chin up delicately with the ends of her fingers. "You see, I'm not going to kill you. I'm going to throw you in this dungeon for the rest of your miserable life. As you rot there, you shall serve as a constant reminder to the people of this palace what happens when a few misguided individuals attempt to betray me. Furthermore, you will never know whether or not your friend Wolf here has actually survived. If he has, it is no thanks to you, and if he hasn't, then you only have yourself to blame. You'll rot, and I hope you remember every day for the rest of your life that you thought you could outwit me, outthink me. Never. You could never have achieved it. You'll be in there for so long that it will be years after your death that anyone even thinks to look in on your remains. Have a nice life, Cade."

She didn't motion him away immediately, but turned instead to look at Wolf. He was, by this point, completely unconscious, held up only by the support of the guards flanking him. His head hung sadly down on his neck, his hair matted to his forehead with a mixture of dried blood and sweat. The cuts he had sustained while Luther was torturing him for information were red around the edges, inflamed, and irritated. Cade tried not to look anymore. Perhaps it would be better if Cira just killed him, just got it over with. He couldn't stand to see

Wolf suffering any longer.

"You, however," Cira purred to his limp body, though Wolf couldn't hear her. "I have special plans for you. I have a sneaking suspicion that it was you who has been scurrying about this palace, gathering up information, spying, and telling Cade everything he needs to know to support his pathetic attempt for my crown. That tongue of yours has been wagging and wagging and wagging, and you've been spilling secrets that were no business of yours." Cira leaned back, a pleasant expression alighting on her delicate face. "See to it," she said in measured tones, "that he never speaks another word ever again."

"Wolf!" Cade screamed and jumped forward, his arms straining against those that held him fast. He was knocked back, and Wolf was dragged off down the darkened tunnel towards his cell. Cade recovered and lunged again and again, pulling as hard as his small frame would allow him. Cira watched Cade's reaction with a look of enjoyment, then she gradually grew tired of his struggling and moved her hand. Cade was knocked on the side of the head and he reeled, stunned, no longer struggling.

"That's better," Cira said appreciatively. "Well, Cade, off goes your friend. All alone now. Your brother abandoned you. Your cousin abandoned you. Ilaina is dead. Your scheming has destroyed your conspirator here. I think you need some time alone to think about what you've done."

She swept her hand to the side, and the guards jerked Cade's arms forward slightly so that his toes dragged for a few inches before he stumbled into step alongside them. He peered down the tunnel for a glimpse of Wolf, but it was as if the black void had swallowed him whole. There wasn't a sound, not a glance. They hit the top of a flight of stairs, and then the guards pulled him down, down, down, into the farthest pit of the dungeons, where there was no hope of ever seeing the sun again. The staircase spiraled around, and the rock walls of the inner cliff were lit by torches so that the guards wouldn't lose their step. Cade gave up momentarily and let himself be dragged along, facing the boredom, facing the horror, facing the fact that Wolf's blood was on his hands.

All at once, there was a horrible cry from the tunnel up ahead. Cade's eyes snapped open and his feet braced against the pull of the guards. "Wolf!" he yelled. "Wolf!" The screaming continued for another fifteen seconds or so, then fell horribly silent, the rushing of stale air replacing the screams with an eerie stillness. "Wolf!" Cade was half-sobbing now. He had lost his poise, his finesse. He was a sixteen-year-old boy begging for forgiveness. "Wolf! I'm sorry! I'm sorry!" He yelled as loud as he could, in case Wolf could hear him. "I'm so sorry!"

"Here," the turnkey motioned, and the small party stopped in front of a forbidding stone door. Cade didn't even register it; he was pulling and fighting against the guards, trying to get away, to wrench himself free. The guard yanked back on the thick handle of the door, the stones grating on one another as they gaped apart.

"I'm sorry!" Cade screamed, and the guards flung him inside. He stopped still and turned around as they began to close the door behind him, suddenly silent, watching them with wide gray eyes. The tiny sliver of light grew smaller and smaller until the stone door closed with a *whooshing* sound, and Cade V was sealed off in his stone tomb.

CHAPTER ONE

TWO FALLS, THREE AND A HALF YEARS LATER

"Is everything all right?" Doyle called down in a hushed whisper. The torch in his hand flickered and cast blue shadows against the planes of his weathered old face. Two reflections of the torch glinted in each lens of his spectacles. "Do you have enough light down there?"

"Yes, there's enough," Errol replied. "Quite enough, thank you."

"I'm going to close up until the morning; it's getting late," Doyle told her. "I'll be back with fresh food and water tomorrow."

"Thank you again," Errol said gratefully. "Good night."

With some grunting and a fair amount of exertion, Doyle stood back and pulled the slab of stone over the opening of the cellar, closing Errol safely in the belly of what was now the skeleton of the former Two Falls library. There were little chunks missing here and there in the upper walls of the cellar, but this was good for ventilation and so that Errol could hear if any guards approached. Such a disturbance was rather unlikely. The library was now a lifeless hulk; Lady Cira's troops had swept through it over two years ago, burning whatever books they deemed unworthy (most, as it turned out), leaving the shell of the building behind to occasionally house Cira's forces before more ample barracks could be built. The building was all but abandoned now, just one of the many ghosts residing in Two Falls.

The bonfires they had made from the books...Errol could still remember the thick, sticky smell of smoke wafting through the rafters of the house where she had stayed...what was it? Four, no, three families ago. It was the small stone house with thatching and wooden trim. She had been lodged in a tiny crawl space in the attic, and had just enough room to peek out between the rafters to the world outside. She remembered that smell and the crackle of flame, the way the ash permeated every possible crevice, settling all over her and her belongings until it looked as though she were a creature made entirely of dust. The blanket of smoke laying thick and heavy over the city as the fires blazed through the days and nights in the central marketplace.

Errol had heard that some of the librarians had desperately tried to save a few precious volumes from the fires, risking their lives by breaking into the forbidden building or by bribing the guards and buying the books away. But what they had saved was nothing compared to what had been lost. Entire lives, entire histories were now forgotten, nothing but pieces of dust left to crumble against the winter wind. She didn't like to think of it.

Errol paced around the cellar a few times, then finally sat in a corner and stretched out her twelve long fingers. All in all, it was much like every other hiding place she had lived in for the past two years: small, cramped, dark, bare. And the cold—that omnipresent cold, the product of four walls constructed of lifeless, joyless stone. Even the past summers had seemed cold to her. She took a few deep breaths and forced herself to think positively, to not let her heart become caged. She reminded herself once again that she was not a prisoner, that this was better than rotting away in the dungeons of Faridor, but in the darkest times she honestly couldn't see a difference between that existence and this. Occasionally, when things became extremely grim, she began to wonder whether or not death was such a bad option, either. In the beginning, these thoughts were few and far between, but now... two years in and with no end in sight, they were coming faster, lasting longer. Bouts of depression without comfort, with only the knowledge that she was alive. Being alive still had to mean *something*.

Freedom was nothing but a faint memory. It was as if the past two years had all but erased the happiness of her previous thirty-seven. She wondered again what had become of her mother and her uncle, whether they had been luckier than her and had managed to escape. She hoped so. Occasionally, she liked to think of them, free, perhaps back in the forest with their relatives. She knew for a fact that Cira had not managed to breach the forest yet. She was glad of it. She could daydream about the freedom of her loved ones without her thoughts being tainted by Cira Kagai.

She stared around at the little room once more, shaking herself from her dark thoughts. She had been surprised to hear that this particular place had never before been used to hide an Ashan; in their brief introductory meeting, Doyle had told her that he had only just recently stumbled upon it. Doyle had been one of those displaced librarians, luckily not an Ashan. He had managed to stay alive and, now that the library was abandoned, was sneaking in nightly and sifting through the remains, trying to salvage any pages or texts that had miraculously escaped the purge. Doyle told her that had the library not been burned, the cellar would perhaps never have been found, but he had come across it after inspecting beneath the rubble of some shelves. The long blank slab had seemed odd to him, so he had tried to move it and inadvertently found the room.

It had been blind luck that Errol had encountered Doyle at all; the events of the past few days had happened so quickly that she scarcely could keep track of them. The Kagaian guards had searched Errol's previous home three times, scaring her latest family half to death before they reluctantly concluded that Errol could no longer stay. It was becoming too dangerous. Errol had nearly resigned herself to being turned out on the street and having to face the guards. The day before she was to leave, Doyle had dropped by the house for a visit with the family, heard of Errol's plight, and offered to hide her in their stead.

Now, here she was, deep in a hidden vault, biding her time while awaiting an unknown future. She shivered and decided that it was safe enough to light the small candle on the table beside her. The golden light gave her a certain amount of comfort, and she stared into the flame as it danced back and forth on the wick. If only there was some way she could get some word, some news from the resistance. Her former host family had told her what they could. There were tales of Ashans being rescued and smuggled out of Two Falls that gave her some small semblance of hope, but here in the cold stone depths of the library, such an outcome seemed highly unlikely. She had heard of demonstrations and sabotage, of spies and secret pamphlets, but her host family, already paranoid that they were being watched, avoided those kinds of things like the scourge and, therefore, had very little to tell.

And what of the Strikers? She leaned back against the wall. It seemed to her that they were everywhere, and they were nowhere all at once. People would whisper of them and then fall silent as soon as a Kagaian guard came into view. There were rumors, rumors that the resistance in Two Falls was led by the Strikers, though others said that they still lived somewhere in the mountains, far away from the city. Perhaps it was all just hearsay, just rumors that Ashans were indeed being covertly shuttled out of the massive fortified walls of Two Falls. But if it were true... Errol could barely comprehend the thought. To be able to walk freely, to see the sunshine and feel the air on the back of her neck. To never, ever, have to be caged in by four stone walls ever again. Errol swore to herself that if she ever got free, she would live in a tent high on the side of a hill, where the wind could blow through her dwelling, where there was always sunshine and the sound of trees and grass whispering. She wouldn't even mind if the snow blew in and piled up on top of her like a blanket. She would gladly take anything besides stone.

She sighed and forced a rueful smile, glancing around her dark, dank surroundings. Then she stood, feeling slightly restless, running thin hands through her short-cropped dark brown hair, down the sides of her nearly skeletal face. A small lump of bread and a flask of water lay on the table, but she ignored them. By this point, she was used to going for long periods of time on very little food and had grown into the habit of automatically rationing what was given her. It wouldn't be time to eat again for a number of hours. She could wait.

She began to walk in tiny circles around the small cellar, hopping every now and again to get the circulation moving through her legs. Years in small, enclosed spaces had taught her that movement was vital for survival. If she remained still, her body would forget how to move, and if an emergency arose she would be completely useless. She ran from one corner to the next, leaping up and landing softly on her toes so as not to make more than a whisper of noise. She was all too aware of the thick knots of Kagaian guards that patrolled the streets at night, keenly attuned to the slightest unusual sound of whispering or of movement.

It was when she turned around again to make another lap that she noticed something unusual. It was small, so small that if the light hadn't flickered just so at the right moment, she would have missed it altogether. She knelt down and crept forward, peering closely down into the corner of the cellar. She reached over and pulled the candle down to her level, throwing the orange light softly over the stone. And there—on the rock farthest in the corner, nestled snugly against the seam of the wall, was a tiny engraving. It was a minuscule star.

Errol cocked her head to one side and sat back, considering. Like many of the older buildings in the city, the library *had* been commissioned by Morthenstar, so perhaps there was nothing unusual about finding her emblem all over it. But here? In a tiny hidden cellar? Perhaps there was something more. Keenly, her excitement mounting, Errol leaned forward and began inspecting the corners of the stone. A chip was missing in one corner, perhaps through age—but no, Errol's finger fell snugly into the groove as if it had been made especially for her, giving her just enough friction to edge the stone ever so slightly forward. As soon as a tiny thread of stone stuck out from the wall, she attacked it with all the grasping might of her twelve spindly fingers, inching the stone forward to reveal a gaping hole in the wall behind it. A hiding place that had remained closed up for centuries.

Errol plopped down, her heart racing and her mind spinning. She tried to shine some light in the hole, but it was only big enough for her hand to slip in, and the ominous darkness of the space beyond chilled her slightly. There was no telling what was waiting within. She half expected some horrible creature to rush out of the wall and start to gnaw on her.

Eventually, however, curiosity overcame her. There was no way she was going to be able to sit in the cellar with the hole open and unexplored. She shut her eyes and slipped her hand into the tiny opening, bracing for the sharp teeth and acid drool that she was sure would meet her. But there was nothing—nothing except the smooth edge of a nearly flat wooden box. Errol blinked in surprise as she felt around and closed her fingers around the side, edging it out of the hole and scanning the surface. It was wood all right, carved with the same familiar image of Morthenstar's star. She smoothed her thumb over the dusty surface, revealing a clean swipe of the reddish polished sheen beneath. There was a clasp on one side of the box, and she gingerly undid it. To her surprise, the wooden slab opened like a book. Within the "pages" were two sheets of parchment. Errol's eyes widened in surprise, and she took the paper between her thumb and forefinger. She had to handle it very delicately, for it was hard and brittle, like old skin, and she was sure that it would crack and crumble if handled too roughly. She eagerly put her candle beside the sheet, anxious to read what it said.

Errol had rather foolishly been expecting it to be written in the modern Common tongue, so she was sorely disappointed. She had never seen anything like the strange markings that stared back at her from the sheet, less like letters and more like shapes with odd squiggles coming off of them. She knew very little about such things, but there was no doubt that this piece of paper was very old and very valuable for it to have been secreted away so thoroughly. She softly closed the wooden slab that protected the two papers and slid it carefully under her table. She had become, by this point, an extremely patient individual, having spent the past years waiting indefinitely. However, for the first time in months or perhaps years, excitement and impatience welled up like a fire in her chest. It would be a long night and day before Doyle returned.

A seemingly interminable span of time elapsed before the small air vents betrayed the small sound of shuffling feet approaching, followed by the grating of stone on stone as the slab was moved aside. A minuscule crack of blue evening light shone at the top of the stone steps of the cellar. Errol, who had alternated between pacing restlessly, sitting restlessly, and twiddling her thumbs restlessly, darted to her feet and practically dashed up the steps to intercept Doyle, who was nearly bowled over by her unexpected enthusiasm.

"I have something for you!" she exclaimed before Doyle could even summon a salutary pleasantry. In the space of a minute, she had described her discovery and breathlessly withdrew the wooden slat. Doyle absorbed the information with a good deal more stoicism than Errol and closely inspected the object while Errol watched with bated breath. Doyle gently sheafed through the two papers, squinting at them as if he were trying to make them out, then replaced them and slowly closed the wooden slab, doing the clasp back up with infuriating calm.

"It seems to me," Doyle said slowly, "that this is one of Morthenstar's papers. We've got to get it to Tarr or Athela. It's our duty."

"The Strikers?" Errol asked eagerly. She felt more alive than she had for six months or more. There was a flush in her cheeks and a bright light in her eyes. "How are we going to get it to them? Do you know them?" *How I wish I could go with you to find them*, she thought wistfully.

"Well, no," Doyle admitted slowly, and Errol could almost see the wheels turning in his brain. "I don't know them personally. But there are ways...there must be ways of getting to them."

Errol fidgeted in her seat while Doyle pondered for a few minutes. Finally, just when the Ashan thought she could take it no longer, Doyle stirred and a slow smile crept across his face. "There's a place in the upper arts districts," he began, "some sort of nightclub or tavern or something. I've never been there, but from what I hear, it's a kind of outpost for the resistance members. The owner bribes some of the Kagaian guards so that he can stay open. And none of it is overt, you understand. Just if forged travel permits...*happen* to exchange hands under a table, the establishment sort of looks the other way. I was planning on inquiring there to see if someone could get you out of the city."

"Get me out?" Errol said eagerly, surprised that Doyle had been making these sorts of inquiries. "You really think someone will help us?"

"I don't know," Doyle admitted. "But it's our best shot."

Abruptly, both of them froze, and Errol instinctively blew out the candle beside them, casting them into darkness. Through the small vents and the cracked-open stone door came the distinct sound of footsteps echoing through the ruined library, growing louder and louder. There were boots heavy with spurs, the swishing of cloaks, and the clinking of metal upon metal.

"I must have been seen when I came in," Doyle muttered angrily.

"They must have seen me."

"Should we just wait here?" Errol whispered. Her breath was coming quicker now.

"What if they saw the candle?" Doyle returned. "Wait...wait just a moment. If they go the other way, they won't see us."

But the boots grew louder, and Errol could hear talking, many different voices, much too many for a weak Ashan and an old, unarmed man to take on by themselves. Through the vents, she saw beams of lamplight shifting from side to side, searching, growing brighter. Errol shrunk back from the wall as if there was somewhere else to hide. Her entire body was tensed up, poised and ready to spring into some sort of action. She had been in houses that had been searched before, but for some reason, the wooden book and the precious papers she had found made the situation all the more dire. Errol had her hand clapped over her own mouth to prevent the sound of her breathing from emanating up onto the floor above. The boots continued to clunk along, their sound magnified a hundred times in the gaping hollow of the library.

"If they come any closer, they'll find us; they're bound to see the cellar opening," Doyle muttered.

Errol remained silent. If they were caught, Doyle had no greater chance of survival than she did. She felt Doyle pressing the wooden slab against her chest, and she clutched at it desperately. The boots were so close now. There was no way either of them could make it.

"Take this," Doyle said. "We must get it to the Strikers at all costs, do you understand? I'm not fast enough."

Errol nodded and realized that Doyle couldn't see the gesture in the darkness of the cellar.

"The club is in the arts district. It's called Orion," Doyle muttered. "Now, when you see a chance, run as fast as you can. Can you do that?"

Errol's heart was pounding hard, but she again nodded, her fingers holding on to the wooden slab for all it was worth. "I'm ready," she whispered. Then she added, "Thank you."

Doyle broke away and clambered headlong up the cellar steps and, with a great heave, threw open the stone on the top of the cellar. A yell went up from the guards, and before she could control what she was doing, Errol was right behind him. She shut her eyes, threw herself out of the cellar, and barreled toward the entrance of the library.

"Another one!" an angry voice shouted. "They're getting away!"

There was the sound of an arrow screaming from a bow and a horrific cry went up, reverberating through the enormous shell of the library. Errol wanted to block the prolonged sound of Doyle's death from her ears but tucked her head and ran on, only too conscious of the soldiers behind her and more arrows screeching through the air beside her head, whistling and plinking off the stone walls. But although the guards were fitter and better fed than Errol, they also were carrying a lot of gear, and Errol had only a few rags on her back and overwhelming fear to add lightness to her feet.

Outside, the cold night air hit her like an abrupt slap in the face, and Errol nearly stopped and shut her eyes to savor the harsh, blissful sensation. But no—first, she must find shelter, find some way to lose the guards behind her. She darted to the right around the corner of the library and saw a small pile of debris lying against the side of the building: crates, barrels, and rags of clothing all in a pile. She slipped around behind the pile and tucked herself into a small ball, sliding her thin body easily into one of the crates, concealing herself from her pursuers. To a passerby, there would be no way a six-foot tall Ashan could fit into one of the small crates, but Errol was, by that point, all angles and thin limbs; though it was snug, she was effectively hidden. To her weak relief, the plodding of heavy boots and the yelling of the guards crashed past her and up the street. She had lost them, for now.

Gingerly, she unfolded her legs and tried to figure out how she would get up to the arts district to deliver the papers. *What was the name?* she thought frantically, then remembered: Orion. In an instant, Doyle's kind, elderly face flashed in front of her eyes, but she shook him away. Like so many others Errol had known, Doyle was now gone and she had to accept it. Doyle had died so that Errol might escape, and Errol was damned if she was going to let that sacrifice be in vain. Now, how to get to the district? She had to keep to the sides of the buildings, lose herself in shadows if at all possible...it would be easier if she had a cloak. She glanced around and saw a piece of discarded fabric in the pile of rubble. She threw it over her head and tucked the ends over her shoulders so that she could conceal her hands and the wooden

52

book under a swath of fabric. In her loose, tattered clothes, she would undoubtedly look like a beggar, but hardly anyone would bother to pay her any mind. She still remembered the way from the library to the arts district, and prayed that the city hadn't changed too much in her years of unofficial incarceration.

As luck would have it, it wasn't past curfew yet, so there was still a healthy gathering of vendors and shoppers in the market squares, though the once vibrant town had all the joyful atmosphere of a funeral. Exchanges were made in grim mutters; money changed hands without a word, and goods were covered up by cloaks and shoved into the bottoms of baskets so that guards wouldn't feel the need to come over and ask about rationing. Food was scarce these days. Two hideouts ago, she remembered the family talking about Cira incorporating outlying villages into the framework of Two Falls, building the city outward, drawing people in like a spider with her web. As the city had grown, farms had slowed production and food had become scarcer.

She crossed the bridge, keeping her head down and stooping to conceal her Ashan height, bending over and coughing when a troop of Kagaian guards marched resolutely past her. She stared over the side of a bridge at the great river that split the center of Two Falls. *How odd*, she thought, *that it should still be flowing along as if nothing had ever happened.* The sound of the guards clanked away behind her. She peered over her shoulder after the guards and continued hurriedly on her way. She had the strangest sensation of an hourglass with the sand running out. She didn't have much time. She had to find the club soon.

Once in the arts district, she debated whether or not to ask someone the location of the club but figured that it would be too suspicious. She didn't know exactly whom she could trust. Instead, she went methodically up and down each street, turning abruptly down back alleys whenever she saw guards, gravitating towards small groups when she saw them, trying to look nonchalant, while in reality she was checking behind herself, her eyes spinning over the streets and the faces surrounding her. But time continued ticking, and she knew that soon it would be the curfew, and everyone had to be indoors unless they had papers that gave them express permission to be out after hours. And these Errol certainly did not have.

She wandered up one street and down another. In her previous life, the one that seemed so hazy nowadays, she had been a tailor, and as such, she had worked down in the market district, but she had had a few bohemian friends who were musicians and who frequently invited her up to their soirées in the arts district. She had once known the place well; now, it was almost unrecognizable. Here and there was the burnt-out shell of a house, the edges of the windows and doors blistered black, shutters swinging off of broken hinges. Doors were boarded up and nailed, and there were a few clubs that Errol distinctly remembered visiting that were now empty and looked almost haunted, their bright, cheery signs now faded and worn, swinging listlessly in the cold wind. She involuntarily quivered and pulled the ragged cloak closer around her shoulders. She wondered where all the people had gone, all the dancers and musicians and painters. Had they fled? Had they all been killed? Or were they, like her, merely biding their time until there was some sort of end to it all?

She wandered from one end of the district to what she supposed was the other, and there was nothing, no signs to indicate where she should go. People were growing scarcer and scarcer, and she began to feel the rise of dread in her throat. Then, finally, she turned the corner of a street (though she was sure that she had been down this one already), and she saw it—a blue sign unlike the others, freshly painted, with a star and the name ORION printed on it. The windows glowed gold, and Errol could hear the sound of music and chatter emanating from them all the way from where she stood. It was glorious, like the breath of life. Errol stood there basking in its light and absorbing its radiance for a few moments before her legs propelled her forward.

"Hey!" came a voice behind her, imperious.

No, Errol thought wildly, *not now, I'm so close, please...*She walked faster, trying to pretend as if she hadn't heard.

"Halt!" yelled the voice again. This time, it was a threat.

There was nothing for it. Errol didn't even bother looking over her shoulder. She broke out into a full run and hurtled as fast as she could toward Orion's front door. There would be seconds, only seconds, between her and the guard. She prayed that the door would be unlocked.

The latch jumped smoothly in her hand, and she flung herself through the doorway. Once inside, she nearly collided directly with a middle-aged man who was standing in front of a pair of curtains that sealed the small entryway off from the rest of the club. The polite, cheerful clinking of silverware from beyond seemed so foreign, so alien to Errol in her state of terror. The man was well-dressed and polished, with dark hair and plunging eyebrows, clearly some sort of bouncer or doorkeeper. Errol was panting, groping painfully for the words. But what could she say? How could she explain? Would this man throw her right back outside to the guards?

"Ashan?" the man inquired, and to Errol's immense shock, he spoke in the Ashan language. "Are you being pursued?"

"I am," Errol panted, nodding, gripping the precious wooden book tighter in her thin hands, hiding it beneath her cloak. "Please, please help me. There is not much time. I have something—"

"Here," the man said curtly and stepped to the side. He pushed one of the walls, and to Errol's surprise, a hidden door swung around as if on a dowel through the center. "Hide in there. I will take care of things."

Errol wanted to thank him and ask him how he knew the Ashan language, but darted into the hiding space and felt the door swing back around behind her. She instinctively threw herself against the farthest wall and cowered, waiting for the end to come. No sooner had the false door clicked shut than Errol heard a commotion at the club's front entrance. She bit her lip to stop herself from crying out; the sound was so close. But nothing happened, no yell of discovery, and the trick door remained firmly closed. After a few moments, Errol tentatively stepped forward and pressed her ear to listen to what was said, only too conscious that the guard was less than three feet away from her.

The guard stalked around the entryway, looking around wildly. His eyes settled upon the bouncer, who was watching him levelly from his post beside the door. The guard strode briskly over and grabbed him roughly by the collar. "You! The Ashan! An Ashan came in here! Where did she go?"

The man gently reached up and firmly removed the guard's hand from the lapel of his coat. He took a deliberate moment to smooth out his appearance before he bothered to make his reply. "What Ashan?" he asked curiously. "I'm sure I haven't seen an Ashan."

Two other guards had come up and were now standing beside their comrade. "I saw her come in here," the first guard snarled. "You two, go search inside and ask the patrons whether or not they have seen anything." The two standing behind him brushed past the bouncer and through the heavy curtains to the room inside.

Listening from within the confines of the closet, Errol turned and saw that on one side of the wall there was a tiny knothole, just wide enough for her to peep through. She placed her eye against it and followed the guards' progress inside the club. At each table, they stopped and checked the customers' papers. The people responded calmly, without fear. Clearly, they were used to this sort of thing. At every table, the guards asked a question and were rewarded with a firm shake of the head. Errol watched them for a time as they grew increasingly frustrated, and couldn't help but smile to herself. She returned her ear to the other wall to hear what was transpiring between the bouncer and the guard.

"What's your name?" the guard demanded.

"Khan," came the unruffled reply. "What's yours?"

"None of your business," the guard snapped. "I'll have you arrested for this."

"I'm quite sure you won't," Khan said evenly, though there wasn't any acidity in his voice meant to provoke the guard. "You'll find it's essentially a big waste of your time. You see, I am rather good friends with your commander, and if he finds that you've arrested me, then I'm afraid you'll lose your job. And don't think about trying to appeal to anyone higher up," Khan said quickly. Errol could almost imagine the guard's mouth opening in protest. "No one will listen, and you know it. They'll have you thrown out. Besides," he maintained, "what on earth is there for you to get upset about? Nothing has happened. Nothing at all. There was no Ashan, as I'm sure your troops will report."

As if on cue, the two guards brushed back in, and Errol could feel the glares being sent Khan's way. "Nothing," one guard said regretfully, shrugging her shoulders. "No one has seen anything. It's improbable that he could have bribed the whole place."

"Shut up," the first guard snapped and wheeled around to bear down once again on Khan, who was watching nonchalantly from his post. The guard shoved a finger up in Khan's face, clearly trying to get a rise out of him so that he could arrest him for causing a fight. "I'm still going to recommend that you be detained and investigated."

"You do that," Khan agreed placidly, not rewarding the guard with any semblance of anger or violence. Instead, he stepped forward and began ushering them genially towards the front door. "Enjoy the paper-work. Goodnight!"

There was a final slam of the front door and Errol let her breath out in a long, relieved *whoosh*. She waited patiently for Khan to give her the safe signal, running and tapping her fingers along the engraved wood of the slab. She thought again of Doyle, but this time, it wasn't with sadness or anger but with vindication. *I did it*, she thought. *I made it.* Though she had only exchanged a few words with Khan, she nevertheless felt as though she were among allies.

There was a soft tap on the door and Errol stood back as Khan swiveled the wall around to peer inside. "Hello," he said cheerily in Ashan as if nothing of much import had happened. "That was a close one, was it not?"

"Yes," Errol agreed, feeling somewhat overwhelmed. "How do you—"

"Do you speak Common?" he asked, and when Errol nodded, he switched languages. "Good. I can't talk long because you never know when people are going to come tromping in or out of the club. But I want you to know that for now, at least, you are safe. I'm going to have to wait until closing time to let you out of here and take you up to our private room, where we can decide what's to be done with you. But it's really all right, because that will give me time to alert some people who can help you. Does that sound like a good plan?"

"I need to speak with the Strikers," Errol told him suddenly and nearly smiled at how farfetched the words sounded. One might just as well ask to speak with a king or queen. "I have something important to give them...I found it...here," she said and began to withdraw the tablet.

"Wait," Khan hissed, waving her back. He tilted his head out of the room and listened for a moment. Someone was coming. "From what I know, the Strikers aren't in Two Falls at the moment, but I have someone who is just as good, very close to them. I'll get a hold of him; he's due to come in later. Will you be all right waiting in here? Do you need a light? Food? Reading material?"

"No," Errol said gratefully. "Perhaps some food later. I'll be fine for now."

"Good," Khan said and quickly stepped back, swinging the trick door closed. A moment later, Errol heard rustling and voices and settled herself back down against the wall. It was comforting to know that she could remain here, safe and unseen, sealed off from any possible danger. All at once, the long sleepless night of anxious waiting and the physical exertion of her escape came crashing down on her, and she fell asleep, conscious only that, for the moment, she was safe.

She awoke with a start to the shrill creak of the trick door swinging open and Khan ducking his head inside once again. Errol glanced wildly around herself until she was finally able to place her surroundings. Then, she rubbed the sleep from her eyes and looked up. It was, by this point, pitch black, and all the lights had gone out in the club beyond. The entire place seemed deserted; all of the patrons had vanished as if by magic.

"Are you all right?" Khan called to her in a whisper. "What's your name, by the way?"

"Errol," the Ashan said groggily. "Is everything all right?"

"We're about to have our meeting," Khan informed her, and there was a smile in his voice. "Care to join us?"

Errol eagerly leapt to her feet, her knees cracking from having had to stay tucked up so long. Khan must have heard it, for he said apologetically, "Sorry I had to keep you in there for all that time. It's Saturday, and that's usually our biggest night."

"It's Saturday?" Errol said blankly.

Khan shot her an unreadable glance, laced with a deep sympathy. "How long have you been underground?" he asked quietly, and led Errol through the curtains into the darkened main area of the club. He kept his hand on Errol's arm, gently guiding her around the tables and stacked chairs. Errol was glad of him.

"Two years," she answered.

"You've managed to stay in hiding for two years?" Khan asked incredulously.

"I've been lucky," Errol admitted.

"You have," Khan agreed. "Usually, the longest someone is able to stay under is six months. Usually, they're found out beforehand."

Errol gulped. "You...you're in the resistance, then?"

"United Resistance of Two Falls," Khan said in perfect Ashan.

"How did you come to speak Ashan?" Errol asked him curiously. She supposed that Khan had had an Ashan friend or had lived outside the city for some time, perhaps in the forest.

"We all do," Khan said, surprised. "A bit, at least. All of the resistance had to learn some basics. Tarr's orders. I picked it up fast; I had a lot of Ashan friends...before."

Errol's mind reeled at this thought. It was a good ploy. It wasn't as though Cira would have many Ashans on staff to do her translating for her. "Tarr," Errol repeated. "You've met him?"

"Watch out," Khan told her quickly, and helped Errol up onto the first step of a staircase. It was pitch black, and Errol tripped and reeled slightly, feeling about with her arms for some kind of banister. After a step or two, she got a hold of her balance and bearings. Once he saw that Errol was all right, Khan responded, rather proudly, "Yes, I have, once or twice. I met him when the Strikers first came to Two Falls. He doesn't come back often, though. I've seen their hideout in the mountains."

"What was he like?" Errol inquired curiously.

Khan paused for a few moments. "Quiet," he said, finally. "And watchful. Mind yourself, this is the last stair." He helped Errol up onto the landing. "Sorry we have to keep it so dark, but we can't let anyone outside know that there are still people in here. And especially after tonight, we're probably being watched."

"I understand," Errol nodded.

Khan led her along a hallway and paused in front of a door. He rapped a few times on it with his knuckles in a staccato pattern, and the door opened a crack. A dim light shone from within, and they slipped in carefully and shut the door close behind them.

Errol blinked painfully in the light and took in her new surroundings. The windows in the room were thickly boarded over, so there was no chance of someone on the street outside noticing the people within. The room was comfortable but sparse, an obvious meeting place with a table, chairs, pitcher, and glasses already set, bookshelves, and a large desk over in one corner covered in papers and pens. It looked like someone's office.

It took Errol a few moments to notice the other individuals standing in the room. There were three of them: two women and a man. One of the women was older, her face a young-looking forty, framed by prematurely gray hair. The other girl was curvy and soft, but her expression was hard; her curly brown hair was braided rigidly along the back of her head. She wore oversized pants held up with a large belt and had her arms folded, dark brown eyes closely regarding Errol as the Ashan studied each of them. The third individual in the room was a big man who looked as though he would only smile under circumstances of extreme duress. He was blond and blandly handsome, and Errol wondered briefly whether this could be Laith, the Striker whose physical beauty had become something of a legend. But Khan had said that none of the Strikers were in the city.

"Please sit," said the big blond, motioning to a chair, and they all settled in. "Your name?"

"Errol."

"My name is Ari," the blond said. "These others are Ella," here, the girl nodded, "and Dev." The graying woman inclined her head, but only slightly. "We are all here to help you. Khan is the owner of this establishment, and Ella is one of my lieutenants here in the Two Falls resistance."

Errol stared at Ella. A lieutenant? Surely, she was far too young for such responsibility. She glanced back around at the others. She had heard of Ari already, of course, who was sort of the Strikers' acting general in Two Falls.

Realizing that the group was waiting expectantly for her to begin speaking, she cleared her voice. She began with her meeting with Doyle and her move to the library cellar, and finally her discovery of the papers in the hidden corner. As she finished, she withdrew the small wooden tablet she'd been clutching in her hands and set it on the table. Ari studied it for a second, digesting all of the lengthy information, then reached forward and gently slid the wooden tablet towards himself. He handled it gingerly, carefully, undoing the clasp and opening it to look at the papers within.

"I couldn't read it," Errol interjected. "I figured it was in some sort of old language."

"It is," Ari agreed, passing the tablet to Ella, who looked it over. "It's very old. It's written in ancient Elyrian, which was the language used in the time of Alder Morthenstar." He surveyed the others, whose expressions were uncomprehending. "Elyrian was primarily a Jelani language. After Kagai was defeated, Common was invented to aid commerce between Jelani, Ashans, and the people of Two Falls."

"I figured the book had to be valuable," Errol shrugged. "If it had been hidden so carefully under Morthenstar's symbol in the middle of her library. I figured it had to be of some importance to you."

"Indeed," Ari agreed. "This could be extremely useful to us. I'm not sure what it is myself, but I'm going to send it to Athela; she's our leading expert on ancient Elyrian translation, and I know she'll be able to decode what's in these papers. Now, may I ask, what became of your friend...Doyle, was it?"

Errol swallowed and looked down at her hands.

"I'm sorry," Ari shook his head. "He must have been a good man to sacrifice himself for you."

"He was," Errol agreed. "I didn't know him well. But he wanted me to give you that," she nodded at the tablet.

"And you have," Ari said comfortingly. "You can rest your mind about that."

Errol shifted uncomfortably in her seat, only too aware that their business was drawing to a close. Her heart was sinking. The excitement of her discovery and the thrill of escape and adventure was gradually wearing away, leaving in its place only an unsettling feeling of uncertainty. *Will I just leave?* She wondered. *Go back out on the street and try to find a new place to stay, to hide? A new family to put in danger? Or will they just keep me locked away here in some new cupboard for two more years? Will I forget what day it is, whether it is light or dark outside?*

While she was thinking, Khan and Dev began conferring quietly on one side of the table. Finally, Dev straightened up and looked over at Ari. "We're going to need a bigger bribe this week," she said. Her voice was strangely accented, and Errol thought he could hear the faintest twinge of native Ashan in her speech. She glanced down to look at Dev's hands to see if she had the telltale sixth fingers, but her hands were concealed beneath the table. *No way she could have survived this long if she were Ashan*, Errol told herself.

"A *bigger* bribe?" Ella demanded sarcastically. "Half of our funds are already channeled into this damn place."

"Ella, please," Ari said sternly, and she immediately closed her mouth, looking slightly abashed. "It's worth it to have a place where we can operate with some modicum of ease."

"Some guards saw Errol come in, came around asking questions," Khan shrugged. "I'm not saying it's definite; I'm just saying we should be prepared for a higher price."

"The commander is getting too greedy," Dev allowed a cold grin to wash over her face. Dev had deep, incongruous dimples on the sides of her mouth when she smiled. "We should teach him a lesson or two about frugality."

"I'd be happy to," Ella said darkly.

"He's still easier to bribe than the last commander, and if we take him out, who knows who we'll get stuck with next?" Khan pointed out.

"We pay the bribe," Ari said with a certain degree of finality. Khan leaned back in his chair, his strong arms crossed over his chest.

Errol waited patiently in her seat, her hands folded on top of each other. After a moment, that unsettled feeling twinged again in her chest, and she glanced uneasily around the table. She cleared her throat, and the others looked at her.

"What...what's to become of me?" she asked in a small voice.

Ari studied her for a moment. "You've been under two years?" he asked.

"Yes."

Ari blinked and set his hand down on the tablet. "You've done a great thing and put yourself at incredible risk by bringing this to us. You'll be moved to the top of our list. I'm going to see that you're kept safely here until arrangements can be made for you to be smuggled out."

Errol's mind went completely blank, and she stared at Ari for quite a minute without moving. Her entire body felt numb and shaky, as if her bones were filled with water. "Out," she repeated hollowly. "Out?"

"Out," Ari affirmed. "Of the city."

"I'll be free?" Errol said in a hushed whisper.

"As soon as arrangements can be made," Ari nodded.

At that, Errol put her face in her hands and wept.

CHAPTER TWO

The short supply train wound its way in a cautious single file through the foothills of the mountains, single file, picking carefully up the slippery rock and threading down through the crevices and escarpments. It bore no banners to signify its allegiance. Every so often, the soldiers would glance up at the looming hills and the dark, imposing trees as if they were expecting something to come bursting out at them.

The captain of the guard rode at the head of the train, silently cursing his luck under his breath. He had been fortunate so far. All of his previous assignments were to accompany wagon trains of munitions and supplies from the Meadows and take them the long way around the forest past Two Falls and back to Faridor. He had so far avoided any unpleasant entanglements. But this time, his orders had changed. Cira urgently needed the supplies and couldn't wait for the long detour around the forest. So they had to come this way, through the north route, and through these blasted foothills. It was the Strikers' domain, and everyone knew it. The captain shivered and hiked his furs farther up his back. It was early autumn but already quite chilly. The winter would be terrible, he was sure. His eyes scanned the horizon for any sign of possible attackers. He had the uncanny feeling that they were being watched.

If only Cira had bothered to allow him reinforcements, more troops! A cavalcade this size never made it through the mountains without being raided by those bloody Strikers. Every time a supply train rounded the north tip of the forest, they risked being turned on their head, their goods scattered like smoke into the depths of the mountains. If Cira wanted supplies so damn badly, she should provide enough security to allow them to arrive safely. He was glad no one could hear his thoughts, as even merely referring to Cira without her title was grounds for a beheading. He glanced around at the rest of the train, counting his soldiers. Nothing yet. They were nearly to the point where they could break to the south and make it safely across the plains. Perhaps they would slip by unnoticed. The captain hoped so. It was either face death at the hands of the Strikers or be forced to return to Cira empty-handed. The captain wasn't sure which fate was worse.

Cira had long ago sent out her own scouts to try and follow the Strikers and their followers, to discover the location of their secret hide-out in the mountains. But she might as well have tried to follow mist over the sea. They vanished as quickly as they came, and all Cira's guards could do was walk around aimlessly in circles over the rocks, finding nothing, seeing nothing, not even footprints or trails.

There was a short hill that plunged them down into a tight alley between two high walls of rock. Here, the captain began to get very nervous. He tried to appear nonchalant while surreptitiously glancing up to the top of the rock every few seconds. His hand crept down to the hilt of his sword and he caressed it with his fingers, gulping down his fear. They were almost through. They were almost through.

All at once there was motion ahead, and the captain raised his head, the train freezing in place behind him.

"Halt!" he called, somewhat redundantly.

Whatever it was—an animal of some sort—flitted through the trees ahead and bounded over a log to come to a stop directly in front of the train. It was a gigantic black dog with up-pricked ears, a long nose, and a bushy tail stuck directly out behind it. A large leather collar was fastened around its neck. The captain felt his stomach turn. He knew whose dog it was.

The dog opened its mouth and began baying at the captain, a deep bass booming noise that was amplified by the surrounding rocks. The dog planted its hind legs and bent forward on its fore as if to get better breath into its bark. Finally, as if signaled by an unseen master, it let out a whine and straightened up, its tail giving an involuntary wag. The captain saw the dog's gaze change focus and, following its direction, whipped around to look over his shoulder.

Standing on the broad slab of rock above them was a small cluster of figures. Three stood at the head, and the captain swallowed anxiously, recognizing them immediately. An Ashan, skin paler than snow, dressed all in black, stood easily with a bow in one hand, an arrow nocked and ready. He had tousled spiky white hair with black tips, piercing golden eyes, long angular features, and a naturally sardonic expression. There was only one person this could be: Archer, the famed Ashan assassin and smuggler-turned-Striker freedom fighter. To his side was a shorter individual, broad and stocky and thick, with shoulder-length silky yellow hair tied half-back behind his head. He had a curved nose, ice-blue eyes, and an ugly scar that split his face from eye to ear. At the head of the group was a Jelani, tall and exceptionally handsome, with dark brown eyes and sandy hair. A thread of discolored white hair ran over his right ear, the remnants of a scar.

Around them, other fighters were materializing seemingly out of nowhere. Laith didn't bother to speak until his entire group had shown themselves, poised at the top of the rock with arrows and swords pointed down at the train. Their movements were like punctuation to an unuttered sentence. The captain's troops were trapped in the worst possible position to try and fight back.

The captain glared at them with as much malice as he dared. Laith and Marc seemed unruffled, whereas Archer appeared to be enjoying himself. "Your swords," Laith said finally. "Drop them beside your horses."

The captain reluctantly turned to his troops and waved his hand, turning back to stare up at Laith. He heard the ripple of leather and of metal hitting the ground as the troops obeyed. He watched the other archers on the top of the rock. There were men and women, young and relatively old. He even thought he could see a few Ashans.

Laith, flanked by Archer and Marc, slid easily down the rock to come and stand beside the captain's horse. Marc grabbed its bit and held its head steady, but the horse could sense the tension in the air. It snorted and bonked its nose into Archer's arm.

"Oy," Archer muttered, swatting at it.

Marc rolled his eyes and soothingly stroked the horse's nose until it settled. He sent Archer a pointed look, and the Ashan made a deprecatory noise in his throat. The captain dimly thought he could hear Archer mutter something along the lines of *"Horses."*

The black dog, who had for all this time remained immobile, barring the exit of the canyon, trotted forward to stand ready behind Laith, who greeted him with a short pat on the head. Laith walked over to stand by the captain's knee.

"What's in the train?" he inquired in his deep voice.

"I don't know, I was assigned at the last minute," the captain lied. It was the first time he had met any of the Strikers, and though his heart was pounding through his chest, he couldn't help but stare at them curiously.

Laith raised a dark eyebrow as if he could sense the deception, and motioned with his head to a few of the Striker troops. The wagons were in the rear of the train, and the captain nearly winced at the thought of his loss. The train was carrying newly-made armor from forges in the Meadows, swords, quivers—not to mention an entire payroll of money to supply troops and buy food and bribes. Why on earth hadn't Cira sent him with more guards?

"Aren't you going to do anything?" came a shout from behind him. The captain wheeled around to face one of his soldiers, who clearly thought that a small case of insubordination would seem fairly petty after Cira was through with them.

"Your captain's currently saving your weaselly behind by *not* doing anything," Archer called out. "I'd be grateful."

"This is cowardice!" the young man yelled angrily. "I signed up to fight, not to roll over and play dead."

"You signed up to *fight*?" Laith asked tiredly beneath his breath, so low that he clearly didn't intend his question to be heard. The captain studied him. There was something weary about Laith, something not physical. His face was young, but his bearing was far older. The captain's gaze slid from him to his bodyguard, Marc. Marc's pale blue eyes were trained expectantly on the guard who had made the outburst.

"Archer…" Laith said in an undertone.

Almost before the captain could think, something from behind him came hurtling through the air in Laith's direction. Laith dodged neatly out of the way, and a knife stuck, *thwack*, into the damp earth beyond him. Almost in unison, Archer whipped up his bow and arrow, tilted ever so slightly to the side, and let it fly. The arrow screeched through the air towards the guard, and the captain let out a yell before realizing that it had only been a warning shot and that the arrow hadn't hit home. The arrowhead merely glanced against the young guard's cheek, leaving an ugly, bloody cut on his face. The young man's hands flew to his face, and he let out a cry.

"Anything else you want to add?" Archer inquired tauntingly, another arrow already at the ready. "I've got more."

The young man shot searing rays of hatred in Archer's direction, but the Ashan was unconcerned. The captain swiveled in the saddle to look around at the young guard. "One more move or word from you, and I'll have you executed right here," he snarled with as much malice as he could muster. "You're already going to be court-martialed for insubordination as soon as we reach Faridor."

"Fine," the young man shot back. Blood seeped through his fingers.

Laith leaned back to survey the other Strikers. "What's going on back there?" he called out. The dog at his side gave out a whine and Laith laid a hand on the black head.

"You should see it!" came an excited cry from one of the young women in Laith's troop. "You should see what they have back here!"

"We'll see it later," Laith called patiently. "Get it out of here. How are we going on the swords?"

"Nearly there, milord," came another yell, this time from an older man.

"You know your way out?" Laith asked the captain, gesturing towards the mouth of the narrow canyon.

The captain stared at him, surprised by the politeness of his tone. "Yes, I think so," he said slowly.

"South is that way," Laith pointed through the trees to his left.

"You'll hit the plains after an hour or so and shouldn't be bothered until you return to Faridor."

"Thank you," the captain said automatically, bewildered by Laith's courtesy. *Aren't we supposed to be on opposing sides?* He wondered. He glanced around behind him at the train. Perhaps it was still just a trap, and they would be shot as soon as they had been cleared of their booty. "Are you...?" he inquired hesitantly.

Laith blinked his dark eyes. "What? Going to execute you and your troop? What bloody good would that do?"

"Fewer soldiers to fight...I don't know..." the captain shrugged.

"You lot keep our people fed, clothed, armed, and funded," Marc cut in, smiling. "If anything, we owe you. Not your fault Cira's enough of an idiot to send you directly through our territory."

Well, we agree on something there, the captain thought wryly, and Archer must have read his expression, for he let go a laugh. "Look," Laith added, "you can tell the other captains if they come through here, they can just think of it as a bit of a traveling tax. They don't try to start anything, we won't do anything either. Can you tell them that?"

"I will," the captain assured him.

A whistle came from the back of the troop, and the captain again stared around to find that the other members of the Striker group had vanished like wind among the rocks and trees. There was not a single one to be seen, not a remaining trunk of supplies in the wagon, none of the discarded swords left uncollected on the ground.

"Thieves," spat the young guard behind the captain.

"Laith," Archer said with some exasperation, "can I just shoot him?"

"I'll take it into consideration," Laith murmured. "You may go," he told the captain. "Give Cira our regards."

The three turned on their heels, the black dog loping along close behind Laith, and in a few seconds were gone, just as if they had just been apparitions, tricks of the light. The captain stood quite still, blinking stupidly for a few moments as he tried to follow where they had gone. Moments before, he had briefly entertained fantasies of tracking them back to their camp, but it was already too late. There was nothing for it.

"Forward," he called, and the train straggled on once again.

"Well, that went well," Archer grinned as the three friends watched the train weave its way slowly out of the narrow canyon and down the wooded side of the hill. They were lying on their stomachs atop a shallow crevasse some distance up the mountain.

"Snippy little guards grow more impertinent every year," Marc griped disapprovingly. "Shows obvious poor training. Not to mention bad parenting."

"Good job with the captain, Laith," Archer complimented.

"Thanks. He won't give us any trouble if he comes through here again. We'll treat him more gently than Cira will. Now that I think of it, why the hell *did* Cira march them straight through here? Apparently, they were carrying quite a valuable load," Laith wondered, squinting his eyes.

"Yeah, I wondered that as well," Archer pondered. "Maybe to see where we would strike."

"That's likely," Laith agreed. "We'll tell the next group not to use the canyon anymore. Get them on the overhang a mile back. They won't be expecting it. If I know Cira, next time she'll lay a trap for us right here."

Once the troop was effectively out of sight, the three stood up. "Breaker!" Laith called and gave a short, curt whistle through his teeth. The big black dog swung around and loped up behind him, and the three Strikers began picking their way back up the hill to where their horses were concealed in a rocky cave further toward the summit.

The interconnected network of underground caves that formed the Strikers' mountain headquarters was humming with activity when they returned. The goods from the supply train had already been cataloged and stored away. Laith walked up to an elderly man who was seated at a desk with a quill pen in his hand, hurriedly scribbling away in a ledger as men and women brought up swords and shields for him to record. The old man was perpetually stooped, and one of the lenses in his glasses was cracked. His eyes crinkled in a hurried smile as he saw Laith and the others draw close.

"You struck gold this time, milord," he said in his quiet voice, counting under his breath. Though Laith had tried time and again to get the army to dispense with the formalities, there was something about the fact that Laith had once been a prince that had taken the fancy of his followers. There was something about his noble bearing that inspired a deeper level of respect in the men and women who fought alongside him. He was invariably addressed as "milord" by his followers, and after a year or so, Laith had stopped protesting.

"What are we looking at?" he inquired.

"Swords, shields, bows and arrows, you name it," the old man shrugged.

Three young women came up, lugging a large, heavy trunk with them. "Guess what's in here?" one asked breathlessly. Her face was beaming.

"Fist-sized hunks of dark chocolate?" Archer inquired hopefully.

The women set down the trunk and opened the top. It was filled to the brim with gold pieces. Even Laith couldn't help but smile at the sight.

"Good grief," Marc exclaimed in awe. "We should have gotten into this racket a long time ago."

"I *was* in this racket," Archer corrected.

"Have it counted," Laith ordered and clapped the three women on their shoulders, walking past them toward the headquarters' upper chambers. The women lit up at his gesture, grinning at one another as baldly as if they had just been awarded a portion of the spoils. Marc saw the exchange and chuckled to himself.

"Good work, all," Marc chimed in and jogged up the stairs to fall into step behind Laith.

They piled into the prince's office and closed the curtained door to give themselves some privacy. Breaker, Laith's large black dog, went to the far corner and curled up automatically behind his chair. The caverns were now constantly filled with people. There were those rescued from Two Falls, recovering from injuries and waiting for word of their families. There were new recruits from the outlying villages and the city being trained to run on raids with the rest of the forces. There were those who were being specially instructed as spies, but they lived apart from the others, closer to Tarr, who was in charge of all the espionage in their operation. The large open center of the cave was the general meeting place, and the honeycomb-like rooms ringing the walls of the circular hub had been converted into everything from offices to first-aid rooms to bunks and private chambers. Farther off down one of the passages was the large room where they had first performed the ceremony to reveal Si as the heir of Morthenstar, and it was here that Laith, Marc, and Athela did most of their fight training with the new recruits. They stabled the horses in yet another long chain of caverns and caves further on.

It had been slow building at first, but as soon as they had re-established their ties with Ari and Two Falls, refugees and recruits began pouring in. There weren't nearly as many Ashan escapees among them as the Strikers would have hoped. Because Ashans and half-Ashans were so easily identifiable by their sixth fingers, they were harder to disguise and sneak past the city wall guards than humans. And though holes in the Two Falls perimeter did occasionally present themselves—a section of disrepaired wall here, a sewer tunnel there—the Strikers had not yet devised a consistently reliable means of escape for Ashans in hiding. Though the Ashans may have been fewer and farther between, there were still plenty of human refugees who fled the city after being targeted for aiding the rebellion or housing Ashan fugitives. They'd often had to set up beds in the open rooms to accommodate the influx of people.

On the days when they found themselves overwhelmed by the surging number of refugees, Laith found himself feeling fervently glad that Cira hadn't yet been able to breach the borders of the Ashan forest. The Strikers' already overextended network would have been almost powerless to raise any resistance if Cira targeted the forest tribes. Fortunately, Cira's army wasn't equipped to deal with cities in the trees, much less creatures who lived in them, and who moved with silence and stealth and attacked with fury when provoked.

"Hell of a catch, eh?" Archer inquired, looking pleased. He unbuckled his quiver and laid it down in a corner, catching Laith's sword when the prince tossed it to him.

"Depends on how you look at it," Laith shrugged. "If we're right, and Cira just planted that morsel so that we would be more likely to jump troops from that position, then it would seem that our winnings today were handed over voluntarily. She wouldn't gamble anything she couldn't afford to lose."

Archer drew up a chair and threw himself into it, looking huffy. "Well, I suppose if she has the entire country's wealth in a stranglehold, not to mention trade agreements with every outlying kingdom that she hasn't knocked over and squeezed dry, I suppose she can afford to lose a bit."

"Sort of depressing," Marc observed.

"Besides," Laith ran his hands through his short, sand-colored hair, "once we divide that money up between food and clothes, weapons, horses, bribes, and travel permits, it's going to dry up pretty fast."

"Calm down, Laith, your cheeriness is overwhelming," Archer raised his eyebrows, hands on hips.

"But it'll help," Laith added quickly. He leaned forward to read a note that had been left for him on his desk.

Marc leaned back in his chair, balancing his foot against the corner of the desk. He moved aside the edge of the curtain and stared down at the hum of activity in the cavern below them.

"Where's Si?" Archer asked.

"Babysitting," Marc replied automatically. "We got three Ashan children in two days ago from Riddleton. So traumatized they wouldn't talk to anyone. Now Si's got them out cavorting around the rocks playing Mountain Goat."

"Good man," Archer said approvingly.

"When do Athela and Tarr get back?" Marc furrowed his brow. "They've been gone for a while now."

"Two weeks yesterday," Laith agreed. "And when they'll be back? It all depends on how well things are going."

"What do you think the prospects are?" Marc wondered.

"We all know that I have a fairly low opinion of the Ashan tribal system," Archer interjected. "Or really any system of government, for that matter."

"You don't say," Laith muttered, not looking up from his paper.

"...so I would say it depends entirely on who they speak to and when. But if I know the Ashans, they're not going to lift a finger to help."

"Seems silly," Marc shook his head. A strand of silky yellow hair fell loose over his ear, and he tucked it back. Two gold studs glinted from his earlobe. "You'd think they'd be more than willing to chip in, seeing as it's their people that are being hunted down and killed."

"Yee-es, but it's not *their* people, you see," Archer corrected. "You're out of the forest, you technically don't belong to them. You're either an exile, meaning you're not even an Ashan anymore, or you've been sent out after the Choosing, like Tarr was, in which case you're supposed to grow up and fend for yourself. *Or* you've chosen to voluntarily leave the tribe and live among humans, in which case you sort of forfeit your official Ashan citizenship. They're not going to go out and fight anyone who isn't trespassing on their land or threatening their tribe directly."

"So let's go in and light a couple of fires and blame 'em on Cira," Marc muttered darkly.

"That's the spirit," Archer said approvingly.

"I just hope they're safe," Laith murmured, finishing up the last of his writing.

"I'd know it if Tarr was hurt," Archer said immediately. Laith glanced up.

Marc leered at him out of one eye. "And Athela? Would you *know* if Athela was hurt?" he asked teasingly.

Archer inhaled through his nose with an air of wounded dignity. "For your information, I know far better than to even *consider* the fact that Athela is not all right. She would strike fear into the heart of a wolverine."

"Amen," Laith agreed fervently and tossed down his pen.

"Just ask her out, Archer," Marc grinned. "Do us all a favor."

"Can't. Too scared," Archer shot back.

Marc rolled his eyes, standing up and stretching his burly arms. The past years had been lean, and Marc was now nothing but a block of solid muscle, all of the excesses of his palace life burned away. Laith rose from his place and pulled the curtain aside, surveying the goings-on inside the cavern. There were few moments where he could stand still like this and be quietly beside his friends. There was always something new to do: someone that had to be saved, food and expenditures that had to be calculated, spoils that had to be tallied. He hoped that Tarr and Athela would be back soon. Even a week or two of their absence was taking its toll; the management of the cavern headquarters had them all stretched thin.

"Rane gets into Two Falls tonight," Archer reminded Laith slowly. "She'll see if there's any news from Ari."

"Right," Laith shook himself slightly. "You all have your assignments for the afternoon?"

"Serve and protect the innocent," Marc responded with a straight face. "How about you, Archer?"

"Eradicate evil," Archer replied.

"My favorite," Laith managed a smile. "Go to it, then."

Marc saluted and clapped him on the shoulder, then was gone.

"I thought your people were supposed to be *peaceful*," Athela hissed through gritted teeth, keeping her hands raised to shoulder height. Ashans swarmed around them, roughly checking them over for any concealed weaponry. Tarr sighed patiently.

"Yes, generally, they are," he conceded. "But, in case you hadn't gathered it, tensions run rather high these days."

"On your knees," the head Ashan ordered them in his native tongue. He was older than them and armed with a forbidding, authoritative stare. He wore the knife of a Kagaian guard strapped to his hip. He clearly afforded Tarr no special trust even though he, too, was Ashan.

They had been intercepted right at the border of the Spruce tribe almost as soon as they had set foot over it, and the swiftness of their discovery gave Tarr a sneaking suspicion that the tribe's borders were being watched extremely closely nowadays. The only reason that they had not been killed directly was because they didn't bear the livery of Kagaian guards.

"We wish to speak with your—hey!" Athela exclaimed, then switched to the Ashan language. "Please do not touch that; it is extremely impolite."

The offending guard stumbled back, startled. "How do you speak Ashan?" he gasped.

"I learned it," Athela sniffed. "A little, at least."

The leader narrowed his eyes at Tarr. "You taught the Ashan language to an outsider?" he demanded. "How dare you violate the laws of our people in such a way?"

"I was not aware that it was an offense," Tarr replied mildly. "We would, however, like to speak with the council of elders. I am sure that if they have a problem with my actions, they can bring them up at that time."

The lead Ashan jerked his head to one side, and Athela and Tarr were shoved roughly forward. Tarr allowed himself to be pushed along. They had been afforded this same sort of hospitality at each of the southernmost Ashan tribes. They had visited the Redwood and the Yew tribes already, and (as much as Tarr wanted to have faith in his own people) he could not deny that the venture had turned out to be, as Athela put it, "like talking to a tree." Their entreaties had gone all but unheard, their pleas for assistance and for volunteers unanswered. It was all a bit surprising to Tarr, as he'd grown up with Morthenstar's story being retold every year in his tribe. He himself had loved it, and he'd naturally assumed that his people would leap at the chance to come to the aid of this newer incarnation of the Strikers. But so far, they'd been without any luck. He had purposefully avoided going back to his home tribe, the Aspen, even though it was located the closest to Two Falls. He couldn't bring himself to face it. He hadn't told Athela that they weren't going back to his old home, and she hadn't asked about it. For that, he'd been grateful.

Once this is over, he told himself. *Once it is over, you'll have a home to go back to.* He wanted to keep the Aspen tribe as it was in his memory, fixed and unchanging. Let the war pass and let him go back, and then he would see what changes had transpired since his childhood. Only then.

Still, in many ways, the first day in the forest had been like a breath of air for Tarr after being long underwater. They had come down out of the mountains and headed south toward Two Falls, skimming along the edge of the valley that dove down to cradle the forest at its base. They had ventured down, deeper into the valley until they at last stood at the base of all those giant, strong trees, and Tarr couldn't help himself. He had excused himself from Athela and climbed as high and as fast as he could to the very top of the tree until he was swinging in the waves of the rolling, rollicking canopy just like he used to do with Juniper as a boy. It could have been his imagination, but the wind smelled sweeter among those trees, and as he clung to the snapping limbs, he closed his eyes and forgot for a few minutes his duties, his responsibilities, the war, the resistance, even the reason why he had returned to the forest in the first place.

It was on those first few minutes of blissful freedom that he ruefully reflected as he and Athela were half-pushed, half-dragged through the belly of the forest to the area beneath the central tree houses of the Spruce tribe. Their escort was something of an improvement on their first foray into Ashan lands, in which one of the Ashans in the Redwood clan had thrown Athela over his shoulder and taken to the trees with her in tow. She had screamed bloody murder and struggled so hard that he had to return with her to the forest floor lest she kill them both with her fighting. It had taken Tarr half an hour of cajoling to get her to voluntarily allow herself to be escorted to the tribal center.

This time, however, they were simply dragged through the forest and then unceremoniously deposited on the floor of the Spruce tribal gathering house, where Athela and Tarr met each other's eyes through an undignified tangle of limbs and belongings. "I won't breathe a word of this to the others, I promise," Tarr vowed as he untwined his legs from the straps of Athela's knapsack and offered her a hand. She gave a sigh and accepted with as much dignity as she could muster. Tarr gave her a comforting pat on the shoulder and reflected on how much she had mellowed over the past few years.

The tribal house was in the same familiar style as the buildings in Tarr's own tribe: charred preserved wood, and doors and windows that had already been exchanged for the heavier, more protective winter screens that blocked out the cool autumn light. By this point, the entire council had gathered, and it looked as though most of the tribe was going to turn out as well. Dozens of curious eyes were trained on the newcomers as they waited patiently in the center of the open meeting area. Tarr hummed a bit to himself and allowed his eyes to wander over the faces of the Ashans around him. Many of them were quite young, and some of the children had managed to elbow their way to the front of the crowd. They were all watching him keenly and with expressions of recognition, occasionally whispering and laughing behind their hands. *At least they've heard of us*, he mused. Beside him, Athela stared stoically ahead. Her long years in the palace had trained her to never betray where she was looking or what she was thinking, but Tarr sensed that she was surreptitiously surveying the village as closely as he.

Finally, the council of Elders took their places at the north side of the circle. There were fifteen of them. The eldest was incredibly frail and thin but had piercing black eyes like a sparrow's. Tarr was well aware that those sharp, dark orbs were trained closely on him.

Etiquette demanded that Athela and Tarr recite their lineage back three generations to explain to the council who they were and where they came from. Tarr had explained this procedure to Athela the first time they arrived in a village. By this point, she was quite good at it; her recitation was almost completely fluent. Tarr followed suit, noting that he had not been Chosen by an Ashan family but listing off his tribe and the names of all the Aspen families he could remember, as well as a few Aspen council members for good measure. The elders followed this with some wise nods and five minutes' conference during which Tarr and Athela waited patiently.

"You are welcome in the tribe," said one of the council members finally. "What have you to say to us?"

"We are members of the Strikers," Tarr explained, and allowed the ripple of whispers and gasps to pass through his audience before he continued. "We are currently fighting a war against Cira Kagai to save the lives of the tribes here in the forest and the other Ashans living in Two Falls. We humbly ask your people to give us aid, either in the capacity of sheltering displaced Ashans, by giving us supplies, or by fighting alongside us."

There was a long silence as the tribe digested this. A cool breeze swung through the trunks of the trees. The council platform, mounted low amongst the boughs of the trees, swayed from side to side like it was rolling against a lapping wave. Tarr enjoyed the familiar motion for a moment or two before the council members stirred and spoke.

"We are against war, Tarr," an elderly woman said sternly.

"As am I," Tarr agreed quietly. "I have no love for war. However, in this particular case, inaction is completely unthinkable. Inaction would result in countless deaths. In a massacre. In genocide. It is already happening."

"We are sorely outnumbered," Athela chimed in. "We need help, any help you can give."

"We do not like to meddle in the affairs of Two Falls," another tribal council member said gravely. "This is not our concern."

"I understand," Tarr couldn't help but sigh inwardly. It was the same conversation, the same pushback they'd been receiving for weeks. "Surely, though, your people could recognize that circumstances have changed? We all live in the same country; we are neighbors. We carry some degree of responsibility for one another. Would you not want the people of Two Falls to come to your aid if threatened?"

The council considered this. "We do not do anything to provoke such antagonism," a female council member pointed out. "The laws of our people are respected and honored. We do not conduct ourselves with the barbarism of humans or of Jelani."

Tarr felt Athela bristle beside him, and was glad that she managed to keep her temper in check. It would do no good for her to get into an argument with members of the council. "When an Ashan commits a crime, he or she is exiled; is that not so?" he asked quietly.

"That is so," one council member agreed, nodding. The crowd was watching Tarr with rapt attention.

"Well, this is not the custom with humans and Jelani," Tarr explained. "And sometimes—not all the time, mind you, but once in a while—an evil person comes along who infects everything and everyone. We must cast them out, by fighting if we must. Like a sickness. We must not merely succumb to it. We must fight back against it. Or lose everything."

A long silence greeted these words. "Tarr," one man said finally, "it is not our concern. Let them come onto our lands. Let them threaten our people. And then we will defend ourselves. Not before."

Tarr's shoulders sagged, but only slightly. He supposed that he had expected this outcome, but he still felt a small wave of disappointment. He paused to gather his thoughts for a few moments, and let his eyes wander around the faces watching him. The older ones looked skeptical, but the younger Ashans' eyes were riveted on him. Tarr glanced over to Athela, whose jaw was set in a firm line, her gray eyes staring straight ahead.

"And what of your...reported association with an exile?" came a small, reedy voice from the back of the council. A ripple of disapproving whispers washed around the tribal house. Tarr swiveled to the side and met that pair of beetle-black eyes. The eldest council member's stare bored into him. Tarr felt a small swell of anger in his stomach and stood up slightly straighter. Athela had stiffened as well. He wondered where the council member had received his information. None of the other Ashan tribes had mentioned Archer before.

"I suppose you are referring to Archer?" Tarr asked.

"He doesn't have a name," the reedy voice countered. The stare never wavered, never blinked. "You admit that you keep association with him?"

"He is my brother," Tarr murmured softly, turning his head slightly and pointing to the family tattoo on his neck, where an Aspen leaf and a Birch leaf lay entwined amid twists of inked calligraphy. This time there was uproar in the crowd, which was only quieted after a few glares from the elder council. The younger members of the tribe were staring at Tarr bug-eyed, and a few mouths were even hanging open.

"Your brother is an *exile?*" a councilwoman gasped.

"You have performed the rites?" another exclaimed angrily. "How dare you!"

"He has saved the lives of many," Tarr said, his back like a ramrod. *They don't know him. They don't know everything that he's done*, he reminded himself. "There is not a day that goes by that he does not regret the life that he took."

"He can never atone," one councilwoman said sharply.

"This is forbidden," the eldest maintained staunchly in that high, whispery voice. "Such a thing is forbidden. If word of this got back to your tribe, you could be exiled as well."

"Archer saves lives while you sit here and let them die," Athela snapped, her patience nearly at an end. "Will you not even offer *refuge* for those who have been driven from their homes?"

The council members, clearly still scandalized at the revelation of Tarr's relation to Archer, talked for a long time while the children watched them, aghast and morbidly fascinated. Tarr avoided looking at them, instead locking grim gazes with Athela. She appeared slightly remorseful for her outburst, but Tarr gave a shrug as if to say, *it's all right, they were bound to refuse anyway.*

Finally, the senior female council member turned around and stood. "If refugees wander into our lands, they will not be killed, but they will not be aided either," she intoned. "This entire matter is no concern of the Ashan people. And let that be noted by all the tribal members present here today," she added, raising her voice slightly so that all the onlookers could hear her. There was a flurry of nodding among the people, and Tarr shifted his weight from one long leg to the other. "Now, begone," she ordered Tarr and Athela. "Once you leave these borders, you will no longer be welcome in our tribal lands."

Tarr gave a courteous bow. "I thank you for your time and for the hospitality of your tribe."

Athela mimicked the bow, though it was a shade shallower than Tarr's. "I do as well," she agreed, a slight edge to her tone.

A few minutes later they were dumped back at the border, and Athela was irately picking twigs out of her curly black hair, glancing bitterly up at the swaying Ashan lookouts, who were watching to make sure they departed as ordered. Once recovered, they started off. She gave Tarr a sidelong look as he marched along in silence. The afternoon was sliding into the gloom of evening, and she thought she saw a few dark figures darting back and forth in the canopy above them, but she couldn't be sure whether they were people or mere tricks of the light.

"We're being followed," she said finally.

Tarr gave a casual glance up into the crown of trees. "I think it's the younger Ashans," he murmured with a small smile. "They'll probably escort us a ways past the border."

"Hmph," said Athela, a bit disgruntled. She fished out a leaf that had become entangled in her black ringlets, tossed it to the side, and sighed. "I'll be glad to get back and see the others. Have a bath."

"Mmm," Tarr assented.

"Oh, hell, Tarr, I'm sorry," Athela blurted out, kicking unnecessarily at a root that jutted out into her path. "I shouldn't have lost my temper like that. It's just...for them to do nothing...and condemn Archer in such a way, when they don't know him and don't even realize the number of people he's saved...how many times he's put his life at risk..." She rolled her eyes. "'He can never atone.' What a load of *balls.*"

"It made me angry as well," Tarr sighed.

"And what about you?" Athela demanded. "Is it true that you could be exiled as well? For fighting with us and for 'consorting' with Archer, or however they put it?"

"I don't know," Tarr answered honestly. The question had been niggling at the back of his brain ever since he'd met Archer. Something about having the Elder say it out loud made it all the more real. *Exiled.* To a certain degree, Tarr felt a deep sense of injustice at the suggestion, because he hadn't done anything wrong. And if merely being associated with Archer was grounds enough...well, then, there must be something wrong with the system. Yet Tarr still remembered the fear and revulsion he had felt those years ago when he first met Archer and learned that he was an exile. Such deeply ingrained societal prejudices were hard to scrape away. He had to be patient with his people.

This did not eliminate his fear, however. He had given only glancing thoughts as to what he would do when the war was over...*if,* indeed, it ever was. He knew better than to make plans for a future that was so uncertain, yet there was always an image in his mind...of Archer, and perhaps of Rane, of returning to the forest, returning home. It was nothing more than a fleeting thought, like a quickly sketched drawing, yet the weight of it struck him fully as he realized that in the event they survived the war, he likely could not have both his loved ones and his home.

Once the war is over, he reassured himself. *I'll figure it out. Just get through the war first.*

"Why didn't you greet them like you do Archer?" Athela asked curiously. She had been watching him, seeing the wheels turning in his head, and was clearly trying to snap him out of it. "You know, the hands on the napes of the necks and the forehead-touching thing?"

"What, other than the fact we were being arrested?" Tarr asked tiredly. "Archer and I do a greeting meant for members of your own tribe. Touching the napes of each others' necks is a way of honoring the other's family."

"Huh," Athela contemplated this, then sent him a sidelong grin. "You still need to teach me how to swear in Ashan. That could have gotten us a bit farther back there."

"Ashan is a lyrical, beautiful language," Tarr sniffed with some dignity. "I wouldn't deign to sully it with obscenities."

"*Si* can swear in Ashan," Athela pointed out.

"Si," Tarr said slowly, "has a gift for that sort of thing."

There were a few steps, silent except for the crunching of leaves underfoot, then Athela tilted her head to one side. "Do you think...that Si...?" her statement trailed off. "Do you think he's ever going to...?"

"I don't know," Tarr replied. "Cheer up, Athela. We did the best we could. You managed not to come to blows with anyone or start any inter-tribal wars. I think, in some ways, our trip was a great success." Unable to help himself, he sent her a teasing leer. "I'll bet *Archer* misses you."

"As if," Athela snorted automatically, though her expression was contemplative. Tarr smiled to himself so that she couldn't see. Athela and Archer's mutual crush was perhaps the worst-kept secret in the entire Striker compound. Tarr and Archer had never discussed it directly, and Tarr knew better than to pry. But there was nevertheless the undeniable fact that Archer, who twice had had to change cities to avoid constantly running into his exes, had in the past three years settled into a life of easy, untroubled, unconsummated monogamy. The only obstacle (and it was a rather large one) was that their various neuroses had aligned in such a way that made it impossible for either to admit their feelings.

Tarr gave a sigh and took a deep breath, letting the smell of the forest and the leaves and autumn fill his nostrils, feeling a smile spread unbidden across his thin face. There would be a day, then another, and another after that. Eventually, they would be back in the mountains, and he would be with Archer again, and Marc and Laith. And Rane. He thought of her long, wavy auburn hair, the way her brow furrowed in her sleep. He hoped, as he always did, that she was all right, that she would return to him safely, and that they would be able to find a few moments to be alone together. That he could look at her lovely face and wonder for the thousandth time what was going on in the mind inside.

Side by side, Tarr and Athela slowly headed south through the darkening forest, black shadows flickering through the branches spreading above them.

CHAPTER THREE

Cira Kagai stood barefoot in a white linen dress, staring out at the blistering desert surrounding the palace of Vireg and its sprawling city. The sun beat down upon her fair skin. She could only be outdoors for an hour or so each day, or her complexion would blister and be ruined. She leaned her head against the carved stone pillar that divided her apartment from the outdoor balcony. This palace was so unlike Faridor, where the icy sea breezes rushed through her rooms each day, where the sun felt soft against her face and where she had to be bundled in furs every evening, except in the height of summer. She squinted slightly. Here, everything was hot. She could feel the moisture beginning to form around her hairline. She blinked. Soon, the negotiations would be over and she could get back to her fortress, back to the benign gray mornings and the thick salt air. She hadn't even wanted to go to Vireg, but King Tarik had refused to make the journey across the sea to meet on *her* territory. He feared for his life, he'd said. Cira smirked at the memory. He had good reason to. Perhaps it was better this way. The negotiations they had conducted had all but secured her throne for decades to come and would ensure her wealth and her position as long as the agreement held. In time, with enough capital, she could always amass an army and take Vireg for her own. Patience. First things first:

quash the rebellion back in her country, seize the forest, and then worry about taking Vireg.

She had scarcely believed it when her royal barge had made anchor at the port. The land by the coast was rocky, with a few spindly trees reaching desperately up to the sky, as if spreading their weight across the searing ground had burned their roots. Across the scattered hills, there was only desert. Flat, blistered, iridescent earth stretched out for miles and then soared up into a constantly seething expanse of white sand dunes, in whose sweep only a few nomadic tribes dared to live. And in the center of it all there was a vast city, the golden color of sand, as if the earth had miraculously come together and condensed to sprout up and form the structures. The palace was located in the exact center, looming, its towers and main buildings all the same rectangular shape, stacked on top of one another.

Cira had no idea what to expect when she walked through the massive doors for the first time. Whatever her preconceptions might have been, she had no way of preparing herself for the richness and luxury of the palace that spread before her, the opulence that glittered in the middle of the desert like a sand-covered pearl. She was greeted cordially by servants with impeccable manners and precisely accented Common language, who guided her up to her new rooms, expansive but not sprawling, with a magnificent view of the city below. The interior of the palace was made of stone so that it remained relatively cool even in the blistering heat, and there were servants who came and waved fans around in the rooms to keep the air moving. The sand had blown in everywhere on her journey: into her palanquin, beneath her clothes, in her eyes and nose, and she had thought it a nuisance. Here, from her perch high in the embrace of the stone palace, she could see the beauty in it.

At night, when Cira went to sleep, there were more servants who drew the light curtains around her bed and offered her sweetened milk to drink if she wished it. She did wish it, and what was more, she wished for a bath to be drawn. When she was presented with an array of scented oils to be added to the bath, she chose the jasmine, and she soaked for hours while handmaidens combed perfumes through her hair. After a few days, she found that the heavy gowns she wore back in Faridor were cumbersome and far too heavy for the heat, and quickly ordered a wardrobe of Viregian dress. At first it had seemed foreign, alien, the many layers of thin, gossamer fabrics making her feel naked and uncomfortable in front of strangers, even though she was in reality quite concealed and modest. But then she began to revel in it, the cool linen, the silk she wore during the nighttime, belted with gold and a gold clasp at the shoulder. She resolved to bring back some servants from Vireg when she returned home. She had asked King Tarik where he got such fine luxuries, and he replied that the land beneath the sand was rich in ore, and that he also had trade agreements with another country to the south. Cira was astonished to hear this, though at the time she hadn't shown it. *Another* country? She had scarcely conceived of such a thing, and made a further resolution to send out scouting parties to the outlying realms when she returned to Faridor. There was so much still for the taking. If Vireg had imported such finery, she could scarcely imagine what the land was like where the goods were made. Her fingertips itched as she thought of it. First, she would take Vireg and assume all of the trade rights. Then, she would take whatever countries supplied it. She would have a monopoly. No one would be able to stand against her. And the navy....with Vireg's navy and the Joymarillian cavalry, she would be feared and respected throughout the world. No one would be able to stand against her.

There were Ashans here and there, but Tarik had done a good job of keeping them out of the way. Cira didn't particularly care about Ashans one way or another. They were a tool, that was all: a tool for her to use and manipulate, to raise prejudices where needed, to light a fire under those unwilling to follow her otherwise. Whether or not the citizens of her country tore themselves apart fighting over whether to kill the Ashans or keep them alive was of little concern to her.

She shifted to one side, feeling the beginning of a burn on her cheeks. She had been daydreaming too long, and the sun was at its apex. She moved back into the dim interior of her apartments, her cobweb-thin gown swishing gently around her legs. She sprawled on her bed and leaned her head on her arms. One of the giant white-striped cats the royal family kept as pets padded silently into the room and regarded her with level amber eyes, then walked by and curled up in one of the corners, blinking at her nonchalantly. Cira would like to take one of them back with her, too. She admired them, their strength and their beauty, the way they were domesticated but still undeniably dangerous. She leaned back, blowing her hot breath onto her arms. She was scheduled to walk with King Tarik in his stables in the afternoon and wasn't sure she still wanted to go. She had already seen the kind of horses they had in this country, and she didn't much care for them: flighty, swift, light as deer, with long ears whose tips nearly met in curving oval halos above their heads. She thought with satisfaction that when the Strikers were dead, she would take Laith's black charger Arfolasth for her own. She had always admired her cousin's horse.

The Strikers. They were like the tiny flies that gathered around an overripe fruit, buzzing into her ears and whispering along the back of her neck. What should have taken a year was now taking twice as long. She had set up the perfect plan: enclose Two Falls, establish it under her rule, and systematically hunt down and destroy all the outlying resistance. But the Strikers had informants in almost every rung of her operations; their network of spies was unparalleled, and their smuggling ring more effective than she cared to admit. When they heard about a raid, they would nimbly dodge out of the way. Sometimes, of course, they were too late; most of the time they weren't. And Cira was getting impatient. She could root out the informants in her network, find the spies, kill them, but that would take time and far more effort than she wanted to expend. Appointing General Grey as Two Falls commander had been a good decision. He had been able to establish at least a modicum of control, which was more than any of his predecessors had managed to do. She was grateful to Tarik for sending him to her.

She sighed and rolled off the bed, moving towards the door where a pair of light sandals waited for her use. She slid her feet into them and walked through the enormous square halls, down the broad staircases where King Tarik had said she would meet servants to take her to the stables. There, she was given a veil to wear over her head and to block out the afternoon sun and the cloying, choking dust. She waited just inside the palace doors, and in a few minutes a covered chariot rolled up outside the carved stone edifice. Cira made her way leisurely towards it, a servant following behind with a parasol to keep the sun off of her pale skin. She flipped her white-blond hair back over one shoulder and climbed up into the chariot beside the driver, who gave her a bow and shook the reins. The team of horses set off at a good pace around the border of the palace. In about ten minutes, they pulled up beside the royal stables, a long row of squat buildings at the rear of the royal court. Cira climbed lightly off of the chariot, the veil drawn over her face. She saw King Tarik waiting for her with his retainers on either side of him. He was a man ten years older than she, small and elegant with dark flashing eyes and an air of cautious intelligence. He did not trust Cira, and for this she respected him.

They walked together through the rows of stables along the boxes of horses used by the lesser nobles of the household. Cira made appreciative noises as the slender, inquisitive faces poked their way out of their stable windows, ears flicking back and forth, recognizing the sound of footfalls on the stone alleyways running between the rows of stalls. Finally, they drew to the last row, where the king's personal favorite horses were kept. There was one of every color: a blood bay, a gray with a dark mane that cascaded across one side of its neck, an ebony black with a snip at the end of his silky muzzle. Here, King Tarik paused and offered his hand to the horse, who snuffled at it with familiarity. Tarik rubbed the horse's poll and playfully grabbed one ear. The horse tossed its head.

"Exquisite," Cira murmured, drawing her veil close around her face. In all honesty, the horse was much too small for her taste and looked as if its legs were so fragile that they would break if someone sat upon its back. But the eyes were wide and intelligent, the neck crested, and the nose slightly dished.

"He is the fastest one in my stables," Tarik told her proudly. "Named for his swiftness of foot. We hold races across the desert every two years; he won as a four-year-old and again as a six-year-old. After that, I put him to stud. You like to ride?" he inquired, turning to her.

"I do, though I am accustomed to mounts slightly taller and stronger."

Tarik laughed. "They do look small, yes, but they are strong, and much faster than any horse you have, I'll wager. It would be interesting to breed some of your horses with ours."

"It would," Cira said in a level tone. *I did not come here to discuss horse breeding*, she growled to herself. Such things were more to Athela's interests. She maneuvered a pleasant expression onto her face. Her negotiations with King Tarik had taught her that he would get to the business at hand when it suited him. Hurrying the matter was seen as impolite and would ultimately result in the postponement of the meeting for another time.

"Well," Tarik said, sighing, finality in his tone. He withdrew his hand from caressing his horse's head, and turned toward Cira, folding his hands behind his back, arched, in perfect posture. "To business, then, I suppose. What you've been waiting for," he added shrewdly, darting a glance at her beneath his dark brow. Cira noticed that his eyes were actually a hazel color. She hadn't seen it before. He was attractive, quiet in his confidence. *Should I seduce him?* She bit her lip, unsure. She *had* been fairly bored, and perhaps it would work out in her favor. Then again, if something went wrong, it could destroy all the negotiations they had gone through up to that point. *I'll try it out*, she decided. *And we'll see how it goes.*

"You have agreed to trade us timber in return for our goods, diamonds, et cetera. Is that how it is?" he began to stroll back along the row of boxes. His retainers were trailing at a respectful distance. Cira noticed them, but paid them little mind. She was used to being shadowed from her many years living in Joymaril. Bodyguards were a fact of royal life.

"That's correct," Cira nodded. "And your navy, should the need arise."

"And where do you plan to get the timber?" he inquired.

"If you ever visited my country, you would see that the land is rich with trees. We have a gigantic forest that is absolutely ripe for the taking. The supply of timber wouldn't be a problem; I have organized a rotation that would ensure the continuation of growth."

"Mm," Tarik murmured. "And what of the Ashans who live in that forest?"

Damn, Cira swore inwardly. *He's not as uninformed as he makes himself out to be.* "In a short period of time, they will no longer be a problem. I plan to take care of the Ashan population in the forest.

Until then, the trees outside of the forest will more than suffice for the parameters set by our agreement."

"I should need security," Tarik glanced up, squinting at something farther down the alley. Cira smiled to herself and tilted her head coyly towards him.

"What, my word isn't good enough?"

Tarik stopped and swiveled to face her, his feet making crescents in the dirt. He studied her for a long while. She stared back, unafraid of any sort of confrontation. She tilted her head up so that her neck looked longer and so that the sun hit her hair. Her eyes dared him to look away.

"Hardly," he murmured. Cira knew that she should take offense at his words, but there was something hidden beneath the word that she was able to pick up on. *Who's seducing who here?* This was a new tone for him to take; their prior discussions had been straightforward and professional—almost suspiciously so.

Tarik turned away from her and continued walking, not bothering to see if she was following him or not. She couldn't help but grin. This was going to be fun, much more fun than the usual idiots she kept around to make things interesting.

She walked up behind him, extending her stride slightly to catch up. He paused again until she fell into step beside him. "The Strikers," he said finally. "There have been reports that they are stirring things up, causing trouble for you."

"Not at all," Cira attempted to look surprised and innocent. Tarik saw right through it.

"Please," he said. "Don't bother."

The façade dropped. "The Strikers are a group of terrorists whose sole purpose is to cause public panic. I am doing my utmost to stop them, though they have a well-organized network of spies and informants. It has been very difficult to land my hands on them. I understand that you know what it is like to have radical organizations threatening your authority. I'm sure you can identify with my situation." Cira leered at him through the corner of her eye. *Serves him right for bringing the Strikers up*, she thought with satisfaction. A few years after he had assumed the throne, Tarik had been temporarily overthrown and imprisoned by a faction of the city that opposed his rule. His allies had been able to quash the rebellion and free him, but the humiliation of his short-term defeat was something that Cira would bet was still a sore point.

Tarik inhaled visibly through his nose, taking the barb in stride, processing it, letting it pass, getting the emotion out of his system before he responded. "I do not wish to begin trading with a country in danger of being overthrown," he returned evenly, knowing how such a comment would sit with Cira's notoriously short temper.

Cira's green eyes widened. "There is no danger of that," she said sharply, flicking her hair back over her shoulder. "They have fled to the mountains. They won't be difficult to eradicate, I guarantee you. There is no reason why our trade cannot begin as planned."

They had reached the edge of the stables where Cira's charioteer was waiting for her. Tarik stopped, musing, his hands still clasped behind his back. "I shall think about that," he said finally, then looked at her. "You are still young, but I think you hold much promise. I am confident that we can conclude these negotiations in the next few days."

Cira stiffened at his paternalistic tone, as Tarik knew she would. She turned away without bowing, a purposeful discourtesy, but Tarik let it go with a smile. *She has spirit*, he thought to himself, watching her dress sway as she walked away and climbed into the chariot. He saw, too, the way she let her hand brush the charioteer's as she stood beside him, not looking over at Tarik. He nearly laughed out loud. *And I think she is a bit dangerous. All the better.*

The evening's heat melted as soon as the moon rose up into the sky. The palace windows were thrown open to accommodate the refreshing wind, and Cira basked in the sensation, her eyes closed against it. A strand of hair slipped down over her bare shoulder and she opened her eyes, brushing it away. Beside her, Tarik slept quietly, and her green stare focused on him for a few lifts and falls of his breathing. Dark hair bloomed across his chest.

Good, she thought approvingly, turning away. *I hate a man who snores.* The entire thing had been quite satisfactory, though Cira would have preferred it to take place in her room instead of his. There was a disconcerting sense of dominance in the fact that she had had to come to *him*, but Cira had debated her options and decided to make the small concession; telling the king of a country to get lost after she had slept with him was probably not the best way to encourage successful negotiations. And Cira never spent the entire night with anyone. That was her rule. She couldn't risk someone else catching her asleep, seeing her in a moment of weakness.

She went back to watching Tarik for a while, then stood and padded across the floor to rifle through Tarik's papers. There was a small ornate writing desk next to one of the windows. Cira stood in front of it, perusing the documents. Nothing of interest. She reached down and slid one of the drawers open. Inside, on the top of a stack of blank parchment, lay a small dagger. *Aha!* She thought. She held the small weapon in her hand, closed the drawer with her knee, and turned to walk back to the bed. The dagger was only four or five inches long, but it was heavy for its size and could certainly do some damage if one knew how and where to use it. She smiled and slid it from its sheath, toying with it in her fingers. Perhaps it would be better if she killed Tarik here and now, assume his power. She felt the familiar rush of adrenaline and excitement at the thought of it, and inadvertently nicked her finger.

She swore under her breath and sucked the tip of her finger to stop the bleeding. *No, it wouldn't do at all,* she decided reluctantly. Much as she would enjoy killing Tarik, she would have a hell of a problem getting back out of the city. Besides, things were going well with their negotiations, especially with this latest development. She had him, as it were, right where she wanted him.

Feeling restless, she stood back up and went to go fetch her gown from where it had been tossed carelessly on the floor. Sliding it back over her head, she realized that it had been ripped slightly in the front, but it would do until she got back to her chambers. She considered for a few moments, eyeing the dagger in her hand. Finally, she smiled and left it on the pillow beside Tarik's head. *That'll give him something to think about in the morning*, she thought with satisfaction.

She slipped out of the doors of his chamber, and the two guards on either side came to attention as she passed. Cira didn't even give them a second glance, but inwardly cursed Tarik for not telling her where the private exit to his chamber was located. Every self-respecting royal had a hidden passageway reserved for smuggling lovers in and out for secret trysts. She gritted her teeth. *But*, she thought suddenly, *let the fool think what he wants. If Tarik believes he is the one in control...it may make him more willing to grant my demands. Let the fool think what he wants.* The thought comforted her greatly.

Hours later, Cira was sitting in her own bed, the curtains drawn. She wasn't sleeping, but was sitting and staring, her hands on her arms. She rubbed them and leaned back, her brain mulling over the various problems she had facing her. She rarely slept anymore.

A few more days and she would return home. She almost didn't want to. Back there were the Strikers, there was rebellion in Two Falls. She had serious business to attend to. Vireg, despite its initial discomforts, had grown on her. She smiled to herself. Once she was in control of it, she reminded herself, she could visit it whenever she liked.

The tiniest noise, no more than an out-of-place scratching on the floor, made her sit up and look about. She cautiously slid a hand under her pillow and withdrew the dagger she kept there, parting the curtains and stepping out into the room. She glanced from side to side and saw nothing. Perhaps it had just been one of the palace cats, or a large insect falling to the ground. But Cira's years of training told her it wasn't. She turned away and headed back to her bed, throwing the curtains wide and crawling on top of the sheets, tucking her feet under her. She waited, her back resting against the ornate headboard, her shoulders slightly hunched, light sheet of hair sliding down the sides of her head and spilling onto her lap.

"Before I throw my knife into your heart," she said evenly, not moving her gaze from directly in front of her, "I'd like to know who exactly has snuck into my room in the middle of the night and thought they could get away with it."

There was no response, but Cira was acutely aware that someone was there nonetheless. She whipped her head around, fingers resting on the dagger beside her leg. Standing against one of the pillars on the balcony was a woman, tall, muscular to the point where every vestige of feminine softness had been lost. She had skin a rich shade of dark brown, and black hair separated into hundreds of tiny braids that were tied back on the rear of her head. She had an oval face, with wide dark eyes that looked intelligent and ruthless, as if she had seen a good deal of cruelty in her time and had had her hand in dispensing some of said cruelty herself. Cira scanned her dark clothing swiftly and saw that she was carrying at least two daggers on her belt and one in her boot. She had an armband on one bicep made of simple black leather tied in an intricate knot. Cira didn't bother to call the guards. She had been half-expecting a sudden onslaught and was relieved that there was only one opponent. She could handle one. She slipped off her mattress, keeping the dagger in one hand, and strode forward. The woman was a great deal taller than she, and was regarding Cira with an appraising sort of level stare, sizing her up.

"Who are you?" Cira asked, flicking the dagger beside her thigh so the woman could see.

"My name is Kai," the woman replied. Her voice was low and slightly husky.

"And what the hell are you doing here? Who paid you to come and assassinate me?" Cira demanded.

The woman laughed in her low voice, a laugh that did not reach her eyes. "If that were the case, you'd be dead without ever having seen me here. That's not why I came. You're here to negotiate business, aren't you? Well, I have a business proposition."

Cira stopped walking and looked Kai up and down. She then looked out to the night sky. Cira was a good ways up in the palace, and the balcony was hard to reach. There was no way that Kai could have gotten into her room from the doors of her apartment, as that would have meant having to sneak past six floors of guards and servants and make it past the sentries at the entrance of her apartments. Not that Cira was about to put it past this strange woman, but it seemed to her that the easiest point of entry would have been the balcony. But no one could have made it to the balcony except for—

"An Ashan," Cira snarled, eyes darting down to Kai's hand, loose at her side. There was the telltale sixth finger. "You're an Ashan."

"That's right," Kai confirmed in a nonchalant voice. "Half-right, at least. But this," She held up her hand, wiggling the extra finger at Cira, "shouldn't matter right now." Cira noticed that Kai had a tattoo in a sprawling, jagged pattern on the last three fingers of her hand, curving around them, spreading diagonally across the back of her hand and curling around her wrist like a bracelet.

"Get out," Cira growled at her, baring her teeth, her eyes flashing green. Kai didn't look impressed by the order, and didn't move a muscle. Cira sprang forward, flicking her knife up and slashing. Kai darted to the side, ducking her upper body backwards to avoid three of Cira's sweeping blows; out came Kai's own dagger, and she blocked two more. She ran sideways up one of the pillars leading out to the balcony and flipped over Cira's head, landing behind her. Without turning around, Cira blocked her stabs, then whipped and smacked Kai hard across the jaw. The Ashan woman grunted slightly and reeled backwards so that her spine touched the ground, then her legs shot her up, and she landed, crouched on the ground, dagger out.

She and Cira circled one another, Kai keeping low to the ground, edging sideways. Cira flipped her dagger expertly so that the blade was pointing down as she gripped the hilt in her fist. She was ready to stab.

Suddenly, Kai stopped. "I didn't come here to kill you."

"So I heard," Cira sneered. "That doesn't make any amount of difference to me. *You* should be killed immediately. And I've been looking for some fun."

"I hear you've been having some trouble getting rid of the Strikers," Kai said, a smile edging up one side of her mouth, an indentation forming there like the end of an arrow. "Been quite the irritation, haven't they? Been rescuing us Ashans right and left, haven't they?"

Cira refused to answer, but her interest was piqued. She kept circling, keeping her eyes steady on Kai's. Neither of them was blinking. Her reaction told Kai that it was safe to continue speaking.

"I could kill them for you. I could kill all of them."

At this, Cira stopped and laughed out loud, throwing her hands down to her sides, relaxing. Kai stood warily, eyeing her. Cira looked at her, head tilted back slightly. "*You'd* kill the Strikers for *me?* Aren't they supposed to be your saviors, you Ashans? Your last and best chance to live? If you think for a moment that I'm going to believe something like that, you've got another thing coming."

"They've saved a lot of Ashans," Kai continued, her tone hard. "But they haven't saved one. The one Ashan they should have saved."

Cira sensed an important chord being struck and leered at her. "What, was it your boyfriend? Girlfriend?"

Kai blinked slowly. "My sister," she said gruffly.

Cira let the memories sink in, wash over her opponent, savoring every second of Kai's pain as if it were a fine wine.

Kai took in a breath. "Your soldiers took her nearly three years ago when you seized Two Falls. I want her back. I've been trying to get passage to your country to try and rescue her, but there's no ship that'll take me now. I nearly made it once, but I was found once I was in Eldrest port, and I was sent back here. Then I heard that you were coming and arranged to meet you. I've come to strike a deal."

Cira made a *tsking* noise in the front of her mouth. "Dear, dear, no one in the whole country to help you find your wayward sister? Can't say I envy the lack of friends you have. What's the matter? Are they all dead, too?"

"I don't have any," Kai said flatly. "Those that I thought I had are gone. But the story of my life is not the issue here. I'm offering you a deal. The heads of the Strikers in return for my sister's freedom."

Cira paused, narrowing her eyes slightly at Kai. She deliberately turned her back on her, as if daring Kai to rush her and strike her down, and ambled over to one of the tables, laden with food. She took a small piece of fruit and began to nibble at the tip of it, perching on the edge of the table. She folded her arms, her dagger still clasped in one hand, looking at Kai appraisingly. "Now, what makes you think that I would need your help in hunting down the Strikers?" she asked shrewdly.

Kai let out a small laugh. "What, you're telling me you're not having problems in that department? How many of them have you killed?"

Cira glared at her silently.

Kai shrugged, uncaring. "Whatever. The point is, they're all skillful, trained warriors. And they've got a network of helpers, spies. You'll never reach them even if you send your entire army after them. They'll vanish up into the mountains, and they'll reappear when you're least expecting it. But if you send me, they'll be dead within three months."

Cira frowned, flipping the dagger around in her hand, catching it by the tip and then again by the hilt. "Why don't you just kill me now, then, and free your sister? Why try and strike a bargain with me?"

"Well, my guess is that you've given orders that if you happen to meet with an untimely demise, the Ashan prisoners you still have will all be executed immediately before there's any chance of them being rescued. Rather a nice shock for any idealistic freedom fighters out there, wouldn't it?"

She's certainly not a fool, Cira mused interestedly. *She saw right through that little scheme, didn't she? And perhaps...perhaps what she says may make some vestige of sense. None of my guards have had any luck so far in capturing the rest of the Strikers. This Ashan could be of some help if she's able to back up her boasting.* Cira couldn't help but let a smile escape her lips. *And, after she kills the Strikers, I can just kill her and whoever her lousy sister is and just be done with it.*

"How do you expect to infiltrate the Strikers?" Cira asked keenly. "They don't just let anyone into their inner circle, you know. There's probably some sort of screening process. They see you anywhere near me, they'll kill you as soon as look at you."

Kai rolled her shoulders around and set one hand on her hip, skin gleaming in the moonlight. "There are two reasons. One, I'm half-Ashan and there's no earthly reason for me to be working for you. Two, I know one of the Strikers already."

Cira looked up sharply. "Who?"

Kai took in Cira's reaction. "One of the two Ashan Strikers. The Brothers, I think they're called now."

"Which one?"

Kai again studied her. The intensity in Cira's voice belied her outward act of calm detachment. "Archer," Kai said slowly.

Cira stood and blinked, glaring at Kai. She paced back and forth a few times as Kai tried to work out what it all meant. Kai was a bit surprised that Archer's name seemed to rouse some sort of personal reaction in Cira, but she kept her mouth shut.

"I don't even know if your sister is still alive," Cira said finally, stopping her pacing and looking up.

"Her name is Rowan; she's from Two Falls," Kai volunteered, a hopeful vulnerability creeping into her voice.

"Do you think I know the *name* of every prisoner rotting in my dungeons?" Cira snapped. "You say you knew this Archer. How do

I know you're not working with him now?"

"You don't," Kai replied mildly.

Cira resumed her pacing, back and forth, back and forth, while Kai watched her movements. "*How* did you know him?"

Something in the odd way Cira was acting told Kai that replying that she and Archer had been lovers wouldn't yield the best results in the way of her goal. "We worked with each other from time to time in Riddleton. Town got too small for the both of us, so I decided to move out."

"All the way to Vireg?" Cira asked dubiously.

"Well, there was an element of official banishment involved as well," Kai admitted, shifting her weight to one leg, hip jutting cockily to one side. Cira appraised Kai's appearance differently now. She supposed that some would find Kai attractive. She had a well-built face, and her dark eyes were an astonishing almond shape, with high cheekbones and full lips. But in Cira's opinion Kai was too much action, too much force, not enough softness and subversive glances.

Feeling slightly better, Cira tilted her head to one side and threw her shoulders back. Kai stood quietly, levelly, the dagger resting still and ready in one hand. "What are your terms?" she said finally.

Kai was relieved, but masked it. She was ready for this. "First, I must be granted safe passage to Faridor. You'll grant me adequate paperwork so that I am not arrested as soon as I arrive. I'll be allowed to see if my sister is all right, and if she is, then you'll release her, we'll go back to Two Falls, and I'll kill the Strikers. If she's dead, the deal's off, and you can rot for all I care."

"Stop right there," Cira hissed, narrowing her eyes once more so that they flashed green in the light from the torches. "What makes you think that I'm just going to let your sister walk free as soon as you march to Faridor? There's no way. I'll grant you safe passage and paperwork, and you may go to Faridor to see if she's still alive. I agree that if she's dead, the deal is off. If she lives, you have two months to kill all the Strikers, and I want proof. I want their bodies sent to me. When they are all dead—only then—your sister and you can go free." *That is, until I have you both arrested and killed, but we'll just leave that as a surprise for you to figure out afterwards.*

Kai was in no hurry to make a decision. She weighed the possibilities. If it were only her life at stake, she would take the agreement in a heartbeat, but she didn't like the thought of gambling Rowan's life as well. It looked, however, as if there wasn't going to be a lot of choice in the matter. "Done," Kai said.

"Oh, and one last thing," Cira added. Kai eyed her warily. She had been expecting additional provisions. It couldn't have been that easy to strike a deal with Cira. "Archer, the Ashan you were talking about before? The one you said you knew?"

"Yes," Kai said cautiously, immediately alert and on her guard. "What about him?"

"You're not to kill him," Cira ordered in a low, silky voice. "I don't want him dead. Beat him senseless, lie to him, trap him, walk him into a ditch, and have him shipped to Faridor in a box; I don't care. But I want him alive, is that understood?"

Kai's mind raced. "Agreed," she replied. "You'll get Archer alive."

Cira paused. "And your personal feelings will not get in the way of your work?"

Kai smirked, glancing down at her boots. "Archer and I did not part on satisfactory terms. It was a long while ago anyway, so what few residual feelings I have for him are all of the negative variety, I can assure you." She could sense that she was close to getting what she'd come for.

"I take it we have a deal, then," Cira said finally. "Remember, though, if they aren't dead in two months, I'll kill your sister, send you her head, and then I'll kill you. Is that understood?"

Kai barely blinked. "Understood."

"Fine." Cira walked out of the room to another table, set with parchment and ink. Kai followed warily, replacing the dagger in its holster beneath her vest. Her heart was starting to pound ever so slightly as Cira wrote the documents, the pen scratching on the papers. On every paper, Cira flipped open the top part of the ring on her right hand, poured a gob of green ink on the bottom right hand of the document, and pressed her seal into it, a snake wrapped around a rose. Kai watched her silently, blinking her large almond-shaped eyes.

Finally, when all was in order, Cira pushed back her chair and presented Kai with the documents. Kai took them and looked them over to make sure that everything was satisfactory.

"Is it all to your liking?" she inquired.

Kai glanced up. Her eyes were a dark violet, rimmed in black; the torchlight caught the rich color and reflected it back. "Everything seems to be in order," she agreed. "I'll send you word after I go to Faridor to let you know whether the deal is on or not. Should I contact you here in Vireg, or should I just leave word at the fortress?"

"Leave it at Faridor," Cira stretched her arms carelessly behind her back. "I'll be done here within a few days." She paused, looking up at her new accomplice, a smile stretching across her face. "I'd get a move on if I were you. Time is wasting."

Kai didn't bother replying. She spun on her heel, strode briskly across the room, and vanished over the balcony, dark skin dissolving into the blue shadows of the night sky, leaving Cira standing alone in the room behind her, nightdress fluttering against her legs in the night breeze.

The night streets of Vireg were teeming with life; seemingly every person in the city had poured out into the open-air markets once the sun set. Vendors hawked their wares from every corner; there was loud, discordant, clanging music, street performers jostling for position, goods and food of every kind dangling from stalls and thrust into the periphery of passersby. Smoke and steam billowed up from fire-bellied cooktops where grizzled merchants tossed intoxicatingly scented piles of sweetly spiced meats and unidentifiable vegetables. Kai walked through the brightly lit city streets, ducking her head. Her stature was so imposing that some of the passersby shot her curious looks as she slid past, but for the most part she went unnoticed.

She went to her small flat on the east side of the city and packed all of her belongings in two bags as the music from the streets below carried up on the wind through her open window. She slung the bags over her shoulder, strapping as many weapons as she could on her legs and arms so she wouldn't have to worry about packing them. She cast her eyes around the dingy one-room affair. She wouldn't worry about paying the last week's rent. She had no inclination to ever return to Vireg.

Back into the street, walking amongst the jostling crowd, Kai kept her eyes straight ahead of her. Images flitted in front of her face: Archer,

Rowan behind the bars of some dank cell at the bottom of Faridor. Her pace increased. It would be easier not to have to kill Archer. The others she didn't give a damn about. She would get her sister and head for the mountains. The rest of the country could burn.

After a long, winding walk, she reached the western border of the port city and slid through some close-sitting buildings to a dock. A man was waiting beside a large ship, which was gently bobbing in the ebbing tide. She slipped him a few coins, flashed her papers, and slunk by him, keeping her face covered, attracting no more attention than a rat scurrying up one of the ropes.

The voyage across the narrow Viregian sea was a calm one; the violent storms that occasionally shook their way down the channel had not begun to gather their full winter strength. For the first three days at sea, Kai did nothing more than sit in the bow of the ship and gaze off towards her destination. She was going home. Her sister was alive; she knew it in her heart. And she would risk everything to keep it that way.

Four days later, Cira stood before King Tarik in the splendor of his audience chamber to bid her final farewells before beginning her voyage back to Faridor. Cira held her head high and bobbed a smooth curtsy, aware that the eyes of his entire court were upon her.

Tarik, outfitted in a resplendent ensemble of deep indigo and embroidered gold, met her eyes coolly and smiled. "Thank you for your visit, your Highness. I would like to offer you a gift in acknowledgment of your departure and as a symbol of our countries' lasting friendship." He turned behind him, where one of his aides handed him a polished ebony box inlaid with a white mother-of-pearl lotus flower. He extended it to her. "I count among my advisors some scholars deeply attuned to the mysteries and magic of the natural world. I am assured that this is an object of great significance, and they advise that I give it to you."

Cira eyed the servant who had handed Tarik the box, but he gave nothing away, just ducked his head in appropriate modesty. Eagerly, she cracked open the box. Within it sat a silver medallion on a bed of crushed indigo velvet (had King Tarik dressed to match his own gift? If he had, she was suitably impressed.) The medallion was engraved with ancient characters that meant nothing to her. She closed the box and gave another pretty curtsy.

"Thank you, Your Majesty," she said, her voice clear. "I will treasure it always. I thank you for a...stimulating visit."

King Tarik smiled.

Later, as her palanquin wound its way through the buzzing market streets towards the city port, Cira found her mind churning over the events of the visit, considering how she could leverage her newfound partnership with Tarik to benefit her in the war against the Strikers. As her entourage drew farther and farther away from the palace, the inlaid box sat in the midst of one of her traveling chests, its existence and its contents quite forgotten.

CHAPTER FOUR

Archer sighted down the shaft of his arrow, one golden eye slightly closed. The wind shifted infinitesimally around him, and he waited patiently as the branch beneath him swayed sideways, then grew still once more. He was balanced like a cat in a low crouch, his form perfectly motionless. About fifty yards away, down the side of the rocky mountain, a deer delicately stepped over a low branch and lipped distractedly at a few blades of grass. It could sense that something was amiss. The large head turned towards him; the brown liquid eyes searched the trees. Then, just as it made a start to turn and run—

Archer's arrow sang through the branches and landed squarely in the deer's heart. Without so much as a cry, it toppled soundly over and lay still. Archer lowered his arms and waited for a few seconds, letting the quiet of the woods fall back over him. He picked his way quickly down the trunk and strode to the deer. He lowered himself to one knee and sharply pulled out the arrow. He had leaned down to heave the heavy animal over onto its side when there was the slightest scuffling in the branches behind him, and he whipped around, arrow ready against the bow. He dropped his hands instantly when he saw what it was. A broad grin bloomed across his mouth.

"Tarr!" he exclaimed, leaping to his feet. "Athela!"

He ran across the clearing and crushed them both into a close hug. Athela, tired as she was from the long journey, couldn't help but relax, and she squeezed him tightly until he released them. He was positively beaming as he looked from Tarr's face to hers.

"Your journey was well?" he asked Tarr in Ashan. He reached out and clasped his hand over the back of Tarr's neck, over the black, looping Ashan tattoo Tarr had gotten when he and Archer had performed the ceremony to become brothers. Archer bore the tattoo on his own neck, too, his birch leaf intertwined with Tarr's aspen, the furls of ink dipping down below the neck of his cloak.

"It was well," Tarr sighed, adjusting the drape of the traditional Ashan traveling cloak that swept down across his front, clapping his hand across the back of Archer's neck. Briefly, they touched foreheads in the traditional greeting. "I will speak of it when we are all together once more in the caves."

"It is good," Archer assented and grinned at Athela once again, switching to Common language. "And you, my lovely, how are you?"

"In desperate need of a bath," Athela couldn't stifle a smile. "And very glad to see you."

"Quite a tempting combination," he grinned and turned back to the deer. He slid his bow over one shoulder and heaved the deer up onto his back. "You just caught me while I was ordering up some dinner. And don't worry," he said to Tarr, "they'll have something for you."

"Good," Tarr said, relieved, eyeing the felled deer with an expression of dismay.

They climbed up through the woods until the trees began to thin out, then they picked their way along the rocky slopes toward the caves. A few guards waved at them here and there from their concealed watchpoints, and one or two shouted greetings to Tarr and Athela. As they turned into the rock entrance of the cave, an eager young woman came dashing breathlessly up to greet them. She was bouncy and energetic, with short-cropped hair and a bad burn on the side of her neck.

"Tarr!" she grinned, fairly jumping up and down. "Welcome home!"

"Hello, Leonore," Tarr replied, his general aura of wary calm a distinct contrast to her exuberance.

"I've been helping everyone with their studies while you've been away," she told him seriously, falling into step beside them. "And we've had one or two new people in who I think would be good additions to the spy network."

"Wonderful," Tarr said, feeling a bit drained by her joie de vivre. *I'll feel better after a good night's sleep,* he assured himself.

"Leonore," Athela said, glancing at Tarr out of the corner of one eye, "Why don't you go run and fetch the others and tell them we're back?"

"Okay!" the girl exclaimed and rushed off to do her bidding.

"Entirely too upbeat," Archer shook his head once she was out of earshot. "Completely unacceptable."

They entered the main cavern, which was a swarm of activity as usual. People were walking to and fro purposefully from the housing to the training centers in the back of the caves. A few smiled at them shyly, and a number even came up to say hello. A few moments later, Marc, Si, and Laith were striding out of the personal quarters towards them.

"You're back!" Si chirped, rushing forward to hug Tarr.

"You're taller!" Tarr exclaimed, holding him back at arm's length. Si had, in reality, not grown since the age of twelve. None of the Strikers had the heart to tell him that he was probably doomed to be five foot two for the rest of his life.

"Thanks," Si sniffed importantly, "I think I've gone up about an inch and three-eighths in the past two months. I'm going through a growth spurt."

There was a pointed silence, broken by Marc clearing his throat. "So, Archer," he raised his eyebrows, eyeing the deer still slung across the tall Ashan's shoulders. "This is a good look for you."

"You like it?" Archer inquired, turning to display his burden from the optimal angle. "It's the latest accessory. I call it 'dead carcass.'"

"It works," Marc nodded approvingly.

They fell into separate groups, making their way back to Laith's office to go over all that had transpired. Tarr dawdled at the rear; Laith stepped beside him and put a hand on his shoulder. Tarr, for his part, was glancing from side to side, hoping to see Rane's soft, oval face and long auburn hair.

"She's not here," Laith told him as if reading his thoughts. "She had to stay in Two Falls. There was urgent business that she needed to see to, and I asked her to stay. I'm sorry."

"I understand," Tarr shrugged, swallowing down his deep disappointment. *At least she's all right*, he assured himself. *You know that this is how things have to be.*

"She's the best we've got out there for that kind of work," Laith reminded him gently. "She's invaluable."

"I know."

"She sends you her love."

Tarr gave Laith an appreciative smile. "Archer filled me in on a bit of what's been going on. Sounds like we've missed a lot."

"Yes, there have been some interesting developments," Laith agreed. He jogged up the last few stairs and went quickly down the hall to his office, where the others were all waiting for them, chatting quietly. They fell silent once Laith and Tarr entered, closing the curtain behind them.

"First things first," Laith began, sliding into his seat, his large black dog lying down directly behind him. "Tarr, Athela, why don't you let us know how your trip went?"

Since the mission had not been entirely productive, Tarr and Athela's recap didn't take very long. Tarr told Laith what he could about the strength of the Ashan tribes and the layout of the forest, but concluded with the admission that it was unlikely they would receive any sort of aid.

If he was disappointed by this news, Laith hid it well. In turn, he gave an overview of the developments of the resistance, what spoils they had been able to take from their raids, and the influx of new refugees. Archer gave the reports from Two Falls, and Marc went over the status of training in the camp.

After this was all done, Laith leaned back in his chair, lacing his fingers behind his head. "That just about covers everything, I think," he mused. "Except..." he leaned beside his desk and withdrew an old wooden tablet. "This was recently recovered from the ruins of the Two Falls library. A welcome home present for you both," he smiled slightly as Tarr and Athela eagerly edged forward to examine it.

"Who found it?" Athela asked, her gray eyes lighting up.

"An Ashan refugee was holed up in a cellar, and she unearthed it and got it to us."

"Any idea what it is?" Tarr inquired.

Laith shrugged. "You two are the scholars."

"Morthenstar's name is cropping up all over the place here," Athela muttered. Tarr could see that her mind was already lost to the world of ancient translation, which—apart from grimacing, riding her horse, and verbally sparring with Archer—was her favorite hobby. She closed the book with an efficient snap and gave Laith a curt nod. "We'll have it done by tomorrow."

"Let's let Tarr get some sleep first, though," Archer suggested, sending his brother a sideways look. "He looks as though he's going to pass out."

Indeed, Tarr felt it. Laith gave his quick assent and the meeting dispersed. Tarr stumbled down the hallway towards his small room on the other end of the caverns. Though by this point it was late in the night, there were still a number of people out in the main area working by candlelight at the long tables, speaking occasionally in quiet voices. It was odd, Tarr reflected, that a place as unnatural as a cave should feel like home, but there was a peace in being in that vast cavern at night, hearing the quiet shuffling of feet on the stone floors or hearing the pounding of snow or thunder in the world above while dozens of people slept nearby.

He barely noticed that Archer was guiding him to his room. He gave Archer a sleepy smile as his brother elbowed him towards his bed and tucked the blankets around his chin as though he were a child. Tarr's room was sparse, his bed neat, and the walls stacked with books and papers. There was a small writing desk in one corner, with pens at the ready. Everything was well-kept and well-ordered. As he gazed sleepily around his chamber, enjoying the sensation of being back in his own bed, he thought suddenly of Rane's swords and how they used to be stacked up in the corner, her cloak hung beside the door, how she felt curled up against him.

Archer was watching him with a lopsided grin on his face. "Sorry, I'm a poor substitute," he joked. "She'll be back soon." Archer blew out the lamp beside Tarr's bed. Even in the darkness, Archer's pale skin glowed almost blue. "I'll try to keep Athela and her translations at bay for at least six hours. You'd better enjoy your sleep."

"I missed you," Tarr murmured gratefully.

"Uh, huh, sure," Archer grinned sardonically. "Good night."

He closed the door behind him and padded back through the hallways to the main cavern. A number of the people working at the tables glanced up and flashed smiles at him. He briefly considered going to bed, then slowly turned on his heel and strode up the flight of stairs to the second floor of rooms. He stopped at a door, gave the briefest of knocks on the threshold, and strode in. Athela started and looked up from over a thick, dusty tome.

"Darn," Archer muttered.

"Hoping to catch me undressing?" Athela asked drily.

"I wouldn't dream of it," He flopped his long body over onto her bed and folded his hands. He watched her for a few minutes until she finally heaved a sigh and glared over at him.

"I assume that you didn't find a substitute person to annoy while I was away."

"No one compares to you, Athela."

"Well, you'll have to hold out a bit longer," she told him shortly. "This new parchment could really be something big."

"I'll behave."

True to his word (and somewhat to Athela's surprise), Archer didn't disturb her for the rest of the night. She scribbled on unflaggingly until the wee hours of the morning, pen scratching along as she painstakingly worked through her translation word by difficult word. Only a sentence or two was completed by the time she finally pushed herself back from the desk and rubbed the sleep from her eyes. Her fingers were stained black by the ink from the pen, and the skin around her face felt heavy. She glanced over and saw that Archer had fallen asleep, his long neck tilted toward her, angular chin jutting down toward his chest. She studied him thoughtfully. She would die before she told him so, but she had always liked the way Archer slept; it was deep and silent like snow falling. It looked as though nothing short of an earthquake could wake him, but Athela knew better. All of the Strikers had spent long nights out in the cold and rain together, so she knew from experience that he would snap awake at the slightest noise.

She coughed lightly, and, true to her expectations, the golden orbs shot open and Archer was immediately awake. "Everything all right?" he asked.

"I'm tired," she said shortly, avoiding his eyes. "I want to go to bed."

He tilted his head to one side. "I'll go," he offered, and stood to leave.

Marc found Laith in the stables at the back of their cavernous compound, leaning on the makeshift stall door of a buckskin mare. Her belly was swollen, and she kept shifting uncomfortably, ignoring the rack of hay in the corner of her stall. Every once in a while, she twisted back to send an irritated look towards her bulging abdomen, then heaved a sigh and switched her heavy weight to the other back leg.

Laith had a peaceful expression on his face as he watched, and straightened up a bit as he heard Marc approach behind him. "What's the update?" Marc asked, passing Laith a steaming mug of tea.

Laith took a grateful sip and shrugged. "I'll be surprised if she doesn't foal tonight. We'll see."

The mare flicked her ears towards the newcomer and then gave another long-suffering sigh. Laith reached out and straightened her forelock between her ears. "Poor old girl," he said soothingly. "Just a short while, and then you'll have all the trouble you can manage, I guarantee you that."

Marc smiled and looked out over his shoulder. The stables were fashioned from a long row of caves with an aisleway in front of them. The wall of the cave opposite the stalls was open, looking out over the spreading scenery below the mountain. This area was sheltered from the wind and was quite lovely in the summer months; now that it was getting chillier, Tarr and some of the half-Ashan recruits had helped build a temporary sliding door to protect against the cold while still letting light in during the day.

The two friends watched the horse for a short while. "Nice to have Tarr and Athela back," Marc observed.

"Very," Laith murmured. "Though it would have been helpful to have any success at all with the Ashans."

"Do you think Cira will go after them soon?" Marc asked. "Burn them out of their trees, like she's promised to do?"

Laith shook his head. "She's sitting on the biggest store of timber in the country. She can't afford to go burning it off. Her greed is, for the moment, our greatest bit of protection."

They fell silent again, watching the restless animal in the stall before them. "She looks like Ilaina's horse," Marc observed.

Laith smiled, but his eyes were sad, and he looked out, considering the mare standing stiffly across from them. "A little bit, I grant you. If Ilaina's horse filled out."

The mare grunted as if in agreement. Marc looked sidelong over at Laith. It had been almost three years since Laith had learned that his wife was presumed dead. All the while, he had stubbornly clung to the belief that she was still alive, that he would have known if she'd been killed. But after so long, with no word of her, not even a whisper, Marc could tell that some part of Laith was starting to lose hope, though he was unlikely to ever admit to it—even to Marc.

"Do you ever wonder where Oren is?" Laith asked suddenly, as if he'd been reading Marc's thoughts.

Marc took a deep breath, remembered his boyfriend's willowy frame, the way he sidled into a room, the sweet expression in his eyes. They, for their part, had barely been able to say goodbye when he'd abruptly been forced to leave Joymaril palace, but at least it had been something. They hadn't expected their separation to stretch on as long as it had. "I do, yes," Marc said. "I hope. I hope that he's all right, that he made it through this somehow. We don't know what happened in Joymaril after Cira took power; the whole city has been locked down. But there's always a chance. There's a chance he survived. That's what I hope."

Laith leaned his beautiful head forward and rested it again on his arms, the mug of tea steaming in one hand. The mare, distracted though she was, reached out her nose and took a *whuffing* inhale of the tea, then decided that whatever was going on in her middle was worth more of her attention.

"Do you feel guilty?" Laith asked abruptly. "About the people we had to leave behind? Not just Oren and Ilaina, but everyone in Two Falls. Ma, having to leave her home because of us. Silva and her brothers.

I don't even know if they made it out. I hope they did." He shook his head, his voice full of melancholy. "Sometimes I wonder if we're not a curse on everyone we touch."

Marc stared at him, trying to mask his alarm. He'd never heard Laith talk like this before and wondered how long he'd been feeling this way. He tried to wrestle with what to say next, to choose his words carefully. "I have to hope," Marc said finally. "I hope that Ilaina is alive." Here, he swallowed. He, like all the others, had basically resigned himself to the belief that Ilaina had died at Joymaril, though he would never tell Laith as much. "I hope that Oren is alive. I hope that Ma is all right, that she survived because we sent her out in time. And Silva and her brothers. I hope they made it up north, and that they've rebuilt a new life for themselves, far away from Cira."

Laith smiled faintly, an expression that did not reach his eyes. "Sounds nice the way you say it, Marc."

Marc shrugged. "It's what I believe," he said simply.

All at once, the mare gave a groan and moved away to the back of her stall, where she began to pace back and forth, looking discontent. Laith straightened, stretching his arms against the side of the stall door. "Marc, go and get Athela," he asked. "I think it's time."

"All right."

Marc turned away and headed back to the main living quarters, his mind uneasy.

"That's him!" Leonore hissed urgently in a not-so-low voice. She nudged the girl sitting beside her. "That's Tarr!"

The other girl narrowed her eyes and watched the tall, thin Ashan as he quietly entered the training room, sunlight streaming momentarily over his face as he passed beneath one of the holes in the cavern roof, walked across the open floor where dozens of others were practicing their hand to hand combat, and strode into his office on the far side of the enclosure. None of the other pairs had even noticed him come in. The door shut quietly behind him.

She shrugged, nonplussed. "He doesn't look like much. Archer is more handsome."

"Just you wait," Leonore maintained staunchly. "You'll see."

The other girl, Imran, was a bit older than Lenore and predisposed to cynicism. She folded her arms dubiously.

Tarr shuffled around the small office adjoining the combat room, sifting through the sheaf of papers and letters that had accumulated since his departure and that Laith had kept safe for him. He was quite methodical; he would carefully open each one, his eyes skimming over the scratchy Ashan characters within. Once he had read a letter through three times and digested its contents, he would carefully place the letter in the crackling stone fireplace in one corner of his room and prod it with a poker until it had dissolved into nothing but ash.

Anyone attempting to rifle through Tarr's office to find incriminating documents relating to his highly effective spy network would find their search to be a short and frustrating one. If there was one thing Tarr had learned, it was that papers could be stolen, and Tarr knew that something as innocuous as a name scrawled on a parchment was enough to sign someone's death warrant. So, he had trained himself to learn everything by heart. He was aided in this endeavor by his naturally photographic memory, as well as his innate diligence and patience. By that point, three years after the beginning of the war, his network consisted of anywhere between fifteen to twenty active agents, all of whom were cataloged away in his memory: faces, names, positions, aliases, code names, missions.

Then there were the ones who had died, whose names he couldn't forget even if he tried. Try as he might to push them aside, to clear up his memory and make space for new faces, new volunteers, new missions, it was the faces of the dead who came back to him most, often on sleepless nights or quiet afternoons. He remembered all of them, not only the ones who had died but the ones who had simply disappeared. There were so many.

He shook his head, trying to clear it of its gloomy thoughts, and focused on the task at hand. The news, as he went through it, was a mixed lot. No new information had been given him. He had reached a stalemate in Two Falls and Faridor; both institutions had become almost fanatically paranoid about his spies, so his agents had to positively creep around or remain immobile in order to avoid detection. Rane was really the most effective spy he had, but he was hesitant to send her into the thick of the fray. Oftentimes, the most dangerous missions were the ones only Rane was qualified for, and the internal conflict between duty and emotion was a daily torment.

Faridor, Tarr reasoned, was his best bet for gathering critical information. There were two avenues of communication within Kagai's forces: the major orders, which came from Cira in Faridor, and the updates about personnel and tactics that were sent from Two Falls. In Faridor, a well-placed agent could possibly receive both. It had been over a month since they'd had a new update about Cira's battle plans and stratagems, and though he'd heard from his agents in the fortress that Cira was away on a political visit across the sea, he'd been impatiently waiting for any possible news of what that trip meant for the resistance. He hoped against anything that she would not receive more reinforcements from whatever kingdom she was visiting; the Strikers' army was already quite sorely outnumbered.

His eyes skimmed across the next decrypted note, which began: *FOX. FARIDOR. HAWK.* This was quite simply to tell Tarr who the message was for (Tarr had been nicknamed "the Fox" by the Kagaian army in Two Falls, and Tarr's own agents had adopted it almost as a point of pride), where the agent was placed (Faridor) and the name of the agent in question (Hawk). Tarr's mind quickly skimmed through his internal list of names and faces...ah, yes, Hawk. She was an older woman who had lived with her daughter's family in Two Falls until they had all been killed in a raid. The grandmother had managed to escape and survive and had gone through a number of channels before she was successfully smuggled out of Two Falls. Though she could have easily waited out the war in the safety and security of the Strikers' mountain stronghold, the day after she arrived at the hideout, she walked up to Tarr and demanded a post as a spy. She had been a most effective one, too; she was set up as a charwoman at Faridor and was privy to all the gossip that flew about. Due to her age and complete believability, she was almost above suspicion. Tarr looked down and read the rest of her note. Translated, it read:

BADGER DISCOVERED. WAIT ARREST. PLACE OPEN UP FOR NEW CHAMBERMAID TO K. ADVISE.

Tarr reread the note a number of times. The only difficulty the old woman had was with the Ashan language, which—along with a smattering of basic words in sign language that Rane had taught them—was mandatory for all his spies to learn. The old woman was far past the age where learning a new language was an easy endeavor, and her notes were choppy at best. "Badger" was another one of Tarr's spies, a groom in Cira's stables. He was a good man, and Tarr had sent him to find out if they were expecting a horse delivery from the country Cira was visiting. If Hawk's note was to be believed, he had been found out. Tarr briefly debated trying to organize some sort of rescue mission but reluctantly negated the idea. It would put too many other lives in jeopardy, and the odds of success were dismal. The dungeons of Faridor were notorious by this point; there had never been a successful rescue attempt or escape. They were located underground and impossible to tunnel through, as the only exit was into the sea outside. The entrances back up into the fortress itself were few and thoroughly guarded, with at least three checkpoints to cross before anyone could go in or out of the front gate. It was understood as a fact of the war that when one went into the dungeons of Faridor, one did not come out.

The other tidbit of information was a bit more positive. "K" was the abbreviation for Cira. A position as a chambermaid in her rooms! Tarr's mind whizzed as he went through his stock of available agents, trying to find the right fit. If someone were to be working that close to Cira, they would have to be someone by whom Cira would not feel threatened. And how best to introduce his new agent into Cira's household? Tarr needed to make sure that if the chambermaid was found out, there could be no relationship established between her and any of the other spies in the fortress. He had another agent, already a servant in Cira's private quarters...but no, she was also too valuable. Perhaps one of his agents in Two Falls, one of the aristocracy, could write a reference letter. Yes, that would do very well. Cira wasn't likely to be too suspicious of a message from an old, respected name.

His brain continued to hum along as he strode over to the fire and thoughtfully poked the letter into oblivion. His concentration on this new problem was broken when he flipped through the remaining letters, all of which amounted to nothing new, especially in Two Falls.

Tarr had hoped that Rane would have uncovered something during her time in the city, something the others had missed.

Two Falls was its own problem entirely. He didn't know whether it had been an incredibly keen move on Cira's part or whether it had been sheer dumb luck, but after her former general in Two Falls had died a year earlier under rather mysterious circumstances (namely, a white and black-fletched arrow to the throat), Cira had appointed a man named Hector Grey to the post.

General Grey, as he was now known, had been a gift of sorts from the King of Vireg. He'd been brought over specially to serve as a war advisor to Cira, and as his capabilities had proved more and more apparent, he had moved higher and higher in her ranks. Tarr wasn't aware of all the details and squabbling that had occurred prior to Grey's appointment as commander of Two Falls, but Cira could not have picked a more shrewd, capable man to run her operations in the city. General Grey was cautious, patient, intensely intelligent, and diligent where his predecessor had been careless. The death rate of Tarr's agents had tripled since General Grey assumed command, and the number of successful Ashan captures had doubled. Instead of the easily bribed guards, Grey began to employ agents and soldiers just as focused and careful as he. Though Tarr loathed him for the bloodshed he had caused and the cool efficiency with which he had uncovered, exposed, and killed his agents, he had to admit that he felt a considerable amount of grudging respect for General Grey. The two had never met; he had never even seen the man, but he loomed as a shadowy figure in Tarr's consciousness. Tarr knew all too well that General Grey was just as aware of *him*; he was rumored to have been the one to first nickname Tarr "the Fox" after some crucial plans had disappeared from the Two Falls headquarters right from under Grey's nose.

Reluctant respect or not, there was not a day that went by where Tarr didn't wish to have a bumbling, idiotic individual in charge in Two Falls, someone who frequently got drunk, left key papers out on their desk, and took frequent long, deep naps at the same time every afternoon. Tarr estimated that General Grey's appointment had prolonged the war by at least a year, and on more than one occasion, Archer had stopped by to express his personal apologies for assassinating the first general at all.

Tarr gave a sigh and shook his head. General Grey could wait. He stood and stretched, then walked out to the training area. Marc was out drilling Tarr's spy recruits in hand-to-hand combat. They were matched up in pairs here and there, grappling and struggling with sticks in the place of knives or daggers. Marc was in one corner, burly arms folded, flanked by Si, who was watching everything with a keen interest. Marc shot Tarr a wink as soon as he saw his friend emerge, then continued to bark in his drill sergeant voice, offering encouragement where needed and sharp criticism whenever an arm or foot was out of place.

Marc was primarily in charge of basic training for the Striker's main forces, but had offered to help Tarr train his spies since it was essential that they had at least some knowledge of basic weapons handling and combat. Marc's approach was to teach them the easiest way to kill and escape a troubling situation, and on more than one occasion, his teaching had saved an agent's life.

Tarr came to a halt beside his friends and watched the agents going through their drills. "How're we doing?" he asked.

"That one is really enthusiastic," Marc nodded towards one corner where a student was throwing herself into battle with more exuberance than skill.

"That's Leonore," Tarr said tiredly.

"Hmm," Marc said thoughtfully. "I'm thinking of teaching her the Si technique and just leaving it at that before someone injures themselves."

Tarr laughed at this. The "Si technique" was to simply go limp when someone grabbed him and then wriggle away as fast as possible. It wasn't perhaps the most dignified approach to combat, but it was effective nonetheless.

He watched the drills for a time, the clatter of practice weapons rising and falling around them. "I'm going to go check on Athela," Tarr told them finally, and left the room as unobtrusively as he had entered.

When the combat lesson was over and the last student had left the training room, Marc gave Si a friendly nudge and walked to one wall where all the practice weapons were kept. Si scampered over and grabbed a staff. "We going to run through those drills again?" he asked in his soft, breathy voice.

"You bet," Marc replied, absentmindedly twirling the staff around his body and over his head. "Now, remember, focus. Try to *react*. React and calculate. All you need is one successful hit, and I'm down."

They began to fight, slow at first, then picking up speed. Here and there, Si faltered or fumbled, but Marc was patient with him and didn't take advantage of the openings Si left. After about five minutes, Marc left his right side wide open, and Si leaped forward, landing a blow on Marc's shoulder. After a moment of recovery, Marc gave him a curt nod, and Si immediately relaxed his stance, letting his staff drop. Marc smiled encouragingly, but instead of returning the expression, Si's face was filled with consternation.

"You let me win," the boy said accusingly.

Marc was taken aback. "I didn't *let* you win. You saw an opening, and you went for it. That took skill," he corrected gently.

"I guess," Si mumbled. He was staring at his feet, aimlessly twirling the staff through his fingers.

Marc watched him thoughtfully for a few moments. "Sit down," he said quietly. Si's gaze snapped up as if his thoughts had been interrupted, but he obeyed, curling down with his legs crossed on the floor. Marc sidled up and sat beside him.

"You started your training much later than the usual beginners' age," he said. "You can't expect to become proficient overnight."

"It hasn't been overnight," Si muttered. "Not even close."

"You've improved enormously," Marc said firmly. "You should be proud of yourself. A negative attitude will get you nowhere."

Si glanced up at him, and Marc was startled to see that instead of defiance and anger, Si's friendly gray eyes were filled with an odd sort of anguish. "It's just..." he began. "When we all came here and we found out it was me, I was so surprised. I never thought it would be me. I thought it would be *Laith* or something. Or you or Athela. But not me. I mean...I'm just *me*, you know? Si. I don't have the training you have or the skills Archer or Laith have. So...I thought...well, if it's me, then maybe I'll get some powers, you know? To help me along a bit. Like, I'll start to *know* things. I'll really be able to help. Or I'll be able to fight well." He stopped, frustration filling his voice. His small hands were clenching in his lap. "So I've waited, and I've waited. And people are dying out there. And *nothing's changing*. I don't know anything more than I used to; I can't suddenly fight well. And people call me by this name, Si Morthenstar, and I don't even know who that is or who that's supposed to be. I've got this name now, this name I never asked for and that I never wanted, and I suddenly have to live up to it. And I don't know how." With an impassioned gesture, he tossed the staff off to one side, where it clattered against the stone and fell silent. Si looked almost abashed at the noise he had made.

Marc's heart ached for him. Though he would never tell Si, he knew that all of the others, himself included, had been waiting and wondering what Si's part was to play in the struggle. Si was improving in his lessons, true, but he showed no raw prodigious talent in the art of combat. He showed no particular adeptness at strategy or tactics or even espionage. He was, in short, a loving, gentle, funny thirteen-year-old boy who was being forced to grow up far too quickly.

Marc cleared his throat and tried to think of the right thing to say. "There's still a lot we don't know about the situation," he began slowly. "A lot of the history and lore and legends. We know there's old magic involved. There could be an entire web of clues we haven't uncovered yet. We've got to give it time and hope that things will unfold for us."

"It's been three years!" Si exclaimed with exasperation. "That's *forever!*"

Marc bit back a smile, knowing that Si, at thirteen, reckoned time rather differently than the rest of them. "Not exactly *forever*, but I know what you mean. You know, Cira's probably wondering what her special powers are, too, right at this very instant."

Si fell silent at this and stared vacantly in front of himself for a few moments. "Do you think she and I will have to meet? You know, to duel or something? The two of us?"

Marc shrugged. "Morthenstar and Kagai never did. Kagai stayed inside the fortress, and Morthenstar was cut down on the battlefield."

"Do you think she's going to kill me?" Si gulped.

Marc couldn't even begin to process such a thought. "No," he said firmly. "She won't. That's why I've been training you, and that's why you've been improving. Besides, Cira's talents were never in combat."

His voice dropped to a low mutter. "*Hand-to-hand* combat, at least."

Si sent him an inscrutable look. "What, you mean she was good at card games or something?"

"Something along those lines," Marc coughed delicately. "She favors a more psychological style of warfare. My point is, Si, that there's still so much we don't know about you or what's going to happen. All we can do is to prepare you as best we can for everything we think could possibly lie ahead. And your job is to do your best until we know more. All right?"

"All right," Si managed a brave smile, his freckled nose wrinkling. They stood up, side by side. "I'll try again. And this time, I want to really try and get you without you helping me."

"That's the spirit," Marc said jovially. "Ready?" His broad right hand gripped the staff and whirled it behind his back to his left in readiness. He needed to work his left arm more. This would be good practice for both of them. But Si wasn't ready yet. He had stopped, the staff slack at his side.

"What is it?" Marc asked anxiously.

"I can't help but feel that if I only *knew* what I'm supposed to do, I could stop this war right now and save all these people," Si shook his head, sending a cascade of copper hair over his ears. "Why was it me? Why was I the one who was chosen?"

Marc had no answer.

Late that night, long after they had eaten dinner in the main room with the rest of the troops, the Strikers convened in Athela's room to hear the report on what she and Tarr had gleaned from the mysterious wooden box from the Two Falls library. As soon as they entered the room, they saw from Athela's expression that it had to be something big. Even though she had gone without sleep for the good part of forty-eight hours after a considerably long and arduous journey, she was fairly radiating uncharacteristic exuberance and goodwill. Even Tarr, whose demeanor generally ran the gamut between placid and mild, seemed not to be able to sit still.

Marc shot Laith a single bewildered look as Athela hurriedly ushered them into her room and sat them down on the bed and in a few chairs that she had arranged around in a circle.

"We've got it!" she blurted out. The bewildered expression around the room deepened. This protocol was unusual; Athela's talks usually began with a prologue and handouts.

"Got what?" said Laith evenly in the voice he used when soothing an overexcited horse. "Is there a clue?"

"Clue? Hell's bells!" Athela exclaimed gleefully.

"Athela, I don't know what that's supposed to mean," Laith said patiently, the soothing tone still intact.

"She means," Tarr cut in, grinning, "that we have the first real piece of evidence that might point us towards finding out what part Si has to play in this whole enterprise."

Si straightened up taller, and Marc felt his heart glow a bit warmer. "What did you find out?" Si asked, his tone slightly more imperious than usual. He was trying to channel Athela and live up to the seriousness of the moment.

"Well, can we tell you how clever we were first?" Athela asked eagerly.

Laith sighed. "Go right ahead."

Athela took a deep breath. "Well, it's not *just* ancient Elyrian as I first thought." With that somewhat inauspicious start, she proceeded to launch into a largely incomprehensible speech revolving around the cross-indexing of different languages and the different taxonomies she had to separate before being able to conjugate the irregular verbs in the archaic coded script on the tablet. She finished as breathlessly as she had begun, and looked around at the others, expecting accolades.

"Well done," Marc said limply.

"My favorite part was the cross-indexing," Archer agreed. "Riveting."

"Well, I couldn't have done it without Tarr here. He's the one who made the big breakthrough," Athela said gallantly.

"So, er," Laith cleared his throat, raising his eyebrows expectantly. "What exactly *is* this breakthrough?"

"You want to do the honors?" Athela asked Tarr, grinning from ear to ear.

Seeing that his friends' nerves were on the breaking point, and knowing Athela's penchant for stretching out the moment of revelation for the maximum possible dramatic effect, Tarr stepped forward. "The tablet," he said, "essentially tells us that the key to Morthenstar's power is located in Two Falls."

The silence was such that they could have heard a pin drop. It continued for a full minute after Tarr's words. "Morthenstar's power?" Laith echoed finally. "Does it say anything about what exactly this power might be?"

"Yeah, does it say?" Si chimed in hopefully.

"Unfortunately not," Tarr shook his head.

"But!" Athela jumped in, lest the lack of specific information put a damper on the moment, "it does give detailed instructions as to where exactly the source is located. All we've got to do is find it." She paused. "Actually, I'm first going to have to decipher the damn instructions. *Then* we have to go find it. And we all know how much fun following Morthenstar's little games can be." This last sentence was said with not a small amount of sarcasm. By this point, Athela had been conducting a centuries-spanning game of hide and seek with Alder Morthenstar's prophecies and personal possessions, much to her vexation.

"I see," Laith said slowly. "So someone in Two Falls is going to have to go around, search for this thing, find it somehow, get it *back* to us somehow, always assuming that this source of Morthenstar's power is something that can be picked up and transported."

"Pretty risky," Archer agreed. "And if there's another bit of puzzling to do in order to get to the source—if whoever's looking for it doesn't have the mental capacities of Tarr or Athela—they're in for it."

"So one of us has to go back to Two Falls," Marc suggested.

"Rane?" Si asked. "She's already there. She's smart, too."

"I would actually like to go and find it myself," Tarr interjected quietly. "Laith's right. We don't know what will face us when we get to the power source. And if our experience with Morthenstar has taught us anything, it's that getting through her clues and puzzles isn't the easiest task."

"Well, if Tarr's going, I'm going," Archer said staunchly, folding his arms.

"Oh, great, the bloody parade again," Marc muttered.

The "bloody parade" was the term that they used to describe the domino effect that occurred whenever one of the Strikers decided to go anywhere. It usually went that if Tarr was going, Archer was going, and if Archer was going, Athela was going (to keep an eye on him, of course), and if Athela went, so did Laith to back her up, and if Laith went, so did Marc, who didn't go anywhere without Si.

"What do you think, Athela?" Laith inquired. "You think this is the real thing?"

"I think," Athela said with a slow smile, "that if we uncover this, we might be able to win the war."

Marc glanced over to Si, whose eyes were alight with excitement. He was immensely glad that the boy felt better, but couldn't quash his own small twinge of fear at what Si might possibly face if they uncovered the power source. And, though he didn't want to admit it to himself, he felt a pang at the thought that Si might not need his protection or guidance anymore.

"In that case," Laith said slowly, "what does everyone think about a change of scenery?"

"Been a while since I've been back to Two Falls," Archer grinned, stretching out his long legs and crossing them in front of him. "I hope that the city has grown sloppy and careless with its jewelry and antique furniture in my absence."

"Agreed?" Laith asked, looking around at the others. There were smiles and nods on their faces. "Fine," he said. "I'll write to Ari straight-away and ask him to prepare things for us. He'll have to find us lodging and a way to get us smuggled in."

"Shouldn't be hard," Athela shrugged. "They're more worried about people getting out than getting in."

Laith stood, his big black dog rising from behind his chair and stalking out of the curtained door after his master. Tarr watched them go with a familiar pang, remembering as he often did the way Wolver, his wolf, used to follow him in and out of rooms. Wolver had vanished from his life as suddenly as he appeared, and though he'd kept a sliver of hope alive and a keen eye out along the mountain range for anything large and white and fluffy, there'd been no trace of him in the intervening years. He looked down at his hands and slowly, unnecessarily, rearranged his paperwork. The others chatted for a few more minutes and then dispersed. The thrill over, Athela gratefully turned to her bed and threw herself on top of the covers, falling asleep almost instantly. Feeling impish, Tarr tempted fate slightly by giving her a gentle prod in the shoulder, but she didn't budge. He chuckled to himself, tugged a blanket over her, and left her in peace.

Upon returning to his own room, however, Tarr couldn't sleep. He was filled with the fire of the possibilities that the tablet had foretold. *Morthenstar's power.* He wondered what it would be. He hoped that Si would be able to handle it. He hoped that the war would be over quickly.

Feeling as though his brain were buzzing with a swarm of bees, Tarr rolled his lanky body out of the cot and walked through the winding stone passageways up to the cool night air outside. Tarr breathed in deep as a shadowy figure moved towards him.

"Identify," the voice said in Ashan.

"It is Tarr," he replied mildly. "At ease."

"Sir," the sentry replied and faded back into the darkness. Tarr wandered out past the entrance and over the slippery rocks to a crag that jutted out of the mountainside. It was a spectacular lookout point (and, in fairer weather, an excellent place for a picnic.) Tarr came up on the occasions when he had a lot to think about, or when he was missing Rane.

The night was an inky, cloying blue, but the air was crisp and refreshing and burned Tarr's throat as he breathed it in. His eyes traced along the barely visible horizon, the sea to the left, and the black speck of Faridor across the sweeping plains. And there, far in the distance, a tiny cluster of flickering yellow lights. Two Falls. It looked so minuscule from his high perch, so insignificant. It was difficult to imagine all the lives, the fears, the death that hung over the city. And somewhere in there was Rane. Tarr rested his hands on the tops of his knees, pulling them close to his chin. It was only a little longer. Only a little while, and he would see her again.

Down the mountain, across those broad, flat plains, through the thick glades of forest and meadow, perched above the spreading waterfalls that marked the southern border of the forest, Two Falls lay sleeping. Sleeping except for Kagai's sentries, guards, and secret police, prowling along the walls and the streets of the city like hungry alley cats; sleeping except for a small band of four who clustered around the corner of a building just across from an eastern marketplace.

"The time isn't right," one hissed. The voice was high, anxious, and worried. "The sentries have just gone by. They'll see us."

"They won't see me," Rane corrected. Her soft voice was hushed. She saw no reason for disquiet. She peered around the corner of the building. The marketplace was deserted, the timing perfect.

"You should go now," a deep voice beside her said. "Throw it, and we'll be able to make the news by morning."

"You can go start printing now, Ari," Rane told him. "It's set, done."

"I'll wait," Ari shook his head. He was always cautious.

"We'll get caught!" the first voice hissed again. "I just saw a sentry, I swear I did!"

"Thank you for your concern," the fourth voice, a woman, snapped. "I'll ask you not to come on any of these missions again if you don't have the stomach for it."

That shut the first voice up for a moment. "You heard what they said they'd do if there were any more demonstrations," he continued in a reedy whine.

"They've been saying that for two years," Rane murmured. "If we listened to every threat they made, the war would have been over a year ago, and we'd all be dead by now." She stood. The young man was starting to try even her extensive patience. She strode out into the marketplace, unafraid. She was clutching something in her hand.

The man behind her let out a gasp. "She's just going to *walk* right out there? What if someone sees her? What if something happens to her?"

Neither Ari nor the other woman bothered to tell him that Rane was perfectly capable of handling herself. She walked across the bare plaza and stopped in front of a row of stalls. She eyed them distastefully. They were the finger stalls, exhibits sponsored by the Kagaian Two Falls government to display Ashan sixth fingers as a way to spread fear and intimidation through the people. They were no less repulsive now—boarded up and closed for the night—than they were when they were bustling and busy showing off their grisly wares.

Rane knelt down to one side. She placed the small bottle of alcohol on the cobblestone beside her and reached into her pocket, withdrawing a flint and tinder. She struck a few sparks until one caught the edge of the damp rag that she had choked into the mouth of the bottle. Quickly, efficiently, she grabbed the bottle and hurled it at the nearest stall.

The bottle splintered into millions of tiny shards, and the alcohol and fire swept together with a massive roar, spreading across the dry, weathered wood of the stalls like waves over the sand. In an instant, the plaza was a blazing inferno of crackling flames and billowing smoke. Rane turned on her heel and walked unconcernedly back to the others. The young man's face was illuminated by the fire. His jaw was agape.

"There's your headline, Ari," Rane remarked. "Better go now if you want it out by morning."

Ari gave her a curt nod and swept his hood down over his eyes, turning in a curve of cloak. Off in the distance, Rane could hear the screams, cries, and yells begin to break out as people woke to see the fire blazing in the marketplace. After about ten seconds, she heard the alarm bell sound off.

"We'd better go," the woman told her. "Kagai's fire brigades will be all over this place in a minute or so."

"You go," Rane told her.

The woman and the young man nodded, the man's eyes still transfixed on the inferno before him. After a moment, the woman pulled him after her and they were swallowed up in the gloom of the street. Rane turned around and ventured out of the shadows, feeling the ripples of heat as they coursed through the cold night air and played out against her skin. For a long while, she stood there and watched the fire burn.

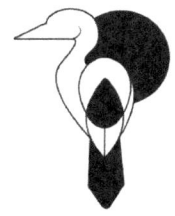

CHAPTER FIVE

"I *beg* your pardon," Archer exclaimed, rising quickly to his feet.

Ari eyed him coldly from across the room. "As I said, we will travel to the meeting in pairs. Marc will be in charge of protecting Si. Laith and Athela will travel as a team. And Ella," here, he turned and inclined his head towards a silent young woman standing a few feet behind him, "will guard Tarr."

"And *why*, might I ask, was I not assigned to guard him?" Archer demanded.

Tarr saw the muscles in Ari's jaw clench and unclench a few times. "Because," he intoned, "Seeing as how he is responsible for the entire Strikers spy network, I prefer to entrust his safety to one of my own lieutenants."

Tarr felt his brother bristle beside him and, out of the corner of his eye, saw Athela give an extremely exaggerated eye roll. Ari's retainers, about five of them, were watching the exchange with rapt attention. Tarr wasn't sure whether there was a wicked streak deep within Ari that enjoyed provoking Archer whenever possible. Whatever the reason, it never took Ari and Archer much more than five minutes in each other's presence to start a fight.

"Is that so?" Archer spat, golden eyes flashing. "You have no authority to give me orders. I outrank you."

"In the mountains, perhaps," Ari said evenly, "but as you might remember, I am the general of operations here in Two Falls, so when I give an order, that's the end of it."

Archer opened and closed his mouth a few times, then narrowed his glittering eyes. "I greatly dislike you, Ari," he said finally.

"That's unfortunate," Ari said in his usual emotionless way.

Archer turned back around and called Ari an extremely rude name in Ashan beneath his breath. Though Ari's Ashan vocabulary didn't extend into the realm of colorful metaphors, he got the gist of what had been said. His eyebrows rose ever so slightly, which for Ari was equivalent to his hand going to the dagger at his belt. There was a horrible, strained silence for a good ten seconds before it was broken by one of Ari's retainers, a young Ashan, who couldn't quite stifle a terrified giggle at the language Archer had used.

"Well, then!" Athela said briskly, shattering the tension like a pane of ice. "Off we go. Archer, for heaven's sake, stop pouting; you'll go along with Ella, and both of you will watch Tarr. Bloody lot of fuss over nothing; the trip to Orion is going to take us all of ten minutes."

Tarr, trying to mask his own amusement, shot a glance over at Ari, who clearly didn't like being overruled but knew better than to try and argue with Athela. "Fall out," Ari ordered and spun on his heel, sweeping out of the room with a swish of cloak and the slight clink of spurs. Ella, the young woman he had assigned to protect Tarr, hung back and waited, looking awkward and uncomfortable. Tarr gave her a warm smile and saw her shoulders relax.

"I'm Tarr," he said. "Ella, right?"

She nodded and swallowed. Ordinarily, Tarr imagined that she was a no-nonsense, self-possessed sort of young woman but was clearly rather starstruck by him. "That's right."

"Are you new?"

"No, I have worked with Ari for over a year," she said proudly. She seemed older than she really was, Tarr thought with a slight twinge.

"That's quite an honor. I'm sure you'll do an excellent job," he assured her and swiveled around to his brother. "This is Arch—"

"Ari looks older since the last time we saw him," Archer interjected in Ashan, still staring narrowly with his yellow eyes trained on the door-frame. "Do you not think that he has gotten older? More haggard?"

"Loads," Tarr said drily, trying to steer the conversation back into a language that Ella could easily understand. Though the Striker troops had all been tasked with learning Ashan, few could keep up with Archer's rapid pace and lilting northern accent. "Ella, why do—"

"I do not think the soldiers respect him," Archer continued, completely oblivious. "That is the first mark of a leader. Respect."

"Archer, why don't you go get your weapons?" Tarr suggested testily. "We're leaving soon; you might need them."

Miraculously, the mention of weaponry pierced through Archer's distracted mind, and the tall Ashan sloped out of the room without another word. Tarr gave a sigh and glanced once more around their surroundings.

The safe house, he had to admit, had been extremely cleverly constructed. Two adjoined townhouses had their backs sealed off into a private, three-story, completely concealed compartment. Outwardly, the structures looked normal; inside, the main habitations were completely unremarkable. But there were secret entrances and concealed doorways that led into the narrow, hidden apartment tucked safely away at the backs of the conjoined house. There was a small kitchen, a lavatory, a meeting room, and six bedrooms, all stacked tightly on top of each other with a staircase threading its way up one side.

Tarr had seen, upon entering, that he had been given a room to share with Rane, though he hadn't yet had a chance to see her. There were signs of her everywhere: her things were already placed neatly inside, one of her swords resting against a wall, her clothes tucked quietly in a drawer, worn leather riding gloves on the bedside table. Her scent was all around the room. It was a bit like cohabitating with a ghost. They had been apart for so long that she scarcely seemed real anymore. But there, with her things and her smell in the room, her presence grew more tangible by the second, and with it Tarr's impatience to see her. Tarr gently picked up one of her riding gloves and rubbed his thumb along the leather before slowly placing it back on the table.

Ari had picked a good night to hold the meeting. Clouds obscured the moon, and the night was dark and thick. Ella, Archer, and Tarr were the last group to leave the safehouse for the club, all heavily cloaked and keeping close to the shadows against the sides of the walls. It had been so long since Tarr had been in the city; here and there were buildings that he dimly recognized, but on the whole, it could have been a completely different place. Windows were boarded up, and the vibrant nightlife he recalled from his first night in the city was nowhere to be seen. Stars that had been carved into the door frames of houses as symbols of Morthenstar's protection had been hacked off years ago, ugly jagged chunks missing from the woodwork. The gaily-colored lanterns that used to be strung across the tops of the streets had been replaced by green Kagaian banners, flapping loudly in the night wind like the heavy wings of crows.

Archer froze and his gloved hand shot out, catching Tarr over the heart and gently pushing him down against the wall. Ella had frozen as well, her spine rigid. In the street ahead of them, a lone Kagaian guard ambled along on his nightly route, spinning his sword aimlessly in one hand. He glanced their way for only a moment, then was gone. Tarr felt Archer relax, and they waited a few more seconds before continuing.

Tarr's throat was tightening in excitement the further they went. *Rane!* He couldn't help but smile. He had been told that she would undoubtedly be at the meeting; Ari had assured him that it would be so. He was excited to finally get to see Orion again as well. He wondered if it had changed. Since the war had broken out, the club had been taken over by Khan, an old friend of Archer and Rowan's, and had become famous throughout the ranks of the resistance. He had often heard fighters returning from Two Falls talking about the nightclub and the people who frequented it. It would be good to get a chance to talk to some of the other resistance leaders as well; though Tarr knew every name of every member of his extensive network, there were a handful he had never actually met in person.

"That's the club up there," Ella said, pointing. Tarr craned his neck around Archer's shoulder to get a good look. From the outside, Orion after closing hours didn't look terribly remarkable. It was dark, shuttered, and sealed up like every other building on the block. They scuttled through the shadows until they were across the street from the club. Ella poked her head out into the street to make sure that the way was clear, and the three of them dashed across the road into the alcove of the front door. Ella rapped briskly on the door with her knuckles, and after a moment, the door opened a crack. Ella whispered an urgent word in Ashan, and the door swung open wider, admitting the three inside.

It took a moment for Tarr's eyes to adjust to the glaring light within. It was a round room almost like an amphitheater, with a raised pillared pathway around the outside of the circle and steps leading down to an inner circle set up as the main dining area and club floor. Though the club seemed completely dead and lifeless from the outside, it was packed to the brim from within, with torches blazing all around the large circular main room. The windows, Tarr saw, were covered by shutters and curtains so heavy and thick that not even a hint of light could seep through to the outside. Tables and chairs had been drawn up, and there were twenty or so individuals standing around chatting in low voices or hovering nervously with their arms folded. Tarr had to pause a moment to take them all in as the faces flicked around to him and Archer, recognition dawning on their expressions. The faces Tarr saw were from every walk of life: young, old, middle-aged, fat, thin, curvy, short, tall, Ashan, half-Ashan, human. Many faces bore scars; some were missing ears or were wearing eye patches, and on many hands, Tarr could see a gap where the sixth finger had been hacked off; unconsciously, his hand went to the nub remaining of the sixth finger on his own left hand, stinging with a sudden whimper of phantom pain. He gulped. Everyone was staring at him. He gave a self-conscious wave and ducked behind a nearby pillar to walk around to the broad table at the head of the room. Archer fell into step behind him. The raised walkway around the circular room was curtained off from the floor below, so Tarr and Archer had a few moments of privacy.

"Bloody hell," Archer growled to him in an undertone, "if Kagai's people happen upon this lot tonight, we can kiss the entire war goodbye."

Tarr remained silent. He was suddenly deeply uncomfortable that he had allowed someone else to orchestrate so important a gathering. Ari had been carefully arranging security for the resistance meeting for weeks, but Tarr still couldn't fully trust that everything had been attended to as stringently as it should have. He had gotten them through the war this far by managing all of their security precautions himself, as much as he was able to. He would have to do better.

Feeling unsettled, he strode briskly beside Archer around the outer curtained pathway to the opposite side of the circular room. Tarr heard Athela's voice call for attention on the floor below, and the crowd on the other side of the curtains quieted.

"Better hurry, mate," Archer said, quickening his pace. But Tarr had seen someone between a gap in the curtains and stopped. Archer halted, swiveling around to stare at him. A knowing, lopsided grin flickered across his mouth.

"Don't be too long," he said impishly, and continued on.

Tarr pulled aside the curtain with one finger. Across the room, leaning quietly against a pillar with her arms folded, was Rane. Her auburn hair fell softly down over one shoulder, and she was watching Athela as she made her opening announcements. Though the attendees were staring raptly at the Strikers at the main table (even breaking out into excited whispers as Archer appeared and took his place beside Athela), no one seemed to have even noticed that Rane was there or recognized who she was. As always, Tarr wondered how it could be that they failed to notice the most beautiful girl in the room.

As if she could feel his gaze on her, Rane's steady eyes flicked up and locked with Tarr's. She gave a shocked start and immediately turned and vanished behind one of the red curtains. Tarr could see which way she was heading and stepped back, a smile shining out over his face as he began to run, the curtains whizzing by, Athela's speech melting into a steady, wordless drone in his ears. And then, in a blissful second, there she was, running towards him, and in another instant she was in his arms, and he was kissing her. He kissed her everywhere—face, lips, cheeks; he even managed to kiss one of her eyebrows. When they parted, her face was shining up at him, and he crushed her to him, her strong arms locked around him, his face buried in her soft hair. They held each other for a minute, then broke apart, and he took her face in his hands and studied it closely. A new scar stood out, ugly and red on her left temple, and her cheekbones glared out more sharply than in his memory, but she was there, and she was alive, and she was safe. Tarr couldn't remember ever being happier.

Knowing that they couldn't spend the entire meeting canoodling behind the curtains together, Tarr took her hand and led her up around the pathway and out of the curtain to the table where the Strikers and Ari sat. Archer shot him a cheeky wink as he took his seat, and there were a few whispers here and there at the flushed expressions on Tarr's and Rane's faces.

"—to directly counter General Grey," Laith concluded. Breaker, his large black dog, lay at his feet, his furry head resting on his paws, pointed ears pricked and watchful. Again, Tarr thought of Wolver, then forced himself back to the present. "We are confident that he will remain unaware of our move to Two Falls for some time. We hope to accomplish as much as we can in that interim. Inevitably, he will find out that we are here, and then appropriate steps will be taken."

"And what of Ashan housing?" came another voice. "We must have more places for our refugees. They are rounding up Ashans and half-Ashans in the outlying country and bringing them here. We have so little room as it is."

"We can't simply conjure housing out of thin air," Laith spread his hands. "Many of those who offered refuge have been arrested. But we're taking steps to reach out to new individuals, to find housing for those who need it."

"I heard a rumor that there was an envoy made to the Ashans in the forest," piped up another. "Is that true?"

Athela opened her mouth to answer, but Tarr cut her off. "No," he said shortly. "That is not true." There was a small buzz at his words, and Athela shot him an incredulous look, but Tarr gave her a warning glance that she seemed to accept. Athela turned back to the crowd.

"What we aim to do," she said firmly, "is push to really overthrow the order of things here. We've been helping Ashans escape, it's true, but we haven't done nearly enough. We need to throw off General Grey. We need to take the city back. We need to take back Two Falls."

Silence greeted her words. "We'd need an army," said one man in the front row. His expression was dubious at best.

"Not necessarily," Tarr said quietly. "We need cunning, and we need strength, and we need unity." *Termites eating away at the wall*, he thought to himself, and smiled.

"And a plan," Archer muttered. A few people in the audience laughed, glad of something to ease the tension in the room. Tarr distinctly heard Ari make a *tsking* sound in his throat at Archer's unprofessionalism.

"That's in the long run," Laith told them. "But we have short-term goals that we're focusing on. Ari," he inclined his head towards the big man at his side, "will continue to organize the publication of our resistance pamphlet. The more information we get out to the people of the city, the bigger presence we have, the stronger we seem, the more likely they will be to join us."

"What of the smuggling?" came a voice. "They've stopped up the walls. Every time we find a new way out, they move in an extra guard, stage a raid, and arrest everyone in the chain."

"It's General Grey," said another, and there was a murmur of assent throughout the room. "He's got a nose for sniffing us out. It's like he's always one step ahead of us."

"I've...erm...actually been working on that one," Archer grinned, leaning back in his chair with one foot propping him up against the table. "I have a couple of ideas in mind."

"I'm going to organize a group to meet with Archer in the upcoming days and to go over and vet his plans," Ari cut in. Archer glared at him.

"Archer will be taking over as head of the smuggling chain," Athela interjected, hoping to head off a public confrontation between the two. "He—"

"Morthenstar!" shouted a woman's voice from the back of the room. Si's head snapped up; Tarr was fairly sure he had been picking at his fingernails for the greater part of the meeting. His face held the sheepish guilt of a child caught daydreaming in the middle of his lessons.

"Yes?" he inquired cheerily, but Tarr could hear unsteadiness in his voice.

"What have *you* done?" said the woman. Tarr could make her out now, an older individual with watery eyes and a severe mouth.

"What have I done?" Si echoed, his mind clearly searching back in time for his last remotely suspicious action. "I...I'm not sure what you mean."

"You're Morthenstar's heir, aren't you?" she demanded.

"Yes," Si mumbled, glancing down at his hands. Marc looked as though he were about five seconds from bolting out of his chair and slugging the woman.

"So what have you done for us?" she said accusingly.

"Leave him be; he's just a boy," said a man closer to the front.

"There is much related to Morthenstar that we have yet to uncover. Indications that may be positive," Laith said, his deep voice soothing yet firm. "And I would remind you that the war is far from over yet. All of us still have our part to play."

The woman fell silent, and Tarr was intensely glad about it. Marc cupped his hand over Si's thin shoulder and gave it a small squeeze, but Si refused to look up from his hands.

The meeting flew by without any further outbursts. This was fine with Tarr; he spoke very little during the rest of the proceedings, preferring to leave Athela and Laith in the roles of authority. The assembly, he knew, was mostly just to show the members of the resistance that the Strikers were there and to establish a more personal connection between them. It was important for morale. He spent the remainder of the gathering alternating between studying the faces of the resistance members, squeezing Rane's thin hand in his own, and daydreaming about the night before them.

Back at the safe house later that night, Athela called Tarr into her room to meet with him briefly. She was poring over some correspondence at her desk when Tarr entered with a gentle knock. She glanced up at him and jerked her head silently toward the bed. Tarr perched there and waited patiently until she had finished her letter.

"How do you think it went?" she asked, throwing down her pen and swiveling around to face him.

"Well," Tarr nodded. "We did what we needed to do."

"Why did you stop me about the Ashan envoy thing?" she asked.

"It would do no good to tell them that the Ashan nations don't stand behind us," Tarr shrugged. "They have enough to deal with without that weighing on their minds."

"Think we can duck General Grey for as long as Laith seems to think?"

Tarr nodded. "It's important that we do. We can get away with a lot if the Kagaian guards here aren't expecting us."

"Yeah," Athela agreed. There was a pause. "Ari did a good job of organizing the meeting," she observed.

"I suppose so," Tarr agreed. Athela cocked an eyebrow, detecting the begrudging tone in his voice. Finally, Tarr spread his hands. "*I* should have done it. If Archer was right, and one detail was out of place, the war would have ended tonight."

"You've got to trust *someone* at some point, Tarr," Athela pressed back gently. "You have to relinquish some control here or there. You can't fight the entire war yourself."

"I trust him!" Tarr protested. "I just con't..." he trailed off.

Athela eyed him. "...Trust him? To not make a mistake?"

"To not be human," Tarr retorted.

"I see," Athela frowned sagely. "And *you're* infallible, are you?"

"So far," Tarr shot back.

Athela rolled her eyes but then began to toy with the lace of her boot. Tarr took a deep breath, steadying himself. His relationship with Athela was what he imagined having a sister would be like. When they disagreed, she wouldn't give him an inch, and he didn't expect her to. He both valued her opinion and occasionally found it infuriating.

She continued this fidgeting for a good minute or two before Tarr ascertained that her mind was somewhere else and that she wasn't going to get to what was troubling her without a bit of prodding.

"Athela," he said slowly, "do you have an emotion you need to talk about?"

"Hell!" she said explosively. "Why does he have to be so *stupid?*"

"Can you clarify a bit more?" Tarr asked patiently. "Are you referring to me, Ari, or Archer?"

"Archer!" she yelled, then caught herself and lowered her voice to a less hysterical volume. "Archer," she repeated. "I can't figure him out. I've known him for years, and I still have no idea whether he—"

"Yes?" Archer's white head poked around the side of the door. "You called?"

"I?" Athela's face went blank with shock, and she began fumbling for words. "I didn't—"

"Just now," Archer's brow furrowed. "I thought I heard your dulcet tones bellowing my name."

"Were you *lurking* outside the *door?*" Athela demanded.

"If you must know, I was off to brush my teeth," Archer said with dignity. "I can't help it that strange women happen to be yelling my name at all hours of the night."

"It was nothing," Athela's jaw was set. "Right, Tarr?"

"Nothing at all," Tarr echoed pleasantly. "'Night."

Archer shot Tarr a narrow, inscrutable glare, but Tarr merely smiled serenely and Archer vanished back around the door. Athela let out her breath through her teeth like steam escaping a teapot. "See?" she demanded in exasperation. "What did that *mean?*"

"I think," Tarr said measuredly, "that Archer heard you yell his name while on his way to brush his teeth and came to see what you wanted him for."

"I suppose," Athela muttered absently. "Why is it, though, the only time I bloody well feel like he's being honest with me is when he's asleep?"

Tarr opened his mouth to speak, then did a double-take. "Athela, when are you two sleeping around each other?"

At this point, she was studiously avoiding Tarr's eyes. He looked at her closely. She seemed to be genuinely vexed. Tarr gave a sigh. She often turned to him for help on this subject, and yet Tarr had the distinct feeling that nothing he said made any difference whatsoever.

"Look," Tarr heaved a sigh of exasperation, the thought of Rane waiting in the room below causing him a twinge of impatience, "if I were you, I would stop looking for nonexistent excuses to put up in the way and just...*get on that*, as it were."

"I...I've never..." Athela began lamely, studiously staring at the floor and plucking at her bootlaces, her cheeks burning with embarrassment.

Tarr felt like heaving a sob of desperation, but took a calm breath and realized that there was literally no one else Athela could go to talk about these sorts of things. He knew what a demonstration of trust it was for her to be open with him at all. "It's all right," he said soothingly. "And I mean that. Just because Archer is more experienced with that sort of thing—"

"*Experienced?*" Athela snorted. "That's putting it mildly. He's only slept with *half* the—"

"That's beside the point," Tarr said with dignity, rising to his feet. Tales of Archer's many conquests had burbled up over the course of the previous few years; it seemed that smuggling, thievery, and assassination weren't his only skills. "If you both like each other as much as I think you do, everything is going to be natural and fine." He walked towards the door and paused, adding, "And it will be a considerable relief to the rest of us."

And with that, he slipped out of the room and headed down the stairs to Rane.

The quarters and offices of General Grey occupied the third story in a building that had once been the Two Falls town hall. The city's prisons, nearly filled, were under the building, and the main barracks stretched from subterranean levels up to portions of the second floor. The third floor was Grey's domain. On that floor, everyone walked swiftly and with purpose. There was almost absolute silence, except when speaking was absolutely necessary. General Grey worked better in a quiet atmosphere.

Lieutenant Allox paused before the broad oak doors and knocked softly. "Enter," came the curt voice from within. Allox quietly pulled open the door and removed her helmet, holding it in the crook of her elbow as she stood at attention, waiting for General Grey to turn and put her at ease.

The General was staring, as he often did, out of the broad windows that overlooked the roofs of the city. It was almost as if by merely looking at his domain, the General could sense what was going on within it. Allox had seen him stand by the window, staring silently out for hours on end, with nothing more than the slightest movement. She hoped, for the sake of her aching feet, that that would not be the case today.

She had little to worry about. After only a few more moments, General Grey turned to face her, and Allox automatically straightened up. "At ease," came the order, and Allox relaxed, stepping forward and setting her helmet on her knee.

General Grey seated himself in a chair beside a small reading table with a few papers and a pen meticulously arranged atop it. Grey was about six feet tall but carried himself as if he were three inches taller, and had the broad, heavy build of a man who had grown up accustomed to hard physical labor. He was nearing his mid-fifties, but there was no sign of a paunch on him; his lifestyle was notoriously austere and disciplined, habits he'd brought with him after serving for years in the King's Desert Guard in Vireg. He had jet-black hair close-cropped to his head, just turning to gray at the temples, and dark skin the color of a plum, almost bluish-purple. His eyebrows were sharp and dove down into creases above his eyes, giving him the perpetually intense expression of a man deep in thought. His watchful, hooded dark eyes, however, betrayed absolutely nothing of what was going on behind them. He spoke little and had only been seen to smile on three occasions, all of them forced. To say that his presence was intimidating would have been a massive understatement.

Allox shifted under the gaze. "Report," General Grey ordered.

The lieutenant cleared her throat before speaking. "No activity, sir."

Grey looked up sharply. "What?"

"There's been no resistance activity reported, sir," she repeated. "None since the smuggling attempt four days ago and the fire at the finger stalls a week before."

"No activity for four days?" General Grey repeated. "This is in all sectors?"

"All sectors of the city."

Grey leaned back in his chair and began to stare vacantly into the space before him. Allox knew better than to expect that he would share his thoughts aloud. Finally, after about two minutes, Grey broke the silence and Allox immediately snapped to attention.

"Get me the officer in charge of surveillance on Orion," he ordered.

Allox snapped a swift salute and spun on her heel, marching smartly out of the room. Grey slowly rose from his chair and walked back to the window, beginning to pace evenly back and forth in front of it, his hands clasped loosely behind his back. In a few minutes, there was another soft knock on the door, and another officer entered. Grey didn't even look to see his salute.

"Give me the report on Orion for the last four days," he ordered.

Surprised, the officer cleared his throat and cast his mind back, knowing that the General would rather have an accurate report than a swift one. "There was a drunken brawl outside the bar four days ago.

The matter was investigated and handled by the local troop. Nothing resistance-related was reported. The next day was quiet, we arrested someone trying to sell forged travel documents. And then the day after that, there was nothing. The club closed early, and our patrols in that sector reported no activity all night. Then," he concluded, "last night we made one arrest during business hours. Someone suspected of selling the wall guard assignments to Striker spies."

Grey digested the information silently. "Get me the officer in charge of tailing Ari," he ordered.

A few minutes later, in walked a third officer who saluted and gave his report. "He's been sighted only once in the past four days. Security has been high. He's taken extra precautions not to be followed. He has not been near his suspected place of residence for two days. We took the opportunity to search the houses, but there was no sign of him. Nothing."

"Thank you," Grey said as a dismissal. The guard saluted and left, leaving Grey deep in thought.

No activity for four days was something too unusual to go unnoticed, he thought. Not a day went by that he didn't get a report of a suspected meeting, a plot to assassinate one of his officers (or him), or news of a new smuggling ring hoping to spirit Ashans out of the city. The details, however, were always infuriatingly vague and only occasionally led to arrests. Ari (and, he suspected, Tarr) had a nose for sniffing out false agents. Nearly all of his spies had been detected and disposed of before they could bring back any really useful information. Lately, there was an uneasiness hanging about the city. He could feel it as he watched the rooftops out his window. He had thought it was just a product of the latest round of crackdowns, of the isolated incidents of arson from the Striker rebellion.

But...perhaps he had been wrong all along. The nervous energy he could sense might have been the result of something else, something bigger. Something of which he was as of yet unaware. Four days. Four days with nothing more than a whisper. And then...Orion closed early two nights ago. Boarded up with no sign of activity all night. *Orion*. Many of his troops couldn't understand why he left it open for business. But they didn't understand the importance of knowing your enemy, of being able to stand up and look them right in the eye. Close down Orion, make a few arrests, and the resistance activity would break apart like a swarm of ants only to converge again in a new place. Dissolve that new meeting place, lose the lives of some of his soldiers, and the cycle would continue. Grey loathed losing his soldiers. Every officer that was killed, every soldier murdered in a raid, was personal to him. After particularly hard losses, Grey barricaded himself in his quarters for days before finally resurfacing, his manner moody and taciturn.

Orion served its purpose, just as everything else did. He could post sentries to survey it, he could make note of the individuals seen entering or leaving, marking who seemed to come and go the most. He could have them followed, leading him steadily through the resistance network to its very core.

Once, when he was a boy, Grey's uncle had traveled with him from the desert to the far, far north, and one night had shown him how water, when frozen, would break apart a glass jar. Grey had never forgotten that image—a splintering from within, from the heart. Bumping off a spy here and there would do no good. He would have to infiltrate all the way to the heart, to split them open from within.

The club would never close for any reason other than a meeting of the resistance. And Ari...Ari, who was second in command only to the Strikers, had been absent from all his known places of work, had stepped up his own security to the point where he had only been glimpsed—glimpsed!—once in four days.

The threads finally began to twine together into a single line. An extremely important meeting had taken place, something that required the utmost care and security, planned to the last detail by Ari himself. The only reason for that would be if they were planning something big—in which case even Grey's spies would have caught wind of something afoot—or if someone important had come to town. Given the facts, Grey was inclined to believe the latter. And given Ari's behavior, Grey had little doubt as to who the important arrival could be.

He broke off his pacing and strode straight to his front door. The retainers guarding the entrance snapped to attention at his approach. "Summon the heads of security for all sectors," he ordered. "And tell them to hurry. The Strikers have returned to Two Falls."

CHAPTER SIX

HOPE!

Fear not, free citizens of Two Falls. There is new hope for our city. Allies from the mountains have joined in our fight against Cira Kagai. With this new aid, we hope to increase our strength tenfold in the coming month.

For those still in hiding—we have smuggled out yet another family from the clutches of the green soldiers. There will be a chance for you. Hope is still alive in Two Falls! Down with Kagai and long live Morthenstar!!

"It's not too much?" the boy asked Tarr anxiously, waiting to see his reaction as the tall Ashan finished reading.

Tarr hid a smile. "No, it's quite good. Very powerful reading. I like the liberal usage of exclamation points at the end."

The boy's tired face cracked into a grin, and he wiped his forehead with his sweaty, ink-stained fingers. "Thank you, sir. Worked on it all night."

"Has Ari seen it yet? You'll have these out by tomorrow morning?"

"I'll show him now. I think so, sir."

"Good work," Tarr clapped him on the shoulder, taking care not to make the gesture patronizing. "And my name is Tarr, not 'sir.'"

"Yes, s—Tarr," the boy said, faintly awed.

"He's a good lad," Ari remarked as they ducked out of the room and clambered up a short flight of stairs to the midday street above. Ari automatically paused and checked to make sure that there were no guards approaching, then he, Tarr, and Archer stepped out into the street, falling into long strides beside each other, the sunshine a welcome change from the dimly lit cellar. "I've put him in charge of the propaganda department," Ari continued. "He works as hard as people twice his age."

"And he's a good speller," Tarr added.

"Apparently, he was one of the brightest students in the academy we had here in Two Falls. His parents were arrested a year after the war began for harboring Ashans. The boy barely escaped alive. He's human, though, so it was easier to find him a place to live. He's been staying with a family in the northern section of the city."

They stepped out into a broad plaza, and Tarr realized with a jolt that the clearing upon which he was standing had at one point been his favorite place in the city. A large, beautiful fountain was set at the center of the square, crowned by an intricately carved statue depicting a man fighting a hideous sea creature. He had whiled away many an afternoon in that plaza perched on the side of the fountain, watching the faces and the bright colors as the people bustled by. Tarr could almost feel the cooling mist on his face as he stepped forward and took in the sight: the statue all but destroyed, dried up and crumbled apart to the point of almost being unrecognizable, efflorescence creeping up the side of the barren pool.

Tarr swallowed and turned back around to Archer, who watched him sympathetically. "Nothing a bit of remodeling can't fix," he offered.

"This is now a favorite meeting place for Kagaian soldiers," Ari informed them.

"So *why* exactly are we now walking towards it?" Archer asked witheringly.

"I merely *thought*," Ari said testily, "That in my overview of the city you would like to see firsthand the strongholds of your enemy."

"Stop it, you two," Tarr muttered, ducking his head as two pedestrians passed by them. He was now in no mood to put up with Ari and Archer's constant bickering.

"Separate," Ari hissed beneath his breath, and immediately the three of them broke apart as a group of five Kagaian guards marched into the square, their green cloaks whispering along behind them, barely audible over the sound of their clanking swords and squeaking leather. Tarr felt, as he always did, the twinge of fear that even now, after three years, he was still unable to completely suppress. He kept his head lowered and his hood up; nothing besides his unusual height would betray him as anything different than the dozens of cloaked, hooded individuals hurriedly crossing two and fro throughout the square.

The guards merely glanced over in his direction and then continued heavily off towards their headquarters. Tarr gave it a few more seconds and then casually sauntered back over to where Archer and Ari were now standing.

"It's easier to operate at night," Ari pointed out as Tarr drew near. "but I wanted you to see what everything looks like."

"I'm glad you did. Here, let's have a look at your map," he suggested, and the three of them drew down an alley and crunched together into an extremely small alcove.

"This is cozy," Archer remarked, his knee digging into what Tarr surmised was his own kidney.

"It's safe," Ari retorted curtly, and drew out a crumpled map and a small bit of charcoal to write with. He spread the parchment open on his knee and gesticulated with the charcoal over areas that were already marked up and annotated. "We've covered these districts. Needless to say, the area around here, near where the headquarters are located, is almost exclusively controlled by Kagai. But here," he motioned with the charcoal, drawing a small loop around the arts district in the southwest corner of the city, "the resistance is the strongest. We're able to operate fairly well there. Now, General Grey is aware of our operations there and keeps it fairly heavily patrolled, but the resistance has better control of the ins and outs of that district than Kagai."

"I see," Tarr frowned. "So southwest is ours, southeast is Kagai's?"

"It's all Kagai's," Ari said grimly, "but our operations are easier in the arts district and part of the northern district, it's true."

"My arm is falling asleep," Archer muttered through gritted teeth.

"Any other observations you want to offer?" Ari inquired sharply. "Perhaps something relating to the *plans*?"

"We should focus our efforts on the plazas," Archer replied, pointing to a few areas on the map with his long fingertip. "They're all in extremely strategic locations. If we can successfully set up operations within all the plazas and squares in Two Falls, we'll have not only places for the resistance to meet and exchange messages, but also be poised to expand outward to the rest of the city."

There was a brief pause and Ari folded up the map, tucking it back into his cloak. His voice was as neutral as ever, but his jaw was working furiously. "Let's go," he announced, and the three of them piled out of the alcove. Ari walked forward ahead of them for a pace or two.

"Be nice to him," Tarr muttered to Archer in Ashan.

"He is a pain," Archer griped back.

"We are fighting on the same side of the war. Please get along with him for now and then continue to hate him *after* the war is concluded."

Archer shot him a petulant yellow glare from within the folds of his black hood and muttered something in the Common tongue along the lines of "pole stuck up his ass." Tarr assumed he was referring to Ari, though he couldn't be certain.

They headed across the plaza and out toward the main marketplace. As they drew closer, Tarr noticed an ever-thickening crowd of black, gray, and brown cloaks. Something was afoot. "Is it market day?" he asked Ari in an undertone.

The big man frowned and shook his head. "No. I don't know what's going on."

A crowd was gathered around the center of the market square where a platform had been erected, stained brown in places by what Tarr fervently hoped was mud. They were at the back of the crowd, and even with their superior height, sightlines were an issue.

"Rooftops," Archer suggested, nudging his brother.

Tarr tugged on Ari's arm, and the three-headed toward the row of buildings closest around the square to the platform. The noise of the crowd had quieted, and Tarr could dimly hear the echoes of a man's voice booming out over the plaza.

"Hurry!" he whispered.

The three made their way up the side of one of the shorter buildings (taking a bit longer to help Ari scale the wall), then ducked their heads low as they ran along the top of the building and huddled behind the ornate ledge of the rooftop that provided some shelter from any prying eyes below.

Tarr leaned up and peeked his head just over the roof's edge. There were screams from the audience below, and to his shock, he saw five or so Kagaian guards winding their way through the crowd as an officer stood waiting on the platform above.

"What are they doing?" Archer asked blankly.

Tarr continued watching. Each guard, after a few seconds, would reach out and grab one of the members of the crowd and drag them, struggling and protesting back towards the platform.

"Oh, no," Ari muttered.

The guards all returned to the platform. By this time, the enormous square was nearly completely filled with people, the plaza a mass of drab browns and grays dotted here and there with the emerald cloaks of Kagaian guards. An unearthly silence hung over the gathering. For so many people in one place, there was not a sound, except for the occasional cry from one of the family members of those who had been taken up to the platform.

The lead officer took a step forward, the line of citizens quaking behind him. There was an old man, a young woman, a middle-aged man, and a young boy; the guards had been working at random when they'd made their selections. The officer raised up his hands for silence, though the plaza already had the eerie atmosphere of a tomb.

"In response to the acts of terrorism perpetrated last week by members of the Two Falls resistance, we have now instilled a new protocol," he announced, his voice booming out over the crowd. "Each week, ten people will be taken at random from their houses in the city. They will be held in the prisons at our headquarters. And," he continued, taking a step, building up steam, "every time we so much as hear of a single Ashan escaping the city, if a single house is burned, if a single officer is killed, we will execute one of those ten."

In shock, Tarr whirled to meet Archer's eyes. The expression that met him was one of barely contained fury. Archer's lips were thinly tightened in a furiously straight line.

At this, a loud buzzing broke out among the people. The officer paused and smiled, clearly enjoying the stir he'd caused amongst them. Tarr whipped back around to Ari. "What can we do?"

Ari's jaw was set. "We cannot stop the resistance. No matter what," he said grimly.

Tarr turned around to face Archer but found him gone. "No!" Tarr cried, scrambling to his hands and knees to scuttle along the edge of the building. "Archer, *no!*"

"Therefore, subjects of Kagai, think twice before you offer a friendly hand to the Ashans or in any way extend aid to a member of the resistance," the officer called out, the crowd quieting down once more. "Your duty, as loyal subjects of Kagai, is to keep the peace. It is your loved ones' lives at stake now. Remember that."

The officer turned to go, and the noise of the crowd surged up behind him like a cresting wave. Suddenly, there was a sharp hiss through the air, and a black and white fletched arrow hit *whap!* in the back of the officer's neck, and he toppled to the ground, clutching at the shaft. A breathless cheer broke out amongst the spectators.

Without missing a beat, the junior officer stepped forward and ran his sword straight through the young boy, who immediately went limp, and the crowd's cheer collectively caught in its throat in a single gasp. The people in the line on the platform cried out and scrambled away from the boy. The officer held the boy's thin shoulder for a moment, then cast him to the ground like a limp rag. A single shriek, a mother's cry, pierced the air and Tarr nearly had to turn away as he watched the woman struggle through the onlookers towards the platform.

"The Strikers!" the officer bellowed. "The Strikers have killed this boy! This is where the path that following them will lead!" He gestured to the heap on the platform with his blade, his eyes boring into the faces of the crowd before him.

"That's precisely what happened," Tarr said tiredly.

A short silence greeted the end of his words. Athela's arms were folded, and her face was a mask.

"I don't need a lecture," Archer snapped after a moment. He was perched in a corner atop one of the chairs, his shoulders hunched over, refusing to make eye contact with the rest of them.

"I'm not going to give you one," she shot back, whirling toward him. "But it was a poor decision, Archer. We're not in the mountains anymore."

"*Poor decision*?" came Ari's booming voice. Even his normally inexpressive face looked angry; he had brewed like a coming storm all afternoon. "It was more than a poor decision; it was *sheer stupidity* that cost an innocent life."

"Funny, Ari, that sounds remarkably like a lecture," Archer snapped, his golden eyes flashing up to bore into Ari's unflinching gaze.

"It's one you need to hear," Ari retorted. "You are careless and reckless, and you kill without thought or foresight. You are a danger to our cause."

Laith quietly moved forward to stand between them, his calming presence de-escalating the tension ever so slightly. "We all become angry by the injustice we see, and we all get emotional," he said quietly. "If we didn't, we wouldn't be fighting this war."

"I could have saved that boy," Ari said beneath his breath. "If you had given me half a chance, I could have saved him."

"The officer is dead!" Archer yelled over Laith's shoulder, leaping to his feet. Laith put a placating arm on his chest, and Marc stood up behind them, ready for trouble. "The officer is dead, isn't he?"

"To be replaced how quickly?" Ari retorted.

"They will waste time, effort, and resources in promoting up some inexperienced junior officer to take his place," Archer maintained stubbornly. "Who will do his job half as well."

"Don't pretend that what you did had any pretense of forethought or strategy, Archer. If it were me, I would have taken the time to *think*," Ari shot back. "To consider my actions and their consequences. Which you've never done."

"What will we do now?" Tarr interjected quietly. "Now that

General Grey has put this decree in order? If we are now so upset about the death of one boy, we must take the time to consider the innocent lives that will be taken if we continue with the actions of the resistance."

"They could be bluffing," Marc suggested tentatively. "About killing those innocent people."

"Or not," Laith shook his head.

"I ask again...what will we do?" Tarr repeated.

This question seemed to drain the air of its anger as Ari and Archer sat back to think. Seeing the situation deflating, Laith gave Archer a quick pat on the chest and stepped over beside Athela, who was chewing her lip and studiously avoiding looking over in Archer's direction.

"We can't stop," she shrugged. "Any cessation in our activities would be admitting defeat. We'd be handing the city over right into Cira's lap."

"Are we in agreement?" Tarr asked, glancing around the circle. Reluctantly, everyone—even Si—nodded their heads yes.

"We won't be able to control the outpouring of anti-Striker emotion from the citizens of the city," Laith pointed out. "Not if we're knowingly putting their families' lives at risk."

Tarr considered this and swiveled towards Ari. "It will be up to you and your propaganda department. Print something saying that we are all fighting this war against tyranny and oppression. That we must not give in to fear if we are to live in peace and freedom again. Something along those lines. Do you think you can manage it?"

"I can try," Ari nodded and turned on his heel, reaching for his cloak. "But I must say one last thing to you," he faced Archer, who glared at him from his seat. Marc once again edged closer. "If it were not for these people who I have come to respect," Ari motioned around to the rest of the Strikers standing in the room, "I would not fight alongside you. I would consider it a dishonor."

"Likewise," Archer spat.

"You are no different than you once were, Archer. These people did not know who you were or what you were, but I did. I lived here in this city while you operated within it, until you were chased out like a dog. They may think you have changed," he swept his hand around to the others, who were watching in stunned silence, "but you never will as long as you have *that* in your hand," Ari indicated Archer's bow, his voice curiously flat and emotionless. He paused, gathering his thoughts. "I'll go now, to try and clean up the mess you have made." And with that, he turned and walked out the door, shutting it firmly behind him.

There was an intensely awkward silence left in his wake.

"Archer—" Athela began, but the white Ashan rose to his feet and walked out of the room without another word.

"Follow him, won't you, Tarr?" Laith asked quietly. "Ari spoke out of turn."

"Archer's ashamed," Tarr told them as he shifted his weight and headed slowly for the door. "He knows he made a mistake. He'll give himself worse than anyone for this. Worse than Ari could give him." He glanced pointedly at Athela. "I wouldn't mention it again."

"I wasn't going to say anything!" Athela exclaimed indignantly.

Tarr shook his head wearily, rubbing the tattoo on the back of his neck with one thin hand. "I'm tired of these arguments. I have an interview in a few minutes, and then I will see all of you again tomorrow morning." He glanced at Rane and gave her a small smile, which she returned.

He walked down the hallway to Archer's room and entered without knocking. Anyone else would have told him to leave Archer alone for a while, but Tarr, who by this point was as familiar with Archer's thoughts as his own, knew that his presence would be a comfort to his brother rather than an imposition.

Archer was sitting with his back to Tarr, fitting new heads onto the shafts of his arrows. Tarr sat beside him and watched for a while, marveling as he always did at how skillfully Archer's nimble fingers worked.

"Do you need any help?" Tarr asked.

Archer sighed but didn't give an inch He shook his black-tipped head. He looked back down to his work, taking a new thread of twine and severing it with a quick swipe of the knife he kept sheathed on his belt. Tarr stayed beside him for a long time, wishing more than anything that he could find the words to tell Archer that he hoped Ari was wrong.

Later, Tarr ducked out of the front of their headquarters. It was pitch black outside; though the moon was full, there was a heavy veil of clouds obscuring everything. Tarr was immensely glad of it. He flipped the hood over his head and waited a few seconds for his escorts to arrive. Once the coast was clear, they came, creeping out of the shadows like foxes. There were two of them, a man and a woman.

"A good night," the man said in gruff Ashan. It was the password.

"A good night," Tarr replied easily and strode off. He would go first while the two escorts hung back so they would not look as though they were in a group. By this point, Tarr was used to hearing people tromp along behind him wherever he went. Since he was not trained in combat as Laith or Marc, he was subject to an armed escort anytime he had to leave headquarters.

Luckily, it was a short walk without any awkward brushes with members of the Kagaian guards, and after about ten minutes or so they drew up outside of a small inn. His escort stepped in front of Tarr and beat the door rhythmically a few times, after which the door creaked open and a shadowy figure admitted them. Tarr glanced around only briefly at his surroundings. The inn, he surmised, would probably be quite cheery during the day, but here at night, with only a single torch burning in a grate, the place was decidedly eerie.

"There," his male bodyguard grunted, indicating a small cupboard tucked neatly beneath the staircase. The door was only about two and a half feet tall, and Tarr was all too aware of how undignified he appeared while trying to thread his long limbs through the opening. The room on the other side of the deceptively small door was almost tall enough to stand in. The female bodyguard passed him a torch through the low opening behind him, and Tarr took it and waved it around at his surroundings, the light revealing a hidden staircase that led, he assumed, to the basement. He glanced back over to his escorts.

"She'll be here in ten minutes," the man grunted. Tarr gave a polite nod and picked his way carefully down the rickety staircase, the cupboard door closing behind him.

The hidden basement had been neatly made up in anticipation of Tarr's arrival. A small desk with parchment and a new ink pen was located in the center of the room, writing implements arranged neatly on the surface. The basement looked conspicuously bare of anything else, and Tarr wondered briefly if it had been a wine cellar. He lit the few candles he could find around the room until the entire place glowed a bright orange. Then he sat down in his chair and waited.

It was this matter of the vacancy in Faridor. A maid's position was open, and Tarr's connections had aligned so that he was in the enviable position of being able to place anyone there that he wanted. The possibilities made the tips of his fingers itch. But it had to be the right sort of person...someone by whom Cira would not be threatened. Tarr hoped more than anything that the young lady about to walk down the basement steps would be a cunning tactician of fifty-six trapped in the body of a nineteen-year-old servant girl.

He hadn't long to wait. Ten minutes later, just as his escort had said, there was a noise at the top of the stairs and the sound of a group of people tromping heavily down towards him. When they drew into the basement, he was able to see her face—or half of it, as the girl was heavily blindfolded. She was tall and thin, and Tarr thought that he vaguely recognized her from his last days in their mountain stronghold.

The blindfold remained in place as the female bodyguard guided the girl down to sit on the chair on the opposite side of the desk from Tarr. Tarr cleared his breath and saw the girl's head snap up the slightest bit at the sound. She was quite nervous, he could tell.

"Don't worry," he began in the sort of soothing, comforting voice he had heard Laith use when he was talking to Athela's horse. "You're quite safe here. My name is Tarr. What's yours?"

"Imran," came the shaky reply.

"Lovely," Tarr said, scratching down the name at the top of the parchment. "I saw you back at the mountain, didn't I? You're a friend of that girl Leonore's?"

"That's right," she said nervously. "I was there for a month, then Leonore and I came to the city with the last group. Leonore—she says she wants to spy for you."

"And you?" Tarr continued, not mentioning the fact that he had interviewed Leonore the previous night. "Why do you want to become a spy for me?"

"I...I want to help you win."

That's good of you, Tarr thought sardonically, but realized that her rather unadorned response could also be due to nerves. "Where are you from?"

"I'm from a village close to the mountains," she said. "Cira's soldiers came through there, and I was separated from my family. There was a small skirmish, and your troops took me out and brought me up to the mountain headquarters. That's how I ended up there."

"And your family?"

"I think they've reached safety; I can't be sure."

"I see."

"I think..." she bit her lip, beginning to loosen up, "if I help you win the war faster, I'll be able to find them faster, you see?"

"Yes, I think I do," Tarr replied. "What was your family trade?"

"My father was a tailor."

"And your mother?"

"Helped in his shop."

Tarr made a small squiggle on the top of his sheet, then leaned back in his chair and studied the girl carefully for a few moments. He remembered the "skirmish" she referred to quite well. An anti-Striker faction had broken out in a formerly neutral town that, unfortunately, lay smack in the middle of the Strikers' own supply routes to their stronghold in the mountains. Marc and Laith had taken a small force and all but reclaimed the town from the control of Cira's troops. The town was technically still under the control of the Strikers. It was an uneasy peace, but it was peace nonetheless.

Tarr once again leaned forward and looked at the girl's half-obscured face. She was bony and angular; her body type could easily have passed for Ashan. She had full lips and black hair that hung straight to her shoulders. But there was something...something about the way she held herself...

"Did you know Laith during your time in the mountain?" he asked. There was a slight stiffening in her shoulders, nothing more.

"No."

"You saw him, though?" Tarr probed in a gentle voice.

"Yes, I saw him."

"What did you think?"

A pause. "He is very handsome."

"Yes, quite," Tarr agreed quietly, leaning back once again in his chair. "I'll tell you what I'm going to do. I think that we have a position here in Two Falls that will benefit from your help. You will be contacted within three days. Take this," he added, sketching the small silhouette of a fox on one corner of the parchment. He ripped off the corner, leaned over, and pressed it into her hand. She jumped at his touch, clutched at the paper immediately, and began nodding. "Thank you very much," he concluded and nodded to the escorts, who stepped forward and took the girl gently by the arms, pulling her to her feet.

"Thank you, sir," she said shakily and allowed herself to be guided out of the room.

Tarr sat motionless in his chair for a few moments, then leaned forward and blew out the candle on the table before him. The flame dissolved into a wisp of smoke that curled in a silver spiral up to the roof of the basement.

"Well, I'll give him one thing," Marc observed sagely as he and Si crouched down behind a box of crates, "Tarr may be limited in some respects..."

"He's really not too great at dancing," Si concurred. "It's a shame."

"...but he can sure as hell smell out a double agent from a mile away," Marc concluded.

They watched as Imran emerged from a side street, tucked inside a large cloak. She glanced this way and that, then trotted forward across the bare plaza in front of the Kagaian headquarters and up the broad, ornate staircase in front of the large double doors of the barracks. One of the door guards came forward and stopped her. After a few seconds of conversing, she took a small slip of parchment out of her pocket and showed it to one of the guards, who immediately stepped back and motioned for the large door to be opened. A moment later, she and the guard ducked inside, and the door was closed behind them.

"That was quick," Si remarked with a muffled yawn. He and Marc had been pulled out of bed half an hour before by Tarr's escorts and had been given orders to tail Imran. "She barely even bothered to go home and put on a cloak before she went to the headquarters. Why do you reckon she did it?"

Marc shrugged a shoulder. "I chatted with Tarr for a second on his way in. He suspects Laith might have been instrumental in the death of her family. Remember that battle we fought in the town near the mountains about a month ago?"

"Oh," Si said, looking down at the ground. "I'm sorry."

"As am I," Marc agreed.

"What'll we do now?"

"Go back and report to Tarr, I reckon," Marc stood up to his full, somewhat diminutive height and stretched, shaking the folds of his cloak back around his shoulders. "Don't worry, Si," he clapped his hand on Si's thin back, "at least now Tarr has a new double agent he can use to our benefit. Better we find out now than after she's been given an important assignment."

"I suppose so," Si said, looking slightly happier. He trotted a few steps to catch up with Marc's long stride, then gamboled over a couple of fallen boards. Marc watched him fondly, then cracked a grin.

"Si! *Attention!*" he hissed. Immediately, Si dove into the shadows on the side of the street, all but vanishing. Marc nodded, satisfied. If there was one area of his studies in which Si excelled, it was stealth. Marc walked by him without breaking his stride. "Now," he said in a low whisper, "See if you can get the paper out of my back pocket without my noticing."

He walked down the street, trying to be as nonchalant as possible. He took the next right and then a left. Here and there were faint scuffling sounds behind him, but on the whole, Si was largely undetectable.

Suddenly, he tripped over something—a board that had all but appeared right in front of his feet. He nearly fell to his knees but managed to catch himself, and in the flurry of the moment he felt a nimble little figure dart up behind him and vanish. Laughing to himself, Marc straightened and whistled low. Si reappeared at his side, slightly out of breath.

"Liar!" the boy panted, his grin visible even in the low light. "You didn't have any papers!"

"Can't always assume your target is carrying what you think they are, can you?" Marc shot back. "Nice trick there with the board."

"Thanks—oh, no!" Si exclaimed. There were footsteps coming rapidly toward them around the corner of one of the alleys, ostensibly in search of the racket. Marc signaled to Si with a curt hand motion that they should refrain from talking and signed to him to split up and find shelter in the street. Si nodded and once again dissolved into the liquid dark of the night. Marc stepped back and tucked himself close to the ground in a small alcove that housed a sewer grate. He held his breath and kept his gaze lowered lest his pursuers see the whites of his eyes. He narrowly flicked a glance upwards as three sets of feet marched purposefully by his hiding place. He waited until they were out of earshot before he slid out from his cover, relieved (as he always was) that no cry had been let out to signal that Si had been discovered.

The boy was beside him again after only a few seconds. "You smell horrible," Si observed matter-of-factly.

"Sewer grate. I'll wash when we're back at the house."

Si grinned and let off a long string of Ashan, which Marc assumed was some sort of verse he had learned from Archer as it rhymed in places. "For heaven's sake, Si, keep it in a language we can all understand."

Si grinned cheekily and avoided the cuff that Marc sent his way. Si had taken to Ashan like a fish to water, whereas Marc's vocabulary extended just as far as the various passwords and codes necessary for him to be a functioning member of the Striker resistance. Anytime Marc tried Si's patience or critiqued his technique, the boy would flash back with a retort in Ashan, which invariably left Marc floundering.

It was very nearly morning; Marc could almost smell the dawn that was about to arise cold and frozen in the east. After the brief adrenaline rush of the night's activities, Si let out another yawn and fell placidly into step beside his friend.

"Marc," he said conversationally, "what did Ari mean today? When he was arguing with Archer?"

"Ari's a very noble individual, Si," Marc said slowly. "He's very proud. He holds himself to a high standard, which makes him less likely to forget and forgive the pasts of others. I think he's always resented Archer a bit for what he was."

Si considered. "He's right, though, isn't he? Ari? It was Archer's fault, wasn't it, that the boy died?"

"The officer who killed the boy was the one at fault," Marc sighed. "But Ari was right in that Archer was wrong to act rashly as he did. I think even Archer knows that."

"What's the difference, though?" Si inquired. "Between Archer and Ari? I mean, Ari's killed people, hasn't he? And I...someday I might kill someone too. In battle, I mean."

"It's a fine line, Si," Marc frowned. "But before, Archer killed for money. That's what Ari has trouble forgiving. He believes only a certain kind of person could kill someone for money rather than in service of a cause." He glanced over at Si's face and saw that the boy was still troubled. "He believes people like that do not have the capacity to change."

"Do you believe that?" Si asked.

Marc considered. "I don't think I can understand the kind of desperation Archer must have felt back then," he said slowly. "From what I have heard, he was taken under the wing of a woman who trained him to do that for a living. I don't think he knew there was another way for a very long time. Probably not until we showed up."

"Oh," Si said quietly. "So we saved him?"

"Maybe," Marc hid a smile. "In a way."

"What if I have to kill someone?" Si asked, his voice very small.

Marc sighed. "Times like this require us to make difficult decisions, Si. We must always make the choices that we believe, in our hearts, to be the right thing. And choosing *not* to kill is every bit as important. You mustn't forget that."

Si thought about this the rest of the walk home. He and Marc spoke only briefly before they parted ways to go to their chambers. As Si wrapped himself up in his quilt and closed his eyes for sleep, a peaceful smile settled on his face. Marc was always able to explain things so that he could understand.

CHAPTER SEVEN

The sentry atop the roof of Faridor squinted down into the gloom below, where he saw a dimly lit shadow pause in front of the gigantic doors of the outer keep. The shadow did not bother to knock; it merely stood there expectantly as if it were perfectly aware of being watched. The sentry turned around to his superior, who had drawn up behind him.

"Orders, sir?" the sentry asked. The captain squinted as well, then shrugged.

"Open the door, we'll see what they want; they might have a message from Lady Cira."

The roof sentry saluted and nodded at the guards on the floor of the courtyard while the captain turned to go down the stairs to the gate and investigate the strange visitor. The keep guards immediately ran forward with ready torches, slipping them into grates by the door hinges. At the top of the wall, a gigantic windlass began to turn, and Faridor's enormous outer doors creaked open just enough to admit the shadowy stranger. The cloaked figure walked into the center of the courtyard, where it was met by the captain. The figure drew back its hood, revealing it to be a dark-skinned woman, tall, with black braided hair.

"What is your business here?" the captain demanded. The woman made no reply but flung the edge of her cloak over her arm with a flourish and extended a sheet of folded paper. The captain motioned for a torch, which arrived quickly, and he read the note by the flickering light. He paused and visibly read it over again, more carefully, on the lookout for any deception. Finally, he seemed to be satisfied and looked up at the woman in front of him. She still hadn't said a word. "Follow me," he ordered finally, returning the letter and spinning on his heel. Kai slipped the letter back into her belt and strode after the captain as he led her into the stronghold of Faridor.

The walk to the dungeons was a relatively quick one, as the captain was well known on sight by all of the house guards, so no one bothered to question Kai's silent presence as they passed through the hallways. Kai looked about her with a cautious interest. The decorations of the hallways were dark and grim: old tapestries and swords, a statue here and there. Kai noticed that Cira had had her portrait painted many times over, for there seemed to be one for nearly every hallway they went through. All of them followed roughly the same theme: Cira posed with a sword and a scepter, her hand aloft; Cira with her foot on the throat of her dying enemies; Cira in the thick of battle with a serene, righteous look on her face.

At last, they went through a door and down a few flights of stairs, the air growing steadily damper and colder with every step. There was an acrid taste to it that made Kai nearly want to hold her breath. The captain stopped in front of a short man seated at the top of another flight of stairs, perched atop a stool with a book propped open in front of him. The captain exchanged a few low words, and the short man flipped through a few pages in his book. The captain turned to Kai.

"What's her name, again? Your sister?"

"Rowan," Kai replied in a low voice. "Her name is Rowan."

"Here," the short man said, pointing to the middle of one of the pages. "Been here for a long time. Was one of the first ones taken. Down three flights of stairs, cell 1265." The short man closed his book with a loud clap and turned away before sweeping back around with a fresh torch for the captain. The captain turned to Kai and inclined his head for her to follow him, which she did through the door and down the three flights of stairs. The cell blocks extended out as far as she could see on each floor they passed, and there was an eerie silence about the place. Kai had braced herself for screams and wails, but she found that the complete lack of sound was far more discomforting. There seemed to be no life in the place, no spark of existence, as if Cira had wiped it out of each prisoner she brought in. *Yet they have to be alive,* Kai assured herself. *They have to be alive, or else she wouldn't be using up all these cells. What would the point be in that?*

On the third flight, the captain stepped off onto the landing, nodding at the guard posted at the head of the main hallway. There was hardly any light except for the one torch located at the checkpoint. The captain led the way down the hallway, followed by Kai and the floor's watchman, who seemed to be rather keen on seeing what someone like Kai was up to in the dungeons of Faridor; it wasn't as if people just showed up wanting a tour. The captain swept his torch from side to side with each of the doors they passed, reading the numbers carved into the stone doors. There were no windows in any of the cells, and Kai was half-glad that she couldn't see the occupants. The eerie silence from above pervaded even these walls; there was no scuffling, no sounds of breathing, only the rhythmic padding of their sets of feet on the stone floors.

Finally, Kai, who was counting ahead of the captain's back-and-forth torch motion, could see their destination ahead of her. Her heart leapt inside her, just as her fear and anticipation lurched, too. It had been a long time since she had seen Rowan. They'd parted on bad terms many years before, but Kai hoped deep within her heart that the old arguments and misunderstandings and resentments wouldn't matter now. She didn't think they would.

Three doors on the left passed in painfully slow succession before the captain stopped in front of cell 1265. He jerked his head over for the floor watchman, who was in charge of the keys, to step forward and open it. Kai wanted to throw him to one side and burst in first herself, but she controlled herself until the lock had turned and the two men pushed the door inward; the captain stepped inside with the torch. Kai followed, biting her lip so hard she tasted the tinny flavor of blood, but she barely even noticed it. She half-hoped, half-dreaded what she would find within.

The cell itself reeked of dirt and ripe, almost animalistic smells, so that Kai caught her breath and covered her face with one hand. There was a wispy candle in one corner burning away, and it took a second for the light of the larger torch to pervade all corners of the tiny area. Kai's violet eyes scanned the cold stone floor, and there, in one corner, curled up in a fetal position, was what was left of her sister, huddled on a threadbare blanket. Kai would hardly have recognized her but for the familiar bloom of the purple birthmark on the right side of her neck. Kai leaped forward and touched her shoulder, afraid that it would be cold, hard, and dead, but instead, she felt a spark of life beneath her fingertips, warmth under the immediate cold of the skin. At first, Rowan did not respond to the touch and remained still, but Kai shook her a bit harder, and something sparked in the dormant skin. Rowan began to move slightly. Her clothes were barely anything, just rags, and they hung off of her skeletal frame like dead leaves on a bare winter branch. Kai felt her heart shriveling by the second as she looked at what had once been her beautiful younger sister.

The thick, shining mane of black hair had been hewn off close to the scalp, and the face that turned around was hardly recognizable. Her cheeks were sunken in, and her eyes were absolutely enormous; the violet color so like Kai's glinted in the torchlight, first uncomprehending, then the expression changed slowly to wonder. Kai moved forward and held her as close as she dared; she half felt that Rowan would break into a thousand pieces if she pressed her too hard. She released her and rocked back. Looking at her sister's destroyed face, no tears came. They hardened in her chest; her anger was growing, throbbing in the air around them, threatening to break through the walls and strike Cira down where she stood hundreds of miles away.

"Rowan," Kai ventured in a low voice. "Do you know who I am?"

Rowan blinked her enormous, rimmed purple eyes. "Kai," she said slowly, her voice breaking. It was huskier and lower than Kai had remembered. "Kai," she repeated, this time her voice growing stronger. "Have you come to save me?"

"Not yet," Kai said, gritting her teeth and supporting Rowan's slight weight when her shoulders sagged. "I can't yet. Not yet, but I'm going to." Kai shot a look over her shoulder and saw that the captain and the watchman were still standing there, looking at them with a sort of morbid curiosity. "Do you mind stepping out of here for a moment, please?" Kai asked harshly. She didn't want them to see her sister like this.

"No," the captain resolutely folded his arms. "I think we should remain here. Whatever you want to say to her, you can say in front of us."

"Rowan," Kai repeated, this time in Ashan, turning back to her sister. "I have come here to see to it that you are alive. I have made a bargain, and very soon I shall return and we can leave this place. You and I will be free, and we will go with our family where these people can never find us again."

"Hey!" the captain barked. "No one said you could speak that here!"

Kai didn't even bother to answer him, but looked back over her shoulder with a stare that nearly froze him where he stood in the doorway. He gulped, glancing down at his feet with embarrassment, and folded his arms. The sentry tried to hide a smirk at his superior's discomfiture. Rowan was still looking at Kai with a deep, unblinking stare. For a minute, Kai thought that Rowan must not have understood what she said and thought fleetingly of repeating herself, but then Rowan slowly opened her mouth.

"You..." she began, then gulped. "You have made a deal with that woman?"

"It is the only way to get you out," Kai insisted firmly.

"You have made a bargain with the woman who has kept me in here for this long, who has starved me, who has beaten me," Rowan's eyes flashed, showing a temporary shadow of the fire she had before. But the fire was extinguished as quickly as it had flickered up. "I have not seen the sun in three years," she told Kai softly.

"You will see it soon," Kai returned, stroking the side of her head.

"Does it still shine?" Rowan asked, her voice a whisper.

"It does," Kai smiled gently, and Rowan laid her bony skull against Kai's breastbone. Kai held her there for some time before Rowan stirred again and looked up at her, the lights of the torches reflected in her glassy violet eyes.

"What is the price?" she asked.

Kai looked at her straight in the face. It wouldn't do to have Rowan know. Once she was free, she would feel the burden of guilt for what Kai had to do to release her. Kai didn't want that for her. She wanted her to be happy. She wanted her to be free of all the pain, all the memories of what had happened. So she didn't answer.

"Kai," Rowan said sharply, an edge to her voice that made Kai's heart ache as she remembered the playful arguments they had had when they were young. "What is the price you are paying for my freedom?"

That entreaty was too much. Kai couldn't lie. "The Strikers," Kai returned hesitantly. "I'm giving Cira the Strikers."

"Alive or dead?"

"Dead," Kai said shortly, hating the word, hating herself.

"Archer?" Rowan asked, brow furrowing, leaning back even further to survey her sister's reaction. "You give her Archer?"

"I have had no love for him in a long time, you know that," Kai countered. "I have had love for you forever."

Rowan didn't reply to this for a while, but Kai could tell that she was unhappy with it. Thinking seemed to exhaust her; she leaned back in the crook of the hard stone walls, resting her head against it, the rings of her trachea showing out vividly through the skin of her arched neck. Kai had to look away; she couldn't bear the sight of it any longer. Her sister had been one of the most beautiful and sought-after women in the country. Kai had never been jealous. She had admired Rowan alongside everyone else, had enjoyed her sharp intelligence and wit. Kai had to try to save the vestige of living spark that was left in her.

"Get me out of here," Rowan said finally, rolling her head back down and looking at Kai. "I want to see the sun again, Kai. I do not care what it takes. I want you to get me out."

"I will," Kai said in the Common tongue and leaned forward, relieved, taking her sister in her arms. She was hard and thin, her torso like kindling wood. "I will get you out of here, Rowan, and we'll go far away. It's too late for the rest. But we'll make it out. I promise you. We'll get our mother and the others and we'll go into the mountains, we'll cross the sea and go to Vireg, we'll keep going as long as it takes. I promise you, I'll make it all better. I'll take care of everything." They stayed like that for a while until Kai felt warm tears running down her arms, and she squeezed Rowan even tighter.

"That's enough," the captain announced behind her and moved forward, laying a hand on Kai's shoulder. Kai flinched it off without letting go of Rowan. It was cruel; it was more than Kai could take to stand up and leave freely while Rowan had to remain in that hell. Perhaps if she clung on tightly enough they would fuse together, and the captain would have to drag them both out of the fortress and set them on the road home. Then they could simply disappear, and Kai wouldn't have to worry about Archer or the rest of the Strikers. She and her sister could go on living with whatever they had left.

"Enough," the captain said in a harder voice, and Kai steeled herself. Getting into a full-out brawl in the middle of the dungeon wasn't going to help anyone. She slowly released Rowan and easily pried her hands from around her waist, setting her sister back against the wall. Rowan watched her tearfully as Kai stood and slowly took a step back.

"I'll come for you," Kai said, and then turned away as the door was shut behind her. She spun around and faced the guard, an unforgiving expression on her face. "Now, you listen," she hissed, getting right up in his face. She was taller than him by two inches, and she used the extra height to her advantage. "I am on a very important mission, as you know, by order of Lady Cira herself. And while I am on this mission I want it seen to that my sister receives the best of care. That means that she is well fed, well clothed, and will be moved to more decent living quarters in one of the towers, not here beneath the earth. A tower where she can see the sunlight. When I return to collect her, I want to be able to recognize her face when I see her, do you understand?"

She intimidated the captain, and Kai could see it, but he swallowed and swung his shoulders around, trying to be cocky. He took a step back so that she didn't tower over him quite so starkly. "Or you'll do what?" he asked insolently.

Kai fixed him with a cold stare. "Trust me," she said in a low voice. "You don't want me to use my imagination. That prisoner," she pointed to the cell door, "my *sister*, is valuable collateral. *I* don't want her damaged. And you can bet that *Lady Cira* doesn't want her damaged. And if Lady Cira doesn't want that, you most certainly don't want it either. If she so much as catches a head cold, your life is forfeit. Do you understand?"

The captain swallowed, and even though he was bearing the brunt of the bullying, the sentry behind him was ducking his head and looking sheepishly at his shoes, no longer enjoying seeing his superior being belittled. Kai moved her violet stare back and forth between the two of them, making sure that they saw she was serious. "I am holding both of you responsible," she told them slowly, and saw the weight of her words fall squarely upon their shoulders where it belonged. Satisfied, she took a step back and released the tension on them. They both visibly breathed sighs of relief.

"Now," Kai announced, striding down the hall towards the staircase. "One of you get me a sheet of parchment and a pen. I've got a letter to write to your Queen. The deal is on."

CHAPTER EIGHT

The lookout at the northern gates had never seen anything quite like it before. An enormous gilt carriage with broad golden wheels sliding evenly along the path, pulled by a perfectly matched team of four blood-bay horses. Their manes tossed and caught blue in the light, and an intricate golden crest emblazoned on their blinkers glittered and winked as they chomped and lathered at the bit, prancing and nipping at one another as the coachman pulled them to a halt at the looming western gate of Two Falls. The four guards looked from one another back to the coach and then back to each other again. The universal expression was one of overwhelming bewilderment.

There was a long period of silence before one of them spoke. The horses stood there shaking their harnesses and pawing. A guard cleared her throat. "Cira...er...Queen Kagai didn't mention that she'd be coming into the city today, did she?" she inquired tentatively to the other guard on duty.

"Not to my knowledge," the other replied hesitantly. "What do—"

All four gave a start as the carriage door suddenly opened and a tall, thin man popped out, a thick envelope clutched in one spindly hand.

"Papers," the head guard snapped, finally remembering her duties.

The thin man extended the envelope with a distinct air of disdain.

His expression implied that there was a general stench surrounding him that he found deeply distasteful. The guard took the proffered paper from him, shrugging off the three other guards as they crowded around her, eager to learn the carriage's origin. There was a blood-red seal on the back of the envelope, emblazoned deeply with a wax crest identical to that on the side of the coach. The guard tugged a few times on the flap of the envelope, afraid to tear it.

"I can't open it," the guard complained.

The tall, thin man rolled his eyes and said in perfectly clipped tones with over-accented *s*'s, "It's a *seal*. You must delicately break the wax."

"Give it here," grunted one of the other guards (who'd had more experience with these sorts of things). He took the envelope, withdrew his dagger, and slid it under the wax seal. Inside was a perfectly arranged sheaf of traveling permits signed and stamped by Cira Kagai herself.

"Hmph," the guard muttered, trying not to look impressed. "And do you...er...do you plan on staying in Two Falls long?"

"*I*," sniffed the tall, thin man with some degree of superciliousness, "am the valet of Count Joris Actaeon. As his papers are in perfect order and his family is favored highly by Queen Cira Kagai herself, he will be remaining in Two Falls for precisely as long as he likes."

The guards craned their necks at the windows of the carriage, hoping to catch a glimpse of the count, but they were heavily curtained and revealed nothing. "Actaeon, eh?" the guard repeated, glancing back down at the papers. "Seems I've heard the name before."

"Quite possibly," the valet intoned snottily, "as his family helped to found this city."

"Look, we're going to have to search the carriage," the guard announced, trying to assert what little authority she felt remained.

"You shall do nothing of the sort," the valet snapped back. "The Count has a travel permit signed by the Queen herself. You have no authority whatsoever to do such a thing."

"Bring out the Count," the guard demanded.

"I shall not!" snapped the valet.

The other guards hung back, half-hoping that fisticuffs would erupt between the head guard and the lanky, slightly effeminate valet. The valet sniffed, stepped back to the carriage door, and rapped lightly with his knuckles. There was the slightest flutter of movement, and then the velvet curtain in the window inched ever so slightly to the left. The guards could see only a ringed, perfectly manicured finger holding the curtain aside from within. Hushed words were exchanged between the valet and the man within, then the valet gave a quick bow and turned back to the guards.

"The Count," he said carefully, "says with all due respect that if you waste his time for one second more, he will personally see to it that you are all imprisoned in Faridor before lunchtime tomorrow."

The guards exchanged glances, clearly convinced that, splendid gilded carriage or no, this entire thing wasn't worth their while.

But the head guard still felt a latent twinge of duty. "Where'll he be staying then?" she asked.

"At the Actaeon mansion near Two Falls Square, of *course*," snipped the valet.

The head guard had had enough. She handed the envelope back to the valet, who sniffed and took an excessive amount of time re-ordering the papers and carefully placing them back in the envelope. He gave an insultingly slight bow, spun on his well-polished heel, and skipped back into the door of the carriage, snapping it shut firmly behind him. The head guard halfheartedly waved them through the gate. The coachman tapped the back of one of the horses with the tip of his whip. The steeds gave a snort and bounded through the doors of the gate, the carriage clattering along behind them.

"Did you get a look at the Count?" one guard asked the other.

"Not a glimpse," his comrade said regretfully. "But if that's his carriage, I'd be interested to see his house."

"Carriage was bigger than *my* house," the first guard said resentfully.

The carriage roared along, the hooves of the four-horse team clattering on the cobblestones, frightened passers-by diving for cover as the carriage sped through the streets past them. Carriages were rare sights those days, especially carriages drawn by a team of four. Yells were stifled and children yanked out of the way by their terrified parents. Every now and again, the single-ringed forefinger would nudge the velvet curtain aside for a few seconds, but the carriage was too fast and the movement too slight for anyone to get a good look inside.

The carriage wound its way to the northeast of Two Falls, leaving a swath of startled whiplash in its wake, snaking towards the affluent district where the towering mansions of the rich and powerful had once stood. Most of them (at least the ones that had belonged to Ashan sympathizers) had been overtaken and converted into cheap housing for many families, but a precious few had remained untouched throughout the years of war. It was up to the largest and most lavish of these that the carriage drew and pulled to a halt. The horses, as though they could sense that their journey was at last at an end, stood quietly, pawing only occasionally on the cobbles. The façade of the house was immense, with carved stone balconies and a grand staircase leading up to the front door, with broad windows on every floor and the name *Actaeon* carved in rigid capitals over the grand front door.

After only a moment, the two front doors swung open and a pair of identically clad servants rushed up to the carriage. The door was opened, and both the servants bowed deeply. The valet extracted himself with businesslike precision from the interior of the carriage and faced the head servant, who bowed again.

"Is everything prepared for the Count?" he asked.

"Everything. We received the letter announcing his arrival last week, and have since been making everything ready for him," the head servant replied with such an efficient tone that the valet couldn't help but give a curt nod in approval.

"Very well," the valet said and waved him away. He stepped back to the carriage, rapped twice on the door, and spoke quietly toward the window. "Everything is ready, sir," he murmured.

By this point, a considerably large crowd of onlookers had gathered, both those who had followed the carriage's progress, wondering at the identity of the owner, and those who had seen the carriage come to a halt in front of the grand house and had witnessed the to-do with the servants. They craned their necks, hoping to catch sight of the nobleman inside the grand carriage. Such opulence was something all but gone from the day-to-day life of Two Falls.

The footman opened the carriage door and pulled down a short flight of retractable steps from beneath the floor. There was a slight rocking to the carriage, and then a single, exquisitely polished riding boot emerged onto the first step, a pristine silver spur glinting at the heel. A deep purple fabric slithered out into the light, and a heavily cloaked figure emerged and strode evenly up the grand staircase, disappearing with a mere whisper of velvet. The doors shut with a quiet finality as soon as the butler and valet had followed. The footman waved the coach around to the back of the house, and that, as far as anyone could see, was the end of it.

The house was well-lit from the sun pouring in through the windows, and the enormous entrance hall echoed with the *clunk* of the figure's heels on the marble floor. The ringed hand emerged from within the cloak to caress the face of a stone bust mounted on a pedestal against one wall.

The valet approached and cleared his throat. "Erm...what now, milord?"

"Now?" came a soft voice. "We have made a suitable entrance. And we wait."

"*What?*" Archer exclaimed, leaping to his feet and upsetting a large pitcher of water in the process.

The others all exchanged expressions of abject shock as Tarr quietly righted the pitcher. Archer, they all well knew, would likely have responded to the news of the world ending with an unflappable, "Oh, balls." This was something else entirely.

"He *what?*" Archer cried again.

"What's going on?" Marc asked with some bewilderment, wandering down the stairs into the dining room. "Why on earth is Archer yelling?"

"I have no idea," Athela said faintly.

"Joris," Archer said, his pale face alight. "Joris is back!"

"Joris?" all of them demanded in unison. Tarr, however, remained quiet. He knew exactly who Joris was from a number of stories Archer had told him, and was unsure of how exactly to feel about the news. Rane glanced at him out of the corner of her eye, clocking his reaction.

"A friend of mine from the old days," Archer explained.

"So, what, he's a male escort?" Athela asked baldly.

Archer assumed a wounded mien. "For your *information*, Athela, an *extremely* small percentage of my former acquaintances were male escorts."

"You think this Joris will help us?" Laith interjected swiftly. Archer grinned and gave a quick shrug.

"I have no idea what he's up to," he said. "but he's obviously here to see us and wants to meet up as soon as possible."

Laith glanced around the circle. Athela gave an exasperated sigh and threw her hands up in disgust. Laith gave a curt assent and leaned towards the door. "Call Ari," he ordered.

An hour after dark, the Strikers were ushered through a secret underground passageway, originating in a nondescript shop and passing beneath the street before feeding into the belly of the Actaeon manor.

Inside the small passage, they found a burning torch waiting to light their way up a winding hidden staircase to the main floor of the house. Archer took the torch from the grate, waved it encouragingly at the others, and began tromping up the stairwell.

"This is right by Nicolas's house," Tarr observed. "Where Pieter was hidden for a time."

"So it is," Athela agreed, glancing about.

"So, again, what exactly does Joris do?" Marc inquired.

"He doesn't really *do* anything," Archer replied. "His family would look down upon him if he *did* ever try to do anything. They're one of the oldest, wealthiest, most powerful families in the human civilization out here. Closely aligned with your lot," he nodded to Laith and Athela. "Legend has it that the Actaeons inherited a good part of Kagai's wealth after he was overthrown."

This stopped them all still. "Come again?" Laith asked slowly.

"Oh, yes," Archer said cheerily. "Kagaian supporters from way back."

Laith, Tarr, Rane, Marc, and Athela stopped abruptly and exchanged glances. Si was busy staring open-mouthed at Archer.

"You are aware," Athela said slowly, "that you are fighting on the side of the Strikers?"

Archer blinked with exaggerated sarcasm. "Wait, I am?"

Athela swiveled around to look exasperatedly at Tarr, who sighed and raised his gaze to the ceiling. She wheeled back to Archer and continued in a measured tone, "And you are currently escorting your fellow Strikers into the home of a known Kagaian supporter because..." she trailed off, raising an arm in an invitation to complete her sentence.

"Ah, I understand your concern now," Archer agreed cheerfully, turning to resume his climb up the stairs. "That's the best part about Joris, really. His family background gives him excellent cover. He can come and go as he pleases without question."

"And Joris's loyalties lie...?" Laith asked slowly.

"Always against authority," Archer smirked. "He'll rebel against anyone or anything who's in power. Comes from being brought up in an overbearingly oppressive, lethargically affluent family. Joris went out of his way to stir up as much trouble as he could, in his own certain way. That's how he met me."

"You being the *apex* of trouble," Athela put in.

"But one thing's for sure," Archer continued, "he'll never side with the ruling power."

"So you trust him?" Si inquired.

"Absolutely," Archer said confidently.

"Unless *we* win and become the ruling power..." Marc said slowly.

"Then we might have something of a problem on our hands," Archer conceded.

"Great," Athela said sarcastically. "I can tell that this is going to be one of our better meetings."

At the top of the staircase was a grate for the torch and the shadowy outline of another door. Archer stuck the torch into the grate and pushed the door open so that a slat of light shone through into the darkened stairwell. Archer peered outside to make sure the coast was clear, then opened the door fully and the Strikers emerged into the brilliant light of the enormous deserted entryway of the mansion. Tarr pushed back his hood and craned his neck at the ceiling. Though the building had looked gigantic from the street, it looked three times as large from the inside. The ceiling arched overhead, and there were pillars along the walls with gold leaf winding up to the ceiling. Priceless works of art hung along the walls, and Tarr stepped in closer to inspect a few. An enormous chandelier twinkled above and dozens of candles flickered in sconces.

"Not too shabby," Si observed appreciatively, his hands on his hips.

"Reminds me of Laith's bathroom," Marc shrugged, nonplussed. Tarr hid a grin. It was easy to forget sometimes that half of the Strikers had been raised in a palace.

There was a slight click and a door opened behind them. The group whirled around, Laith's hand going to the hilt of his sword. But it was only a tall, thin valet who approached, fussily pursing his lips as he looked them over.

"You're here to see the Count?" he inquired.

"Yep," Archer replied. "Good to see you again."

"And you," the valet replied, though his clipped tone sounded insincere.

"How's the knee?" Archer asked cheekily. "I still feel terrible about that, by the way."

"It's *fine*," the valet snapped. Then, struggling to recover his dignified composure, continued, "This way, please. He sniffed and motioned them off to their right.

Please let there be a hidden door, Tarr hoped inwardly, remembering the other mansion in this district they'd once visited. His wish was granted. The valet placed a hand beside a large portrait of a man on horseback and gave a gentle shove. The painting swung open, revealing a quiet sitting room lined with books and with a fire roaring away in an enormous carved fireplace. Delighted at the secret entrance, Tarr clambered over the threshold and revolved slowly on his heel to take in the full scope of his new surroundings. The valet bowed and swiveled the painting shut behind them, leaving them quite alone in the room.

"You are sure of this?" Tarr asked Archer in Ashan, his tone quiet.

"I..." Archer began, but he was cut off.

"Archer," came a deep voice from one of the chairs. The Strikers turned around in one motion as a young man rose and turned to them.

His face was unlike anything that Tarr had ever seen before: androgynous and almost otherworldly. A pale visage framed by a mop of dark black curls and unearthly features—so feminine that if it wasn't for the deep, distinctly male voice Tarr had heard a moment before, he wouldn't have been sure whether the person facing them was male or female. His eyes were large, a light gray-green; the curve of his nose was slightly rounded so as to give him a rather foreign look, and a pair of extremely full, sensuous lips curved into the slightest hint of a smile. A moment later the smile cracked open fully, and Tarr was shocked to see the grin transform his face from odd femininity into outright boyish charm. He was perfectly dressed, from the scarf tied neatly around his neck to the bottom of his nearly reflective riding boots (Tarr looked sheepishly down at his own boots, which were caked in about three weeks' worth of mud from the street.) After a moment, Joris stepped forward and clasped Archer in a close hug; he was taller than he looked from afar, nearly six feet. Tarr hung back, making a calculated decision to watch and consider rather than participate in any discussion.

Archer and Joris parted, and Archer turned to present his friend to the others. Tarr had to choke down a laugh once he caught sight of Si's expression; the boy had never been capable of subtle reactions, and he was staring at Joris with his mouth open slightly and one eyebrow raised up to comically disbelieving heights.

"Everyone, this is Joris," Archer announced, and introduced them all one by one. To the men, Joris inclined his head slightly and offered a polite, firm handshake—his manners were perfect, and even Tarr's untrained sensibilities could sense that he had been impeccably brought up. To Rane and Athela he gave a deeper bow and the slightest brush of his lips on the backs of their hands. When it was Rane's turn, Tarr felt the oddest bristling inside as Joris's pale green eyes snaked from her hand to her face, and the slightest glimmer flicked across his lips. Though Tarr was by no means a jealous or hot-tempered individual, he had to resist the temptation to stride over and give the young man a vigorous shove, for whether Joris's expression was natural or calculated, the effect was the same: that smile could turn anyone's legs to jelly if he chose to deploy it with its full power.

They took seats in a circle around the living room, Rane sliding in close beside Tarr on one of the loveseats. She met his eyes for the briefest of seconds and, in that fleeting moment, communicated an unmistakable message: *I don't trust him.* Tarr gave her hand the slightest squeeze. *Me neither.* When he looked back up, he saw with a jolt that Joris was watching them quietly from across the circle, that enigmatic smile playing around the corners of his full lips. Tarr swallowed, feeling unsettled.

"So," Laith began, "what can we do for you?"

Joris's curious smile widened a bit, and he spread his hands slightly. "I would like to help you."

Immediately, Tarr found himself trying to pinpoint Joris's odd accent. It wasn't native to Two Falls, that was certain. He assumed that Joris had been schooled outside of the city, perhaps in some distant exotic land.

"And in what *way* could you help?" Athela demanded, an edge to her tone. She sounded absolutely certain that Joris wasn't capable of so much as lifting a dish, much less spearheading any sort of military campaign.

Joris seemed to sense this and fixed his unsettling sphinxlike gaze on Athela. He looked quite unperturbed by her sharpness. "Well, as you may or may not be aware, Lady Cira returned to Faridor Island earlier this morning."

The sentence dropped like a stone into the room, and every one of the Strikers swiveled around to face Tarr, who sat as still as he could while inside, he seethed. He himself had only received word of Cira's return just before they had left for Joris's mansion and had been planning to bring it up once they had gone back to the safehouse. None of the servants in Faridor (his spies among them) had been alerted to her return lest someone try to attack her ship as it arrived. *How could he possibly have known?* Tarr wondered angrily. He was so used to being three steps ahead of everyone else that it perturbed him greatly to be on the same playing field as someone as unknowable as Joris.

Joris, for his part, seemed to be greatly enjoying the minor commotion he had caused. "Well," he purred, "in any case, she *has* returned, and I have an idea or two about how I could help the cause. You have spies in her household, yes?"

The eyes once again swept to Tarr, who sighed a little. Though he loved them all dearly, subterfuge was not his friends' strong point.

Joris tilted his head from side to side. "I could provide you with information straight from Lady Cira herself," he said calmly. "I am willing to do this."

"You?" Marc asked blankly. "A spy?"

"Me," Joris smiled faintly, almost to himself. "A spy."

There was a long silence, nothing but the fire crackling merrily beside them and the low, distant howl of the cold wind outside. Joris reached to the table beside him, picked up a glass, and swirled the scarlet liquid around inside.

"Well, I think it's a great idea," Archer agreed enthusiastically.

"Let me get this straight," Laith said slowly. "You will find a way to get inside Cira's household. You will somehow be appointed to some sort of high position, earn her confidence. And you will feed us information from there?"

"That's correct," Joris replied.

"And, if you don't mind my asking, if you are in a position so close to her, why don't you just kill her for us?" Laith inquired bluntly.

Joris's green eyes swiveled around to Laith. "I," he said slowly, "am not an assassin. This is something I shall not do."

"That's convenient," Athela sneered, crossing her arms.

"Do not be so quick to judge," Joris said. "I have invited you here, to my house, and offered you help. I shall not do murder, and you are not in a place to comment upon that."

Athela opened her mouth to speak, but shut it again quickly. "Sorry," she conceded grudgingly. Si let out a gasp, which she ignored.

"So, what?" Marc asked, "You get yourself appointed Chamberlain or something? Master of the Bath?"

Joris's full mouth pulled farther into a mischievous grin. "Not quite," he sipped his glass. "My interests...lie elsewhere. Somewhere more intimate."

There was a universal moment of confusion, then realization dawned over every face except Si's. "Would you give us a moment to discuss amongst ourselves?" Laith inquired politely.

Joris inclined his head in a gesture of respect towards Laith and unhurriedly stood, taking his glass in his hand and sauntering towards the trick door. Once it was quietly closed behind him, Athela leaped to her feet and spun around. "Where on *earth* did you find this piece of work, Archer?"

"Calm down," Archer said placatingly, holding up both his hands.

"And keep your voice down," Tarr murmured.

"I mean, *really*," she growled. "He's volunteering to go up and seduce my sister?"

"Wait, *that's...*?" Si mumbled wonderingly, realization dawning. "*Oh...*"

"Well," Archer said delicately. "It's one idea."

"And what the hell was that about Cira being back?" Marc demanded, turning towards Tarr. "Did you know that she was back?"

"I knew," Tarr sighed. "Found out right before we left and wanted to wait and bring it up later."

"How did *he* know?" Si wondered.

"I don't know," Tarr said honestly. "He is certainly well-informed, that's for sure."

"What do you think?" Laith asked him. "About Joris?"

Tarr considered, not wanting to say anything that would upset Archer. "I'm not certain. There's something that I can't quite put my finger on, and I'm not sure that we can trust him. Moreover, I'm not sure we can trust his ability to actually pull something like this off. But," he said quickly, before Archer could interject and protest, "if we are looking for a spy to get into Cira's household, we couldn't find one with a more secure background. From a well-to-do family that is known for its support of Kagai. Intelligent, observant, cautious. He was sizing us all up the minute we walked in."

"So he's smart," Athela allowed. "But he has no training for this sort of thing. What if it comes to combat? He said himself that he can't fight."

"Not everyone in this war needs to be able to fight," Tarr said quietly. "And we know that even if we killed Cira tomorrow, the war wouldn't be over. The odds are that General Grey would be appointed to take her place, and the whole thing would continue. Or Vireg would invade us and take over. We've got to dismantle all of it."

Athela looked momentarily abashed, but recovered quickly. "Besides, I've never known Cira to respect any of her lovers enough to confide in them. Odds are she'd keep him in a separate room, feed him twice a day through a slat in the door, and he'd never find out a single useful thing."

"Leave that to him," Archer insisted. "I'm telling you, he has this way...he's got a way about him that I myself have never been able to fully understand." He paused, wrestling to fully articulate his meaning. Finally, he shook his head. "Let's just say he's *extremely* good at this sort of thing." There was a tone in his voice that held a certain implication. Tarr bit his lip to keep from grinning.

"But consider this," Athela pointed out. "Best circumstances here: Joris succeeds and becomes extremely close to Cira. She starts to bestow him with land, titles, riches, power, everything. What, he's just going to continue working for us? Forget all the temptation?"

"Remember what I said earlier?" Archer asked. "He *has* money and land and a title. I've known him for over a decade and never have I known any of those things to have the slightest impression on him at all. He's never particularly cared for them."

"You'd never know it, the way he dresses," Athela grumbled.

"He looks like a mop," Si agreed. Marc barely stifled a snort.

"It's an *image*. What I'm trying to say is he already has ample means to sustain the lifestyle he likes. And he'll do whatever it takes to thumb his nose at his family," Archer insisted. "He could be an asset to us."

They took a moment, pondering the options. "Well, Tarr, it's up to you," Athela said finally. "You're in charge of the spy organization, what do you think? Should we bring him on?"

Tarr frowned and mused for a second or two. "We'll bring him on. We tell him nothing that could betray any great secrets. We can lose nothing by it; at the very worst, Cira will discover that we have moved back to Two Falls. He knows nothing of where we are staying or any other information about those in our organization. What could we lose?"

"It is decided then," Laith gave an efficient nod.

"Some conditions," Tarr said quickly. "I will keep him on a tight leash. I will not divulge the identities of any of my agents."

"How will he get information out to us?" Archer asked.

"I doubt he'll actually pull this off, much less learn anything useful," Tarr shrugged. "But once we have confirmation that he is in place, I will alert my agents to his presence. The other condition is that he will deal solely through Laith."

"Why?" the prince asked.

"He's more likely to relate to you as an equal or leader rather than me. He defers to you as a fellow noble. " Tarr said flatly.

Marc looked impressed. "Yeah? What am *I* thinking now?"

Tarr laughed. "You're thinking I'm slightly terrifying and wondering whether I'll get what you're thinking right."

"Dead on," Marc nodded.

"*Wow*," Si breathed, awestruck. "Tarr, what am I—"

"Bring Joris back in," Laith interjected, nodding to Archer, who skipped out the side door and exchanged a few words with Joris, who reappeared a few seconds later. Again, in his completely unhurried style, he sauntered up to the mantle, where he took down a decanter, uncorked it, and languorously poured himself another glass. It took so long that it was almost comical.

"Well," he said, once he had settled again in his large armchair, "what did you decide?"

"We'd like to accept your help," Laith replied. Tarr saw Joris's eyes dart over to his own face, then back to Laith.

"I am glad to be able to help," Joris said, matching Laith's formal, courteous tone.

"It will be dangerous," Laith pointed out.

Joris smiled placidly. "So I hope."

"If you are caught, you'll be executed," Athela warned.

"This is not my first time courting danger," Joris returned.

"Will you require any assistance in setting up a meeting with Cira?" Laith asked.

"No, I think I shall, from this point on, operate outside your jurisdiction," Joris suggested. "This will be an enjoyable challenge. I think the farther I distance myself from the Strikers, the better. I have enough information to create a suitable introduction."

"If you don't mind my asking, how did you know about Cira coming back?" Marc asked. Tarr was glad. He'd been wondering himself.

"My parents," Joris smiled. "She wrote them herself to tell them the suggested date of her arrival. I had one of my servants confirm the arrival of her ship early this afternoon."

"Handy, isn't it? To have parents like yours?" Tarr asked shrewdly.

Joris shifted. "On some occasions, yes."

So the parents are a sore spot, Tarr confirmed, feeling slightly more reassured now that he'd found a pressure point.

"And how do you propose I relay information to you?" Joris asked Laith.

"Once you are in place, we will devise a suitable communications system," Laith said without missing a beat *Good old Laith*, Tarr smiled to himself. *No one can spin words better.*

"That is acceptable," Joris said in his curiously formal way. "If you, in turn, wish to reach me, I shall set up a system of communication through my valet. I assure you that we can trust him implicitly. He has been with me nearly since I was born, and his own nursemaid was an Ashan. His sympathies are even more deep-seated than mine."

"Your valet had a nursemaid?" Si asked blankly. "How many servants do you—"

"I'm glad to hear he's loyal," Laith cut in, rising to signal that their meeting was drawing to a close. Joris stood and grasped his hand. Each of the Strikers cycled through and met him in a handshake. When it was Tarr's turn, Joris clasped his hand tightly and stared at him with his pale gray-green eyes.

"Do you speak Ashan?" Tarr asked him.

"I speak a number of languages," Joris replied in Ashan so perfect, Tarr wouldn't have been able to tell his accent from that of one of the other tribes. "I am able to write and read as well."

"Excellent. I wish you luck in your enterprise," Tarr replied, and released the handshake, leaving Joris to once again touch his lips to the backs of the ladies' hands.

"I'll catch up with you in a second," Archer called to them, motioning them back towards the secret door in the hallway where Joris's valet was now standing in attendance, eyeing Archer warily from his post. Archer stepped forward and caught Joris by the elbow, pulling him over to the side.

"Glad you're working with us," he said quietly so that the others couldn't hear. A grin of remembrance flashed. "Just like old times."

"Yes," Joris agreed, his pale green eyes twinkling with genuine affection. It did not go unnoticed by Tarr, who was watching them closely from across the entrance hall.

"Why did you decide to join us now? Now, after so long?" Archer asked.

"Affairs in the country kept me busy," Joris shrugged. "My parents. You know. It was amusing for some time, but then I grew incredibly bored. I have been following your exploits, however. Quite impressive. It seems that many of our fellows were wrong about you, Archer."

Archer shrugged uncomfortably. "Perhaps. Perhaps not."

Joris's smile was deadly. He glanced over at Athela. "She has lovely eyes," he observed, inclining his head towards her. "Do not tell me that you have retired from the chase."

"It's been three years of chase," Archer sighed.

"I've never known you to have such difficulties."

"You're about to experience them yourself," Archer smirked. "She's Cira's sister."

Joris's eyebrows rose. "I did not know that. It will be good to finally have a challenge."

Archer clapped him on the back, then looked at his friend more closely. "Good luck, Joris," he said quietly. "Be careful."

Joris shook his head and smiled. "Don't worry, Archer. I am always careful."

Rane pulled her hood over her head and glanced out from beneath the roof. The rain that had coursed so steadily down for the past two days had finally subsided, leaving thick vats of mud in the many sections of road where the cobbles had been turned up and left in disrepair. The denizens of the city were still reluctant to venture out into the open, even though the weather had cleared to some extent, so for the most part, Rane found herself alone as she began her rounds near their safehouse. Though there were plenty of volunteers ready and willing to patrol in her stead, Rane had quietly insisted on carrying at least one shift herself. This was both because she liked the time to be alone, but also because her eyes were trained to notice things that the average recruit would miss.

She made her first pass up and down the street, taking care to space out her course so that no one would take notice of her. The sky glowered overhead, and she shivered a bit; winter was coming far too fast, and with it would come thick drifts of snow that would blanket the land and effectively slow down the smuggling rings and underground supply trains they were operating.

She was unsure of what to think about the situation with Joris. She had briefly spoken to Tarr about it after their meeting with him, but Tarr had been strangely closed off about the entire thing. Rane didn't press the matter. Tarr, in his own quiet way, was rather protective of his relationship with Archer, and any person from or reminder of his past was viewed with more than a small twinge of jealousy.

She ducked inside a doorway and blew on her fingers to warm them, thinking fondly of the kettle of tea she would put over the fire once her shift was over. She thought of Athela, holed up in her room with the door bolted shut, poring over paper after paper and book after book, hunting for anything relating to Morthenstar's legend that could help them decipher the new documents they had uncovered. She thought, not for the first time, of the countless volumes, the wealth of knowledge that had been lost to them when the Two Falls library had burned. Centuries of stories, wisdom, memories had evaporated into the south wind in a matter of hours. The full impact of that loss hadn't fully been grasped, not even by Tarr and Athela.

She glanced to one side and wondered whether Marc and Si were out on patrol themselves, whether she would see them on their way back to the safehouse.

A cloaked figure exited one of the nearby doorways and jogged across the street, carefully protected against the oncoming inclement weather. Rane chanced a peek up at the sky. She had about fifteen minutes until the rain would start again. Time enough to make another pass or two.

She stepped out onto the cobbled street and walked back down the path, crossing in front of their house. It looked so quiet, so unassuming. She hunched her shoulders up and briefly looked down to the ground as she crossed the stairwell entrance to the building across the street from their safehouse.

Then she noticed something and stopped still, staring at the trace of a mark on the ground. It was almost nothing, yet...she furrowed her brow and glanced over her shoulder to make sure that she was not being watched. She bent and examined the mark.

It was a footprint, squarely imprinted in the mud where a few cobblestones had been turned out of the street, facing directly towards the front door of the safehouse. On the surface, it was nothing special, just one of thousands of such prints that could be found throughout the city. But there was something about its presentation that struck Rane as odd: it had been placed so squarely and clearly at the center of the little patch of mud, as if care and thought had been given to its making. The imprint was deliberate, crisp, almost like it had been stamped into the earth. There were no other similar prints around it, no indication that it had actually been made in the course of someone walking across the street. Rane was suddenly struck by the sensation that she had found someone's calling card, like a bouquet of roses left for her at her front door. Someone wanted her to know: *I was here.*

She backtracked and studied what she had found from a distance, then walked back up to examine the print more closely. Even Rane might have missed it had she not chanced a look down to the ground at that precise moment in time.

Like a dog on the hunt, she cocked her head to one side and narrowed her eyes, looking to the left, where she assumed the prints had originated. They *couldn't* have just dropped there beside the stairwell. She whirled around and ducked down the small side alley, which, as she expected, was rough and partially unpaved. The rain had transformed it into a washed-out tub of muddy glop, and she winced slightly as she took her first step off of the cobblestones into the mess. She offered up a silent prayer that the rain would hold off for a while longer, then stepped into the alley, picking her way carefully along, careful not to disturb any of the tracks she found there, just in case they belonged to the unknown person she was tracking.

And there she discovered what she was looking for: a fresh, clear print. There was a deep heel, the imprint of a riding boot. The footprints were large; they belonged to someone on the taller side. It was impossible to determine the person's gender, but Rane had a gut feeling that they belonged to a man. She took a few steps back, tracing the path of these new prints. A few paces back down the alley, she found something that stopped her cold. She squatted down and gently touched the earth, then rocked back on her heels, trying to piece together the puzzle in her mind.

There were two deep muddy holes, almost six inches deep, close beside one another near the wall. They were footprints, but of a different kind than the others. Rane tilted her head to one side, trying to put herself in the place of the man who had been there. Then she looked up, and felt fear like a stone dropping into the pit of her stomach. The way they were pointing aimed the view of the individual directly towards the Strikers' safehouse.

And then, all at once, the scene fell into place, almost as if she were witnessing it transpiring in front of her. This man had walked up the alley and stood motionless, watching their house throughout the rainstorm that had taken place earlier that afternoon. He hadn't moved even while the alleyway had turned into thick, muddy slop all around his feet. Finally, when the storm had ended, he had pulled his boots out one after the other, creating a deep hole in the earth where each boot had been. He had then walked forward up the alley and stood for another long period of time beside the stairwell, still watching their house, unmoving. Then he had walked away, leaving behind the one careful, intentional print in the mud for her to find. He had left no more than half an hour ago, she calculated, judging from the time the rain had stopped and the start of her patrol. And, with a prickling on the nape of her neck, she realized that there was a high probability that this man could still not be too far away. In a rush, her senses went into overdrive. She began filtering every single noise in the streets to try and gauge whether there was a threat. But everything was almost eerily quiet.

She made a cautious move back to the original "calling card" print and studied it anew. She glanced up. The roof overhang was low. He must have caught it, swung up, and spirited off that way.

He can't have been a member of our patrol, she told herself, mind racing. *Our patrols are always told to keep in motion, to never remain in the same place for too long to avoid being spotted and attracting attention.* Besides, there was a strange malevolence in the threads of the scene she had woven together, something sinister. He had not merely watched the safehouse. He wanted them to know he was watching them.

Rane was not easily frightened, but she found that she could not bear to stay in the cramped, claustrophobic alleyway for one second more. She strode forward out of the area, her hand creeping almost subconsciously to the hilt of the sword she had hidden under her cloak. Off to her right, a horse let out a high-pitched whinny almost like a scream, and Rane nearly jumped a foot in the air.

Steady, she said firmly. *Get a hold of yourself. Take steps to address the problem and overcome it. Double the guards on patrol. Have them be vigilant for anyone matching the description you've come up with. Immediately report to Laith and Athela what you've seen.*

But even with that, setting her jaw in a confident line, she couldn't help but walk a bit faster back to the secret entrance to the safehouse. For she still had the strangest, unsettling feeling that she was being watched.

The riding party blazed across the open land, streaking through the meadows and the small forested glades threading over the plain. Cira set the pace while her two ladies-in-waiting and their ten bodyguards rode slightly behind, understanding full well that Cira wouldn't take kindly to anyone trying to pass her. Her hood flew back from over her pale hair, and she shut her eyes, leaning forward into her horse's mane. Her eyes watered with the sting of the cold wind, and she reveled in its familiar feeling against her face. The sail home had been excruciatingly long and almost unbearably cramped. A good, fast ride across open country felt like a fresh breath of air after weeks underground.

She slowed as they approached one of the smaller glades. She frequently hunted here when the season was in; it was one of her favorite areas to stop and take a rest. Her horse's nostrils heaved as they broke into a walk, the party behind her matching her pace stride for stride. She stroked her horse's neck and twitched her hood back over her head. One of her ladies-in-waiting drew up alongside her. Cira barely acknowledged her. She was the pretty niece of a well-to-do Riddleton family and had been sent to Cira's fortress only a few weeks before as a token of their goodwill.

"Would you like some water, Your Majesty?" she inquired in a soft voice. Cira waved her away. *If I wanted water, I would have asked for it, stupid girl*, she thought irritably. The young lady-in-waiting immediately reined in and fell back to ride behind her, leaving Cira free to choose the path they took.

All at once, a thought occurred to Cira, and she pulled her horse to the left, breaking into a canter, her entourage following close behind. They went deep into a stretch of forest before Cira again broke her horse into a walk. They made their way up a steep, small hill until the sound of softly rushing water could be heard a little ways away, and shortly thereafter the group came upon a small waterfall rushing gently into a large open pool of clear, cold water. Cira stopped and wheeled her horse about to face the others.

"I wish to stop here. Guards, go out of eyesight and stay alert. Ladies, stay with me."

Her group quickly obeyed, dispersing in their various bidden directions. Cira's ladies dismounted and came to help her down from her saddle. Cira was heavily swathed in cloaks and her riding habit, but she eyed the pool of water somewhat breathlessly as she fumbled with the clasp of her outer cloak.

"Help me off with this," she ordered curtly.

The two ladies exchanged bewildered glances. "Your Majesty, what are you going to do?"

"Go for a swim," Cira replied shortly. "Your duty is to get this cloak off and not ask irritating questions."

"Yes, Your Majesty," the girl said, looking abashed, working quickly to undo the clasp of the cloak.

"Won't you catch cold, Your Majesty?" the other inquired, giving an involuntary shiver as the freezing wind whipped through her hair and down the back of her cloak.

"I shall do nothing of the sort," Cira snapped. "But I tell you what I shall do. I shall send you packing back to Riddleton immediately if you dare to question me again."

"I was just expressing my concern for Your Majesty's health," the girl murmured with a deep curtsy. "I meant no disrespect for Your Majesty."

"Stand up, stand up," Cira said impatiently, eyeing the water. When she was younger, she would often go for dips in the lake outside of Joymaril in the dead of winter, partially to scandalize the court, but partially because she liked the feeling, the self-control it took to fight against the overwhelming cold. There was something almost like daring death in submerging oneself beneath water that was only a moment or two from freezing.

The cloak was finally swept off from around her shoulders, and she set about undoing her riding habit (it was one of the most glorious things she owned, gossamer skirts and a buttery leather bodice—quite lovely, but it wasn't as if anyone would notice it, what with the heavy winter cloak covering it all the time). She pulled off her riding gloves and layers of petticoat after petticoat until finally she stood barefoot in the clammy, damp leaves and mossy loam, wearing only her barest underdress. A sharp blade of wind cut through her, but she refused to even shiver. Her ladies stood back and watched her with wide eyes as if she were a strange and dangerous animal. *Let them look*, she thought. She liked the idea of shocking them, thought about them repeating this story in hushed, urgent whispers all throughout Faridor that night and for days after. How Queen Cira walked half-naked into a freezing pool of water. She rather liked the idea of being thought mad.

She pulled her white-blond hair down out of its combs and let it tumble down in a shining sheet around her shoulders. She took a step forward (glancing over her shoulder to see if any of the guards were watching; she rather hoped they were) and touched her toe right into the edge of the icy water. It was so cold that it burned. She reached down with one hand, gathered her skirt up above her pale knee, and placed her whole foot into the water. It bit and stung at her like a live animal, but she gritted her teeth and waded right in without a second's hesitation. The mud below sucked at her feet and she pulled them away, striding forward into the pool until the water was up to her hips. She chanced a look at her ladies-in-waiting, who were clutching at one another in terror, not knowing what they could possibly do. She hid a smile and looked back to the fall, then stifled a scream and nearly fell back.

A man astride a horse was standing and quietly watching her across the water, nearly obscured by the tumbling falls.

Her ladies, startled by Cira's sudden movement, instinctively leaped forward, then let out full-fledged shrieks and turned, rushing out of the clearing to alert the guards. This gave Cira a few seconds to collect herself. She was quite unafraid; if he had wanted to shoot her, he would have done so already. She could kill the guards for being so careless, for standing by and letting such a thing happen. But no matter. She tilted her head to the side, trying to peer around the waterfall to get a better look at him. As she did so, he moved his horse forward, stepping around so that, for the first time, she was able to see his face. Neither of them moved for what seemed like an eternity.

"Your Majesty! Your Majesty!" the younger one of her ladies screamed as the entire troop crashed belatedly over the hill. Cira had only the vaguest notion of disappointment that her dramatic tableau had been destroyed, but she was still transfixed by the creature standing in front of her.

Two guards drew bows and arrows and aimed them at the man, who glanced at them, completely unconcerned. The rest of her body-guards rushed forward to drag him from his horse, who snorted and started. "Stop!" Cira commanded in her most imperious voice, and they fell back, circling the stranger like a pack of wolves.

By this point, the other girls had taken a good look at the stranger's face and were transfixed as well, their mouths positively hanging open. It was a beautiful, feminine, almost angelic face framed by a head of thick dark curls, pale gray-green eyes, and a full, sensuous mouth that was curving ever so slightly into the beginnings of an ironic smile. Cira was all at once aware of the cold, the water still up to her hips, her white underdress, her bare arms and neck. She ever so slowly edged back to the shore, her dress sticking and clinging to her legs as she emerged, leaves and weeds plastered against her feet and ankles, never taking her eyes from the young man on the horse. At once, her ladies walked forward and swathed her in a heavy fur cloak. They made motions to step protectively between her and the intruder, but she shrugged them off and stepped towards him, finally remembering to blink.

"*What*," she said in a low hiss, "may I ask, do you think you're doing?"

"Riding on my property," came the reply in a voice so low and masculine that it was a blind shock to hear against the femininity of his features. "And what, might I ask, do you think *you're* doing?"

The guards automatically lunged forward at him. "Back!" she snapped at them. "*Your* land?" she demanded heatedly. "Have you no idea who you are addressing? This *country* belongs to me."

"I take it you are Queen Cira, then," he said in an easygoing tone, which sent a flame of resentment flickering within her stomach.

"I am. You are welcome to dismount immediately and kneel before me," she ordered silkily.

"My parents have already knelt to you; I think their obeisance carries down to me as well," he shrugged.

"Your parents?" she snapped. "Who are they?"

"I am Count Joris Actaeon," he replied. "My parents are the Count and Countess Actaeon."

Cira had been fully prepared for this brash young man to actually turn out to be a complete nobody, so no one was more surprised than she at this information. His parents now lived in a distant county, but they had one of the oldest mansions in Two Falls, swaths of rich lands south of the Meadows, and paid her a handsome sum every year in deference. "Actaeon," she repeated slowly, catching the hint of satisfaction on his face as he realized she had recognized his name after all. "And tell me, are your parents aware that you're about ten seconds away from talking yourself into execution for insubordination?"

"I was merely stating a fact, my Lady."

"Your *Majesty*," she corrected sharply.

Joris's unreadable smile held for a beat, and then he slowly inclined his head in a bow. "I beg your pardon. Your Majesty."

Cira studied him for a moment, then turned away. "Take him," she ordered, and immediately the guards leaped forward, wrestling the young man from the saddle. She glanced back to watch, enjoying herself more than she had in weeks. She almost hoped that he would put up something of a resistance, but this seemed to be far from his mind, as he was outnumbered eight to one. The guards dragged him over and forced him to kneel before Cira, which he did without outcry or visible complaint, though she could see from his eyes that he dearly wanted to lash out. He seemed to be possessed of a great deal of self-control.

She took a step closer to him, almost daring him to strike at her, but he remained still. She loomed above him, emphasizing the difference in height between them. He was even more beautiful from a foot away, his face almost startlingly feminine. She slowly reached out a finger and stroked it along his cheek—it was perfectly soft. His chest would be smooth as well. She swallowed and stared straight back into his pale gray-green eyes as he watched her unblinkingly. She ran her finger along his jaw and then gently brushed the pad of her thumb over his full lips, parting them ever so slightly. His breath warmed her hand, and she drew back.

"Because of my respect for your parents," she told him, "I shall not execute you for the insolence you have shown me today."

"Thank you, Your Majesty," Joris replied.

"You'll be brought back to the palace with me," she continued, and, seeing the flicker of triumph on his face, smiled and added, "and thrown into the dungeons for three days." Here, she stretched her arms and almost purred. "So that I'll have time to sit back and consider what I want to do with you."

Even though they had just met, Cira knew better than to expect this strange young man to utter a cry of protest or beg to be spared. He merely smiled a small, enigmatic smile and gave a slight inclination of his head. "Whatever you wish, Your Majesty. I am commanded by your will."

"Not yet, perhaps," Cira murmured beneath her breath. "But you will be."

He must have heard her, for that strange sphinxlike smile increased by the slightest bit as she turned on her heel and heard him being pulled to his feet behind her. She would not bother to speak to him, not even to look at him again, until they reached Faridor. She would see him locked up. In a few days they would take him out, and she'd find out if there was any change in his character.

She mounted up and rode back to the fortress without a backwards glance, all the while conscious of a pair of gray-green eyes searing through her.

CHAPTER NINE

"It just doesn't add up," Athela groused, lifting up one of the sheets on her desk and squinting at it. "Any way you look at it. Vertically, diagonally, backwards…"

Tarr stared at her. He had never before heard Athela make a joke pertaining to her decoding duties, and reminded himself to ask Laith whether or not there were any long-term mental effects of sleep deprivation. "Give it here," he said soothingly, holding out his hand. "You *have* been staring at all these documents for about five days straight. A pair of fresh eyes will do you good."

Athela heaved a sigh and collapsed into her chair. "Well, that's just the damned frustrating thing about this, Tarr. I've brought it this far. I went through *that—* " here, she pointed at a stack of documents piled high on one corner of her desk, each paper at a different stage of decomposition, "and now I've got it translated down to these three. All we've got to do is put them together, and that's what's got me stumped."

Tarr smiled sympathetically and looked over the papers before him, spreading them out on the desk. Already, his brain was starting to happily click away, eager to have a new puzzle to work on. As Athela had noted, there were three documents laid before him. One was a small sheet with what looked to be a map of Two Falls drawn upon it. The river split the page down the middle, and major buildings and landmarks were outlined in a stern, definite line. Tarr lifted this up and indicated it. "Two Falls?"

"Yeah," Athela replied wearily, pinching her sinuses with her thumb and forefinger. "One of the documents turned out to be step-by-step instructions on how to draw the map. Incredibly precise. What size paper to use, exactly where and what and how everything should be marked."

Tarr looked down again at what she had drawn. It must have taken Athela ages. "But nothing mentioning the location of Morthenstar's power?"

Athela shrugged. "Everything I read is there. Believe me, I went over and over it again, trying to see if I had missed something. That's all there is."

He turned to the third page. On it were a few lines in Athela's handwriting, having obviously been translated from another text. They read:

The city in his hand
The right palm atop the star
At the point of his destiny the sun sets
On the source of his power

Tarr read it again to himself, brow furrowed. Athela watched him with amusement. "The original poem rhymed," she said helpfully.

"Thanks." Tarr leaned back in his chair and steepled his fingers under his nose. After a few moments, something clicked. "Si?" he suggested hesitantly.

Athela sent him a withering look. "Yes, Tarr, that is the current topic of conversation."

"What if Si's the key to the map?" Tarr said eagerly.

Athela regarded him quizzically for a few moments, then her expression cleared. "It's not fair," she protested. "You only had to look at it for twelve seconds."

"Fresh eyes," Tarr said apologetically. "You did the hard bit."

"'The point of his destiny...' Si doesn't have any points, unless it's like his elbow or something."

"I highly doubt Si's power *or* destiny is located in his elbow, Athela."

"Don't you take that patronizing tone with me, Tarr. I'm thinking aloud."

"His right palm..." Tarr mused. "Where's Si?"

Athela arose. "Living area, I think," she replied. "I'm still not sure what you mean when you say that he's the key."

Tarr shook his head. "Hold on a minute. If I'm right, you're going to love this. Or hate it."

"It's such a fine line," Athela agreed, sighing.

They found Si curled up in an armchair with a book in his lap. Marc and Laith were quietly talking in one corner, and Breaker, Laith's large black dog, was lying at his master's feet. The dog perked up as Athela and Tarr entered.

"Si," Athela began with a businesslike tone.

"It was Breaker," Si said automatically, starting and snapping the book shut. Tarr made a mental note to check on the state of all of the lamps and furniture.

"Si, come here for a second," Athela commanded. Si gave a shrug and hopped out of his chair, striding over to them with swinging arms and trusting raised eyebrows.

"Give me your right hand," Tarr told him, laying the piece of paper down on the floor. Si sent Tarr a strange look, glanced at Marc for assurance, and did as he was told.

"What's going on?" Marc asked.

"Tarr might have figured it out," Athela informed him, looking begrudgingly pleased.

"Just lay your right hand here," Tarr instructed Si, pointing at one of the city squares. Athela leaned forward, frowning.

"That's the town square with the big star statue, isn't it?" she asked.

Tarr nodded, grinning. "'Right palm atop the star.'"

With Si's hand squarely on the image of the town square, he spread out his hand so that each finger lay atop one of the main roads feeding into the square. It was a perfect fit.

"Impressive," Laith commented. "Now what?"

Tarr read back over the verse that Athela had translated. "The point of his destiny has to be his star tattoo. Lay your forearm flat against the map, Si." The boy obeyed, his arm naturally resting atop the line of the

Two Falls river. "The sun sets to the west, so…"

"West is here," Marc indicated with a tap on the paper.

One of the points of Si's star tattoo pointed due west. Tarr sketched an invisible line through the air from the tattoo to a small inked square building on the map. The star's point seemed to be aimed directly at it.

"There," Tarr pointed. "That's where we search."

Silence fell over the group. The hum of excitement and discovery seemed to dim ever so slightly.

"Hang on," Marc frowned. "How on earth would whoever drew that four billion years ago or whatever have known what size hand Si would have?"

Tarr shrugged, slightly deflated. "Magic?" he asked hopefully.

Marc wrinkled his nose in distaste and opened his mouth to reply, but Laith cut him off. "Where is that?" he asked, squinting. "I don't remember a building being there."

"Well, we've got to account for the fact that these documents were put together hundreds of years ago," Athela pointed out. "Probably none of the original buildings remain, except the library, and that's way over here."

"Underground," Tarr suggested. "Whatever we're looking for is probably underground."

"Excellent, shall I order some shovels, then?" Marc asked cheekily.

At that moment, Archer strode past the door, then stopped and did a double-take when he saw his friends huddled in a cluster together. He backpedaled and strode into the room. "Afternoon, all. Been out on patrol. What's all the excitement about?"

"Tarr and I have decoded the information about the location of Si's supposed powers," Athela informed him. "It's apparently here in this building, but we can't figure out exactly where that is."

Archer, who knew the city better than any of them, took the sheet and cocked one eyebrow. "The cobbler shop?"

"Cobbler?" Athela wrinkled her nose.

"Yeah, that's the cobbler shop, run by that dodgy little man…what's his name?"

"I know who you're talking about," Laith agreed. "I've seen him before, been by his place. That's it for sure."

"Wait a minute..." Athela said slowly, swiveling around to Tarr. "A cobbler shop. You mean...the shoe store? Si's shoe store?"

Tarr gaped at her. Si had long insisted that he'd found Morthenstar's sword hidden in a shoe shop in Two Falls, but none of them had believed him.

"I told you!" Si said eagerly, breaking the silence that had fallen on all of them.

"A *shoe store*," Athela growled, rounding on Tarr accusingly.

"*I* didn't make the prophecy, Athela," Tarr pointed out mildly.

"I miss the old days," Athela sighed, collapsing into the chair. "When things were buried in mausoleums or temples and were afforded some shred of dignity."

"So, what's the plan?" Marc asked brightly.

"Yeah!" Si exclaimed. "What do you think my power is going to be? Am I going to have to jump into a well or something, and then when I come out I'll be really strong? Am I going to turn into Laith?"

"I hope not," Laith murmured faintly.

"We'll head out immediately after dark, find a way into the cellar, and go from there," Tarr said. "We find out tonight."

Si nodded, his young face shining.

The wooden door to the cobbler's cellar gave way almost immediately. Unfortunately, it did so with what seemed like an inordinately deafening *crash*. Athela let out a low hiss through her teeth, and immediately the seven Strikers scattered, ducking under cover and behind corners, keeping low to the ground below eye level. Sure enough, two minutes later, a group of Kagaian guards came up to investigate the sound. Tarr kept his breath low and even, crouching behind Archer's shoulder in a dark adjoining alleyway. He felt Rane place her hand on the small of his back and smiled at the touch. From his vantage point, he could overhear the officers' conversation.

"Doesn't seem like anyone's here," one of them observed.

"Who'd want to kick open a cobbler's cellar door?" another wondered.

"Whoever it is is out past curfew," came a third voice, gruff and authoritative. "Come on. They can't have gone far. Public drunkenness, more than likely."

With the clanking of boots and the slight rustling of their cloaks, the officers vanished down the street. As they had been instructed to do beforehand, Tarr and Archer waited a full minute in darkness before creeping back across the road and convening with the others. Off to their left, the river glinted in the moonlight, and the quiet rushing of water filled up the silence of the sleeping city.

"Right, we have to be fast before they double back again," Athela whispered. She motioned to Marc, who stepped forward and gave the door a hearty tug. It swung open without protest. The door was angled on the ground directly beside the wall of the cobbler's shop, and the darkness below gaped at them unwelcomingly.

"Well, then," Athela said, eyeing the cellar and sounding uncertain. "Who wants to be first?"

The Strikers looked around at one another. No one volunteered. "I'll go," Laith said finally, stripping off his cloak and handing it to Marc.

"That's the spirit," Marc said approvingly. "Way to set a good example."

"Should we leave someone here to guard the entrance?" Tarr inquired.

Laith swung around. "Breaker'll stay and watch. He'll be less noticeable than one of us, anyway. Breaker," he ordered, and immediately his black dog appeared out of the gloom. "Lie down. Good boy."

Laith sat at the edge of the opening and tentatively stuck a foot into the inky blackness. "No stairs," he grunted. "Just going to have to jump and hope for the best." He slid his other foot over into the opening of the cellar.

"Is any sort of monster devouring you?" Si asked with interest, peering over the edge.

"Yes, Si," Laith replied drily. He pushed himself forward a bit and gave a hop; Tarr found himself holding his breath. There was silence, then the sound of him hitting the floor.

"All right?" Athela whispered urgently.

"Fine. Bit of a drop. Hand me a light," came the reply. Archer unclipped a tiny lamp from his belt and handed it down to him. In a few seconds, a small beam of light shone out, just enough for the others to see, not enough to attract any notice.

Tarr and Archer went after Laith, both landing springily and easily with their natural Ashan agility. They turned and helped the others down after them. Rane descended light as a feather and gave Tarr a quick smile before turning to take in their new surroundings. The cellar was small and utilitarian, with boxes and supplies and half-finished works neatly tucked away into the corners of the room. A small flight of stairs on the other side of the cellar led presumably up into the shop itself.

"Where now?" Archer wondered.

"Must be another passageway around here. Start looking, but try not to put anything too out of order," Tarr told them. The Strikers spread apart and immediately began to search. The walls were stone; the room in which they were standing must be very old. Tarr wondered what building had stood here in Morthenstar's time.

"Here!" Rane's quiet voice called out, and immediately they all rushed to her side. She indicated a small marking on one of the stones of the wall—a six-pointed star identical to the one on Si's arm.

"Good eyes," Tarr said proudly.

Athela shouldered her way to the front of the pack and began to probe questingly around the corners of the stone with her fingers. She gave a quick push, and the stone withdrew from her touch with the sound of rock grating upon rock. In a few moments, the other stones began to pull back as well, until there was an opening just large enough for someone to stoop through. An inky black passageway yawning open on the other side.

"Give me the lamp, I'll go first this time," Athela ordered, and Marc passed the small lantern to her. She slid the lantern through the opening and stuck her head inside, peering around for a few moments before scooching forward and vanishing. "It's bigger on the other side," she called. "I can stand up. "Looks like no one's been in here for a while."

Makes sense, Tarr thought with a grin. His heart was beginning to pound faster. Until Rane had found the engraving on the wall, there was a chance that they were looking in the wrong place. But now they were almost there. Tarr glanced over to Si, whose small face was pale and uncharacteristically drawn in the dark flickering shadows. Tarr could barely fathom the sorts of things that must be going through his mind.

Marc gave the boy's shoulder a comforting squeeze, and Si seemed to snap out of his trance. "You come after me," Marc told him, and Si nodded anxiously. It was a tighter fit for Marc than it had been for Athela; though they were about the same height, Marc was much broader than she and had to contort himself to squeeze through. Si came after, followed by Laith, then Rane, Archer, and Tarr.

The passageway on the other side was, as Athela had described, considerably old. The air itself smelled of mildew and tasted dank and stale, so much so that it stung Tarr's eyes. Cobwebs choked the walls of the arched hallway, whose roof wasn't tall enough for Laith, Archer, and Tarr to stand up straight. Awkwardly hunched over, Tarr stared about himself, openmouthed. There were carvings on the wall—what looked to be ancient inscriptions in a hieroglyphic text that he had never seen before. They almost appeared to be dancing in the flickering orange light emanating from Athela's lamp. Tarr wished more than anything that he had parchment, a pencil, his translation texts, a cup of tea, and a long afternoon to while away within the passage—imagine being the one to discover an entirely new ancient alphabet! He ran his fingers over some of the words, trying to imagine the people who had carved it all those years ago, knowing that this secret place would be sealed up, possibly undiscovered for the rest of time. And he thought, too, about what might lie ahead of them.

Marc's hand was clapped squarely on Si's shoulder as they inched through the passage; Laith and Archer almost comically stooped over to avoid bumping their heads on the roof. Si's back was resolute—though Tarr could see, even from the back of the line, that the young man's hand was shaking.

"Do you think it's going to be like it was in the cave when we found out I was Morthenstar's heir?" Si asked suddenly. "Like, there'll be a flash of light or something, and then I'll be different?"

"I don't know," Tarr replied honestly. "I've read nothing about what can be contained here, nothing about what exactly your power is supposed to be. All I've read points to where it is."

"You'll be all right," Laith chimed in, his deep voice soothing. "We'll take care of you." He sounded like the essence of calm, but Tarr could see the prince's left hand tensely gripping the hilt of his sword.

"Another door," Athela called out ahead of them. "And Morthen-star's symbol is on the stone."

"Try pushing it," Tarr suggested, knowing Morthenstar's affinity for pushable stone barricades.

"No good," Athela said after a moment. "And I can't see anything else. Looks like a dead end."

"I'll try," Si offered, squeezing past Marc and Athela. He took a deep breath, steeled himself, and pressed his hand against the engraved star. At once, the door split in two and seemed to pull apart, revealing a larger room ahead of them. Rane craned her neck around Archer's arm to try and get a better look. Athela nudged Si to stand behind her again and held out the lamp as she stepped inside.

"What is it?" Archer called out to her.

It was a long time before she replied. "You're not going to believe it." Her voice was stunned. Tarr gave Archer and Rane a forceful push, berating himself for being relegated to the end of the line. They poured into the room, lit only slightly by the light of Athela's lamp.

"So, what is it?" Archer demanded impatiently. "I can't see."

"Wait just a moment," Athela implored him. "We've got to get some more light..."

"There are torches on the walls," Laith told them. "Here, hand me your lamp for a moment; I'll get them lit." He took one of the torches out of the brazier and lit it with the light of the lamp. Tarr came close beside Athela. Her face was alight, ecstatic.

"What?" he asked, completely bewildered.

"Tarr, *look*," she breathed, gesturing as light began to fill the room. The glow moved to a large tablet of stone that was centered in the room, very close to where Tarr and Athela stood. The light wavered and finally spilled over the likeness of a woman carved into the top of the stone tablet, the shadows cutting together and blending into the planes of a face. The woman's eyes were closed, and her hand was crossed over her chest, her visage familiar. Tarr could feel his heart skip a beat and his mouth fall completely open as Laith lit the last torch, sending the entire room into golden illumination.

"So?" Archer demanded. "Where are we?"

"Archer," Tarr swallowed, trying not to suddenly break out into dance, "We're standing inside Alder Morthenstar's tomb."

His words fell like stones into the echoing expanse of the room. The others all stared at him for a long time with nearly identical expressions of shock and disbelief. One by one, their gazes broke away to appraise and absorb their surroundings with fresh eyes.

"Underneath a *shoe store*," Athela muttered disbelievingly.

It was a surprisingly cavernous room for being located so far underground, with high arched ceilings and pillars in the ancient style. The walls were carved as well, and Tarr moved away to get a closer look. Half-statues of men, women, and animals emerged from the walls, eerily lifelike, with blank, expressionless eyes. Tarr imagined that some of the faces belonged to Morthenstar's Strikers; some were gripping weapons, and all of the carvings were captioned underneath in the same strange hieroglyphic text he had seen in the passageway. Tarr felt so exhilarated that he could barely contain himself, so he turned and looked once again at the tomb in the center of the room. Morthenstar's coffin was made from an extremely large block of stone, with a short flight of steps at the bottom of the dais. Morthenstar herself was carved into the top of the rock, so lifelike that it almost seemed as though at any point she might sit up, stretch, and smile around at them. Hieroglyphic texts were written on either side of the coffin, and it was ornately decorated with winding leaves and images of horses. On the side of the coffin closest to Morthenstar's feet was engraved a coat of arms: her own star emblem and three other symbols Tarr didn't recognize.

"Do you know what those are?" he asked Laith, pointing.

The prince stood beside him and squinted at the crest. "Those are crests of some of the houses of the Jelani," he replied. "You see there, the ivy is the symbol of the house of Cade, my family, the egret is the symbol of Joymaril, Athela's side, and the lotus...actually, that's the house of Esson. Rane's a member of that house, on her father's side—though technically, we refer to her as a member of Joymaril because that's her mother's house."

Tarr's head was swimming. "With the design of the room and the care and elaborate decoration I see in the stonework, as well as this Jelani iconography, I think it's safe to say that Daemun built this tomb for her after she died."

"Wouldn't her tomb be more of a big deal?" Marc asked. "Like, wouldn't people want to visit it? Say, from the street level?"

"Not unless the other Strikers were trying to hide something with her," Tarr shook his head. "There are plenty of statues up above where people pay their respects."

"I agree," Athela chimed in, her nose hovering two inches from the side of the tablet. "Look at this text, will you? Tarr, have you ever seen anything like this before?"

"No, never," Tarr said eagerly, crouching down beside Athela to examine the carvings on the side of the coffin. "What do you think it could be? Funeral rites? Some sort of prayer to take her to the underworld?"

"We don't have an underworld in Jelani religion," Laith corrected. "We have only a spiritual world, sort of a next-step destination."

"But it could still stand for—" Athela continued.

"Do you think Morthenstar's still in there?" Archer wondered aloud, standing off to the side with his arms folded thoughtfully. "Like if we look in there, we'll find her skeleton? Or even better, her mummified remains?" He sounded almost hopeful.

The others paused and considered the coffin with fresh perspective. Rane's nose wrinkled. "I suppose so," Tarr agreed, aware that only he and Athela would likely be excited about finding Morthenstar's mummified remains.

"I bet we could sell bits of Morthenstar on the black market," Archer mused enterprisingly. "As long as we could prove it was her. There's tons of loonies out there who would love to have one of her fingernails or whatever."

"Hey!" Si exclaimed. "That's my ancestor you're talking about!"

Archer made a conciliatory gesture. "My apologies, Si. Although, from what I've seen of Morthenstar in our communal visions, I think she'd be perfectly fine in giving up a toe or two in order to help the cause."

"Archer, you are *unbelievable*," Athela rolled her eyes. "You—"

"Look," Marc cut in, his hands on his hips. "We're getting sidetracked. Where's the source of Si's power? Let's find that, and *then* Tarr and Athela can hole themselves up here for the next week, and Archer can dig up Morthenstar and sell her for parts."

"You're right," Athela agreed. "We've got to find the source first."

"Unless it's already happened," Laith suggested, turning to the boy. Si looked a bit vacant; Tarr supposed that he was still thinking about mummified fingernails. "Si, do you feel any stronger? Any change at all?"

Si closed his mouth and appeared to be concentrating very hard. After a few seconds, he shrugged. "Nope," he chirped. "Still the same."

"So it's not the *place*..." Tarr muttered to himself, biting his lip and frowning. "It must still be something hidden in this room. Some sort of key, or hiding spot, or trigger we have to find to activate it."

"Want us to search the room again?" Rane inquired quietly.

"Might as well," Tarr shrugged.

This time, however, their search was fruitless. One of the walls was plainer, with long stones jutting out haphazardly here and there, but there was no star engraved on any of them. None of the figurative statues were conveniently pointing in any particular direction. Tarr even caught Marc hopefully poking away at bits of rock in the hopes that he would trigger something and it would move.

"Nothing," Athela griped as they all drew together in the center of the room. "She's got to stop *hiding* things like this!"

"Si," Laith mused, turning to him. "Let's try this. You're a Morthenstar. You're Alder's heir. You want to hide something very important in a place where no one else would look. Where would you hide it?"

"Hmm," Si frowned deeply, his freckled nose wrinkling slightly. "I would hide it...." Suddenly, the thought came to him. "On the ceiling!" he exclaimed.

"The ceiling?" Athela asked, bewildered.

"Athela," Tarr said with a grin, "He's right."

They all craned their necks upwards. Directly above Alder's coffin was an engraving. It looked to be Morthenstar's symbol enclosed in a circle with writing around it, with an arrow pointing to one corner of the room, right beside the plain wall with the funny stones jutting out here and there.

"Well, they certainly are related," Marc remarked, squinting up at the ceiling above them. "No one else in their right mind would think of that."

"There's another brazier over here!" Laith called to them. "I missed it before; it's sort of hidden back here."

"Light it," Tarr said eagerly, the flood of excitement coursing through him as he felt them narrowing closer to their goal.

A few moments later, the torch was lit. Laith stared expectantly, and Archer cocked his head to one side. "I don't see anything *too* funny, do you?"

"Possibly," Tarr frowned. *This must be it...but what could it be?* He stepped back, trying to take the scene in from a wider perspective. And suddenly...he felt it making a little more sense. He took another step back...it was becoming right... "Put out the other lights!" he exclaimed.

The urgency in his voice was such that the others didn't even bother to stop and ask him why. They rushed quickly around the room, dousing the other flames until the only light remaining in the room was that from the brazier that Laith had just lit.

"I don't see it," Marc admitted.

"Stand back here," Tarr told him, unable to keep the grin from his face. The other Strikers came to stand beside him.

The light from the torch was cast at such an angle and the jutting stones in the wall were arranged in such a way that a pattern was made by the dark shadows thrown by the firelight. Together, they created a circle with four lines inside—four lines all pointing to the same stone, the very center of the circle, and one with no shadows falling on it at all.

"That's the one," Athela breathed. "It's in there. Whatever it is."

None of them dared move. Finally, Si swallowed and took his first tentative step forward. He slowly inched his way towards the wall, as if afraid that it would suddenly explode in front of him. He extended his arm. With a deep breath, he stopped and touched the stone in the middle of the wall. It sank back and up, revealing a dark space beyond. Si visibly steeled himself and reached inside, his eyes squinting shut. Tarr felt his own knuckles aching as he gripped Rane's arm.

Suddenly, Si relaxed. There was the slightest chink of metal upon stone. Something caught the light, gleaming silver as Si withdrew it from the hiding place. The boy held it up to his face, his back still turned to the others as he examined it.

"Well?" demanded Athela, fairly bursting with anticipation. "What is it?"

"Some sort of...necklace," Si replied, turning to them, his eyes still on the metal piece in his hand.

"And?" Marc asked curiously. "Is it glowing or getting warm or anything?"

"Emitting sparks or smoke?" Archer added.

"Nope, nothing," Si shook his head, looking relieved that the wall hadn't exploded on him and anxious at the apparent lack of spontaneous magical emissions. He walked over to the others. "Here, you look at it."

Athela eagerly rushed forward and took it from his hands. "A medallion," she said with audible surprise. "It's some sort of medallion."

Something clicked in the back of Tarr's mind, but he remained silent as the Strikers passed it around the small circle from hand to hand until it came to him. He inspected it closely. It was engraved on both sides with strange markings not unlike the mysterious hieroglyphs decorating the tomb. Morthenstar's symbol was on the center of one side. It hung on a nondescript chain of ordinary-looking metal.

"We've seen this before," he reminded them. "The vision we had when Si was named as the heir. Morthenstar was wearing it around her neck."

"Good memory," Laith said, impressed.

"Yes, of course!" Athela exclaimed, snapping her fingers. However, her excitement faded as the medallion continued to placidly dangle on its chain without any demonstrable sign of magical power. She gave it a few halfhearted shakes and passed it back to Si. "Here, you hold it again. Concentrate. Try to get it to work."

"What am I trying to get it to do?" Si asked dubiously.

"I don't know, *something!*" Athela said impatiently. For Si's sake, Tarr wished that Athela could keep a cool head, but at the same time, he could understand her feelings. They had come this far, had moved all the way down to Two Falls to find this medallion. None of them wanted to admit that they had gone to all these lengths to discover a completely normal item of jewelry with absolutely no remarkable attributes whatsoever. But if it *was* just a regular hunk of metal, why had it been so elaborately hidden?

Si gripped the round medallion in his small hand and closed his eyes, trying to concentrate. For half a moment, Tarr thought that something would happen—the metal would glow or turn some sort of color, and at last, Si's destiny would be fulfilled. But nothing happened. After a minute or so, Si opened one eye and shook his head, sheepishly avoiding Athela's gaze. Tarr's heart ached for him. He knew that Si would feel personally responsible for Athela's disappointment.

"Feel any stronger?" Archer inquired hopefully. "Here, punch Marc."

"Yeah, punch me," Marc agreed.

Si debated, then shrugged and dealt Marc a hefty blow in the arm. "Nope," Marc replied. "Nothing."

"You could have at least pretended," Si muttered, staring at the floor. Laith put his hand on the young man's shoulder.

"Si, none of this is your fault," he said firmly. "Athela is not angry with you, is she? Are you, Athela?"

"Absolutely not," Athela agreed, hands on her hips, cobwebs trailing through her curly black hair. "I'm just a bit frustrated with the damn medallion, that's all."

"As are we all," Laith leaned down, trying to meet Si's eyes.

"Maybe we were wrong all along," Si mumbled. "Maybe you got the wrong person. Maybe I'm not the heir after all. Maybe I'm just some ordinary kid."

You and me both, Tarr thought to himself.

"Look at me," Laith ordered. Si faced him, his expression plainly distraught, lines of worry creasing his brow. Laith took his finger and pointed to the star on his arm. "This mark is not a mistake. Out of all of us, you were the one named as the heir. This is who you're meant to be. You've already done things that no one else your age would be brave enough to do, and you've fought alongside us for the past three years. Just because this," he took the medallion and held it up in front of Si, "isn't the answer we were looking for—or that we don't understand it— does not mean for an instant that we have any doubt in you or the part you're going to play in all this. Do you understand me?"

Si's lip quivered ever so slightly, and his gray eyes met Laith's. Finally, he nodded. "Yes, I understand."

"Good," Laith straightened up and looked around at the others.

"Well, we've got what we came for. I suggest we get out of here and back to the house, where at least the air is a bit less stale."

"Hear, hear," Archer agreed. "Lead on."

Much later, after Si had gone to bed, the rest of the Strikers drew together in the living quarters. Athela, unsurprisingly, was the first to speak.

"Well, that was it. Dead end," she said curtly. "We've got to start looking elsewhere. I should have known better than to believe in any of that outdated hocus-pocus."

"That 'outdated hocus-pocus' has stood us in good stead in the past, Athela," Laith pointed out. "I wouldn't be too quick to dismiss it."

"We don't know for *certain* that it doesn't work," Tarr added, though he was inclined to agree with Athela.

"Look," Athela spread her hands entreatingly. "Last time, and all the times before, we followed her damn clues, looked far and wide, and at the end of it—*boom*—a big flash of light, and we're given what we came for. This time, nothing. Do any of you want to try to explain that?"

There was silence throughout the room. Rane suddenly looked over at the door and stared at it, deep in thought.

Athela spread her hands. "Things were different back then. If Morthenstar did possess particular powers, they could have just been *her* natural attributes, and in order to explain them, people just started saying that it was the medallion that was the magical thing. It could have just become part of the legend, and the medallion could actually be meaningless."

"It's possible," Laith admitted. "So where does that leave us now?"

"We have to stop relying on the thought that Si is suddenly going to be able to save us and win this war outright," Athela said bluntly. "We have to just resign ourselves to think about him as we always have—a boy, nothing extraordinary."

"That's unfair," Marc cut in, bristling angrily. "Si—"

Athela held up a placating hand. "Marc, you know exactly what I mean. Si is a wonderful person, but he's not a gifted fighter and shows no skills as far as tactical maneuvering."

"He's *thirteen*!" Marc exclaimed. "You can hardly expect him to—"

"But I *can*, Marc," Athela interrupted. "I'm not interested in the warrior he could become when he's twenty, the tactician he could develop into in his thirties. The war is happening *now*, and he is a thirteen-year-old boy." She gave a shrug. Even Marc could think of no argument to counter her.

"Fighting isn't everything," Tarr pointed out defensively.

"Si isn't a problem solver like you, Tarr," Athela spun around to face him. "He isn't good at organizing spies or puzzling things out."

"But remember what I said earlier," Laith said quietly. "I wasn't lying when I spoke to Si in the crypt. He *was* marked as Morthenstar's heir. There may yet be a destiny waiting for him of which we are unaware, some part he has yet to play."

"We know nothing about the ancient magic, Laith," Athela maintained. "Those arts died out centuries ago. No one practices them anymore. How are we to know how they work? Maybe back in Morthenstar's time, this war was predicted to happen later than it has, or Si was supposed to be fully grown when he was named the heir. How should we know? All we can know now is what is in front of us. And that is, though he may be heir in name, Si can have no real part to play in this war. It's up to us to see him safely through this. That's the best we can do." She broke off and turned away, wiping her forehead. Tarr could see that she was simply trying to face the situation as practically as possible. She turned back around entreatingly to them. "Please understand...I love Si, but..."

"I know," Laith agreed tiredly. "Marc, are you all right with continuing his training?"

"Of course," Marc said firmly. "I still believe you all are wrong."

"I hope so," Athela shook her head. "But we have to be prepared."

"I have patrol again tonight," Archer stretched and cracked his neck. "See you all tomorrow afternoon."

"What were you looking at?" Tarr asked Rane in a low voice as they all stood and prepared to leave. She shook her head, her eyes still trained on the closed door of the room. Suddenly, in three swift strides, she crossed the floor and threw it open, looking up the stairs just in time to see a small shadow disappear around the corner of the landing above.

"Si," she said quietly. "He was listening at the door."

CHAPTER TEN

It was three days before Marc judged that it was all right for Si to come back out with him on night patrol. By all outward appearances, nothing with the boy had changed: he was cheery and pleasant to all and made his usual silly jokes whenever they were called for. At one point, Archer remarked to Tarr that Si seemed to be taking the entire situation surprisingly well. Only Marc, who knew the boy better than anyone, could sense the differences. Instead of merrily skipping up the stairs three at a time, he took them slowly, running his hand up the creaky wood of the banister. When it was his turn to do the dishes, he no longer hummed quietly beneath his breath. He stood at the sink, silently pumping water into the basin, the rusty squeak filling the empty air.

"Almost ready?" Marc asked quietly, poking his head into Si's room. The boy was lying on his bed, staring at the ceiling with his hands folded pensively across his thin chest. It was a moment before Si snapped out of his reverie and glanced over, the familiar smile springing into place.

"Yes," he replied immediately, swinging up into a sitting position. "I'll just be five minutes."

"Good," Marc smiled. "I'll be downstairs. And don't forget your dagger this time."

"I just wanted to see if I could take them down unarmed," Si boasted with mock bravado. "You know, really put my training to the test. See if those lessons you've been teaching me are really all they're cracked up to be."

"Rest assured, Si, my teaching methods are perfectly sound," Marc rolled his eyes, stepping back into the hall and closing the door.

Once Marc wasn't looking, Si's eyes went down to his hands, the smile falling from his face like rain. He reached under his bed, pulled out his boots, and tugged them on, taking more time than usual to lace them up. For the past few days, he'd had the strangest sensation of floating. He would drift up and down the stairs, in and out of rooms, and when he spoke to the others it was almost as if he were watching himself from a distance. Si didn't completely understand it, nor the odd heaviness he now felt in his chest, around his heart. He had been sad before, certainly, but it had never felt like this.

It was quite a minute or two before Si realized that his boots were on and neatly laced up to his knees. He shook his head to clear it, then, as he was standing, he glanced over to the small bedside table beside his leg. With one finger, he pulled out the drawer and withdrew the medallion from within. The chain dropped with the slightest tinkling of metal, and Si cocked his head. He smiled as he flicked the medallion around, watching it twinkle in the lamplight. *Seems a shame to waste it*, he thought to himself. *Tomorrow, I'll go out and find someone to sell it to on the black market. We can probably get a good sum for it, maybe pay for a few new travel permits. I was just hearing Tarr say the other day that they've changed the permit and don't yet have a new one to copy. Yes, tomorrow I'll go. And if the others ask where the medallion's gone, I'll say that I'll lost it. They'll believe it.*

His mind made up, Si moved to replace the medallion in the drawer, but something stopped him. He looked once more at the trinket. *After tomorrow, I'll just go back to being plain old Si. No more Morthenstar, no matter what they call me. I might as well wear this and see what it feels like. One night, that's all.* He inspected the medallion a bit closer and saw that it was actually made up of two circles of metal pressed against one another. Interested, he gave the top one a twist and was pleased to see the way it rotated.

A tiny chill passed through him and was gone.

He paused and looped the shiny chain over his head, then passed the medallion down his shirt where it bumped against his breastbone, resting cool and silver against his skin. Si took a deep breath, reached for his jacket, and went down to meet Marc.

It was brighter than usual that night, the moon hanging like a dewdrop in the western sky. The constellations glittered overhead, and three times Si walked into the backs of Marc's heels craning his neck up at them. In the home he had lived in as a young boy, one of the older girls told them all the stories of the constellations every night as bedtime stories. Si knew them all by heart.

"Focus," Marc hissed in his best drill sergeant tone, and Si stumbled over his toes a bit before coming to attention. They drew up to a corner and sank down to the ground.

"We've had a tip-off about a possible informant coming to meet with one of the officers tonight. There," Marc nodded to the deep overhang of one of the nearby buildings.

"What are we going to do?" Si asked.

"See who it is, and then you're going to track them back to where they live. We'll get all the information we can on them before Ari and Tarr decide whether to make an arrest or see if we can use them to our advantage."

"Tailing, eh?" Si grinned. "That sounds like fun."

"It'll be dangerous," Marc warned. The moonlight cast a shadow over his scar, throwing it into even greater relief. "I'm not going to follow you this time. You'll be on your own."

Si hid a smile, knowing full well that, in reality, Marc would be shadowing him from twenty paces the entire time. "I'll do my best," he said, trying to sound confident. Marc gave him a small pat on the back.

"You're all right?" he asked, trying to sound casual.

"Fine," Si said firmly. "I'm fine."

Marc fell silent, and they waited. Si was accustomed to this; their nightly outings were only about three percent action, and the rest was silence. If they were in a safe area, occasionally they would talk or joke around or Marc would instruct Si in some sort of fighting maneuver. Once in a while, he would ask Marc about his life at the palace, and every so often he would get a story. Marc didn't like to talk about it much for some reason. Si could never quite figure out why. Sometimes it was hard to believe that Marc was actually a member of the royal family. The idea was silly. Almost as silly as finding himself named the heir of Morthenstar.

Marc gave him a slight nudge, and Si knew that their target had been sighted. They crouched towards the ground like a pair of cats. In a few moments, the door of the nearby house opened and a shadowy figure exited. No lights were put on in the house, no sign to give their appearance away. The figure paused and Marc and Si waited, their eyes trained on him. Si glanced over at his friend, profiled in the moonlight. Marc's flaxen hair was hidden under a dark knit cap, but his ice-blue eyes shone out pale in the darkness. Suddenly, Marc's body tensed, and Si again looked to the door. There was another person now, approaching carefully across the black street.

The exchange between the two was brief. The approaching figure (from what little Si could see) did most of the talking before curt nods were given, and the two parted ways. Marc gave Si a wink and nudged him forward.

Si took a deep breath and edged forward ever so slightly, pausing to see that the way was clear. The figure ahead of him made a slight indication left, so Si feinted, predicting where the man would go. He waited at a corner, and sure enough, a moment later the man passed by. Si let him get a good twenty feet ahead before he darted out into the road—

From out of nowhere, Si felt himself being grabbed roughly from behind, a heavy arm wrapping around his neck. Without being able to think, he let out a terrified yelp as the arm choked the air from his throat. His arms flailed helplessly against his attacker, who was as tall as Laith and as strong as Marc. Si's gray eyes searched helplessly in the gloom as two, then five, then ten, then fifteen figures appeared in the darkness and drew closer. *An ambush!* Si thought in terror. *Did Marc really not follow me this time? Did he really not follow me? Am I alone?* He tried to clear his head, tried to remember what Marc had taught him about fighting, but there was nothing but blinding, blinding panic.

"You got one!" one of the soldiers said, laughing. "Which one?"

"I hope it's Athela," another one sneered. "Here, hold 'er up."

Something quick to the left caught his eye, and in another moment

Marc barreled into the alleyway, whipping the broadsword out of the scabbard on his back. The officers scattered, and amidst the shock of Marc's sudden appearance Si felt the officer's grip on him loosen ever so slightly. He wrenched his head back and bit down hard on the officer's hand. With a cry and a round oath, Si felt himself being dropped to the ground.

"Get him!" one of the nearby officers hissed, but Si dealt the guard a swift kick to the shin and scuttled backwards, finding the shadows. The officer wavered, making a motion to go after Si, but Marc let out a low, animalistic growl and lunged forward, sword out and at the ready. The officer put his hands up to try and defend himself. Si winced slightly in anticipation, but before Marc got to him, three of the other officers had pounced on Marc's back and dragged him away.

Si let out a strangled scream, but Marc's heavy shoulders shrugged the officers off as if they were flies. He whipped around, sword cutting through the air with a whisper before crashing, metal against metal, with the weapons of the other officers. In the darkness, Si could see the orange flecks of sparks bursting from the blades. Marc dealt a heavy blow against an enemy sword, the sheer force sending him reeling back a few feet. Marc rocked back to prepare another strike; he ducked and, with the back of his fist, hit the other guard soundly across the jaw, sending the man toppling like a pile of bricks. Si bit his lip so hard he tasted iron and blood, his hand clenching in a fist.

The guards were more wary now and backed away to regroup, all their swords bristling. They circled Marc like cats around a fallen bird. Marc kept very still and watched them only with the movements of his eyes. Si's mind raced, wondering whether he should run and get one of the others—Laith, Archer, *anyone* who could help. But part of him couldn't leave Marc alone. It would take too long to get back to the safehouse, too long to summon any aid. Si briefly considered yelling for help, hoping that there was a Striker-friendly building nearby, but there was a high likelihood that all that would do would attract other Kagaian guards.

A guard lunged and Marc was ready for her, parrying the blow and dodging another with expert ease. It was a good thing that the street was narrow, as it forced the guards to form ranks so that they could not all attack him at once. Another blow came and was blocked, but a guard darted up behind him and managed to swipe his blade across Marc's leg as Marc turned to him.

"No!" Si heard himself cry, then clapped his hands over his mouth and immediately scrambled to the side in case one of the guards had heard. Marc let out a grunt of pain, his left leg buckling beneath his weight. One hand held up his sword, still at the ready; the other clasped his leg, and Si nearly cried out again as he saw blood seep through Marc's fingers, black in the light of the moon. Marc sank down like a wounded deer, his lips drawn back over his teeth in a grimace. He stumbled against the wall, and the guards edged closer, still wary of his sword. Marc leaned his back against the stones and tried his best to stay upright. The wound in his leg was deep, and his nostrils flared as he tried to steady his breathing.

"Which one is this?" the head guard asked in a gruff voice, peering down at Marc.

"Lord Marcus," a voice rang out from somewhere down the street.

"So that must have been Si Morthenstar I had," the guard grunted, mostly to himself.

"Morthenstar mustn't be far away," another voice chimed in. "I'll wager he's still nearby."

"Lord Marcus," the guard mused, then took a step forward towards Marc. "Very interesting indeed. You, my friend, are no use to us. We'll kill you immediately. We'll find that boy, never fear. We'll bring him to Faridor, and the next time he comes back to Two Falls it will be just his head on a *pike*."

In an instant, Si could see what would happen next. He could see the rage in Marc's eyes build to a breaking point. He saw Marc rear up and hurl himself at the guards, and then in another instant, Si could see the dozens of swords that would go plunging into his friend from every angle. Fear and rage, more potent rage and hatred Si had never felt before, filled his eyes. Before even Marc was on his feet, Si threw himself forward, hoping to do anything to stop them, to put anything between those swords and Marc. His mind was blank; all he felt was a burning sensation sweeping from his stomach all the way up into his throat, felt the anger flow down through his arms to his fingertips.

Marc was just about to lunge at the guards when suddenly Si was between them, his arms outstretched, clawing and reaching like a wildcat.

"*NO!*" Marc bellowed, knowing that in an instant Si would be thrown to the ground and it would all be over.

But that was not what happened.

The first things Marc was conscious of were sounds: an earsplitting *crack* and then screams; long, horrible screams, and for a split second he thought that Si was surely dead. But then he realized that the screams were lower in register; the voice belonged to someone much older than Si. In the confusion of the night and the jumble of bodies crowding the street, Marc could not make sense of what was happening; his ears filled with the horrible, elemental sound of abject pain and fear. All at once a body dropped, and then another, and then another, and he could dimly make out Si's small form moving from side to side like some sort of possessed creature in the fray of the guards, yet there was no weapon in his hand.

Almost as soon as it had begun, the fury stopped. The last guard dropped with the sound of cascading metal and creaking leather and then all was silent, the horrible echoes of the screams still fading off into the distant towers of the city.

Marc's eyes were wide and unblinking with shock. With one hand, he pulled himself up the side of the wall, his left leg useless beneath him. Blood seeped down his trouser leg in an even stream, but Marc barely took any notice. Before him stood Si, looking frail and thin, his head slung low on his neck like a tired animal. His small hands hung limply by his sides and littered at his feet were the bodies of the guards. Marc could see no weapon in either of his hands.

"Si?" he asked, his voice cracking. "Si, what happened?"

At the sound of his voice, Si stirred and looked up as if waking from a dream. "Marc?" he whispered, and then looked down at his feet, at the forms carpeting the cobblestones. Dazed, Si turned, then tried to take a step but found that he couldn't, for the body of a guard was draped over his feet. He turned and looked and looked, then raised his hands and gazed at them for a long while. "Marc...my hands."

"You're hurt," Marc grunted and hobbled forward, dragging his leg behind him. He reached forward and tore a few strips from Si's shirt. The boy had been cut above the elbow; not serious, but Marc needed something to do to give himself time to think. He tightly wound the bandage around Si's arm and tucked the ends in, then repeated the process to his own leg to attempt to stem the flow of blood.

"What happened?" Si asked wonderingly, still staring down at the ground around his feet.

"You don't remember?" Marc asked sharply.

"I remember..." Si said vaguely, "but how..."

"We have to get out of here. That racket we caused, I'll be surprised if half the Kagaian guard doesn't show up in the next five minutes to have us arrested," Marc snapped. The shock of the fight, the fear for his friend's life, the overwhelming confusion of Si's actions had left Marc a bit shell-shocked, but his soldier's brain elbowed through the fray and told him to do one thing: *find safety, ask questions later.* "Come on," he ordered. "I can't walk well on my leg; you'll have to hold me up with your good arm. It'll take a long time, but we'll make it back."

"Are they dead?" Si whispered, the reality beginning to dawn on him.

"Si—"

"*Are they dead?*"

Marc swallowed and met Si's eyes in the dim light of the moon. The boy's face was no longer sleepy or dazed; he was returning to himself, and the horror of the situation dawned brighter in every passing moment. Slowly, Marc knelt and felt for the pulse at the neck of one of the guards and, finding none, reached another. He briskly stood and jerked his head. "Hold me up," he ordered sternly.

"They're dead," Si's voice was hollow with wonderment. "I killed them. How? How did I do it?"

"*Hold me up,*" Marc snapped, and Si moved forward numbly, tripping over the bodies. He slipped beneath Marc's outstretched arm and guided him towards the wall. His face was trancelike. "Look," Marc told him firmly. "You're going to get me home. You need to get me home. I'll have a look at that wound, and I'll give you something to sleep. Then in the morning, we can tell Tarr and Athela what happened, and they'll sort it out for us. This isn't normal, is it?"

Si mutely shook his head in response.

"Exactly. If it's not normal, then there has to be a reason that this happened, and Tarr and Athela will go about finding the answer for us. And that'll be the end of it."

"I killed all those people," Si whispered, his eyes like black holes. "I thought they were going to stab you, and I killed them."

"We don't know that," Marc shook his head, shifting his weight painfully.

"My hands..." Si whispered.

"*Now*," Marc barked, and Si gave a small shudder, lurching forward down the street. They were silent for the rest of the painful, arduous walk home, but all the while, beneath the weight of his arm, Marc could feel Si's shoulders trembling like a leaf in the wind.

In another three hours, Si was safely asleep in his own room. He had been in such a state that Marc had had to put some of Rane's sleeping herbs into a drink and give it to the boy. He then awakened the others and explained what had happened as Rane sewed up the gash on his leg. Her auburn hair was twisted atop her head and out of her eyes, sleeping shirt hanging loosely off her neck and exposing one shoulder.

"Are you sure they were dead?" Athela inquired.

"I know when someone's dead, Athela," Marc replied gruffly. "All of them—and there were at least twelve."

"Si?" Archer asked disbelievingly. "Kill twelve soldiers?"

"And you say he wasn't armed," Laith frowned.

"No, he wasn't."

"He's not strong enough to hurt someone just by hitting them," Athela pointed out.

"Marc," Tarr said, speaking up for the first time. "Was he wearing the medallion?"

Five sets of wide eyes swiveled around in Tarr's direction. His words hung like an echo in the little room. It was a long while before someone else spoke. Marc said hesitantly, "I can't remember...I think I did see something around his neck. I can't be sure."

"Easy enough to check," Tarr suggested.

"You really think that's what it is?" Athela asked in a whisper.

"Well, I can't recall a time *before* we discovered the medallion when Si was suddenly able to kill a dozen soldiers with his bare hands," Tarr remarked evenly.

"So it works, after all!" Archer exclaimed.

"*Works*?" Marc demanded angrily, starting up from his chair.

"Sit still," Rane told him in a low voice. "You'll pull the stitches."

"Works?" Marc demanded again, glaring at Archer. "You weren't with him back there. Whatever happened to him, that wasn't Si."

"All I'm saying," Archer shot back, "is that all this time we've been hoping that something would enable Si to be able to fight up to whatever potential we imagined Morthenstar's heir could fight. And it looks like that's happened."

Archer had been able to cut straight to the truth, much to the visible discomfort of the others. All of them remained silent and still, except for Rane, who reached over and snipped off the end of thread from Marc's wound. She quietly packed away her supplies in her small medical bag and glanced up at Tarr.

"Well, none of us thought it would be like this," Athela muttered. "None of us could have known..."

"We expected *something* to change. And whatever happened, it would have changed Si," Archer pointed out. "He wouldn't have been the same person, however his powers happened to manifest. If he was suddenly able to fight, to lead, to win the war, that's not the person we know and love."

Athela suddenly stood up from her chair and strode angrily to one corner of the room. For a moment, she stood there, her shoulders tense, and then she whirled back around to the others. "Well, then, that settles it. We've got to get rid of that thing."

"I agree," Archer agreed. "I want Si the way he is."

"Shouldn't Si have some say in the matter?" Marc asked tensely. Tarr found himself silently agreeing.

"It's not just Si," Athela maintained, as if she were trying to convince herself that her motivations in getting rid of the medallion extended past personal feelings and into the realm of duty. "It poses a danger to all of us. We have no idea really what it can do or how to control it."

"Agreed," Marc said immediately.

"We must be careful, though," Laith interjected. "An object of this sort of power shouldn't just be disposed of haphazardly. What's to say that this medallion won't have a similar effect on anyone else? We can't afford to have it fall into the hands of anyone on the opposing side."

"We'll keep it close," Tarr agreed. "Laith's right."

"I hate to bring it up," Rane said softly, "But we know so little about this medallion and its power. What's to say that even if we keep the medallion away from Si and see that he doesn't wear it, he will ever be the same again? What if it has triggered something in him, and he will always be this way? Like a key opening a door?"

"I don't like to even think it," Laith shook his head, tiredly rubbing a hand through his short-cut sandy hair.

"And we still don't understand what happened or why," Archer pointed out. "Has anything you've read given any indication of the type of power this medallion is supposed to harness?"

"No, nothing," Athela folded her arms. "I never even knew it was a medallion until we found it in the crypt the other night."

"Maybe I can go back to the tomb and see if I can decipher any of those hieroglyphs," Tarr volunteered, trying not to sound too hopeful.

"We have quite enough trouble going on right now without losing you or Athela down a bloody hole for two weeks," Archer retorted, knowing full well Tarr's true ulterior motives.

"But if it will help Si..." Marc suggested.

"We'll have a look," Athela told him firmly. "But we will control ourselves. Won't we, Tarr?"

"Yes," Tarr agreed.

"What to do about the boy?" Archer asked.

"Marc," Athela rounded on him, "you must keep an extremely close eye on him. Get the medallion away from him, but try not to let him know that anything is seriously wrong."

"Don't you think the twelve corpses might have already tipped him off?" Archer inquired sarcastically.

Laith shot him a look. "Obviously, Si will be very upset for some time to come. But we must all do our part to treat him no differently than usual and to keep him as calm as possible. We don't know if or when something might set him off and whether or not he will be able to control himself."

The group unhappily considered the prospect of treating their friend as they would a barely tamed animal. "He kept saying it was something in his hands," Marc muttered, almost to himself. "Like there was something in his hands that let him kill all those guards."

"You're saying he was able to kill them just by touching them?" Tarr asked.

"I don't know," Marc said, looking strained. "That's what it sounded like. What it seemed like."

"We'll take care of him, Marc, don't worry," Laith said comfortingly, his deep voice soothing. He clapped his friend on the shoulder. "Come on, then. Let's get some sleep."

Tarr waited in the room until almost all of the others had gone. Rane stood across from him, her auburn hair down her back. "Are you coming back to bed?" she asked in a soft voice.

"In a minute," Tarr murmured, giving her a wan smile.

"Do you think he'll be all right?" she asked.

"I don't know," Tarr replied honestly. "I don't know."

"Tarr..." her voice trailed off, as if she were debating whether to speak or to remain silent. "I saw tracks the other day. Someone has been standing by this house. On the street for hours. We're being watched."

Tarr looked at her sharply. "Cira? General Grey?"

"I don't think so. They'd have acted by now."

"Have you found out who it is? What they want?"

She shook her head. "Not yet. But I will. I just wanted you to know. We may want to consider switching safehouses."

She stepped forward, kissed him softly, and went out the door. Tarr slouched down in his chair, sticking his long legs all the way across the floor. Someone was watching their house. And this awful business with Si. It had seemed so easy when they had talked about finding Morthenstar's hiding place, following the clues, confident that what they unearthed would help them win the war and restore peace to the country. It was incredibly unpleasant to admit that when it came down to it, he had no idea exactly what they were dealing with. And what was worse, he was unsure whether Si would ever be the same again.

Night descended across the country again like a soft violet blanket. The lights in the fortress of Faridor glittered out across the ocean like smattered clusters of tiny stars. Cira Kagai paused beside the window at the top of the stairwell and gazed out across the sea. The lighthouse she was planning to build on the clifftop near Faridor would soon be finished and would be a symbolic step towards the completion of her trade negotiations. With the riches of Vireg to back her, the war would soon be over. She could choke the life out of the rebellion without even batting an eye.

It was a quiet evening except for the slight whisper of her slippers against the stone floor. She wound her way down the curving staircase towards her private dining chamber, where, as was her custom, she would eat alone next to a pile of work papers. The guards beside the door of her dining room bowed as she entered, their armor chinking. A chair was moved back for her from the table and she seated herself at one end. Her servants padded around her in silence. She abhorred any sort of distractions during her meals, and her mind was already deep into the trade treaties that had been sent to her that afternoon.

After five minutes or so, a guard entered, bowed, and approached. "Your Majesty," he said softly as he came up beside her and bowed again.

"Do not disturb me," she snapped at him.

"Your Majesty, as you ordered, I have summoned the prisoner up from the dungeons to see you now."

Cira glanced up at him. *Prisoner?* Then she remembered with a delicious rush of anticipation. *Joris Actaeon.* It had been three days since she had met him in the forest. She wondered whether he would be as insolent now after his stint in her dungeons. "Oh, yes," she lowered her paper to the table. "I remember now. Fetch him in."

The guard bowed and withdrew. Cira straightened up, arranging her features into an expression she hoped was aloof and cool. No need to show him any excitement. Perhaps she would pretend to be reading her papers...yes, that was right. Make it look as though she couldn't care less whether he was back in the dungeons or standing right in front of her.

She heard him approach but let an inordinate amount of time pass before she bothered to glance up and look at him. There he stood, flanked by two guards, his wrists shackled together. Three days of imprisonment had caused surprisingly little difference in his appearance. He was slightly dirty, a bit disheveled, but looked far from conquered. His mop of dark hair curled over his forehead, and his pale, sage-green eyes studied her calmly from across the room.

"Joris Actaeon, is it?" she asked.

"Yes," he replied in the strangely deep voice that belied his feminine features.

"Yes, *Your Majesty*," she snapped. He refused to say the words, merely inclined his head of curly brown hair ever so slightly, the amount of deference one would give to a lady-in-waiting, not a Queen. She glared at him, and he stared at her impassively with his light green eyes. Finally, Cira relented. "Unchain him. Give him a place at the table," she said finally. The guards did as they were told, and Joris moved automatically to sit at the other end of the long table opposite her. He rubbed his wrists slightly as plates and food were brought out for him.

"Tell me," he said conversationally. "Is it your habit to keep your guests locked up for three days in your dungeons, or am I just particularly lucky?"

"You are not my guest," Cira shot back. "You were blatantly disrespectful and disobedient. If you like, I could easily have you executed instead."

"If I am not your guest, then why am I now enjoying the pleasure of your company?" he inquired.

"I wanted to have another look at you."

"And?"

"I believe this is the last time I will allow someone so low and dirty to sit at my table," Cira said smoothly. "I'm afraid your appearance has caused me to quite lose my appetite."

"What a shame," Joris replied, looking unfazed. He began to eat, seemingly oblivious to Cira watching his every move. He must have been hungry, having had little to eat for the past three days, but he consumed his food at a polite rate and with impeccable table manners.

A servant approached and poured wine into a goblet, leaving the bottle beside Joris's plate. Joris drank deeply, then looked up to Cira. "You have a good wine cellar."

She sneered. "You would expect any less?"

He merely smiled. "Your glass appears to be empty."

"I suppose so."

Joris filled his goblet and stood, then walked up to stand beside Cira. She could feel the heat from him as he set down the cup beside her plate. She glanced at it, then slid it away, staring challengingly into his face.

"I'll bet you've poisoned it," she murmured, never looking away.

"What, between my seat and yours? Don't be ridiculous."

"Spies have ways of doing these things."

"I'm not a spy."

"I don't trust you."

Her eyes were wide and accusatory as she dared him to make the next move. After a moment, a placid smile flitted across his full lips. "Here, I'll prove to you that it's not poisoned," he murmured. He leaned over, picked up the cup of wine, and drank it deeply. When he returned it to the table, he leaned down so that his face was only a foot or so away from hers. Cira was vaguely conscious of goosebumps on her arms, but swallowed hoarsely and tried to control them. She glanced over into the cup without moving her head, refusing to pull away from him and concede any ground.

"You drank it all," she said accusingly.

The enigmatic expression returned to his lips and he leaned forward, pressing them against hers for only a moment. They were warm and soft and tasted of wine. Before Cira knew what was happening, Joris was sidling nonchalantly back down the table to his chair and seating himself with the same infuriating half-smile playing on his features.

Cira's stomach felt as if it had rolled into one large knot, and she found that her hand was clenched. As her senses returned, she slowly flattened her hand, took a deep breath, and leaned back in her chair. "How dare you take such liberties?" she demanded.

"I apologize if I offended Your Majesty," he replied, not looking sorry at all.

"How dare you think that I would allow someone as dirty as you to touch me?" she hissed.

"Something tells me," he said carefully, "that you wouldn't mind one bit."

Cira stiffened, and her green eyes narrowed into slits. "I've had your family investigated, you know," she said.

"And?" he asked.

She didn't reply. He seemed to know full well that any incriminating evidence against his family was not to be found. They had been one of her most ardent supporters, bestowing monetary gifts every year that she had ruled. His family's support of Kagaian rule ran back hundreds of years. She found it hard to believe that they had been able to exist through the pro-Morthenstar era that had come after.

"Why were you in the forest that day?" she snapped, her impatience momentarily getting the better of her.

"Inspecting my family's lands," he replied. "I had been away."

"Tell me the truth."

"That *is* the truth."

"Why are you *here*, then?"

"*You*," Joris pointed out, "brought me here. Against my will, I might add."

"Do you wish to leave?" she inquired.

Joris studied her for a moment, smiled, and folded his hands. There was something in his expression that said all she needed to know.

She pushed her chair back from the table and stood. Joris mimicked her action automatically out of well-bred courtesy. "I am tired and wish to go to bed," she announced. He inclined his head slightly, and she brushed past him towards the opposite door. Behind it was the short staircase that led directly to her chambers. Without a backwards glance, she swept up the staircase and out of sight, leaving the door open behind her.

Joris stared at it for a moment, then smiled conspiratorially. He crossed back to Cira's place at the table, filled the cup, drank it down in one gulp, then walked across the room and followed Cira through the door. With a rather cheeky backwards glance at her chamber guards, he closed the door firmly behind him.

The next night, a cold winter wind gathered over the sea and blew across the country, breaking across the walls of the Strikers' safehouse.

Whether he felt the wind or not from within his room, Si, wide awake, gave a small shiver and turned over in his bed. Marc was snoring peacefully in an armchair in one corner of the room, his big hands folded over his stomach. Si had always admired Marc's ability to sleep sitting up. He assumed that it was a habit left over from his soldiering days as a boy.

For about half an hour after Si woke up that morning, he was sure that the horrific events of the previous night had simply been a dream. But the minute he caught a look at Archer's and Laith's strained faces over the breakfast table, it all came flooding back to him: every horrible sensation, every sound. But there was a distance from it, too, as if he had watched someone *else* in the fight instead of himself. Marc and Tarr had spoken about it with him later that afternoon, and Tarr explained that he assumed it was something to do with the medallion, and that they would soon figure out what was going on.

"But I need to know exactly what happened," Tarr said. Si shifted uncomfortably in his seat. He liked Tarr very much, but it was different talking to him than it was to Marc. Tarr was almost like a doctor trying to diagnose him.

"I don't remember much, just sort of sounds and feelings," Si shrugged. "It seemed as though every time I touched them, they sort of withered up and fell to the ground."

"What were you feeling?"

"I was angry. I thought they were going to kill Marc."

"You shouldn't have stayed," Marc interjected sternly. "You should have immediately gone to safety. You're too important to risk yourself that way."

"Why am I important?" Si demanded. "You're the better fighter."

"You are more important to *me*," Marc barked, his icy eyes flashing and his voice taking on a tone Si had never heard before. "And I'm your teacher. So you must promise me you'll never do something so foolhardy ever again."

Si bit his lip and looked down at his feet. Tarr tilted his head to one side and met Marc's eyes. "Si, we're going to do whatever we can to help you, I promise," he said comfortingly.

"Have you heard anything about this before?" Si asked hopefully. "In your books?"

"No," Tarr confessed. "But trust me. I will do whatever it takes."

Si thought about Tarr's words as he sat up in his bed late that night. He trusted Tarr implicitly, knew his intelligence, knew that he had solved deeper problems than this. *But it takes time*, he thought to himself. *It always takes a few weeks before he or Athela can find anything. What if it happens again between now and then? What if I hurt Marc?* He looked anxiously over at the shadowy form of his friend in the corner. The situation was still so strange. The words "killed twelve people" had no meaning when they were applied to him. He had never killed anyone.

Their faces. Here, he cringed and almost shrank into himself. He could just make out their faces. Glimpses of eyes and gaping mouths... he clenched his eyes shut and held the heel of his palms up to them until his vision dissolved into a flurry of color. He hadn't dreamed the previous night, and assumed it was due to the heavy sleeping draught that Marc had given him. But now he was afraid to. He was horribly, horribly afraid, and the worst of it was that it wasn't anything external that he could shrink from. It was something inside himself.

Feeling restless, he hopped out of bed, and Marc awoke immediately. "Going to the loo," Si assured him. "Go back to sleep."

Marc nodded, and, in another instant, he had drifted off. Si padded down the stairs to the bathroom, where he pumped some water into his hands and splashed it on his face. There, hunched over the water basin, he felt the stirrings of rebellion deep within his chest.

No, he thought to myself. *I'm not going to be enslaved to this thing. I can be strong enough to conquer it. It belonged to Morthenstar, didn't it? It was put in that tomb for me to find and wear. Well, I'm a Morthenstar, too, and I'm not going to be beaten by some centuries-old hunk of metal. I can wear the medallion, and I can control myself. I won't let anything happen. Now that I know what to expect. That's what happened last time—I just wasn't ready for it. I didn't know what to expect. What happened before was an accident, nothing more.*

The word "accident" sounded hollow even in his mind, but he felt better nonetheless. *I'm going to fight it, and I'm going to win*, he assured himself. *Those twelve people who died last night were trying to kill Marc. Laith would have done the same thing, and would have done it with a sword, too, and no one would have thought anything more of it. The girls in the marketplace would have gossiped about it and would probably have liked him even more for it. This is just something I have to beat, that's all. Like one of Marc's training drills.*

His mind made up, he straightened and marched firmly up the stairs (and wasn't aware until the last few steps that his resolve was translating into some fairly loud stomping). He went more quietly back into his room and tiptoed to his bed. Marc's steady breathing halted only for a moment as he registered Si's return, then he snuffled comfortably, turned a bit, and was back asleep. Si waited until the snoring had resumed its usual cadence, then walked up beside Marc to where his scabbard and pack lay on the floor. His nimble fingers had been trained by years of pickpocketing, and it was only a few instants before his grasp closed around the cool metal of the medallion. In a flash, he was back in his bed, listening warily. Much to his relief, the snoring went on uninterrupted.

Si held out the medallion in front of himself and took a deep breath. He thought for a moment about whether he should say something or pray, but as he had never prayed before and was not entirely sure to which religion Morthenstar belonged, he decided against ad-libbing a prayer for fear of blaspheming. Wincing preemptively, he looped the chain over his head and sat very stiffly on the edge of his bed, waiting for something to happen.

Nothing did.

After two minutes or so, Si became conscious of his own nervous breathing and made a decisive effort to calm down. Nothing was happening the way he thought it would. He wasn't in the grip of any homicidal urges; he had no desire to run over to Marc and skewer him with his own sword. *This isn't so bad*, Si thought to himself. *Not so bad at all.* He moved slowly and lay down on his mattress, staring at the vast emptiness of the ceiling above. He was completely aware of the medallion resting lightly upon his chest, the cool metal against his skin. Five minutes, and he still didn't want to kill anyone. No one at all. *I'm not dangerous after all*, he assured himself. *It must have been a fluke. I must have hit pressure points on all of those guards last night, ones that killed them straight away. I must have absorbed more from*

Marc's teaching than I thought I did. It's all just become instinct, just like he said. And now I can be as great a fighter as he is. Maybe even as great as Laith. Or Archer.

He was starting to feel pleasantly drowsy, and was dimly aware of the feeling of slipping away into sleep. But he still wanted to test the medallion and his own willpower, so he roused his mind to wake back up. *Come on*, he told himself. *Snap out of it.* But the slipping feeling still persisted. He felt as if he were falling, and the edges of his vision began to blur into blackness. But none of it was sleep. This was nothing like falling asleep. He tried again to wake himself, to stir himself out of it. But he was helpless, as if a great tide had rolled in and had taken hold of him and was dragging him under. Si tried to move an arm but found he could not; he tried to claw and fight against the forces overpowering his mind, but was unable to.

"Marc!" he managed to cry out before everything in his field of vision went black.

Am I dead? He wondered to himself. There was the sensation of physically moving his eyes from side to side, but everything was deep in darkness. *I don't feel like I'm dead...but then again, I probably wouldn't know what feeling dead was like.* It was a small comfort to realize that he could still have these conversations with himself. He tried to locate his own heartbeat, but could not. It was as if he were floating, weightless, without any physical body.

And then...things gradually became clearer. Just a small speck in his field of vision grew lighter and lighter until forms began to take shape. Si blissfully clung to that glimpse of light, thinking that perhaps he was seeing images of his room and that if he focused on them hard enough, he would be plucked out of the nightmare and placed back in his bed. *If I make it back*, he thought to himself, *I'll never, ever touch the medallion again. I promise. Please don't let me be dead. Please don't let me be alone.*

The area grew lighter and lighter, and now Si could make out an image. It wasn't his room, but something wonderfully recognizable. It was a cup, just an ordinary cup like the ones they had in the kitchen. And Laith! He could see Laith now, and he almost shouted for joy. He tried to call out, but the prince made no notice of him, and he realized that he had no voice. He was trapped without a body, without a way of communication, just a spirit and a consciousness. Laith was smiling in the almost sad, reserved way that he did nowadays. His hair was cropped short as it was now, and Si could see the white scar over his right ear from when they had nearly been executed in the alleyway back in Two Falls. The cup he'd noticed before was in front of Laith, and as the vision grew clearer, it looked as if he were sitting at the Strikers' dinner table having a meal with the others. It was incredibly realistic, completely unlike a dream. The dreams Si remembered had all been hazy and vague, but here he could make out every hair on Laith's head, watch the prince's characteristic head tilts and mannerisms. It was almost like a play Si had seen before at one of the festivals in Riddleton. And something...something told him that what he was seeing hadn't happened yet, but that it *would* happen. As if he would wake up and walk down the stairs and see Laith at the table, just as he was now. Such a thing seemed natural. *I'm seeing the future*, he realized, and began to feel less terrified and more excited. He hoped that he would see Marc in the vision. If anyone could hear him or see him when he didn't have a body or a voice, he was sure Marc would.

The vision grew hazy, and Si felt a painful sensation behind where his eyes used to be. His focus drew in on the cup, and he watched, stunned, as a hand extended into the picture. He couldn't see who the hand belonged to, but it held a small vial with a stopper in it. The hand undid the vial and poured the contents (what looked like only a few droplets of liquid) into the cup. And then it was almost as if Si were looking *through* the cup into the liquid contents inside, and he could feel the drink swirling around with the droplets and knew that something very, very evil was inside of it.

And then came the painful twinge behind his eyes, and the vision shifted again, growing hazy and then clearer once again. He looked up from the cup to the hand above it and then to the face. It was Marc.

Marc? Si wondered incredulously, his joy at seeing his friend halted at once by his confusion. *Why is Marc putting bad things in that cup?* He could feel anxiety welling up inside of him as Marc picked up the cup and placed it in front of Laith. The prince looked at Marc and smiled, trustingly.

"No!" Si yelled. "Laith, don't drink it!"

But Laith couldn't hear him. He raised the cup to his lips and drank deeply. Si began screaming soundlessly over and over for Laith to stop. But even as he did, Laith's hand dropped the cup, his dark eyes rolling back in his head. In an instant, he was bucking back and forth and a horrible black liquid was seeping from his lips. Si knew beyond a doubt that Laith had drunk poison and was surely going to die. *And it was Marc...it was Marc who gave it to him...*Si cried out over and over again without so much as an echo. The vision became blurry and confused, and he once again felt as though he was falling extremely fast and had no way to stop himself. He flailed, wanting nothing more than for the horrible images all to end.

And then at once it was as if he had fallen from his bed and hit the floor very hard. His nails were digging into his palms...*his palms!* Si shot up and looked around. He was lying on the floor of his room, and he had hands...and a face...and eyes again. The lamp in his room had been lit, and everything was a glowing orange. He blinked a few times and made out Marc's anxious expression hovering an inch from his face. But instead of welcome, Si felt fear. He started back, staring at Marc, who held up his hands placatingly. The vision still felt *real,* not as easily dismissed as a dream would be. This was different. Si had seen the future; he was sure of it. But the future he had seen was so horrible, so terrifying, that he could scarcely conceive of its true meaning.

"You...you killed Laith!" he gasped, his breathing ragged and uneven.

"I what?" Marc asked, bewildered.

"You killed Laith!" Si shouted. "Stay away from me!"

"Si, I would never kill Laith!" Marc said urgently. "Laith is fine. Now, for heaven's sake, calm down and tell me what happened. You were dreaming. You were dreaming, and then you started yelling my name, and you kept yelling it. What happened to you?"

"I will *not* calm down!" Si screamed, tears streaming down his face. "How could you...why would you ever...put poison in his cup? Are you working for Cira? Is that why this is happening to me? Did you want this all along?"

Marc's hands dropped and he stared at Si, his eyes round and disbelieving. Even as Si said the words, he realized how bizarre they sounded, but he couldn't reconcile what he had seen in his vision to what he knew to be true. "Si, please. Please just take a moment and talk to me. I want to help you." His voice was entreating, kind, but it simply made Si cry even harder.

"Go away," he sobbed. "Please go away."

"No," Marc said quietly.

"Go away!" Si cried.

"I won't," Marc replied.

Furious, Si flew across the bed and past Marc out into the hallway. Laith was already running towards Si's room. He had his scabbard in one hand and hadn't even taken the time to throw a shirt on. Si flew past him, practically shoving the astonished prince out of the way. He could hear Marc's footsteps behind him and ran even faster, even harder, flying down the staircase.

"What the hell is going on?" Laith shouted.

"I don't know, stop him," Marc yelled back, but Si shut his eyes and blocked their sounds from his ears. He reached the lower landing and could see Archer's door starting to open, but he charged down the hallway and banged on Tarr's door. A moment later it opened, and he toppled into the room, bending over double, panting in ragged breaths.

When he looked back up, he saw Rane in one corner with her hand on her sword. She wore a simple sleeping shift, her auburn hair down past her shoulders and her face as alert as a hawk's. Tarr was sitting on the bed beside the lamp without a shirt, the tattoo on the nape of his neck burning black in the golden light. His face was groggy, but it sobered as soon as he took his first look at Si.

The boy looked up, barely registering the sounds of the others coming up behind him in the hallway. His voice was quivering and unsteady as he met Tarr's deeply concerned eyes.

"Tarr," he mumbled shakily, "I think that I must be going mad."

CHAPTER ELEVEN

Cira stirred and rolled onto her side. Her head was heavy, and the light outside felt far too bright. She squinted and tried to clamp a hand over her eyes. It was no good. She sat up in bed, twisting her limbs and stretching. It felt very late indeed.

As her eyes adjusted to the light, she realized that across from her in the bed was a mop of dark curls. Instantly, everything came rushing back to her, and she let out a hiss. *He spent the night here*, she thought furiously. *How dare he?* She reached over and pulled out one of the daggers she kept beneath her pillow and lunged towards Joris's sleeping form. She shoved him over on his back and leveled the dagger at the base of his throat as he struggled into consciousness.

"Oh," he grunted as the pale green eyes flickered open. "Hullo."

"What are you still doing here?" Cira snapped.

Joris looked entirely unperturbed. He glanced at Cira, at the blade, then squinted over at the curtained windows. "I do not respond to death threats before ten in the morning," he told her firmly. With that, he pushed her off of him, rolled over, and went back to sleep.

Cira sat there stupidly, not entirely sure of what she should do. Finally, she put away the dagger beneath her pillow and grumpily folded her arms, staring vexedly at the back of his head until her maid came quietly through the door to dress her.

She had already bathed and was swathed in a dressing gown when Joris finally rolled out of bed. One of Cira's maids kept her eyes demurely downcast as she held out a robe for him. Joris barely glanced at her as he took the garment; he was accustomed to dealing with servants.

He hadn't had much of a chance to take in the layout of Cira's rooms the previous night, as other matters had taken precedence. Her chambers were an extremely large circular room with sections curtained off around her bath and her sleeping area. The rest of the apartment was furnished as a spacious living area. On one side was her writing desk, immaculately neat. Everything was richly appointed, as if Cira had taken every opulent or lavish trinket she had ever come across and scattered them carelessly throughout the room. A twisting ivory vase sat in one corner, a beautiful inlaid box perched on her desk; what looked like an enormous sapphire suspended in a small glass case had been tossed almost haphazardly into an open drawer. Joris was ambling casually towards the desk when he heard something behind him and turned. Cira was approaching rapidly, eyeing him warily as if she wasn't sure how to treat him after what had transpired the previous night.

"I attend to business matters in the morning," she told him without any attempt at courteous preamble. "You may remain here for now. One of my counselors may be meeting with me, in which case you will be shown out."

"You take your state meetings here?" Joris asked, surprised. "In your rooms? Not your council chamber?"

Cira eyed him narrowly, and at once, Joris understood. Her private rooms were just that: private. It would be too easy for important information to be overheard in a more public, accessible space. *Clever of you*, Joris thought appreciatively. "Fine," he said. "Is there any breakfast?"

Cira indicated a small table in the lounge area of the room, laden with a plate and a number of small dishes. "You may serve yourself for breakfast," she told him. "I shall go and work now."

Joris gave her an ironic bow, and she swept away without saying another word. He settled in for a comfortable breakfast, looking outwardly lethargic while his eyes scanned every inch of the room. He was determined not to waste a moment.

The instant Cira sat down at her desk, all of her maids quietly whisked out of the door as if on cue, leaving only the guards standing at the chamber entrance. No one was close enough to look over Cira's shoulder, and as Joris casually surveyed her workspace across the top of his toast, he saw that each desk drawer was carefully padlocked. Cira was remarkably cautious about her paperwork being overseen or stolen by any of her household staff, more careful than she was with any of the expensive jewels or trinkets she had strewn around her room. Joris felt an almost unwilling sense of respect welling up in the back of his mind as he watched her work. She was completely absorbed in whatever she was reading and, after a moment, she drew a blank piece of parchment toward herself and began scrawling a reply. He briefly debated sidling up behind her and trying to be affectionate as a way of catching a glimpse of her writing but quickly decided that it would be too much, too soon. Cira would see through him instantly.

There was a light rap on the door, and it opened. Joris swiveled around to gauge the appearance of the newcomer, eager to see the face of the counselor or official who was coming to meet with Cira. To his disappointment, it was just a young woman clad in the robes of one of Cira's household staff. Her step hesitated ever so slightly as she caught sight of Joris, but a moment later she bobbed him a light curtsy and continued inside. Joris was confused. The other maids had exited as soon as Cira sat down at her desk and it was obvious that Cira didn't wish to be disturbed. Yet as he waited, Cira completely ignored the presence of this new maid as she set about her work, tidying around Cira's bedchamber and starting to put the sheets back in order. Joris furrowed his brow ever so slightly. Something funny was going on. It wasn't common (at least in the levels of high society in which he operated) for servants to go about their cleaning in the presence of their employers. Rooms were straightened, fires lit, sheets replaced, all as if by magic. The mark of a good servant, at least in his experience, was invisibility. But, he reasoned, if it was Cira's habit to take her state meetings and conduct her business from within her personal chambers, there wouldn't be a great deal of time for household staff to see to the cleaning. Perhaps Cira didn't mind.

He watched, expecting something to happen, and didn't have long to wait. After about five minutes of silence, he saw Cira glance up from her paperwork, catch sight of what the maid was doing, and slowly curse underneath her breath. She drew a new sheet of paper before her on her desk and quickly jotted down a few words. She stood and walked over to the maid, whose back was turned as she pulled a blanket tight around the foot of the bed. To Joris's surprise, the maid made no acknowledgment as Cira's footsteps approached. She made no sign that she heard Cira at all.

Cira tapped the maid on the shoulder, and the girl whirled around as if startled, then ducked into a deep curtsy, her eyes lowered to the floor and her hands clasped behind her back.

She's deaf, Joris realized.

Cira handed the maid the note she'd written, and the girl quickly read it. She gave a short nod and bobbed another curtsy, then began to pull aside the blanket she had so carefully arranged.

Cira strode back across the room to her desk. Seeing that Joris had watched the exchange with interest, she explained, "I want her to use the heavier linen. It's getting far too cold now for the summer linen." Cira seated herself at her desk and once again busied herself with her papers.

Joris looked back to the maid, this time with keen interest. The girl was of medium height and extremely thin; she obviously hadn't had good nutrition during her childhood. She had a sharp, intelligent face and strong features: dark flashing eyes and deep brown hair that framed a long jaw, giving her the look of a fox. She went about her work with a sort of single-minded intensity, and though Joris was able to observe her closely from his vantage point across the room, not once did he see her eyes stray over to where Cira worked. And except for the first startled glance he had received when the girl had entered the room and seen him standing there, she did not look over at him.

Joris made a great show of selecting a book and arraying himself decoratively atop one of Cira's couches. The maid finished in the bedchamber and moved into the bath; the only sounds she made were the occasional gentle clinks of metal upon metal and a soft splash of water on the floor. Joris could easily see why Cira didn't mind her presence. It was as if the girl wasn't even there at all.

A loud knock sounded and the door opened, admitting an

important-looking elderly man flanked by two guards.

"My Queen," he said in a booming, genial tone, sweeping into a ridiculous bow that, in Joris's expert opinion, would have had him laughed out of most of the elite social gatherings of Two Falls. "I have so looked forward to meeting with you today." Joris narrowed his eyes, analyzing the man's appearance with expert acumen. *Well-to-do, was a member of the old establishment when Cira appointed him to this position. He clearly thought that he was in for it and is well aware that he owes Cira his life, hence the overly ingratiating manner.* Joris inspected his perfect nails. This newcomer was precisely the sort of person he couldn't help but despise.

"I'm interested to see what ideas you have come up with," Cira agreed with a surprising amount of courtesy, even allowing the counselor to brush his lips over the top of her outstretched hand. "First, though..." she glanced pointedly over at Joris, a faint smile playing around her lips, as if to say *I've caught you.* Joris couldn't help but smirk back at her. *Damn*, he thought to himself. *I'd hoped she'd forget I was here.* The guards took a step towards him to show him out.

"I can just go out and read on the balcony," he suggested with a casual shrug of his shoulder, thanking the heavens that the day was a fair one. "Will that please you, Your Majesty?"

Cira considered between them, glancing from her counselor and back to Joris. She inclined her head and motioned towards the light-filled balcony, where the sounds of the sea filled the air. Joris dipped her a perfect bow, glancing over at her counselor as if to say, *and* that's *how to do it.* The counselor glared at him a bit as Joris sauntered out into the sun.

Cira's balcony wrapped its way around almost the entire tower. He chose a bench that put him closest to where the maid was working. The doors had been thrown open to admit the rare fall sunshine, with light white curtains billowing in the soft wind. He couldn't hear anything of what Cira and her counselor were speaking about over the crash of the waves, but he positioned himself so that if he turned his head in one direction, he could see Cira and the counselor; if he turned slightly in the other direction he could keep an eye on the movements of her maid. There was something about that girl that was sending off a chime in the back of his mind. He had good instincts about people and had learned to follow them. The maid was certainly in a unique position within the household. She was granted access to Cira's inner sanctum in sensitive moments because her deafness made it impossible for her to overhear anything of what was said.

He wondered also who the counselor was. Through his contacts and his movements in the upper echelons of society, Joris knew most of the Kagaian officials in Two Falls and Riddleton. If only Tarr had given him access to the spies in Faridor, he would have some sort of way to cross-check the names and faces he came across. But Tarr was merely being cautious, the same way Joris would be if their positions had been reversed. Joris had a lot of respect for what he had heard and read of Tarr and his methods. Besides, there would always be ways of finding out names and positions. He just had to make sure that it was Cira who volunteered the information, never he who asked for it.

Joris stretched his legs out idly before him and wondered how long the meeting would run. He could gain no more intelligence on the content of Cira's conversation and was eager to see something of Faridor besides the dungeons, the dining hall, and Cira's chambers.

He couldn't help but grin to himself. That had been an efficiently executed mission, if nothing else. He had been worried at first when Cira had had him incarcerated, but there was nothing for her to find out as far as his family was concerned, and he had been relatively sure that that was as deep as she would look. The days in the dungeons had been uncomfortable, but he had been subjected to less hospitable accommodations in his time. From there, it had been a fairly straight shot to Cira's bed, which had been altogether enjoyable.

He glanced over the top of his book. He was half-reading it, intently enough to be able to recount the plot and characters should Cira ask him about it later, but lightly enough that the slightest bit of movement within her chambers would snap up his attention. The curtain billowed in and out of the doorframe, obscuring his vision from time to time, but generally he had a good view of the interior where the maid worked. She had come out of the bath and was now in the living area. He saw her moving quietly through the room, tidying and dusting where she saw fit. Her silhouette moved against the curtain, and then Joris became aware of her figure growing still. He leaned forward and peered with more intensity through the door frame, cursing the curtain that was now obscuring his view. Finally, a large gust of wind blew along the balcony, and the curtain swept up.

The maid was standing almost motionless at a large table resting against one side of the room. A mirror was mounted above the table, and though her back was to him, Joris had a perfectly clear view of her face in the mirror. Though her hands were moving automatically along the objects resting on the table, and her polish rag never stopped circling, there was something in her expression that made him look closer. Her face was tilted down, and her eyes were looking into the mirror with an almost unblinking stare. She wasn't looking at herself; she was staring into something off in one corner of the mirror.

Interested, Joris glanced over the top of his book in the opposite direction, where he could just barely see Cira at her desk. Cira was pouring wax on a piece of parchment and pressing her seal into it; it was clearly some sort of official document. She handed it to the counselor, who folded it and slipped it safely into the inside pocket of his coat. Joris swiveled his eyes back over to the maid, who had stopped watching through the mirror and was once again tidying Cira's things as if nothing unusual had happened.

Cira stood with an air of finality and moved out of Joris's line of sight towards the front door. Intrigued by what he'd just witnessed, he decided to gamble a bit and stood, walking back to the balcony entrance where he could once again see the entirety of the room.

What followed next happened so fast that if Joris had not been watching carefully, he would have completely missed it. The maid had (intentionally, in Joris's mind) happened to be walking with a large basket of linens past the door to the apartment as Cira and the counselor approached. The maid deferentially stepped to the side, lowering into a curtsy, her hand on the door handle. The counselor bowed to Cira, then turned to leave. As he did, the maid stepped forward, basket clutched in one arm, under the pretense of politely opening the door for him. As he went past, she bumped him ever so slightly with her basket, and Joris barely glimpsed her other hand lightly darting into his coat pocket and withdrawing the letter, her action shielded behind her hamper. A moment later, Cira was already halfway back to her desk, the counselor was out the door, and the maid was calmly fetching fresh towels from a nearby closet, the letter nowhere in sight. It was so neat and so deftly done that Joris almost laughed aloud at the sheer audacity.

Then, almost as if the maid felt Joris's eyes resting upon her, she looked up. Their eyes locked together. Softly, so that only she could see, he silently gave her a round of applause. The blood drained from her face, but rather than fear, he saw resolve in her expression. Her long jaw lifted ever so slightly in an attitude of defiance. *She'd fight her way out of here if she had to*, Joris thought to himself. He respected that. Quickly, he raised a hand in a placating gesture to tell her that it was all right. He placed his hand against his chest and gave her a short nod. *I'm on your side*, he thought, hoping she would understand. A moment later, she gave a curt jerk of her head and went back to her tasks. She did not look back up at him again.

Well, well, Joris mused, chuckling inwardly. *Looks as though I've found one of Tarr's spies. And a crafty one, at that.*

He ambled back out to the balcony and continued to pretend to read his book. A short while later, Cira appeared at the balcony entrance, now fully dressed in a pale silver gown, her white hair blowing up in the wind. Joris had to admit to himself that she was really quite beautiful, with her wide-set catlike eyes. She watched him for a moment.

"All done," she announced finally, and Joris stretched and stood. He took care not to touch her. *Keep her guessing*, he thought. "How is your book?" she asked.

"Quite good, actually," he admitted.

"I like it, too," she agreed. "Sorry that took so long. Counselor Jacks always likes to speak a lot more than necessary. Uses three adjectives for every noun."

Joris held aside the curtain and followed her inside. *Counselor Jacks*, he thought with satisfaction. "Was it productive, at least?"

"Finally got those damned trade..." Cira glanced at him and decided against continuing on. "Yes," she said. "It was, rather."

"I rather fancy a ride," Joris mused airily.

"Perfect," Cira assented. "Go and change. There are clothes for you downstairs. I will meet you down at the stables in an hour."

She showed him to the door and shut it behind him. Joris was not terribly surprised that there was a guard waiting on the other side, seemingly to escort him to change his clothes. She was taking no chances and was clearly choosing the distantly cool approach to him, which was just as well, as this was his own chosen mode of operation. Two people playing this sort of game was always more interesting than one. He found himself whistling as he sauntered down the twisting staircase. This was going to be much more fun than he thought.

"These are fresh," Laith grunted, mostly to himself, as he leaned down and examined the footprint Rane indicated. She nodded mutely and glanced up at Archer, who was surveying the street behind them with his sharp yellow eyes. The day was cold and gray, and there were fewer people out than usual.

"Whoever it is, he's been keeping this post for weeks," Rane informed him in a low voice. "I wanted to see if I could get a cohesive trail, but there's been nothing until today. Usually just a single impression in some churned-up bit of mud."

"He wants us to see them," Laith murmured, his brow furrowing. "Why would he want us to see them?"

"I thought the same thing," Rane assented.

"Guards behind us," Archer hissed in a low voice, and immediately Laith and Rane turned away and separated. There was the clink of armor and the stomp of heavy feet, and a patrol of green Kagaian guards swept past the alleyway. They gave the troop a few seconds and then turned back to examine the print once again.

"There have been no signs of him coming in or leaving until today," Rane muttered. "Just calling cards left here and there for me to find. I wanted to bring you over to have a look with me, to see if you have an idea of how he could be doing it."

Laith squinted up at the building above. "Over the roofs, perhaps?"

"Possible," Archer agreed. "It'd be a tricky climb for anyone who wasn't Ashan."

"The roof was the only way I could see, too," Rane agreed.

"Why would an Ashan want to post himself across from the house, often in broad daylight?" Laith wondered. "Danger, threat of discovery. Seems a foolish thing to do."

"Laith, whoever it is has been standing in one place in a tiny alleyway undetected for hours at a time," Archer said laconically. "I'm not sure rationality is going to be a big factor here."

Laith grunted under his breath and glanced down at Rane.

"These marks have been here for weeks?"

Rane nodded. "I first saw them about three weeks ago. I've been monitoring them daily, and decided to report today when I saw a change in his pattern. Whoever it is hasn't come close to the house or made any advances or threats."

"A spy, perhaps," Archer suggested. "We should switch safehouses."

"Not much he'd be able to see from across the street, and if it were just to get our location, it seems as though he would have reported it, and we would have seen some action on General Grey's part," Laith countered.

"Which begs the question, how did he find our location to begin with?" Archer added. "Only Ari's top officers know the precise location, and the bodyguards have all been with us since the beginning. I can't see any of them turning to Cira's side, not when most of them have lost families to her."

The three friends stood in contemplative silence for a few moments, weighing all the possibilities the strange footprints portended. Finally, Archer gave an impatient shrug. "We should follow them, I think."

"Be on your guard," Laith warned. He didn't like the fact that he had to travel without a sword during the day; the better he could pass unnoticed by Kagaian guards. And there was something about this business—the prospect of a silent, seemingly unmotivated, ghostly watcher—that chilled him to the heart.

The three moved smoothly out of the alleyway and immediately separated out to cover the street, Rane on the far left, Archer in the middle, and Laith on the far right curb, moving with the unspoken coordination of a flock of swallows. Rane, who was fluent in sign language, had taught all the Strikers a few basic words and was able to direct Laith and Archer with covert signs, almost impossible for outsiders to detect. They went down one main street and into another, stalling for a moment as Rane struggled here and there to stay on the trail amid the maze of muddy prints that stained the cobbles. Finally, she gave a final sign, and the three drew into a small doorway that was safely out of the view of any guards who would pass by.

"Where did he go?" Laith asked in a low voice.

"In the alley opposite," Rane nodded to a shadowy passage that, even in the daylight, looked dark and foreboding. It was so dark, in fact, that it was impossible to make out the end of the street. The path was covered, narrow, and cramped; it was certainly not the ideal location for a fight if a fight was to be had. Laith didn't like it.

"Do you know what it is?" Laith asked Archer.

"A dead end, for one," Archer said grimly. "A long, narrow dead end."

"Ambush, if you ask me," Laith said immediately. "Archer, check the roofs again, make sure there's no one up there waiting for us."

Archer gave a short nod and, in a few blinks of an eye, had scrambled up the wall to the roof. A minute or so later, he landed back beside them, featherlight on his feet. He shook his head. "I surveyed the roofs; there's no one hiding. Could see behind the chimneys and everything—if he's setting up an ambush from above, he'd have to be invisible."

Laith rolled his shoulders and looked at Rane. "What do you think?"

Rane thought. Caution dictated that they should turn around, regroup, and try to formulate a plan to get a more advantageous position. But Rane was irritated by the cryptic, teasing trail left by their mysterious prey. She was impatient to unmask them, to put the threat to rest. She glanced up at her two friends.

"They won't be in any better position to fight than we are," she pointed out. "And there's three of us."

"There aren't any windows lining the alley where they could shoot at us," Laith mused.

"I have to say, I am really loving the truly reckless turn this mission is taking," Archer grinned.

Laith squared his shoulders. "Right, then, everyone stick together. Archer, you're a mid-guard. Rane, bring up the rear."

The other two nodded mutely and readied themselves. Laith peered around the side of the alcove at the dark, narrow alley opposite. It was lucky that the streets were largely empty. They would have had a hell of a time accomplishing anything with troops of guards passing by every two minutes.

Laith went first, striding across the street and placing his back against the opposite wall. The entrance of the alley was just beside him. Rane and Archer slid up next to him. Laith slipped his hand beneath his cloak and closed his fingers around his knife. He waited for the other two to do the same, then caught both their eyes and nodded. Nothing for it.

He took a deep breath and darted around the corner and back, throwing the dagger long and hard into the wood of the house, blocking up the other end of the alley. They waited, ears straining for any sound, a cry from someone concealed in the shadows. None came. No daggers were flung back at him, no arrows shot. Laith met Archer's eye and nodded again. He felt Archer's hand press against his back, the signal that the Ashan was ready. Laith tapped the wall twice, and the three of them whirled around the corner and into the alley.

Archer's golden eyes adjusted to the darkness faster than Rane's and Laith's, and before Laith was even sure what was happening, Archer's knife was up and speeding through the air beside him. Suddenly, Laith saw a form, something human, leaning against the far wall. Archer's knife landed a hair's breadth from the side of the person's head, and whoever it was didn't flinch. It was unnatural. Laith blinked again and saw that it was a woman, and she was propped up against the wall, her head hanging limply down on her neck, long rose-gold hair spilling over her shoulders.

The three Strikers glanced at one another and ran forward in unison. Archer's white hand stole out from his black cloak and felt beneath the girl's neck. "Dead," he said curtly. "But still warm."

Rane made a hissing sound through her teeth and whirled, scanning the alleyway with sharp intensity and latent frustration. *He's still near...* There was no way up; the walls were sheer and slick with rain, and there was no sign of any disturbance on the shingles or the tiles of the surrounding roofs. Finally, her eyes traveled down to the back of the house at the end of the alley. There was a small window, ever so slightly ajar. Without a word, she took off with lightning speed, throwing up the window and disappearing into the gloom of the house. Archer and

Laith watched her go a little breathlessly.

"If he's to be found, she'll get him," Archer said certainly. "Here, help me, she's propped up on a peg or something."

The two easily picked the girl up and laid her on the ground. She was barely over twenty by the looks of it. Laith's throat caught. There was something familiar about her. "Poor thing," he said, pushing some of her hair to the side. "What a senseless, evil thing to do."

"We'll catch him," Archer said again, almost as if he were speaking to the girl. His eyes glowed intently from beneath his black hood. "We'll catch him. Laith, what do—"

But Laith was frowning down at the girl. There was something... something strange glittering from beneath a fold in her dress. He reached down and unpinned it. It was a jewel, a pendant in the shape of a lily. It was gilded with all manner of precious stones, winking and glinting, completely out of place in the dank street.

"Pretty bauble," Archer remarked. "Odd for a girl like that to have that sort of jewel on her. She seems like more of a shopgirl or whatever from the way she dresses. Do you—" But again, Archer stopped short, for he caught a glimpse of his friend's face and saw that all of Laith's color had drained away, leaving his skin a clammy, bloodless white. "Laith!" he yelped and rushed forward as Laith rocked to the side. He steadied Laith's shoulder and looked in astonishment at the prince's ghastly expression. "What is it? What happened?"

"This..." Laith began. "This..."

Archer glanced over his shoulder as if hoping for Rane to reappear. Turning back, his golden eyes focused on the wall where the girl had been hung. There was a tiny piece of parchment nailed to the wall, folded with a neat crease. Archer ripped it off impatiently and read it. In a deliberate, slanting script, he read:

For Laith

He furrowed his brow. Laith looked up at him with unseeing eyes. "Archer," the prince finally managed slowly, "this was my wife's pendant."

Archer gaped at him. "*Holy* hell!" he exclaimed, leaping to his feet as if stung. He looked again at the note in his hand, then back to Laith's palm, which was limply clutching the jeweled lily. He paced back and forth a stride or two, wishing that there was something concrete to do. He wished fervently that Rane would come marching back around the corner at that instant with the culprit firmly in tow.

"Can you be sure?" he asked Laith finally.

"I had it made for our first anniversary," Laith replied, his voice low. "There's not another like it. I'd know it anywhere."

"*Holy* hell," Archer said again, this time through gritted teeth. Since there was nothing to do and no one to hit, he figured it was time for some intelligent thought. "All right, you have to think. Who could possibly hate you this much? It's obvious whoever it is is targeting you specifically. I don't see this as being related to Cira." He turned away and resumed his pacing. "Just what we bloody well need at a time like this: a killer with some personal vendetta against *you.*"

"I don't know," Laith said simply. "Other than anyone in the Kagaian army, I can't think of any enemies. Not like this. Nothing this... personal. None that are out and walking around freely, at least. And I can't see why any one of Cira's soldiers should hate me so specifically."

"Family member you killed, perhaps," Archer suggested.

"Perhaps," Laith agreed slowly, though his thoughtful tone implied that such a thing sounded unlikely. The immediate shock was beginning to wear off, and his hand gripped the pendant more tightly.

"Why this girl, though?" Archer gesticulated at the young woman's prone form. "It doesn't make any sense."

"Something tells me rational thought is not going to be a factor here," said Laith, ironically echoing Archer's earlier observation. "But there is a reason."

"What reason could that possibly be?" Archer demanded.

"She looks like my wife," Laith said quietly. "My wife is about her height and age and has wavy hair like hers. Faces are completely different, though. I thought she looked familiar at first, and I realized that that's why."

Archer's hands dropped, and he felt deflated. "Oh, mate, I'm so sorry."

Laith shook his head. "Don't pity *me.* This girl is not Ilaina. This girl died completely senselessly. But she does tell us a few things about whoever it was that did this." He rose to his feet, and Archer felt relieved to see that he was recovering from the shock. "Ilaina is all right," Laith said with force, as though he were single-handedly propping up a crumbling wall. "She's out there, somewhere. I'd know. I'd know if she was gone."

"I believe you," Archer said quickly. "But who do you think did *this*?"

Laith held up his fingers and ticked them off. "One, whoever it is must have come from Joymaril. No one else would know what my wife looked like or have been able to lay hands on the pendant. Two, all of this—this setup, the footprints outside our house, the elaborate trail, the girl, the pendant, the note— tells us that this person is highly theatrical. If he comes after us, it will be with some grand dramatic gesture. Three, that kind of drama means that he wants attention. He wants to be found, wants to be confronted. That's the way we'll get him in the end. He'll be so eager to get caught that he'll get careless. Four, as you probably have already guessed, we are dealing with an extremely sick, deranged individual." A cloud passed over Laith's face as if a thought had occurred to him, but after a moment, he shook his head and it dissipated.

"Here's a novel idea. How about we change safehouses?" Archer suggested again doggedly.

Laith considered it. "We probably should. But it will take time. Something tells me he'd find us again right away. That kind of large-scale move will make us vulnerable to Kagai's spies, will draw attention."

"What if he reports us to Cira?"

"He hasn't yet." Laith sighed. "For whatever reason. It's a gamble."

Archer agreed grimly. "It is. And we're stretched thin. We have the exchange for those stolen travel papers that I've been organizing tomorrow night, and Tarr is focusing on the upcoming raid. We won't be able to start working on a safehouse move until after the exchange, at least."

Laith shook his head. "This person is good enough to have come and gone without even *Rane* being able to see how he did it. More patrols here or there aren't going to make a whit of difference. Any extra guards we put out are just being sent into danger. Odds are he'll kill some of them just to create some sort of macabre tableau for me to stumble across."

"Point taken," Archer conceded. "So you can't remember *anyone* back at the palace who could do this?"

Laith considered, expression darkening once again. "Perhaps...it would be nearly impossible, though. He's been locked away. Unless..."

Archer stared at him expectantly, eyebrows raised. Laith looked down at the sad form of the girl and ruefully shook his head. "It's hard to imagine anyone capable of such a thing." He tucked the jewel beneath his cloak.

Rane appeared behind them, and Archer wheeled around, clearly hoping for someone to punch. He looked disappointed, yet somewhat unsurprised, to find that she was alone. Rane shook her head grimly, almost unable to bring herself to say the words. "I lost him."

She stopped and stared down at the girl, her eyes widening for a moment. She caught herself and shook her head. "For a moment, I thought..." she began, almost to herself.

"That it was Ilaina," Laith agreed. "I know."

Rane glanced between the two of them, at the grim set to their mouths. Archer motioned to Laith. "You fill her in on what's going on," he said. "I'll see that the girl is looked after."

And with that, they parted. Archer waited until they were gone, then pulled his hood up farther over his face as it slowly began to rain.

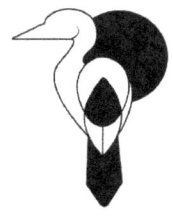

CHAPTER TWELVE

The young captain shifted uncomfortably in her high-backed chair and stole another furtive glance at the silent figure of General Grey, sitting perfectly erect and unblinking a few feet away. The captain's back was beginning to cramp, and she flexed her shoulders a few times to no avail. She had only recently been promoted; her predecessor had been picked off during his afternoon lunch by one of the Strikers' hired assassins. *Served him right,* the captain thought to herself, not for the first time. *In these dark times no one has the luxury of eating scones by an open window in broad daylight.* It was a rather gloomy way to climb the ranks—but then again, sometimes that's simply the way things had to go. She had fully readied herself to enter this new realm of responsibility with a clear head and a positive attitude (not to mention the good sense to eat her meals in some dark, secluded corner), but nothing she had previously experienced could have prepared her for this: the first dragging minutes of the fourth hour of one of the longest conferences of her life.

She squinted up at the paper at the front of the room but still could make neither heads nor tails of it, so she sighed and folded her arms. If the other officers gathered in the room were feeling as restless as she, they were doing a better job of hiding it (even if one of the lieutenants was looking a little *too* intently at the paper.) The captain could tell by the intensely furrowed brow of her colleague that in all likelihood, the lieutenant was still slightly drunk from his previous night off, not having counted on the mandatory attendance required of such a gathering.

Damn Strikers anyway. It was just like them to cook up a plan like this and drag every self-respecting officer in Two Falls out of their beds at three in the morning. Somehow, some (likely Ashan) thieves had laid their hands on five sets of travel papers, signed and sealed by Queen Cira herself, and were in talks to sell the papers to the Strikers. It was a devastating blow. Such papers, and the individuals holding them, were beyond questioning, even if they had an Ashan sixth finger on display for all to see. With the papers in their hands, the Strikers could churn out all manner of almost unidentifiable forgeries before new official papers could be designed and distributed. How the papers had been lost had been something of a shaky story, but the captain had noticed a few new heads adorning the main gate, and it was not difficult to assume that the new décor and the hiccup in security were somehow related. In any case, their Kagaian spies had been working overtime to unearth any information that could lead to the recovery of the documents, to no avail...until that morning.

Which, unfortunately, still left the captain cold, tired, and with a knot between her shoulders. General Grey's council chambers were large, drafty, and echoed magnificently, magnifying the sound of any cough or a squeaking chair. Though the rooms were large, Grey kept them spartan. Apparently, General Grey had served in some sort of foreign army that frowned on wall hangings and tasteful floral arrangements. The captain fought down the urge to scratch at her nose and shifted her weight, causing a painful wooden squeak to reverberate around the lofty chamber. She felt a few sidelong glances and tried to arrange her features into a stern, contemplative expression. It didn't seem as though a break was imminent, so she tried hard to think.

It certainly didn't appear to her as though their spies had turned up anything particularly useful. Apparently, the Strikers were being remarkably careful, and much of the puzzle had yet to be decoded. She read once more down the list of words, copied in heavy, blocky handwriting on the paper before her:

MOON ~ SNAKE ~ LILY ~ BULL ~ ASPEN

Below it were written the names of five pubs in the old arts district of Two Falls:

THE OUTSIDER PUB AND EATERY
SEVEN HORSEMEN BAR
THE LOVELY LASS
STOUT BAR
TWO SISTERS BREWERY

From what the other officers had presented earlier in the meeting, these pubs had each been given a code name, and only one of them would be the exchange site for the travel papers that night. The spies had no indication of which name went with which location—or which location, for that matter, would be the dropoff site. This, the spies assured them, was the same information that had been given out from the top Striker command to their operatives, with the difference being that the Strikers would likely know the code and the dropoff site, whereas all the Kagaian troops had to go on were the baffling list of names.

It all seemed fairly hopeless to the young captain. They could crack the code all they wanted and figure out which name went where, but they would still be no closer to figuring out the dropoff site. And forces were stretched thin, far too thin, to post a substantial guard at each pub and wait for something to happen; the Strikers were good enough fighters that without a substantial troop to counter them, they'd be able to just claw their way out of any small confrontation with the papers intact. No, the only way to beat them was to head them off by *force*, the sheer brute force of an entire column's surprise ambush, and that possibility was sliding further into the distance with each passing moment. The captain concluded this thought mere moments before she realized that she had to go to the bathroom.

She was just working out how best to phrase her request when, for the first time in an hour and a half, General Grey stirred and spoke. "Do we know which of the Strikers will be heading up this operation?" he asked in his low, quiet voice. Some of the soldiers started visibly at the sudden sound, and the captain was smugly pleased with the supercilious looks she was able to shoot them. Two commanders, the ones who had presented the report in the first place, glanced at each other, and one cleared her throat. "We believe that Lord Argolaith is heading up the operation, with support from Ari, Archer, and Lord Marcus on the security end, Tarr on the tactical side."

"Very well," General Grey said in a conversational tone. The captain could feel the room beginning to slide back into its customary torpor after the momentary excitement of human speech. But Grey wasn't done. His ramrod back straightened the slightest bit more; he slid his boots beneath his chair and announced, "The exchange will be held at The Lovely Lass, code-named Lily. Prepare your teams; I want everyone ready." There was finality in his tone, but when he stood, no one followed suit.

The bewildered expressions on the faces around him were so comical that the captain nearly forgot her own astonishment in her struggle to fight down a laugh. "How...how did you reach that conclusion, sir?" one lieutenant asked meekly.

Grey halted and looked around at the expectant faces. They seemed to all be waiting for some flourish, a grand reveal of a hidden magic trick. But there was none.

Grey nearly smiled to himself. The answer had been obvious to him. He had found out everything—*everything*—he possibly could about each of the Strikers. When they captured a Striker agent, they were interrogated for hours and hours, seemingly trivial information: inside jokes, nicknames, best friends, birthdates, lovers past and present. He had ordered scrolls sent to him with the Jelani Strikers' family histories. So, the solution was obvious: Lily was the sigil given to Laith's deceased wife, Ilaina, upon the occasion of her marriage into the royal family. Laith would be leading the campaign. It would stand to reason that the operation would be structured in honor of his late wife.

He shook his head. It was too easy; this, ironically, was what had tripped him up at first. He had been certain that the code name assignments would be more complex, so he had had to systematically think through and exclude any other possibilities. He was almost disappointed. This operation didn't have Tarr's distinct stamp, his meticulousness. Tarr should have acted alone; this was the work of an amateur. Grey sighed. Tarr should have kept a closer watch. He should have been more careful.

General Grey let the silence hang a moment longer. "Assemble your teams," he ordered at last, with no further explanation to his officers. "Report back here in four hours. The Strikers will not get away with this tonight."

Tarr stood in the corner with his thin arms folded as Laith, Archer, Marc, and Ari had a last-minute conference to go over the final details of the handoff. The curtains, drawn heavily over the windows, were somewhat unnecessary, as it was pitch black outside. They kept their voices low, and the business was concluded at last with a series of brisk handshakes and a few "Good lucks" in Ashan. A single paper rested on the small table in the center of the room, and as Marc and Ari turned to leave in a rustle of cloaks and the sound of leather strapped to leather, Laith carefully held the paper over the open flame of the lantern until it was burned completely to ash.

Archer stopped beside Tarr, sensing something amiss. His golden eyes searched his brother's face, and he raised his eyebrows in the form of an unspoken question.

"Nothing," Tarr told him in Ashan, shaking his head. It was unlike him not to be completely honest with Archer, but he could not put to words exactly what was making him uneasy. "Nerves, that is all. Keep yourself safe. Get us those travel papers. Think of all the Ashans we can get out of the city."

Tarr could tell that Archer was not completely convinced, but he let it go. He clasped Tarr's head in his hand and, in another moment, was gone, off to assemble the rooftop team that would provide outside security for the handoff. As the door quietly clicked shut, Tarr and Laith found themselves alone.

"Laith," Tarr said on sudden impulse, "we shouldn't go tonight. We must call it off. We sent the codes to the captains too early."

"Do you think someone gave up the codes?" Laith asked, alarmed.

Tarr shifted. It had been something of a risk, but Laith had needed his captains to scout the five bars to assess any security risks. "No, I don't think so. And even if the Kagaian troops did manage to get a hold of them, the odds of their being able to decipher them are slim. I just..." he trailed off, frustrated at his inability to express his thoughts.

"Only you, Ari, Archer, Marc, and I know the final location of the dropoff," Laith reminded him. "Their teams won't know for sure till they get there. It's about as secure as we can get."

"I know," Tarr said unhappily. "I have a feeling. I don't trust this. Something is wrong."

Laith's mind was visibly racing. "I can't contact our source to change the location. And she might be less inclined to give us the papers if we stand her up." He stopped. "Tarr, think of it. Absolute authority from Cira herself, and who knows how many forgeries we'll be able to produce and send out before the troops get wind of it."

Even Tarr had to smile. It had been an extraordinary stroke of luck, one that was much needed in the dark, unhappy weeks that had recently transpired. Si was withdrawn and had fallen into bouts of silent brooding; Marc was torn between his active duty and his worry for Si. Athela had had to relocate to assist in a high-profile raid, and the only times Tarr had been able to see Rane were a few fleeting hours when she slipped into his bed after her night shift and before daybreak, and then she was too tired to do anything but cling to him in her dreamless sleep. Tarr glanced up at Laith's face, drawn and unsmiling as it had been for so long. They were tired, all of them, tired to the bone. Winter was coming with a dank chill that seemed to permeate every rafter and brick of the house; food was becoming more and more scarce now that the bounty of the summer was running out, and Tarr woke up feeling every morning as if there would never come an end to this dreadful war.

"Just be prepared for anything, especially an ambush," Tarr told Laith finally, wishing he had something more comforting to say. "I just don't trust General Grey to roll over." *I should have been the one to set the code for the dropoff,* he thought. *I should have done it, not you. I've just been so busy with this business of getting the new maid set up in Faridor and the raids that Athela is running...*

Laith rubbed a hand over his head and down the back of his neck. "I'll be on the street. Archer's running security," Laith reminded him.

"Archer can outfox just about anyone."

True, Tarr thought, and it did give him some measure of comfort. Not to mention the fact that Ari and Marc, the closest equivalents they had to brick walls, would be present in the club, with Ari overseeing the handoff himself. He managed a smile and clasped Laith's shoulder, which the prince returned with a flicker of his old self. "I'll take care of it," he assured Tarr. "See you back here in an hour."

And after Laith had closed the door, Tarr set about tidying the contents of their office, too anxious to be able to sit. He had no proof that the code names had been leaked, much less deciphered, and though it had to be done, he wished that they had never been written down or given out at all. He knew Grey had spies in his operation, just as Tarr did, and though he liked to think that he was usually two steps ahead, he had no way of knowing for sure.

He didn't like it. He didn't trust it. He should have planned this on his own.

Finally, he made a few desultory adjustments to a sheaf of parchment, then sat. He wished he had something to do other than wait.

The Lovely Lass was a quiet, unassuming place on the south side of the old arts district. Its owner barely managed to scrape by after the fees and monthly bribes were paid out, but the doors kept opening and there was an intermittent trickle of patrons coming in and out. That night, for one reason or another (and much to the landlord's surprise), the place was uncharacteristically full.

Marc's soldiers had been filing in regularly for the last four hours, dressed in their most unassuming street clothes and not visibly armed. They were stationed at strategically selected tables around the single circular dining area. Ari himself was heavily cloaked and had been nursing a beer at a table for the past hour. As a rule, he didn't touch alcohol, so to keep up the illusion, every now and again he would lean to one side, and a few tablespoons of ale would splash onto the wood beside the heel of his boot. The place was sparsely furnished; wooden tables and patched-together chairs filled the area and spoke volumes of the difficult times. The only real effort in the way of decoration was the place's namesake: a portrait of a lovely, plump girl with shining golden ringlets seated in an almost nauseatingly bucolic meadow beside fat, torpid-looking sheep. She rested above the bar with an expression of simpering benevolence, and Ari eyed her distastefully as he swirled the beverage around in the tankard beneath his nose. The barman was clearly not used to dealing with such a high volume of customers and was rushing to and fro with a harried air. He knocked into Ari's elbow as he passed and huffed out a cursory "Sorry" as he went. Ari breathed out of his nose. A higher-strung individual would have gone reaching for his knife, but Ari was too patient and too calm for such nonsense. It would all be over soon.

The handoff was set for midnight. Ari had the purse at his waist and kept his eyes peeled, not acknowledging when Marc and one of his soldiers entered and sat at a table beside the bar that lay directly in Ari's eyeline. *Good.* This meant that the Strikers were all in place and that everything was as ready as it would ever be. The minutes ticked by slowly, and he flicked a piece of dirt off the corner of the table.

A small, nervous-looking woman entered, pushed back her hood, and immediately made a beeline towards Ari. His mouth tightened in annoyance. He had explicitly told her to take her time in choosing a seat. Some people could never keep their heads. Something caught his eye—a face. Someone he recognized? Gone now.

The woman who quickly dropped to sit across from him was middle-aged, with a dark, feline visage. Ari wondered how she had come across such important documents. She positively radiated nervous energy. He wished he could somehow reach out and calm her.

"Money," she demanded hoarsely.

At least this won't be a drawn-out transaction, he thought wryly. Wordlessly, he placed the purse in her hand beneath the table. Something moved in the corner of his eye. It was the face again. He knew it at once. A Kagaian guard who usually worked at the main gate, young and stupid and too eager. Gave the ambush away. *The ambush!* Movement everywhere—

"Strikers!" Ari bellowed and turned over the table with a heavy crash, dragging the stunned woman down with him, the room erupting furiously around him. An arrow thudded into the wood of the table inches from his head, and the woman let out a scream. Ari couldn't see nearly as well as he wanted to. One of his big hands shoved the woman's head down out of harm's way, and the other felt beneath his robes for the knives hidden in his vest. They hadn't been able to smuggle swords in—stupid and clumsy.

A body crashed into the table beside them, and Ari forcibly shoved it out of the way, darting out with his knife and pausing only slightly to make out the identity of his quarry. Their time was running out, and it was easier to carry papers than it would be to drag this woman with him. He whipped around to her. "Give me the papers!" he bellowed. She shrank back, terrified, but her quicksilver hands were darting around to the spilled coins on the floor. Ari was seized with fury, the sight of the hard-earned rations and supplies for his troops being gobbled up by this greedy creature.

Someone grabbed him from behind, and Ari twisted backwards, trying to protect his throat from the blade. He shoved an elbow haphazardly into his attacker's gut and was satisfied with the grunt of pain as it connected. He whipped around and knocked the man to the ground, then glanced about, trying to gauge his surroundings. It was utter pandemonium, and he could see with only a cursory glance that they were sorely outnumbered and would certainly not last long. They had to retreat, but no one was going to make it out of there alive without at least a bit more firepower. *Damn you, Archer,* he thought, not for the first time. *Where the hell are you?*

As if in response, Archer himself came crashing through the pub's door and onto the floor, already locked in combat with two doggedly persistent attackers. He was struggling mightily, one Kagaian guard's hands around his long throat, white skin of his face cut and drenched in startlingly scarlet blood. Ari could see that Archer's troops were similarly occupied outside the door—Ari's heart sank at the sheer *number* of Kagaians. He spun around to the woman still cowering behind him and caught sight of the leather strap of a rucksack across her chest. He darted forward with his knife and sliced the strap in half, pulling her bag to him before she had time to protest. He must get the bag out of the bar if there was to be any hope for them at all.

He crouched low as the next onslaught came rushing and breaking over him like a wave. He caught their force with his shoulder and toppled two of them over, his knife out and slashing haphazardly through the air. "Get your Strikers out of here, Marc!" he bellowed, but the din was so overwhelming that even he could barely hear his own voice. "Get out!" he cried again and turned around to where Archer was finally managing to kick the dead weight of his opponent off of him. The Ashan's face was an almost unrecognizable bloody mess; Ari was almost sure that his nose was broken. Archer twisted around, blinking the blood from his eyes. "Out!" Ari waved at him, and Archer coughed, nodding, bent almost double from the pain.

Ari took a step and almost slipped—there were so many bodies, not so many fighters anymore. The door was blocked, there were too many troops standing between him and Archer, and Archer almost certainly could not make it over to him. He twisted, dodging a blow from a large woman with a brandished sword, kicking her leg out from under her as she recovered from her strike. Marc was faring the best of all of them in a corner with a small knot of fighters that he had somehow managed to assemble into some sort of battle formation. A soldier to the last. He looked over just as Ari waved to catch his eye and gave a nod of understanding. *Retreat.*

Ari could wait no longer. The closest exit was a window, and after swiping once or twice more, he tucked his head and shoulder and crashed through the glass, his bulk shattering the panes. A cry went up behind him, and he scrambled as fast as he could to his feet, trying to recover from the shock of his landing and the scraping of the shattered glass in his hair, blood trickling down the side of his head. But he was up, up on his feet, and the bag was beneath his arms. Shadowy forms flocked around him like crows, but he dodged and flailed his knife, and somehow they backed away, and he was running, hoping that some of his fighters had been able to follow.

It was a long while before Ari realized that he was just running without direction and that if he was going to make it home alive, he would have to slow his pace and appear to act normal. He forced himself to walk, his hands clutching at the bag beneath his arm. He became aware that he had been going in the completely opposite direction of the hideout and slowly adjusted his direction. It would become more and more dangerous the longer he was out; the bulletin would be posted for Kagaian patrols to be on the lookout for Striker stragglers trying to find safety after the fracas.

His legs felt like rubber, and he lost almost all sense of time or direction. The minutes stretched interminably. Finally, he found himself in the alley beside the safehouse. He gave the knock and collapsed to his knees, unable to stand any longer. The door opened a crack, no light behind it.

"Oh, no," came a hollow voice. *Tarr*. Ari slumped over, and all was darkness.

He awoke in the largest room of the safehouse, now converted into a sick bay. He became conscious so suddenly that he jerked upright with a snap, going straight for his knife. "Quiet," a soothing voice told him. "You're all right."

He was most certainly not all right, but he lay back obediently and looked around. The other Strikers were there: Tarr, Rane, Si bending over Marc, whose arm was tied in a sling around his neck. Tarr was next to a tightly blanketed bloody mess that Ari could only assume was Archer. He wondered whether the Ashan had been killed, but no—he could see the bloody pale hand was clasped, strong and alive, around Tarr's. Tarr was speaking in a low voice and was even managing to smile somehow. Ari couldn't understand it, but then again, he couldn't understand a lot about those two. He had a great deal of respect for Tarr, but the same could certainly not be said for Archer.

Archer's right eye was swollen completely shut, but his other was a sliver of gold that was lucid and alert. It gave Tarr hope. "We'll get you cleaned up soon," Tarr told him in a low voice, "though this current appearance is something to behold." A squeeze from Archer's hand. "Glad you agree." Rane moved beside them and gently pushed Tarr's arm out of the way, sponging herbal medicine across Archer's face.

The door quietly opened, and all fell silent as Laith entered, his presence heavy. His face was cut, though not nearly as bad as Archer's, and had already been bandaged up. "When you are able, I wish to meet with my officers in the chambers," he announced with formal stiffness, and withdrew to the other room.

Rane nodded to Tarr, who stood and went to follow Laith. Ari, completely ignoring the protestations of the young man tending to his wounds, struggled to his feet and hobbled after Tarr, feeling as though he still had glass lodged here and there. Archer's second-in-command followed, with Si and Marc trailing behind. The door closed behind them, and Tarr looked around at all of them, his expression grave.

"What happened?" he asked hollowly.

"Ambush," Marc said flatly. "They knew we'd be there."

Laith's eyes flicked over to Tarr, who remained silent. "My team was intercepted on the street before we could get into the pub to help Ari and Archer," Laith told him.

"The papers," Ari croaked. "We have the papers, don't we?"

Slowly, reluctantly, Laith turned around and picked up the knapsack Ari had recovered. Ari swallowed, and Laith turned to show him a huge slash across the side of the sack, splitting it almost in two. Ari felt his legs almost give way. It must have happened during one of the scuffles as he fought his way out of the bar. There was no way any of the contents could have remained in the bag after that, certainly not after his leap out of the window or all the running he had done. After all of that, after all of the fighting and death, the papers were probably being trampled into mud on the streets of Two Falls. Ari forced himself to stand up straight, unblinking.

"How many did we lose?" Marc asked hoarsely.

"The numbers are still coming in," Laith told him. "We lost a great many."

"Were..." Archer's second-in-command ventured, "Were we able to retrieve any? Any of our wounded?"

Laith grimly shook his head, and they all had a moment of silence to ponder the fate of their friends. They knew what it meant. Those injured or still alive would be taken back to headquarters or thrown in Faridor for interrogation or torture. The bodies of their fallen comrades would be taken, their heads would be cut off and mounted on pikes above the Two Falls gate. The Strikers would be forced to look at them whenever they passed.

"They gave their life for this cause," Laith reminded them, his deep voice somehow comforting even amidst their despair. It was one of Laith's great strengths, imparting courage to others when they desperately needed it. "They knew the risk going in, and they went because they were brave and because they believed in what we do, believed in it enough to die for it. What Kagai chooses to do with them after death is her own evil, and she will pay for it in the end, mark my words. We must remember them as they lived, and why they died, and what they died for. Now," he sighed and motioned them all to sit, which they did. "I want to hear everyone's full report."

Tarr went out to take a walk just as the dawn began to break over the rooftops. It was normally not allowed, but he had assured Laith and Marc that he would be safe, and indeed, he was dimly aware of the presence of two bodyguards as they trailed behind him in the shadows. Archer's blood was starting to dry and crumble off of Tarr's hands as he climbed up to the top of a nearby building and settled down flat on his back to watch the clouds roll back towards the distant mountains.

There was no other way about it: he had been bested. He never should have let anyone else plan the exchange; Laith's involvement had left too many openings, too many gaps that could be filled in by their enemies. He should have just done it himself. He was the only one he could truly trust. They had gambled their friends' lives and only some of them had survived. It was his own fault.

It was a small miracle that Archer had made it out of there alive. A lesser individual would certainly have fallen under the injuries Archer had withstood that night, but his stubbornness extended to the physical level as well: he had a tenacious heart that simply refused to stop beating, and Tarr had never been as relieved as when Archer's hand had reached up to grip his with it sinewy, wiry strength. Tarr wondered, not for the first time, what it was that caused one being to harbor love for another so completely and unconditionally.

He had to end this war. He had to do it soon.

He needed someone new in Faridor. Joris, according to his spies, had been admitted to Cira's inner sanctum in what seemed like a shockingly short amount of time—even faster than it had taken for Tarr to send a message alerting his spies there to the young count's presence. Tarr almost felt grudgingly impressed with Joris's progress, despite his doubts as to his ultimate usefulness as an agent. If they were going to bring Cira down, they would need a two-pronged attack. He had his best agent there, Cicada, but eminently capable though she was, she alone wouldn't be enough to turn the wheel on the war. She needed more support. He had to shift his focus from solely resting on Two Falls.

He knew who needed to go, but once again simply couldn't bring himself to do it.

The thought of sending Rane into Faridor, the thought of waiting day after day as she stalked the halls of that dreadful, cold fortress—not to mention the fact that even with her training and guile, there was still the possibility that she would be recognized by someone from Joymaril—the thought of the horrific, unspeakable things that would be done to her if she were found to be a Striker...it was impossible. Cira had grown more and more ruthless and cruel during her reign, especially towards her defeated opponents. It no longer sufficed to kill; now, she had to maim and defile as an example to all who opposed her. The thought of any of the things he had seen done to other captured spies being visited upon Rane was simply too much for him to consider. And what if she made a mistake? What if she was caught in the wrong room at the wrong time? What if she let herself fall into a trap?

He couldn't do it. He would have to choose someone else. People made mistakes, and if someone were to make a mistake in Faridor, it wouldn't be the woman he loved.

The familiar cold hand closed about his chest as he contemplated this, his next move. He thought of the risks. Thought of the very high probability of failure and the death of an innocent life. And, as he had done so many times before, he steeled himself and made his decision. The sky opened up, impartial and cold, above his head.

"Leonore," he said a day later, forcing himself to look at the youthful, eager face watching him, her hands folded neatly in her lap and her eyebrows raised in rapt attention. "I need you to go to Faridor. Are you ready?"

"Yes," she replied breathlessly. Something in the solemnity and silence of Tarr's demeanor caught her in the midst of her excitement, and she took a pause. She had wanted so long to work for Tarr; had been dogging his steps like a puppy for months. "Yes," she said again and punctuated it with a firm, decisive nod.

"Good," Tarr continued. "I have many spies in Faridor, but you will be known to only one or two of them at the most. I'm hoping that because of your young age, you won't be as likely to fall under suspicion. I don't want you to take unnecessary risks just to impress me. Your bravery is evidenced in your sheer willingness to participate in this mission."

She nodded again, and Tarr was relieved to see that she was looking a bit more serious. "You'll be sent back to our mountain camp for a month of intensive training before you're transferred to Faridor. I'm going to have you placed as a maid. We have many such positions already filled, but you are to take on one single mission." He waited for her nod, and when it came, he continued, "Cira has been cementing ties with foreign powers, either for protection or trade or both. I want to know exactly what sort of deals have been finalized. I want to know details of money, supplies, troops, and whatever else you can find. Do you understand?"

Leonore nodded again, and Tarr could almost see the wheels visibly turning in her head. He waited for about a minute, waiting for the news and thoughts to settle, then smiled gently and asked whether she had any questions.

"Will I have to kill anyone?" she asked.

"I hope not," Tarr replied honestly. "I can't be sure. But know that you'll be trained to protect yourself if any such situation arises. You're a soldier now, like the rest of us. You're just going about it a slightly different way."

"Like you."

He smiled softly. "Like me. And I'll be listening for news of you, and if at any point we feel that your situation is becoming compromised, I will make every effort to withdraw you." He had said this many times before because he knew it was a comfort to new spies going behind enemy lines. It was reassuring in a precarious, completely unstable situation to think that there was someone out in the distance looking after their welfare. Tarr knew all too well, however, that he usually found out far too late to do anything to help his agents and could only sit back and strike the file from his record. If he was lucky, he notified the relatives if there were any left.

Leonore managed a shaky smile. It was a lot for someone so young to process, and she had a rough couple of weeks ahead of her. "What I want you to do now is not speak of this to anyone, not any of your friends, but I want you to take three days and do exactly what you want to do. At the end of the three days, you'll be taken to the mountains for your training. Now, if you have any reservations about the mission you're about to undertake, please speak up now, and we'll forget the whole thing."

Leonore barely hesitated and nodded her head. "I'm ready."

Tarr smiled and extended his hand. She grasped it, and he let it hang there for a moment before they parted. He turned and quietly left the room, shutting the door behind him. An elderly woman, whom he recognized as one of Laith's aides, was waiting for him in the hallway.

"Give her a minute," Tarr told her, motioning with his head towards the room where Leonore sat. "Had to spring it on her rather quickly."

"Yes, sir," the woman replied. "Archer would like to speak with you."

"Is he all right?" Tarr asked, instantly on the alert.

"Yes, he's *fine*," she said, rather snappishly. "A little *too* fine for his own good, if you ask me."

Tarr tamped down a snort and went past her down the hallway, then around and up the stairs into Archer's bedroom. Archer rolled his head over, his one non-swollen eye crinkling at the sight of Tarr. A freshly made "Get Well Soon" card in Si's unmistakable scrawl was propped up beneath his bedside lantern; as he sat, Tarr could see that the subheading on the card read: "Hope your face improves." Tarr hid a smile, stifling the churning in his stomach at the sight of Archer's broken nose, trying to adopt a stern demeanor. "Archer, have you been tormenting your caretakers again? We've only got so many people left who are willing to come in here and spoon-feed you."

Archer adopted what could be construed as an innocent expression, which was difficult to discern with half of his face out of commission. "She's a stern, saucy, irresistible minx," he muttered between his gritted teeth.

"How are you feeling?" Tarr inquired, though he knew it was a rather stupid question.

"Like a daisy," Archer deadpanned. "I have something for you. A way out without the papers."

"What are you talking about?" Tarr asked.

Archer reached painfully over to his bedside table and fumbled with the cover of a book. "I'll get it," Tarr said hurriedly and took the book from him. Archer slumped back, looking exhausted. Tucked inside the pages was a folded piece of paper. Tarr withdrew it and smoothed it out. To his great surprise, it was a rudimentary sketch of a boat. He looked up to Archer, brow furrowed.

"The city gates are too well guarded, they have officers too eager to be really thorough with paperwork. But boats...boats are harder to check," Archer grunted. "And there are so many cargo loads coming in and out of the city every day by the river..."

The sketch, the more he examined it, was rather brilliant. The boat was designed to only be slightly larger than a skiff. All manner of small cargo could be loaded onto the shallow boat, but the real trick was located at the stern. A short stack of boxes, all outfitted with false bottoms or sides, would be stacked atop and beside one another on the surface of the boat. By all outward appearances, the boxes would appear to simply be freight; the tops could be loaded with objects so that they would appear completely full. But Archer had designed it so that someone could slither down through the topmost box and curl up in a small hidden compartment made by adjoining hollowed-out boxes beneath. It was only a short ride from the northern gate of Two Falls to a safe disembarkation point at the edge of the cliffs before the falls. It was highly risky, but Tarr knew that anyone who really longed for freedom would accept that without hesitation. He started to get excited.

"Archer, this just might work," he said, looking up at his brother. Archer managed a smile.

"Did it with my bad hand, too," he grunted. "But if this works, Tarr, we can get Ashans out, papers or no papers."

"How long will it take you to heal?" Tarr asked.

A shadow of the familiar grin flitted across Archer's face. "Dunno. How long will it take you to build the thing?"

As it turned out, it took Tarr's crews two weeks to build an appropriate model (after a few initial mishaps) and have it ensconced in the dead of night at a quiet, unassuming mooring in the center of town. During his daily rounds, Tarr couldn't help but wander past it once or twice, looking for any signs that he felt could be detected by Kagai's guards. But it was really rather good, and he reflected how lucky he was that they had so many excellent craftsmen and carpenters working for them.

Archer, spurred by some combination of excitement and hard-headedness, made a recovery that shocked most of their medical staff into disbelief. His face was still horribly bruised, and his broken nose had been set as best it could, but he was fully limber and functional enough to demand unequivocally that he be posted to the head of Operation Glub, as he liked to call it. ("We can't call it that," Athela had complained. "It makes it sound like someone's drowning." Archer had replied cheerily, "If things don't go to plan, it could be quite apropos.")

Laith had wanted to do a few trial runs before attempting to extract their priority refugees, but Tarr intervened. Errol, the Ashan who had found the documents about the medallion hidden in the Two Falls library, had been waiting long and patiently for her chance to escape to freedom. Tarr had personally spoken with her on a number of occasions. Out of everyone the Strikers were attempting to help, they owed Errol the most.

The escape was set to take place a week after the boat was placed at the dock. A local merchant who was sympathetic to the Strikers' cause had been secretly smuggling out a small amount of supplies for them every week (including parcels of mail bound for the mountains) and had leapt at the chance to help spirit refugees out of the city. The merchant was elderly and was afflicted by back pains that made actual fighting nearly impossible; the most he could do was to get on and off the dock and steer his boat through the water, so Tarr was glad to give him the extra opportunity to support the cause. In any case, the merchant had made a few dry runs in and out of the city with the boat, and all had gone well; the cargo had been searched, and the guards had noticed nothing amiss.

Archer and Athela were heading up the execution of the plan together. Athela had recently returned from commanding a raid and had subsequently been tied up with managing a few squabbles and vandalism attempts in the western part of the city. She was growing restless and had requested a change of pace. She was waiting outside of Archer's room when the Ashan finally exited, clad all in black with a mask hanging at the ready around his neck. He met her with a grin, one eye still grotesque and puffy, his long nose looking ever so slightly crooked, but on the whole, he was back to normal. Athela hoped her relief didn't show every time she looked at him. It had been difficult, more difficult than she cared to admit, to see him lying in a bloody heap in medical quarters.

"Ready?" he asked her, and she stirred.

"This had better work," she told him sternly, as if it were all up to him. It came out more harshly than she had intended; to her relief, Archer merely laughed and caught her in the crook of his arm for a quick hug.

"Dear Athela," he said fondly.

They trooped down the stairs together towards the cellar where Errol was waiting for them. Archer gave three quick raps with his knuckles, and he and Athela were admitted. Errol was sitting beside Tarr and shot to her feet as Archer and Athela entered. Her expression was a twisted mixture of hope and anxiety.

"Now, do you all know what to do?" Tarr inquired.

Errol nodded mutely, swallowing. Her hopes had been so high when she had heard about the plan to recover the transit papers, and had been crushed when the exchange and recovery had turned into a Kagaian ambush. It was almost too much to wish that this new scheme, Archer's boat plan, could actually work. But still, she was actually *out* doing something, not pacing the walls of some cellar waiting for news. She had a sneaking suspicion that it had been Tarr who had put her up to be the first beneficiary of this new plan, and she wondered how best to express her gratitude. Perhaps she didn't have to. Tarr seemed to be the sort of person who could understand such things without having to be told. As if he had heard Errol's thoughts, Tarr caught her eye and offered a reassuring smile before stepping over to speak with Athela and Archer about some last-minute security measures.

"I have someone waiting on the other side to help orient Errol and hopefully reconnect her with her uncle and mother," Tarr informed them. "I've already explained the situation to her. We don't have assurances that they're still out there, but we're hoping they sought refuge on the outskirts of one of the forest tribes. Barring that, there are towns beyond the forest that are aiding refugees and are ready to take her in."

"I'm impressed," Athela said approvingly. Tarr ruffled his hair, looking tired.

"When was the last time you slept, mate?" Archer asked him.

Tarr shrugged a thin shoulder. "I'll sleep after this goes through and we get everyone out."

"Next year, then?" Archer ribbed him gently.

Errol's hands were twisting together as the three Strikers rejoined her. She was wearing all black, thin and form-fitting fabric. It would make for a chilly ride, but the secret compartment didn't have enough room to accommodate bulkier winterproof clothing.

"Remember," Tarr told her, "One hour to daybreak, then the boats can start running, and it's just a half-hour ride from there. Just an hour and a half from now, there'll be warm clothes waiting for you on the other side. And you'll be free."

Errol could barely reply. She made some sort of noise in the back of her throat and felt herself nodding hurriedly, mouth cracking into more of a grimace than a smile. Tarr firmly clasped her on the back of the neck, and almost at once, Errol straightened up and stopped visibly shaking.

"Our quiet, meek little Tarr," Athela said under her breath so that he couldn't hear. "Who'd have thought it?"

Archer smiled in agreement.

Archer and Athela personally escorted Errol from the base through the streets of Two Falls down to the waterfront where the boat was kept at its mooring. It was pitch black, just as Tarr had calculated it would be. Athela and Archer's bodyguards hung back beneath a nearby bridge, keeping their eyes peeled for any danger. A few of the other merchants were coming down to ready their light, slim boats for the early-morning shipments; by law, the boats could only run after the first light of dawn. This left an hour for them to wait before they could push off and make their bid for freedom. It was still so dark that Archer had to guide them down the dock to the end where the merchant and his son were waiting at the ready. Athela spoke to the merchant and introduced him to Errol, who had resumed shivering, either from fear or from the cold.

"Everything's set," the merchant told her.

Athela turned to Archer, who, to her surprise, wasn't even looking at them. He was staring off into the blackness with the keen alertness of a hawk.

"What is it?" she inquired.

"Nothing," he said quickly, looking back down at them. "Errol, are you ready?"

Errol, too, wasn't listening. She was looking down at the inky black water. Archer put his hand on Errol's shoulder and spoke a few quick words to her in singsong Ashan. Errol's head immediately snapped back up, and in the dark gloom, Athela thought she could see the slightest ghost of a smile. "Now, be as quiet as you can," Archer whispered in Errol's ear.

A low whistle sounded; it was an alert from one of Archer's troops. "Guards coming," Athela hissed urgently. "Now, Errol, slip into the compartment."

They hunkered down at the very edge of the pier and steadied Errol as she stepped onto the boat, which rocked gently with her weight. The merchant held open the trick box, and Errol stuck one foot inside. After a few moments of finagling, she slid her body through the false bottom of the box and disappeared into the hidden compartment underneath. The merchant immediately set about replacing the box's false bottom and filling it up again with cargo.

Archer and Athela stood back, heads cocked to the side, admiring Archer's handiwork. Even though they knew the design of the compartment, it was hard to believe that there was room in there for anyone to hide.

"Well, I'll be damned," Archer said appreciatively. "This just might work."

"Hurry!" the merchant's son exclaimed. The light of the night patrol's lantern was coming closer and closer along the edge of the river. "There's no time! You two! Get into the boat."

Archer and Athela moved as fast as they could, sliding into the prow and curling up beside each other. The merchant haphazardly covered them with a thick sheet of canvas and a few spare pieces of rope. In the few breathless seconds that followed, all that could be distinguished was the slightest knock, the signal that Errol was settled safely in the hidden compartment. Archer breathed a sigh of relief and clasped his hand over his own mouth, nudging Athela to do the same. They heard footsteps as the guards stopped at their dock and came down the pier towards the boat.

"Early shipment, then?" asked the guard.

"We like to get a good start on the day, sir," replied the merchant.

"Papers," the guard demanded automatically, clearly done with the pleasantries. There was a heavy rocking of the small boat as the merchant stood and rustled about in his bag for the requisite permits. A few seconds of silence followed as the guard read them.

"We had reports of individuals sneaking around these parts after hours," he said. "Have you seen anything?"

"No, sir, but then we haven't been looking much toward shore. We've been loading up for the past half-hour or so," the merchant replied.

"Hmm," said the guard. "And the boy?"

"My son. He's certified as well; it's written just there."

He's not going to leave, Archer realized with a jolt. His mind started to race. He only had his knives; he was better with a bow and arrow, but it was much too close for that. And Athela didn't have her sword...

"We're going to search your cargo," the guard told him. "Step off the boat."

A few hopeless moments trailed by, and Archer felt Athela's body stiffen close beside him. Archer's heart felt as though it were beating up into his throat.

CRASH! All at once, a loud sound was heard, followed by whooping and laughter far off in the distance.

"What the—!" yelled the guard, and Archer could hear his footsteps pound away back up the pier.

"Vandals, sir! On the bridge!" another voice reported breathlessly. "It might be some of the Strikers!"

"Bunch of drunks, at the very least," replied the guard in a dark voice. "Hurry, we'll catch them."

The loud clinking of footsteps and metal roared past them and sped off into the distance. The whooping, laughter, and taunting continued, trailing far away in the opposite direction. Archer let his body relax ever so slightly and felt Athela do the same. There were a few more prolonged seconds before the merchant urgently tapped them on the feet and threw back the canvas.

"They won't be back around this way for a while, I think. Someone set fire to the bridge over on the far side," he nodded in the direction of the blot of roaring flames on the other side of the river.

"The Strikers' Arson Division, always punctual," Archer quipped, neatly springing off the boat and helping Athela clamber slightly less gracefully back onto the pier. "We'll watch you till you're safely past the gate."

"Good luck," Athela said, and she and Archer ran as quickly and as quietly as they could off the pier and down the edge of the river. They took refuge in the shadowy cover of the nearby bridge, hiding in the structure's framework, a roost that offered both cover and a clear view of the merchant's boat.

"I don't envy Errol," Athela muttered, shivering.

"She believes she's going to be free," Archer said. "What could be a better feeling than that?"

Athela looked over at him curiously but said nothing more.

Partially out of necessity, neither of them spoke much as they crouched in the darkness, waiting for the first light of dawn. They hadn't been alone together in quite a while, and Athela couldn't help but enjoy herself, even in his silent company. Much to her relief, it seemed that the Strikers' fire diversion had worked like a charm, and not a single other patrol came down the edge of the river, diverted elsewhere. After a while, Archer started to hum an odd, melancholy tune beneath his breath, and though her initial reaction was always to tell him to shut up, in this instance she found it rather comforting.

"Think she'll make it?" she asked finally.

"Yes."

She thought. "What was the song you were humming?"

"Folk song." The golden eyes swept up the length of the river.

"From the forest?"

"The Meadows. We didn't have music in the forest. Mostly atonal chanting and some erratic drumming."

She smirked at the thought, then blinked soberly. "You miss it very much? The forest?"

"Do you miss Joymaril?" he asked.

She considered. Not for a moment did she miss the people or the backstabbing, sycophantic nature of the court. But she missed the waterfall, the quiet lake, the riding trails through the forest, the sights and smells of the city, how exciting it had been the first time she had leapt the walls of the palace and blended into the crowd of people, completely anonymous. "Sort of," she replied lamely.

He let her words hang there, and the two of them waited on in complete silence. Finally, a lone bell tolled the break of dawn, and, softly as the flutter of wings, lanterns were lit along the edge of the river in the prows of all the waiting merchant boats, and one by one, they began to push back and head down the river.

"It's time," Archer nudged her and quietly climbed down from the underbelly of the bridge, Athela close behind. They waited until their boat had pushed back.

"So far, so good," Athela muttered.

The two of them stole along the edge of the river, keeping to the darkness as they went. Shopkeepers were starting to head out to set up their stalls and stores, and it seemed to be growing ever lighter by the second. They reached the northern gate just as the light turned a deep bluish-gray and silently took up a post on a roof overlooking the river guards. Boats slid past them in the water, pausing to be inspected before being admitted through the passage and out of the city. Archer scanned each with his golden eyes; to Athela, the people were just a blur. Finally, he nudged her and inclined his head towards one particular boat.

"Is that them?" she whispered, and he assented.

Archer gripped the edge of the roof as hard as he could as the inspecting officer spoke to the merchant and his son and sheafed through the papers. He attempted to budge the largest one, the one with the trick bottom. There were only a few inches of wood separating Errol from the officers. The officer attempted again to move the box, and when it wouldn't, he spoke sharply to the merchant, who shrugged and gesticulated a bit. The officer opened the top of the box and peered inside, and Archer nearly burst out laughing.

"What?" Athela demanded.

"He's filled the trick top with slabs of iron," Archer told her. "The sort of thing Cira would certainly need as far as supplies go, but the last thing in the world some lazy customs official is going to want to go through to get to the bottom of that box. Oh, he's a clever one."

The officer replaced the lid of the box and spoke a few last words to the merchant before waving him along. Archer squeezed Athela's hand tight as the boat gracefully slid past the post, through the gate, and out of Two Falls.

"They made it," he breathed, hardly daring to believe it himself. "They actually made it."

"Now, just as long as Errol made it too and isn't freezing under there like a large Ashan ice cube," Athela replied.

"It's what attracted me to you in the first place, Athela, your unwavering sense of optimism," Archer flashed back and slid down the roof, landing neatly at the bottom. "Head back and tell Tarr that so far, it's so good."

"What are you doing?" she asked curiously.

"Going for some shopping." When she didn't move, he made an entreating gesture with his hands. "I promise, I'll be right behind you."

Athela muttered something but begrudgingly acquiesced. Archer watched her go, then slowly turned around.

"Kai," he said in a low voice, "it's been a long time."

Like a panther slinking out of the darkness, a tall, athletic figure suddenly dissolved into plain view. Kai squared her shoulders and stared him down, unsurprised that he had called her out. The two took stock of one another, and Archer found himself automatically running his eye up and down the small street on which he found himself. It wasn't the best place for a fight.

Outwardly, Kai looked no different than he had remembered. Yet there was a determined, ruthless set to her mouth that he hadn't remembered before. She was tall, much taller than Athela, he realized. Funny. He hadn't really made the comparison before.

"Why are you here?" he asked.

She spread her hands. "Take a guess."

He pondered. "You're here to kill me for some reason or another?" His expression darkened. "On behalf of Cira Kagai, perhaps?"

She grinned, a flash of white teeth. "You're getting the spirit of the thing."

He reconsidered. "To kill the Strikers? Obviously, you're here to kill someone, Kai, since that's all you've ever been good at, but what I'm wondering is why exactly you decided to come out and betray your cover this way. Seems a bit premature."

"I've already overheard *many* useful things over the past few weeks," Kai smiled conspiratorially. "It's been particularly useful breaking into the apartments beside your safehouse at night. One can hear many things through an apartment wall. Interesting, all that stuff about Morthenstar's medallion. Do you think it's really magic or that your friend Si is truly losing his mind? I could always take the medallion off your hands for you, too, give you a good price..."

Archer had to restrain himself from lashing out at her. Her knowledge was dangerous, far too dangerous. *How had she heard them talk about the medallion? How could she know?* "Indeed," Archer said measuredly, then conversationally added, "By the by, have you been stalking our safehouse, and did you kill an innocent girl for fun and pin a creepy note to her and address it to my friend?"

Kai's brow furrowed, and he could see that she was genuinely puzzled by the question. "Not recently," she said.

"Aha," Archer murmured. "Just thought I'd check."

Kai sent him an inscrutable look. "I wanted to speak to you because I have a question for you. A riddle that's puzzled me lately."

He was surprised but hid it. "What might that be?"

"Why would Cira Kagai want *you* alive? You, of all people?"

Her question seemed to give him pause. "I have no idea," he replied honestly. "Maybe she needs a new court jester."

She glared at him. "Made some improvements to your face, I see," she observed.

He took a step forward, letting his sheer proximity provoke her. She narrowed her brilliant violet eyes at him but didn't budge. He took another step. They were now standing only a hair's breadth from one another. The moment hung in the air. She bared her teeth and lunged; in another breath, Archer had flipped her over and was holding her to the ground, pinning her wriggling form beneath his hand and knee, his knife out and poised to strike. She stopped struggling and waited, staring at the tip of the blade.

Archer looked down at her. It would be the wise decision, he knew, to just be done with her here and now. Whatever feelings had been between them had been over long ago. What he had perhaps once considered to be love, he now recognized for what it was. But he heard a nagging voice in the back of his mind, a voice that sounded distinctly like Ari's, a voice that accused him of killing indiscriminately without any thought or foresight. He looked away. There were years between them, and there had been good times as well as bad. Both he and Kai were of the same breed: they had long ago sold whatever soul they once had to make their way in the world. And though he didn't like to think of it, Archer couldn't help but see Rowan when he looked down at Kai and the dark fate to which she had almost certainly been delivered years before.

"Why don't you do it?" Kai hissed at him, and Archer was confused to see a trace of desperate panic in her eye. That was unusual. Kai was usually unwaveringly cool, even in the face of an oncoming arrow.

"What's happened?" Archer asked again, but this time, his voice was softer, almost entreating. "Why are you here?"

Kai's eyes flickered for a moment, but she wasn't about to give in. She gritted her teeth and pressed against his shoulder, refusing to reply. "Are you a new man, is that it?" she demanded. "Got your tribal tattoos, an Ashan brother. Even got a new lady friend, do you? She's not terribly pretty, from what I saw of her. Your standards have slipped since I left."

"One of the bodyguards," he told her curtly. "Nothing more." Betraying any feelings for Athela was the quickest way to mark her as a target, but he felt his hackles rise at Kai's insult.

"You were holding her hand," Kai sneered.

"I'm afraid of the dark," Archer retorted with a careless shrug. "You know that better than anyone. Now, Kai," he said, shifting his weight, "This reunion has certainly been stimulating. What I want to tell you is this." Here, he reached forward and grabbed her jaw, holding it firm so that she was forced to stare into his piercing golden eyes. "I am going to let you go this once. You get this single chance to pick up and walk away. You may not believe it, and I don't expect you to, but I have a life now. If you so much as look at one of my friends in a way I don't like, even passing by on the street, I will *end* you faster than you can imagine. Your mothers were kind to me, and so was your sister. I'm doing this for them. So make the intelligent decision and leave. Now." With that, he released her face and stood back up, replacing the knife in his belt.

Kai lay on the ground a bit stunned, then sprang to her feet and brushed herself off. His words and his manner had shocked her completely, but what was even more confounding was that she could see he had meant everything he'd said. Without another sound, she turned away from him and vaulted up onto the roof, disappearing like a breath of smoke on the other side.

Archer stood in the alley alone as the sun rose higher and brighter behind him. He hoped that he would never have to see Kai's face again. He hoped he had made the right decision in letting her go. Finding that his hand was bunched into an involuntary fist, he released it, stretched out his fingers, tucked the black mask over his face, and headed back to headquarters.

CHAPTER THIRTEEN

Marc, Si, and Tarr sat together at the breakfast table a few days later, scraping the last bit of their ration of butter across a fresh loaf of bread. Si ate hungrily, and Tarr reflected that the boy had been given little food the previous week. Though he himself was feeling the sharp stabs of hunger, he pushed over the last half of his bread to Si, who inhaled it with a grateful, silent nod. Tarr leaned back and gathered a sheaf of papers in his hands, proofs of the latest propaganda pamphlet to be papered across Two Falls.

The door opened, and Athela stalked in. She poured herself a glass of water. "Morning," she said, and the others nodded. Marc had been on late patrol the night before and had managed one, perhaps two hours of sleep and was not in a terribly talkative mood. "I'm going out to survey the east movement," she told them. "Anyone care to come along?"

Tarr held up the thick stack of papers and frowned an apologetic no. The door opened, and Archer sloped through it. He gave quick nods all around and clasped Tarr on the shoulder as he passed. Then, the small room lapsed into a curiously awkward silence, punctuated only by the sounds of water being poured, swilled around in a cup, and then swallowed. Tarr saw out of the corner of his eye that Si had stopped eating and was watching the two of them with unabashed fascination.

"Well, I'm off," Athela announced loudly and strode purposefully out of the room. Archer watched her go, then paused for a beat.

"Going to go check out arms manufacturing," he announced. "Any takers?"

Mute refusals came from all around. Archer chugged the last bit of water in his cup and walked out the door. Tarr, Si, and Marc all glanced at one another.

"They're in love, aren't they?" Si observed.

Marc and Tarr exchanged looks. Tarr raised his eyebrows, as if to say *this is all you, friend.*

"Well, Si," Marc declared, clearing his throat with what Tarr recognized immediately as his "father hen" manner, "love comes in all manner of forms. Archer and Athela are simply working through what we call the 'undeclared, blaringly obvious and socially awkward' phase."

"What are some other kinds of love?" Si asked curiously.

Marc glanced in Tarr's direction, clearly hoping again for some form of assistance, but Tarr merely folded his arms and raised his eyebrows higher, interested to see where the conversation was going. Marc cleared his throat. "Well, there's familial love. The kind that keeps me from murdering Laith when he leaves the top off of the milk jar."

"Oh, yes," Si agreed, clearly familiar with that particular form of love.

"There's friendly love," Marc continued, hitting a comfortable pedagogical stride.

"Like when you and Archer get into fights about arrows versus swords," Si chimed in. "Sometimes you grab him in a headlock."

"Er...yes," Marc agreed. "Headlocks can be a part of it. And then there's romantic love, which sometimes crosses over into the boundaries of...erm...physical love."

"Physical love?" Si wrinkled his nose.

There was silence. Marc was trapped. His mouth remained open as he glanced alternately at Tarr and the door, clearly hoping for some form of escape. Tarr took a deep drink of water and gave him a placid, encouraging nod. Marc gritted his teeth and doggedly launched into a monologue that made little to no sense even to Tarr, who was by that point well versed in such things. At the conclusion, Si looked bewildered and a bit frightened. Marc folded his arms and attempted to appear fatherly.

"Is it really like that, Tarr?" Si asked in a hushed voice, his eyes wide as saucers.

"More or less," Tarr agreed vaguely and went back to his paperwork, leaving Si sitting disconcertedly staring at the table.

Unrelated to the talk he'd received at the breakfast table, the boy found himself unaccountably restless for the rest of the day. The other Strikers seemed consumed with work and duties, and for once, he could find nothing to occupy himself. Even Ari, who usually brought him along on some errand or packing mission or another, was occupied in the north of the city. So Si put on a cloak, begged permission from Tarr, dutifully notified two of his bodyguards, and decided to take a walk.

Since the incident with the medallion, the others had treated him the same as ever—exaggeratedly so, with an almost strained heartiness— but Si could feel something hovering around like a cloud. He couldn't be sure whether he was imagining the whole thing, whether his loss of control had made him paranoid and self-conscious. Those around him eyed him with caution, like he was a firecracker that could be triggered to go off at any moment, and if Si were being honest with himself, he could understand why. Tarr had the medallion safely locked away, and Marc watched over him like an overprotective brother. Si had to face the fact that he simply couldn't trust himself anymore. It was a frightening and uncertain headspace to occupy.

Si was so deep in thought that it was a few minutes before he was aware of a curious, cold feeling creeping up the back of his neck. It was so tangible that he almost raised a hand to swat it away, then stopped still and swiveled around. The street was empty, except for the two bodyguards trailing behind him at a safe distance. Si's brow furrowed, and he slowly turned again. He had been tracing a familiar path from their hideaway around the center of the city, but as he gazed around the street, it seemed almost alien; there was a cold mist hovering in the air, and the damp seemed to hush the sounds of the city. Everything was strangely muted. Si held up his hands in front of his face and rubbed them together just to be sure that he wasn't dreaming or in the midst of another bizarre vision. When all seemed to be normal, he took another step forward, but the feeling didn't recede.

He veered away from his initial course and skirted the downtown area of the city, wandering up one street and down the next. There were very few people out, and the pervading feeling of unease didn't leave him as he walked. The mist seemed to grow heavier and heavier, and the only sounds he could make out were the curiously loud echoes of his bodyguards' steps. And then suddenly, he heard something else. A fourth pair of footsteps, then a fifth, and a sixth. Si whipped around and ducked into an alcove, then waited until his bodyguards came in beside him.

"What is it?" one of them asked.

"We're being followed," Si muttered urgently, craning his neck out into the street and gazing around.

The two bodyguards exchanged concerned looks. They clearly hadn't noticed anything unusual. Si wasn't sure whether stories about his strange visions had reached anyone outside the core Strikers, and he began to feel anxious that they wouldn't believe him. One of the bodyguards looked down towards Si. "There's no one," she told him slowly. "We've been keeping a good look out. We've seen nothing."

"I heard them," Si frowned. "Footsteps. At least three others!"

"There was no one, sir," the second bodyguard told him, his expression leery.

Si was starting to feel alarmed. Either the bodyguards were lying, or they were all being followed and were in terrible danger. Or, of course, Si's mind was once again starting to play tricks on him. He thought about running back to the headquarters, locking himself up in the safehouse, and never leaving again. He had heard stories about people who had lost their minds and been committed to the dungeons and prisons of Two Falls and would never have dreamed that such a fate would befall him. He wished that he had never set eyes on the medallion.

Or, he reasoned, *quite possibly, the sound I heard was just an echo or three little old ladies coming down the street after an afternoon of shopping. Calm down.*

"It was probably nothing," he announced to the two bodyguards. He tried to assume his best coolly authoritative Laith impression. "We'll just loop around quickly and then head back to the safehouse."

He set out again, trying to ignore the prickling at his back. He kept his head ducked and kept to the smallest, narrowest passages he could find. The hairs on the nape of his neck were standing straight on end as if a chilly wind were blowing down the back of his collar. The distant, echoing footsteps started up again, and Si knew that there was no way anyone else in the street could be making them. They were being followed by someone or *something*, of that he was certain.

He whipped around as fast as he could and, for a split second, caught a glimpse of a tall, thin figure in a long scarlet cloak standing at the head of the alley. Almost as soon as Si could blink, the figure was gone. The two bodyguards turned to look in the same direction, but it was too late for them to have seen anything. Si opened his mouth to call a warning, but realized that saying anything more would convince them he was going mad. But *he* was certain. There was someone there, someone who didn't want to be seen.

Si's small, pale hands clenched into fists, and he cursed himself silently for having come out unarmed. He knew better than to think he could really outdo anyone much bigger than him in a fight. But he was fast, and he was cunning. He could outrun them. He knew the streets well. His breath came faster as he held his fists at his sides, lengthening the stride of his walk until he reached the end of the street. And as soon as there was room to run, he bolted off as fast as he could.

He heard a cry from one of the bodyguards as he started away, but they were too slow to keep up. With the speed of a fox, he darted around one corner and saw a large pile of debris blocking his way. He dropped to his belly, shimmied under the large planks of wood, and took up running on the other side. *That should lose someone*, he thought to himself. It was freeing, in a way, to be left to his own devices. Not to have to worry about proper form or the way to handle a sword. Just to have the ability to run and hide.

Maybe he would keep running as far as he could. Away from Two Falls, away from the others, away from everything.

Out of the corner of one eye, he spied a long gutter pipe that led up the side of an apartment building to a thin balconied corridor on the third floor. He sprang up to the pipe and scaled it with the agility of a squirrel, swinging over the side of the balcony and bolting down the corridor. He stopped at the end, crouching down in the shadows and peering down into the street below. There was no one. He had left his own bodyguards far behind, and there was no further sight of the strange scarlet-cloaked figure he had seen at the head of the alley. The curious prickling feeling still tickled the back of his neck, so he remained on his guard. But for the time being, he felt that he was safe enough to take a moment and think.

He had heard what the others had said about the mysterious footprints that Rane had found around their house and remembered that a girl had recently died under extremely bizarre circumstances with a note for Laith pinned to her. Was the scarlet figure he had seen the same person who had been shadowing the safehouse? The thought that he was being stalked by some sort of homicidal maniac was not exactly thrilling. He wondered how he could get word to the other Strikers or whether he'd be able to make it back safely to the house on his own. Once the bodyguards realized that they'd lost him, one would stay out and search while the other would go and notify the other Strikers. *Marc will find me*, he thought firmly. *He won't stop looking until he does.*

His feeling of unease grew the longer he sat still, and he felt the overwhelming urge to move his location. The alleyway was narrow, and he knew enough from his thieving days to be able to gauge the distance. He swung up on the side of the balcony railing and then hopped across the void to land somewhat heavily on the railing on the opposite side of the street. He scaled down the side and thudded down to the ground, then took off running and skirted the wall before whipping around the corner.

To his dismay, he found himself mostly sealed off in a courtyard. With a lurch in his stomach, he heard the echo of a footstep off in the distance, then another, then another. They were coming closer. The mist was gathering on his unmoving eyelashes, and he wiped his eyes with a shaking hand. He spun around, cornered, searching for a sure way of escape. There was none. He kept low and scurried across the courtyard, then slipped through a door into a dark room that turned out to be some sort of storage shed. He quietly closed the door behind him and hunkered down beside one of the windows, out of view of anyone who happened to be passing outside.

Minutes stretched into an eternity. Si was desperately conscious of the heaviness of his breathing, how loud it seemed in the muted silence of the dark room. The Strikers must surely be on their way by this point. As long as Rane or Archer were with them, they'd be able to find him, he was certain. Perhaps he had been stupid to leave his bodyguards behind like he had. He chanced a look out the window, and his heart nearly stopped.

A red figure stood in the center of the courtyard, bathed in the damp silver sunlight. It wore a scarlet cloak with black lining that rippled in the quiet, misty wind. It stood perfectly still. Si only glimpsed it for a split second, then ducked back down beneath the sill. Perhaps it hadn't seen him. Perhaps it would leave him alone. Si couldn't remember being so terrified in his entire life.

Almost against his own will, he forced himself up on his elbows and looked out of the window again. This time, he let out an audible cry of fear and terror. The figure had silently stolen forward so that it stood only a foot or two away from the window. Si could see the figure's face. They were at once neither male nor female, their forehead wrapped in some kind of black covering. The face was clearly old but was oddly unlined, as if they had spent their entire life indoors out of the glare of the sun. Their skin was thin yet soft, and their eyes were pale and sickly blue. The stranger's presence was deeply unsettling, so much so that Si's stomach twisted, overwhelmingly afraid that he couldn't will his limbs into motion. And there was something about the figure's expression, something almost *familiar* about the way in which the person regarded Si. Si, for his part, was sure he had never seen them before in his life.

Slowly, the figure's hand went from their hip up to their hood and slowly pushed the fabric back from their head, revealing the deep black lining beneath. Their head was wrapped now only in a tight black fabric that obscured everything but their major features. A long, skeletal hand pulled back the wrap from their forehead, and Si watched in abject astonishment as the person's head was revealed. Their head was entirely shaved, round and white as an egg with aging and liver spots speckling it here and there. But the thing that stopped Si cold was the person's forehead: it bore a red tattoo of Morthenstar's emblem, the six-pointed star, almost identical to that on Si's arm.

Si felt his hand leap almost unbidden to touch the marking on his arm, his mind swimming in confusion. *Who is that?* He wondered blankly. *Is it me? From the future?*

Other than contributing to his complete bewilderment, the star tattoo proved to comfort Si, if only to a tiny degree. No one with a Morthenstar tattoo could conceivably want to hurt him, could they? Si's thoughts were re-forming through the haze of fear, and he began to mentally scan his surroundings, looking again for a way out. He wasn't sure what the person's next move would be, but he didn't want to remain there to find out. The stranger had barely even blinked, and took a step forward. Si tensed his body to run.

All at once, the figure whipped around as if they had heard something. Their skeletal, pale hand tensed at their side, then they jerked the red hood back over their head and, without another motion, disappeared into thin air.

Si's jaw fell open. They had actually *disappeared.* They hadn't run, hadn't jumped away. One instant, they were there; the next, they were gone. Si wished he could understand what was going on.

He struggled wobbly to his feet and tested his stance to make sure that he could remain upright. When he could, he took a step forward, the adrenaline pouring down his arms and into the tips of his fingers so that they tingled quite unpleasantly, and he nearly fell forward. Another figure was running down the alleyway into the courtyard, but it was someone he recognized, and he almost shouted for joy. Rane.

He slipped out of the door to the shed and gave her a small, friendly wave. Rane's eyes were wide and extremely anxious, and she slid to a halt in front of him, immediately reaching out to touch him on the shoulder. "Si," she said quietly, "are you having one of your visions? Can you speak to me?"

"No, I'm fine," Si assured her. "But let me tell you, there is some *weird* shit going on around here."

Rane laughed. "Watch your language," she chided, but it was more relieved than scolding. "Let me walk you back home, and you can tell all of us what happened."

Tarr listened to the entire tale with his fingers steepled beneath his nose, and his long legs thrown out and crossed at the ankles. Marc paced back and forth behind Si and occasionally made low-pitched, disgruntled guttural noises whenever Si said something like "I jumped off the roof" or "I left the bodyguards behind."

When Si got to the part where the mysterious figure vanished into thin air, Laith's dark brows came together, and Athela pinched her sinuses between her thumb and forefinger.

"Then Rane showed up," Si concluded with a helpless shrug. "And now here I am. I can't explain any of it."

"It's lucky you weren't *killed*," Marc growled. "That was an intensely stupid thing to do."

"Is there anyone *not* stalking this bloody safehouse?" Archer wondered aloud.

"Why didn't your bodyguards hear them?" Athela wondered aloud.

"Do you think it actually was me?" Si asked Tarr. "Like, me from way in the future?" A few months ago, the question would have sounded ridiculous, but by that point, so many strange things had happened that he could no longer be sure of anything. "They had a tattoo, too, but on their head. They didn't really look like me." Si remembered something and brightened. "They had blue eyes! They can't have been me." It was a relief; whoever the person was, they clearly hadn't aged well.

"How could they have simply *disappeared* like that?" Archer wondered.

"You believe me, then?" Si asked them anxiously.

"Why wouldn't we?" Tarr asked equably. "You are many things, Si, but you're not dishonest."

"Except for the whole thief thing," Athela pointed out.

"Yes, well, there was that," Tarr conceded.

"I was never dishonest about *being* a thief," Si pointed out.

"Do you think that they're the person who's been stalking our house and killed that girl? Laith asked Tarr.

"Honestly, it's surprising that our various stalkers aren't *colliding* into each other on the street outside at this point," Archer rolled his eyes. "That's three different people so far."

"Three?" Athela asked, gaze narrowing suspiciously.

"Two," Archer corrected himself hurriedly and a bit evasively. "As long as this person isn't the one who killed the girl in the alley."

Tarr frowned. "We don't know who this person is, or what they want, or why they were following Si. But they made no move to harm Si in any way, whereas we know that the person who killed that girl is homicidal in the extreme. And we know that the killer has, for one reason or another, decided to target Laith, so it seems most likely that if he were to make contact, it would be with him."

"Again, I must insist in the most animated language that we *change safehouses*," Archer said exasperatedly.

"Yes," Tarr said distractedly, his mind still roiling. "Yes, we should."

"But the person I saw *disappeared*," Si continued. "Who do we know who can do that kind of magic? You told me magic died out long ago, Tarr."

"As far as we know, yes," Tarr agreed.

"'As far as we know,'" Athela scoffed. "It seems to me like we know less and less as the days go by."

No one disputed that statement. Si, for his part, was extremely glad that none of his friends seemed to think that he had lost his grip. It seemed so much easier, discussing what had happened here in the quiet of the safehouse with the other Strikers surrounding him. But the image of the stranger's face would not leave his brain anytime soon. And though he wanted to forget about the entire thing, he had a feeling that it wouldn't be long before he saw them again.

CHAPTER FOURTEEN

"Now!" The Kagaian commander cried eagerly, feeling a surge of excitement as he reared back and kicked down the heavy wooden doors of the storeroom. He had always wanted to kick down a door. He had also always wanted to be the one to march Lord Argolaith up to General Grey in chains and announce that the threat to Kagaian law in Two Falls had effectively been eliminated. Now was his chance.

He and his troops had lain in wait until just the right moment and had burst forward in a surge of power towards the unsuspecting cellar. He hoped that Argolaith and Marc and maybe even Archer would be sitting there, perhaps playing cards. Yes, that was it! Playing cards. What a funny scene that would be. Their looks of astonishment as he drew his sword, aimed it at them, and announced that they were now his prisoners.

So caught up was he in his reverie that he was nearly run over by a few of his more eager soldiers. He quickly recovered himself and lurched to the front of the pack. The rickety, narrow cellar stairs were not built to support the weight of twenty armored troopers, so they had to slow down the pace as they picked their way into the belly of the cavern. *Yes, here it is!* The commander thought in a rush. *Perhaps they'll be playing cards on a hill of ill-gotten Striker gold!*

With a fierce battle cry, he slid to a halt, sword out, ready to face all comers. His soldiers were at his back. The blood was up. They were ready for anything.

A very startled raccoon gave an indignant screech in a dark, far corner and scurried out of sight. One of the commander's men let out an effeminate yelp behind him. At first, the commander thought that his eyes were having trouble adjusting to the dimness of the cellar. But then it dawned on them. With the raccoon gone, the cellar was completely bare.

"What?" blurted a woman to the commander's left.

"Shut up," he snapped peevishly. "Who was in charge of navigation?"

"Me, sir," came a shaky voice.

"We're..." the commander swallowed. "We're in the right place, aren't we?"

"Yes sir!" the voice said meekly. "We've had it staked out for a week! We watched a new supply shipment come in here yesterday."

The commander narrowed his eyes and swiveled on his heel, glaring at each and every one of his dumbfounded troops. *"Then where—the hell—are they?"*

Unsurprisingly, no one seemed to be able to answer his question. The commander turned back around, his dreams of Striker-capturing glory swiftly being replaced with images of his attempting to explain this botched raid to his superiors. *They must have found out...somehow,* he reasoned. *That's the only way we can explain the supplies being here one day and then gone the next. They must have been tipped off.* This comforted him somewhat. If there had been an informant, that would mean that some of the blame, at least, was shifted from his shoulders.

Suddenly, the commander thought he heard something, like a whisper or the scratching of a footstep—or even (he imagined fancifully) a barely repressed giggle. His eyes narrowed, and he straightened his shoulders, desperately attempting to retain whatever dignity he had left.

"The situation has been compromised," he announced. It was something he had once heard his lieutenant say, and it had filled him with a sense of urgency and import. "We must clear out at once and report back to headquarters." With that, he smartly stepped forward, and the troops hesitantly followed him, clearly anxious about the possibility of any lingering raccoons. There was the sound of boots clomping heavily back up the staircase, and then the door was ponderously shut behind them.

The sound of tromping feet on wood gradually began to fade away in the empty, echoing space. In its place grew the unmistakable form of deeply repressed laughter.

"Will you be quiet?" Marc demanded, though he, too, was having trouble keeping a smile back from the twitching corners of his mouth. "They nearly heard you!"

Archer let out a full guffaw, swinging down from his hiding place atop the ceiling beams to land like a feather on the ground. "The only thing that could have possibly made that better would have been if the stairway had collapsed. Or the raccoon had bitten one in the face."

"Their expressions *were* priceless," Marc conceded as he and Laith swung down from the ceiling to stand beside Archer.

"We made a neat job of it," Laith commented, glancing around the room. They had worked furiously through the night, displacing the supplies to a hideaway beneath the floor. His shoulders ached, and his body felt as though it were dragging him down, but he squared his back like the soldier he was and forced himself to be alert.

"Handy little informant you've found yourself, mate," Archer said to him. "Saved us all a lot of trouble."

"That she did," Laith murmured.

A small trapdoor stirred in the corner of the room, and two pairs of eyes peeked out anxiously at them. Marc waved them forward. "Come on, the way is clear. Though next time, you should really wait for my signal."

"Yes sir," chorused a reply, and two retainers, both green recruits not much older than Si, scurried from a hiding place and came to stand beside them. They were girls, sisters, and were still overcome with awe at everything the Strikers said or did,

"If I may say, sir, *very* well put together," one announced breathlessly, her eyes on Laith.

"A triumph of subterfuge and execution," the other put in, clearly not wanting to be outdone. Archer rolled his eyes but tried to make it look as though he were examining the ceiling beams.

Laith moved his shoulders around in a circle and cracked his neck. Marc watched him out of the corner of his eye. He knew exactly how hard Laith had been working and how well he was trying to hide it.

"You go home," Marc told Laith lightly. "I'll clean up here. See that all the ends are tied up."

Laith looked to be on the verge of protesting but gave a sigh and then nodded. "I'll be up and about later tonight," he assured Marc.

He took steps towards the door, and Marc motioned one of the retainers over with a crook of his finger. He dropped his voice down low. "If he is woken up at all before well into tomorrow afternoon, you are fired."

The retainer looked startled, but Marc gave a gentle laugh and touched her on the shoulder to show that he was only joking. The girl gave a nervous, coughing chuckle and turned to scurry off after Laith. Archer shook his head and muttered something beneath his breath, then headed over to the cleverly concealed trapdoor to check the contents below.

Marc stood silently for some time, looking at the spot where the shadow of his friend had disappeared from sight. Almost unbidden, a memory flashed in front of his eyes: Laith, many years before, running heedlessly through a sunlit field of billowing grass.

General Calchas drew back the curtain of his tent and stepped out into the gentle warmth of the early evening sunshine. His eyes traveled across the softly rolling silhouette of the hills against the golden sky, the purple trees dotting the land here and there, the blue mist beginning to settle in for the night. And the grass, waving sea-green oceans of grass, blowing in shining ripples whenever there was the slightest gust of wind. Though this was his fortieth tour of duty in the Meadows, he was still struck anew by its beauty every time he walked outside.

But it only took a split second for him to recall the rolled-up parchment he clasped in his left hand and the terse, non-negotiable language of the orders within. He sighed heavily and took a moment to breathe in the clean, sweet-smelling air.

"Argolaith!" he bellowed, his voice carrying out over the wind. It was the seasoned bark of an aging soldier, he reflected wryly. A bit past its prime, but not completely devoid of power. Not yet.

He waited patiently, knowing that he would not have to call again, and in a few seconds' time he spotted two figures running up and over the nearest hill. The other soldiers, tending to their horses and their kits along the neat rows of tents, gave the two a cursory glance and turned away. A few campfires were being lit; the rosy golden glow in the sky was going fast.

The young prince was tall for his age and strong—though a little thin—but Calchas was quite sure that he would grow into his long, coltish legs and square shoulders. He came barreling up with a gleeful, impish look on his face and a grin stretched over his mouth, and slid to attention a respectful step or two in front of Calchas, chest heaving as he tried to recover his wind.

His companion was slower to arrive. Square, short, and stocky, with a low center of gravity that, even at the young age of fourteen, made knocking him over a difficult prospect, Marc jogged up to stand beside Argolaith. Calchas hid a smile at the sight of them. Their difference in height and proportion was undeniably comical. Marc's yellow flaxen hair was cropped short to his head, and his smooth, boyish face radiated his inner good nature.

"Well, then," Calchas began slowly, scratching his jaw with a weathered, callused finger, "who won that race, I wonder?"

"I did, sir," Argolaith said serenely.

"Laith," Marc interjected. He had begun to call Argolaith "Laith" a few months before, and it had stuck. "When I said, 'Shall we race?' I meant it as more of a *suggestion* than a challenge."

"Liar," Laith retorted. "You said, 'last one back to camp has to clean the other's kit.'"

"I remember it differently," Marc maintained stolidly.

"Silence," Calchas barked with mock severity, trying again to hide a smile. He had brought many of the young royals through their training in the Meadows, but he had never been quite as fond of a pair as he was of Marc and Laith. He couldn't remember a single actual argument between them, even in their very early childhoods.

"Argolaith, I need to have a word," Calchas nodded towards the boy. Laith turned and clapped Marc on the shoulder.

"Great, Marc, you can go get started oiling my saddle. I rode through a particularly muddy river the other day, so it should be a lot of fun."

Marc walked off, muttering to himself. Laith grinned cheekily and walked beneath the flap of Calchas's tent into the dim, sparse interior, standing at attention in front of the general's table. Decades of nomadic patrolling life had left Calchas little opportunity to accrue worldly possessions. Next to an oil lamp were a few books and maps; on the floor was a comfortable rug, and across the tent was his cot. In another corner was displayed his full battle armor and a few of his favorite ceremonial swords. Everything, including the tent, could be packed up and ready to move in less than ten minutes.

Calchas sat at the table, smoothing his wispy gray hair back with one hand. For a long time, he studied the boy standing in front of him. Calchas had been good friends with Argolaith's parents, and he could see more of them in the boy every day. The large eyes, the tendency towards darker coloring, and the aristocratic nose were his father's; the mouth and the delicate bone structure were his mother's. At fourteen, he was an undeniably handsome youth, and Calchas could only imagine how he would be when he grew into himself a bit.

In a sudden rush, Calchas found himself remembering the first year the boy had come to him. Laith's father had died in a battle in the Meadows when his small troop had been completely overwhelmed by a band of outlaws that had been pillaging the nearby towns. Shortly after that, at the traditional age of four years, Argolaith had been given into Calchas's care. Argolaith's mother, always in delicate health, died the year after her son left following a short, sudden illness. Argolaith barely had any recollection of either of them.

Calchas remembered holding the child in front of him as he slept in the saddle, his small golden head bobbing tiredly with each stride. Many of the youngsters cried for weeks after they had left the palace and the comforts of home, but Argolaith never had. He had taken to the lifestyle as naturally as he had taken to walking. It was a life lived constantly out of doors: in the rain, the snow, the sleet, often sleeping on the ground or in the mud. There was constant danger and the threat of attack, and from an early age, Laith had shown a knack for combat, particularly in swordplay, which had been introduced to him as soon as he had come under Calchas's tutelage. He had been carefully schooled and his body had been sharply disciplined, and had grown into an intelligent, healthy young man. He had been given none of the privileges or pampering that being a prince implied; when the troops huddled outside in the freezing cold, Argolaith was right there alongside them. When the others were forced to run barefoot up steep rocks bearing their kit on their backs, Argolaith was expected to be at the front of the line. The other soldiers dutifully referred to him as "Prince Argolaith," but Calchas was quite sure that the boy's grasp of what his title actually meant was dim at best.

While Calchas was thinking, the boy stood quietly in front of him, well aware that when Calchas wished to speak, he would do so. The odd thing about Argolaith was that even with his youthful exuberance and energy, he never moved unless he had to; there was a preternatural stillness about him that was out of place for a boy of his age. It was one of the natural traits that made him a clever fighter and a difficult opponent to best.

"Prince Argolaith," Calchas began. Argolaith cocked his head to one side. There was a strange tone in the General's address. Something was up.

"I have here," Calchas continued slowly, in his low, rumbling voice, "a message from the palace. As you know, your fourteenth birthday has recently come and gone, and with it your tenth year serving with me. Therefore, it seems, your time here in the Meadows with us is at an end. I have been given orders that you shall return immediately with the royal guard back to the palace, where," he finished heavily, "you shall live and begin your royal duties."

Argolaith digested this information. He had seen the group of emissaries ride into camp earlier that day, wearing the royal purple cloaks emblazoned with the family crest of Joymaril, their banners flapping tautly in the wind. They had looked at him strangely as they'd passed, and he'd wondered why. Finally, he nodded. "Yes, sir," was all he said.

Calchas leaned forward, lacing his fingertips together. He was every bit a soldier, and was not given to showing great wells of emotion. But he felt as though he needed to communicate something very important to the boy, and was unsure of how best to do it. "I feel, Argolaith, that I must offer you some advice. You've lived out with us nearly all your life, and I think that you will find that living in the palace is something quite different than you're used to. Here, your title means little—the troops like and admire you because you're a good lad, and you're respectful to your elders. In *general*," he added, with the twinge of a wrinkled smile, which the boy mirrored. "But in the palace, they will love you *only* because of your title. Or because of your face."

My face? Argolaith wondered, somewhat bewildered. *What's wrong with it?*

"My boy," Calchas continued. "Here's the hardest thing. Just because they like you or give you attention for these things does not for an instant mean that you should stop being every inch the young man I have taught you to be so far. They will give you respect and affection without you ever having earned it. But you must *never* stop *trying* to earn it anyway. Do you understand?"

"I think so, sir," Argolaith replied slowly, his handsome brow furrowed.

"Good," Calchas sighed again, feeling older by the second. "I've taught you as much as I can. They will teach you other things: deception, double-dealing, double-crossing. To survive, you must be familiar with these sorts of things, but that doesn't mean that you need to become a virtuoso in them." His weathered eyes met Laith's. "I'm very fond of you, Argolaith. As fond of you as if you were my son," he said, feeling slightly abashed at the sensitive nature of the words. "I have a strong suspicion that you are going to turn out to be a good man. This will be both a gift and a curse to you. I imagine that you will be faced with a great deal of difficulty as time goes on. The world isn't kind to good men or women, Argolaith, but it needs them desperately." He paused. "Do you understand me?"

It was a long time before the boy responded. "Yes, sir," he said softly, and Calchas knew that he had taken the words to heart even if he couldn't completely grasp their meaning.

"Good lad. Dismissed."

Argolaith saluted and walked towards the door, then paused and turned. "Sir," he said hesitantly. "What about Marc? Is he coming, too?"

"Marc will go with you," Calchas nodded with a smile.

Argolaith looked relieved and disappeared out into the gloom of the evening. Calchas stared after him for a long while before turning back to his table and taking out a sheaf of paper to write Prince Argolaith's official letter of introduction to the Queen.

Court life proved to be every bit as baffling as Calchas had made it out to be, and Laith (as he was now known throughout the palace) on more than one occasion found himself fervently thanking his teacher for his few carefully imparted words of advice. The deception, the lying, the backstabbing had all taken him completely by surprise, but he remembered Calchas's words and realized that he must think of them merely as other forms of combat, like swordplay or javelin-throwing, skills to be understood and studied in order to be overcome. Over time, he watched and learned and became a master of diplomacy, of calculated control, never stooping to the level of his opponents but emerging ever more often as the victor in the social skirmishes that were the day-to-day life in the palace. He was envied by his peers for being exceedingly handsome, bright, and well-bred, but he was so generally pleasant and unpretentious that their sniping was mostly unfounded and eventually developed into merely the occasional bad-tempered remark.

Adolescents his own age, Laith soon discovered, were something else entirely. Even when he was only dimly aware of them, they were constantly fluttering around him, whispering behind his back, giggling, flirting with him. To one and all, he was polite, charming, and courteous (seeing no other way to behave under the circumstances), but the fact that they paid so much attention to him without actually bothering to get to know him first never failed to confuse him. (Marc, who was similarly taken aback by the behavior of Laith's admirers in the palace, once remarked to him that "for all they know you could be a crummy idiot, albeit one with good cheekbones.") But still, Laith remembered Calchas's words, and with more than a little childlike innocence, he strove to win each of them over and be friendly to all so that they would have something to whisper about other than the length of his eyelashes. He had been completely blindsided by the amount of attention paid to his looks when he had first arrived. In the Meadows, surrounded by the other soldiers, no one had ever mentioned it. He couldn't understand the uproarious fuss it created at court. His view was very practical: he had been born to two conventionally attractive parents whose facial structures had complimented each other. Besides, he reasoned, people would also stare at him if he had an extra hand growing out of his forehead, so there really was no reason to let any of it go to his ego.

He was reunited with his younger brother, Cade, who, it was said, looked very much more like their mother's side of the family than their father's. Cade, due to early childhood illnesses, was deemed to be too weak for the ten years in the Meadows that had been ordered on Laith, and instead had spent his youth at court, mastering the more social forms of combat which Laith was hurriedly trying to acquire. Cade preferred to read and study, whereas Laith was used to an active outdoor lifestyle and felt claustrophobic if he remained inside the palace for too long. As a result, the two brothers never became terribly close, and if there was a slight twinge of jealousy on Cade's part at having his older, handsomer brother suddenly home and at the center of attention, it went unsaid and unexpressed.

The strangest animal of all those he met—and the most frightening—took the diminutive shape of Laith's cousin Cira. He had first met her on his second day at the palace, just before he was scheduled to be presented officially to the Queen (his father's sister) and the other nobles of the court. He was having trouble finding his way around the palace and still got lost in the vastness of his own apartments; Marc had joked that he needed to leave a trail from the front door to his bedchamber just so he could make it out for breakfast. On the morning before the royal audience, he made a wrong turn down a passageway and found himself face-to-face with his cousin, whom Marc had pointed out to him at an official gathering the previous day. She was as white-blond as his younger brother Cade, with wide-set green eyes like a cat. She was very pretty, but she had a disconcerting maturity and calculating air about her that belied her young years.

The first few seconds of their accidental meeting were very awkward for Laith; she stared at him with a curious look on her face. Laith felt rather like a delicious sweet: something to be devoured rather than savored. It was an odd sensation.

"I'm Laith," he said finally, then corrected himself. "Prince Argolaith, I mean. You're my cousin Cira, aren't you?"

"*Princess* Cira," she corrected, though her mind was obviously still elsewhere.

"I'm afraid I'm lost," he said apologetically. "I must have taken a wrong turn. I'm trying to find the audience chamber."

"I'm going there now," she replied. "We can walk there together if you'd like."

"Thanks," he said, and offered his arm, as he had been taught to do. It was an old-fashioned courtesy, and Cira's eyes glittered as she put her small hand on the hook of his elbow.

Immediately as they entered the hall together, hundreds of heads swiveled towards them, and the courtiers began to whisper and chatter amongst themselves. Laith knew then why she had suggested they walk in together—not out of kindness, but out of concern for her own standing at court. Somehow, his presence had served to boost her status.

Laith swallowed down the indignity of being reduced to a prop for his cousin's ego, and waited before the King and Queen as Cira left him to go stand at the hand of her mother. He made all the proper courtesies and was welcomed coolly by the Queen, his aunt. Then the court converged together, and he was introduced to dozens of nobles, seemingly all at once. Their names ran together in his head until he couldn't remember a single one. All of them commented on what a fine young man he had grown up to be and asked if the stories of his swordsmanship were true. How much like his father he looked! How much like his mother! What good friends Count so-and-so had been with his parents, how sad they were when they had passed away. Perhaps the young prince would want to come to their apartments and play cards at some point?

Laith smiled and was as polite and winning as he could be, all the while forming an assessment of his family. The King, he realized, seemed to be only dimly aware of his surroundings and communicated almost exclusively in monosyllabic grunts. The Queen was cold, and Cira was disconcerting. But there was someone missing…he vaguely remembered that he had another cousin. Where was she? Why was she not introduced to him along with all the others?

He collapsed down into a heap on his bed two hours later (actually, he had to climb *up* onto his bed and then collapse, for it was as tall as he) as Marc looked on in sympathy.

"Rough time?" he asked.

"And where were *you*?" Laith demanded accusingly, his voice muffled in the thickness of the mattress.

"The kitchen, actually," Marc replied easily.

Laith turned his head and glared at him. "I might've known."

"Balls," Marc said loftily, tossing his head. Marc had taken to saying "balls" at every opportunity now that there weren't any commanders around to censor their language. "It's all a part of my bodyguard training. All the gossip, the news, the plots, they get overheard by the servants and brought back to the kitchen, and that's where I find them out. It's for your own good."

"And if you get a meat pasty thrown in for free, so much the better, eh?" Laith muttered.

"Isn't the king great?" Marc asked with a grin.

"Yeah," Laith murmured. He was fairly sure that the King had called him "Leaf" when he'd gone up to be introduced. "Does he have any...hobbies?"

"Gardening," Marc replied vaguely.

"Oh," Laith searched for a response. "Good for him."

"He has to make his own fun with a family like that," Marc agreed. "Did you meet Cira?"

"Yes," Laith replied uncomfortably.

"Isn't she creepy?" Marc asked delightedly.

"Overwhelmingly so," Laith sighed. "Doesn't she have a sister or something?"

"Someone equally as creepy, I'll reckon," Marc shrugged.

"But she wasn't at the reception," Laith furrowed his brow. "Come on, Marc. Let's go for a ride. I need to get some air."

"Sounds good," Marc hopped down from the edge of the bed. He headed for the door, Laith close behind.

The two boys settled into their new life, adjusting to the daily routines of the palace. They still spent as much time as possible outdoors or continuing their training at the Academy, but found that more and more they had to meter off time for Laith to keep engagements and invitations from various people at court. Oddly, many invitations were from parents who had daughters around Laith's age.

One afternoon, Laith made his way to the stables without Marc, who had been called to the Academy for an exam in basic combat. Laith felt rather lonely as he walked along the rows of stalls, missing Marc's amiable chatter about the latest news from the kitchens.

Glossy, wide-eyed equine heads poked curiously out at him as his footsteps echoed along the cobbled corridor. The stables were located at the far back of the palace, where they led into open paddocks and training rings and further up into a vast network of trails cleared through the forest for the royals to ride. Laith stopped to scratch a cheek here and there or stroke an ear or twiddle a silky nose. The horse he rode was getting along in years (he had been given her as a present during his time in the Meadows), but she was still a fine animal: a tall red roan with a no-nonsense head and a willing spirit. He motioned away the groom, who had automatically come forward to saddle her up for him. He liked to do these things himself.

Shortly thereafter, he found himself on one of the back riding paths winding through the forest, shedding all the worries and confusions of the court behind him like a cast-off cloak. This was his favorite trail; it led down across a river and then through the woods into a broad grassy flat that was excellent for a free gallop. Horse and rider wove their way through the mossy trees at an easy canter, speeding through the golden shafts of light sifting through the broad branches of the forest. At the entrance to a small clearing, he squeezed his heels tight against his horse's middle, and she stretched out her stride into a full gallop. Laith bent forward over her neck, rising out of the saddle, enjoying the exhilaration of motion and the wind tearing at his face and clothes.

With a start, he realized that he was not alone. Looking over his shoulder, he saw a horse and rider come streaking out of the woods behind him. His hand went to the scabbard on the front of the saddle, but when he looked back again, he saw to his surprise that the rider was a young girl about his age. She had wild black hair, unlike anything that he had ever seen before, which blew out behind her like a cloud. Her strong face was set into a fierce look of competition.

Grinning, Laith turned and urged his horse on even faster. His mount took the cue and flattened out her neck, reaching for all she was worth, but it was not fast enough. The other horse, a dark bay, came right up alongside them, so close that the riders' stirrup irons were almost clinking against one another. The dark-haired girl tucked her compact body close to her horse's neck and made the slightest flick with her heels. The horse sped past them and vanished into the forest opposite a good five lengths ahead.

Once out of the clearing, Laith pulled up his horse, her sides heaving and her neck slicked with sweat. He was disappointed in losing this impromptu race but was more overcome with curiosity as to the identity of the mysterious rider. *And what a rider!* Laith thought admiringly. She had been perfectly balanced in the saddle, as if the horse was merely an extension of her own limbs.

The girl and her horse were a few yards away, just within the cover of the forest. The girl was walking her horse around in circles; he had apparently become rather over-excited as a result of the race. Laith studied her face. Her coloring was incredibly strange for a Joymarillian: dark skin, wild black hair, and strong dark brows. Her eyes were light gray, rimmed with dark eyelashes like kohl. She wasn't necessarily pretty, but hers was a face full of strength and character. Though her expression was distrusting and even aggressively challenging, Laith liked her right away.

"I want a rematch," he called out, smiling. To his surprise, the smile was not returned, and the face that regarded him remained as antagonistic as ever. "What's your name?" he called out.

Without a word, the rider whirled her horse and sped off into the forest, skimming along the trail and into the brush, leaving an astonished Laith watching her dust filter through the shafts of afternoon sun.

"Athela," Marc said the next day as they walked along one of the balconies. "I asked around, and she fits the description you gave me. I mean, besides, who else here has huge black hair and a chip on their shoulder?"

"So that's her," Laith mused. "I wondered if it was."

Marc glanced at him archly. "Do you *like* her?" he asked teasingly.

"Don't be gross, Marc," Laith said aloofly. "She's my cousin."

"Well, if you wanted to get in another look at her, word is she spends most of her time in the stables," Marc suggested.

"And why doesn't she ever show up at the family gatherings?"

"I guess she's out of favor with the King and Queen. The general feeling is that she's sort of...weird."

"Why?" Laith inquired.

Marc shrugged. "Dunno."

"Dunno" didn't seem like reason enough for Laith to steer clear of her. He resolved to find her again at the nearest opportunity.

That opportunity came later than Laith had anticipated. He happened upon her quite by accident after he had nearly given up hope of running into her again. Laith's horse was standing in its paddock, and he was in the middle of procuring a halter to catch her when he looked over to the corner of the enclosure and was quite startled to see that Athela was sitting only a few feet away from him. She was propped up against a fence post, hunkered down so far that she was almost invisible unless one was standing a short distance away. She was watching her bay horse graze, a soft, peaceful expression on her face and a long piece of grass protruding from her mouth.

Laith fiddled with his horse's halter, taking a long time to unbuckle it and slide the headstall over her ears. He could sense that he was being watched sidelong by his cousin's cold gray eyes.

"Hello," he called to her finally, leading his horse up to the fence. "Want to go for a ride with me?"

"Did Cira send you?" Athela snapped. It was the first thing she had ever said to him. Her voice was deeper than most girls her age. She leaped to her feet. He saw that her boots were old and worn but were well cared for. The underarm of her shirt was ripped and was a few sizes too small for her. He could tell that she had been wearing it for a long time. She stared at him, her eyes wide with challenge.

Laith stopped beside his horse, confused. "Cira?" he asked blankly. "Why would she send me?" *And why would I do what she says?*

Athela glared at him, clearly unsure of whether or not she could trust him. Laith could see that she was growing angry and decided to slowly walk away. She was like an animal: cornered, ready to fight. *And*, he mused, *she may also be frightened, as many cornered animals are. I wonder why.*

"People only like you because you're good-looking!" she yelled at his retreating back.

He stopped and turned around. "That's not true," he retorted evenly. "People also like me because I'm polite and good-natured."

With that, he walked away out of earshot, smiling at having gotten in the last word. For a long while, he could feel the force of her stare on his back.

Her words about Cira had piqued Laith's curiosity to the point where, a few days later, he actually invited Cira to his chambers for lunch. She had leaped at the chance with indecorous enthusiasm and had been sure to spread the word about his invitation to all the other young people of the court so that their jealousy followed her like a cloud wherever she stalked.

By that point, Laith thought that he just about had a handle on his cousin. Mere ambition he could have understood. But there was something different in what was driving Cira: a desire to devour, to consume, a gluttonous need to take and continue taking. If a bauble caught her eye—be it a trinket, a horse, the adoration of the court—she *had* to have it. Laith wondered, even then, whether she would ever be satisfied. He didn't dare imagine the horrors she would commit in pursuit of that satisfaction.

They lunched on his balcony overlooking the lake and the water-falls at the front of the palace. Cira did most of the talking for the first half-hour, chatting away through different stories making their way through the court gossip chain. Most of the tales she told were care-fully designed to flatter her in Laith's eyes. She wasn't stupid, Laith knew. That was the main problem. If she had been stupid, he could have excused at least some of her behavior. She would have been an annoyance, nothing more. But her intelligence added an extra layer of undeniable, calculating cruelty to everything she said or did.

"You have the most *beautiful* apartments," Cira sighed, pushing herself back from the table and staring around. "You'll have to come and see mine sometime."

"That'd be very nice," Laith agreed, regretting it. From inside his chamber, out of Cira's range of vision, he saw Marc make a gagging expression, and bit down a laugh. "I was in the stables the other day," he said conversationally, "and I ran into your sister."

Cira laughed haughtily, and for the first time, a flash of outright cruelty crossed her face. "It's amazing you were able to wash the smell off," she said. Laith's mouth fell open slightly at this, but he masked his surprise.

"Why is she never at parties?" he asked.

"Who'd want her there?" Cira asked, as if it were the most obvious thing in the world.

This is productive, Laith grimaced inwardly. "I'm new here," he said in an apologetic tone. "I'm still trying to figure out who goes where and with whom."

Cira smiled again, pityingly. "Of course. Well, for one thing, she *looks*...I mean, you saw her. Have you ever seen anything as ugly? Her hair looks like a scraggly bush. It's the color of ink. And her eyes are like a snake."

Laith felt the urge to begin defending Athela. She wasn't ugly by any means; she was attractive in a different, less conventional way than Cira. Not overtly feminine, not delicate, but strong and slightly wild. He held his tongue. "Well, looks are hardly everything," he managed.

"Easy for you to say, I'm sure," Cira purred. "Mother and Father never liked her, though. It's a good thing I'm a girl, or else she'd still be the heir to the throne. They changed it, you see, the order of succession. Once I came along."

"But why?" Laith asked, still uncomprehending.

"Bad luck," Cira said, leaning forward. "It's bad luck to have a child who looks like her. One comes along every once in a while, and they always mean bad things. Besides, it's a good thing Mother's rid of her. She's *so* impolite and ill-tempered. She's rude and conceited and is terribly strange."

Laith felt a rising warmth and an incredible sympathy towards his unwanted cousin. *If she's strange and bad-tempered, it's clearly not through her own doing*, he thought. He was beginning to wonder how to ask Cira about Athela's strange words to him when she suddenly beat him to it.

"You know what," she said, with the cruel smile of a child squashing a small insect beneath her thumb, "I had a bit of fun with her a while back. I got two girls to go up to her and make friends with her—took them forever; she's got no trust in anybody."

I wonder why, Laith thought wryly.

"They convinced her that there was a ball she was invited to, and they got her all dressed up in these hideous clothes with all that hair piled on top of her head, and she walked through the middle of the palace and right into the main entrance hall, right in front of everyone at court!" Cira was overcome with mirth at the memory. "You should have heard the laughter....and you know what? She started *crying!*" Cira dissolved into giggles.

Laith wanted to vomit, or at least forcibly eject Cira from his apartments and scrub clean the place where she had sat and the plates from which she had eaten. He resolved firmly to never have anything further to do with her, and his mind was made up that he would try his best to befriend Athela. *If anyone needs a friend,* he thought, *it's her*.

"How...funny," he said stiffly. Cira quelled her laughter as she realized he didn't find it as amusing as she did.

"You had to be there," she suggested. "May I have more wine?"

"You two are *related?*" Marc shrieked in disbelief as soon as Laith had escorted Cira out of his apartment. "I'm tempted to break off my friendship with *you* just by association."

"I know," Laith rubbed the back of his head disbelievingly. "Calchas said this place would be strange, but I had no idea."

Marc was hurrying around the room, pulling on his boots and reaching for his jacket. Laith watched him wonderingly for a few moments. "What on earth are you doing, Marc?"

"To find your cousin, of course!" Marc said, as if it were obvious. "She's gone fifteen years already without having the winning sunshine of my personality beaming through her life! There's not a moment to lose."

"I like your thinking," Laith agreed, catching his jacket as Marc tossed it at him.

"Plus," Marc added contemplatively, "If we happen to irritate that rat of a cousin of yours in the process..."

"...So much the better," Laith concurred with a smile, holding the door open for him. "After you."

Try as they might, Athela's defenses proved to be as impenetrable as a fortress. Every attempt at conversation was gruffly rebuffed; when she saw Laith or Marc approaching, she would glare at them and refuse to respond if spoken to. But the boys were not easily put off. Marc in particular came at "Project Friendly Cousin" with a gusto that surprised even Laith. Though he undoubtedly meant well, Marc's ever-escalating attempts to win over Athela began to cross over into the extreme (leaving flowers and baked goods at the foot of her chamber door) so that after about a month or so of his behavior, Laith was privately convinced that Athela believed Marc to be incurably deranged.

As it turned out, Laith found his way through to his mysterious cousin quite by accident. A new spring came, and with it the Joymaril-lian horse market, one of the biggest non-religious festivals in the city. Horse breeders and dealers brought in their stock all the way from the Meadows; barges came from across the sea, landing at the southern port town and bringing horses up to Joymaril to be sold. The royal family had first pick of all the best horses, and it was expected for Laith to be spending day after day wandering in the city streets (flanked by Marc and two other bodyguards, of course), looking through the newly-erected temporary corrals that choked the alleyways and filled the public plazas.

Laith had never seen anything quite like it, and was almost over-come with excitement each time he stepped foot out of the palace. Here was something vibrant and alive, completely unlike the cold, plotting atmosphere of Joymaril. Every night, pageants and theatrical perfor-mances were staged in the open areas of the city; he and Marc donned cloaks and masks and snuck out of their palace apartments at sundown to watch them. Everything had been decorated with gay pendants and garlands of the newly bloomed spring flowers; the entire city looked like a garden. Auctions were held every hour; horses of all kinds were led trotting and snorting through the cobbled streets: slender hunters for the royal families, draught horses with hooves as big as Laith's head ready to work up in the forests. The most prized animals were festooned with flowers and traditional celebratory paint and were exhibited for all the crowds to see. The entire city was messy and raucous and free, and Laith had never felt more at home since his return.

Knowing Athela's fondness for horses, it was perhaps surprising that Laith had not expected to find her at the market. The celebrations and parades and pageants had temporarily driven her from his mind, which was to be expected for a boy of fifteen. But one afternoon, he and Marc were separated on opposite sides of a street while a procession of two-year-olds was being paraded through the city on the way to the auction block to be sold. The young animals were prancing and tossing their heads, skittishly skirting towards the curbs as people threw flower petals into the golden air. Laith had stepped back, craning his neck and searching for Marc, when his eyes slid to a figure partially concealed in a doorway, eyes staring hungrily out at the street. It was his cousin Athela. She hadn't even bothered to conceal her appearance, and there were no signs of bodyguards anywhere. Part of Laith wanted to stride up to her and scold her for being so careless with her safety; then he remembered that he himself was in disguise and had purposefully slipped past the two adult bodyguards assigned to him. He sidled up alongside Athela, whose rapt expression never wavered as he drew close. She gave no indication that she was even aware of his presence. He followed her gaze out into the street, where one horse in particular was causing quite the commotion.

It was a dapple-gray colt with a jet-black mane and tail and a black muzzle. He was doing his best to completely pull his head away from the two handlers now desperately clinging to his halter. He was crow-hopping and rearing up on his tightly coiled back legs and shaking his head violently back and forth. But, Laith noticed, none of this seemed to be done out of sheer bad manners or fear; it was almost as if the colt was thoroughly enjoying the trouble he was causing. Laith grinned and glanced back over at Athela, whose face was as soft and warm as if she were looking at a kitten playing gently in the sunshine. There was no doubt about it. She was in love.

"Any notion of his breeding?" Laith inquired, hoping that in her altered state Athela wouldn't realize he was actually talking to her.

"He's half desert horse," she replied in her strange, low voice, never taking her eyes from the colt. "His breeder says he's the fastest one he's ever seen. I asked if I could ride him, and he said no one can ride him until they've bought him. He also said that no one's been able to stay on him for longer than five seconds."

Laith bit back a grin, knowing that what might have sounded like a deterrent to other purchasers was a positive boon for Athela. "He's got good, clean lines," he observed. "Short back, strong legs. You going to buy him, then?"

"I can't afford him," Athela mumbled, and suddenly, she seemed to realize that she was conversing with someone. She glanced suspiciously over at him. "Why are you asking?"

Laith shrugged. "Just wondering."

"You're going to buy him for yourself, aren't you?" she demanded, her brow furrowing angrily.

"I don't think so. I prefer a horse I can actually *ride*," Laith replied mildly. "Why can't you afford him?"

"I haven't much money of my own," Athela replied, scuffing her shoe on the ground.

"Can't you ask your parents?"

"They wouldn't give it to me," Athela shrugged, her voice wistful. Her eyes once again slid over to the retreating horse, who was now merrily squealing and attempting to bite a chunk out of his handler's shoulder.

"When's he up to be sold?" Laith inquired.

"Anytime between now and the day after tomorrow," Athela shook her head, then snapped back to look up at Laith, her gray eyes turning icy cold. "Never mind about it. Leave me alone. And tell your friend to stop leaving crap around my door. It's weird."

Without another word, she swept into the street and was swallowed up by the crowd.

Though Laith kept his eye out for Athela all the rest of that afternoon and night, there was no trace of her. He had the distinct feeling that Athela was purposefully avoiding him.

The next morning, he happened to be in a drawing room with the

King, Queen, and Cira (and, of course, the usual bevy of courtiers) when one of the guards came up to the Queen.

"Lady Athela to see you, Your Majesty," he intoned, and immediately the entire room went silent. Laith's head snapped around, and there she was. She was standing awkwardly in the doorway, visibly uncomfortable at being in the room. So dark and otherworldly was her appearance that it again struck Laith how odd it was to think that she was actually related to anyone in the royal family. Her eyes were ducked low, and her hands were twisting behind her back as she shuffled sidelong in the room, occasionally darting glances at her sister and parents as if she expected them to leap out at her. Laith glanced over at Cira and saw that her face was steeped in a haughty, fiendish delight.

"Well?" the Queen demanded, as if irritated that Athela could be presumptive enough to interrupt her after-brunch gossiping.

Athela made an attempt at a curtsy, which looked somewhat like a stork trying to retrieve a fallen object. "I...er...your Majesty...mother," she swallowed and finally, bravely raised her eyes to the others, her cheeks visibly flushing red under their scrutinizing gazes. Laith tried to catch her eye and give her an encouraging smile, but she avoided him. "I was wondering if I could have some money."

Cira let out a barking laugh. "Money?" she shrieked delightedly. "What on earth could *you* want money for? New *clothes?*"

The Queen silenced her with a look, but Cira continued to look smug. "What do you want money for?"

"A horse," Athela blurted out eagerly. "At the market."

"I see," the Queen frowned.

"I'll pay you back!" Athela exclaimed, her words spilling out all at once. She had clearly prepared what she was going to say. "I'll work in the stables and earn the money to pay you back for him. It's just that he's going to be sold, and I...I've simply got..." She glanced around at the bemused faces throughout the room. "I've got to get him," she quavered, again looking down to study the toe of her boot.

"*My* daughter? Work in the stables?" the Queen demanded, as if such a thing were unheard of. "Certainly not. I forbid you to do so."

"But," Athela mumbled, not looking up, "how else will I be able to get him?"

"I'm afraid that means you won't. There are plenty of horses in the stable for you to ride," the Queen said in what outwardly sounded like a kind, comforting tone, masking the sting within. "You are dismissed."

Laith half-expected Athela to burst into tears on the spot (he had seen others their age do so under much less stressful or humiliating circumstances), but she simply performed another awkward half-curtsy and turned, walking dejectedly out of the room, her shoulders hunched over and her head hung low.

"Have you ever *seen* anything quite so pathetic?" Cira crowed as the door shut behind her. "Imagine, working in the *stables*." She turned her green cat's eyes over to Laith, trying to sense what he was thinking. She slunk over to his side and tucked her small hand inside his arm. "Don't you agree, Laith?"

"Quite," he said noncommittally, and Cira grinned like a wolf baring its teeth.

Laith found Athela the next day back in her usual spot out in the paddocks. It was a beautiful sunny day, but to see her, it might as well have been pouring rain down on her head. She had her back to him as he walked up to her, toying with a piece of grass at her feet. He made sure that she heard him approach, offering a casual "Good morning" as he passed. He stopped nearby to inspect his new horse, a four-year-old he had purchased at auction the night before. The horse came from the Meadows and had impeccable lineage; he was jet-black and enormous, his manner quiet and gentle and level-headed. Laith had seen him, and the two had bonded immediately. Laith had decided to buck the usual tradition of naming his horse after a type of music and had instead named him after the ancient Elyrian word for wind, *arfolasth*, (although Marc had pointed out to him that the name really sounded like "Sound-one-makes-when-one-sneezes.")

Arfolasth whickered softly and meandered over to his master as Laith approached and climbed up onto the rail of the paddock to rub his nose. Arfolasth scratched his forehead on Laith's knee, and the boy glanced over to his cousin, half-expecting her to be glaring at him. But though she was watching him, her expression was more sad than anything.

"What happened to your horse?" he inquired.

"Sold," she replied curtly, tossing the two halves of grass onto her boot. Laith clambered back off of the fence and walked over to stand beside her.

"Do you still want him?" he asked.

She squinted up at him, trying to gauge his meaning. "Of course I do, but it's not going to happen." She shrugged a shoulder, visibly trying to overcome her disappointment. "At least I still have the training horses to ride."

Laith studied her. He had never liked her more than he had at that moment. "Athela, I want to be your friend."

The guard went back up. "Why?" she demanded.

Laith shrugged. "Do I need a reason?"

"Why don't you want to be friends with Cira instead?" she hissed.

"Because I don't like her. And because I can't go riding with her without her worrying about getting her shoes dirty," Laith rejoined, and almost saw the flicker of a smile cross Athela's face. "Now, come on."

Athela studied him for a minute. "All right," she said hesitantly, standing up and brushing the grass off her old, ratty riding breeches. "Hang on a moment; I'll go see if any of the training horses are free."

"Wait," Laith stopped her. "I'm going to go ride my new horse, and I need you to be able to keep up."

Challenge flashed in her gray eyes, and they narrowed into slits. "What do you mean? I'm faster—" she began. Laith smiled evenly and inclined his head back towards the barn, where Marc was attempting to lead a dapple gray colt towards them. He was being jerked almost off his feet with every step. His bulk was the only thing preventing him from being tossed into a nearby paddock.

"Oh!" Athela gasped, forgetting herself momentarily and clutching at Laith's arm, her grip vise-like. A moment later, she had leaped forward and was running towards the colt, fairly elbowing Marc out of the way in her eagerness to get to the horse.

"Thank heavens," Marc grunted, rolling his shoulder painfully and handing her the silk leadrope. "Dotty animal nearly jerked my arm out of the socket."

Laith approached, unable to stop himself from grinning. An incandescent smile was beaming forth from Athela's face, and with that in place of her usual glower, she looked enormously pretty. The flighty colt sniffed at her hand and squealed shrilly as she rubbed its dark nose, but he had quieted considerably in her presence. Marc eyed the animal warily as Athela looked breathlessly over to Laith.

"You bought him!" she exclaimed. "I'm almost glad it was you; at least now I can see him. Can I ride him sometime?"

"Whenever you want," Laith shrugged with a pleased grin. "He's yours."

At this, a wash of almost heartbreaking hope flooded her eyes. Her mouth positively fell open, but a moment later it closed again, and her expression hardened suspiciously. "I'll pay you for him. I don't care what my mother says; I'll work in the stables whether she wants me to or not."

"He's a gift," Laith told her firmly.

"I don't want to be in your debt."

"You're not in debt if someone gives you a gift."

"What's the gift *for?*" she demanded.

He considered. "Your birthday."

Her eyes narrowed. "That was last *winter.*"

"Late birthday, then." He smiled winningly. Athela looked from him to Marc (who was beaming as well) and then back to the horse. Slowly, Laith could see it begin to dawn on her that she had been given something she desperately wanted with no strings attached. That someone had been kind to her without any ulterior motive. She swallowed and began scratching the horse between its ears, which pleased the colt so much that he began pawing the ground up with his sharp hoof. She let out a deep laugh of pure happiness and turned back around to the boys.

"I'm sorry if I was..." she said hesitantly.

Laith waved his hands dismissively.

"You are...?" she asked, turning to Marc.

"Marc," he replied, twinkling his fingers, smooth face beaming. "Guy who's been leaving crap around your door."

She actually laughed and looked back at the horse. "Aria," she said firmly. "He was one of the first great racehorses. I'm going to name him Aria." She looked back at the others. "You up for a ride, then?"

"Be right back...erm...are you sure he's broken in and everything?"

Marc inquired, looking at Aria with some concern. The colt, as if he had understood, gave a hearty spontaneous buck then stood still, eagerly looking around at them as if expecting a reward. Athela patted his neck, positively delighted.

"I don't think it's going to make much difference with this fellow, unbroken or not," Laith murmured slowly. Marc raised his hands to the sky in an expression of prayer, then jogged off towards the stables.

"Here, give me a leg up; I'm going to run him up the field!" Athela said eagerly. Laith looped the leadrope around the halter, making a pair of makeshift reins for her, then moved to the horse's shoulder where Athela was waiting. He cupped her knee in one hand and threw her lightly onto Aria's back. The horse reared and Laith dodged neatly out of the way, but before the gray could completely burst forward into a dead run, Athela had one heel stuck in his belly and had tightly pulled his head around so that Aria found himself making tiny circles around Laith.

"He's a handful," Laith observed, dodging a dark foreleg and attempting not to get run over.

"He's wonderful," Athela laughed, her black hair tumbling down from its comb, falling loose over her shoulders. Her face was alight. They made a few more loops before she managed to pull him to a quivering, eager halt. She had quiet hands and a steady seat, and Laith could see that her sense of calm would do well for the horse. She patted the dappled neck and looked down at Laith, who had his arms folded over his chest and was smiling serenely. "Laith..." she trailed off, clearly unused to having to express her feelings. "Laith, I...he..." She thought for a moment. "Thank you."

Laith shook his head. Those two words meant more to him than any of the false compliments he had received from anyone in the palace. He patted Aria's shoulder and flashed a grin up at his cousin. "I'll get my horse. Don't wait up."

"Don't worry, I won't!" she exclaimed. In another instant, she had wheeled Aria around, dug her heels into his flanks, and before Laith had time to blink, horse and rider had flashed across the green field and were flying up like a gray bird into the hills.

CHAPTER FIFTEEN

It was a strange night, the kind that kept people tossing and turning restlessly in their beds. An unusually warm wind was blowing down the streets, and the silver slip of the moon hung low over the rooftops as if it, too, were afraid to show its face. Something was afoot. Tarr could feel it in the prickling hairs on the nape of his neck and the way he found his hands subconsciously clutching themselves into fists whenever he wasn't thinking. For a while, he had been pretending to sleep, but when he realized that Rane was in the grip of the same insomnia, they had both got up, put on dressing gowns, and Rane had gone downstairs to make some tea. Tarr wished that he had a window to open to let in some fresh air. It was overbearingly stuffy in their safehouse. He felt smothered.

He and Rane were sitting back in their room, silently sipping disinterestedly at their tea, when there was a soft knock at the door. Tarr was surprised to find that he had almost expected the interruption. He rose immediately and went to the door where he was startled to find Si, who looked ashen and shaken.

"Are you all right?" Tarr inquired, immediately ushering him into the room and protectively shutting the door.

"Yes," Si replied, clearly trying to get a hold of himself. "I had that dream again. The one with Marc."

Tarr immediately remembered the dream he was talking about, but he urged Si to recount it to him again as Rane sat beside him on the bed, resting a comforting arm around the boy's shoulders.

"We're seated at a table, and Marc...he's not Marc anymore, he's, like, evil. He pours something into Laith's goblet, and Laith drinks it then falls over, and I know he's dead," Si recounted in a hollow, empty-sounding voice. "You said that I should come and tell you if anything happened again."

"You were quite right to," Tarr assured him comfortingly. "You haven't been anywhere near that medallion again, have you?"

"No," Si shook his head, frowning. "Not at all. And it wasn't as bad this time. Last time it was...*real*...this time it felt more like just a dream."

"But it was the same vision?" Rane inquired.

Si nodded, looking troubled. "Exactly the same."

"You think you'll be able to go back to sleep?" Tarr asked.

Si shrugged, then wrinkled his freckled nose. "Something's...a bit weird tonight, isn't it?"

Tarr laughed gently. "Yes, Si, things are a bit weird. Who knows? Could be an odd southern wind..."

The suggestion of strange winds seemed to do little in the way of comforting Si, but he gave a firm nod and rose to his feet. "Don't worry. I can fall asleep anywhere," he announced gamely. This was true. Tarr had literally once seen Si fall asleep in the middle of a riot.

Si strode from the room with a "Goodnight" that was hearty to the point of being bravado. Rane watched him go affectionately and stood, pausing to run her fingers through Tarr's hair. "There's some sort of dark force at work tonight," she murmured, and though neither Tarr nor Rane were prone to romanticism or overreacting, Tarr was inclined to feel that she was right. "Are you hungry?" Rane asked. Tarr wasn't, but he was feeling cooped up inside their room. He stood and stretched and, just for good measure, checked that the cupboard containing the medallion was securely locked, just the way he had left it. Satisfied that it was safe, he followed Rane out the door, noticing that she was incongruously wearing her sword buckled over her nightgown. Even in his anxious state of mind, the sight of it eked a small affectionate smile.

The two of them traipsed out the bedroom door, waving hello to the hall guard on duty, and went down the stairs once more to the kitchen. Tarr set about collecting the used tea leaves into a small pile to brew another pot as Rane cut two pieces of bread, even going so far as to slice two precious sliver-thin pieces of cheese to lay atop it. They ate in silence, leaning beside the iron stove for warmth. With his spare hand, Tarr thoughtfully toyed with a strand of Rane's auburn hair.

Then there was a sound, a sound so slight it could easily have been someone turning over in bed or a mouse scurrying along one of the wooden floorboards, but Rane was instantly on the alert. Her eyes focused on the room directly above. Their room. Her hand flew to the hilt of her sword. She silently waved Tarr back, indicating that he should follow her at a safe distance. She crept quickly and silently through the kitchen and up the stairs back to their room, Tarr creeping forward as fast as he dared, not wanting to make a sound that would give away her position. She crouched low like a fox, out of the expected eyeline, and nudged the door open. She peered inside, her sword already half-drawn. Tarr swallowed, hoping that his heart wasn't making too much noise as it drummed within his chest. She crept around the corner and vanished within. A split second later she reappeared, her face completely ashen.

"The medallion," she said. "Gone."

Tarr leaped to his feet and pushed past her, all pretense of stealth gone, and darted into the room. The cabinet door was shut as he'd left it, but when he tried the handle, he found that it was unlocked and the contents within had vanished.

"I checked it," he whipped around to Rane, searching for validation. "I checked it, and it was locked."

"I know," she said grimly. "There's someone here. In the safehouse."

"You go alert the hall guards," Tarr told her. "I'll wake the others."

Both of them bolted off in opposite directions. Tarr went first to Laith's room, where he found the prince already awake. He was stretched out on his bed, fully dressed, his dark eyes boring holes into the ceiling. His sword was within reach. He swung upright as Tarr entered.

"Trouble?" he asked, seeing the expression on Tarr's face.

"Someone took the medallion," Tarr told him flatly. "Someone is in the house."

Laith was immediately on his feet, and an instant later was jogging down the hall to Marc's room to get him up. Tarr went to Archer and Athela, both of whom, he was surprised to find, were already awake as well. They met in the hallway beside Si's door. Rane joined them, her jaw set in a thin, strained line.

"Have the guards seen anything?" Laith demanded.

"Nothing," she replied. "No sign of anyone. No forced entry. All the outer doors are still bolted and guarded from the inside."

Laith narrowed his dark eyes and swiveled around to look at the others. "Marc, you've got to wake Si and warn him that he should be on his guard."

Marc nodded and disappeared into Si's room. A few moments later, they heard the comforting low tones of his voice.

"I've looked around; I can't see anything either. No signs of forced entry." Archer told him with a twinge of frustration. His white torso was glowing gold in the lamplight. "For the love of the fates, we have *got* to change safehouses."

"They can't have escaped," Athela pointed out.

"We don't have evidence they were even here in the first place," Tarr pointed out. "Except that the medallion was *definitely* here and then was *definitely* gone in the space of about five minutes."

"Split up," Laith ordered tersely. "Search every inch of the place. Marc will stay here to guard Si. If someone has found their way inside, our entire security may be completely shot."

The Strikers did as they were bid, fanning out silently down the hall. Tarr was reminded of a game he used to play at night back in the forest with the other young Ashans. Two opposing teams would try to cross enemy lines to steal a prize and take it back to their own side. It was only played in the dead of night with no moon, so the players were left wondering if the figures they dimly saw flitting about in the black trees were allies or enemies. Tarr had never much cared for the game then, and didn't particularly care for it now. The way the safehouse was structured, with rooms and hallways stacked on top of one another to the right and the stairwell leading straight through from top to bottom on the left, made it nearly impossible for Tarr to keep track of the location of his friends. He picked his way rather stupidly along the dark hallway, fully aware that if he were pitted against an armed, dangerous intruder, the battle would be short and the result not in his favor.

He came to the end of the hallway and tentatively threw open the door to the last room, Athela's. There was nothing—at least, he *thought* there was nothing. There was a dark shadow in the corner that could easily be the shape of a man. He fumbled around frantically for a lamp and finally found it, cranking the oil up until the room was bathed in the eerie, dancing light. There was nothing. Tarr had been mistaken. But the dark, prickly feeling on the back of his neck refused to go away.

When he headed back out into the hallway, he was relieved to see Athela coming towards him. Her gray eyes were flashing angrily, and she was stalking the corridor like a panther on the prowl. The familiar sight of her displeasure (especially now that it was being channeled towards some other entity) was almost comforting to Tarr. If anything large and ominous leaped out at them, Athela would be more than pleased to immediately chop said large, ominous thing into tiny bits. He decided to stick with her for the time being.

"Nothing?" he asked.

"Nothing," she growled. "I hate this."

Tarr hated it, too, though not for the same reasons. Tarr was afraid, undeniably afraid, and worried for the safety of his friends. And the dread of what would happen if the medallion was not recovered, if a power of that magnitude fell into the hands of the wrong individual, had not yet fully settled on him. Athela, on the other hand, hated the situation because she did not have anything tangible to hack apart or verbally abuse.

Suddenly, there was a yell. Below them, far below. A cry of alarm, of fear, but not (Tarr was relieved to hear) of pain. Athela whipped around so fast she nearly struck Tarr in the face with her flying hair, then went darting down the stairs like a hound on the scent. She leaped clean over the side railing and hurled herself haphazardly through the air to land on the lower floor's landing. Tarr took a slightly more conventional route and went down the stairs, leaping them four at a time with his long legs.

The ruckus was centered on the main floor, right by the kitchen. The small area was crowded with bodies. Tarr arrived, panting, sliding to a halt where he saw that all the others, save Marc and Si, had gathered after the alarm had been sounded.

"What's up?" he asked breathlessly.

"Ella saw something," Laith said curtly, motioning with his head towards one of the hall guards, whom Tarr recognized as one of their more levelheaded, seasoned fighters, not given to flights of fancy.

"What was it?"

"A figure, cloaked. Couldn't tell if it was a man or a woman. Saw it at the end of the hallway, then it disappeared," she reported in her economic way.

Something unpleasant began to nag at the back of Tarr's mind. He slowly turned and stared back up the staircase. He remembered something...

"What, Tarr?" Archer asked sharply.

"I don't know..." Tarr replied slowly.

Up in Si's room, Marc was standing at the alert directly behind the door with his broadsword out. If anyone attempted to force entry, he could easily kick the door in and attack them with an onslaught of strength. Si was perched like a nervous bird right at the tip of his bed. The tension was so immense that even though Si wanted to, he didn't dare speak to distract Marc's attention. He strained his ears, trying to listen for anything like footsteps or someone creeping up the passageway outside. But he heard nothing. *Maybe it's nothing*, he thought to himself. *Maybe the medallion was stolen a while ago, and Tarr just dreamed that he locked the cabinet door.* But this didn't seem likely, and there was something about the night, something about the atmosphere of the room, that refused to allow him to relax. He tried to settle himself by keeping his eyes trained on Marc. As long as Marc stood beside him, nothing bad would happen to him. He was certain of it.

All of a sudden, he felt something at his side, something cold, as if he were sitting next to a block of ice. He slowly looked over, expecting nothing. Instead, he felt himself releasing a terrified cry.

"It's *them!*" he screamed.

It was the stranger—the cloaked figure he had seen in the street, whose scarlet hood was lined with black and who bore the star tattoo on their forehead. Si squinted his eyes shut and darted back, sure it was a dream, but when he opened them back up, the person was still there, and in their hand—*the medallion!*

Marc had frozen for a fraction of a second at the sound of Si's cry, but after only an instant, he gave a low growl and barreled towards the figure. Quicker, quicker than he would have thought possible, the emaciated, liver-spotted hand darted out and threw the chain of the medallion around Si's neck. Si was caught in the moment between frozen fear and galvanizing motion, and he turned to Marc, his childish gray eyes filled with overwhelming fear.

"Marc!" he cried and reached out a hand. Marc, mid-attack, stretched out to touch him.

But faster than both of them, faster than Marc's eyes could register, the stranger snaked out their pale, spotted hand and took Si's arm. With nothing more than a whisper, the two of them disappeared into thin air.

Marc lost his balance and crashed headlong into the opposite wall, disoriented and frustrated. When he shook himself and looked back up at the empty room, the guttural, anguished howl he let out froze the rest of the household in their tracks and sent a physical chill racing up Tarr's back.

"*Marc!*" Laith shouted, and like a rolling thundercloud they all charged up the stairs to Si's room. Laith nearly ran headlong into Marc, who was swinging out of Si's bedroom with a wild, almost unrecognizable look on his face.

"They *took* him!" Marc bellowed. "Hurry, not a moment to lose; they might still be around here somewhere! We can still find him!"

"Took him?" Ella asked, bewildered. "How? Who?"

But the others didn't even waste the time to ask that question. They ran off in groups, rushing from room to room, opening closet doors and cupboards, and tearing the place apart in the hopes of finding Si. But there was no trace of him anywhere. Tarr went about the search almost halfheartedly. With each passing second, a part of him realized that Si was gone. He had been taken, and Tarr had absolutely no idea how they were going to get him back. And what was worse was that whoever had taken him had Si, *and* they had the medallion.

After the house had been combed from top to bottom, they reconvened in the living area on the bottom floor. Laith called the hall guards together, where they stood at attention before him. Though he was in his bare feet, loose pants, and a nightshirt, Laith had a way of commanding their respect as though he were fully outfitted in battle armor. "We're putting the entire Striker force in this city on high alert," he told them sternly. "Ella, I want you to immediately go and get Ari. Find him, wherever he is, and I want you to personally tell him what has happened. I need to see him as soon as he can be reached and brought here."

"Yes, m'Lord," she nodded and flew from the room.

"Vynce," he ordered the other, "You must immediately organize a search party and start combing the streets for Si or any sign of those who might have taken him."

"Tall, old, in a cloak with red lining. Tattoo on their forehead," Marc told them dully. Tarr could almost feel the waves of frustration and anger radiating out of him.

"I do not want a single moment of time wasted. You understand? For all we know, these people want to kill the heir of Morthenstar, and they have him directly in the palms of their hands." Laith's voice left no room for misinterpretation. "But remember, you *cannot let anyone outside the immediate Striker guard know the details of what has happened*. If civilians or, the fates forbid, Kagai learns that Si has been...abducted...it could be absolutely catastrophic for our cause. The enemy would think us crippled. The people would lose faith. Do you understand me?"

"I understand completely." In another moment, Vynce and the other two hall guards were gone.

With only the Strikers left in the room, the atmosphere seemed to deflate. Archer collapsed in a chair, rubbing the sides of his angular nose. Marc began to pace back and forth like a caged animal.

"We'll get him back," Athela assured him.

"You don't know that," Marc snapped, the first time Tarr had ever heard him speak so harshly. "He's just a boy."

"You've trained him well," Archer pointed out, though they all knew that if Marc had been overcome by the mysterious figure's power, there was nothing Si could do against them, training or no. "Maybe he'll steal his way out," Archer reasoned. "If there's one thing that boy has up his sleeve, it's trickery."

"How could anyone just *disappear* like that?" Marc demanded.

"Like, out a trapdoor?" Athela wrinkled her nose.

"Into thin air!" Marc exclaimed with a short movement of his arm, so violent that he nearly sent a nearby chair toppling over.

"Like Si told us," Rane pointed out quietly. "The day that he felt something and hid. He saw the person you described, Marc. And he said that they vanished into thin air."

Silence hung over them for a moment. "We should've..." Athela began.

"We have *nothing*," Tarr said tersely, "*nothing* that can fight against that sort of power." He hesitated to use the word "magic," but the others sensed his meaning.

"That sort of thing...this sort of power...was supposed to have died out years ago," Athela said dubiously.

"So what, the effect of the medallion on Si, that can all be explained *logically*?" Laith asked, spreading his hands. "If you have any plausible theories, I would love to hear them. I certainly don't have any."

"This is beside the point," said Athela, clearly itching to take some sort of action. "We have to be out searching. Disappearing into thin air or not, Laith's right; we can't waste any time. How do we know how far they can go? Maybe they can only disappear for a short distances. Come on. We'll find them."

The others filed out the door, Marc fairly bursting past them. Tarr trailed behind them at the end. The others would be faster, more thorough than him. They had been trained for this sort of tracking. Tarr needed time to think.

The search that ensued was so complete that there was not a single loyal Striker fighter who was exempt. They kept the news of Si's abduction a secret and instructed their troops instead to search for any sign of the strange scarlet figure. The Striker forces complied, hunting through every attic to every cellar that they could. Those who worked undercover used their day jobs to entreat entry into strange houses, to look at the foundations of the buildings for false bottoms, hidden rooms, or antechambers where Si could have been stolen away. But the search was fruitless. Si had vanished like a gust of wind, and there were no traces of the person who had stolen him. No one recognized the description of his abductor or had heard tales of any such individual being sighted in town.

Tarr pored over book after book, but nothing was revealed. He looked in every tome of Kagaian lore he could come across, but there was no mention of the type of mysterious figure Marc had seen. Marc, for his part, had barely rested for more than an hour from the moment Si had vanished. On two occasions, he had been half-dragged back to the safehouse by his soldiers, too spent and physically and emotionally exhausted to go any further. Tarr ached for him, and his heart ached for Si, trapped and alone somewhere. He had to be alive. Tarr knew that he had to be alive.

He hoped he was alive.

They gathered back together three days later at Orion, which had been closed (at least according to the outside world) for minor repairs. Security at the club was at an all-time high, and each of the Strikers came armed and prepared, even Tarr. Every square inch of street in a three-block radius was being carefully watched, and an elaborate warning system was set up. After Si's abduction, Tarr had taken the Strikers' security firmly into his own hands and was taking no chances.

Orion's open central room had been closely curtained off so that no one on the street outside would be able to guess that there were people within. Only a single table had been set; the others were swept clean, with their chairs balancing upside down on their tops. Marc was the last to draw up a chair. Khan had done his best to scrounge up a good amount of food for the Strikers' meal, but even the successful club was showing signs of the lean times.

They passed around plates of bread and cheese and the last remnants of the fall fruit harvest. A large, sweet pat of butter was shared between all who sat at the table. A bottle of wine sat at the center of the table. The Strikers were joined by Ari, Khan, and Ella, a roaming security detail passed in and out of the central curtained room. Tarr kept track of them and thought he had seen roughly eight or so different security officers. It was completely secure, and yet something was bothering him. Something that reminded him of Si...though to his immense frustration, he could not identify exactly what it was.

"All right, Ari," Laith said tiredly, "better give us your report."

Ari proceeded to tell them precisely what Tarr had supposed he would. Yes, his soldiers had been thorough in their search; no, they had not recovered any sign of Si. Tarr felt his mind wandering away from the conversation. Something was familiar about their setting, almost as if he had seen it before.

Off to one side of the room, Tarr saw a young security guard come rushing out of the curtains and stride up to Ella. The two began to speak in low tones, with the younger guard looking urgent and Ella trying to brush her off. Tarr was interested.

"Excuse me," he mumbled for a moment and pushed his chair away from the table. Most of the rest of them were involved in the conversation with Ari and paid Tarr little attention as he left. Tarr sidled casually up to the two guards, who immediately straightened with respect as he approached them.

"What's going on?" he asked.

"Nothing at all, sir," Ella answered him. Tarr turned away and looked expectantly at the younger guard, his eyebrows raised. She bit her lip and glanced down at her feet.

"I thought...I thought someone unlatched the kitchen door just now," she whispered. "Back there in the kitchens. It was locked only a moment before, I'm sure of it."

Ella shook her head sternly. "There are people in the kitchens preparing food. Of course, people may latch or unlatch the kitchen door."

"But we had orders to keep it closed!" she persisted.

"It's all right," Tarr said, and the gentleness of his manner had a visibly soothing effect on the two people before him. "I'll let the others know. It's probably nothing, but it's always better to be safer. Especially now."

He turned and walked slowly back towards the table, taking in the scene before him. They all sat at the long rectangular table, and a server was coming to refill the main wine jug at the center of the table and bring in a load of freshly baked rolls. Ari and Archer, unsurprisingly, were arguing about the merits of expanding their search outside the city limits, and the Strikers seemed divided on what exactly was the best course to take. Marc reached out to the new bottle of wine and began to pour some for Laith, who was sitting to his right and was deep in conversation. Tarr watched him carefully, the wheels in his brain clicking away. He couldn't shake the strange feeling that he had been there before, like someone had described this meeting to him as a bedtime story long ago.

Marc put down the bottle silently, and Laith reached for the cup, ducking his head in a quick, soundless thank-you to Marc. He brought it to his lips. Tarr turned and looked back over his shoulder to the kitchens. Then everything came together, and his heart nearly stopped. He started forward but the wine cup was already at Laith's lips.

"*Archer, Laith has been poisoned!*" Tarr screamed in Ashan, and Archer cast only a split-second look at the prince before bolting out of his chair and out of the room. The others were frozen in their seats. Athela's mouth fell open in shock.

"Tarr—" she began.

Laith only managed a quizzical look towards the place where Archer had vanished before he looked straight ahead again, his body giving an involuntary shudder. And, in a horrific torrent, blood spurted from his mouth and down his chin, and he toppled back in his chair, the wood crashing and splintering beneath him.

"Laith!" Athela shrieked and dived across the table to her cousin. Marc scrambled across the floor to get to him, but Laith cried out as if the pain he was experiencing within was more excruciating than anything any of the others could possibly imagine. The room was gripped in a state of abject pandemonium. Guards drew swords but stood around, looking completely lost.

"Search the entire club!" Ari bellowed, drawing his own sword and charging out of the room. Laith's cry was cut short as another burble of black bile, and blood poured out of his throat. His body began to shake wildly, and Tarr realized very quickly, as if it were a punch to the stomach, that Laith was about to die, and what was more, he was going to die very fast. The prince's face had faded to a bleached white, as pale as Archer's, and his brown eyes were rolled up in his head, his body bent like a bow as his limbs flailed wildly on the ground, blood gurgling out of his mouth more and more with every breath that tried to escape.

Athela was crying but didn't seem to notice it. She was lying over her cousin's body, her teeth gritted, trying to stifle his thrashing, and Marc had thrown himself over one of Laith's arms, his hand behind Laith's head to prevent him from smashing the back of it open as he bucked and pitched on the floor.

"What do we do?" Athela cried. "Please, please, what are we going to do?"

"Laith!" Marc yelled, but Laith was clearly beyond all hearing by that point.

Where's Archer? Tarr screamed in his mind, and at that very moment, his brother burst into the room and elbowed Rane roughly aside, shoving Athela back with one of his arms. He had a small bottle in his hand, as well as some black powder in a vial.

"Hold his arms down," Archer yelled, and the others obeyed. Tears were beginning to stream down Tarr's cheeks without his even realizing it. Marc's shoulders were shaking, but he had the look of deadly focus in his eyes Tarr recognized when he was fighting. Archer sat atop Laith's stomach and lifted his head up as another wave of blood came pouring out of the prince's mouth, soaking his hands and his clothing, but Archer barely seemed to notice. He freed one of his hands and picked up the vial of dark liquid, pulling the stopper out with his teeth and pouring the liquid down Laith's throat, closing his mouth and forcing him to swallow. Laith choked and retched, his body still thrashing. Archer then took a large pinch of the powder, grabbed Laith's tongue, and sprinkled some on the back of it, closing his mouth again. Laith screamed in absolute agony and fell back, his body writhing so hard that Archer was nearly thrown off of him.

"You're killing him!" Athela screamed, beating at Archer with one of her fists, but Tarr pulled her away from him, exerting all his strength to restrain her. "Archer, stop it, you're killing him!" she sobbed again, giving up fighting as she watched her cousin's convulsions. But Archer paid no notice to her and merely laid one of his hands on Laith's chest, muttering something under his breath. Tarr couldn't hear exactly what was being said, but Archer was clearly either praying or trying to coax Laith back from the brink. Tarr didn't know what to do; he just clung to Athela's shaking shoulders as much for his own support as her restraint. Perhaps Archer had merely given him another dose of poison to make his end go faster, spare him what little pain he could. Laith dead—he couldn't even conceive of it.

Laith's spasms subsided slightly, and he began to grow still. His arms slumped limply to the side, and Marc gently released his hold. Tarr could barely stand to look at him.

"Oh, no," Marc said, his face going gray. "Oh, no, oh, *please,* no." He frantically scooted up beside Laith, fairly pushing Archer off of him, and gathered the prince up in his arms. "Oh, Laith, I'm so sorry…" He bent his head down into Laith's chest, his shoulders shaking. Laith's beautiful head lolled sadly back on his bent neck, his eyes half-open, pupils rolled back, his chin and chest stained with dark black blood.

Tarr looked over to Archer, who was watching motionless, expressionless, as if what he was feeling couldn't possibly be translated into any sort of outward emotion. The white knuckles bunched and released on the floor. Athela grew quiet, and Tarr loosened his grip. She slid forward only an inch or so before slumping slightly as if someone had knocked her wind out. She stared at her cousin, gray eyes sightless.

Suddenly, Marc's head shot up. "Archer!" he whispered huskily, hurriedly. "Archer, I hear something!"

The Ashan straightened up and shot forward, pushing himself in front of Marc and laying his head against Laith's chest. It was faint, distant, and irregular, but there was an unmistakable sound. Archer could have let out a triumphant whoop but stopped himself. Athela's eyes had widened, her face heartbreakingly hopeful.

"I thought I was too late," he told them. "I thought he had—but he's alive. There's a heartbeat. There's a heartbeat!" He could have laughed. He leaned back and ripped Laith's shirt open. There was the shallowest hint of a breath, a millimeter rise and fall. Archer leaned him up and scooped him into his arms. "We have to get him upstairs," he informed the others. "Got to get him upstairs

"He's alive?" Athela asked blankly, as if she could barely believe it to be true.

"Yes," Archer said.

A few of the kitchen staff, who had heard the commotion and had rushed into the grisly scene, came hesitantly forward, carrying pitchers of water and fresh cloth. Athela grabbed water and a rag and began cleaning the blood from Laith's face and chest. He was still pale as a sheet, but no longer had the look of death on his face.

"How did you know?" Marc swung around to face Tarr, still visibly in a state of shock. "How did you know the wine had been poisoned? You knew as soon as he took a sip."

"Si warned us," Tarr told him, his voice shaking. "You remember the vision he had? Where he thought that Marc had poisoned Laith?"

The others stared at him.

"He told me that in his dream he saw you uncork a vial of poison at a dinner table, pour it in Laith's wine glass, and hand it to him, then Laith died," Tarr told him.

"I didn't poison anything!" Marc exclaimed, more bewildered than indignant.

"I know that. But you poured him the poisoned wine today and handed it to him. It just...the whole thing seemed *wrong*, somehow. It was almost like Si was right behind me, trying to tell me what was going on."

Marc shook his head. They made their way slowly up to the office above the café and laid Laith down on a mat, stripping him of his clothes and wrapping him in a warm blanket. His lean body was covered in sweat, and he was beginning to shake. Rane knelt beside his head and placed her cool hand on his forehead, brushing his short, sandy hair back. They stood in silence around him for a moment and watched his chest rise and fall. The sight of it comforted them.

"It's going to be rough, isn't it?" Rane asked Archer, who nodded mutely. "What was the poison?"

"Some sort of Erifax extract," Archer shook his head darkly. "Fast. Brutal. Effective."

"And how did *you* happen to have the antidote?" Athela demanded accusingly.

Archer glanced up at her. "Things like this used to be my stock in trade, remember?" he asked mildly. "I always carry basic medical supplies and a kit of antidotes at the bottom of my quiver. Standard procedure."

"This doesn't seem like an ordinary poison," Athela said darkly.

Archer shrugged. "It's not common, but it was quite popular with a friend of mine long ago, to the point where I just started carrying the antidote around with me anyway. She always..." he trailed off into silence, and his eyes became glassy. He glanced over his shoulder as if he thought to find someone there behind him.

"You know," Athela accused him, her voice in a deathly growl. "You *know* who did this."

Archer made no reply, but his expression said it all. Marc's shocked demeanor shook away, and he sprang to his feet, his ice-blue eyes boring into Archer with barely contained fury. "*Who was it?*" Marc demanded icily, and Tarr was almost sure that Marc would have easily struck his friend to get the answer.

At that moment, Ari burst through the door. "We have tracks," he told them breathlessly, craning his neck over to see Laith. "Is he—"

But Marc was already pushing past him out the door. Archer turned away from Laith and leaped to his feet. "Stop," Athela ordered, and Archer paused. "You'll never be able to call him off of whoever did this. Nothing, not hell or high water, can stop him."

"You could," Archer told her.

"Why would I *want* to?" Athela demanded, rising angrily to stand before him, her gray eyes flashing like thunderclouds and her dark curls spilling over her shoulders. The front of her dress was covered in her cousin's blood. "Whoever it was nearly *killed* Laith. Does that mean anything to you at all?"

"How *dare* you even ask me that?" Archer snapped furiously, meeting her stride for stride.

"Because you're doing a fairly good impression of not giving a shit at all, Archer!" Athela spat, her hands balled into fists at her side. "Who was it that did this?"

Archer was silent but did not break his golden gaze away from her. Athela turned away from him in utter disgust, refusing to say a single word more. She knelt beside Laith and took his large hand in hers. Rane was pointedly refusing to look at Archer either and was crushing herbs with a mortar and pestle, speaking in low tones to one of the kitchen maids who had come up to help. Archer looked helplessly from Athela's rigid back to Laith's ashen face, to Tarr.

"Do not desert me too, brother," he said in Ashan. "It is not so simple."

"I will not desert you, brother," Tarr replied.

In another moment, Archer was gone, the door shut fast behind him.

At the sound, Athela leaped to her feet, grabbed a cup of water on a nearby table, and hurled it furiously at the wall opposite, where it crashed to the floor. The kitchen maid visibly jumped at the sound but ducked her head, wanting to avoid any offshoots of Athela's wrath. Tarr looked at his friend as she stared, nostrils flaring and chest heaving, after Archer. Tarr unfolded his long legs and walked beside her. Even in her greatest rage, Athela would do nothing to harm Tarr.

"Laith is alive," he assured her quietly.

"How could he?" Athela breathed, and her words caught in her throat. Tarr could almost feel the pain radiating from her.

"I believe," Tarr said slowly, "I *truly* believe that Archer is trying to do the right thing."

Athela snorted. "The *right* thing." She shook her head and turned to look down at Laith's dormant figure. "He'll never be able to call off Marc. Not after he's had to deal with Si, and now this..."

"That is up to him, and it is up to Marc," Tarr told her. "We must stay here with Laith and make sure that he is able to come through this. And we've got to start planning for what's to come. Laith will not be able to fight for a long time. We've got to think of a place we can keep him. We've got to move safehouses immediately."

Athela nodded slowly, the wheels in her mind almost visibly turning. She sat back down beside Laith and placed her hand flat on his belly, staring at it as it slowly rose and fell.

Archer ran faster than he had ever run before, hurtling through the twisting alleyways and around corners like a speeding arrow. Luckily, Marc hadn't bothered to cover his tracks and the trail was an easy one. Archer's arms pumped with every stride he took, his keen yellow eyes honed in on the footprints in the freshly thrown mud. He was lucky; dark clouds were gathering ominously over the city, and it seemed as if the whole place was preparing for a terrific winter storm. Windows were bolted, and the few people who were out and about were hooded and too preoccupied with their own work to pay him any heed.

The trail banked suddenly to the right, and Archer skidded to a halt. There, far away at the end of an alleyway, he could see two small figures locked in a frenzied, anguished motion. Praying that he wasn't too late already, Archer took off towards them.

Kai, probably out of desperation, had allowed herself to be cornered at the dead end of one of the alleyways. She was crouching down, as dangerous as a baying dog; her lips were drawn up over her teeth in a ferocious snarl, her chest heaving. She had run hard and fast to escape him. A long, thin knife was gripped in one hand. Marc, on the other hand, showed no trace of emotion on his face. His hands were empty and his body was relaxed, but his eyes were burning a cold ice-blue, full of such fury and hatred that they could almost have melted Kai to the ground.

"Marc!" Archer cried out.

Kai's eyes darted toward him, and in her moment of distraction Marc took his chance. He barreled towards her with the force of a toppling boulder, pinning her against the opposite wall and crushing the air out of her chest. Instinctively, she brought up the knife, but Marc caught her hand with his, and as easily as if he were tossing a bag over his shoulder, he flipped her over so that she was lying on her back, completely exposed and defenseless. She growled and slashed the knife towards the tendons at his ankle, but Marc casually sidestepped and brought his boot down hard onto her wrist. Kai yelled out and kicked up at him, but he leaned down, snatched the knife from her hand with seemingly no effort at all, and pressed his boot down on her throat. His teeth were gritted and the malevolent expression upon his face held no trace of the person Archer knew.

Kai's breathing became ragged as Marc pressed down harder on her throat. Her hands came clawing up at his ankle, but Marc was much too strong for her. He held the knife point down over her face with a distinct air of satisfaction, then lunged back—

Wumph! Archer catapulted as hard as he could into Marc, and they both went tumbling over in a tangled knot of arms and legs. Kai scrambled to her feet, but Marc was already up and after her. He caught her foot and she came down hard onto the cobblestones, already slick with newly falling sleet. Kai let out a yell of fury and tried to get away from him, but Marc yanked her back towards him as easily as if she were a protesting kitten. Archer grabbed him from behind, using all the power in his body to stay Marc's knife.

"Get *off!*" Marc bellowed furiously, trying to kick Archer away.

"Marc, stop!" Archer shouted, locking his elbow against Marc's. Marc's arm was like a steel rod; Archer had never before experienced firsthand just how strong he was, and it was all the Ashan could do to keep the knife from inching forward toward Kai.

"Please, Marc," Archer said quietly, leaning in close to his friend's ear. "Please, Marc. Stop, now."

With a howl of fury, Marc tossed Archer off his back and stood, his hands loose and helpless at his sides. Archer quickly moved to Kai, pinning her down to the ground. By this point, even with the fear coursing through her blood, she was far too exhausted to protest. She watched Archer narrowly with her brilliant violet eyes as the rain dripped down and pooled on her face.

"What do you want from me?" Marc cried. "Archer, she tried to kill him! She tried to kill Laith!"

"I know," Archer said, trying to keep his voice even and calm.

"She deserves to die!" Marc shouted. "Tell me you know that! Tell me you know that she does not deserve to live!"

"I know," Archer said again. "But Marc, this is not a life for a life. Laith is still alive. That big heart of his is going to go on beating, and he's going to get better, and he's going to live. You should be with *him* now. Not here."

Marc's shoulders sagged, but his rage was still palpable. "She'll try to do it again."

"She won't," Archer retorted, and he looked down at Kai, whose caged eyes searched him for an explanation. "Kai," he said slowly in Ashan, and she blinked in surprise to hear the language coming from his mouth. "Kai, if it were my decision, and certainly if it were the decision of Marc, you would surely be killed. Yes?"

"Yes," she replied hoarsely in the same tongue.

"I know what will be achieved with your death. But I think that more can be achieved with your life. Yes?"

"Yes," she assented, still eyeing him narrowly.

"I am being merciful to you," he told her, and they both paused for a moment, letting the gravity of that statement sink in. "I am not a merciful person. But I will be merciful to you. For your mother, who saved me, and for your sister. I gave you a chance before, and you did not take it. I am not giving *you* a chance this time." Then he spoke a word, the ancient Ashan word for life. It was a transaction as ancient as the Ashan people, one seldom invoked and never spoken lightly. It was the most holy word the Ashans possessed.

Kai's eyes snapped into his, and she stared unblinkingly at him. Archer repeated the word to her. "You know what this means," he said to her slowly. "I have spared your life not once but twice. It belongs to me now. You are half-Ashan, and you have respected and lived the laws of your mother's people. You sang at the death of every tree. I have seen you do this with my own eyes. These laws run in your blood. Do you hear me?"

"Yes," Kai grunted reluctantly through gritted teeth, hating it.

"Your life is mine. Say the word."

"My life is yours."

"My law runs in your blood."

"Your law runs in my blood," she repeated, cementing the exchange of life. Archer's shoulders shifted above her, and in the dim corner of her eye, she saw Marc standing taut and at the ready. She saw that he could not understand the words that were being exchanged between them.

"You were hired by Cira Kagai?"

"Yes."

"Then," Archer breathed through his mouth and relaxed his hold on her ever so slightly. "As the owner of your life, I command you to return to Faridor and kill Cira Kagai...or be killed yourself."

Kai stared wide-eyed at his face and saw without a doubt that there could be no room for negotiation. Archer was right. Though she had lived her life among humans and committed countless crimes, she had always been taught to adhere to the basic codes of the Ashan people. And the life debt was the most binding pact one Ashan could make with another, as important a relationship as a mother to a child or a seed to a tree. Kai had no choice but to obey his word and fulfill the agreement that had just been made between them.

Slowly, Archer moved back away from her and rose to his feet.

Stiffly, Kai brushed the pooling water from her face and clambered slowly to her feet to face him. There he was. Archer. They had spent most of their childhood and youth together. They had fought, of course. She wondered whether they had ever really loved each other. Oftentimes, when she was younger and more romantic, she had tried to picture what their final goodbye would be like. In a blaze of glory, perhaps, or a hail of arrows. But she had certainly never pictured anything like this, freezing sleet pouring down their faces as they stared at one another, breath steaming in the cold.

"Cira Kagai or my life," she told him flatly and turned to walk away. For a fleeting moment, she wondered whether Marc would let her go, and part of her almost wished that he would come charging at her and finish what he had started. But there was no noise—nothing. She took a deep breath and squared her shoulders as she walked. It was a curious feeling, as if a door had closed behind her. She would not be able to make another attempt on the lives of the Strikers, even if she wanted to. Half-Ashan though she was, the life debt was binding. Betraying the pact she had made with Archer would dishonor her mother's people and would almost inevitably result in her own death.

All that mattered now was Rowan. Having failed in her attempt to kill the Strikers, her next step was actually very simple: she would have to take it upon herself to rescue her sister from Faridor. There was a high probability she would never come back. She would have to take time, time alone to prepare herself for everything that was to come.

Marc and Archer stood in silence until Kai turned the corner and vanished. Marc turned a pair of helpless eyes to Archer. "Please believe me, Marc," Archer said. "I'm your friend. Trust me that she is gone, and we'll never see her again."

Marc shook his head, but the fire had gone out of his eyes. The freezing rain was streaming cold down his face.

"Come on," Archer clapped him on the back. "Let's go see Laith."

CHAPTER SIXTEEN

Laith's recovery was extremely slow, and his absence only emphasized just how great a part the prince played in the resistance. Ari stepped up his shifts to the point where Tarr began to doubt whether he slept or ate at all, and Archer was working double-time to try to continue getting Ashans out via their trick boat before the river froze over for the winter. Their rescue endeavors ground along slowly, far too slowly for Tarr's liking. Resources seemed to be dwindling away, with fewer and fewer supplies arriving from the mountains and food growing more scarce. Tarr had a sneaking suspicion that Cira was trying to starve them out by limiting the amount of food allowed into the city at all, and he began developing plans to target the food supplies sent to the Kagaian headquarters instead. The reports Athela received said that Cira was changing her routes and stepping up security around the Two Falls wall to the point where it was nearly impossible for their Striker allies in the mountains to smuggle food and arms to them. Tarr knew that the Strikers would continue doing everything they could, but there was no denying that they were turning down a long road that led to starvation and defeat.

Every now and again, alone in his room, Tarr's mind would wander back to the forest, to the steaming baths of hot water the Ashans would draw in winter, watching the snow fall and the mist rising around them. Tarr remembered lying on his cot in the communal sleeping quarters, the light gray and blue as it filtered through the winter screens of his treehouse, gentle hushing sounds of the snow crowning the trees above him. These memories were like a warm, comforting blanket; as soon as he snapped back to reality, the harsh cold set back in and it was all he could do to place one foot in front of the other to get through the day.

As if to mimic Tarr's general mood, the winter weather finally set in with a full week of freezing sleet that clung to the rooftops and plopped to the ground in large sloshy heaps that melted at midday and left a thick coating of mud over all the increasingly torn-up roads of the city. Rane pointed out that this could actually help them keep an eye out for any unfriendly footprints, but Tarr would have given anything for a balmy spring day and a good meal. Though he was thin, he had a high metabolism and hunger gnawed at him from morning until night until it became as familiar as the tired ache in his bones.

After the consecutive disasters of Si's kidnapping and the attack on Laith's life, not to mention the deadly taunts of the mysterious assassin haunting their safehouse, Archer got his wish and the Strikers finally split up into separate hideouts, changing residences on a rotating basis. It was safer, to be sure, but although Tarr was one of the major proponents of the housing change, their new situation was considerably more lonely. He didn't wake up to hear the night watch changing or walk past Archer's room to see him polishing his bow, didn't see Athela bent over maps of Two Falls at the breakfast table. He missed the sound of Breaker's claws as the dog followed Laith up and down the stairs from one room to another, the memory of Wolver close behind.

One morning, Tarr awoke in the belly of Joris's lavish manor in the affluent district of Two Falls. The house had been taken over as one of the Strikers' new hideaways almost as soon as they had made the decision to move. Joris had dismissed his servants to a distant family estate after his relocation to Faridor, and the mansion had been summarily packed away and carefully shut up; there it stood, empty and unoccupied, almost waiting for someone to move in. Archer had been the first to suggest using Joris's residence as a new safehouse, reasoning that Joris would be delighted by the thought of his family's ancestral residence being used for such anti-establishment purposes. There were secret entrances aplenty and a plethora of rooms within to harbor Striker agents should the need arise. The house's furnishings, considerably more plush than the other shelters they'd established (where a good night's sleep meant a hardwood floor and perhaps some straw with a blanket drawn over it), meant that in short order the manor was the most coveted safehouse assignment in the entire Striker operation.

Tarr rubbed his face in his hands and thought momentarily of Pieter, the city councilor they'd managed to sneak into hiding before the war had fully broken out. He'd lived for a time in his nephew's home, a manor quite similar in its appointments and proximity to Joris's. Cira had been quite keen on the idea of stamping out all vestiges of the previous Two Falls government, and her troops had been very persistent in carrying out her orders. Tarr had suspected Pieter's nephew of betraying the Strikers to Cira, and Ari had captured and removed him years ago. The Strikers continued to keep Pieter in hiding, moving him from place to place every few months. They'd need Pieter if they ever managed to take back Two Falls; none of the Strikers knew the first thing about actually *running* a city. (Though, Tarr conceded, none of them had known the first thing about running a resistance organization either, and they were managing all right so far, imminent starvation notwithstanding.)

Though he had no window, his body told him that it was eight-thirty in the morning and that the daily reports, if there were any, were to be dropped off to him soon. He turned round in his chair and stared at the four-poster bed where Rane was sleeping peacefully, her smooth bare back turned to him and her auburn curls spilling out over the pillow. He couldn't help but smile. After an extremely brief internal debate, he got up, hopped over the cold floor in his bare feet, and dove back under the warm covers, feeling that anyone who came to deliver his mail would just have to go ahead and be scandalized.

Though Tarr knew without a doubt that he must have felt a great deal like a tall, rail-thin ice cube, Rane instinctively turned and moved closer to him, nuzzling her head into his bony ribcage. He stroked her hair and felt himself drifting pleasantly back off to sleep, reflecting groggily that these mornings with Rane invariably inspired him to write extremely bad poetry.

Tarr was halfway back to sleep again when there was a curt knock at the door. Both Rane and Tarr started and sat up, but Tarr motioned her back with his hand and stood. Rane nodded sleepily and curled up again facing the wall. In the few instances she was able to have a full night's rest, she could sleep for ten hours or more. Tarr tugged the curtain closed to give her more privacy, then hop-frogged back across the freezing floor in his bare feet and opened the door.

A woman was standing outside, muffled and cloaked almost to the point of nonrecognition, but Tarr gave her a warm smile nevertheless. "Just the Faridor report?" he asked.

She nodded and handed him an unobtrusive flat envelope. "Just that. That was all I was given."

"Thank you for your trouble. Stay warm," Tarr advised her. "If you have time, you're free to rest here, eat something. It's better supplied than the other safehouses."

"Thank you, sir, I might do that." The eyes above the wrapped scarf twinkled tiredly, and the woman turned to go.

Tarr shut the door and walked over to his desk, turning up the light in the lamp and closely inspecting the envelope for signs of tampering. Seeing none, he reached into the desk and withdrew an inlaid letter opener (Tarr had been amused at first by how ostentatious it was, but admitted to himself after a few days that it did make the mundane task of opening the day's mail feel a bit more exciting), opened the envelope and read what was inside.

Tarr sat motionless for a long time after he had finished, the open letter balanced like a feather on his knee. Slowly, he looked down and reread the letter, then almost without thinking took out a piece of parchment and ink and began to scribble.

The scratching sound filled the room, and after a short while Rane stirred restlessly and rubbed her eyes. She slid her feet onto the floor, grabbed a blanket from the bed, and tiptoed over to Tarr. She kissed him lightly on the tattoo on the nape of his neck, but he barely seemed to notice. "What're you writing?" she asked, sliding to sit on the desk. Her eyes went down to the letter in his lap. "You got the Faridor report?"

Tarr nodded wordlessly, handing her the parchment. Rane's brow furrowed as she scanned the words with her lake-blue eyes. It was triple-coded, of the utmost secrecy. The insignia drawn at the top of the page was the sign of one of their best spies in Faridor, codenamed Cicada. The letter read:

> HAVE JUST LEARNED THAT CIRA IS BEGINNING NEGOTIATIONS WITH OVERSEAS GOVERNMENTS TO SECURE A WEAPON TO USE AGAINST THE STRIKERS. WE ARE NOT AWARE AT THIS TIME WHAT SUCH A WEAPON MAY BE, WHETHER IT IS A POISON, PIECE OF MACHINERY, OR SOMEHOW RELATED TO THE OCCULT. NEGOTIATIONS ARE TOP-SECRET, SO IT WILL BE DIFFICULT TO UNCOVER MORE. REQUEST SUPPORT.

"Has she made contact with Joris?" Rane asked.

"I think so," Tarr confirmed. "Contact, nothing more. I hope he's enjoying himself."

Rane stood quietly, pondering, then looked down at the page Tarr had been writing. "What's this?" she asked, picking it up. Tarr looked rather sheepish.

> *THINGS TO DO:*
> *FIND SI*
> *ELIMINATE INDIVIDUALS WHO TOOK SI*
> *FIND ASSASSIN WHO IS STALKING US*
> *GET LAITH BACK UP TO FIGHTING STRENGTH*
> *FIGURE OUT WHAT WAS GOING ON WITH THE MEDALLION*
> *FIND MEDALLION AGAIN*
> *FIND CIRA'S WEAPON*
> *TAKE BACK TWO FALLS*
> *KILL CIRA, TAKE FARIDOR*
> *HAVE BREAKFAST WITH RANE*

"I wrote the last one on there so that I could cross it off in an hour and feel better about myself," Tarr said morosely.

"I love you," she sighed and put the paper back down before him. "What's this weapon she's got?"

Tarr shook his head tiredly. "You read the note; could be anything.

I trust Cicada, she's the best we have."

"She requested backup, who are you going to send?" Rane asked. Tarr refused to meet her eyes.

"I've already taken care of it," he said evasively.

"Tarr," she said pointedly.

"We need you here," he retorted.

"I speak sign language!" she exclaimed angrily. "There is literally *no* reason—"

"The last time I checked, I'm the head of the spy ring; it's my decision to make."

Neither Tarr nor Rane were familiar with such an uncharacteristically assertive attitude, and for a moment Rane looked taken aback. "It is your decision," she agreed. "But I have told you before. There are too many lives at stake for you to let *this*," she motioned between them, "get in the way of rational judgment."

Tarr grunted noncommittally.

"You have to trust me," she said. "You have to trust me to take care of myself. You have to give up one ounce of control and let me handle things myself."

Tarr opened his mouth, closed it, and turned away. She reached out a hand and caught him by the arm.

"I'm serious, Tarr," she said fiercely. "These decisions could be the difference between us winning the war or not. If you do not assign me to Faridor, it had better be for a damn good reason."

"I *have* a damn good reason," Tarr answered. "Laith is out of commission, Athela is focused on tending to him, Si is missing, Marc and his team are scouring the city looking for traces of the person who took him, and I'm not about to try to call Marc off. We need you here. Ari, Archer, and I can't fight the battle for Two Falls on our own. You leave, Cira will win."

Rane threw up her hands with barely contained frustration. "So who? Who did you send in my place?"

"No one you know," Tarr lied.

"*Who?*" Rane insisted, not letting him get away with it.

"Leonore," Tarr said in a low voice.

Rane gaped at him. "*Leonore?*" she breathed. "That girl has absolutely no training whatsoever, Tarr. She has no business being in Faridor. You'll be sending her to her death for sure. Cira will sniff her out in a heartbeat."

"If Joris is doing his job correctly, Cira will have more important things on her mind than a housemaid," Tarr countered. "She can run errands for Cicada, do whatever's necessary. She's keen. She's been wanting to work for me for a long time."

"She'll die," Rane said simply. "I can't believe you are consciously making this decision. *You have to trust me*. Let me do this."

"What about you?" Tarr shot back, tension in his voice. "You lived in Joymaril for years. What's to say that Cira won't recognize you the moment you walk in? Or someone else in her household, for that matter? You'd be every bit as much of a liability as Leonore. And if she discovers your identity, you're dead *and* you'd possibly take half the resistance down with you once she realizes you're a Striker and tortures the names out of you. You don't know that you won't give them up any more than I do. I can't risk having the information you know falling into her hands, Rane. I can't."

Rane opened her mouth to retort, but instead shifted to the side. Tarr's tilted green and brown eyes gazed back at her calmly. He was so good at it. So good at arguing and making it seem as though he were completely detached, that everything he said was based solely on logic.

"You're a better liar than you used to be," she said finally, with just the barest edge of bitterness.

Tarr barely blinked. "It's my job, Rane. Those are my reasons, and as your commanding officer I ask that you respect them. I will accept the consequences."

"You'll have to," Rane said. "They won't be anyone else's fault but yours."

And with that, she turned and left.

Marc pounded his fist three times against the frozen wood of the door and took a step back, turning his cloaked head to look through the sleet. No one was behind him. A cold trickle of water slid through his cloak and down his back. He shivered. A moment later, the door opened and Marc was ushered inside.

It was a small house on the northwestern outskirts of the city, owned by an old couple whose adopted Ashan son had died in one of the early raids. Though the house itself was only big enough for the couple, they had an extensive cellar that they had offered up for the Strikers' use. It was not the most concealed or fortified safehouse the Strikers had ever had, but it was unassuming and far enough away from the Kagaian headquarters that they were reasonably sure they would not be disturbed as long as basic precautions were taken.

"Hungry?" the old woman asked Marc as he came inside. He managed a small smile, remembering Ma and the times when they'd come tromping into their old house and she'd ask them the same question. He was glad that Ma had safely gotten away before everything had gone bad. He walked past their old house sometimes; a new family was living in it, and it was hard to pass without painful memories of the old days.

"Thank you. In a little while, I'll have something," Marc smiled. "I'm going to check in with the others first."

"Potato soup," she said enticingly, and Marc's stomach growled. He hadn't eaten yet that day. "I found a beef bone to make broth with, too," she told him proudly. Marc didn't even want to know what the old woman had had to do to get such a delicacy. Usually, their potato soup was thinned with water.

"I'll be back up, I promise," he assured her, and she smiled in a comforting way, taking his sopping wet cloak and handing him one of their old, worn towels to dry off. "Archer is here, too," she informed him.

Marc headed down to the cellar, reflecting on how tenuous it was that an old couple and a worn wooden door were the only things standing between them and the Kagaian guards.

The cellar was damp and cold, but Athela and the others had done their best to make it livable. They had stuffed the corners of the room with straw for insulation and had scraped together every spare blanket in the city to keep Laith warm and comfortable during his recovery. The prince was fast asleep on the thin cot drawn for him in the far corner of the room. His head was turned away from the doorway. Athela and Archer were sitting quietly together beside him. They looked up, startled, as Marc entered. Three other Striker soldiers were sleeping huddled together across the room.

"Anything new? Any sign of Si?" Athela asked as Marc sat beside them. The tone of her voice was heavy; she knew better than to expect anything.

Marc shook his head silently and leaned over to look at Laith. Since the poisoning, Laith sported a deathly pallor that rivaled even Archer's. His dark brows and lashes stuck out in sharp, garish contrast to his skin, and when he spoke, the inside of his mouth was a crimson red against his white lips. He had lost an incredible amount of weight, and the finely curved bones of his face stuck out against his skin, giving him the appearance of a living skeleton. Marc was almost glad that he was unconscious. When he was awake, the sight of his physical weakness was almost too much for Marc to bear; even the act of sitting up left Laith panting for breath. He had never known the prince to be so feeble in any regard. But he was alive. And while he was alive, there was hope.

"I hope he doesn't get sick," Athela murmured, pulling the blanket up closer to Laith's chin. "I hope he makes it through the winter. A damp cellar isn't the best place to keep him."

"We could move him to the townhouse," Archer suggested.

Athela shook her head. "Too close to Kagaian patrols. This is the farthest safehouse we've got. We can't risk Cira's soldiers finding him, not with him in this state."

Marc laid his hand on Laith's head, and the prince stirred, inhaling deeply. "He'll be all right," Marc assured them. "His heart just goes on beating."

Suddenly feeling exhausted, Marc slid down to lean his back against the wall. He tilted his head and closed his eyes, his silky yellow hair falling about his face. Archer reached into his pocket and withdrew a flask, nudging it against Marc's side.

"You *would*," Athela rolled her eyes. But then she stopped and considered, the silence punctuated by the sound of freezing sleet outside, and after a moment, held out her hand.

Marc gratefully took the flask and gulped down a deep swig, feeling the fire surge through his belly and down his limbs, warming him to his toes. "Thanks," he said, wiping his mouth and passing it over to Athela's outstretched hand.

"Better eat something, or you'll be dancing on the tabletop in five minutes," Athela told him.

Marc shook his head, staring ahead into space. It seemed as though Si had disappeared from the face of the earth without leaving so much as a trace. Marc couldn't remember the last time he had felt quite so discouraged.

"We'll find him," Archer said, as if reading Marc's thoughts. "We've got to find him."

"They haven't even sent a ransom note," Marc shook his head. "If they want to give him up for money, they'd have told us by now. If they'd wanted to deliver him to Faridor, we would have heard of it through Tarr's spies. It doesn't make sense. He just *vanished*."

"We've got to face the fact that he might not be alive anymore," Athela said gently, but Marc shook his head.

"He's alive. I know it. I'd know if he wasn't. I can't explain it. But that's the strange part...I know he's alive, and yet we've had no word from him. Or of him."

"They could have gone anywhere, really," Archer pointed out. "If that pale person with the robes and the questionable face tattoos grabbed him and was able to disappear, there's no telling what they could be up to."

This seemed to do little to comfort Marc, who seemed suddenly restless again. "I am feeling rather lightheaded. I think I'll go up and see about that soup," he said, standing up. "Will you be here all day?"

"No, we're both relocating...Archer has some things to do in the east side, smuggling-wise. But Kali, over there," Athela nodded towards one of the sleeping figures across the room, "has been half in love with Laith for a year and might be even more in love with him now that he's incapacitated. She dotes on him more than any of us. Never worry."

Marc nodded silently and trudged back up the stairs and out of sight. Athela and Archer watched him go. Athela was on the verge of saying something about Si, then glanced over at Archer and happened to notice (not for the first time) that his eyelashes were a pale dove gray. Neither of them spoke for a while; the air seemed somehow thicker, and the silence was louder. The comfortable peace they'd been sharing together had shifted perceptibly.

"What's going on?" Athela wondered aloud, never one for subtlety.

"We're alone again," Archer said, leaning his head against the wall and gazing up at the ceiling. "And unless I'm mistaken, you're giving me the eye."

"So what?" Athela demanded.

"Nothing," Archer replied with an easy shrug, not even bothering to look at her. "Go ahead and admire. Many do."

Athela rolled her eyes. "The subterranean vapors are having some adverse effects, I see."

Archer cocked an eyebrow, folding his arms casually across his chest in what Athela found to be a particularly infuriating manner. "I'm sorry, by the way," he said suddenly.

Athela was taken aback. "For what?" she asked. "You'll have to be a bit more specific."

"For Laith. For the argument we had."

"Oh," Athela considered. "I still think you were being an ass."

"And that's your prerogative. But I..." Archer groped for words. "I was trying to do the right thing. You may not agree. But I was trying."

Athela sighed. "That's what Tarr said."

"Oh yes?"

"Yes. And I..." Athela stirred. "I'm sorry for what I said, too. I still don't agree with what you did, but...I'm sorry anyway."

Archer nodded, and a pleasant, peaceable silence enveloped them.

"In the spirit of righting past wrongs," Archer said abruptly, "there's something that I have been meaning to do for a long time and haven't yet."

"Oh yes?" she asked, her guard back up. "And what is that?"

Archer smiled at her, and Athela felt a flutter deep in her core. "I've needed to kiss you."

"Kiss?" Athela gawked at him. "Me?"

"It's usually done with the lips," Archer said pleasantly, leaning back against the wall again.

"Shut up," she snapped automatically. "What are you talking about?"

Archer looked directly at her. To her horror, his expression was... vulnerable. Full of need. Of longing, even. This frightened her more than anything. His arms were tighter against his chest, and Athela wished that the stampede of horses parading in the pit of her stomach would give it a rest.

Athela bit her lip angrily. "You can't do this!"

Archer looked puzzled. "What?"

Athela groped for some semblance of her usual common sense, but articulation, it seemed, had flown out the window. "You...you're *flirting with me* and we're in a *cellar* next to my half-dead *cousin* and *three sleeping adolescents!*"

"There's a time and a place for everything, I suppose," Archer rejoined, glancing around. "There's just something about this cellar tonight..." he waved his hand with a flourish, "that invites romance. Maybe it's the mildew."

Athela swallowed. Her hands were shaking, and she tried to hide them behind her back, but Archer merely looked at her with his easy half-smile. She forced herself to meet his eyes.

"What's the matter?" he asked gently, his manner genuine and disarming. "No games. No tricks. No jokes. What's the problem? You know how I feel. And I have my suspicions that beneath that healthy protective layer of disdain, there may be something resembling warm feelings on your end as well."

Athela stared at the ceiling, hoping for support, but none came. She couldn't meet his gaze anymore, so she looked down to the floor. "I've never..."

"What?" he asked softly. "Been with someone?"

"Not just that..." she said lamely, aware of just how pathetic she sounded. "Never had...a boyfriend. Girlfriend. Kiss, whatever."

She expected Archer to crack some sort of derogatory joke, but none came. "Their loss," he shrugged. "My gain."

"It matters to *me*," she said, surprised at how heated her own voice sounded. It was as if her words had been clasped in a jar that was beginning to pour out onto the floor. "It matters to me, Archer. No one kissed me when I was younger, and now I'm too old, and everyone is going to think I'm weird because I have had no experience with such things, and you are the *last* person I should be telling all this. It's *embarrassing*."

He was listening quietly, his face expressionless. "Is that it?"

"I can't trust you," Athela spread her hands. There was a pain in her voice she didn't anticipate. "I can't. You can say exactly what anyone wants to hear to get your way. How can I trust that? How do I know you're not coming after me just to get me and then walk away with another notch on your belt?" she sighed.

"I should be insulted," Archer said quietly, "by how low your opinion of me seems to be."

She stared at him, shocked.

"*Do* you like me? At all?" Archer asked. Athela turned away, her eyes feeling curiously hot. Mutely, she nodded.

"Well, that's something, at least," Archer murmured. "Look at me."

Athela did as he asked. The expression on Archer's face was so sincere. She desperately wanted to believe him. "I won't joke about it. I won't make fun. Ever. I promise."

Athela fiddled with her hands and nodded again.

"Now," Archer said briskly, straightening up against the wall. "All that aside, there's one thing I think we can take care of right now."

Athela was instantly on her guard. "What's that?"

"Your first kiss," Archer said easily. "Wouldn't it be nice to get it out of the way?"

"'Get it out of the way?'" she echoed drily. "The romantic prelude every girl dreams of." A soft, devilish smile had returned to Archer's eyes, and she felt one of his hands reach out and pull her closer. "Hey!" she exclaimed, pulling back, her arms shaking.

"All right. We don't have to," Archer said pleasantly, releasing her and looking unperturbed.

"What?" Athela demanded, suddenly affronted. "You're giving up?"

Archer stared at her for a moment and laughed. "Athela, you are an immensely complicated woman."

Athela's throat felt prickly, and her stomach had turned from stampeding horses to jelly. She figured that it wouldn't be romantic if she threw up, but then she noticed again how graceful his neck was and what a nice mouth he had, and how it curved up at one end when he looked at her. She felt her nerves quieten. She half-hoped Laith would awaken and break them up. She gave him a second or two, but he slept on. There was nothing for it.

"All right...what do I do?" she said squarely, facing Archer as though they were about to duel.

Archer laughed. "Come here."

He pulled her toward him so that she was sitting on his lap. She had never been so close to Archer before and couldn't bring herself to look him in the face. He smelled like green leaves after a fresh summer rain. He raised one hand and gently touched the side of her face, his skin cool against her cheek, smooth like marble. The other he set gently against the curve of her waist.

"You can touch me too, if you like," Archer suggested. He said it nicely, probably realizing that she felt too petrified to move. Athela swallowed and moved a hand to the slope of muscle at his shoulder and then to his neck. She realized suddenly that she had always wondered what it felt like to touch him. His skin naturally seemed to be several degrees cooler than a regular person's, but the sensation was bracing and refreshing; she found herself tracing the black curve of the tattoo at the nape of his neck. Archer's golden eyes were half-closed, enjoying the sensation. This took Athela aback. She hadn't quite understood that it was within her power to give pleasure to Archer as well. She quickly removed her hand, placing it upon his chest, where she knew his green leaf tattoo to be. Shocked, she looked at his face. Underneath her palm, his heart was pounding as hard and fast as a drumbeat; he must have been as nervous as she. He hid it well.

Archer cupped her head in his large hand and drew her lips to his. A thrill ran through her entire body, startled by his warmth and how...*pleasant* it was. After a second or two, he released her and assessed her expression. "Was that all right?" he asked.

Athela stared at him, wide-eyed.

"I'll take that as a yes?" he eyed her narrowly, one eyebrow arched.

"Yes," she breathed, trying not to sound too eager. *Finally,* she thought. *I can see what all the fuss is about.*

He slid his arm around her waist, hugging her closer, and she felt herself relax and bend with him. He threaded his fingers in her hair and pulled her lips to his. This time it was different—Athela felt herself relax and let herself begin to move with him. She felt as though there were hands pulling her dizzyingly down; she sank against Archer, following the warmth and sweet taste of his mouth with her own. It was unlike anything she had ever experienced. She felt suddenly ravenous; all the worries had flown, all she was conscious of was Archer's mouth and his hand gripping her hip hard against him. Her passion surprised even her; never before had she imagined herself kissing Archer like this, both her hands laced through his black and white hair, pulling him closer to her, frustrated that somehow it still wasn't close enough. The spinning sensation grew greater and greater in the bottom of her stomach, and finally she forced herself to break away. Archer was breathing hard, looking at her wide-eyed in amazement.

"Well," Athela said brightly. "Glad we got that out of the way."

Archer grinned and reached out to pull her in again, but Athela froze, the momentary interlude cutting her conviction asunder. If she began to kiss him again, she knew that she would not want to stop. That she might not be able to stop. And where could they go from there?

"No," she said. "No...I..." For an instant, it looked as though she might change her mind, but she pushed herself away from him and stood. For a few seconds she stood there, confused, then whirled and went running up the cellar steps. Archer slumped back against the wall, trying to catch his breath, and after a minute or two, stretched his long legs and meandered his way back up the stairs and out into the weather. A long, cold walk would do him good.

Marc came back down to the cellar to check on Laith one last time before he headed back out. He sat next to the cot and laid his hand against Laith's forehead. To his surprise, Laith's dark lashes fluttered, and something resembling a grin flitted across the prince's face.

"Marc," he croaked, sounding as though he were near death. "Archer and Athela just made out."

Marc straightened immediately and nearly punched him in the face. "*What?*" he asked, absolutely stunned.

"Yeah," came a muffled voice from across the room. "They were really noisy, too. A lot of slurping."

"Don't say 'slurping,' that's disgusting," Marc called, then lowered his voice and peered back down at Laith. "You're kidding."

"I'm not," Laith whispered huskily, eyes closed but delighted. "And it sounded like Athela enjoyed it."

"Of course she did; Archer has to have his technique honed by now."

"It was really...rather sweet," Laith winced and shifted. "I think he really likes her."

Marc shook his head. "I tell you though, Laith, if we make it through this war, today's going to be declared a national holiday."

Laith smiled for the first time in weeks.

CHAPTER SEVENTEEN

Si awoke in the darkness. It was a strange darkness, whose smell he didn't recognize. He was cognizant of a small cot beneath him, a light blanket covering his shoulders. *Marc!* He thought. *I have to find Marc!* He dimly remembered Marc yelling, reaching out to him. He remembered the medallion and the strange figure...

I'm kidnapped! he shrieked inwardly and leaped up off the bed. *Help!* The moment of panic blossomed, then died. *But I'm still alive. That's a good start.* Something told him he'd been asleep for a very long time. If whoever had captured him wanted him dead, he would be dead already. He sincerely hoped that he wasn't in Faridor, that he wasn't about to be tortured for names. He tried to remember what Marc taught him to do in the event he was abducted, but the only thing he could remember Marc saying was something along the lines of "do your best," which wasn't a great deal of help to him at that moment. *Be brave*, he told himself. *Be brave and make your friends proud of you. You're a Striker, and you're Morthenstar's heir, whatever anybody thinks.* So Si steeled himself and sat on the edge of his cot with his hands folded in his lap, waiting in the dark.

It was only about a minute or so before Si saw a small light appear and move towards him. He stiffened automatically, bracing himself for whatever was about to come. *I don't* think *I'm in Faridor*, he thought again. The light grew and filled the room to the point where Si was finally able to make out his surroundings. To his surprise, he didn't seem to be caged at all. He was in what appeared to be an underground cavern, with cots tucked here and there among the rock formations. It wasn't unlike the Strikers' own hideout in the mountains. Puzzled, Si touched his feet to the stone floor and stood up. The single pinpoint of light, which he had originally thought to be from a lantern, had inexplicably spread and now filled the entire space. Si stepped forward out of his nook and looked up to the roof of the cave, catching his breath as he did. The entire soaring dome was made of glittering, shining stalactites that gleamed like the sun. Si's mouth fell open and he gazed up, revolving around in circles, trying to take it all in. Any feelings of dread he had about his abduction were beginning to fall away and were replaced by a feeling of profound curiosity. *Where on earth am I?* he wondered.

A footstep sounded behind him and Si whirled, reaching for his hip where Marc had taught him to keep a knife. Unsurprisingly, there was none there. Fear gripped Si's throat, and he took a step back, facing the elderly figure with the scarlet star tattoo on their forehead.

"Who are you?" Si demanded. "Where am I? Why have you taken me?"

"Si Morthenstar," said the person. Their voice was curiously high-pitched and slightly eerie. "Please have a seat."

"Where—" Si began, then looked down by his right arm. A chair had appeared, seemingly out of nowhere. Si folded his arms and faced the stranger, looking stubborn and petulant. "I am not going to sit down until you tell me how you're able to appear and disappear things."

"I'm about to, if you sit down," they returned patiently.

Still keeping his face as uncooperative as possible, Si took a seat. "What's your name?"

"Elder," said the stranger.

Si's brow furrowed. "Elder...like an Ashan elder?"

They shook their head. "There are many elders in many different cultures. I am no Ashan. This is merely the name I have chosen."

"If you're an Elder, does that mean there's a Younger?" Si joked. The stranger forced a rather painful smile.

"Yes," they sighed. "I expected as much. The first Morthenstar had a sense of humor as well." The words "sense of humor" were said with immense distaste.

"You knew Morthenstar?" Si wondered, gray eyes wide.

The stranger smiled patiently, and then, as if Si had blinked and missed it, a chair appeared before them in the center of the cavern. Elder glided forward and took a seat, steepling their long, thin fingers in their lap. "I knew Morthenstar very well."

Si felt as though insects had begun running up and down his arms. He shuddered. "Are you...human?" he whispered.

"Once," Elder smiled enigmatically, the wrinkles on their wizened face cracking slightly. "We have given ourselves to something beyond time. Beyond age. We have made a pact with the stronger forces of the world."

"What forces?" Si asked dubiously.

"Good. Evil," Elder shrugged dreamily. "We are servants of that which keeps the world turning and the people in it moving."

Si felt as though he were in the midst of a deep fog. "Meaning?"

Elder sighed, brushing an invisible speck from the knee of their scarlet robes. "We were once human. We were students, followers of the Unspoken Art. Persecuted by many. But with power few could imagine. We saw the coming of Morthenstar, of Kagai, of the first war that split this land. So, to protect it, we made the ultimate sacrifice. We gave up the gift of mortality to better serve the cause of good. To see that the imbalance, the unnatural concentration of good and evil in the world, could be restored to a proper order."

Si was certainly relieved that they hadn't made a pact with evil, and it seemed, for the most part, that they were harmless (except for the chairs appearing and disappearing). Si narrowed his eyes dubiously. "What's the Unspoken Art? Magic?"

Elder sniffed rather primly and lowered their voice to a mysterious growl. "There is no way to explain what it is."

"It's magic," Si said blandly.

Elder preened. "Some more crass individuals might refer to it as that. But it is so much more. The mysteries of the infinite...the thread connecting every dewdrop to the sheer interwoven fabric of space and time..." their voice drifted off dreamily.

Si coughed, seeming to startle Elder out of their reverie. "Sounds great!" he said cheerily. "Why kidnap *me*, though?"

Elder looked disgruntled and leaned forward. "Because it was your *time*. Because you had found...this." They turned their hand, and in their palm lay Si's medallion. "Because your powers have been unlocked, and your journey towards the infinite has begun. We were summoned from the farthest depths—"

"Hey!" Si exclaimed angrily, leaping up and snatching at the medallion. "Give that back!"

"Sit down," Elder ordered irritatedly.

"Give it *back!*" Si bellowed.

"Sit," Elder snapped curtly, and Si shut his mouth, returning to his seat, wishing that the searing rays from his eyes would pierce Elder right through their old, spotted face.

"We knew, of course, the moment that you uncovered this medallion," Elder told him, tones soothing. "And we knew it was time for you to come to us."

"Cut the nonsense," Si grunted, his eyes flashing. "I don't want to hear any more of this mumbo-jumbo." He stopped, ashamed both of his rudeness and of the fact that he had used the term "mumbo-jumbo" in a sentence, wishing something more mature had come out of his mouth instead. "Look, I'm sorry to have to be impolite, but you took me away from my friends and kept me here for who knows how long, and they probably all think I'm dead by now, and you took my medallion, and you're still not giving me answers about how you made that chair appear."

"We had to consult the stars," said Elder dreamily, staring up at the glittering ceiling. "We had to keep you asleep until we were sure that the time was right for us to reveal our presence to you. But we have been watching. We've been watching you for quite some time."

"How long have I been here?" Si asked.

"Time is meaningless," Elder replied superciliously.

"To *you*, maybe," Si retorted.

"Weeks?" Elder waved their hand dismissively. "Months?"

"Hang on," Si demanded. "Did you hurt a girl and leave her in an alleyway for Laith to find? Have you been leaving creepy tracks and notes for my friends to find?"

"No," said Elder, with the self-satisfied air of someone who knew exactly who *did* do it.

"Well, then, who's this *we* who's been watching me?"

"The Serpens," Elder replied. "We were the stewards of Alder Morthenstar and have been the guardians of eternal secrets for thousands of years. We may choose our messengers, our vessels, and we send them where we wish to carry out our work. People, even animals. But you, Si, you out of all others, were chosen by forces even greater than us. Your particular alignment of cells and molecules, your singular placement in the fabric of time and space. We, who know the mysteries of past and future and good and evil, are here to serve you and to teach you."

Si groped for words. He didn't have a firm grasp on what cells or molecules were, so rather than try to engage Elder on an intellectual level, he opted for evasive politeness. "Thanks very much," he said rather lamely. "You said there's more of you? The...Serpens?"

Elder leaned back in their chair and waved one of their pale, skeletal hands in the air. All around them, in a sudden ripple of light, Si saw rows of black-robed individuals, skin pale, scarlet stars on their foreheads. They watched him silently. Si swallowed, and with another wave of Elder's hand, they vanished.

"Oh," Si said weakly. "Can I...can I ask where those people might have gone?"

"We do not exist in the temporal realm," Elder blinked, their eyes misty. "We are servants of the south wind and the purveyors of..."

"There's a back room, I'll bet," Si concluded shrewdly. "I saw that trick at a fair once."

"We are here to teach you," Elder informed him curtly, a little put out that their monologue had been cut short.

"But Marc's my teacher," Si said automatically. Elder regarded him thoughtfully.

"Yes, Marc. He's a tricky one. Fashioned himself as a brother...a father...a guide to you, hasn't he? We saw his thread as the world spun, saw it shining and glowing as the strands intersected. We knew he would make it difficult for you."

"Make what difficult?" Si asked.

"...and in the far-out reaches of the depths of time, how the blossoming life-threads wove together and sprang forward with new force..." Elder continued in their sleepy, dreamy monotone.

"It must be a pretty wild place in that brain of yours," Si observed.

"You cannot know the infinite vastness of the universe," Elder intoned.

"I know," Si agreed, sounding perfectly fine about it.

"The first step towards your destiny requires a choice, Si," Elder said, their eyes focusing with a sudden sharpness that took Si aback. "You must make a choice. We cannot hold you here against your will."

"Really?" Si asked excitedly. "You mean I can go back whenever I want?"

Elder considered thoughtfully, as if they were planning their next strategic move. "Let me ask you this. Why do you have strange visions? Why was it that when you wore the medallion and touched those Kagaian guards, they died without you ever having drawn your sword?"

Si felt his mouth falling open. "How..." he breathed. "How could you possibly know what happened?"

Elder smiled, looking pleased with themself. "We know everything, Si. Everything from the tiniest decibel in the deepest ocean crevice to the soundless explosion of every supernova."

"What's a supernova?" Si wrinkled his nose.

"Why do these things happen to you, Si? How did you know that Marc would poison Lord Argolaith?" Elder asked.

Si started and stood up, pushing his chair back in his haste. "He what? He didn't really poison Laith, did he?"

"Sit down, they're all quite fine...Rane, however..." Elder shook their head.

"Rane?" Si exclaimed.

"Forget that I said anything," Elder brushed it away. "Can you tell me why these things happen?"

"I don't know," Si said helplessly. "I guess...magic?"

"The Unspeakable Art," Elder corrected primly.

"If it's unspeakable, why are you talking about it?" Si asked shrewdly.

Elder made an unbecoming noise in the back of their throat. "Your powers have been unlocked, and only we can provide you with answers, with guidance. *You* don't know the answers, do you?"

"Tarr is going to find out!" Si exclaimed angrily.

"That is impossible."

Si opened and shut his mouth a few times, but no sound came out. He couldn't think of anything to say that could shake Elder's seemingly unflappable certainty. And all at once, Si felt a tiny twinge of doubt deep in the pit of his chest. *What if Tarr doesn't find out?* he thought. *What if he can never help me? Do I just lose my mind? Do I destroy the medallion? If I destroy the medallion, do I give up everything that makes me Morthenstar's heir? What sort of powers is this person talking about? Was this all one big mistake?*

"It was no mistake," Elder said. Si jumped, surprised that the thoughts had been picked from his head with seemingly no effort whatsoever. "You are Morthenstar's heir. Your path will be shown to you before long. But without an understanding of that power, it may be wielded for good...or for evil. It will never be within your control if you are without a full understanding of its nature. And once you have that knowledge, there is no limit to what you can achieve. Even Alder Morthenstar herself only *began* to tap into her complete power, her absolute potential. Over the years, that power has concentrated and boiled away. It is now channeled into *you*. With our guidance, you can go even further than she."

Si felt himself growing more and more frustrated. "But there's got to be something—some book, some ancient scroll..."

Elder smiled in an infuriatingly patronizing way. "These arts far predate any written word, and the secrets have been jealously guarded by the members of this order. If it's your destiny that you wish to fulfill, it is here that you must find it."

"Yeah, right!" Si exclaimed, conscious of the fact that he sounded every inch the thirteen-year-old he was. "Learn with *you*? You'd probably just go yabbering on about the stars for forty-five minutes..."

Elder drew themself up, incensed that Si had dared to insult the cosmos. "You speak of what you do not know," they said coldly. "Which, at this point, is rather a lot. Si Morthenstar, you were the one chosen.

You may go...or stay...I have said my piece. The decision lies with you now."

And with that, Elder vanished into the dark. Si blinked stupidly, then quickly glanced over his shoulder just to make sure that Elder wasn't standing behind him. The cavern was empty. He was alone. Si had never felt so conflicted; hot tears of anger rose in his eyes, and he gritted his teeth and clenched his small fists into balls. He wanted to hit something, to break the stupid spindly chair beneath him. He leaned back and tilted his head up towards the ceiling, trying to control himself. The stalactites glittered and gleamed down at him like a dome of crystals. The sight was oddly soothing. He took a few deep breaths, just as Marc had advised him to do when he needed to calm down.

Here it was: his chance to learn everything about his newfound powers, about his birthright. *That is, provided Elder has been telling me the truth*, he reasoned, Tarr's skeptical sensibility worming its way into the back of his thoughts. *I have really no proof that they are who they say they are. Except that they know about the medallion...and they have not harmed me...yet. What if I refuse? Will they really allow me to go?* Si couldn't be sure. Another less important factor in his decision was that he wasn't sure he could put up with Elder's dreamy cosmological musings for more than an hour or two.

On the other hand...Si had to face the fact that Tarr knew just as much as he did about the secrets of Morthenstar and the mysterious medallion, which amounted to very little at all. *Sometimes it just takes time. Finding the right book in the right place. Putting two and two together. If anyone is able to do it, it's Tarr. Unless*, piped up the nasty voice in the back of his mind, *Elder is telling the truth, and these secrets predate any written text.*

But you've got a lot more to go on now, Si countered himself. *You know who took you. The Serpens. You know about Elder. You've got more clues to give Tarr. Maybe one of those will amount to something.*

Or maybe not, the voice sneered. *And you would have given up everything. Your destiny...the one chance you have to actually make a difference in this war. And for what? Because you're homesick?*

Si reluctantly had to admit it. He missed the others. He had only a vague sense of how long he had been gone, but it felt like an eternity.

He missed Athela, missed Tarr pursing his lips while reading missives beside his morning tea, the sound of Laith's reassuring footstep going past the door. Most of all, he missed Marc—missed being able to ask him for advice, missed the way Marc could always make him feel useful and important, help him feel as though he were standing on solid ground.

That's it, he decided, his jaw set stubbornly. *I'm going back. I'm going to tell the others what I know, and we're going to figure this out together, just as we've done from the beginning. I won't be giving anything up by going back. I'm a Striker, and that's the way it's going to stay.*

He leapt from his chair and faced the gloom. "I want to go back!" he called out. His voice echoed around the cavernous room. He pushed his copper hair away from his eyes. "Do you hear me? I want to go back!" Almost as soon as the words were out of his mouth, he caught himself. *The medallion!* he thought quickly. *I've got to get it back before—*

"*Wait!*" he cried.

There was a low whoosh, and Si felt himself knocked off his feet; he was whirling, tumbling, as if he were caught underwater by a crashing wave overhead. He tossed and turned, his arms billowing in the force of the gust, then all at once there was cold wind on his cheeks, a loud splat, and Si was deposited unceremoniously in the middle of a street in Two Falls, cold rain falling hard on his face.

CHAPTER EIGHTEEN

Laith was up on his feet for the first time in weeks, leaning on Archer's shoulder as the two of them hobbled around the safehouse cellar. Laith's breathing was steady, and his stride grew more and more even as his muscles unkinked. "Thank goodness," he breathed with relief. "Everything still works. Arfolasth will be so happy. He's probably gone out of his mind being cooped up this much."

"Athela's taken him out once or twice when the way was clear," Archer assured him, shifting the prince's arm higher on his shoulder. "Upsy-daisy, there we go. Look at you; you'll be out wreaking havoc in no time." Archer cleared his throat nervously. "Speaking of wreaking havoc, I had something I wanted to talk to you about."

"You kissed Athela," Laith replied matter-of-factly. "And given the noises I heard, 'kissed' is a fairly generous description."

Archer nearly dropped Laith on the floor. "How did you know?"

"I was there, remember?" Laith said.

"But..." sputtered Archer, "you were unconscious!"

"I," said Laith patiently, as though he were explaining to a small child, "was *pretending*."

"Are you going to kill me?" Archer winced, one of his golden eyes half-closed, as if bracing for the blow to come. Laith stopped and faced him. His handsome face had regained some of its usual color, though his skin was pale from having spent so much time inside. A tiny hint of a smile played at the corner of his lips.

"Well, aside from the slurping sounds, *of which there were quite a few*," Laith said with mock severity, "you were altogether quite decent to her."

"If I'd known we had an audience, I would have put on more of a show," Archer grinned as they began another lap over the cold flagstones of the cellar floor.

"We can be thankful for small miracles, I suppose," Laith muttered.

Suddenly, they heard footsteps behind them on the stairwell. One of the upstairs guards came flying down the steps so fast that she nearly tripped and fell flat. Her face was as white as a ghost. Immediately sensing trouble, Archer darted across the room to where his bow and quiver were leaning against the wall, Laith a few wobbly steps behind him.

"My Lord," she said, nodding to Argolaith, opening her mouth to continue.

"What is it? A raid?" Laith demanded sharply.

"Have they breached one of the safehouses?" Archer asked.

"It's...Si..." she managed, and her face bloomed into a wide smile. "He's been found."

Halfway across the city, Si was sitting guiltily on a velvet sofa, desperately trying not to drip mud all over the rich furnishings. He had gone straight to Joris's hideout the minute that he had appeared, somewhat disoriented, onto the streets of Two Falls, figuring that some Striker agent or another would be at the hideout and could help him get back to his friends. The guards at the safehouse had immediately summoned runners to comb the city for the other Strikers.

Athela and Tarr were already beside him. Tarr was pouring hot water for a pot of tea, and Athela was furiously pacing, clearly trying to resist the urge to throw her arms around Si and burst into incoherent sobs of utter joy.

"It's..." she cleared her throat unconvincingly, "...a good thing you came back because I've had to take late watch with Marc for three weeks."

"I missed you, too," Si said seriously, not fooled for an instant. "I honestly never thought I'd come back."

"He snores a lot," she informed him.

"I was really scared," Si agreed.

"The food around here is horrible," she grumbled.

"You're right, we're all together again, and that's all that matters," Si replied soothingly.

Athela returned this with a masculine-sounding grunt, but when she turned around, Tarr could see that she was smiling. He poured a large, steaming cup of tea for Si and set it down in front of him. "You get some fresh tea leaves as a bit of celebration," he ruffled Si's copper hair affectionately.

"I was about to say...old tea? My companions are just the *dregs* of society," Si joked merrily. Athela whirled on her heel and fixed him with an iron stare.

"Is it too late to send him back?" she asked in a dark voice.

But before the matter could escalate, the door burst open, and in came Laith and Archer, panting but overjoyed.

"I'm back!" Si announced jovially, as though he had just been on a long vacation.

"Where? How?" Laith breathed, but Archer had already grabbed the boy and lifted him up to his immense height to hug him fully. Si's legs dangled a few feet above the ground, and he seemed to be having trouble getting air.

"Well, don't *kill* him now that we've just got him back," Athela said crossly, and Archer put him down, beaming delightedly. A significant look passed between Athela and Archer, a look which did not escape Si's attention.

"Did they finally kiss?" he asked Tarr excitedly.

"I—I never!" Athela spluttered and stalked from the room, sending a sharp glare in Archer's direction as though it were his fault that Si had found out. When Archer was sure she was out of earshot, he and Si hit a covert high-five.

The door flew open, and Marc stood framed in the doorway. Si tore himself away from Archer and ran to Marc, who blinked for a moment as if he couldn't quite believe it himself. He crushed the boy in an enormous hug, his face pressed against Si's hair. After a moment, he pulled Si away and held him at arm's length, looking him over for any sign of hurt or abuse. "Who did it?" Marc demanded. "Who took you?"

"It's a long story," Si shook his head, his eyes beaming with happiness. "I'll tell you all about it. They won't take me again, though. I promise."

"Rane's out on patrol," Tarr said softly. "Let's all sit down and get something to eat."

Though the dinner was just a loaf of bread between them and a bowl of thin cabbage soup, they ate as though it were an enormous feast. Gradually, Si pieced together the snippets he could remember. His kidnapping, the medallion, Elder's strange words, the existence of the Serpens. "But," he concluded. "I figured that anything they could know, Tarr could find out too. So that's why I came back. And I missed all of you so much." He grinned around at them.

"The Serpens," Tarr mused. "Remember, we'd heard of them already. Back when Si was marked as the heir, in the vision of Morthenstar we saw. She mentioned the Serpens, but I didn't know what she meant."

"Did they feed you?" Marc asked sharply.

"I guess so," Si mused. "I don't *think* I felt hungry."

"When I find them..." Marc growled.

"Marc," Tarr said placatingly, "from what Si's told us, these people don't mean us any harm. They allowed Si to return to us. Besides, I don't think that they're going to be easily found."

"Probably too busy thinking about the mysteries of the damn universe," Si muttered.

"Language," Marc said automatically.

"But you'll find out, right?" Si continued, as if he hadn't heard Marc. He swiveled in his seat and looked at Tarr with hopeful eyes. "You're going to find out what all of this means, and how I can control my power and all that, right? Even though they took the medallion away from me?"

Tarr looked down the table and saw all five pairs of eyes turned toward him, wide and expectantly hopeful. "Yes," he said, trying to sound absolutely certain. "Yes, of course we are."

CHAPTER NINETEEN

Overnight, the sleet turned into a freezing hail that pelted furiously against the shuttered windows of Faridor. Beneath a mound of silken, embroidered sheets and thick down coverlets, a figure stirred and emerged into the morning gloom. Joris rubbed his hands sleepily through his tousled curls, blinked a few times, and glanced around. Cira was already up and about; the now-familiar signs of her were absent. Her silk robe was gone from its usual chair, her slippers were missing from her side of the bed, and through the slightly cracked bedroom door, he could see one of her maids enter and start to tidy up the rest of the apartment. He stretched as luxuriously as a cat and slid reluctantly out from under the plush sheets.

The door opened and the maid walked in, then stopped short when she realized he wasn't wearing clothes. "My lord!" she stammered, averting her eyes modestly. "I'm terribly sorry, I thought—"

"Calm down," Joris said in his purring, deep voice, grinning as he saw the flush of color rise in her cheeks. "Nothing you haven't seen before." He languorously fished a shirt from the pile of clothes on the floor beside him and pulled it over his head. "Where's Her Majesty this morning?"

"She had her breakfast downstairs, M'Lord," the maid bobbed a curtsy, clearly eager for him to be out of the room so that she could go about her business.

"Very well," Joris yawned again and pulled on a pair of trousers. He sidled out of the room, leaving the maid to recover her wits. *Breakfast,* he sighed to himself. *Typical.* If he knew Cira, it was breakfast with a side of paperwork, the contents of which were always kept safely hidden from his prying gaze.

Even after the long months they had spent in each other's company, Cira was extremely careful never to slip, never to let any strand of information pass by his ears. Joris was patient, but things were reaching a head. His surroundings were rich, to be sure, the food excellent, the wine superb, and he and Cira had immediately discovered that their relations were mutually satisfying. But Joris had grown up in splendor, and he had been with many beautiful people. Where others may have been tempted to stray and forget their purpose in exchange for a life of ease, Joris was generally unimpressed. Besides, luxuries aside, he was, in essence, nothing more than a kept pet: Cira had tethered him to a suffocatingly short leash. He could roam about her rooms well enough, but was always under guarded supervision the moment he walked through the door.

Cira's stringent precautions in this regard struck him as both infuriating and, as her opponent, somewhat admirable. Reluctantly, he had to admit that he had found things to respect in her. She was entirely self-possessed, with a cool efficiency that melted into warm ardor given the correct coaxing. He liked the way she walked: light-footed like a cat, her green eyes flashing whenever she was displeased, and her pale blond hair blowing back behind her like a sheet. He even enjoyed the way she would hold him at arm's length for a week or two before allowing him back into her bed. She kept things interesting, and she knew how to play his sort of games. Joris had to concede that they were a pair well-matched. It was a shame, in some ways, that they were on opposite sides of the battle.

"Late!" a voice hissed behind him as the door banged open. Cira breezed into the room, her midnight blue robe swishing about her legs as she walked. "How *dare* they be late for an appointment with me?"

One of her counselors was trailing anxiously behind her, and Joris was amused to see that the man literally seemed to be wringing his hands. "There was snow on the roads through the mountains, your Majesty," the counselor said apologetically, "but we've sent lookouts, and I promise you that they are due to arrive here at the palace any minute."

"Call me when they've arrived," Cira told him without turning around to look at his face. "Go!"

The councilor ventured a harried glance at Joris, then withdrew from the room, shuffling awkwardly beneath the weight of his ceremonial winter robes. Joris eyed Cira from where he stood, sizing up her mood like he was reading a familiar book. Finally, he strode across the room and stretched out on one of the couches, picking up a book and holding it loosely in his hand.

"Aren't you going to get up and do anything useful?" Cira barked at him from the window.

"Like what, your Majesty?" he asked impudently.

"You laze around all day and do nothing," Cira snapped.

Joris blinked his large eyes innocently at her, and a smile darted across his lips. "Not *nothing*, certainly, your Majesty. In fact, you are present during most of my most strenuous daily activity."

Cira snorted derisively despite herself.

"I can withdraw to Two Falls if it pleases you," Joris suggested.

Cira slowly swiveled around to look at him, her green eyes narrowed. "It pleases me that you should remain here."

"I hope Your Majesty will forgive my lethargy, in that case," he returned insolently. "I live but to serve."

At that, Cira's façade broke and a smile flashed for a moment upon her face. She swished across the room and sat beside him, toying with the open front of his shirt. "I keep you locked up here in the tower like a prisoner," she mused, running her finger along the buttons. Her voice was no longer mock-angry or even playful. "You understand, though, why I cannot allow you to go back?"

Joris smiled evasively. "I was under the impression that you favored my company."

Cira shook her head. "You can never go back, now. Knowing what you know. I can't allow it."

"I know nothing," he insisted.

Cira didn't budge an inch. "Even so."

He shrugged, pretending nonchalance. "As it pleases you. I am happy here."

This seemed to take Cira by surprise. "You are? Happy?"

"Certainly," Joris replied. "My needs...are well provided for." He stroked a finger up the inside of her white forearm. She gave a small shudder and turned her head away, staring out of the window for a long moment.

"You have riches where you come from," she pointed out.

"Yes," he agreed. "But you're here."

"What do you mean?" Cira asked.

"I like you," Joris answered. It wasn't entirely untrue.

Cira stood immediately and turned, walking towards the balcony. Joris rose to sit on the green couch, carefully setting his book to the side.

"What was all that about?" he inquired, jerking his head in the direction of the door, trying to sound innocent.

"Field report from scouts in the Meadows," she answered, her mind clearly elsewhere. "Our next campaign must be in that direction." Realizing that she was on the verge of breaking her cardinal rule of not divulging information, she whirled. "I should like to ride today," she announced to him.

Joris glanced at the weather outside the floor-length windows, looking uninspired. "It's filthy outside."

"Then I shall command it to be sunny," she told him starchly, and Joris could see that she was only half-joking.

A moment later there was an urgent knock, and an older man walked in, clearly having come straight from a hard night's ride and up to the tower without pausing to even wipe his feet or catch his breath. He bowed as low as he could manage in Cira's direction and then collapsed into a nearby chair. His dark hair was streaked here and there with gray, and there was a thick layer of mud caked all the way from his boots up to his knees.

"What did you do, *wade* here?" Cira inquired disdainfully, elegantly arraying herself in a nearby chair. The man was still panting, but managed a weak smile.

"The Meadows aren't as safe as we thought," he grunted. "My

party was waylaid by a large battalion of…"

"Oh, come now, come now, catch a breath," Cira cut him off before he could say precisely *what kind* of battalion had beset them. "Joris, would you be so good as to fetch us a jug of water? I've sent all the servants out for the moment."

Joris knew that this was merely an excuse to get him away from her advisor and that any protest from him would raise her suspicions. *Besides,* he thought to himself, *there is probably little of interest for me in a report from the Meadows.* He lazily stretched one leg out after the other and sauntered across the room, taking his time as he went. There was a pitcher of water in the bathchamber and he retrieved it, pondering how best to make his re-entrance. If he stalled and tried to listen in on their conversation, there was a high probability that he might pique Cira's suspicions, and then the game would be up. No. Best to just barge right back in, uncaring, and hope that they were saying something interesting.

That was precisely what he did. As Joris walked back into the living area, he saw Cira's eyes widen and her mouth fly open slightly. Her officer was in the middle of saying, "—look forward to meeting him at last. Has he made many trips to Faridor since he assumed command?"

"Er—no," said Cira, staring at Joris out of the corner of her eye as he poured a glass of water for each of them and set the jug atop a nearby table. The guard didn't seem to catch her hint and continued to talk.

"I suppose it is too dangerous for you to travel there right now," the officer continued conversationally, clearly oblivious to Cira's discomfort.

"Very good," she cut him off. "Have some water. You must be thirsty."

Joris was all too conscious of the fact that Cira's eyes were darting back and forth from him to the officer like those of a cornered animal. *What is going on?* He wondered. *What can they possibly be talking about that's as terribly important as all of that?*

"Have you had any word from the armory?" he asked Cira abruptly, hoping to divert her alarm. "My new shipment of ivory handles from King Tarik should have come in by now."

Cira seemed to relax, but only slightly. "Go and see for yourself.

There's a guard outside who can take you there." She seemed glad for the opportunity to be rid of him.

Joris made a great show of getting up and going out; Cira was careful not to resume her conversation with her advisor until the door was shut. A green-cloaked guard was waiting impassively outside, and together, Joris and the guard began to wind their way down the spiral staircase beneath Cira's apartments.

Once they had gone down one flight, Joris paused, pretending to search his pockets. "Wait for me a moment; I forgot the armory order," he told the guard. He jogged as noiselessly as he could back up and around the twisting stairwell to the entrance of Cira's room. He checked to be sure that the guard could not see him on the landing below, then he placed his ear against the door, figuring that if what was being said inside was so almighty important, then it might be worth being eventually beheaded.

"That's right. For three days, a week from tomorrow. I want no papers; I want no information about this written anywhere. I want you to go yourself. Tonight." Cira said, her voice slightly muffled.

Joris didn't dare wait a second longer. He fairly raced back down to where the guard was waiting. "Had it all along," he said curtly. "Come on, I haven't got all day."

As they went, Joris tried his best to maintain a haughty, detached exterior while inside his mind raced. *A week from now something is going to happen. It will last three days. Someone is coming to Faridor.* He racked his brain, nodding distractedly to one of Cira's courtiers as she brushed past him in the hall. *The officer said he'd be pleased to meet him. Someone important. From the Meadows? Unlikely. The counselor just came from there. Somewhere unsafe for Cira to travel...*

Then it hit him like a load of bricks, so startling that he stopped stock still in the middle of the hallway. *Two Falls. And the man they're talking about is General Grey. General Grey is going to leave Two Falls in a week to come to Faridor and meet with Cira for three days. It's going to be done in secret so that no one knows he's gone, and so that the Strikers will have no time to plan an attack.*

Two Falls will be unguarded. The fox can take the henhouse.

He forced himself to keep walking and suddenly realized that he had gone straight past the door of the armory; the guard was waiting for him a few steps back. He forced himself to push all thoughts of Grey from his mind and went in to converse with Cira's armorer about the shipment of engraved ivory. The handles were indeed quite fine, and even Joris was impressed with the craftsmanship. On a typical day, the pieces would have occupied him for hours, but his newfound knowledge was gnawing away at the back of his mind with every second that ticked by. He needed to be alone to think. So, after a few minutes' inspection, he ordered a few new daggers to be made and walked back up to Cira's chambers. She was at her personal writing desk, scribbling away with her back turned to him, an unspoken signal that she wished to be left alone. Joris arranged himself on his usual couch with a book pulled up in front of his face. And then he thought of what to do.

He needed to pass along the information as soon as he could. He wasn't even sure whether it would be *that* useful to the Strikers; after all, it was only three days, and even though he was ostensibly working for them, he had little actual knowledge as to their military strength. But he had spent so long in Cira's keep at arm's length that the mere prospect of being able to tell them anything was immensely rewarding.

Who to pass it along to? He couldn't escape the fortress; he was barely allowed out on Cira's apartment stairwell. Writing was far too dangerous. He had no knowledge of any of Tarr's codes, and he was fairly sure that any of his correspondence would be immediately read and screened by Cira's spies. Tarr hadn't trusted him enough to give him any of the passwords or codes usually used by his other agents. *Tarr probably didn't have a lot of faith in my success at all, come to think of it,* he mused.

Then he remembered.

The girl. Cira's deaf maid, the one who came in to clean on the days when Cira's council members came up to her chambers for discussions. She must have ways of getting information to Tarr. Could he try to find some way to meet her outside of Cira's apartments? No, that was impossible. He couldn't leave without being seen, and besides, it was too great a risk to ask for her personally in the servant's quarters, regardless of whether or not he could come up with a convincing excuse for needing to find her. It would have to be done in Cira's apartments.

He frantically raced through Cira's schedule, frustrated that in his indolence, he had forgotten which day of the week it was. "What's the date today?" he asked Cira.

"Second day," she grunted, not turning around.

He was in luck. The girl would be in the next morning.

Joris took a deep breath and tempered his excitement. He was going to have to watch himself. If he was right and somehow the Strikers were able to get the information and use it, Cira's suspicions would naturally come to fall on him. So, he would have to be twice as sure to give her no reason to think that he was the spy. He was determined to come out the other side of this clean.

Joris liked to believe that he made it through the next day without giving any hint as to the flurry of nerves and impatience that had built within him. He spent the day in his usual ways: loitering about, eating, reading. He would have liked the weather to have cleared up so that he could go out hunting and distract himself.

He slept only a few hours, and had to pretend to be asleep after Cira woke and got dressed so that he wouldn't appear more lively and alert than usual. When he could no longer take it, he wandered out in a semi-dressed state, hoping that a member of the household staff would be there to be appropriately scandalized. But there was only Cira, who gave him an unaffected glance and went back to her writing.

There was a polite knock at the door, and Joris gave a small jump that he tried to mask by pretending that he had an itch on his ribcage. To his disappointment, it was only one of Cira's ladies-in-waiting, who had brought in a few fabric samples. Cira waved her over, and the two of them began discussing possible designs for some sort of festival. *Not like Faridor is going to get terribly cheery, even for a holiday,* Joris thought, and found himself wondering vaguely if this meant that he had to look into fabric for an outfit as well. After a short time, Cira dismissed the maid and resumed her writing.

Right as Joris's mind was about to drift off into a pleasant world filled with expensive brocades and meticulously embroidered waist-coats, the door opened again, and the deaf maid walked in, her head ducked and bearing her usual air of single-minded purpose. Her dark dress hung loose on her extremely thin frame, and she had pulled her deep brown hair back to a bun at the nape of her neck. At the sight of her, Joris suddenly felt a burst of excitement like a firecracker in the pit of his stomach.

Smooth as silk, he set down his book, rose, and glided across the room to kiss Cira on the side of the neck. She shrugged him off, annoyed, blotting a spot of ink that had fallen on her stack of parchment. Joris took the hint and backed away, striding purposefully towards the balcony. "I might see if anyone wants to go for a hunt," he called. "Even with the weather."

"Please do not bother me," Cira snapped. Joris couldn't help but hide a grin. Across the room within the bedchamber, the maid was collecting a few items of clothing that were strewn on the floor near the bed.

"Wait," Joris called out loudly. "Girl! I need you to take my riding boots to be cleaned."

"She's deaf, you idiot," Cira snapped. "She can't hear you. Go show her what you need."

Joris made an annoyed sound in the back of his throat, as if having to cross the room was the biggest imposition he had ever endured. He approached the maid, who must have felt a change in the air behind her, for she whirled and faced him. He saw a flicker of surprise cross her features, followed by a calculated wariness.

"Girl," he said again loudly, as if this would make any difference in her comprehension, "my boots are dirty. Take them to be cleaned." He pointed to a pair of mud-caked riding boots propped up against the wall.

"Would you please be quiet?" Cira barked.

The maid's eyes followed his pointing finger to the pair of boots, and though she looked a bit puzzled, it was easy enough for her to understand what Joris was talking about. She made a motion to go and collect the boots, but Joris caught her arm and stopped her. At his touch, her confusion visibly gave way to suspicion and alarm. Joris glanced over his shoulder at Cira, who was still immersed in whatever she was writing. It was now or never. He fixed his expression into one of deadly urgency and mouthed, *I have a message for Tarr.*

The girl's countenance changed abruptly, face clearing and eyes widening with surprise. For a second, Joris thought that all was well, but a moment later, she shook her head. Quietly, she raised her hands and mimed a writing motion. It was obvious what she meant: she knew he wanted to tell her something important, but needed it to be written down.

Joris stopped and surveyed the room, searching for something, anything that could be of help. The maid pushed him to the side, collected the boots he'd indicated, and went to set them next to the apartment door. Joris stood dumbly in place, his mind racing. The maid widened her eyes at him and made a shooing motion with her hands. *Get on with it*, she seemed to be saying. *Act like everything is normal. Don't let Cira get suspicious.*

"Wretched girl," Joris said aloud, slouching onto one of Cira's couches. "I can't understand why you keep her around."

"She's better at following orders than you, for one thing," Cira hissed. "I told you to shut up."

So ordered, Joris allowed himself one loud disgruntled *hmph* and settled himself back. The maid had resumed her cleaning, her sharp, observant eyes darting about, looking for some sort of solution to their predicament. Joris watched her closely. She met his gaze again and pointed quickly at Cira.

It took Joris a moment to understand, but then realization dawned. The only place with available pen and ink was Cira's writing desk. *This is mad*, he thought. *Should I wait until Cira has left me alone, perhaps later today, and then try and write a note to the maid?* But there was no guarantee that such an occasion would arise. The message had to be delivered now. Joris looked back to the maid and shook his head helplessly.

The maid considered for a moment, then raised her hand and pulsed it a few times. *Wait a moment*, she seemed to be indicating. *I have an idea.*

Joris decided to take the opportunity to offer up a few heartfelt prayers to whatever fates might be looking down on them. The maid, seemingly in no hurry, made her way slowly around the room, dusting various surfaces and polishing tabletops. She crossed behind him out of his field of vision, and began quietly moving about in Cira's curtained-off sleeping chamber.

All at once, there was an almighty crash and the sound of something shattering into pieces. Cira disgustedly threw down her pen atop her piece of parchment and, with a mighty oath, pushed back from her desk and whirled around.

"What the hell is going on this morning?" she shouted. "Do I need to throw everyone in this bloody tower into the sea in order to get some work done?"

She strode off in a cloud of seething fury to see what had broken, and disappeared behind the curtain sectioning her bedchamber off from the rest of the room. Her voice lifted into sounds of displeasure at whatever the maid had knocked over. Her desk stood unguarded. It was Joris's chance.

He leapt to his feet and dashed to Cira's desk. He snatched a blank sheet of parchment and her pen and furiously wrote, hoping that the maid would be able to decipher his frantic handwriting: *Grey at Faridor in 1 week. Gone 3 days.*

Heart racing so hard he felt almost lightheaded, he flung down the pen and fairly hurled himself back onto his couch, trying to slow his breathing down to a reasonable rate. An instant later, Cira reappeared and took her place at her desk. Covertly, he folded the paper and hid it on the couch beneath his knee.

All right, Joris thought tensely. *Now the maid just needs to come back around and I can hand this to her and...*

"I can't focus anymore," Cira complained, pushing back from her desk and swiveling around to glare at him. "You all have ruined my concentration."

Turn back around, dammit, Joris swore, but he kept his composure as unflappable as ever. His full lips parted in an innocent, winning smile, and he shook his head so that one of his dark curls of hair fell forward in front of his pale gray-green eyes. He could almost see Cira melt a little in her chair. Behind him, he was conscious of the tinkling sounds of shards being swept up and collected.

"Let's go for a walk," Cira said abruptly. "I need some fresh air."

"Of course," Joris responded evenly, though his stomach gave a fresh twist. *Should I hide the note somewhere around here for the maid to find? How will she know that I've hidden it? How will she know where to look?*

All at once, Cira waved her hand at someone distantly behind him and realized that she was trying to catch the maid's attention. The girl must have re-emerged from Cira's bedchamber. Joris didn't dare turn around, and focused instead on picking a minuscule speck of dirt from one fingernail.

"Leave now," Cira ordered, with a dismissive gesture towards the door. "We're going out." She pointed to herself and Joris and indicated the door again. The maid must have confirmed her comprehension, for Cira stood, looking satisfied. As she moved, Joris took the opportunity to rise to his feet as well.

Hoping the maid was watching him, and remembering her nimble sleight of hand from months before, he covertly slid the note into the back of his trousers, with the top sticking out. Cira walked towards him, smiling coolly and extending her arm for him to take. He did, and as they turned together towards the door, he felt the faintest brush against his back, then saw the maid walking quietly off in the other direction to gather her cleaning supplies and pick up his dirty boots.

Cira waited and saw the maid safely out of her room before she and Joris left the apartment themselves, flanked by two guards as they strode down the stairs. It was only once Cira was walking in front of him down a long, narrow corridor that Joris finally dared pass a hand over the back of his trousers. The note was no longer there. The maid had done it. A thrill shuddered through his throat and down each of his arms. *They had done it. They had gotten away with it.*

He realized that since they'd left Cira's room, his breath had been coming in short bursts. His hands were shaking. *I wonder whether anything will come of this*, he thought. *I suppose eventually I'll find out, one way or the other.* Ahead of him, Cira flicked a strand of hair over her shoulder, her delicate features momentarily in profile. He rolled his shoulders to loosen them, forcing himself to clear his head, to fully bring his attention back to the present. He had to be patient. He had to wait.

It was much harder than it had been before.

It was a day later when Cira's counselor found himself standing opposite General Grey, who was seated in the large chair behind his ornate desk. The General listened quietly as his guest spoke. The counselor, in turn, tried not to feel unnerved by the General's expressionless yet curiously piercing stare.

"...and so her Majesty wishes for you to visit her in Faridor and make your report at that time," he concluded, shifting uneasily. The floor emitted a loud creak that shattered the stillness of the grand room, and the messenger cringed inwardly.

"Why must I go to Faridor?" the General asked in a quiet voice.

"Her Majesty wishes it so," the counselor replied. *It's not exactly as though Cira explains herself to me.*

The General rose to his feet and slowly walked across the room. He did not like such an order, and he had not left Two Falls since he had taken over after his predecessor's assassination. He knew the city now, knew her like the back of his hand. He knew her alleyways, her hideouts, her clubs, her denizens; kept a running list in his head of those he could trust and those he couldn't. He maintained order. But, he consoled himself, it would only be for three days. The Strikers were without a centralized army. Even if they attacked during his absence, there would be no way that they could overcome the Kagaian forces in Two Falls. And Grey had heard rumors that Laith had been severely injured or perhaps even killed. Si, Morthenstar's own heir, had not been sighted or spoken of in weeks, and there was a rumor that he had gone missing. The Strikers were in no shape to attack.

But even so...He paused and turned back towards the windows behind him. Somewhere out there, somewhere in some cold room hidden away in the belly of the city, was Tarr. And the mere fact that Tarr would remain in Two Falls while he himself left filled the General with anxiety. *We will have to take extra precautions*, he thought firmly. *Assume they will attack. Prepare for anything.* But all his inner assurances could do little to assuage the gnawing unease in his chest.

"I will comply with her Majesty's wishes, of course," he said finally, strolling back towards his desk.

The messenger, who had been standing politely while General Grey slowly paced the length of the room and back, let out a sigh of relief.

It wasn't as though Grey had any choice in the matter, but he would have been loath to report even the slightest hint of negativity back to the Queen. If there was anyone prone to killing the messenger, it was Cira. "Very good, sir," he said aloud. "Shall I make arrangements for your journey?"

"No," Grey replied, sitting down at his desk and withdrawing a pen and ink. "I shall make my own preparations. Go now; you may tell her that I am coming." With that, the General began to scratch out a message across the parchment, and the counselor took the hint. He rose and bowed (even though the General was clearly no longer paying attention to him) and backed away with as much dignity as he could. After he was safely out of the room, he let out an involuntary shudder. There was something about General Grey's silent intensity and those sharp eyes that gave him the creeps.

Grey finished scrawling his message and rang his bell. The door opened promptly, and one of his secretaries walked in. Grey casually handed her the parchment, which the secretary rolled and tied without reading. "Take a note," Grey ordered, and the secretary brought out a small writing plate and parchment and waited, her pen poised. Grey began to pace again, with the slow fluid motion of a cat. The scribe watched attentively.

"The following is a top-secret order," Grey began and swiveled to face the scribe, who was a young, eager, skinny young woman of about twenty-six. "This means that I will know exactly who comes into contact with this message, and should there be any slip-ups, the most dire consequences await the guilty parties." He began to walk again. The scribe waited until his back was fully turned to swallow nervously, starting to realize how hot the room suddenly felt.

"For three days beginning on the high moon of the month, unofficial command shall be taken of Two Falls by my second officer, Lieutenant General Allox. I will be relocating temporarily to a safe house on the other side of the city to receive a debrief by senior Faridor officers." *That sounds convincing enough*, General Grey thought to himself. "No public word shall be given of my temporary relocation. Lieutenant General Allox will handle all inquiries and Two Falls business at that time, and any business for me will be directed to Allox or delayed until my return to headquarters. Is that understood?"

"It will be done, sir," said the scribe smartly, finishing her last transcription with a flourish of her pen. "Shall there be anything else?"

Grey listed his four most senior officers and gave strict instructions that the directive was meant solely for them and that it should not be distributed to anyone else. His duties complete, the scribe withdrew to leave Grey in moody contemplation by his fireplace. Lieutenant General Allox was an intelligent, capable officer and was more than able to hold down the fort for three days without incident. She had a good group of troops. Everything would be fine.

But nevertheless, General Grey was unhappy.

CHAPTER TWENTY

Tarr blinked, rubbed his eyes, and read the coded letter for a third time, just in case he was still asleep and dreaming. His heart started pounding, and he sat straight up, energy surging through his limbs so quickly that he sprang to his feet and nearly ran across the tiny room. He glanced down and read the code again.

The young woman who had delivered the note stared at him with an unsure look. She couldn't tell by his reaction whether the news was good or bad. "What is it, sir?"

Tarr started as though he had forgotten she was in the room with him. He rushed forward, his brown and green eyes wide with urgency. He took her by the shoulders and stared into her face. "When was this sent?"

"I brought it myself, sir. From Faridor, just last night."

Tarr could barely breathe. "I need you to get a team together. Comb the city and bring all the Strikers and Ari back here with me. Even Rane. I need you to find them *as fast as you possibly can*. Are you able to do it?"

The gravity of the unknown situation was not lost on the girl, whose mouth tightened into a resolute line. She nodded solemnly. "I will find them, sir."

"Good. As fast as you can." Tarr turned away as the girl flew out the door. He could hear her footsteps pounding away down the hallway. Unable to sit still, Tarr quickly started walking the length of the room with his long, lanky strides, his mind firing like a sparking machine. He was suddenly brimming with energy.

It was nearly three hours before all the others, about fifteen in total, had been rounded up and crammed into Tarr's room. Tables had been set up, and chairs dragged in, and looking around at the faces, Tarr reflected wryly how delighted Cira's guards would be if they happened to stumble into the room at that moment; nearly every resistance captain was present, arms folded, eyebrows raised. Archer, Laith, Athela, and Marc stood just behind Tarr. Si was perched on one corner of the table. Ari, who had just come off of a two-day shift, was looking rumpled and exhausted, but his eyes were trained keenly on Tarr, waiting for him to begin. The room was hushed, expectant.

"I have just received intelligence from Faridor that in one week, General Grey will leave this city for a private meeting with Cira," Tarr said. "He will be gone for three days. If we're to take back this city, that will be our best opportunity."

Tarr's words fell like a stone into water. A few of the younger officers' mouths dropped. The older ones stared at him gravely. "Has this been verified by our sources in the Two Falls Kagaian headquarters?" Ari asked.

"No," Tarr shook his head. "I only received this information a few hours ago. We've had no word from the headquarters." He considered for a moment. "Though if what I know of General Grey is true, this meeting is probably entirely Cira's idea, and Grey is trying not to let word of it get out."

The room lapsed into another prolonged silence. After a moment, one of the younger girls in the room timidly raised her hand. Tarr smiled encouragingly at her, and after letting loose a nervous cough, she said, "Still, General Grey is only one person. Even if he leaves, what difference will it make? Kagai's army is still much stronger, better equipped, and better fed than ours."

"That's a completely valid point," Tarr agreed. "What we've always had on our side are cunning and the kind of guerrilla tactics against which it is difficult for them to fight outright. But General Grey has managed to stay in step with us. He's a smart man, one of the smartest I've ever encountered. He not only has the brute force of the Kagaian army, but he's got an army of spies and informants to match our own. He recognizes the importance of each." Tarr slowly walked around the corner of the table. "To have him out of the way, even for as small a period of time as three days, is more of a chance than we might ever get again. Whoever takes over as second in command cannot possibly hope to be as well prepared or have as good a handle on the spy network... or have that sixth sense the way that General Grey does." He paused and shrugged a thin shoulder. "It's a chance. It's as good a chance as we'll get."

Athela swiveled around to look at Ari and Rane. "Who would take over as his second in command?"

Ari and Rane regarded each other for a moment. "Lieutenant Allox," Ari answered.

"What's she like?" Athela asked.

"Smart," Rane replied. "Capable."

"We've got to get rid of her," Athela decided, looking back at Tarr.

"Assassination?" Archer suggested.

"Too obvious," Laith countered. "If we're going to get this to work, we can't let on that we know anything about what's happening."

"What if we get rid of her the first day that General Grey is gone?" Si piped up from his perch.

"That'll cut down on the amount of time we have to put a plan into action," Ari frowned.

"Anyone know who'll take over for Lieutenant Allox if she is indisposed?" Athela asked the group.

"The second lieutenant is a man named Elgin," Ari replied.

"I know him," Archer agreed. "Luckily for us, he's sort of an idiot. He was chosen to replace one of the officers my snipers picked off about a month or two ago."

"If we can somehow occupy Allox's attention," Laith mused, "to the point where Elgin is put in command of the Two Falls headquarters, that's stacking the deck pretty highly in our favor."

Tarr nodded in agreement and turned to a quiet, older-looking man who was seated with his hands folded in his lap. He had run an old bookstore in the main section of town before his wife, an Ashan, was killed and his shop was destroyed by Kagaian troops. He was one of Tarr's top forgers. "Do you think you can get us some sort of official order that's urgent enough to get Allox out of our hair but non-threatening enough not to raise any suspicions?"

"I think I can," the old man replied, pushing his glasses up a bit farther on his nose.

"Good," Tarr said firmly. "Work with Marc and Archer and see if you all can't concoct a nice little trap for Lieutenant Allox. I want it run by me first before we execute."

Marc and Archer grinned at one another, and Marc gave Si a nudge with his elbow. Tarr looked around at the others' faces. There was fear, excitement, and, for the first time in a long time, something resembling hope.

Ari, however, still looked unsure, and after a moment spoke up. "Tarr, I agree that this is a chance we have to take. However, the issue still stands: even if we get Lieutenant Allox out of the way, *we will have no army*. Our soldiers have been starving all through the winter. We have no supplies and very limited weapons."

Tarr sighed inwardly. He knew that Ari was right and was just trying to be logical, but it was still rather deflating. A sidelong glance at Archer confirmed that his brother was trying to figure out how to surreptitiously kick Ari in the shin. "Then we are going to have to figure out a way to succeed without the use of excessive force," Tarr informed them levelly. "Until then, we have a very short time to do a great many things. To those of you who have not been assigned a mission, I want you to form groups and do reconnaissance work as best you can. I want to know what Kagai's total force is here in Two Falls, estimates of their supplies, and what we have to work with. Without calling too much attention, we must try to recruit as many new agents as we can. Is that understood? Good."

Tarr nodded, and the room immediately burst into a flurry of action as individuals broke into groups and headed out of the door. Tarr waited behind, and soon, the room was empty except for the seven Strikers and Ari.

"Do you have any *actual* ideas about how to execute some sort of plan?" Ari inquired tiredly as the door closed. Archer silently shot him a nasty look.

"Not yet," Tarr replied equably. "But I'm sure something will come to us."

Athela pulled out a large map and unrolled it on the tabletop. It was an intricately detailed map of the city, with color-coded buildings indicating Kagaian and Striker strongholds. The scarlet areas looked pathetically small.

"Well, *that's* depressing," Archer sighed.

"Not necessarily," Athela countered. "We're smaller, harder to find. More difficult to eradicate."

"Like bugs," Si agreed.

"An apt metaphor," Marc smiled.

Athela's face looked strained as she turned to Tarr. "We're outnumbered, Tarr. Comically, ridiculously outnumbered."

"Then we need to find a way to even the odds," Tarr replied. "Use every trick we have up our sleeves to divide them, confuse them, pick them off wherever we can. Get them where we want them and swarm them." He paused, smiling reflectively. "Like bugs."

"Sounds great in theory," Marc agreed. "Any ideas *how* exactly we can do that?"

For that question, however, Tarr did not have a ready reply.

"Si, any chance you can summon those powers of yours and call in some reinforcements?" Archer joked with a sidelong wink. Si smiled, but there was a strained edge to it. A moment later, a faraway, vacant look crossed his expression, and Tarr thought to himself that the boy must, in fact, be saying some sort of prayer.

"This is all we've really got to go on right now," Laith acknowledged. "Everyone mull it over. For now, let's try and survey every possible asset we've got left in this city. There may still have been some things that we missed. We'll meet back here at midnight tonight, and we *will* have come up with a plan by then." His tone left no room for misinterpretation.

The small group broke up and shuffled out of the door. Tarr stayed behind, sliding into his favorite chair and steepling his eleven long fingers beneath his nose. His sweetly tilted eyes blinked up to the muted gray light sifting in from a high window. *What do I have?* he thought to himself. *I have spies.* His mind immediately flicked over to Leonore, the young girl he had just assigned to Faridor. Something stirred in the back of his memory. *She had a friend. A young friend...* He closed his eyes and thought deeply, as if he were churning the contents of his brain with an oar or paddle. *Imran.* The face clicked into place. Full lips, dark, shoulder-length hair. Bony, angular, tall for her age. Could easily have passed for Ashan. Tarr remembered that he had had Marc and Si follow her and that they had discovered that she was working as a double agent for Grey. He had kept her around anyway, just in case. Perhaps there was something there...perhaps.

The hours slid by as Tarr sat motionless, assessing the cards he held in his hand, trying to conjure up a way to take back the city of Two Falls.

What they needed, Tarr realized, was a miracle.

Midnight came, it seemed, a mere split second after Tarr had registered the sun setting outside his single window, the light fading gradually from gold to orange to dark lavender and finally to black. Other than a few vague assassination plans and the trump card that was the young Kagaian double agent Imran, Tarr had come up with very little. Feeling disconcerted and frustrated with himself (but determined not to show it to his friends), he stretched out one long leg after another and stood by the hidden entrance, waiting for the others to show up. Si and Athela were first, then Rane and Archer. When the white Ashan entered the room, he raised his gray eyebrows questioningly at Tarr, who could only roll his eyes in self-exasperation. Archer chuckled hollowly, and Tarr knew that Archer had been no more successful than he in coming up with something brilliant.

The next quick rap at the secret entrance admitted Ari, who was followed by a strange woman Tarr did not recognize. The woman was older than all of them, well into her forties by the look of her, and had the build of someone who was used to riding long distances in a saddle. She was obviously some sort of soldier, outfitted in ornate but light-fitting traveling armor and a purple cloak the likes of which Tarr had only seen a few times before. *Is she Jelani?* he wondered. The cloak was worn and old, with splattered mud caked around the hem, but was made of a rich material that suggested wealth. Her face was weathered and sunburned, and her pale shoulder-length hair pulled back into a tie at the nape of her neck. Her eyes were small and seemed almost permanently squinted shut, with a premature burst of crow's feet at the corners, but Tarr surmised that they were light blue or gray. Tarr regarded her with frank curiosity and sent a searching look to Ari, who was, as usual, infuriatingly indecipherable.

"I'll explain," he said flatly. He moved inside, followed by this strange guest. *Must be his version of a surprise. Charming,* Tarr thought to himself as he closed the door behind them.

Archer was staring incredulously at the unknown visitor as Tarr passed into the meeting room. Tarr could tell that he was itching to ask Ari who she was and what was going on, but as a rule, Archer didn't speak to Ari unless under extreme duress. Si, obviously fascinated by all the hidden dynamics, kept peering up at the strange soldier's armor, then glancing between Archer and Ari, as if hoping Archer would start a conversation that would lead to some sort of physical altercation. Tarr had once overheard Marc and Si constructing an elaborate wager about which of the two would win if their mutual animosity ever came to actual blows.

Laith and Marc were late to arrive; ten minutes after midnight, there was a quick knock at the secret door, and Tarr moved back to admit them into the awkwardly silent room.

"How goes it?" Marc asked briskly, striding inside and brushing the late-night mist out of his flaxen hair. Laith ducked under the doorframe behind him and gave Tarr a quick smile and nod, stamping the mud from his boots before continuing into the meeting hall. Tarr figured that he'd let Marc and Laith see Ari's surprise for themselves and followed them in.

Though Tarr's piqued curiosity had prompted all sorts of suppositions as to the soldier's identity in the intervening minutes between Ari's and Laith's arrivals, he was not quite prepared for what actually transpired. Marc, then Laith entered the room, and no sooner had the strange soldier clapped eyes on them than she had strode forward and bent to one knee in front of Laith. Laith, for his part, looked as if he had seen a ghost.

"Prince Argolaith!" said the soldier, her head still bent.

Laith froze in his tracks. His eyes grew wider, and his mouth opened and closed a few times. He glanced at Marc, who looked similarly flabbergasted. "Lady Burton?" he asked incredulously.

The woman Laith called Lady Burton arose and gripped Laith by the arms; then the two shared one of the most enthusiastic, soldierly embraces Tarr had ever been privileged to witness, with much pounding of backs and clapping of shoulders. Tarr glanced over to Ari, who was watching the proceedings with about as much emotion or interest as if he had been watching a livestock show at the market. When Ari noticed that Tarr was studying him, he gave a half-shrug.

"I figured if Laith didn't recognize her and she wasn't who she said she was, we could all just kill her," he said calmly, by way of explanation.

"Ah," Tarr murmured faintly. "Good thinking."

By now, Marc and Lady Burton had exchanged a similarly enthusiastic greeting (though Tarr noted with an inward grin that Marc had to stand on his toes to be of an equivalent height), and all three turned around to face the others, beaming with the welcome surprise of seeing a long-lost friend. "This," Laith said, placing a hand on Lady Burton's shoulder, "is Lady Burton, with whom I served many years during my training with the Joymarillian mounted division in the Meadows."

Lady Burton gave a curt bow to each of them as Laith went around the room and made the appropriate introductions. "Now," Laith began, as they settled down into chairs drawn up around the meeting table, "what on earth are you doing here in Two Falls? How did you find us?"

Lady Burton explained that the same division with whom Laith had served had left five years ago on an exploratory mission to the undiscovered western hinterlands of the Meadows. They were making note of the peoples and cultures they encountered on the way, and to see whether, during the term of their travels, they could reach a body of water similar to that which rested on the eastern shores between their country and the desert regions of Vireg. They found such a body of water after two years, spent a year traveling up and down the coast mapping the regions they discovered, and then, according to the royal directives they had been given, began traveling back to the palace of

Joymaril.

"So wait," Athela cut in after she had reached this point in her story, "you mean to say that no one in your division was aware of anything that's happened? Cira's takeover? Our exile?"

"Nothing," Lady Burton shrugged. "But that is not unusual, especially considering the far-reaching scope of our mission. We did receive extremely intermittent dispatches for the first year, but after that we ranged too far for anyone to find us."

Athela settled back into her chair, looking overwhelmed. "All right, then," she said. "Continue."

Burton continued. A month ago, they'd stopped at a post town in the Meadows, a settlement out just at the edge of the wilderness. To their astonishment, a yellowing, brittle letter had been waiting for them there, addressed to Lord Calchas from Laith's brother Cade. The letter was short, stating that Laith and the others had been banished and that Cade suspected Cira was about to stage a coup. He requested Calchas's aid.

"Three years," Marc shook his head, bewildered. "Three years the letter was there."

"Tucked inside the desk of the postmaster," Burton agreed ruefully.

Tarr glanced over at Laith, whose face was unnaturally pale, clearly digesting the unsettling news about his brother. Tarr found himself wondering what had happened to Cade after the letter was sent. Had he been captured? Executed? Survival seemed unlikely after so long.

Lady Burton continued her account. After the letter had been found, Calchas immediately moved them out toward the direction of Two Falls, intending to stop and investigate the situation in the city before proceeding to Joymaril. Only about a week before, just as they were nearing the Ashan forest, a small advance party of their division encountered a band of troops marching under the green Kagaian banner right on the borders of the Meadows. Words were exchanged, blows were threatened, and the Kagaian troops (who, it seemed, were escorting some kind of dignitary or official) managed to get away.

"So," Lady Burton concluded in a remarkably nonchalant way, "we came as fast as we could to see if we could find Lord Argolaith and offer our services." She gave an ironic half-grimace. "Sorry we were late."

"We're glad to have you here," Laith assured her faintly, clapping her on the shoulder once again. "Your timing is impeccable."

Tarr considered Laith's words for a moment. The timing was, indeed, almost impossibly impeccable. There they'd all been, standing around and beseeching the fates for some sort of miracle, and a mere few hours later, one had turned up. Tarr thoughtfully turned around to look at Si, who was staring with unabashed excitement and curiosity at Lady Burton: wide-eyed, innocent, and unassuming. The thought was incredibly farfetched, but Tarr couldn't stop himself from wondering whether Si had, indeed, pulled some sort of cosmic string to summon the troop to their aid. A moment after the idea had crossed his mind, Tarr shook his head and dismissed the notion as pure folly. *Coincidence*, he reassured himself. *A lucky break.*

The other Strikers stared around at each other in bewildered silence. "But, erm," Archer said, clearing his throat delicately, wresting his eyes away from Si, "as you all are soldiers of Joymaril, and Joymaril is currently under the control of Cira, doesn't that make you loyal to her?"

Lady Burton blinked as though she thought Archer was rather slow. "We served the true Queen," she said flatly. "I swore no oath to Lady Cira, nor any other pretender to the throne. Besides, we rode with Lord Argolaith and Lord Marcus for years when they were young," she looked fondly over at the pair beside her. "And, no offense, Lady Athela, but your sister Cira was always a bit of a...snit."

"None taken," Athela said breezily. She had, as Tarr knew first-hand, called Cira far worse things than a snit.

"So," Tarr cut in, hoping that he wasn't sounding too rude. "How many of you...are there?"

"Not very many," Lady Burton frowned. "Only two hundred or so."

Tarr had a sudden urge to either dance or vomit, or possibly both at the same time. *Two hundred?* An army it wasn't, but a troop of two hundred trained, fed soldiers was far more than they could ever hope for. "That's...good," he said, trying to sound seasoned and professional and utterly nonchalant. One sidelong smirk from Rane told him that he hadn't fooled her for a second.

"It's still not enough," Ari grunted, ever the optimist.

Archer shot him a filthy look. "It's a far sight better than what we had six hours ago," the Ashan retorted.

"Who's in command of your division?" Laith asked.

Lady Burton gazed at him levelly. "Why, General Calchas, of course."

Laith shifted ever so slightly, his eyes lightening. Tarr could tell that the name meant something significant. The prince turned to face the others. "I'm going out to meet with the troop tonight. Tarr, Athela, see if you can figure out what to do with all this. Where are you stationed?" he asked, turning back to Lady Burton.

"We're hidden on the southwest outskirts of the forest, well out of sight of any of the wall patrols," Burton answered. "You can come back with me if you'd like. It wasn't too much trouble getting in, despite what all those guards seem to think."

"It's getting *out* that's usually the problem," Archer remarked.

"I'll come too," Marc volunteered. "We'll find a way, find someone to bribe."

"Or Archer's boat," Athela said sarcastically.

"You dare scoff at my boat," Archer shook his head disapprovingly. "However, if we're looking for a *slightly* less aquatic means of egress, one of my squad found a backed-up sewer line yesterday that leads outside the city. Shouldn't be *too* disgusting."

"Fine," Laith stood quickly. He suddenly seemed to be in a great hurry to visit the troops. "Let's meet back in the morning, then."

Tarr stretched tiredly, but his mind was buzzing. It would be another night with only an hour or two of sleep, but this time, he felt alive, ready for it. As much as he hated to admit it, Ari was right. Two hundred wasn't enough, not *nearly* enough, but it was something. He would have to get creative, that was all.

Laith, Lady Burton, Ari, and Marc departed soon after, and Si went and fetched the city map again. They stared at it numbly for a few minutes before Tarr tilted his head to one side and asked, "Athela? Have I told you about a young lady named Imran?" Puzzled, Athela shook her head. A slow smile began to creep in at the sides of his mouth.

"Friends," he said, "I think I just might have an idea."

Laith and Marc kept a few strides behind Lady Burton as they wove their way down the side of the hill and into the shadowy gloom of the outskirts of the forest. Laith peered over his shoulder and squinted into the darkness every few feet, trying to catch a glimpse of any sort of camp.

"Here," said Lady Burton, and they halted.

"Where's the camp?" Marc whispered. Laith was relieved to find that he was not the only one feeling bewildered.

Lady Burton let off a low whistle like a bird call; after a few seconds, it was returned. The coast was clear. Burton motioned to their right, where the trees sloped up towards the curtain of stars above a small embankment. There, tucked within the crevices of the slope, were a number of tents, cleverly hidden by a rock wall. There were no lights outside the tents, but Laith could make out a dim, curtained glow that suggested life within. Laith swallowed, his heart pounding harder.

Burton led the way down the rows of tents, then stopped in front of a tent in the center. She paused for a moment, then held the flap aside. A soft, orange light emanated from within. Laith glanced at Marc, who smiled reassuringly, and they stepped inside.

The tent was just as Laith remembered it, though the fabric was slightly more worn and aged since he had last been inside. It seemed smaller, too: the ceiling seemed lower, and the sides of the tent pressed in, whereas in his boyish memory the tent had seemed vast. The curtains were all a deep, rich, reddish-purple trimmed with gold and silver braid, and on the ceiling there was a fabulous design of the sun, moon, and constellations. Laith suddenly remembered the nights when he and Marc were boys and had come into the tent to hear the stories of those stars and the heroes who were honored there. A flood of memory and emotion washed over him, and he swallowed again.

There were about ten men and women, each attired in the traditional garb of Joymarillian commanders and lieutenant generals, seated in the tent. All rose as they entered.

"Prince Argolaith, sir," Burton intoned, "and Lord Marcus."

Laith swept the faces before him. Most of them were younger, nearer his age than not (including one or two he thought he remembered as having served with him when he was a boy). There were a few older officers, some completely new faces. But the man seated in the middle, whose hair was now a pure white, whose weatherbeaten face crinkled ever so slightly, was the one he had wanted to see.

"Prince Argolaith," said General Calchas and slowly, stiffly, sank to one knee. The others beside him did the same.

Laith was overcome at the sight of his teacher. "Rise, please, all of you," he said quickly, and strode forward. Calchas rose creakily to his feet, one hand on his knee to help himself up, a smile creased into the lines of his face.

"Let me look at you both," Calchas said. His voice was raspy, like two stones grating against one another. He held Laith and Marc at arm's length and regarded them. Marc's hair hadn't darkened as much as Calchas had anticipated it would. He had the same frost-tinted blue eyes, the stocky build of a boxer, the same kindness and good humor on his face. A pale scar divided his face diagonally in two; he would have to ask Marc to tell him the story of that particular wound. And Laith...Calchas had brought up many youngsters in his years, but Laith had always been a favorite. He was a fine young man, well-built, with nobility and innate intelligence apparent in every gesture and expression. He had also, Calchas noted with a bit of a smile, become every bit as handsome as everyone had predicted he would be. But there was something else: a tired expression in the eyes, a sadness that had not been there before. The recent years had not been kind to Laith, Calchas saw, and the realization pained him greatly.

Calchas stepped back and motioned for leather folding stools to be brought and set, and the group settled themselves in. Stories were exchanged, the groups were caught up. Every now and then, a rolling peal of laughter filled the tent; laughter, Calchas noted, in which Laith did not take part. After an hour or so, Marc and Laith began to fill the commanders in on the circumstances in Two Falls: their precarious position, and their need for backup and supplies.

"It's a dire situation," Laith concluded. "We will not be able to make it through another winter. Cira is starving and weeding us out, one by one."

"You've received no aid from Joymaril?" Calchas inquired.

"Not a word," Laith shook his head. "It's been completely closed off. There's been no word from anyone. No news. We can't even get close to the city."

"And I doubt we could rely on the Ashans for help," chimed in one of the lieutenants.

"We reached out to them with largely negative results," Laith shrugged.

"Still, I highly doubt that there are none still loyal to you and your family at the palace," Calchas pointed out. "What of your brother? Other than that letter, I've heard nothing."

Laith shook his head again hopelessly. "Nothing. I don't even know whether he's living or dead. I have a feeling he's alive; he's always been a clever one. But if he is, he has made no attempt to contact us."

"We'll see if we can get any word from the inside," Calchas motioned to a young woman sitting next to him to make note of the order.

"Your presence here has changed things," Marc pointed out.

"Are you willing to help us?" Laith asked.

Calchas glanced around at his commanders. "We will do whatever we can," he announced. "Your cousin, Athela, is the elder sister and the rightful Queen, and we will support her claim to the throne." He rose to his feet, and in a single motion, the others did as well. "I would now like to have a few words with Prince Argolaith alone."

Marc raised an eyebrow at Laith, who nodded. Marc clapped one of the other soldiers on the back, and they headed out of the tent, closing the flap behind them. Calchas returned to his seat and faced Laith. A comfortable silence passed.

"I remember the last time you stood here, my boy," said Calchas, pointing to the center of the tent, "before going back to the palace."

"How old was I?" Laith smiled. "Eleven? Twelve?"

"Fourteen," Calchas shook his head wonderingly. He paused. "A few years ago, we received word that you were married. I would have liked to come to your wedding. We drank a toast to you and to your bride."

A cloud seemed to pass over Laith's face, and his voice grew quiet. "You're right; I am married," he confirmed.

"What is her name?"

"Ilaina." Laith's eyes had a faraway look to them. "We were separated when we had to flee Joymaril. She's still out there, somewhere.

In hiding, probably."

Calchas was quiet for a moment and pretended to flick a piece of grit off of the arm of his chair. "I had a wife as well," he said finally. "When I was much younger. She died in childbirth many years ago."

Laith blinked in surprise. "I'm sorry," he said, realizing that Calchas had had a life he'd only been dimly aware of when he was a boy. "What did you do?"

Calchas gave a self-mocking laugh. "Spent my years wandering around the wilderness on horseback," he said.

Laith managed a small chuckle, then fell quiet. "She's still out there," he said again. "She has to be. She won't just be...*gone*."

"I hope so, my boy," Calchas said, though his voice was tinged with sorrow.

A long, heavy sigh escaped Laith's lips, then he straightened up and squared his shoulders. He met Calchas square in the eyes. "It's good to see you, sir," he said, every inch the soldier again.

"You as well, my lad," said Calchas wistfully. "Now, then, what's this plan your friends are concocting?"

"I'm not sure yet," said Laith. "Whatever it is, it'll have to be soon."

"We'll be ready," Calchas assured him. "We'll fight alongside you, my boy. I promise."

Laith smiled, but his dark eyes were sad.

Four days later, under cover of darkness, a small contingent of Kagaian riders quietly slipped out through one of the back gates of Two Falls. Though they began riding east, their path eventually began bending north, sliding up along the coastline towards the fortress of Faridor. They passed the wall without being detected, but Tarr had stationed lookouts along the road to Faridor. By the time the gray morning light began to creep over the city walls, they had reported back that it was true: General Grey had officially left Two Falls. It was now or never.

Tarr called an early meeting at the Strikers' headquarters. A few of the junior members of the Striker forces were summoned as well and were commanded to carry out some small tasks while the important meeting was taking place. One of these was the young girl Imran. Tarr assigned her and another girl to copy some maps one room down from the strategy session. After an hour or so, the other girl was called out of the room to assist the medical team with rolling fresh bandages for the wounded, leaving Imran alone in the room beside the Strikers' secret meeting.

After the meeting, most of the other Strikers cleared out of the building. Tarr himself strode casually into the map room to check on Imran's progress. The girl's head snapped around as he entered, and she gave him a rather forced smile. She had been dawdling a bit in her work, trying her best to overhear what had transpired in the adjacent room.

"Everything going well?" Tarr asked kindly, peering over her shoulder at the half-finished map.

"Sort of," said Imran in a low voice. "I'm not very good at this."

"Don't forget the lake there," Tarr suggested, tapping the original map with one long finger.

"Oh, right," said Imran distractedly, shaking her dark hair over one shoulder. "I'm sorry about that."

There was a swift rap on the door, and Archer poked his head inside. "Tarr," he said, then halted as soon as he saw Imran. "I...er... could I speak to you about...?" he trailed off.

"Oh, right," said Tarr hurriedly. He turned to Imran. "I'll be right back."

Tarr moved out into the hallway, closing the door behind him. "What is it?" he asked.

"We've got word of the troop," Archer said in a low voice, grinning.

"Archer!" Tarr snapped, no levity in his tone. He looked pointedly to the door of the map room. "Not here."

Tarr led him a few paces down the hallway and around a nearby corner. "Now, look, Archer, you can't say those kinds of things while we might be overheard," he hissed, frustrated.

"No one's listening," Archer said dismissively. "Just got word back from General Calchas. Their troop is going to move camp to the northwest side of the wall. It's a little less steep there; he thinks it'll be easier to attack the wall from that position."

"Fine. Are they all outfitted?"

"As far as I can tell," shrugged Archer. "A small group, but we'll have surprise on our side."

"Good. Meet up with Marc this afternoon; we'll reconvene tonight. You sure it'll be a full moon for the attack?"

"Bright as a lamp," Archer assured him. "Talk to you later."

With that, Archer turned and headed down the passageway. Tarr watched him go, a feeling of anxiety twisting in his stomach. As softly as he could, without making a single whisper of sound, he turned on his heel and padded to the corner of the hallway. He peered around, and just as he did, he saw the door to the map room slowly latch shut, as though someone had just closed it. There was no doubt about it. Imran had heard them.

Tarr smiled serenely to himself and turned to go.

Rane stretched luxuriously, slipping pleasantly into consciousness after the decadence of six hours' sleep. She awoke, squinting away the bright light through the window, and grabbed her sword. As she did, she noted rather sadly that it had shared her bed far more often than Tarr in the past month, especially after their argument about whether or not she should be assigned to Faridor. It was a quiet morning, and there were no sounds from the streets outside, so she decided it was safe to walk out of her hidden sleeping chamber and into the main kitchen of Joris's house. Her auburn hair fell in a loose braid down her back, and she strode quickly through the house, listening for signs of the other Strikers. There were none. *They must all be out finalizing preparations before the attack*, she thought.

She was barefoot and still in her loose sleeping clothes, her feet slapping softly against the tile as she walked. She carried her sword along at her side; she had more than once tried to buckle the sheath to her pajama pants, but they always fell down in an extremely unseemly way.

She made her way to the kitchen and pumped a cup full of cold, fresh water, then leaned against one of the counters, drinking it and staring through the broad window that opened onto the street outside. In ten minutes, she counted only two or three people passing by; between the coldness of the oncoming winter and the fear that pervaded the city, it was rare that anyone left their house unless in case of emergency.

It felt to her like the calm before the storm; with General Grey gone, the fate of Two Falls would be decided in the next two days, one way or the other. There was only one day before their plan was put into action, and though she could feel her nerves jangling, logically, there was very little she could do at that moment in her pajamas.

As she took another contemplative sip, her eyes once more scanned the street. Her breath stopped short.

It was almost like an apparition: where a moment before the street had been empty, suddenly there was a figure there, facing her; a figure clad in black clothes and a black cloak. He stood directly across from her, on the other side of the street, beneath an awning. She could not see his face.

Rane straightened, her eyes trained on the figure, and slowly set her cup down on the counter. She knew who it was, knew by the prickling of the hairs on the back of her neck and by the feeling in her gut. It was *him*. The mysterious man who had been haunting them, who had left his tracks outside their headquarters, who had killed the girl in an attempt to taunt Laith. He was there, and he was *looking straight at her,* as if he could see her through the window, waiting for her to come out.

Slowly, Rane picked up her cup, finished the water, and drew her sword.

Rane opened the front door of Joris's apartment and padded down the front steps in her bare feet. The icy wind cut through her shirt like a knife, and the freezing stones burned her feet, but she shrugged the pain away with the discipline she had been taught since childhood. The winter gusts began to blow her auburn hair free of its braid, locks of hair flying like burnished red flame against the dull, neutral colors of the winter-soaked city. The figure was still across the street, a dark blot against the gray of the buildings. Rane advanced slowly, raising her sword into an attack position. And then—like that—the figure had vanished. But not by magic this time. She had seen where he'd gone.

Rane bolted forward like a flash of light, darting down the thin alley with her hair flying around her shoulders. Knowing better than to rush into a potential ambush unguarded, she slowed and raised her sword before her, training her ears for any possible whisper of sound. The alley was empty as far as she could see, but there was no way any human being could have run down it that fast. He had to still be there... somewhere.

There was a dark alcove about twenty feet in front of her. She lowered herself into a crouch and pressed her back against the wall, advancing forward. Ten feet...five feet.

Suddenly, there was the swooping sound of fabric behind her, and she whirled. He had dropped out of nowhere. Temporarily off balance, she stumbled backward and swept her sword towards him. It crashed against his with a deafening sound, and luckily the force of it sent him back an inch or so so that she had time to recover. He was much taller than her, almost the height of Laith. His lower face was covered, and there was a heavy hood over his head, but in that split second, she caught a glimpse of a pair of eyes, coal black, so deep that they were like falling into an empty void. His eyes were filled with the absence of life. For the first time in a long time, Rane felt genuinely afraid.

She swept her sword up and back, and he matched her movements perfectly. The alleyway was much too narrow for a fight like this; their swords clanged off each other and off the stone walls of the building with showers of sparks. He lunged at her, pushing her back a few feet; she crouched and swung as hard as she could at his legs, but he dodged like a feather and brought his sword down at her head. She rolled back, somersaulting squarely onto her bare feet, red hair flying, feeling the point of his blade miss her temple by a hair's breadth. *He's been taught at the Academy, as I was*, she thought to herself amid the frenzy of the moment. *That's the only way.* Rane was not as artistic or graceful a swordsman as Laith, but she had been trained to be deadly and efficient. This man was not only as good as her...he was *better.* She cursed herself for being foolish enough to walk into this fight unguarded, unaided. He had the advantage while they were in this confined space; his height and relative strength gave him the upper hand. She needed to be free to move around. *Lead him out of here*, she thought. *Get him out in the open.*

Slowly, Rane began to pull him out of the alleyway, knowing that there was an open plaza behind her. Inch by inch, she led him backward, coaxing him towards her, trying not to get lost in those fathomless black eyes.

They burst into the plaza, and Rane darted away, swiping her sword at his shoulder as she went; he bent backward and the blow barely grazed him. She could hear shutters and windows latching as the inhabitants of the houses turned a blind eye; duelists in broad daylight meant trouble, trouble that they wanted no part in. *Focus*, she told herself sternly. *Weak points. Get it over with.* He had a tendency of leaving his right underarm exposed—if she could just slip her blade in under his guard...

His striking arm came near her, close enough that she could aim a blow with her fist, if not her blade. She felt it connect, felt the give as the wrist cracked right at the joint. She expected a cry of pain or frustration, but he made no sound. She could barely hear him breathe. He was silent except for the rustle of his cloak, the slap of his boots on the uneven cobbles. Then, much to her surprise, he swiped at her with his deadened hand, knocking her off balance. She instinctively clawed at him; they were close enough that her fingernails caught the covering on the lower part of his face and pulled it down. Rane was taken completely aback. She had never seen such a face before; it was narrow and pointed, bore no scar, no outward sign of trauma, but there was unmistakable madness written in his eyes and around the corners of his mouth. With a fresh stab of fear, Rane realized she knew exactly who he was.

She started surveying her possible means of escape. Perhaps fleeing outright would be her best option, but she remembered how quickly he had been able to disappear down the alley. It would be difficult to run and make it. One of the houses? All were bolted shut. No one would admit her.

She parried his next three advances, their swords flashing lightning quick as they danced into the center of the small plaza. This time, he was pushing her; she was no longer leading him anywhere. She darted to the side, trying to break his control; he kicked at her, and she dodged beneath his leg, bringing her sword down to his back. He was too quick, and his blade was already up, but he was off balance in his attempt to block the blow, so she lunged forward. He managed to dodge the force of it, but her blade caught him in the flesh of his stomach. Seeing a chance, she leaped again at him, overeager and careless in her haste. She went past him, off-kilter in her attempt to land a blow. He spun and caught her in the back of the head with his fist, sending her flying against the wall of a nearby building. She kept her feet and her sword and turned towards him, rallying to be ready against the next onslaught. But he was fast, too fast for her to be prepared. She tried to turn her head away.

The last thing she saw was his smile before he cut her throat.

Rane sank down with a gurgled whimper, crumpled against the side of the building as warm blood poured from her throat over her clasped fingers. He was gone, gone like a breath of wind. His work was done. She pressed as hard as she could against her neck, but there was so much blood...too much blood. Her vision grew hazy, and she forced herself to crawl inch by brutal inch towards the door of the nearest house. With her last ounce of strength, she pounded as hard as she could against the wooden door and collapsed, her crimson hands sticky against the wet ground.

A few seconds later, the door creaked timidly open. "She's dead," came a female voice, older, maternal. "Who is she?"

"Get bandages as fast as you can, string, hot water, soap," came another voice, younger, male. The door opened wider.

"Leave her outside!" said the woman's voice. "There'll be nothing but trouble if we take her in. She could be one of the Strikers, and we'd all be killed."

"It wasn't a Kagaian guard she was fighting," the young man maintained. "Hurry, clear off my work table."

Rane was scooped from the cold earth and borne into the room, the workshop of a cobbler's house. A roaring fire heated the room from one corner, and the woman fretfully cleared off the cobbler's table, heating his needles and thread, bringing piles of fresh towels to the bench.

"We'll have no way to explain away all this blood," she chided her son as he mopped away at the crimson stream. "You just try and explain it away when the Kagaian guards come."

"He missed her major arteries," the cobbler replied, ignoring his mother and squinting down at Rane. "I was watching. She turned her head." He was a pudgy, freckly young man with a keen eye and long, nimble fingers. He had done his fair share of stitching up wounds for his friends, among them carpenters and blacksmiths, and since the war began, he had tended to the injured as much as he could. Doctors had become scarce, and the need for new shoes had declined. "Heat that needle and hand it to me. Now keep your hand here and keep pressure on it."

Focused and purposeful, the young man worked to close the wound and stem the bleeding. His mother, after keeping up her chiding tirade for the first hour, had fallen silent and had begun efficiently cleaning around the wound. The young auburn-haired woman had lost so much blood...there was no way she could possibly survive. And yet...her chest kept rising...and falling.

Finally, the young cobbler sat and rubbed a towel against his damp forehead. "That's all I can do, I suppose," he sighed. He and his mother regarded the prone form on his worktable, the bandage wrapped tight around her throat. "Who do you think she is?"

It was evening when Archer and Tarr, heavily cloaked against the cold night, picked their way through the small alleyway. Rane had been reported missing when she had uncharacteristically missed her shift, and Archer had been called in to track her. Tarr, at his side, was coursing with a thick combination of sleep deprivation and adrenaline; their plan to take Two Falls was to be set in motion the very next day, and there they were, wandering through the city in search of their missing friend. Tarr's mouth was set in a thin line, and Archer could tell that he was primed to explode.

Archer surveyed the small plaza with his golden eyes, then saw the crimson stain on the wall of the house opposite. He swallowed and glanced over to his brother. Tarr hadn't seen it, or at least hadn't registered its meaning. As calmly as he could, Archer strode across the plaza and knocked at the door.

"Archer, what's that?" Tarr asked slowly, pointing at the dark red discoloration.

"I don't know," Archer replied, keeping his voice pointedly even, though his heart had leaped into his throat. "Stand behind me, Tarr," he ordered, closing his fingers around the hilt of the dagger at his back.

"Archer, what *is* that?" Tarr asked again, a bit unsteadily.

The door opened a crack. A young man's eye peered out at them. "Who's there?"

"Don't let them in!" came the audible whisper of a woman behind him.

"We're the Strikers," said Archer shortly. There was no time for subterfuge. "We're looking for our friend. Rane, young woman, brown hair."

"Auburn," Tarr corrected automatically.

"Auburn. You seen her?"

There was a small scuffle and a hissed altercation between the young man at the door and the older woman behind him. "Yes," he said finally, still eyeing Archer warily. "Yes, she's here."

Archer extended an arm to prevent Tarr from lunging forward and barging through the door. "Wonderful. May we get her?"

"How do I know you are who you say you are?" said the young man.

"I'm Archer," said the Ashan. "You've heard of me?" He pulled back his hood, revealing the white skin, the flashing yellow eyes, and the black-tipped hair. The young man behind the door paused and stared at him for a moment, debating internally, then admitted them into the room.

With a low cry, Tarr leaped forward and bent over Rane's still frame. "Is she alive?" he gasped. "What happened?" His hands floated over her, afraid to touch her and do more damage. Tenderly, he examined the sides of her face with the tips of his long fingers. Her skin was as cold and smooth as porcelain.

"She was in a fight with someone. Didn't get a glimpse of him. He cut her throat, but I've patched her up. We managed to stop the bleeding; it wasn't deep enough to kill her, I don't think. She's still alive, at least." The young cobbler stood back, fascinated by the anguish on Tarr's face, the incongruous fact that the Ashan brothers, the Strikers, were standing here in his workroom. His mother had half-hidden herself in a closet and peered fearfully around the corner at them.

Gently, Tarr placed his hand over Rane's chest and closed his eyes. He hadn't slept for nearly two days, and the room began to swim before him. But he forced himself to be calm, to be comforted by the persistent rise and fall of Rane's breathing beneath the flat of his hand.

"It was *him*," Tarr growled in Ashan. "It was the one who killed that girl in the alley. The one who's been watching us."

Archer nodded. "In all likelihood." He turned to the cobbler and said in the Common tongue, "Thank you for your help. We owe you for her life."

The cobbler shrugged carelessly, but felt pleased with himself. Tarr gathered Rane up into his arms, wrapping his cloak around her. A thick fog had descended on the city streets, and as they slipped from the cobbler's house across the small plaza back to their safehouse, no one saw them go.

In short order, the Strikers were again assembled. Tarr was alternately pacing around the room and pausing by Rane's cot to check on her. Si was perched beside her, his small hand resting atop hers. Laith regarded Tarr levelly, fearing that he might be near a mental breaking point.

"You should get some sleep," he advised.

"We have to call off the mission," Tarr said, not breaking the stride of his agitated pacing. "We can't do it. We can't do it."

"It's our last chance," Laith reminded him levelly.

"Two of our best fighters are down," Athela pointed out. "You're still not up to your full strength, and now we've lost Rane."

"We haven't *lost* Rane!" Tarr snapped.

Athela blinked in surprise at the ferocity of his tone. "Of course not," she said soothingly. "I meant that she will not be up and ready to fight tomorrow, that's all."

"We can't do it," Tarr repeated.

"Tarr," said Archer calmly, "Rane is all right. We can station someone to change the dressing on her wound, to clean it and make sure it does not become infected."

"What about the pain?" Tarr demanded.

A curious expression was on Si's face, slightly dreamy. "She's not in any pain right now. She's asleep. She's getting stronger. You can take comfort in that."

As Tarr rounded the room again and paused beside the bed, Si reached out and reassuringly touched Tarr on the hand. Tarr looked down at Rane's lovely, quiet face and felt the anxiety begin to drain out of him. He sank down onto the cot, his head in his hands. "How could this happen?" he muttered.

"She's still alive," Marc reminded him. "And Rane is tough. She'll make it through all right."

"What if she's unable to speak again?" Tarr whispered.

"Then we'll deal with that when it happens," Laith told him firmly. "You need to take a sleeping draught and get some rest."

Tarr nodded miserably and walked from the room towards the kitchens. Once he was gone, Si curled his legs beneath him and regarded the others in the room. "Are we still going to go ahead with the plan?" he asked keenly.

"Like Laith said, it's our only chance," Athela shook her head. "General Grey will be back the morning after tomorrow."

"What about the man who did...this?" Archer inquired, inclining his head towards Rane.

"We focus on tomorrow, then we deal with him," said Laith firmly. "And trust me, he *will be dealt with.*" The tone of his voice left no room for doubt.

Silence enveloped them. "Are we ready, then?" Athela asked quietly.

No one replied. Rane moved slightly in her sleep.

At the Kagaian headquarters of Two Falls, a young girl came tentatively up the main passage. She cowered under the watchful stare of the two soldiers escorting her up to the main offices. Imran's long, thin arms hung nervously at her sides, and she glanced up every now and again to the officers beside her. The torches lining the walls flickered back and forth as they passed, each footstep echoing cavernously in the hall. Finally, they stopped in front of a large oak door. One of the soldiers knocked, and they were admitted.

There was a secretary seated behind a desk, who was scratching a quill pen against a curling sheet of parchment. She glanced up at Imran and the guards, then went unconcernedly back to writing. They waited for a full thirty seconds until the secretary neatly laid down her pen. She laced her fingers together and raised her eyebrows inquiringly.

"I wish...I wish to see General Grey," said Imran nervously. "I'm a spy for him...against the Strikers. And I have information."

The secretary's expression remained unchanged, though her eyebrows raised slightly higher. "Do you have the code word?"

"Yes," Imran bit her lip and repeated the strange phrase just as she had been taught. The secretary regarded her narrowly.

"You'll report to Lieutenant Elgin tonight," she announced, pushing her chair back from the large ornate desk.

"Where is Allox?" Imran asked, anxious. "If Grey is not available, then I usually report to Allox."

"Allox has been called away," the secretary said evasively. "Come."

Imran glanced at her guards and followed the secretary to another door on the opposite side of the large, well-appointed room. After a brisk knock, the secretary stepped inside, shutting Imran out. The girl heard a few words being exchanged on the other side of the door, and then it swung open.

It was a smaller room than she was used to; in her previous interactions with the Kagaian forces, she had typically been taken to General Grey's own quarters. Lieutenant Elgin approached her and gave her a cursory look up and down. He was in his late thirties, with a thin mustache and a decidedly arrogant air.

"Well? What is it?" he demanded, as if she'd interrupted something very important.

Imran took a deep breath. "The Strikers are planning an attack tomorrow night. They have a force waiting outside the city walls, and they're going to move on Two Falls."

Elgin and the secretary exchanged glances; then he eyed her narrowly. "What *force*? How do you know this?" he asked suspiciously.

Imran began fumbling for words. "I was at the headquarters, and I heard them planning something in the next room, but it just sounded like they were going to try to raid the armory. Then afterwards, I heard Tarr and Archer talking, and the whole meeting was just a ruse. They have soldiers waiting outside the city gates to the northwest. And they're going to attack on the full moon, which is tomorrow night."

"How many?" Elgin asked.

"I don't know...not many," Imran stammered. "They said there weren't many."

Elgin paused to contemplate the information. "You're sure of this?" Imran nodded fervently.

A slow smile crept across Elgin's twitchy mustache. "Good girl, you've done well and will be rewarded."

Imran bobbed a small curtsy, then looked at the secretary, unsure of what to do. The secretary, whose unflappable demeanor had been visibly rattled by Imran's information, shakily showed her out.

Elgin was secretly crowing inside. What a lucky couple of days! General Grey leaving, then Lieutenant Allox was called away, and he... *he!* was put in command of all of Two Falls. And now, like a plump apple falling right into his lap, this new information had arisen. The Strikers had been decimated down to an ounce of their former strength and influence. And if General Grey rode back to the city in two days to find out that he, Lieutenant Elgin, had single-handedly wiped out what was left of them, had carried out a military intervention, and delivered the Strikers to him in chains...Elgin could barely wrap his head around the riches, the estates, the accolades that would be heaped upon him by not only General Grey but Cira Kagai as well.

The girl had said a small group was waiting to attack. That was easily dealt with. He could wait for them to charge, certainly, and would take pleasure in laughing at their futile attempts to breach the wall. But it would be so much more satisfying—a more impressive show of strength—to catch them unawares, surprising them in their own ruse and stamping them out before they even had the chance to attack. He would summon together all of the Kagaian forces in the city (many of them inexperienced; this would be good practice) and march them out to startle and overwhelm the Strikers where they sat, waiting for him like sitting ducks. It was really all too delightful.

He let the satisfaction wash over him for a few more moments, then rang the bell at the table, its light tinkling sound filling the stuffy air of the office. A few moments later, the secretary appeared.

"Summon my captains of the guards," he ordered. "And be quick."

CHAPTER TWENTY-ONE

The night faded seamlessly into a crisp gray morning. Tarr wasn't conscious of having slept at all but must have drifted away at some point, for he sprang up with a start, his arms and torso resting on the thin cot beside Rane. Blearily, he rubbed his face with the back of his hand and, seeing Rane, immediately reached out to check her breathing and pulse, terrified that she may have quietly passed away during the night. But to his relief, her pulse was there—a pale fluttering beneath her skin. Her chest rose and fell almost imperceptibly, but she was breathing. Tarr could have cried with relief. Her skin was as pale as chalk, and her auburn hair stood out almost garishly against the pallor of her face and the white of the crisp bedsheet beneath her. Tarr leaned over and gently kissed her cheek. The bandage on her neck had a thin crimson line soaking through the fabric, but Tarr was relieved to see that she hadn't completely bled through. Hopefully, they had been able to stem most of the damage. Hopefully. Not for the first time, Tarr found himself saying a silent prayer of gratitude to the cobbler who'd saved Rane's life.

He rocked back in his chair, lowering his head tiredly into his hands. He had suddenly remembered. *Tonight.* Tonight, they would attempt to take back Two Falls. The trap would spring, and all things would be decided. The fate of the city they had fought so hard to save would be sealed. Tarr nearly laughed aloud at the irony of it all. For all he knew, he wouldn't even live to see the next morning. There was a chance that one of his friends could be dead. It all seemed so incredibly unreal. If he allowed the doubt and the fear to seep into his mind, then, like a poison, it would consume him. He had to believe they could pull it off somehow. He had to have hope.

There was a soft knock at the door, and a young man, one of the Strikers' attendants on duty, entered. He bore with him a steaming bowl of hot water, a poultice of precious medicinal herbs, and a towel. He gave Tarr a friendly smile. "I'm part of the medical team," he explained. "I'm here to tend to Rane."

"Tend away," Tarr said quietly, sliding back in his chair and offering up his place to the young man. "What time is it?"

"Midday."

Tarr's stomach lurched, and he cursed himself in anger. *So late.* "Are there any other Strikers in the house right now?"

"As far as I know, they've been out all night preparing the troops for battle," the young man answered, setting down the bowl and bending down to examine Rane. Tarr felt a pang of guilt. *They were doing what I should have been doing*, he chastised himself. *They shouldn't have let me stay here, shouldn't have let me fall asleep like this.*

"I'll be around the house if you need me," Tarr told him and walked out of the room, closing the door behind him with a quiet *click.*

Tarr washed his face with a bowl of freezing cold water and subsequently started to feel slightly more alive. There was a small noise behind him, and he turned to face Ari, who was still clad in his clothes from the night before. Ari was possessed of the infuriating ability to look completely placid in the face of utter catastrophe: blond, dully handsome, and utterly humorless. Tarr was immensely glad to see him. There was something comforting about Ari's indefatigable stoicism.

"I fell asleep," Tarr said apologetically. "I'm sorry."

"We've handled most of the preparations," Ari shrugged. "Laith and Athela and the others are readying their teams and trying to spread the word as covertly as possible. We've done all we can. Now we just have to wait until nightfall." He crossed the room with a few long strides and splashed a bit of water against his neck. He paused reflectively, dripping steadily into the basin. "This, from what I've been told, is the hard part."

Tarr, feeling suddenly antsy, crossed the room and looked out of the window. "I can't help but feel that I've forgotten something. That this entire thing may not even work."

Ari stared at him levelly. "*Did* you forget something?"

Tarr rolled his eyes. "You're a lot of help, Ari."

Ari shrugged again, as though he didn't particularly care whether Tarr thought he was a help or not. "Whether or not you've forgotten something, nightfall will be here in a few hours, and we'll find out."

There was a quick stride in the hall behind him, and Archer entered. "Tarr, I—oh," he said, with a tone of disappointment as he caught sight of Ari. "I came to see how Rane is doing."

"Still alive," Tarr sighed, managing a small smile.

Archer stared at Ari, clearly trying to make him uncomfortable enough that he would leave the room. Ari, as ever, was immune and instead began deliberately washing his hands. Exasperated, Archer turned to Tarr, purposefully excluding Ari from their direct conversation by lapsing into Ashan.

"We have prepared everything, brother. All is in place. Where will you be during the battle tonight?"

Tarr, not wishing to be as passive-aggressively immature as Archer, replied in the Common tongue so that Ari could understand. "I will stay here, in the safe house. With Rane. If things..." he swallowed. "If things do not go as planned, I want to be here with her when the time comes."

Archer nodded, his golden hawk eyes softening as he placed a long hand on Tarr's shoulder. He turned to leave, shooting Ari a barely concealed glare as he did. Ari blinked unresponsively.

"What will you do until tonight?" Tarr asked him.

"Read," said Ari vaguely. He stood. "The others will be back shortly." With that impassive pronouncement, he made his departure. Tarr wondered idly what Ari could possibly read that might divert his attention away from the oncoming battle, but realized it was pointless to speculate. He had a sneaking suspicion that Ari's tastes in literature didn't run very far past dry historical nonfiction.

Archer shook his head disbelievingly at Ari's retreating back, as if he had never quite seen the like of him before.

Perhaps it was something in the air, perhaps it was a result of the whispers that had begun to run rampant around the city, but not a single citizen of Two Falls set foot outside their home that entire day. The town appeared almost deserted: the fading beauty of the broad streets of old town, the narrow alleyways of the densely packed eastern neighborhoods, the curving hills of the arts district. A quiet mist blew this way and that down the streets; white gusts of air licked up the sides of the brick buildings and filtered through the grates into the sewers below. The air was cold and sharp enough to cut like a knife; doors and windows were fettered against it. Thick billows of smoke blew from the chimneys along the rows of neatly tiled rooftops, mingling with the dusky clouds above in the low-hanging sky. Everywhere, there was the feeling of anticipation, of a strange tide about to crash onto the city and wash everything clean.

The other Strikers gradually made their way back to Joris's old townhouse. Each of them stopped to check in on Rane and then proceeded up to one room or another to prepare or to get some much-needed sleep before the night fell. Si sat alone at the kitchen table, staring into vacant space ahead. The normally bright room was shuttered, casting it into a deep, heavy gloom. Si's young face was uncharacteristically solemn, his copper hair hanging loose around his neck and jaw. He felt old, far older than he ever had before.

A quiet step behind him heralded Marc, who took a seat next to him. Silence hung between the two for a long while. "This part is always difficult," Marc said finally. "Have you eaten anything?"

"Couldn't face it," Si mumbled, staring down at his thin hands. "Marc, how many battles have you been in before? Real battles, like in a war?"

"A few," Marc said evasively. "Not any for a long while." He patted his stomach benevolently. "Got used to the palace living, you know."

"You'll be all right, though?" Si said anxiously, not meeting Marc's eyes. "You know what to do so you won't be killed?"

"Of course," Marc assured him, hiding a smile. He kept his voice calm, trying to allay Si's fears. "Besides, I'm pretty hard to knock over, if you hadn't noticed already. A low center of gravity is a big asset in times like these."

"Yeah," said Si. He gave a small sniff, and Marc saw the hint of a tear roll down the boy's freckled cheek. Marc didn't want to embarrass him by calling attention to it, but silently reached into his pocket, withdrew a handkerchief, and pushed it across the table to Si, who accepted it without a word, dabbing at his nose.

"I'll take care of myself, and I'll take care of Laith. That's my job," Marc told him firmly. "You know how some people's jobs are to be plumbers or herd sheep? Mine is to go into battle and to come out the other side and drag Laith out along with me."

Si mumbled something along the lines of, "But water pumps don't attack the plumbers when they go to fix them."

"Point taken," Marc smiled and patted Si's shoulder. "You'll be safe throughout the battle. Whatever happens. If things look like they're going to become too dangerous, we have people who are going to get you out of the city and will take you to the mountains where you'll be safe. They'll take care of you."

"I wish I could fight," Si broke in, the sting of frustration in his voice. "I wish I wasn't so...*useless*."

"Tarr won't be in the fighting either," Marc pointed out. "He's not useless."

Si debated whether or not to go on arguing, but relented. It was the same old debate he and Marc had been having for three years, and it certainly wasn't going to be resolved that night. He managed a mute nod.

One of Marc's Strikers poked her head around the corner of the wall. Her arms were full of a few large boxes. "We've got it, sir," she said.

"Excellent," Marc said.

"What's that?" Si asked curiously, craning his neck at the mysterious parcels.

"You'll see," Marc gave a wink and rose to his feet. The woman was struggling to keep the boxes aloft; their contents appeared to be very heavy. Marc easily scooped a box from her arms and smiled at Si. "Have some food, you'll feel better. Then you can come up and see what I've got here."

Si managed a wan grin and waited until Marc's footsteps had faded across the house. He wandered aimlessly out of the room, tracing his fingers along the polished wood of the walls, around the edges of the portrait frames that hung along the hall. Finding himself beside Rane's room, he pressed his ear to the door to listen for signs of movement, and hearing none, he went in. He wanted to say goodbye to her, too, to wish her luck.

Rane was alone in the room, her reddish-brown hair fanned out against the sheet. Si moved to sit in the chair beside her cot. She looked so delicate; the dark curve of her eyelashes, the peaceful set of her mouth. Her hands had been placed gently at her sides. Si reached out to touch her hand.

The instant his skin touched hers, a wave like an electric shock rippled through him. It was like a flashing burst of light: Si gave a yell and toppled out of his chair as faces and images and words and whispers went hurtling through his brain like a rolling sea. He wasn't conscious of ever hitting the floor, but when his eyes finally snapped back open, he realized that he was flat on his back, staring up at the blank face of the ceiling above. Panting, he groped about himself and confirmed that he was lying on solid ground. *What happened?* He reached up and touched his legs, chest, face. *All there. I appear to be all right.* Si struggled up to his elbows and surveyed the overturned chair. He hoped no one had overheard. *What happened?*

All at once, Si realized that he was not the same. Something had happened when he touched Rane's hand...he *knew* things. Things he hadn't experienced, people he had never met. It was just as it had been before with his visions about Laith and Marc, or his terrifying experience with the Kagaian soldiers in the street. The blinding heat of energy, the rush of uncontrollable power through his body...but this time, there was an assurance, a certainty. Si knew the answers to questions he could barely comprehend. He didn't understand how he knew them. But he felt the truth of what he had seen.

His heart pounding, Si quietly rose to his feet and righted the chair as silently as he could. He backed towards the door, praying that he had not disturbed Rane. Feeling sick, he shut the door and ran as fast as he could to his temporary bedroom before bolting and locking himself inside. He took a few steadying breaths and then, with a feeling of dread, knowing what he would see before he actually looked, he went slowly to the top drawer of his dresser and opened it. Inside was the silver medallion, placed there by some unseen, unknown hand. It winked back at him innocently.

He threw the drawer shut and flung himself onto the bed, wrapping himself up tightly in the stale bedclothes, shoving a pillow firmly over his head, just as he had done when he was little. There was nowhere he could go, no one he could talk to. Not even Marc. Hot tears sprang from his eyes and flowed silently down his cheeks as he muffled his sobs into the unfeeling pillowcase. The other Strikers had far enough to deal with that day without the news that he had almost certainly lost his mind.

Upstairs, Athela was pacing restlessly from one side of her room to the other like a caged animal. She had tried to sleep, even tried to read (Ari had made it look so easy), but to no avail. Solitary for almost her entire life, all at once, she didn't want to be alone. She felt pulled in dozens of different directions.

Unable to stand the confinement of her bedroom any longer, she opened the door and padded barefoot out into the hall. Every step she took let out a complaining creak, and Athela winced at the sound. She wished it were nightfall, wished that it was the next morning, wished everything was over already. They had gone over the plans dozens of times, but there was still the note of uncertainty...if their scheme hadn't worked, if things hadn't gone according to Tarr's outline...well, there was no way of knowing that until their time was up. Somehow, the thought wasn't terribly comforting.

Athela suddenly halted, realizing in a rush that her meandering hadn't been as aimless as she'd thought; she had unconsciously walked to stand directly in front of Archer's room. Something in the pit of her stomach gave a raucous lurch. *Behave yourself*, she told it sternly. *You have lived, eaten, and slept on floors beside that stringy Ashan for nearly three years. This fluttery, girlish nonsense is completely uncharacteristic and unbecoming of a woman of your independence and maturity.*

Thus reassured, she told herself to take a step forward but found that there was some form of connection missing between her brain and her feet. Her mind slipped unbidden back to their kiss in the cellar. The only sensation Athela could compare it to was the thrill of speeding across a broad, flat plain on the back of her horse. The memory of it filled her with a rush of uncaring, impulsive recklessness.

Archer's door was open a crack, and a thin shaft of light fell across the hallway at her feet. Athela leaned forward and peered into the room. Archer was walking around the back of the bed, chest bare, dressed in a loose pair of black pants drawn with a string around his slender hips. He seemed completely oblivious to her presence. As she watched, he retrieved something from behind the bed, then walked around to the other side nearest her and sat, the mattress moving slightly with his weight. The light fell softly over his long, lean frame as he reached for his bow and began to fiddle with the end of it, intently manipulating the wrappings with his deft fingers and stretching a fresh string from one end to the other. Her eyes traveled from his face to his shoulder. Athela had never been quite so struck by his strange, otherworldly beauty as she was at that moment.

Perhaps it was her quick intake of breath or perhaps some sort of sixth sense that alerted him to her presence, but he suddenly glanced up, and their gazes locked together. Athela swallowed and took a preemptive step backward. As if recognizing something in the expression on her face, Archer silently set aside his bow and stood, crossing the floor in three long strides and opening the door fully to face her. Athela straightened and tried to look haughty, daring him to tease her or call her out for spying on him. But he just stared down at her from his great height, his hands loose at his sides, that same disconcerting air of vulnerability on his face as had been there that day in the cellar. Athela grappled with the overwhelming urge to reach out and touch him—she knew that his skin would be smooth and blissfully cool beneath her fingers.

Athela raised her chin and, with the feeling of someone diving off a high cliff into dark water, stepped forward and slid her arms around Archer's waist, laying her cheek against his bare chest. She could feel his body's tension relax as she touched him, even as she heard his heart begin racing wildly against her ear. She felt his hands slide into her hair and felt him press his face against the top of her head, his breath warm and enveloping. She had the strangest sensation of coming home.

She pushed him back, wrestling internally for a protracted few seconds. She was surprised at the look of consternation she saw flicker across his face.

"I'm sorry," he apologized immediately. "I—"

Without letting him say another word, she reached up and pulled his lips down to hers. Part of her wondered whether their second kiss could be anywhere near as good as their first—whether that had just been a fluke, the result of three years' pent-up feelings—but almost immediately, those doubts were put to rest. After a moment of surprise and hesitation, Archer responded to her with an intense, almost overwhelming ardor, as if he'd been physically released after holding himself back.

Again, she felt the wonderful sensation of spinning and sinking all at once. She clung to him hard, conscious only of his hands at her waist and the salty, sweet taste of his mouth as they sinuously moved against each other. Dimly, she felt him reach beneath her and lift her effortlessly up onto his hips, pressing her back against the corner of the wall as she twined her legs around him. She pulled him as close as she physically could, thrilled by the feeling of his weight and all his strength bearing down on her. Her hands threaded ecstatically through his soft hair as he kissed her jaw, her neck, lightly bit her shoulder.

"Archer," she whispered urgently, and he halted immediately.

They met each others' eyes, both out of breath, cheeks and throats flushed. An unspoken question passed between them. Athela nodded ever so slightly, brushing his nose with hers, and kissed him again softly. He leaned back and gazed at her tenderly, gently brushing a dark curl back from her cheek.

"This won't change anything," she said as firmly as she could. Even to her, it sounded more like a plea than a statement of fact.

A smile flickered across the corners of his mouth. "Yes, it will," he said quietly. Still holding her, he stepped back into the room and shut the door behind them.

Having been summoned by Marc, Si sat quietly on a couch in one corner of the small second-floor sitting room. A fire was crackling in the hearth beside him, and a few long candles were lit in sconces around the room; it was cheery and more pleasant than it had been alone in his room. A large painting within a gilt frame hung above the mantle. The image was of rolling hills, chirping birds, a stream alight with spring color. It all seemed so very far away. Si could not remember a time when it hadn't been winter.

He drew his knees up to his chin and wrapped his arms around his legs, glad that he had forced himself to get back up, to act as though everything was normal. He didn't want the others to be worried. Marc, Laith, and a young Joymarillian woman whom Si didn't know stood in the center of the room. Laith and Marc were both attired in simple undershirts, riding trousers, and boots. Marc laid down his mysterious box in the center of the floor and began removing its contents. Si craned his neck to see.

"Armor!" he exclaimed, trying to sound like his usual, enthusiastic self. "Neat!"

Marc glanced up and shot him a quick wink, then raised a finger to his lips. Si was instantly abashed, and recoiled against the wall. He understood at once the gravity and the ceremony of the scene before him and felt suddenly foolish and awkward. He was unused to Laith and Marc moving with such weight and decorum and grew all the more conscious of his intrusive presence in the stillness of the room. Although he was fascinated, he fought the urge to slip quietly away. *Marc invited me to watch,* he reminded himself. So he would.

The young woman, whose brown hair was pulled in a tight knot at the back of her head, was already dressed and armed for battle. She held up a steaming basin of water, a towel draped over one of her arms. Laith dipped his hands in the water and splashed it over his face and neck, rubbing vigorously. Marc took the towel and held it out, and Laith dried his face, hands, and hair.

Marc retrieved a folded piece of cloth from the items on the ground. It was a leather tunic, slightly worn but visibly tough, with laces up the sides. Laith stood quietly, his arms outstretched, as Marc expertly threaded the laces through and tied them in knots at the ends of the tunic. Next came a shirt of intricately laced chain mail that shimmered in the firelight and moved with a light metallic clinking sound as Marc raised it and lifted it over Laith's head. After the mail came a light red cloth that tied like a handkerchief and was tucked into the leather shirt, followed by a thick leather collar that fastened over the mail and the red cloth, protecting the prince's neck.

This was all done in complete silence, and Si realized that he was witnessing a ceremony that Marc and Laith had enacted many times since they were soldiers his age. Their lives in Joymaril, the lives they had led before, were so alien to him that he began to feel the strange sensation that he was looking at a pair of two completely different people, that his friends had vanished and been replaced by this strange ancient warlord and his knight.

The battle armor itself was jet black and had been recently polished so that it reflected the firelight like a dark demonic flame. Laith moved his head slightly as the breastplate was fitted against him; Si, though he had not had a great deal of experience in these sorts of matters, ascertained that the armor was not Laith's; it hung just a little too loosely to have been made especially for him. But Marc cinched the breast and backplates in at the shoulders and sides as tight as they would go, the slap of leather sounding sharply through the quiet as he tightened the straps and slid them into their buckles. Laith squared his shoulders as the pauldrons were fitted and buckled across his chest at the front and back; with them, his shoulders acquired a full three inches in width.

Laith spread his arms, and Marc first laced a light cloth over Laith's forearms to protect him from the chain mail. Then on went the braces at his bicep and forearm, with an extra piece on his left elbow to protect his shield arm. Lastly, Marc kneeled and buckled armor over Laith's thighs so that they glinted like black steel with every movement. Laith relaxed his arms and turned, the long strips of black leather hanging from his breastplate shifting slightly with a heavy, stiff sound. Marc reached back into the box and withdrew the final item, a long, thick cloak that was of a brilliant blood-red scarlet, the color of the Striker flag. Laith ducked his head so that Marc could slip it over his head, then Laith rolled his shoulders forward and threw the cloak over one arm so that it hung down in a long swaying ripple along his back. He silently held out one hand, and Marc pressed two black leather gloves into them as he raised the prince's sword and scabbard and buckled them at his hip. Laith slid the gloves over his hands. With that final touch, the only visible part of him that was still *him*—not this creature of black metal—was his face.

He turned slightly towards Si. The bulk of the armor on top of his natural height made him loom within the small room like a giant shadow. The blood red of his cloak clashed like an open wound against the shining black of his armor, which danced and gleamed with each leap of the glowing fire. It was a chilling effect; Laith looked nothing less than an avenging angel, a mixture of unearthly beauty and the unspoken promise of imminent death.

Si was terrified and felt himself unconsciously shrinking back.

Marc dressed quickly in his own armor, assisted by the young woman, who had laid down the basin in order to fasten the buckles. His was a dark brown, embossed here and there with gold thread, and though the armor made his already bulky shoulders increase in size, the effect was not nearly as stunning as Laith's. He swept the same scarlet cloak over one shoulder, just as Laith had done; it was clearly the style favored by Joymarillian warlords. Then, the two faced each other and knelt, bowing their heads and placing their right hands on each other's left shoulders. Laith spoke quietly and quickly in a language Si couldn't understand, which was followed by a response from Marc. Then the hands came down off the shoulders, were clasped against their own hearts, and then on the hilts of their swords. They rose, and the ceremony was complete. With a quick motion, Laith flipped the hood of his cloak over his head so that his face was obscured by a dark shadow, and he swept from the room, passing by Si with a gust of cold, steely air. Si did not recognize the look on Laith's face, or any other part of his friend at all. The young woman followed Laith out. But Marc stopped beside him at the door and gave him the old familiar smile.

"Marc," Si stammered, "L-Laith..."

"Be glad he's on our side, Si," Marc grinned with the wink of one ice-blue eye. He reached out a gloved hand and clasped Si's neck. "It's about time for us to get into position. I'll be back in a few hours."

Si nodded mutely, feeling as though his heart were being torn in forty different directions. He lunged forward and hugged Marc around the neck, the strangeness of the cold, hard armor so different from Marc's usual warm comfort. Si released him, wishing that he could find a way to tell him to be careful, that he was the teacher, the brother, the father Si had always wished for, and that he would not know what to do if Marc were gone. Si groped for the words, then steeled his thin shoulders and gave a short nod.

"See you in a few hours," he said firmly.

Marc ruffled his hair and vanished.

Tarr stood outside the door, waiting for the war party to leave. It felt strange to stand out in the open this way. The moon was a misty orb still low in the sky, the color of a burning ember. It would cool to a blue-white as it rose higher in the sky. It would travel in its arc one more time, and at the end of its descent, all their fates would be decided. Tarr took a deep breath, felt the numbing freeze of the stone beneath his bare feet.

Hearing a noise behind him in the house, Tarr turned and quietly stepped back inside. The soldiers, all outfitted in identical scarlet cloaks, had assembled in the entryway. No one was talking much, and the looks on most of the faces seemed to be more scared than anything. Tarr felt eyes on him and smiled in what he hoped was a comforting way.

The crowd in the house parted slightly, and Athela strode forward, outfitted in full riding gear, with lightweight armor that would allow her to move on horseback but would protect her from arrows or the swipes of enemy swords. A red cloak was pulled up over her ebony hair. She paused in front of Tarr, who surveyed her narrowly. Something about her was different.

She gave him an extremely pointed look and raised her eyes. Abruptly, as though she couldn't contain it, she gave him a slow grin, completely incongruous with their circumstances. He furrowed his brow, puzzled. Then it dawned.

"You *didn't!*" he muttered. "*Tonight?* I do not *believe* you two."

Athela's mouth silently opened and closed a few times. Then, a sheepish, girlish smile split her face fully. After a moment, she recovered and forced the grin back down. She jutted her chin defiantly in the air. "Yes. I did. It was my decision, and I'm glad I did it." She paused for a beat, a bit of the bravado slipping. Conspiratorially, she whispered, "And I'm going to try not to die tonight because you and I have a lot of things to discuss."

"I'll bet." Tarr shook his head exasperatedly. Knowing that Athela would shrink from anything so familiar as a hug, he reached out and rather formally clasped her arm. He was happy for her. She may not have made a wise decision, timing-wise, but he was happy for her nonetheless. Athela beckoned to her small team, all outfitted in riding gear, and walked a few paces from the door to exchange a few final preparatory words.

Archer was next. He strode across the threshold with an undeniable swagger, black from head to foot, his quiver buckled over his red cloak, bow in hand. His yellow eyes flashed as he walked up to Tarr, turning his back so that the soldiers in the entryway couldn't see. Then, in a moment, the façade fell and anxiety etched itself across his face.

"Tarr," he said in a strangled voice, "I think I'm in love."

"*Now*?" Tarr hissed, fighting down the urge to strangle him. "You idiot. You're about to go into battle!"

"Stupid, I know," Archer muttered desperately, a hunted look on his face. "But Athela and I—"

"I know," Tarr cut him off with a hurried wave of his hand. "Please, I beg of you, spare me the details."

Archer was taken aback. "You *know?* How—?"

Tarr rolled his eyes. "Honestly, you two spend three *years* dancing circles around each other, and you choose *tonight* to..."

"Did she say anything?" Archer exclaimed, his eyes lighting up.

"Would you *focus?*" Tarr nearly shrieked, then glanced to the side. A few of the soldiers had begun to stare at them. "Archer," he began again, more slowly, this time in Ashan. "My brother. My dearest brother. You must put these things from your mind for tonight. There is work to do."

Archer nodded soberly and tried his best to look penitent. "I know. I know. Battle. Two Falls. Got it."

Tarr laughed despite himself. He clasped his hand on the back of Archer's neck, over their entwined tattoos, and brought Archer's forehead to his own. He felt Archer do the same. Archer squeezed his neck in his long hand, then released him and beckoned to his troop.

As Archer stepped out of the house, Athela stopped her

conversation with her team and watched him for a few moments in the gloom of the street. He didn't realize she was looking at him. He listened intently as a member of his group asked him a question, his long, clever hands tightening the quiver buckled across his chest. He turned, broad shoulders tapering evenly into his slim waist. Athela realized she was holding her breath, and a jumble of memories from the past hours flooded unbidden through her mind, dizzying and heady. Her world, she realized suddenly, had shifted ever so slightly. Archer, once so familiar, was now a strange, exciting new entity.

A wave of conflicting emotions rocked her. The longing she had once felt for Archer—and had been able to tolerate, if not ignore—had counterintuitively increased its intensity tenfold. So many tenets she had once regarded as foundational to her being now seemed like they belonged to a completely different person.

And then she remembered where they were, and that Archer was about to walk into battle. That, like Ilaina, in the span of a few minutes he might simply be gone and never come back. That the door would close on a world of possibilities that she had only just tantalizingly been able to glimpse.

Her stomach twisted unpleasantly and swelled heavily with a deep, sinking feeling of dread. The power of it was crushing, intolerable, unbearable. With the discipline she had honed since childhood, she forced it back, tamped it down. She turned away from him and walked towards her waiting horse.

Back in the safehouse, the light buzz of conversation around the door suddenly fell deathly quiet, and Tarr turned to the sound of heavy footsteps. The group swept apart, leaving a wide walkway for the last three figures to leave. Argolaith, his face darkened by the hood and his body glinting like a black blade of steel, strode silently across the room, his cloak rippling blood red down his back. Flanking him, similarly hooded and cloaked, strode Ari and Marc. Almost unconsciously, the soldiers in the room bowed as they passed, and Tarr felt himself stepping backward to give Laith a wide berth. Laith met Tarr's eyes, and none of the prince's warmth was recognizable within them. His beautiful face was as cold and hard as stone. He turned at the door and faced the remaining soldiers.

"Tonight," he said quietly, his deep, silken voice filling the hushed void of the room, "we free the city of Two Falls." With that, the door was opened, and he walked out into the blue night, followed by Marc, Ari, and the rest of the troops. As they left, Tarr saw that the fear on so many of the faces had been turned into determination and awe in the prince's wake.

The room empty, Tarr felt almost comical closing the door after them, as though he were wishing them well on their first day off to school. He glanced behind him and saw Si's small, frightened face peering through the banister of the stairs.

Tarr smiled and motioned him down. "Come on, Si, let's check on Rane."

There was nothing left to do but wait and see what day would dawn. Or if, indeed, they would live to see it at all.

"The troops are ready, sir," intoned the officer, and Elgin wriggled in gleeful anticipation. They had waited until the cover of night. It was the perfect time to march out and catch the band of Strikers unawares.

"Send them forward," commanded Elgin with a triumphant stroke of his mustache. "You know what to do." He had no intention of riding out with them. He would deliver the news to General Grey when he returned, and had no desire to get his hands dirty in the process.

The officer nodded and retreated. A moment later, Elgin heard the order go up, and he strode across the wide office to the window. The troops, led by the green and silver banner of Kagai snapping in the cold wind, marched out in a rank that was four soldiers wide and countless soldiers long. Moonlight glinted like water off their armor, and the green cloaks shimmered as they walked in practiced unison toward the north gate. Elgin couldn't help but smile in eager delight. It was a nasty surprise, slithering through the streets towards the pitiful Striker camp outside the city walls like a glinting green serpent.

In the empty night, the footsteps behind the city walls sounded like thunder in the distance. For the small camp of Jelani warriors outside the west wall, it was a sound that only gradually became clear as it approached. A cry went up around the camp, and General Calchas swept out of his tent as Lady Burton thrust his helmet into his waiting hands.

"Sound the horn!" Calchas ordered gruffly. "Douse the torches!"

His orders were hurriedly obeyed, and the alarm was raised. The silvery sound blared out, sounding a warning to the Jelani troops. The horn carried across the city where the citizens of Two Falls huddled in their homes, waiting for the thunderous footfall of Kagaian soldiers to break into an outright storm. Athela heard it where she and her riders stood saddling their horses. Archer and his sharpshooters stopped their progression across the roofs of Two Falls. Marc turned to Laith, his voice tense.

"That's a Jelani horn," he muttered. "Do you think that the soldiers have—" he trailed off, leaving the question unanswered. Laith, his face hooded and expressionless, gave no reply.

The west gate of Two Falls wrenched open with a complaining groan, and the troop of Kagaian soldiers poured out onto the night-blanketed hillside. They fanned out so that the hill was covered with a shifting swath of troops and armor. The commander, seated astride a roan charger, rode to the head of the company with her soldiers.

"Search them out!" she called. "Destroy them! Forward!"

She wheeled her horse, and as one body, the enormous fan of troops moved down the hill towards the Jelani camp where General Calchas and his fighters waited, steeling themselves for the strike. The soldiers broke into a run, and their voices rose in the fierce cry of battle.

"Take cover in the rocks," Calchas called to his warriors.

The thunder on the ground grew to a deafening roar.

"Jelani, arise!" Calchas and his commanders called in unison.

The wave of Kagaian troops crashed against the rocks like a breaking sea.

It was an hour, maybe two, after the Jelani horn had first sounded. All of Two Falls lay still. The moon, as promised, had shed its orange glow and climbed to a great height, hanging heavy and blue like an engorged pearl in the sky.

The distant roar and clash of battle at the north wall of the city had grown silent. In every house, the people waited for a sign: a cheer, the sound of a trumpet. But none came. The heavy west doors again groaned their way open, and a green river of Kagaian soldiers—fewer now, much fewer—covered in mud and blood and dirt, cloaks and armor stained and torn, marched their way back into the city. At their center was a small thicket of Jelani troops, hands behind their heads, in a state of complete surrender as they were marched back to the Kagaian headquarters to await their fate. General Calchas, hands tied in front of him, walked at the head of the small remaining group of Jelani, his jaw set and his eyes boring holes in the space before him. His face was smudged, and a wound on his forehead trickled blood down the side of his cheek.

The citizens of Two Falls closest to the west wall peeked out of their windows to see the sorry procession. At once, the news began to ripple across the city: the Strikers had failed. Their last attempt at an army had been decimated, and Kagai had won. It was over so quickly.

Elgin, who had been pacing the length of the office, peered out of the window and saw his troops returning. His heart leapt with greedy anticipation. That was it! Two hours, nothing more, and they had won. They apparently had lost quite a few soldiers, but, well...that was war, after all. Cira would give him a title, give him land, maybe even a relative of hers as a wife...nothing would be too much for him to ask. He fought the urge to twirl and skip his way down the stairs two at a time, then caught himself and stopped short. He peered down at the troop and cursed under his breath. *Why did they take prisoners? I gave no order to take prisoners.* But then he saw a richly attired officer at the head of the group that he assumed to be the Striker general. *Maybe not a total loss...we could use him for bargaining if he's worth enough.* Elgin turned and, barely suppressing the grin on his face, strode swiftly out of the room and down to meet his officers in the broad entry room of the Kagaian headquarters.

The returning troops were nearly all assembled in the cavernous, arching hall when Elgin arrived. He tossed his hair and strode up to the lead commander. The green cloak was tattered and muddy, and there was something about her that seemed...odd. It was probably the bloodstains. Elgin shook the feeling off. "Well?" he demanded.

"The battle was successful, sir," the commander reported. "We have taken many of the officers prisoner so that they may be dealt with according to the wishes of Queen Cira Kagai."

"Let me see the Striker general," Elgin ordered, eager to gloat over the man he had just beaten. An old man, the one Elgin had spotted from the window, stepped forward through the crowd. Elgin sneered at him.

"Bit old to be playing a young man's game, aren't we?" he asked. Then, to his commander, he asked, "Were there any signs of the lead Strikers amongst them?"

"No," the commander reported.

"Did they pay you to fight for them?" Elgin asked the general. The old man merely stared at him. "Speak, dog!" Elgin demanded, raising a hand to strike the old man in the face.

"Sir!" came a cry.

"What?" Elgin snapped, turning away. One of his home officers, positioned beside a nearby window, was pointing at something outside in the street.

"I think it's one of the Strikers!" he exclaimed.

A murmur broke out amongst the troops. "Silence!" Elgin barked. Casting Calchas a dirty look, he swung on his heel and walked to the window. Standing outside in the street, in a beam of open moonlight, was a lone rider on a dapple gray horse. The horse was leaping about in circles, and the rider was craning her neck, obviously trying to get a look at the troops inside the headquarters. The hood flew back, revealing the long mane of thick, curly black hair.

"It's Athela!" Elgin shouted gleefully. He couldn't believe his good luck. He would crush the strength of the Strikers *and* capture their leaders in a single night. Once she was taken, it would only be a matter of time until she was tortured into giving up the secret hiding places of the others. He turned to the home officer. "Alert the cavalry and all the rest of the night watches. She was foolish enough to come and see if the Strikers' plan worked. We won't let her escape this time. We'll send every spare troop we have after her. Go!"

Breathlessly, the officer fled in the direction of the stables, and a few moments later, the alarm bell was ringing, sounding out across the city. Elgin glanced out of the window and saw that at the first sound of the bell the excitable horse had reared and leaped as if it would try to fly onto a nearby rooftop. With amazing balance, Athela kept her seat, then wheeled the horse north and took off into the dark. A few moments later, there was the deafening clatter of hooves on cobblestone as the entire Kagaian cavalry took off down the street after her, a flurry of horses and riders and motion.

Elgin whipped around to face the Strikers' general once again. "And you..." he trailed off, his eyes sliding sideways over to the returning Kagaian commander. He suddenly realized what had bothered him about the woman's appearance. Around the soldier's left elbow was tied a bright red piece of cloth. He looked around at the rest of the returning Kagaian troops, and around each of their elbows was the same scarlet band. The color of the Strikers.

His eyes narrowed and his voice came out in a hiss. "What is the meaning of—"

"NOW!" bellowed the commander, and at once, the room erupted into chaos.

The troops threw off their green cloaks and drew their swords in a ripple of frenzied motion. General Calchas easily tossed away his shackles and caught the sword thrown to him by one of his warriors. In another moment, he stepped forward, the sword swung with a screaming arc, and Elgin thudded onto the floor, his face still bearing its comical expression of astonishment and bewilderment.

It was a few seconds before the other home officers in the room knew what was happening, and by then, it was too late. The disguised Jelani troops cut through them like a scythe, fanning out through the halls and rooms, sweeping over everything in sight. When the entry room had been cleared and only Jelani still stood, Lady Burton and another commander walked up to Calchas for orders.

"Find the armory and then go to the dungeons. Free and arm whomever you find there," he ordered curtly. Lady Burton nodded and disappeared. "You," he said to the other. "Light the signal."

"Yes, milord," she assented, and took off running towards the staircase.

"The rest of you, finish searching this headquarters, then leave a small troop here to set up an infirmary. I want the armory cleared out and cots for the wounded set up. Find whatever medical supplies you can and bring them there," he shouted. A short, disciplined bark of confirmation was returned to him, and his soldiers scattered expertly in every direction.

A group of twenty or so, swords out, threaded their way into the dungeons, down a wide, curving staircase that sloped slightly into the cold, musty ground beneath the city. Finally, the staircase flattened out, and though torches flickered on the walls, there was no sign of a guard or anyone on duty. The lead Jelani officer, a woman with a thick braid of pale hair that splashed across the back of her armor, nodded to her troops to go carefully and quietly and to stick in defense formation. There was not a lot of room to fight. She pulled a small dagger from the top of her boot and held it at the ready. Behind her, her second officer stood with his shield up, ready to defend her at a moment's notice.

There was a sudden, wild shout that echoed deafeningly through the cold stone hallway, and the Jelani commander stifled a cry of surprise. Instantly, she threw herself forward shoulder-first as a barrage of concealed Kagaian soldiers launched themselves around the corner at her. It was too tight for any kind of elaborate swordplay, so the Jelani fought forward, stabbing here and there where they could, fending off blows as the clash of the swords against armor and shields was magnified to an earsplitting din by the stone walls.

In a few minutes, it was over. While the Kagaian recruits had numbers on their side, they were no match for the seasoned Jelani warriors, who had done little else than ride and fight in the last ten years. The group of Jelani rounded the corner, finding themselves at the head of a long, winding cell block.

A small man was cowering behind a rickety desk. The Jelani commander strode forward and seized him by the throat, wrenching him to his feet and pressing the dripping blade of her dagger against his neck.

"Open all the cells," she hissed through clenched teeth, her pale blue eyes searing into him. "*Now*."

She threw him to the ground as he stuttered incoherently and immediately scrambled to his feet, fumbling for keys and making his way down the cell block, unlocking door after door after door.

"Listen to me!" she called. "We are here at the order of the Strikers. Those who wish to arm themselves and help to fight for freedom this night may follow us. Those who are too weak or sick to fight, follow us upstairs and we will tend to you."

There was a moment of silence after her words; the only sound was the turnkey's frenzied footsteps and the clink and squeak of opening locks. Then, gradually, the doors of the cells began to inch open, and one by one, the prisoners crept out. Some were so grizzled and thin that they looked more like shadows than people. The Jelani commander swallowed but maintained her stoic composure. "This way," she called, and the prisoners began to shuffle towards her.

"Where do I get a sword?" croaked a voice beside her. It was an old man with a gray beard down his front. But there was a fire in his wrinkled eye that told the commander she had no right to question his readiness.

"Our troops are waiting upstairs in the armory," she informed him.

The old man nodded and took the first step toward the light above.

Athela could hear the deafening clatter of the hooves behind her. Aria's ears kept flicking back and forth, intent on outrunning them and infuriated that Athela was not letting him do so. Athela kept his nose in check, but he kept lengthening his stride, so much so that Athela was worried that she would lose her pursuers completely. She banked a hard left down a narrow alley and, frustrated with the cumbersome cloak pulling at her neck, reached up and undid the clasp, sending the scarlet cloak floating up behind her into the night wind like an autumn leaf. In order to tail her down the alley, her pursuers would have to thin their line and slow down. Good. That would buy her some time.

At the end of the alley, she released Aria ever so slightly, and the horse gobbled up the free rein, surging forward and into an open market square near the city's center. Athela glanced over her shoulder, saw no one, and pulled Aria to a halt. She stood up in her stirrups and swiveled around in the saddle, clutching Aria's mane as he furiously danced around in place, aching to run.

There—there it was!

A beacon of flame lit the top spire of the Kagaian headquarters across the city. The green flag was burning. Calchas's soldiers had done it. Athela turned again to the sound of metallic clattering hooves as the entire Kagaian cavalry charged out of the alleyway and poured through every street into the marketplace after her. And there—she turned again—Kagaian footsoldiers, the night watch, were arriving in force, summoned by the alarm bells at their headquarters. Aria snorted, bouncing up and down on his hind legs. "Almost," Athela muttered through gritted teeth. "Almost." She looked to the tops of the roofs and towers dotting the edges of the market square. In one, she could faintly see the liquid movement of a black shadow against the blue sky.

Athela urged Aria forward, veering past a lamppost. She lunged out of the saddle and whipped the burning torch out of its enclosure as she passed. Aria galloped towards the Two Falls river, whose bank formed the western edge of the square. She pulled Aria to a halt where the square's flagstones dropped off at the river's edge, the eerie silence of the frozen river heavy in the night air. She glanced around. The marketplace was choked with Kagaian troops surging up after her from the east and the south. *Here goes nothing*, she thought, and threw the torch onto the frozen ice of the river.

To the shock of all, the river burst into flame. The fire licked its way like lightning up the stream to the northernmost bridge. And there, on the western bank, suddenly illuminated by the burning river, were the Strikers. Marc, Ari, and Argolaith were at the head of the group on horseback. Each wore a scarlet cloak.

As one, the Kagaian soldiers abruptly froze and surveyed the scene before them. Argolaith, face obscured by a red hood atop his enormous black charger, glinted like a demon in the flame. A few of the Kagaian troops felt themselves involuntarily taking a step back. Beside the black horse, Argolaith's dog, Breaker, was baying wildly and darting back and forth, eager to leap into the fray.

Argolaith, without moving, quietly said, "Attack."

Marc, his voice lowered into a full, booming bass growl, bellowed the word aloud so that its sound rang out over the rooftops. The cry was taken up and volleyed back by the hundreds of voices filling the square. Athela reached for the scabbard on the back of her saddle and drew her sword into the air, releasing Aria's rein as Laith and the wave of Strikers pounded past her over the bridges towards the Kagaian troops. Aria reared up on his haunches and spun around, bolting forward to join the surge of Strikers and horses sweeping across the cobblestones.

Just then, the air started to sing with loud, terrible screams as arrows from the rooftops began to fly through the night air and Kagaian cavalry officers toppled like stones from their saddles.

From his vantage point high in one of the bell towers, Archer reared up, sighted down the length of his arrow, and let it fly. A moment later, a soldier who had been about to charge into Ari toppled to the ground. The sniper beside Archer narrowed her eye and loosed her arrow—a miss, but a close one.

Athela kept Aria back in a chokehold so that he held the rushing line stride for stride alongside Laith and Marc. Breaker was keeping a bounding pace a few lengths in front of the line of horses, darting this way and that as arrows sang through the cold and clattered off the cobblestones beside his paws. Athela could feel her voice unconsciously raising in a roar as the seething mass of dark Kagaian shapes began to take human form, the bristling steel blades winking in the dim light. She twisted her hand in a hunk of Aria's dark mane and raised her sword to the side, anticipating the rush of the first explosive clash.

With a deafening clatter of metal upon metal, the two sides fell against each other, and in an instant, everything lapsed into a curious moment-by-moment speed of action and reaction, only the barest thread of thought. A few of the horses went down with shrill screams, their riders swallowed up by the sea of fighters. Laith, flanked by Athela, Marc, and Ari, cut a swath through the thick of the Kagaian forces. No one seemed to want to approach Laith's glittering black figure atop the enormous horse, and Athela could visibly make out the faces of a few of the Kagaian soldiers as they took dubious steps back, the grips on their swords suddenly unsure.

A cry rose up behind them, and the leader of the Kagaian cavalry urged his soldiers to group together. Once massed, they careened towards Argolaith and the others, troops from both sides scurrying to avoid the crushing sea of hooves. They came quickly, but Laith and Marc were ready for them. Marc barked out a warning and alerted the soldiers near them just in time. Breaker slithered in between the charging hooves, biting and snapping as best he could to keep the opponents' horses distracted and uneasy. Laith swiveled Arfolasth to one side and brought his sword down with a crushing blow against the commander's shield. The black charger danced in place, raising himself up onto his hindquarters and shifting Laith out of the way at exactly the perfect second to avoid a hit. The riders circled each other, their blows a show of brute force rather than any sort of artistic swordplay. There was desperation in the actions of the Kagaian guards, who knew exactly what they were up against and exactly what kind of outcome would result from a loss.

"Laith!" Marc barked. A soldier was coming up behind Laith on the ground, his knife out, clearly aiming to cut Laith at the back of his knee or heel and incapacitate him. Laith took up the reins, and for a few bouncing steps, he and Arfolasth hovered together, then the black horse leaped into the air and fired out with his hind legs, catching the approaching soldier clear in the chest and caving in his ribcage with one brutal stroke of his enormous hooves. Then Laith's sword was out, and the black horse whirled again, cleaving the way through two riders.

Up in the tower, Archer hunkered down to refresh his quiver. "We're running out," he called to the girl beside him. "Shoot as carefully as you can." He leaned back over the railing and chanced a look down at the square. He could clearly make out Laith's glittering black form and scarlet cloak, and could see Marc and Ari beside him, but couldn't quite see Athela from where he sat. As he turned to nock an arrow to his bow, he happened to glance to the left, and at once, his golden eyes caught the tiniest flicker of movement. There were people on the roof, clutching torches—people that he was almost completely certain were not members of the Strikers.

"Hold fast!" he called to the astonished girl beside him. He leaped to his feet, slung his bow over his head and shoulders, and threw himself off the side of the tower. He could just hear the faintest wisp of her scream as he hurtled through the cold air and easily landed on all fours on one of the rooftops lower down. As nimbly and as quickly as a cat, he ran straight across the ridgepole of the roof, then sprang across the thin gap separating the buildings and skidded to a halt down the slope of the far roof, his white hand extended for balance. The figure he had seen from the tower blinked at him in unabashed shock. It was a Kagaian guard after all, torch in hand.

Oh, no, Archer thought grimly. *They're going to try to burn the roofs and send a warning sign to Faridor.* The island fortress was too far away for any lookouts there to notice a few fires burning in Two Falls, but an entire city's rooftops set aflame were bound to attract attention. Recovering, the guard swiped at him. Archer ducked a blow from the torch and easily sent the Kagaian soldier toppling to the ground. He caught the flaming torch in his hand and twisted, narrowing his brilliant eyes at the silhouette of the city against the night sky. Yes—almost like invading insects, he could see pinpoints of light here and there making their way up to the rooftops. They had to be stopped. The rooftops were slippery and coated with frost; the already damp wood would be difficult to set alight. It would buy them a little time, at least.

Archer smothered the flame of the torch in the gutter and tossed the useless length of wood down to the ground below. He nimbly ran along the thin beam of the roofs until he reached the next sniper lookout point and silently scaled up the stone face of the tower as easily as if he had been climbing a tree. He heaved himself up over the side and grinned as the faces of three shocked snipers whipped around to face him and then relaxed once they recognized who it was. One of the snipers was half-Ashan, a tall, thin woman in her mid-fifties with a wiry build and a naturally wary look in her eye.

"I need all Ashans and half-Ashans to immediately take to the roofs. They're trying to set them alight, to send a warning to Faridor," he told her. "Spread the word as fast as you can."

With a curt nod, she laid down her weapons and vanished over the side of the tower. Archer breathed a measured sigh of relief. "And keep your eyes out to the rooftops as well," he told the others. "We can't risk letting that lot giving away our game, can we?"

As if comforted by Archer's presence, the other snipers managed small smiles, then turned back to sight down the shafts of their arrows towards the pandemonium below.

Argolaith was on the ground now, back-to-back against Marc. Together, they faced a circle of cautiously advancing soldiers. Laith's eyes narrowed as he surveyed them and kept his eyes peeled for any flash of red around him, but it seemed like there was nothing but an impenetrable wall of green armor. The Strikers had lost warriors, that was certain—a great many warriors. But the battle wasn't over yet.

His sword was light and balanced in his right hand, and he communicated with Marc at his back through a series of largely invisible cues. Marc shifted to the left, and Laith mirrored his action, knowing that the Kagaian soldiers must be coming up behind him. Marc's elbow nudged him, and without hesitation, Laith whipped around, the blade suddenly singing through the air, connecting with the steel of a young Kagaian officer. It was a frenzy of action as the two Jelani parried and retreated, facing the thick forest of bristling swords and swinging green cloaks. *Come on*, Laith thought to himself, keeping his face carefully impassive. *Come on.*

And suddenly, like the wind changing, he could feel it. The heads of the Kagaian guards began to ripple towards the far side of the town square. Figures materialized from within the alleyways. There were swords flashing in their hands, pitchforks, large pieces of wood. Some ran straight toward the Kagaian guards with nothing but their fists clenched. The citizens of Two Falls had risen up as one. Calchas's troops and the released prisoners from the Kagaian headquarters came pouring in, and together, they had the Kagaians pinned in on all sides in the city square. Archer's snipers were covering the rooftops, and there was no chance of escape now that a new wave of Striker fighters had materialized out of the night mist.

A few of the Kagaian fighters broke away and turned around to try and face this fresh onslaught. Though in numbers they were still somewhat superior, they had suffered extreme losses; it was nearly impossible to turn around without finding a green cloak slumped over on the stones. They were demoralized, and they were tired. The released prisoners and General Calchas's troops had had a few minutes to gather themselves, which the Kagaian troops had not. There was the flurry of a skirmish on the far end of the square as Calchas's soldiers pushed the Kagaian fighters back towards the center of the square, but it died down like the last spitting gasp of a dying ember.

And then the first sword was dropped, hitting the stones with a high-pitched clang, almost like a bell tolling the end of day. One Kagaian guard stopped in his tracks, eyeing the wall of horses and riders and footsoldiers and swords. He saw the desperate determination, the fierce loathing in the eyes of the prisoners. The soldier raised his hands behind his head and sank to his knees in surrender. His commanding officer, spotting him out of the corner of her eye, took a step forward and opened her mouth to order the soldier back to his knees, but before she could, another sword had clanged to the ground. Like a wave, the Kagaian troops looked at one another and sank to their knees.

After a few moments of the dense metallic chiming of the swords being cast down, an unearthly silence stole over the city center, the echoes of the din of battle still reverberating off the far walls until it faded into silence.

Laith, who stood beside Marc and Ari, slowly lowered his weapon and swiveled around, gaze passing over the cowed Kagaian troops. Deliberately, he straightened and sheathed his sword. A long red cut bled on his forehead, but he was otherwise unscathed. Quickly, he looked to Marc and Ari, who nodded that they were all right, then he glanced up to the nearest tower, trying to catch a glimpse of Archer, but the Ashan did not appear to be at his post.

The clatter of hooves sounded behind them, and Athela rode up on Aria, skipping off his back and landing like a feather on the ground beside them. Her left leg nearly buckled; she had been injured, but she steadied herself against her saddle and shook her head at them, assuring them that everything was all right. Aria's flanks steamed and heaved, and for the first time in recent memory, he stood quietly as she held his bit.

Laith, followed by the others, walked through the lines of kneeling Kagaian soldiers and up to the nearest commander. He glanced down at her. She looked back at him with a narrow stare of abject hatred. Laith couldn't help but give her a pleasant smile, then he raised his head and addressed the entire square.

"You have all surrendered. Keeping your hands on your heads, I want you to stand up and form lines by the central fountain. You will then be escorted back to the Kagaian—excuse me, *Striker* headquarters."

He turned away as the Kagaian soldiers began to stand and assemble as he had instructed, slight clinking here and there as their boots collided with the discarded swords littering the ground. Calchas's officers filed forward to surround them.

"We've won!" cried one of the freed prisoners, a club clutched uncertainly in her hands. "We've won!" She turned to the others around her, clearly intent on inciting some sort of cheer or public celebration.

"We do not celebrate yet," Laith barked loudly, and any burgeoning cheers were immediately quashed at the sound of his voice. "We still have to make it through the night. I want no celebrating, no flag-burning, nothing until we give the orders. We do not take down the Kagaian flags over the gates of the city. I want the one at the Two Falls headquarters replaced immediately and flown at full mast. Those of you who are injured will be taken to the infirmary we have set up at the headquarters. The rest of you, I want you all to fan out over every inch of the city walls. *No one* is allowed to get in or out, not a dog, not a person. If you see a carrier pigeon released, I want it shot out of the sky. That is crucial. Nothing must appear to have changed. Does everyone understand?"

There was a dull murmur of assent. It was obvious that the people had thought the entire battle was over and were somewhat disappointed that it wasn't. Laith seemed to sense this, and his voice grew gentler. "The sunrise is almost here," he assured them. "We just have to make it through the night."

After a few seconds, the square slowly began to shuffle into motion as the soldiers did as Laith had instructed. A few moments later, Archer and a few of his snipers jogged up towards them. A large smile was etched over his face.

"Glad to see we all survived," he remarked, glancing around at all of them, eyes resting for a beat longer on Athela. His smile faltered as he gave Ari a perfunctory glare, but then the bounce was back in his step. "I have my snipers clearing the rooftops, and then I'm having them position on top of the city walls to try and keep anyone from running off to warn Cira."

"Good," Laith nodded and clapped him on the shoulder.

"Someone should go and fetch Tarr for this bit," Marc suggested.

Archer flashed them a wolfish grin and loped off into the night.

General Grey and his entourage had set off as early as they could from Faridor to make the journey back to Two Falls. The meeting had been effective, he supposed. Cira had seemed rather distracted by a very flashy, effeminate-looking young man she had lounging about her chambers. General Grey had long ago given up trying to understand women's tastes. The young man looked as though he had never even had to wipe his own nose.

He was almost relieved to find that the city walls were still standing, black and impressive against the gray morning light. The green Kagaian banners still flapped and cracked in the wind, and he spotted two of the sentries on duty staring down at him, black smudges against the cloudy winter sky. His small party drew up their muddy horses to a halt in front of the gate.

"General Grey returning to Two Falls," called Grey's lieutenant. "Open the gate."

"Yes sir," came back the gruff reply from above, and one of the smudges disappeared out of view.

Something prickled at the back of Grey's neck, something he couldn't quite put his finger on. The gates creaked open, and the other members of his party began to ride forward into the city. Grey hesitated, on the verge of ordering them to halt, but realized it would look rather foolish if he, the commander, hung around reluctantly outside the gate while his troops rode in. He nudged his horse forward and entered. The place appeared to be quiet, deserted. He felt his grip tighten as he cast about with his dark, hooded eyes, looking for signs of danger. The gates creaked back to a close behind them.

The instant the doors clanked shut, a horde of shadowy faceless figures behind them darted out and swooped the other officers beside him off their horses. The horses screamed in terror and bolted as their riders were wrestled to the ground. Gray started and reached for his sword, wheeling his horse around to face any attackers, but as soon as he saw the party walking towards him from one of the nearby houses, he halted resignedly and took his hand off of his sword. He pulled his horse up and waited quietly as the Strikers approached him. *They did it*, he thought to himself dully, almost shaking his head. *They somehow managed to do it.*

The Striker at the head of the group was tall and sandy-blond, with dark brown eyes and an innately regal carriage. This one must be Prince Argolaith. He glanced at the others in the group following the prince and sorted them out: the white Ashan, Archer, who had killed four of his best officers, as well as his own predecessor. Lady Athela, sister to Queen Cira. The stocky blond with shoulders like a wrestler must have been Lord Marcus. There was no sign of the young man, Si Morthenstar, or the other Jelani woman he'd heard about.

Argolaith drew up beside him and laid a hand quietly yet firmly on Grey's bridle.

"We have taken Two Falls," he told the general, his voice deep and measured. "And you, as of now, are a prisoner."

Grey took a slow breath, then swung his leg over the back of the saddle and dismounted. He stood eye to eye with Laith.

"Which one of you," he said slowly, "is Tarr?"

There was a flicker of the heads in the group as they glanced over their shoulders. The small crowd parted slightly, and Gray found himself staring at a tall, thin, unremarkable Ashan with dark brown hair and a bony, rectangular face. His hands were loosely held in his pockets as he stood unobtrusively at the back, a melancholy, wistful tilt to the edges of his eyes. Gray almost wanted to scoff in disbelief, but then he met the Ashan's gaze, which was regarding him searchingly with a quiet, reserved fascination. The expression was sharp and brilliant; it belied his unassuming appearance. He didn't miss a movement or a breath. Gray realized that this must indeed be the Ashan who had outsmarted him, who had taken back the city right from beneath him. He certainly didn't look like much.

Gray gave an infinitesimal nod and, without another word, was led away through the streets by a large group of flanking guards. Laith and the others watched him go, and as soon as he was gone, the prince turned to face the others. A smile began to creep across his face.

"Open the gates and raise the Striker flags!" he called. "Two Falls is ours!"

And with that, a cheer rose from the throats of those beside him. It spread through the streets and the houses until the sounds of celebration covered the city like a cloud whose thunder could be heard all the way across the sea.

CHAPTER TWENTY-TWO

"Well, what do you think?" Cira asked, not turning around from the window.

Joris took great pains not to let his utter surprise register on his face. He ran a hand through his dark curls and forced himself to sit back farther on the richly embroidered divan. "I thought," he said measuredly, "that you were intending to marry King Tarik. To secure the trade routes and ensure his military support when you invade the West."

Cira gave a dismissive flutter of her hand and turned to face him, her wide-set green cat's eyes piercing. "What's the point of being Queen if I can't do as I like? Do you not want to?"

Joris's mind raced, and he adopted a casually sardonic tone. "This is all so sudden," he said. Cira rolled her eyes and made a noise in her throat. She swept across the room, her robe fluttering around her feet as she went.

"I was thinking," she continued, ignoring Joris, "That we could announce the engagement on the anniversary of my coronation. We could even go on a small celebratory tour, if you like. Visit Joymaril and go down the coast, maybe see some of my future lands in the West. What do you say?"

Joris finally began to understand that Cira was being serious. "I'd be King?" he asked dubiously.

"King Consort," Cira corrected. "But yes." She was fiddling with a small box over on the table where she stood, some trinket or other she must have brought back from her visit to Vireg earlier that year. She opened the box, toyed with what lay inside, then stepped back from the desk and continued to stride about the room. She glanced up to look at him, a seemingly apprehensive smile playing about the edges of her mouth.

"King Consort," she repeated, as if dangling the title in front of him.

"I was born with a title," Joris said lazily.

"King is still a step up," Cira pointed out sharply.

"What of the Strikers?" Joris asked. "What will we do about them while we're off on our grand engagement tour?"

Cira whirled angrily, tossing her hands up in the air. "General Grey will worry about it," she snapped. "I'll kill him myself if their heads are not on a platter at my front gate in a month. They make it all so dreadfully *boring*." The last word escaped her with considerable venom. "We have to stay cooped up in here because they keep launching their damned attacks. I didn't build myself up to all of this," she motioned about the magnificently apportioned room, "just to be locked up inside it like a prisoner. They don't see what I'm trying to build. They don't understand."

"We go hunting," Joris pointed out mildly, flicking an infinitesimal piece of dust off of the back of the divan. "We ride across your lands. We're not locked up."

Cira snorted and resumed fiddling with the small box. "If they were *dead*," she said, almost to herself, "just think about how perfect everything would be."

He supposed he should have felt pleased with himself for how effective the job had been. He would be willing to take this step, if only because of the interesting layer of complexity it would lend to the project. The only thing that nagged at him was that title...*king*. He had always detested any form of leadership or establishment, and while his title and nobility had often come in handy for him as far as gaining entrance to functions and sidestepping tiresome bureaucracy, the thought of being even further ensconced in Cira's organization made him want to vomit. His parents (he shuddered) would be so *proud* of him.

Cira was still waiting expectantly for his answer, her eyebrows raised. He opened his mouth to reply, when suddenly there was an enormous pounding on her chamber door, and before Cira could even command an entrance, three envoys piled into the room, looking wind-blown and utterly terrified. So startled was Cira at their abrupt entrance and harried appearances that she nearly forgot to be incensed at their unceremonious arrival.

"Your Majesty," gasped one of the envoys.

"What is it?" Cira said slowly. Joris realized instantly what was about to be said. He felt a sharp thrill of satisfaction followed by a dark current of fear. His life was about to get slightly more complicated.

"My lady, the Strikers have taken back Two Falls," the envoy breathed. "They've taken General Grey prisoner, and they have taken back the city."

"They've raised the scarlet flag over the city gates," another envoy chimed in, his eyes darting from Cira back to Joris, as if searching for some form of protection.

Cira's face blackened into an ice-cold thundercloud. She swayed ever so slightly, leaning on the table for support, and Joris fought down a fresh swell of victory that threatened to bloom into a smile on his face. He thought instantly of the deaf maid who'd helped him. *We did it,* he thought. *She did it.* Cira was silent for a full minute, and when she spoke, her voice was barely over a whisper.

"When did this happen?"

"They captured the General yesterday," the envoy babbled. "They took the city the night before; they had reinforcements waiting outside the walls of the city..."

"*What* reinforcements?" Cira snapped, like a knife cutting through paper. "I thought we had starved them to extinction!"

The envoys glanced helplessly at one another. They were merely messengers; they had no knowledge of Cira's tactical maneuvers.

"And I suppose," Cira said silkily, "that my Kagaian troops just *sat* there and let them take it? What, may I ask, do they think they're doing *now?* Do they expect me to believe that they're just *standing* there and letting the Strikers take over *my* city as easily as all that?"

"There was a battle, Your Majesty," one of the envoys informed her hesitantly, crushing his riding hat between large, awkward hands. "Many of the troops were scattered, others were killed."

"We outnumber them *four to one*," Cira shot back. "Were they not *told* how to use their swords?"

Again, the envoys glanced at one another for support. "We have word that there are a few remaining pockets of loyalists who are attempting to regroup and launch an attack from within…"

"Leave," Cira ordered curtly, turning away from them and walking back across her chamber. "Send in my captain of the guard."

While the guard was fetched, Joris waited in silence, realizing that there was absolutely nothing he could do or say. He watched Cira's mind whirling, saw her visibly calculating how to discover who executed the takeover and how best to wreak her vengeance upon them.

I have to get out, Joris realized. *Her paranoia will know no end. She'll start at the fringes and eliminate every single person of whose loyalty she is not utterly certain. I'll be immune for some time because of her liking for me, but sooner or later, she'll come to me and that will be it. I'll have to leave tonight, somehow. Tomorrow at the latest.*

The captain of the guard arrived, looking warily across the room as he entered and bowed. "Your Majesty, I have just been made aware of the situation in Two Falls."

"'A situation,'" Cira echoed in a sneering voice. "Yes, I suppose you could call it that. How soon can you rally an army together to take the city back? The mere thought of the Strikers thinking for an instant that they've got the better of me…"

She trailed off, and the captain glanced from her to Joris, looking as though he had something to say but that Cira was certainly not going to like it.

Cira sensed his hesitation. "Out with it!" she barked.

The captain shifted uncomfortably and took an unconscious step backward so that he was nearly out of the room. "The wall of Two Falls…" he began awkwardly. Cira's face darkened even deeper so that her throat was crimson red with fury. Joris couldn't help but marvel at the irony. The wall, the impenetrable wall that Cira had spent so long building in order to keep the denizens of Two Falls *in,* was now the main barrier keeping her out. And Joris could see the captain's point. Two Falls was strategically located on high ground. Any sort of assault on the city would be extremely costly, both in terms of expense and equipment and in the lives of her troops. As much as it infuriated her, the sensible thing for Cira to do was to concede temporary defeat and focus her energy elsewhere.

Like a shadow, Joris watched the realization pass over Cira's face. "Fine," she said, her voice dark and foreboding. "Fine. But to have organized the attack, they must have known that General Grey would be out of the city that day. There's no way they could have achieved this while he was on watch. Grey was the only one in Two Falls who knew of the order. So we must have a leak inside Faridor itself." She drew herself up to her full height, her eyes boring holes into the captain. "I want you to lock down the fortress tonight. No one, not even a cook, comes in or goes out. I want every single servant, maid, guard, and soldier in this household arrested and questioned. Question them *harshly.* Execute anyone who takes longer than two seconds to think of an answer. Any shred of suspicion is grounds for beheading. Is that understood?"

The captain's mouth fell open, and it was only through years of practice that Joris prevented his from doing the same.

"My...my lady?" the captain stammered.

"What part of my order did you not understand?" Cira demanded.

The captain shot Joris another helpless look and backed out of the door, closing it shakily behind him. Cira shot a look at Joris, as if daring him to challenge her. Joris turned away and walked to the window opposite, staring down at the stormy gray sea crashing against the rocks, feeling the walls of his prison closing in ever tighter.

The first floor of the Kagaian headquarters of Two Falls had been repurposed into a makeshift infirmary for those who still needed tending to after the battle, and also served as a processing center for the dozens of prisoners they had collected after the conclusion of the fight. There were so many Kagaian surrenders, in fact, that there was some trouble deciding exactly what to do with them. They would barely fit into the prison cells, and Tarr couldn't help but feel that it was inhumane to pack them in together four at a time.

Against Tarr's wishes, they came up with an offer. Those who still declared loyalty to Cira would be released into her care, banished from Two Falls, and sent to Faridor. Those who had families in Two Falls and had taken jobs as soldiers to support their livelihoods were offered a pardon, providing that they registered their names and addresses and vowed never to raise arms against the Strikers again. Tarr expressed, in no uncertain terms, that such a bargain was bound to result in a Kagaian resistance being formed almost immediately, but the others, exhausted from the fight, tired of the killing, had outvoted him.

"Have some faith in people, Tarr," Marc had told him.

Tarr hadn't replied and had retreated into a stony silence. Tarr knew exactly what people were capable of. His missing finger was a constant reminder.

They gathered together two days after the Battle of Two Falls in what was formerly General Grey's office. The curtains had been pulled back, allowing the winter light to spill in over the floor. Someone, in a desperate attempt to bring some semblance of life to the room, had arranged a few sprigs of holly and pine in a small jar on the central banquet table. Tarr stood by the window, staring out at the streets below. He smiled to see that there were people gingerly venturing out, walking to and fro as if they weren't quite sure whether such liberties were permitted. Already, there was word that volunteers were clearing out the town square, the site of the main battle, preparing for the market to be reinstated. Tarr couldn't help but feel pleased.

He turned from the window and faced the others. The order of the day was to parse together some sort of ruling plan, some way to get Two Falls back on its feet. Ari, his arm bandaged and held in a sling, sat at one end of the table. Laith stood nearby, his fingers steepled under his nose and Breaker sleeping beneath his chair, the dog's large glossy black head resting on his paws. Beside Laith stood Pieter, the city councilor who had been safely brought out of hiding after nearly three years lived underground. The time spent in hiding had aged him even more; he was wrinkled and quite grizzled, but his advice would be invaluable as they attempted to reinstate order. General Calchas, half of his face obscured by a large bandage, stood at the opposite end of the table from Ari, flanked by two officers Tarr didn't recognize. Lady Burton, his second-in-command, had fallen while retaking the headquarters. There were another five or six individuals, representatives from various trade organizations, and a few who had helped see to Ashan welfare during the occupation, who had been recommended by either Ari or Pieter as having valuable opinions to contribute. Before them lay the almost insurmountable task of attempting to rebuild a city that had been all but crushed by the past years of war.

It was no easy proposition; that was plain for Tarr to see. The Strikers began, filling the makeshift council in on exactly where the city stood as far as food, supplies, and medical aid were concerned. For some reason, the situation sounded even more dire when the city's desperate needs were listed all at once. Calchas seemed to be more interested in the city's fortifications, especially safety around the wall, and volunteered his officers as new heads of security.

"If I know Cira," Laith said wryly, "the very first thing she's going to want to do is to get back at us. We should be prepared for an attack."

"If there are any brains among the lot of them over at Faridor," Calchas shook his head, "they'll know that unless they can get together a considerable army, there's just no tactical advantage to trying to take back the city. Cira did a good job building this wall, and the fact that it's on high ground works to our advantage. If she attempts anything of that nature, it'll be her loss, not ours."

"We know that she has connections to the lands across the sea to the East," Athela reminded the council. "If she's angry enough, there is the possibility that she may raise an army with their help."

"Trade is one thing. Borrowing an entire army is another. She'd be in Tarik's debt," Tarr shook his head. "I think we're safe on that front for a little while at least. That will be her last resort."

"And what do we do about passage in and out of the city?" asked one of the newcomers, an Ashan woman with long white hair. "The shoe is now on the other foot, as it were. We can't know that people coming in or out aren't working for Cira. Are we going to keep the gates closed, as she did?"

Tarr gave a sigh. It was ironic, really, now that the situations were reversed. He would have to develop an entirely new sense of paranoia, have to recalibrate his mental maps of the city towards defense rather than offense.

"We'll have to require some form of identification," Ari maintained. "Some way of verifying that we're not letting a whole host of spies into the city."

Tarr shook his head. "Laith is right. At least for now, Cira is going to be angry and vengeful. Her mind is going to leap to a military campaign of some sort, some kind of big, dramatic gesture to show that she's still in control. She isn't going to immediately turn to some campaign of espionage or subterfuge. It will give us some time to work out a system. I want the city to be open. We didn't do all of this work just to lock the doors back up again and pen people in."

"Ari's right, however," Pieter chimed in. "We need some sort of travel documents."

In another few moments, the task of drafting some sort of identification paper was given to one of the younger soldiers who had worked in Tarr's forgery division. Tarr thought ruefully that now *he* was going to have to be the one to keep his eyes sharp for faked documents, to come up with some clever way to keep Cira's spies from smooth-talking their way inside the city gates. After brainstorming for a few minutes, Tarr came up with an idea for some sort of stamp with a hidden code so that the document could be held up to the light to verify its authenticity. The young officer promised that he would work on it, and seemed rather excited at the prospect.

The meeting stretched on for hours, and lunch was brought in at noon. Even in just a few days, the difference of having an open city had made its mark. As news of the Strikers' victory had spread to the surrounding lands, donations of food and supplies—whatever could be spared—were slowly beginning to trickle in. Some marvelous soul, who owned vineyards just to the west, had immediately sent in a wagon filled with casks of wine. As Tarr raised a glass to his lips and inhaled the deep, woody aroma, he sent a silent grateful prayer in the vintner's direction.

They debated next about the best way to set up the city's infrastructure. Pieter suggested reinstating the town council, in which officials from the various city neighborhoods would meet once a week to discuss issues with the city's planning and government. Tarr nearly laughed when he pictured what Archer's expression would be after he realized that he'd helped reinstate the old government of Two Falls, an organization that had all but chased him out of the city many years before.

Finally, Pieter pushed his chair back from the table. The old man was unused to talking for so long and was visibly exhausted by the duration of the meeting. "Friends," he said, his voice raspy from overuse, "I thank you all for taking the time to meet here today. I feel that we have made great strides, and that all the decisions presented today will have positive results for the future of our city."

"Have we thought about attempting to reach out to Joymaril?" one of Calchas's officers asked.

Tarr and Laith glanced at one another. Laith cleared his throat. "We have had no contact with the palace of Joymaril since the war broke out," he informed the group. "We have no idea what the situation is in the city, who is in charge, whether the loyalty there still leans towards Cira. Any attempt at communication with the people of the city has failed, and any attempt to infiltrate it or slip inside has also..." he trailed off, shooting another guarded glance towards Tarr, "failed."

Tarr shifted his seat. Those "failures," as Laith so delicately put them, were, in fact, the lives of three of the Strikers over the past two years, who had been shot down by Joymarillian snipers before they could even get close to the lake.

"We are reluctant to attempt any further communication until we have intelligence as to the situation in the palace," Tarr asserted. "Our focus has been directly on reclaiming Two Falls. It seemed to be the logical thing to address Joymaril at a later date."

"That later date may be now," Pieter pointed out. "If Cira is as angry as you say she is, we're going to need all the help we can get. Joymaril could attack at any moment with their cavalry. If they breached the wall, we'd be done for."

And with that, he stood up from his chair, acknowledged the rest of his colleagues, and walked from the room—presumably for a long nap. Tarr glanced out the chamber door as Pieter opened it and saw Si, who had been sitting against the wall opposite. Si leaped to his feet and gave a quick wave. Tarr winked at him, wondering how long the boy must have been sitting outside waiting for the meeting to end.

The others took Pieter's exit as a signal that the meeting was over and began saying their farewells in quiet twos and threes. Out of the corner of his eye, Tarr saw Si make motions to approach them, but before he could, Calchas strode up to Tarr and Laith, and Si fell back. Tarr waggled a covert finger at him, telling Si to wait just one more minute.

"I am glad to hear that Rane is doing better," Calchas began, with a nod to Tarr. "I hear that she's even able to sit up and walk about a bit."

"Thank you," Tarr replied. "She's still unable to speak or move much, but it's a relief that the most dangerous part is past."

"I was told there's been intelligence about a secret weapon that Cira is working on," Calchas continued. "Do you have any further information about that?"

Tarr and Laith glanced at one another. "Not yet," Tarr shook his head. "No idea, really. We've lost contact with our spies at Faridor since the battle. It's likely that Cira is rearranging the household, shaking things up. As soon as it all settles down, we intend to order all our spies to focus on uncovering whatever that weapon might be."

Calchas frowned. "If it's something that could threaten the security of this town, I'm going to need to know about it as soon as possible so that we can take steps to prepare."

"Yes, of course," Tarr assured him, feeling somewhat exasperated as his head began to spin. *Of course we'd tell you if we bloody well knew anything*, he thought crankily. Out of the corner of his eye, he saw Si bouncing impatiently up and down on the balls of his feet as if he had to go to the bathroom.

"Anything else?" Tarr asked hurriedly, thinking that it wouldn't be very professional-looking if the heir of Morthenstar wet himself in the middle of the Two Falls council chambers.

"Yes," said Calchas slowly. "Archer and a number of my officers have been monitoring the presence of the remaining Kagaian support within the city. We have a presentation that we'd like to give to you in one of the adjoining meeting rooms."

Tarr felt himself already reeling from the extensive six-hour meeting they had just endured. He exchanged a rather helpless glance with Laith.

Calchas scowled at them, as though they were schoolboys shirking their work. "Unless you have anything more important to attend to than the city's security?"

"No, of course not," Tarr assured him, thinking inwardly *only a square meal and a few hours' sleep.*

"Good. I'll expect you there in five minutes," Calchas nodded curtly and swept from the room. Laith sighed apologetically.

"Advance, advance, never retreat," he clapped Tarr on the back. "We'll have time for sleep when this entire blasted war is over."

"The extra meeting was probably Ari's idea," Tarr grumbled, realizing that he was starting to sound a lot like Archer. "He lives for unending meetings."

Laith laughed and shrugged helplessly He walked out of the room, casting a concerned look towards Si, who appeared to be about to burst. As soon as Si and Tarr were alone, Si bolted forward and accosted Tarr with a maddening bombast of buoyant, youthful energy. Tarr suddenly felt three times as tired.

"Tarr!" he exclaimed with a bright, freckly smile, his copper hair bouncing. "We've taken Two Falls!"

I noticed, Tarr thought tiredly. "Yes," he agreed, as pleasantly as possible.

Si blinked at him for a few seconds and realized that Tarr was clearly not on the same wavelength. "The medallion!" he exclaimed. "All of my powers and things. You said we'd be able to start figuring all of that out as soon as we'd taken over Two Falls!"

Tarr couldn't bring himself to wipe the smile off of Si's face by forcing him to face the realities of government bureaucracy. *And I did promise.* He thought that he had been tired *before* the Two Falls victory, but this...Tarr straightened his thin shoulders and adopted an air of unquestionable confidence. "We will," he assured Si. "We're going to figure out all of that, *and* what it all means, *and* I'll bet there's a fantastic buried treasure or code somewhere that'll tell us all about it."

Si's smile brightened even more, and he opened his mouth to add something when suddenly Ari poked his head around the door. "Meeting's starting, Tarr," he called. "We'll need you."

Si's expression faltered, and he looked up to Tarr, searching the Ashan's face with his wide gray eyes. "I promise, Si," Tarr said again, trying to sound as convincing as he possibly could. "We've just got to get all of this under control."

He patted Si's shoulder and walked briskly out into the hall, leaving Si standing alone in the council room, the smile gradually fading from his face.

Dark clouds rolled in from across the sea that night and settled low over the land, effectively blocking out the morning sun so that the transition between day and night was nearly imperceptible. The snow began slowly at first, then began to fall more and more rapidly. It promised to be one of the biggest blizzards in recent memory.

A single figure approached the bridge at Faridor, wrapped heavily in a fur cloak. The guards, huddled together at the end of the bridge, were instantly on the alert.

"Papers!" one demanded curtly, and papers were proffered. They were, as far as the guards could tell, all in order. The figure, whose face was still obscured by the thick cloaks and furs, was ushered over the bridge under the guards' suspiciously watchful gaze.

As she approached the front gates of Faridor, Kai pushed back the hood from over her face and took a deep breath. The fortress loomed out of the dark, the snow swirling and spiraling around it in furious gusts. Kai knew that she would never walk back out of the fortress alive, and the thought was oddly calming. She had had time to prepare, and she was at peace with it. She had only to do two more things before her time was done: she would free her sister. And she would kill Cira Kagai.

Since her botched assassination attempt on Laith and her subsequent life pact with Archer, she had struggled to decide on the best course of action to take. She could take advantage of her freedom, certainly: run away, and Archer would never be the wiser. But that would leave her sister rotting away in the dungeons of Faridor, and that thought was simply intolerable. So, she had faced the inevitable and had traveled back to her mother's tribe. The voyage had taken a great deal longer than she had expected, as some of the Ashan tribes had taken to a rather nomadic existence, forsaking their comfortable tree cities and moving around so as to avoid being spotted by any of Cira's renegade troops, some of whom had taken to conducting raids and abducting unwary Ashans for rewards back in Two Falls.

Kai had found the Redwood tribe and said her farewells, such as they were. Her mother had been a favorite daughter of the tribe, even when youthful indiscretions and wanderings had resulted in a frowned-upon marriage to a woman from Two Falls, which itself resulted in the adoption of Kai, Rowan, and various other siblings. When the marriage to Kai's human mother had fizzled, Kai's Ashan mother returned to her people. Since her Ashan mother's passing (and given Kai's mixed parentage, not to mention her chosen lifestyle and occupation), she had been regarded as having only the most peripheral connection to the tribe. Still, Kai supposed the tribe was all the kin that she had, and the thought of them made her slightly less lonely. She left word with them to be passed to her remaining brothers and sisters in the event that they made contact. She had settled what few affairs she had left and had resolutely turned east and traveled back through the forest and up across the wide plains towards the sea. And now, like something out of a dream, she stood before the front gates of Faridor, which gaped open before her and closed her within like the maw of an enormous beast.

Again and again, she produced her papers when asked by various guards at the many checkpoints leading into the fortress. At one door, they searched her for weapons (which was almost comical in its futility; Kai had effectively been concealing weapons on her person since she was twelve years old) and, with a great deal of ado, was shown up the stairs to Cira's tower.

Something had changed—Kai could feel it. There was a tension in the air, a fear and discomfort that Kai hadn't sensed during her earlier visit. She began to wonder what it could be.

"I want to see my sister," she told one of the guards. "Take me to her."

"Your sister is held at the top of the north tower," he replied sternly. "You see Her Majesty first."

The staircase wound up and up and up, and Kai's heart began to beat a bit harder. She felt the dagger on the inside of her boot and pictured pulling it, leaping forward at Cira, and ending the war once and for all. Or perhaps, if the situation was right, she would take Cira hostage and force them to release Rowan before she finished her off. Yes. That was the better way.

Finally, at the top of the tower, Kai was motioned to stop. The guard knocked on the door and was admitted. After a few moments' conversing within, the guard returned and fixed Kai with a narrow glare. "Her Majesty will see you now," he growled and showed her in.

Kai walked to the room, each stride measured, and ducked under the doorframe, filling the space like a tall, dark shadow. A huge fire roared in the fireplace. A large tray with wine and glasses was laid on a small inlaid table in front of the fire, and a number of large pillows were propped up on the floor. Clearly, Kai had interrupted something of a private romantic night.

Cira was standing before her, small and delicate, pale sheet of blond hair cascading over one shoulder of her dark lace-edged dress. Her arms were folded, and her eyebrows raised. Clearly, she had only allowed Kai to enter so that she could get the chance to upbraid her about her failure to eliminate the Strikers.

"*You*," Cira hissed. "I'm surprised you had the nerve to show your face to me again. I should kill you myself, right here."

Kai made no response. She stepped forward and ambled slowly through the room, taking her time, letting Cira seethe behind her. She wanted no sudden movements, no rash decisions; she wanted to choose her time wisely.

"Speak!" Cira commanded again.

Kai walked over beside Cira's desk, glancing casually down at it. On top of the desk lay a small open box with a lining of blue velvet. And there, in the center, was a silver medallion, glinting dully in the low light. Kai recognized it and was so caught off guard that she momentarily forgot herself.

"When did you get Morthenstar's medallion?" she asked curiously. *I would have seen, I would have heard,* she thought to herself. *I watched them. I listened so closely.*

"What are you talking about?" Cira snapped, her eyes flashing. "*Morthenstar's* medallion?"

Kai's attention jerked back to the matter at hand. Cira was still seething, and Kai would have to act quickly She began to calculate just how far she would have to leap to strike Cira down, or to wrestle her to the ground and take her as a hostage. She was alone, unarmed as far as Kai could see. It would almost be too easy. But the angle wasn't good. She had to keep Cira talking, to move around so that Cira wouldn't be able to take shelter behind one of the nearby pieces of furniture. The closer she could get, the better.

"I was able to poison Laith," Kai told her casually. "He survived, though." She took a tiny step to her right. Cira made no move. Perfect.

"I would think that with your supposed reputation, you would consider actually using a poison that *worked*," Cira said sarcastically.

Another tiny step. "They outwitted me."

"Apparently not so hard to do," Cira snapped. "And for that, both you and your sister will die tomorrow morning."

"Can I see her first?" Kai asked.

Cira's green eyes flashed with the pleasure of denying Kai her wish. "Absolutely not. She's in the north tower under heavy guard, and there's absolutely no way you'll make it. She'll be executed there."

Kai took another tiny step. It was just about perfect...

Suddenly, there was a movement out of her left periphery. A young man, slender and with a mop of unruly dark curls, walked out of an adjoining room. He stopped, looking up at her with surprise. To Kai's intense shock, she realized she *knew him*. It took her a moment to sort him out, to place the person she knew in this strange, unnatural setting. But there was no mistaking the beautiful, almost feminine features, the large gray-green eyes.

"Joris?" she exclaimed. "What...what are you doing here?"

An instant of shocked silence greeted her words. Joris's mouth fell open for only the hint of a second, and then he recovered his air of nonchalance. His eyes, however, were darting frantically. Cira's face had gone an eerie, stony shade of white, and she slowly revolved on her heel, looking from Kai to him.

"You know this Ashan?" Cira asked him, her voice deathly quiet.

Joris's answer came quickly, too quickly to be as reassuring as he wanted it to be. "Yes, I know her from the days when I lived back in Two Falls. At my parents' private city home."

"You betrayed Archer too, then," Kai spat in disgust. The shock of seeing Joris, of realizing what they had both become, drove every thought of subtlety from her mind. She was angry. She was especially angry at herself. "We both did. I should have known that you'd become the bought dog of this woman," she jerked her head towards Cira, whose head snapped sharply back around to stare at her.

"What are you talking about?" Cira whispered, her eyes sharp as knives.

Kai ignored her and continued speaking directly to Joris. She felt revulsion, both at herself for having stooped to becoming Cira's hired assassin and at Joris, whose own betrayal had instantly brought hers into startling clarity.

"Does Archer know? Does he know that you agreed to become Cira's pet?" She laughed ruefully. Cira's face looked frighteningly blank. "I tried to kill him, you know. Always said I would. We always joked that only one of us was going to make it out alive. But you...you were his *friend*." She shook her head with disgust.

Cira's head revolved around to Joris, who raised his eyebrows as if nothing Kai had just said had impressed him in the slightest. "She's lying," he said easily. "I have absolutely no idea what she's talking about."

Something strange happened to Cira's face. It was almost as if a door closed behind her eyes. Kai glanced between the two, unable to fully understand what was going on between them. Cira looked back to Kai, and suddenly, Kai knew exactly what would happen. The guards would be called. She would be outnumbered. She wasn't in a good position to fight them off, and Rowan—she had to get to Rowan. The only way to Rowan was through Cira. She lunged, catching her dagger up in her hand.

Like lightning, Joris darted across the room and pushed Cira out of the way. Kai fell off balance and rammed into the tray of wine, sending it to the floor with a crash, the drink soaking into the carpet like blood. At the commotion, the door flew open, and two of Cira's guards sped into the room.

"Get her!" Cira bellowed, gesturing to Kai, who was still squabbling on the floor with Joris. She dealt him a heavy blow with one balled-up fist, and he released her with a low grunt. She paused, assessing the situation. She had lost her chance to kill Cira. The guards were already flying towards her. *Rowan.* With one backwards glance at Cira, she darted across the room and threw open the balcony doors. An enormous freezing gust of wind and snow billowed into the room, and like a dark flash, Kai was up and over the edge of the balcony, falling through empty black space, Cira's furious shouts fading into the distance behind her.

The air howled in her ears as she fell blindly; then, like a cat, she felt the stone roof of one of the buildings coming up beneath her, and she tucked herself up, rolling into her landing to break most of the damage to her bones. She had her mother's Ashan fearlessness and agility, but because of her weight was not able to shake off a landing as easily as her full-Ashan brethren. Dazed, she shook her head to clear the wind and cold from it, then squinted through the dark, tumultuous snow to orient herself to the sea. Yes—there it was; she could hear it and could, even in the glowering night, see the muted white caps of the waves crashing against the rocks around the base of Faridor. There was the bridge. So the north tower was...that one. Even amid the roar of the wind and the sea, she could hear the alarms sounding all around the fortress. There wouldn't be very much time. Cira would know where she was heading.

Kai took off at a run, only her half-Ashan agility preventing her from slipping and careening off the ice-slick roof to break her neck on the stones below. She skipped from roof to roof until the north tower rose dark and imposing before her. She crouched low, staying as far out of sight as she could, as all around her the bells continued ringing and more and more torches were lit. Kagaian soldiers were pouring out onto the rooftops, balconies, and walls, searching for her.

The tower was eight stories high, and there were lights gleaming in almost every window—except for some of those on the sixth and seventh floors. The sixth floor, she saw, had bars on all the windows. *Aha*, she thought. *There you are.*

She leaped forward onto the tower wall and began scaling up the sheer, slick stones. To anyone without Ashan blood, it would have been an impossible ascent, but almost as if by magic, her feet found safe holds and her hands hauled her up, foot by foot, into the piercing cold wind and the whirling snow.

Finally, on the floor below Rowan's, she paused. There was a slight overhang of rock just above the glass-paned window and no bars to cover it. It would be easier to break in here and run up one flight of stairs, rather than try and work her way through the iron bars on Rowan's windows.

She shifted her handholds so that she was hanging in front of the window, then coiled up her long, powerful legs and kicked them through the glass panel, which shattered like thin ice onto the floor inside. She kicked again, clearing out the remaining jagged shards with the toes of her rugged boots, then swung herself into the room, landing gracefully on two feet in the middle of the empty interior. She surveyed the dark chamber, made out the outline of a door, and dove for it, catching up her dagger in her hand. She peeked her head out into the torchlit hall of the north tower. There were footsteps, but they were still distant. She bolted out into the hall and careened up the spiral staircase, twirling her dagger between her fingers.

On the next floor she came out onto the landing and ran headlong into a strained-looking man with glasses and a quill pen in one hand. She knocked him over and held the dagger to his neck. "Bring me to the Ashan woman's cell," she hissed at him, and when he paused, she cut a vicious nick onto his cheek. "Bring me to her!" she demanded again, her violet eyes flashing.

As she had surmised, the man was both a turnkey and a coward, and he immediately nodded, clasping a thick hand to his wounded cheek and regarding her with an abject expression of fear. She moved her knee from the pit of his stomach, and he scuttled backward. The floor of the circular tower was made up of three cells, and the man took her to the second one, fumbling with his keys. Kai stalked behind him like a cat.

"Rowan!" she called as the guard fitted the key into the lock. As soon as the door was open, Kai dealt him a crushing blow on the back of the neck, and the man sank to the floor with a groan.

"Kai?" came a hoarse voice from within. Kai darted inside, grasping around in the darkness. Her hands felt a bony wrist and fingers like icicles. She grasped the hand and pulled her sister out into the dim yellow gloom of the torchlit hallway.

Rowan blinked against the unfamiliar light, her eyes sunken and hollow, skin an unnaturally pale shade, contrasting sharply with the dark purple birthmark on her neck. She looked like a tattered skeleton. Kai could barely stand to look at her.

"We don't have much time," she said, pulling the dazed Rowan behind her to the stairwell. Kai shrugged off her cloak and wrapped it around her sister's frail shoulders. "You've got to get out of here. Cira is after me. There's an open window on the fifth floor. Get out, then jump, swim, run...whatever you have to do to be free. You have to be strong; you have to get out of here. I'll distract them for as long as I can. Go."

She half-dragged Rowan down to the room on the next floor and pushed her inside. The sound of footsteps was closer now, the shouts echoing off the stone walls of the stairwell. Snow and wind gusted in through the broken window, and Rowan looked dubiously from it to Kai, who seized her sister by the shoulders and shook her.

"You have to survive," she told her firmly. "You have to. You have to be strong. Go. I love you."

With that, she hugged Rowan fiercely and shoved her towards the open window. Rowan stood for a moment, seemingly unsure of which foot she should place in front of the other, then edged to the window and glanced down. A steely resolve settled across her face, and she looked back at Kai.

"I love you, too," she said. She slid over the edge of the windowsill and out of sight, the dark black gloom and white sheet of snow swallowing her up.

Kai let out a long breath and closed her eyes. Then, slowly, she turned to the door and plunged through it, hurling herself down the stairs and into the wall of waiting Kagaian soldiers.

In another half hour, there was a curt knock at Cira's chamber door. She was pacing back and forth, guards posted at every corner of the room. Joris sat quietly behind her on one of the couches, his eyes fixed, unmoving on the slowly darkening stain of red wine on the carpet. They hadn't spoken a word since Kai left.

Cira's head snapped up at the sound of the knock at the door, and nodded to the bodyguard to open it. A soldier, tattered and bloodied, walked in and saluted sharply.

"Well?" Cira demanded.

"The Ashan assassin is dead," she reported. "As you assumed, she was found in the north tower."

"And the prisoner?" Cira asked.

"She escaped," the soldier said uncomfortably. "The Ashan woman was able to hold the soldiers off long enough that the sister had a good head start. We're not sure where she is now, but we've already begun to form a search party."

Cira waved her hand dismissively. "A half-dead prisoner shouldn't be hard to find, especially in this weather. She'll have to swim for shore. Bring her back here when you find her. She may still be of some use in the future."

The soldier nodded and withdrew. Cira turned to look down at Joris, who was sitting mutely behind her. Two of the bodyguards glanced at one another.

"Now that the threat is over, my lady..." the most senior bodyguard began, "...would you like us to stand by?" The others had already started walking towards the door. Joris looked up and met her eyes.

"Wait," Cira ordered, and the bodyguards paused, staring at her. Cira didn't move a muscle.

Joris, his hands folded in his lap, regarded her levelly, his face open. It was all over. "I saved you," he murmured wonderingly. The words were not a plea for clemency; instead, he seemed surprised with himself, almost bemused. He shook his head. There was a hint of his disarming smile at one corner of his mouth.

"I saved you," he repeated.

Cira regarded him coldly. "Then you're a fool," she told him. "Guards," she snapped loudly, straightening up. The bodyguards, startled, paused at the threshold and walked up to await her orders. "Arrest this man. I want him taken to the dungeons immediately."

Dubiously but obediently, the guards made a motion to take Joris by the arms and lift him off of the couch. He waved them away, the same curious smile flitting about his mouth. He stood, adjusting his perfectly buttoned cuffs and smoothing the front of his sleek blue shirt, then reached over the arm of the couch for his purple velvet coat, shimmying the soft fabric over his shoulders and adjusting so that it fell just so. He glanced to the mirror hanging over the mantle and gave his hair a few final swipes, then faced Cira and gave her the slightest ironic bow. Then he straightened and allowed himself to be led away.

Laith lay on his bed in the new Striker headquarters, reading quietly as the snow raged outside. Breaker lay on the floor beside his bed. How much nicer it was, Laith thought, to know that it was safe outside. He turned a page of his book and realized that he hadn't actually been paying attention to anything he'd read since the last chapter. He sighed and glanced down at the large black dog lying beside him. Breaker raised his head, ears pricked. A moment later, there was a slight knock and Si's face peeked through the crack in the door.

Laith smiled warmly and lay the book down on his chest, glad for the interruption. "Come on in, Si," he encouraged him. Si entered and gave Breaker a pat on his silky black head, then drew up a chair to sit beside Laith. Si seemed unsure of where to begin and seemed somewhat conflicted about saying whatever he had come there to say. So the boy pointed at the book on Laith's chest.

"Whatcha reading?" he asked.

Laith looked down and shrugged one of his shoulders. "Something General Calchas brought with him about military campaigns and the like. Not terribly interesting. I was trying to bore myself to sleep, but so far, it hasn't worked."

Si laughed. "General Calchas is pretty funny," he observed. "He always acts like he doesn't approve of what I'm saying or doing, but then I catch him laughing at me a lot. In a nice way."

Laith hid a smile. The description sounded extremely familiar. "He's spent more of his life raising boys and girls like you than he has fighting wars," he told Si. "I'm sure he likes you very much."

Si seemed gratified but, after a beat of silence, still seemed unsure of how to begin. "Si," Laith prompted him gently. "What is it?"

"Well, I..." Si looked troubled, then grasped for a way to start. "Laith, you know how sometimes I just...I just know things? Like when I thought Marc was going to poison you?"

Instantly, Laith was on the alert. He straightened up and swung his legs over the side of the bed so that he and Si were staring face to face. "Go on," Laith urged him. "Have you had another one of your visions?"

"Sort of," Si said uncomfortably.

"Is something going to happen?" Laith asked seriously, his dark brown eyes grave.

"No, not really," Si's face was anguished. He met Laith's gaze. "Laith...I think...I think I know who killed your wife. It was the same person who attacked Rane."

Laith didn't know what he had been expecting, but it certainly wasn't *that*. He swallowed, feeling a sharp pain in his chest, and a knot grew deep in the pit of his stomach. "What do you mean, Si? My wife isn't dead."

"I saw..." Si groped for words. "Well, I didn't really *see*...and I wasn't asleep this time. But it was the same sort of feeling. I was sitting next to Rane, right, and I touched her arm, and all at once, there was this *flash*...and it wasn't even so much that I had this vision; it was more like I suddenly had a memory that hadn't been there before. Not Rane's memory even, but...just something that felt like a memory. Do you understand?"

Laith couldn't possibly hope to understand, but he could visualize what Si was describing. He nodded, and Si, encouraged, continued.

"And this memory was of that place, in front of the big palace where you and Marc and Rane and Athela used to live. That bridge underneath the water. I remember there was a woman on horseback there, and Cira was there, and this man. And the woman was your wife, I'm sure of it—we met when I was at the palace, do you remember? And then, the man stabbed the woman after she got off the horse. I..." he trailed off, seeing the look on Laith's face. "I'm sorry, Laith."

"What did this man look like?" Laith asked slowly, trying to ignore the fierce drumming of his heart. *It's not true,* he thought to himself. *She wouldn't have gone without saying goodbye. She can't just be gone.*

"He was tall and thin, and he was wearing a mask. But I know... somehow, I know that he has pale hair, but his eyes..." Si shuddered. "His eyes are *black*. Like pits, with no light in them. And I...I know his name. Rane knew it, too. She recognized him when he attacked her."

Laith was barely able to form the words. "What is it?" he whispered hoarsely, though he realized he probably already knew.

"Lord Seth," Si replied, and Laith's blood froze cold.

The name of Lord Seth, the psychopath condemned to rot in Joymaril's prisons for the remainder of his life, fell into the air and hung there. He remembered the day that Lord Seth had given Marc his scar, how he'd stood there watching them with detached interest as Marc's blood dripped from the end of his sword. An accident, they'd said. Laith never believed it. Nor had Marc, who'd had to bear the weight of that blow the rest of his life. Seth had simply *stared*—curiously, as if he were observing the behavior of some strange foreign species—as Marc had howled in pain.

Trying to appear calm, Laith cleared his throat. "Si, can you tell me anything else? Anything else you might know?"

"Do you know him?" Si asked anxiously.

"Yes, I do," Laith replied in a low voice. "Anything else you can tell me?"

Si glanced down at his hands. "He's the same one who killed that girl in the alleyway," he said.

How on earth could you know this? Laith wanted to demand, but pushed the urge away. "Thank you, Si," he said instead. "Thank you very much. Now that we know what we're up against, we can take steps to protect ourselves."

Si smiled, relieved, and stood to leave. He paused at the door and turned around to look at Laith. "Laith," he said slowly, "I'm scared of him."

Laith managed a wan smile. "So am I, Si."

Looking troubled, Si left the room, closing the door behind him.

He's wrong, Laith told himself firmly. *He's wrong about Ilaina. He must have seen things wrong, must have misunderstood his vision. He envisioned me dying, and I'm still here. Ilaina can't just be gone.*

A floor below them, in Rane's room, Tarr sat sleeping with his hand on his head beside her bed. Rane stirred and opened her eyes, and at once, Tarr snapped to attention, attuned to her every movement. A happy smile spread across his face.

"Hullo," he said, relieved. "Nice to see you awake and lively."

"Lively" was a bit of a stretch, and they both knew it. Rane smiled at him, and then her face grew grave. She turned her head—painfully, because of her neck, and glanced towards a short stack of letters on the table beside her. Reports from Faridor from their various spies. The reports had not been good.

"I know," Tarr said heavily. Cira, as they had predicted, had made her dramatic show of retaliation, though she had focused inward rather than aiming her wrath at Two Falls. She had executed dozens of her own servants, effectively wiping out any individual who had joined her house within the last month. Among those killed had been two of his newest spies, including Leonore, the young girl he had sent off in search of Cira's secret weapon. She was dead. More names, more faces to keep him up at night.

"Cicada is still alive," Tarr reminded Rane. "And Joris. We still have plenty of eyes and ears inside the fortress."

Rane's eyes closed for a beat, and then, with great effort, she managed a coarse whisper. The pain and effort it took for her to speak was almost unbearable to hear. "Cira will be more dangerous now than ever before," she croaked. "I doubt Joris will last much longer. She'll be looking for spies everywhere she turns. No one you send in there will be remotely safe."

"They weren't before," Tarr pointed out. He could already see where Rane was taking this conversation, and he wasn't going to have it. Not with her lying there. Not with her having just survived such a brutal attack. Not when she was still so weak and unwell, and not when he still loved her so very much.

"Tarr, we've taken back Two Falls, but this war is still very far from over," Rane pointed out in her raspy whisper, reaching out and taking his arm. "Cira is more than able to summon an army against us. To join forces with the kingdoms across the sea and march on us. To raise the Joymarillian cavalry. To burn the forest to the ground, if she wants, and all the Ashans with it. She may do it just out of pure spite. And if there is, in fact, some sort of weapon she's concocting that we know nothing about, it could spell death for every last one of us."

Tarr stood and turned away from her, unable to listen to any more. He had made difficult decisions during the war, many of which he still had yet to fully process, but this was next to intolerable. He couldn't bear to look at her.

"Tarr," she continued, her voice rattling like dry grass, "you need your best spies in Faridor. Your best spies are me and Cicada. She and I can work together."

"I won't do it," Tarr snapped. "I won't do it." He sat back down beside her in a rush and gathered her hands into his. "Rane, we've *just* found a modicum of peace. We've taken back the city. We don't have to be apart every day; you don't have to be on patrol every night. We can go *out walking* together. In the *daylight*. I can hold your hand, and it won't matter who will be able to see us or not. You can't..." he struggled with the words, fighting down the surge of panic. "You can't go to Faridor. You *can't.*"

Rane regarded him, her eyes soft but determined. She formed words, swallowed painfully. "I can. And I will," she said simply. "As soon as I'm well enough."

"I won't allow it!" Tarr said sharply. "As the head of the spy organization of the Strikers, I am still your commanding officer, and I will *simply not allow you to do this.*"

"Tarr," she croaked. "Your judgment in this matter is not sound. It is no longer up to you."

"Rane, look at you!" Tarr exclaimed, pushing back from her. "Lord Seth nearly killed you. You're not infallible."

"Neither are you," she replied quietly.

I've kept us alive so far, Tarr felt like shouting back, but he remembered Leonore and stopped short before the words could leave his lips.

She took a calm, considered breath. "I am going, with or without your permission."

Tarr turned away from her.

Rane watched him, still calm, still composed. She was well aware that Tarr's fury and frustration and blustering were only because he realized that she was right. She had to go. There was no one else left.

Tarr buried his face in his hands, and his shoulders grew slack. Rane reached up with one of her hands and passed it through his short brown hair.

CHAPTER TWENTY-THREE

The next dawn was cold and sharp as the blade of a knife. It hung, glittering, over the sheer white expanse of land beneath. Small gusts of swirling snow on the hillsides were swept up by errant twists of wind, and the trees sighed and creaked beneath their heavy burdens. The dead of winter had settled over all things.

That morning, Count Joris Actaeon was led out to the central courtyard in the middle of Faridor's keep. The icy wind bit at his ears and nose, slashed through his velvet coat. The square was empty except for the block; straw was scattered about it, presumably to catch his blood. Two executioners stood by, hooded all in black like shadows against the gray stone of the fortress and the slate of the sky. Joris tried to ignore his heartbeat as it mounted.

He glanced around, expecting to see Cira watching at one of the windows. Seconds passed. He was led to the block, pressed down to kneel, made to lay his head upon the freezing wood. He thought wanly to himself, *perhaps a reprieve will come.* The thought almost made him laugh. No pardon came.

I saved her, he wondered. *Why did I save her?*

It was the last thought he had, just as the blade came swishing down through the air towards his neck.

As the blade fell, Cira was standing beside the desk in her room, her fingers running absentmindedly along her things. Her eyes traveled down to the little inlaid box she'd brought back from Vireg, to the silvery medallion that lay within crushed folds of cobalt-blue velvet.

Morthenstar's medallion, Kai had called it. The Ashan had seemed genuinely bewildered that she had it. She didn't think that Kai was lying when she'd blurted the words out.

Cira opened the box wider and took out the medallion to inspect it. It didn't seem like anything of great importance. She turned it in her hand, admiring the weight of it. It seemed to be two circles of metal lying atop one another. She gave the medallion a small twist, pleased to feel how smoothly it turned.

A small, strange chill ran through her body and dissipated into the air.

Odd, she thought and laid the medallion back down in its box.

The news of Joris's execution was not made public. The Actaeons were a powerful family with a great deal of wealth at their disposal, and even Cira was wary of angering them. A month into the new year, word spread of a cargo ship that had sunk on a crossing to the desert country of Vireg. The young Count was among the passengers listed on the roster. Cira sent personal condolences to Joris's family upon receiving the news of the sinking, and if the family harbored any suspicions about the circumstances of their son's death, they were never voiced aloud.

Snow fell for a solid two weeks after the day of Joris's execution, right up until the eve of the new year. Usually, this was greeted by a wave of celebration in the city of Two Falls, but that particular year, the holiday was considerably subdued. There were no parties, no parades, no candles lit in the windows and on the street corners, no late-night carousing or singing. Perhaps it was because families were still desperately trying to contact loved ones who had managed to escape the city while others were rebuilding their homes after the battle in the square. Everyone seemed relieved to be alive and more in need of a long rest than a party.

The lights burned, however, from the torches in front of the Two Falls headquarters. The Strikers had officially moved in; each had his or her own separate room, offices, and a seemingly endless line of duties that needed attending to and problems that needed sorting out. Tarr had been buried under a large pile of paperwork: coded messages that his spies had confiscated from the Kagaian files left in the headquarters upon their takeover. Tarr and his team had been decoding the messages for nearly two days straight, and though Tarr knew that it was unlikely they would find anything of real value (the most important messages had probably been burned after they were read), they pressed on nonetheless.

After spending three hours decoding a particularly worthless message regarding Cira's wish that her troops be fed a diet of whole grains and complex proteins, Tarr realized that his left shoulder had developed into a large, painful knot. He pushed his chair back from the table, gave the other workers an apologetic nod, and stepped out of the cramped room to get some air. He rolled his shoulder around in its socket and, just as soon as he started to feel slightly more relaxed, saw Ari walking towards him with the calm, businesslike set to his blandly handsome face that signified a desire to speak about something important. Tarr heaved a small, weary sigh. He had, by this point, developed a certain expertise in deciphering all of Ari's distinctly inexpressive expressions.

"What is it?" Tarr asked as Ari approached, not bothering to be particularly polite.

"We have word from our street patrol. There is a meeting place designated for the remaining Kagaian loyalists in the city," Ari informed him.

Kagaian loyalists, Tarr thought furiously. *We never should have let her soldiers go. Never should have shown any clemency. The others should have listened to me.*

"They're meeting tonight in about an hour."

"Send someone, then," Tarr shrugged. "Send Archer."

Ari blinked slowly and then coughed. "Don't you think Archer would be slightly...*obvious*?" he asked delicately.

Tarr stifled a small laugh. Ari had a point. Both in appearance and actions, subtlety was not Archer's strong point. "What's Laith up to tonight?"

Ari considered. He had a great deal more respect for Laith than he did Archer. "I'll ask him," he said.

"Don't you worry that Laith might be recognized?" Tarr mused.

"Not as easily as Archer. And for all we know, the loyalists may be masked to protect their identities. Laith could be, too." Ari shrugged. "I'll go with him."

"Good. Scope it out, and if it looks chancy at all, then get out of there. We just want a general idea of what's going on, what's being said. If they're asking for secret handshakes or passwords, don't do anything that will get you into any trouble."

Ari nodded and spun on his heel. Not for the first time, Tarr wondered if Ari actually ever slept at all.

Laith and Ari set out later that night and found themselves standing in front of a small, unobtrusive pub called the Broken Door. Laith tucked a scarf over his mouth and nose and gave Ari a small wink.

"Come out if there's any trouble," Ari cautioned him.

Laith nodded imperceptibly and swept into the pub. His arrival attracted a few glances, but most of the individuals in the extremely crowded room were already in the midst of conversation and paid him no notice. To his relief, Laith saw that he was not the only one being cautious with his appearance. Though the pub was warm and there was a large fire flickering in the hearth on the east side of the room, many of the individuals at the tables had left their cloaks up or their faces partially obscured by scarves, old habits from the Kagaian occupation. After pausing at the door and kicking some of the snow off of his boots, Laith gave a small cough and spotted a table in one corner, with one other person seated at it, his back turned towards the door. Laith could see no other open table, so he walked across the room to the empty seat and pulled it out.

"Mind if I sit here?" he asked, trying to disguise his voice by keeping it hoarse. The individual gave no reply. It was a man; Laith could tell by the breadth of the shoulders. He was hunched over a mug in front of him, cloak pulled over his head.

Laith settled himself in the seat and glanced around, loosening his cloak and trying to appear at ease. He gave another glance around the room, scanning for any faces he might recognize, keeping a jocular tone in his voice. "I just heard about this a short while ago. Is this just a meeting place, or is there going to be an official program of any sort?"

He glanced back to the person sitting across the table from him, who had still not looked up or acknowledged his arrival. Was he asleep? Laith leaned to the side, trying to catch a surreptitious glimpse within the man's hood to see whether he was, in fact, awake.

Then the individual stirred, the head rose, and the hood fell back. Laith found himself staring into a pair of dark, expressionless eyes, pits so deep that no light seemed to shine out of them. Though it had been many, many years since they had last stood face to face, Laith instantly recognized the sharp bones and delicate hands, the pale hair.

Lord Seth.

Seth smiled at him, a slow, playful smile that did not reach his coal-black eyes. And all of a sudden, as unblinking and hollow as death itself, Laith *knew*.

He knew that it was true, that the very worst fear he'd harbored, the thought he'd pushed down and down inside his heart, was true all along. Ilaina was gone, plucked from the earth, erased from his life for that day and every day that would follow. And he hadn't felt her leave. He'd felt nothing at all.

The face of her killer smiled back at him.

Something in Laith's head snapped. It was as if someone were screaming inside his ears, so high and so loudly that he could burst. Laith had never felt anything like it before in his life; he was consumed by a rage and a fire that flooded from his chest through his arms and down deep into the pit of his stomach. In an instant, he lunged, going straight for the dagger at his hip, his teeth bared like an attacking wolf.

But Seth's hand found Laith's under the table and halted him, his fingers like thin steel cables around Laith's wrist. His dark eyebrows arched, and one slender, delicate finger rose up to his pale lips. He glanced across the room, still smiling playfully. Laith followed his gaze, taking in the scope of their surroundings. Like a wave, he reeled and realized the situation. He, Laith, one of the leaders of the Strikers, was literally cornered inside a room filled with Kagaian loyalists. If he attacked Seth, if he revealed his identity, there was no way that he would make it out of the room alive. And Seth was a fighter—a good one, nearly as good a swordsman as Laith himself—and would not be felled by any random, desperate blow Laith could dole out in his fury. Like a flame slowly flaring and rising, Laith realized that he could do absolutely nothing. With almost unimaginable effort, he wrestled his rage back down.

Slowly, still tensed, still furiously debating whether to strike out or whether to remain motionless, Laith sat back. He released his grip on his dagger's hilt and leaned against his chair, his eyes boring blistering holes into Seth's skin. His fists clenched so hard they felt like iron balls rather than hands. He had never wanted to hurt anyone so much. He thought how fast he could have his dagger out, how fast he could cut Seth across the face, how fast he could wipe the smile from his lips. It would not be fast enough.

Seth's smile widened, and he wagged a thin finger at Laith as if chastising him for thinking such reckless thoughts. Laith realized that he was breathing like a cornered bull, each breath shaking his entire frame. His head was swimming and he felt fire tingling in every finger. All he could think about, the only thing that consumed him, was the face before him. The smiling, smug face, the expressionless black eyes like the depths of the earth.

Without saying a word, Seth slowly pushed his chair back and stood, shaking out the folds of his black cloak around his thin frame so that Laith could see. *He hadn't even come armed.* The smile widened, and Seth slowly came around the side of the table and placed his hand on Laith's shoulder. It was a caress, almost loving. Laith recoiled against the back wall, his dark brown eyes spitting fire at the figure in front of him. Then Seth gave a small, sweet nod and turned away. Laith knew what it meant. *I'll be seeing you.*

Should he follow? No, it would attract too much attention if they left together. Let him get to the door, let him get to the door...

Laith sprang up, shoving his chair back with a loud screech that caused a few nearby individuals to glance in his direction, but Laith was past caring. He swept past the tables, jostling a few elbows here and there, then burst out of the stifling, cramped warmth of the pub and into the cool, sharp night air. A moment later, his dagger was drawn and Laith was barreling forward, towards nothing but the dark. *I will find him. He's near, he's very near...*

Someone collided with Laith and threw him back against the wall of a nearby building. Laith, filled with adrenaline, bellowed and struggled for a moment, thinking it must be Seth, it must be...

"Have you lost your senses?" Ari's voice, uncharacteristically concerned, hissed in his ear. "What are you doing with your knife out? Do you want to get us both killed?"

With an enormous heave, Laith shoved Ari off of him. "Where did he go?" Laith demanded in a deadly whisper. "Where?"

"Who?" Ari asked blankly.

"A man came out of the pub right in front of me!" Laith hissed, spinning from left to right, searching for a sign, any sign. The snow had been cleared just in front of the pub. There were no footprints around it. Nothing. Nothing...how could it be?

"I saw no one," Ari said slowly, beginning to sound concerned.

"What?" Laith snapped, pushing Ari back, his dagger still gleaming in the moonlight. Ari raised both hands, trying to placate him further. "I saw no one," he insisted quietly.

Laith turned again and looked up to the cold, uncaring sliver of moon above, the dark night sky, and the overwhelming emptiness of the small clearing. Other than Ari, there was no sign of life. No tracks. Nothing.

Laith's breath came out in fast, frozen puffs of steam, his shoulders tensed and eyes glaring blankly out into the darkness, as if he were ready to lunge at anything that moved. Ari slowly reached out and touched Laith's arm. He was shaking, quivering from head to foot. Whether it was from fear, sorrow, or rage, Ari couldn't say.

Back across the city, a single light was shining from Athela's bedroom on the second story of the new Two Falls headquarters. She had arranged the room exactly as she liked it: books on her bedside table, a single candle burning, a fire in the grate. She had found it difficult to relax that night, unaccustomed both to having time off and especially to sleeping in a room with windows. The Strikers had lived in hiding for so long that it was extremely odd to have a proper room, to be able to step out into a city street without having to worry about being seen or attracting attention.

Perhaps it was the coming of the new year that was making her restless. She had tried reading, but had turned the same three sentences over and over for half an hour before she had decided to stop. She had debated relieving Tarr of his decoding duties, but he and the other spies had looked far too miserable for her to want to subject herself to any such thing. She had finally gone out to visit her horse, but Aria's energy wasn't exactly soothing, even on the best of days. So she'd brought in his tack and some saddle soap and had set to work scrubbing the riding equipment clean. It was an activity that usually calmed her, but she found her mind going unbidden again and again to those few stolen hours before the battle.

Almost as if she had conjured him, there was a soft knock at the door, and something in Athela's chest made a very curious leap. She knew who it was before she said, "Come in."

Without turning around, she heard Archer's long, lanky frame come in and settle on the bed. "Missed a spot," he said ironically, watching Athela's furious motions as she soaped the stirrup leather of her saddle.

Athela heaved a sigh and faced him. He was grinning at her in his wonderfully disarming way, leaning on his elbow with his long legs trailing over the end of the bed like an invitation. He looked...happy. There was an intimacy, a knowing in his eyes when he looked at her now that made the blood rush to her cheeks. His black-tipped hair was tousled as if he had just come in from the cold. Athela had never seen anything that looked quite so wonderful.

Abruptly, she looked down at her hands, the grease and dirt from the leather in the creases of her palms and beneath her fingernails. She couldn't find the words to say what she needed to.

"Athela," Archer said quietly behind her. "Look at me."

She met his eyes, and immediately his smile fell. The golden eyes searched her expression and saw all that there was to see. He pushed himself up so that he could sit on the edge of the bed. Gone was the playfulness.

"Looks like you and I have two choices: we either do this for real, or we end it right now. I can't go halfway." he said.

"What do you want?" Athela asked, looking back down at the

saddle in her hands.

"I want you," he said simply. "I want to be with you."

She felt buzzing in her ears. "We could still die tomorrow. You or I."

"I don't care."

She looked up at him. "I do. I can't, Archer. I can't have you today only to have you taken away from me tomorrow."

His golden eyes looked grave, his lips growing tense. She wanted so badly to kiss him. "That's your decision?"

"Yes," Athela replied, hating herself.

"Aha," Archer brushed off his hands and briskly leaped to his feet, going to the door. "Well, in that case, I'm going to go see what Tarr is up to. The bachelor life for me and all that." He stopped and looked back at her. For a moment, Athela thought that he was going to protest, to try and change her mind.

Instead, he looked at her, his eyes sad. "You deserve to have good things, Athela," he said. "To be happy. I wish you knew that." An instant later, the jaunty expression was back in place, and he left her.

As the door shut behind him, Athela wondered why doing the responsible thing could possibly make her feel so wretched. She went back to scrubbing the saddle, her mouth dry and her eyes burning in an unfamiliar way. *You deserve to have good things.* What on earth did he mean? She scrubbed harder.

She did not see Archer's smile fall away as he strode down the hallway, and didn't see the hands tuck deep into his pockets, or the head fall to stare at the ground as it passed by. Archer didn't stop at Tarr's office. He continued walking until he was well outside the headquarters and stood alone, without a coat or a cloak, in the silence of the bracingly cold winter night.

Perched on a pile of rocks in the middle of the gray, crashing sea, Faridor stood frozen like an ice palace, icicles hanging down from the turrets and the window panes, wide patterns of frost coating the outer walls as snow teetered in drifts atop the rooftops. The furious sea wind had torn two of the Kagaian flags to shreds outside the front gates, but no one had braved the elements to replace them. All was quiet. As the midnight hour approached, a few covert glasses of wine were poured in the kitchens and in the guards' quarters, but otherwise, the fortress seemed as still as a tomb.

A lone figure, dressed conservatively in the uniform of a maid, walked down one of the red-carpeted hallways holding a small pile of folded bedclothes, the flames of the grated torches dancing in her wake. Hers was a face strange to those halls, but she did not bother to glance up at the portraits and priceless swords as she passed them. The neck on her dress was high, and if her walk was slightly weak and a little wobbly, her face perhaps a bit pale, her expression was nevertheless resolute. She paused by a small door and gave a curt knock. The door opened a crack, and she stepped inside.

The maids' quarters were the size of a large closet. In the room, two beds stood close together: one neatly made, the other bare. There was nothing—no paper, no books, nothing where any secret material could be hidden. Rane nodded in satisfaction and laid her pile of bedclothes down on the bare mattress. She turned around to the young woman who had opened the door for her.

"My name is Rane," she signed, spelling her name out with her fingers. "Are you Cicada?"

The girl was shocked. For a few moments, she looked suspiciously at Rane, gauging whether it was some sort of trap. But then, slowly, tentatively, she raised her hands. "Yes, I'm Cicada," she replied hesitantly.

"I'm one of Tarr's agents. With the Strikers." Rane told her. "I'm here to work with you."

Cicada's face relaxed. She took a step back and considered Rane anew. The two women sized each other up. "It's about time," Cicada said forcefully, and Rane was surprised to see her expression break into a sly grin. "It's a lot of work, bringing down this fortress all by myself." She was an extremely fast signer and vocalized slightly as she spoke.

"Once more, a bit slower," Rane begged. "You speak so quickly. And I haven't signed with anyone in a while."

Cicada made an impatient noise in the back of her throat but did as Rane requested. This time, Rane understood perfectly and nodded her comprehension.

"You're hearing?" Cicada asked curiously.

"Yes, I'm hearing," Rane replied. "My father is deaf."

"That makes sense," Cicada nodded briskly. "Now, how much do you know about what's going on here? About the weapon Cira supposedly has?"

"Not much," Rane admitted. "Just what you've communicated to Tarr. All our other agents here are gone."

If Cicada was at all concerned to discover that she was the only surviving spy remaining at Faridor, she didn't show it. If anything, her jaw tightened. Rane fleetingly reflected on the immense pressures Cicada must have withstood to make it through Cira's recent inquisition alive.

"Have a seat, then, and I'll tell you everything," Cicada gestured toward the empty bed. When Rane had settled herself, Cicada raised her hands and began to sign.

Halfway across the fortress, Cira sat alone in her throne room, slumped in the high-backed chair, her finger against her temple and the edge of her porcelain jaw cupped in her palm. Her green eyes stared vacantly at the floor before her, then slowly her gaze traveled upwards. Shadows from the torches danced across the large, sloping ceiling and across the shining obsidian floor, twisting and darting into grotesque faces and shapes. The emerald Kagaian banners hung lifeless from the pillars that marked the length of the room. A long red carpet ran like blood from the end of Cira's throne to the large, arched double doors at the opposite side of the room. Every single sound inside the room was magnified to an enormous degree, so when there was a small knock at the door and it creaked open, the noise shattered the enveloping silence like a peal of thunder.

A servant bearing a goblet on a tray timidly made his way down the red carpet to where Cira sat on her throne. The servant bowed before her and looked up at her, high on her perch atop the throne.

"Your Majesty, it..." he swallowed, searching for words. "I hope you will forgive the impertinence, but it has just passed midnight. It is the new year, and I thought Your Majesty would like a glass of wine to celebrate."

"Is it poisoned?" Cira asked in a low voice.

The man looked instantly alarmed, his eyes darting from side to side. "I...no...I..." he stammered, looking over his shoulder at the empty room for any assistance.

"Taste it," Cira ordered in the same dull tone.

The man's mouth opened and closed, and then he slowly took the goblet and raised it to his lips. He took a sip and swallowed, and when nothing happened, he offered her the goblet on the tray, his eyes large and frightened.

Cira swept the goblet from the tray and waved the servant away. He backed up a few steps before turning and fairly running from the room. The doors groaned shut, and once again, everything was wonderful, delicious silence.

Cira took a slow sip from the wine and held the cup loosely in her hand. Her eyes traveled to the ceiling back to the floor and up again. *The new year*, she thought to herself. She took another sip of the wine and traced the serpentine carvings on the arm of her throne. They were cold to the touch, hard.

Her grip loosened ever so slightly on the goblet of wine and it toppled from her hands, clanging down the steps of her throne and spilling out dark and red onto the flagstones. Cira was startled for a moment, then she looked at the pool of red on the floor and began to laugh.

"You are not alone," came a low voice behind her.

Cira shot out of her throne, the smile evaporating from her face. Her green eyes flashed as she searched for the origin of the voice she'd heard, her hands shaped into claws, ready to protect herself.

"Show yourself," she commanded, her voice resolute.

There was a shimmer in the air in front of her, and two people clad in the darkest emerald green stepped out of nothingness and stood before her. Cira's mouth fell open, and she stared at them, hardly daring to believe what had just happened.

"What..." she breathed, "...who are..."

"Here to show you the way," said the figure who had spoken before. It sounded like a woman, but the face that spoke was so ancient and withered that it was impossible to be sure.

Cira regained some of her composure. "You must kneel before me," she commanded. "I am your Queen."

"Not yet," the figure replied, its horrible, green-tinged, puckered face stretching uncomfortably into a ghoulish approximation of a smile. Cira shuddered despite herself.

"We sent you Kagai's medallion," said the second figure, the voice deeper, masculine.

"*Kagai's* medallion?" Cira asked sharply. "Not Morthenstar's?"

"No," the woman said shrewdly. "Twin keys for twin locks. It is Kagai's medallion that holds the key to your power, and you have turned it. You have now tapped into a well of energy beyond your wildest imaginings, but you must learn to control it."

"Oh, *must* I?" Cira snapped. Her shock at the sudden appearance of the two figures was rapidly giving way to annoyance. How *superior* they sounded.

"You must," the other figure said simply. "Come with us. We will teach you."

"I need no *teacher*," Cira snapped haughtily, drawing herself up. Her eyes cast about for any of her guards, but they all seemed to have vanished. It was beneath her to throw these strange people out of her throne room by herself, but they were leaving her very little option. Besides, she didn't like the look of them, nor the way they had appeared seemingly out of nowhere.

"You have only just begun to step beyond your world," the figure said. "And your power will grow greater and greater by the day. The universe beyond will expand for you. But unless you learn to harness this power early on, it will run away with you. It will take you and pull you down like a current in the ocean."

Cira considered. She certainly liked the idea of power growing greater and greater by the day, but she had really no idea what these strange cloaked figures were talking about. She could feel her impatience mounting.

"Who am I?" she asked rhetorically, narrowing her brilliant eyes.

"Cira Kagai," replied the desiccated old woman. "A young woman with potential. But who has not achieved greatness yet. The greatness of Kagai is at your fingertips. Come with us."

"Oh?" Cira drew herself up. "I have not achieved greatness yet? Look around you. I have taken Joymaril, I took Two Falls, I sit on the throne of Faridor. The riches of the world are mine for the taking. I have achieved all this without your help." She sneered. "I need no teacher. I need no instruction. Everything I have, I have taken myself. I do not need you."

She thought she saw the woman's face tighten ever so slightly, but it was hard to tell. She felt an inner surge of satisfaction, felt the pleasure in provoking a reaction from the people before her. *How dare they tell me what I can and cannot have? How dare they presume to tell me what my powers are?* She could feel a tight rage begin to build in her chest, almost as though it could flow out of her hands, blast through the ends of her fingertips. *Whatever power I have is within me, not them. They know nothing. They can tell me nothing. They can teach me nothing.*

"Stop," said the woman sharply, as though she could tell that something was growing, that the light was starting to change. "*Stop.*" The edge of fear was starting to creep into her impassive voice. Cira could see her eyes getting wider.

Cira nearly laughed, enjoying the roiling feeling in her throat, churning like a raging sea. She lifted up her arms wide open, as if she were about to embrace them to her chest. She took a step forward and was pleased to see the two figures fall back, unsteady. The woman held up her hands, as though to try and resist; Cira could feel the burning growing to a breaking point, and then, all at once, she closed her eyes and—

An earsplitting *crack* exploded throughout the room, and a sharp beam of light shot out like a flint being struck to tinder. The Kagaian banners were ripped from the walls and billowed heavily to the floor; the atmosphere in the room seemed to break in half. Cira opened her eyes, breathless, overwhelmed by the sensation. She saw what lay before her and nearly gasped in shock.

Before her, on the ground beneath her throne, were what looked like blackened, charred remains, so twisted that it was nearly impossible to tell what they had been before. Thin wisps of smoke blew off them and up into the air, where they hung for a few seconds and then dissolved.

Cira slowly stepped down from her throne platform and approached one of the blackened piles. She nudged it with the tip of her slipper, and the husk dissolved into ash. A slight gust blew through the empty room, and some of the ash was swept up into the air, where it hung for a few seconds and then dissipated.

Cira stood there watching for a few seconds more, then withdrew her foot and noiselessly backed up the stairs to regain her seat on the throne. Her hands were shaking slightly as they slid comfortably over the armrests, and she looked out, surveying the expanse of her empty throne room. A slow smile crept over her face.

CHAPTER TWENTY-FOUR

Marc and Si sat together on the slant of roof above Marc's bedroom window. It was just big enough for the two of them, and the walls on either side shielded them against much of the cold winter wind. Both were wrapped up in thick cloaks, hoods drawn up so that only their faces were exposed.

"What's that one?" Marc asked, pointing at the carpet of stars above. He traced a circular shape with a dot in the center.

Si wrinkled his freckled nose and squinted. "That's the Holy Bread Roll of Tiris Mornath," he answered easily. "The legend says that the god of thunder ate it before he smote the great tree-king of Usgarth."

"Ah," Marc mused.

"It was the breakfast that gave him power, you see, so he decided to immortalize it by hanging it in the stars," Si told him wisely. "Your turn."

The game of Comic Constellations had been born after a particularly boring night on duty when Marc and Si sat stargazing. Marc quickly realized that Si was making up the name and backstory of every single constellation he outlined. As the game developed, the names, constellations, and stories had gradually grown more and more ridiculous.

Marc followed the wild motion of Si's gloved finger. "The Immortal Spit-up of Arsgard, King of Muldarn," he said casually. "It came up after he wed the Queen of the Sea-People and ate her ceremonial wedding cake."

"Too much seawater in the ceremonial wedding cake," Si agreed solemnly.

Marc stole a glance at the boy. Si had been acting strange that day. He'd been hanging about with Marc all evening, almost as if he were afraid to let him out of his sight. It had been Si's idea to come up on the roof. By all outward appearances he seemed completely normal, yet Marc, who knew Si like the back of his hand, could sense that something was amiss. He knew better than to pry, and hoped that Si would bring up whatever was wrong in his own time.

Across the city, there was suddenly a dull cheer, the sound of voices raised together in celebration. "Must be near midnight," Marc observed, pushing himself up into a sitting position. "Another year come and gone. We've done well, eh?" He nudged Si, whose smile and nod came a bit too quick. Marc continued, speaking rapidly to allay the discomfort he felt. "Here we are, sitting on top of the Kagaian headquarters at Two Falls. Whod've thunk it, eh?"

Si rose up beside him. He stared out at the city spread beneath them, his arms slung around his thin knees. He looked despondent. On the street below, he saw Laith and Ari returning to the Striker headquarters. Laith took long, urgent strides, and Ari jogged to keep up with him. Something was wrong. But Si couldn't think about that right now.

"Next year, we'll be sitting on top of Faridor," Marc nudged him again, then his face fell as Si gave no reaction. "And after that, somewhere far away, away from the war. Si, what's wrong?"

Si looked up at him. It was some time before he spoke. He looked afraid; nervous and unsure of himself. But there was a steely bolt of resolution at the back of his gray eyes that threw Marc. "You know I'll be alright," he said finally. "Whatever happens."

This confused Marc even more. His brows knit together in concern, and he tucked a strand of his straw-colored yellow hair behind one ear. "Of course, Si." He placed one hand on Si's shoulder.

"I have to leave for a little while," said Si, who began to fumble with something at his throat.

"Have to leave?" Marc said blankly, his ice-blue eyes darting down to Si's hands and back up to his face. "What are you talking about?"

"I'll be alright," Si said again, stopping his fidgeting and looking straight into Marc's face. "Don't worry about me. I'll be fine."

"Si," Marc said slowly, his eyes resting on the hand clasped at the base of Si's throat, "where did you get the medallion? I thought it was gone." Then, his eyes narrowing slightly, "Why are you wearing it?"

Before Marc could react, Si's hand darted out and clasped the side of Marc's head. He didn't know if this would work—he only knew that it *had* to. *Sleep.* Si thought, closing his eyes. *Go to sleep, just for a minute or two.*

And suddenly, he felt a warmth, an energy bloom in his stomach and rush up through his arms and out of his hands. There was a short burst, and suddenly, Marc's astonished face went slack. He collapsed onto the roof, unconscious.

Si anxiously reached out and felt Marc's pulse, hoping that this power, whatever it was that he had done, hadn't overdone it and killed his friend. But no, Marc was just asleep. The slant of the roof and the ridge at the end would prevent him from falling off. It was time. Si squeezed his friend's shoulder for the last time, then turned on all fours and scrambled up the slick side of the roof, scaling like a cat to the very top until he was balanced on the peak of the roof.

Si wasn't as sure of himself at great heights as an Ashan would be, so it was with great caution that he slowly raised himself from a crouch to his full diminutive height. As he became more sure of his footing, he allowed himself to look around at the city below him. It seemed so peaceful and so quiet. The brilliant canopy of stars curved above him, and the twinkling lights splayed before him in the houses of the city seemed to reflect the dome above. There were brilliant colors to be seen: the pale blue lilac of the drifts of snow on the rooftops, the dark cobalt and purples and indigos of the night sky and the surrounding land, rising up to the foothills and dusky pale mountains in the distance. Si wondered whether he would ever experience another night like this one. If he came back (and Si wasn't sure whether he ever *would*), perhaps he would be completely changed. Perhaps he would lose his sense of sight, his sense of feeling. Perhaps he wouldn't be *himself* anymore.

But you know that that is what you have to face, he reminded himself sternly. *This is what you have decided to do. You are going to take your fate into your own hands. You are going to become exactly who you need to be. You are going to learn who and what you are.*

Si took a deep breath. It was now or never. Marc would be awake in a few short minutes and would begin tearing the entire city apart looking for him. He loosened the cloak and let it fall behind him in a soft heap. Si's copper hair ruffled a bit in the wind, and he let an involuntary shiver shake his body. He took out the medallion from within his shirt and held it loosely in his hand. He stared at it for a long moment, then squeezed it tight inside his small fist.

"I'm ready," he said aloud, and closed his eyes.

The medallion began to glow with a soft, warm light. Si could feel it heating his hand like a living thing, and could dimly see its light through his clenched eyelids. He gritted his teeth, and then, in the wisp of a moment, he had vanished into nothingness. A small gust of snow was sent spinning and swirling and twisting up in his wake. And then the snow fell slowly down through the air, settling back upon the rooftop, and once again all was still.

EPILOGUE

THE PALACE OF JOYMARIL, EARLIER THAT DAY

Lady Vera stood at the expansive balcony outside of the sleeping chamber of her room and began to twirl a strand of her pale reddish hair around one finger. Abandoning that, she started to chew on her fingernails, staring down at the lake at the base of the cliff. In the distance, she could see snow starting to fall over Two Falls. The lake below seemed to be winking cheekily up at her in the cold winter afternoon, so pert and sparkling she wanted to spit at it, but instead, she just kept biting her nails right down to the quick. Finally, she desisted and turned away, striding back into her room, her gait slightly awkward and less impressive than she imagined it to be. She stopped in front of her desk and glanced down at a sheet of paper lying open, creased twice. She considered ignoring it for a moment, then plopped down in her chair and took it closer.

Her eyes scanned along the rigidly spaced, formally lettered words. After a minute or so, she tossed the paper down to her desk once more and made a noncommittal noise in the back of her throat. She wished that one of her servants would walk through the room so they could see how irate she was and offer her some sort of supplication. When none came, she pushed her chair abruptly back again, nearly falling as it skidded harder than she had intended. There were no more nails for her to bite, so she began pacing, thinking of what a dramatic scene she would make when someone entered. She paused, stared at the door. No one came through.

She made the same noise at the back of her throat once again and sat down heavily on the bed. Where was everybody? Didn't anyone *care* about her? Wasn't this the reason she had servants? She bit her lip, considered abandoning the element of a surprise discovery, and finally called out, "Nadia!"

After a few moments, the door quietly opened, and her hand-maiden entered, keeping her eyes lowered to the ground. She curtsied politely, clasping her hands in front of her. "What is it, my Lady?" she inquired demurely. Nadia never spoke much, but she seemed to listen fairly well, which was all that Lady Vera required of anyone. She liked to do most of the talking.

"I've had *another* letter from Cira," Lady Vera whined. "*Another* one, and it's been less than a month. She wants me to send over even more of the trainees from the Academy when I *told* her already that we're running out, and she can't keep demanding this from me as though I were a factory! Besides," she pouted, fiddling with her hands for a moment, "what about my own personal safety? I'm important too, you know. Cira appointed *me* to rule Joymaril in her place while she's in Faridor. What if one of the Strikers wants to come after *me?* I need protection!" Vera kicked her legs against the side of the bed. Though she was nearly twenty-two, she looked every inch a spoiled child.

Nadia took a deep breath and slowly walked forward. She had served Lady Vera for three and a half years. Three and a half of the longest and most arduous years of her life. Every day, she remembered what it had been like with Lady Ilaina and found that the memories didn't fade with age. How could they, when every day she was confronted with Vera's tantrums, her whining, her gossiping? Ilaina could quietly enter a crowded room, and immediately everyone would be aware of her presence. Vera usually stomped into everything from formal gatherings to her own bathroom, and was barely noticed in either circumstance.

Nadia recalled the way in which Ilaina would ask her how her day was, listen carefully, profess sympathy when necessary, encouragement when needed. Lady Vera hadn't asked her a single thing about herself in three and a half years.

Ilaina had kept her rooms light and airy, with drapings of silver, fresh lilies in a vase on her bedside table. Vera had decorated her apartments in the most visually assaulting shade of fuchsia that the dyers could manage to produce. Many of the other household servants had been offended when Nadia was promoted to the role of head handmaiden; she had only served Ilaina and one other lady beforehand. They felt that Nadia was lacking in the necessary experience to take care of a Queen. Nadia herself had nearly left the household when she received the order; there was a world of difference between serving a queen in spirit and manner and a queen in title. But, as she had soon discovered, taking care of Vera was fairly simple, if enervating. Sort out her tantrums, coddle her when necessary, and make sure that she took the occasional bath. And if there was one thing Nadia had learned from a lifetime of servitude in the royal family, it was how to keep her mouth shut. So she kept it shut and kept her eyes open for any pathways that might lead to her liberation. And never far from her mind was the thought of Prince Cade, Prince Argolaith's younger brother, locked away in the dungeons. She didn't know whether or not he was alive or dead, but he was the only small amount of hope she had.

Nadia sat down beside Lady Vera and patted her on the hand. "She really doesn't seem to treat you very fairly," she said comfortingly. "You have every reason to be upset."

"She thinks that I'm a *child,* and I'm not!" Vera exclaimed hotly. "She has no right, no right at all. She just thinks that I'm her...her... *puppet!*"

And you are surprised...? Nadia thought wryly, but forced a sympathetic smile. "What are you going to do about it? You could write her back and tell her that you are concerned for your own safety."

Vera sniffed. "I *suppose* I could." But, realizing that such a solution would cut down on the amount of whining she would be able to accomplish, she quickly took another breath and continued, "But you remember last year when I wrote to her and asked her if I could throw a festival to celebrate the day that I was officially crowned Queen regent? I mean, it was the best idea anyone around here has had in years, and what did she tell me? No. She said that it was frivolous. *Frivolous.*" Vera shook her head blankly at the thought that dancing, flirting, and gossiping could possibly be considered frivolous. She bent closer to Nadia with a conspiratorial whisper, though they were alone in the room. The other servants only entered when absolutely necessary. Nadia leaned in, trying to look interested. "You know," Vera said in hushed tones. "I just think that Cira isn't comfortable with me trying to assert myself as Queen. She doesn't like me doing anything that *she* hasn't thought of first."

Not bad, it's only taken you three years to realize it, Nadia thought, but raised her eyebrows as if in surprise. "You really think so?"

Vera nodded fervently. "I'm positive."

"Well, I think you're right," Nadia said guardedly.

All at once, Nadia felt a curious rush within and paused. She began to see a way. If she could just begin to plant the seeds...slowly, cautiously, without Vera noticing. She had to keep talking, to keep Vera on the hook. "She does tend to order you around quite a lot. What does she think you are, one of her advisors? Or are you a trusted confidante to whom she gave the throne?"

"That's right!" Vera exclaimed, taking the bait and running with it, just as Nadia had anticipated. Nadia was quite sure that prior to her being appointed Queen Regent, Vera and Cira had perhaps exchanged three words with one another, but there was no limit to Vera's capacity for self-delusion. "She appointed *me!*" she exclaimed. "What does she want me to do, sit around here all day?"

"Unless there's an errand she wants you to run," Nadia added sympathetically. "But, my Lady, if I may be so bold...you *are* Queen. You do not necessarily have to ask for permission for everything you do."

Vera turned her eyes to her handmaiden. The thought seemingly boggled her mind. Nadia hoped fervently that Vera could manage to keep up. "I think you're right," Vera said slowly, then the idea began to catch hold. "You're very right!" she exclaimed, leaping up. "I can do whatever I want! And what is Cira going to do? Is she going to come all the way over from Faridor to send me to my room? There's nothing she can do to me! Plus, I've got the entire royal army on my side! I'm probably stronger than her, anyway! What if I took control of Joymaril for myself? Then where would she be?" Lady Vera looked more excited than Nadia had ever seen her. The dull, plain face was fairly alight with energy. *Now, if I can only channel it in the right direction...*Nadia thought. *Carefully, carefully.*

"But you must make some gesture, Milady," Nadia said delicately. Lady Vera's face fell slightly as she contemplated this. *Great, I've lost her.* "Some gesture to really set off the chain of events," she elaborated, more slowly this time. "You must establish that you are different from Cira, that you are a better ruler than her. That you are not cruel. That you are merciful and wise. The people will support you. Cira has given them little love. She has been here only once or twice since she seized the throne. How are the people expected to swear loyalty to someone they barely see? But you, they see you every day. They could rally behind you."

"I don't need you to tell me what to do," Vera said crossly, upset that Nadia's brain was working much more quickly than her own. Nadia bit her lip, shutting back the anger.

"I'm sorry, Milady, I was merely suggesting," Nadia said courteously. Vera began pacing back and forth until it made Nadia quite seasick to watch her. She finally halted and looked up.

"What sort of gesture do you think I should make?" she asked.

Careful, guide her into this one, Nadia thought. She shrugged, trying to roll the thoughts around in her head. "Well, what is Cira known for?"

Vera looked up at the ceiling, like a small child searching for the answer to some academic test. "She took over the country," she said dubiously. "She's built lots of things. She's strong."

"She *is* strong," Nadia conceded. "But is she *kind*?"

"No," Vera mumbled.

Nadia spread her hands and sat back, as if to suggest an obvious answer. But when Vera stared at her blankly, Nadia stifled a heavy sigh and continued. "Well, it is as I said. You must set yourself apart from Cira. Perhaps if the people saw a ruler who was kind, just, and...merciful. One who was forgiving to those who wronged her. They may give you the love that they never showed Cira." She waited, hoping that Vera would make the connection. And for a frantic few seconds, it looked as if she wouldn't. Then Vera's face brightened, realization dawning.

"I have an idea!" she exclaimed. Nadia held her breath. "Who do we have in the dungeons right now?

Nadia's heart began to pound harder, but she gave a casual shrug. "Just some political dissenters, mostly. The ones Cira put away when she came to power. A few murderers, but you needn't worry about them."

Vera nodded. "The political dissenters were those who opposed Cira taking power?"

"That's right."

"Then they're sure to support *me*," Vera said, smiling. "When I take over." This statement was so illogical that if Nadia hadn't desperately been trying to guide Vera to a certain point, she would have reflexively contradicted the statement. "I mean, if we are going to show Cira who's really in charge of Joymaril, who will they support? Me. I mean, I am Queen, after all. What I want to do is to pardon those political dissenters in the dungeons," (here, Nadia's heart gave a loud *thump*) "and a month from now, I want to throw a grand party for the entire city, whether Cira likes it or not, in which those that I've pardoned will come up and swear fealty to me. That way, everyone will be able to see how much better of a ruler I am than Cira!" She smiled and looked hopefully at Nadia, searching for approval. In that moment, Nadia almost pitied her stupidity.

"An excellent plan, Milady," Nadia smiled, and Vera gave a visible sigh of relief. "No one would ever dream of Lady Cira showing such mercy to her enemies. You will be loved above all other rulers."

Nadia could see how this thought pleased Vera. She stood up again and began tugging at the ends of her strawberry-blonde hair. The ridiculous robes of state she always wore in an attempt to make her image more imposing and regal clashed uproariously with the fuchsia wall hangings and bedclothes. She strode back and forth, arms swinging, clearly envisioning the pleasurable sight of freed men approaching her on bended knees and swearing their loyalty. Nadia could understand the appeal this held to Vera. Even the most unscrupulous of the social climbing men at court had studiously avoided her ever since her reign had begun. Perhaps it was an aversion to her character. Or, perhaps, they took her for what she was: Cira's puppet, with no will of her own that they could influence to their advantage.

Nadia watched her, praying that she wouldn't remember Cade trapped in the dungeon, recognize the danger of him living, and change her mind. Finally, Vera stopped and turned again. "Send for my advisors; I shall make this plan into a decree. The prisoners shall be released at sundown. And it's the new year!" she brightened. "It's perfect. It was meant to be."

Nadia stood measuredly, trying not to leap to her feet and rush off in search of Vera's desired advisors. "Remember, my Lady, that Cira still holds your advisors under her thumb. They may try and sway my Lady to change her mind."

Vera bristled at the thought. "My mind is made up," she said, trying to infuse her dull voice with some of the glacier-like cold that pervaded Cira's, to a distinctly humorous effect. "Send for my advisors immediately."

Nadia gave a perfect curtsy. "As you wish, your Majesty," she said. She rarely called Vera "Majesty," and when she did, it was only when she meant to inflate her ego even more. She turned and walked with great control out of the room. But once the heavy door had closed behind her, she began to run. She ran as fast as she could, not caring whether any of the other servants saw her and began to gossip amongst themselves. Nadia felt freer than she had in all those long years. If only there was some way she could get word to Cade that tonight he would be free...

A young man of twenty lay on his back, facing the stone roof of the cell. He had, by that point, lost all track of time. He wandered through his thoughts and imagination often for days at a time. He was pulled out of his trances only by the circadian pangs in his stomach, which signaled him that it was time to eat the meager meals dumped unceremoniously through a small slat in the stone wall of his cell. His white-blond hair had been chopped off a number of times during his incarceration to keep it out of his eyes. He had found nothing to keep back the bleached stubble that was shining on his chin and cheeks. He was small for his age and looked as though he would have been much taller had he been allowed adequate nutrition and had been able to run and be outdoors during the crucial years of his development. The slate gray eyes hadn't lost their brilliant spark of intelligence, but after so long in a cell, they were apt to wander, to grow unfocused. When the boredom had overcome him, Cade had surrendered and retreated into the depths of his own mind, where he existed more peacefully than he ever could have had he spent his days mulling over his dark fate.

The day had begun uneventfully. Cade forced himself to eat, and then lay, as he often did, on the stone floor and stared up at the rectangular slabs of stone that made up his roof. His mind drifted away until he was outdoors, under the sun, running through the forest. He remembered things that had happened to him far better now than he had before. Without the distractions of everyday life, he was able to call up memories that had long been dormant in his subconscious.

From time to time, Cade thought of Wolf, his bodyguard, who had been taken into custody the same day as he. If Wolf had survived whatever mutilation Cira had visited upon him, there was a high likelihood that he would be mentally lost after his imprisonment. Cade didn't like to think of that. He did, however, like to think of his revenge. Occasionally, his mind would become so fevered with the heat of it that he would have to snap out of his reverie and stand up and pace around the cell to work off excess energy. His chest tightened when he thought how sweet it would be to stand in front of Cira, to see her eyes narrow with fear, to see the dawning realization on her face that her time had come and that Cade was the one who had brought it. Cade could drive himself dizzy with his plotting, but nothing gave him as much pleasure as that mental image of Cira realizing her doom was approaching. Though he was not physically fighting, he had not, by any stretch of the imagination, given up.

That night, Cade was still staring at his ceiling. The cell was dark and it must have been near nightfall, for his body was tiring. He had no window and could not see when the sun rose or set; the only clock he had was his body, which had set him up in a fairly routine schedule of sleeping and waking. His sleeping was not very unlike his waking, but Cade didn't mind much. Whatever normalcy he could retain, he would.

There was a small sound at the door, then a larger scraping, which startled Cade more than anything. He shot straight up, spinning around, gray eyes wide, his heart throbbing in his chest. The only sounds he usually heard were the occasional passing by of booted feet and the clang of his dinner being delivered and his empty plate retrieved. This was none of those things. Never before had anyone even made a motion to open the door. He scuttled to a corner like a frightened insect and stood, trying to regain control of himself, and suddenly, a brilliant light shone straight into his eyes. A torchlight! Cade covered his eyes to shield them from the blinding but could have cried out with joy. He wished that he could put his hands around the dancing light, the brilliant contrast to the blank blue-gray slabs of stone that made up his world. And behind the torch there were *people*...Cade had almost forgotten what they were like. He watched in wonder as they hesitated, then walked forward towards him; he reached out to touch one of them, but they roughly pushed his hand away. One grabbed him roughly behind the elbow, and the contact, the warmth of the touch, the grip of fingers other than his own was so powerful that Cade's legs gave out beneath him. He was hauled roughly to his feet once more and dragged out of the cell. So entranced was Cade that he had been pulled for a good twenty yards before it occurred to him to wonder why he was being taken out of the dungeon.

"Am I..." he asked, his voice cracking, deeper than even he had remembered it. He coughed a few times. "Am I to be executed?" *Bloody odd time for it*, he thought vaguely. *Was Cira just bored today?*

"No," one of the guards growled. Cade nearly cried out with joy. *A human voice. It is a human voice.* The gruff tones, the clipped words, the inflections were like a song to his ears. "You're being released and pardoned. Bunch of you are. Lady Vera's orders."

"Damn strange, you ask me," the other guard snarled. "But you better count your lucky stars, your *highness.*" The two guards sniggered. "And better watch yourself, keep your head low. Attract as little attention as possible; Cira might forget you even exist." The other guard snorted at this.

Cade's mind was spinning fast, and he stumbled over his feet again. How odd it was to be so unused to something as normal as *walking*. *Released?* He turned the word over and over in his mind. *Released?*

Did that mean what he thought it did? Was he to be allowed to walk about the palace freely? Would he be able to see the stars again? Feel a fresh breeze on his face? Go running as far as he wanted for as long as he wanted? Would he be able to hear the sound of music, of laughter? He wanted it so much that he hardly dared hope for it. But the guards had said it—they had said the word. *Released.*

He let the guards pull him forward and chanted it over and over again. He hardly noticed where he was being dragged; he just watched pillars and torches go sliding unfocused past his vision in a dreamlike blur. The palace smelled the same; his senses were assaulted with memories. *Released*, he thought again. There was no way that Cira would ever have allowed Vera to do such a thing. Did that mean that Cira had been defeated? Had Laith and Athela finally beaten her? But no...that couldn't be it. One of the guards had said something about Cira not finding out. What was going on?

They stopped suddenly, Cade's legs wobbling beneath him. A door was opened, and he was put inside. Cade glanced around, vaguely remembering the room. It used to be his. He had been returned to his old apartment. The guard to his left glanced around as well and smiled cruelly. "They gave away some of your things," he sneered, nodding his head to where Cade's handsome bookshelves used to rest, his desk, his rug, and tapestries. "Some of the families who support Cira got them. No way you'll get those things back." He laughed, but Cade would have shrugged had he been able to. Books he could replace. Desks, tapestries, rugs, he didn't need. All he needed now was the night sky. The guards were watching him expectantly, searching for some kind of angry reaction, but when all they got was a numb silence, they lost interest and turned to go. Cade stood on his shaky legs for a few moments, then whipped around.

"Wolf!" he said, his voice cracking again. The guards turned and eyed him. Cade gulped, trying to wet his dry throat. "Has Wolf been released? Is he still alive?"

Seeing a sensitive spot, one of the guards smiled cruelly. "Not that I'm aware of. Find out soon, though, won't you?" The guards laughed again and walked out of the door, leaving Cade standing alone in the dim room.

All of it seemed to hit him at once, and he slumped to the floor in a heap, his head spinning, his limbs weak. He hadn't realized how long it had been since he had had to walk freely, to stand and reach his arms up above his head and not be able to touch the ceiling. He crawled over to a nearby couch. It was hard and uncomfortable, but it felt like eiderdown. He pulled his small body onto it and sat, his thin chest heaving with the effort. He closed his eyes and then looked up and saw the roof and felt a surge of hatred like he had never felt before. He no longer wanted to see roofs above him. He needed the sky.

Body coursing with adrenaline, he heaved himself up and walked unsteadily to the nearby balcony. He pushed his way through the thin doors and out into the open, where a blast of freezing night air burst across his face like a bracing splash of water. He gripped the stone rim of the balustrade, half afraid that he would lose his orientation and fall off. The wind was cold, chilling him through his tattered shirt down to the very bone. He closed his eyes and took in a deep breath. The cold air sifted through his nose and mouth and circled his lungs, clearing out years of dust and stifling must, wiping his mind clean, brushing away the shadows from his eyes. He looked up at the twinkling stars nestled in the purple sky, the moon glinting a deep red-orange above the entwining black threads of the tree branches silhouetted against the brilliant light, streaked here and there with traces of recent snow. He sank down again, his energy finally giving out, feeling the wind around his ears, ruffling his hair. He closed his eyes.

I must be dreaming, he thought.

What seemed like a short while later, he heard his name being called frantically from within his apartment. He stirred, lips parting, and looked up again at the sky to make sure that it had not all been a dream, that he was, indeed, free. The moon was now directly above him, no longer orange but a creamy pale yellow. He smiled at it and didn't look away until the voice sounded again from within. It was a woman's, vaguely familiar.

"Lord Cade!" There was movement behind him. "Lord Cade!"

"Here," Cade tried to croak, but his voice was so unused that barely a thread of sound came out. There was another loud movement from within his room, and a woman's figure appeared in the doorway.

"Lord Cade!" the woman shrieked and rushed towards him. There were hands on his face, on his arms. Cade felt himself melt, his eyes half-closing as he soaked in the touch, the warmth. But he was being pulled again, back inside. He tried to struggle, to tell whoever it was that he never wanted to go inside again, but she was much stronger than he was. He opened his eyes as she lit a lamp nearby, and he cringed for a moment, eyes burning, then saw who it was and recognized her.

"Nadia?" he asked, and when she turned around, he saw that there were tears in her eyes.

"You're alive, my Lord," she whispered, and the way she smiled told Cade that she had not truly smiled in a very long time. "We must get you cleaned up now. I'll run a bath."

"Nadia, where's Wolf?" Cade asked, voice tripping as it came from his throat.

Nadia looked down at her hands. "I don't know if he has been released yet, my Lord. But the minute he is—if he is—I will tell you."

Cade slumped back against the nearby couch as Nadia left the room and began to fill a tub in the other room with hot water from the kitchens. She pulled him into the bathroom, undressed him quietly and efficiently, and helped him into the tub. He was too weak to scrub, so she did it, cleaning away the dirt and grime until the pale shade of his skin could be seen through. Cade was at first embarrassed at Nadia seeing him naked, but her attitude was so businesslike that he relaxed and enjoyed the feeling of the hot water, his tears silently comingling with the water streaming down his face as he basked in the sensation of being touched by another person.

She helped him out of the bath, sitting him down, shaving him, and cutting his hair while he hung in the chair like a rag doll. She wrapped him in a warm robe (his filthy, tattered clothes were thankfully nowhere to be seen) and took him from the bathroom back into the main chamber. Cade straightened up as he sat down, feeling, an inch at a time, much more like the person he had been years ago instead of a caged animal.

Nadia quietly walked up behind him and handed him a mirror, which he took and flipped up towards his face. The reflection that stared back was like a strange, distant echo of the visage that he remembered.

He resembled his brother more than he had before; his jaw had broadened some, and the small bit of baby fat in his cheeks had been whittled down so that his cheekbones and brow curved smoothly beneath his skin, creating a small dip from which his slate eyes glimmered. His straight white-blond hair, still drying, brushed around the outline of his face, contrasting with the dark lashes rimming his eyes. It was the face of a man, and what was more, it was a man who Cade didn't completely recognize. It threw him. He lowered the mirror and stared straight ahead. He didn't want to look anymore.

Nadia sat down opposite him and regarded him closely. He was physically weak, but she could see no sign that there was anything mentally wrong with him. That was good. She, like Cade, was also surprised by how his face and air had matured, even if his stature had remained small. She realized that across the intervening years, she had thought of him only as the young teenage boy he'd been when he was arrested.

"Why have I been released?" Cade asked in his new, strange low voice after a long silence.

"Lady Vera— " Nadia began, then started again. "I have been Lady Vera's handmaiden for the past three years, and she has grown increasingly dissatisfied with Cira's stranglehold over what she feels is her rightful rule, even though it was Cira who put her in a position of power in the first place. Today, she decided to enact a small sort of rebellion, which took the form of showing clemency to a few of Cira's political dissenters. You, as one, have been released."

Cade eyed her narrowly. "This decree was, I have a feeling, encouraged somewhat by you?"

Nadia modestly lowered her eyes in assent, and Cade leaned back. This raised Nadia up into a higher estimation in his mind. "Has Vera married?" he asked.

Nadia nearly laughed. "No, she hasn't."

"I'm surprised."

"Really?" Nadia asked blankly. "Come, now, my Lord, you've spent over five minutes with her, haven't you?"

"Unwillingly," Cade conceded, and smiled. Good. It would be easier without an annoying, power-hungry husband trying to get in the way of what was about to happen.

"My Lord, what is it that you intend to do?" Nadia asked, holding her breath at his reply. If he responded that he was going to give up all his claim to the crown, retreat into the woods, and become a landscape painter, she knew that without a doubt she would walk straight out onto the balcony and over the railing. But Cade merely tilted his head from one side to another.

"I won't know until I've been able to ask you a few questions. And until I've learned whether or not Wolf is alive."

Nadia nodded, dimly remembering the nature of his evasive answers. She wasn't put off by them. There was a knock at the door behind them, and she whipped around, her eyes wide. Cade knew immediately the danger that she would be in if a servant found Lady Vera's head servant conspiring with a recently freed political dissenter. Cade jerked his head to the right, and Nadia rose, slipping off into another room in the apartment.

"Come in," Cade said as loudly as he could, but the door didn't open. They hadn't heard him. He took a deeper breath. "Come in," he said, barely audible this time. The door opened. There was a servant, who seemed to debate whether or not to bow to him, then decided to go for the safe route and inclined his head a few inches.

"I have been sent to inform your Lordship that your former bodyguard Wolf has been released and is alive. Servants are seeing to him now, cleaning him up. He is in another wing of the palace." The servant bowed again for good measure.

Cade tried to stifle the shout of happiness that welled up within him. "Have him brought here *immediately* after he has been cleaned up. He will stay with me from now on, do you understand? I want a room fixed up as soon as possible."

"Yes, your lordship."

Cade slumped down in the seat, unable to stop himself from grinning as the door closed quietly behind the servant. Nadia stepped back out of the shadows, looking carefully to see whether the coast was clear. She sat down again opposite Cade.

"He is alive, then?" she asked.

"Yes," he replied. "He's alive. He's alive."

"Would your Lordship like me to leave?" she asked hesitantly.

"No, stay here. I want to talk to you two as soon as possible."

"Perhaps it should wait until you and Wolf have had a good night's sleep?" Nadia inquired delicately, noting with concern the way Cade lay on the back of the couch for support. But the prince shook his head firmly.

"I've slept enough," he said shortly. "I have thought of this day more often than you could possibly imagine,"

"I doubt that very much, my lord," Nadia said softly.

Wolf sat like a coiled spring, silently regarding Cade beneath heavy-lidded eyes. If he was relieved to have been set free—overwhelmed by joy, bewildered, shocked—his steely expression did not betray him.

His face had changed, not only with the advance of age but in the expression he bore. Cade remembered him as always having a smile close at hand, but the person who sat before him looked as though not even a threat of death or torture could drive him to move his mouth from the thin, tight line in which it was held. The mottled pelt of blond, auburn, and gray hairs atop his head now had distinctive streaks of white around the temples and at the nape of his neck. The clear blue eyes that bored straight into Cade's showed none of the warmth of humor they had years before. It was perfectly possible for Cade to recognize him, and yet it seemed as if a completely different person was facing him. Unlike Cade, whose stature had suffered from his incarceration, it seemed that Wolf had spent his four years exercising as well as he could in the tiny cell in which he spent the duration of his imprisonment. He had grown a good three to four inches, broader across the shoulders, any small amount of softness to his face or body chiseled away by his struggle to survive. There were a number of scars on his face and throat, remnants of the day he had been imprisoned, souvenirs of his fight to the death with his former mentor, Luther. Cade swallowed. The memories were impossible to cast aside, but every time Cade relived that day, he became sick to his stomach and slightly dizzy.

He shook the thoughts from his head and looked back to what had been his friend. Fleetingly, he reflected that perhaps Cira had, in fact, succeeded in killing him; at first glance, there was no discernible human life in his eyes. They were metallic, still. But as Cade watched, he realized that something burned beneath them. Cade could see it. He recognized it. Revenge.

Nadia leaned down beside him, placing her hand behind his head on the back of the couch, leaning close to his ear. "My Lord," she whispered. "Wolf...the day that you were taken...Cira..." she trailed off. Cade glanced at her impatiently, and Nadia took a deep breath. "Wolf is mute, my Lord. He cannot speak. She...she cut out his tongue." Nadia leaned back, looking anxious, and Cade let her words hit him. He wanted to look anywhere, anywhere but in Wolf's vengeful eyes, but found himself unable to do so. His stomach twisted unpleasantly as screams echoed in his mind, Wolf's cries as he was led down the passageway. He knew now what Cira must have been doing to him to make him scream like that...as Cade was being led away, unaware, unscathed. He took in a shuddering breath, his hands beginning to sweat. He wished Wolf would blink.

Surely, Wolf blames me for everything as well. I'm surprised he hasn't tried to kill me already. At that moment, Cade would have preferred that fate to any other. The guilt clawed at him like a wild beast. There was no reason why Wolf should have had to suffer like that. *Your fault, your fault*, a nasty voice within him repeated.

"Nadia," Cade said cautiously. "I have changed my mind. Would you excuse us for a moment? Oh, and...bring a piece of parchment and a pen before you go?"

Nadia glanced between the two, then rose and did as she was told, stealing out of the room as silently as a shadow. Once the door had shut quietly behind her, Cade turned his gaze back to Wolf, who still hadn't blinked or moved a muscle. All at once, Wolf stirred. He motioned for Cade to hand him the parchment and the pen. The gesture so startled Cade that he nearly dropped the bottle of ink he was holding, but recovered and handed them to Wolf, who took them silently and began to write. For a few seconds, there was no sound in the room except for the scratching of the tip of the pen on the brittle paper. Then, Wolf straightened up and handed the paper to Cade, watching him unblinkingly. Cade read:

I do not blame you for what has happened to me

Cade looked up, hardly daring to believe it. Wolf nodded ever so slightly, then took the paper from Cade's still hands and wrote some more before handing it back.

You were in a cell as well as I. You have suffered as well as I

"It doesn't compare," Cade said quietly. "It doesn't remotely compare, what she did to you..."

Wolf cut him off with an impatient flick of one hand, then wrote:

You did what you had to do to try and save us both and I did what I had to do. I do not hold you accountable. And, for one reason or another, we failed. We were too slow, too careless, or perhaps she was too quick. But my loyalty is with you.

Cade looked up, scarcely daring to believe the words. Wolf's expression had not softened even somewhat, but Cade had the writing before him. He said nothing and hoped that his silence would convey his relief and gratitude more than any words could. Wolf shifted ever so slightly, as if he understood exactly what Cade was feeling. There was a beat between them before Wolf took the paper from Cade's hands and wrote:

But now I take it that the situation has changed slightly?

"Yes, somewhat," Cade replied, after he had read it.

And we may use it to our advantage?

Cade paused. "I think we may. We will start tomorrow. There are people we will need. A good deal of luck. A good deal of cunning and planning. But we will not make any of the careless mistakes we made last time. You are the only one I trust, so you will be the only one I communicate my true intentions to. And," he thought carefully before he continued, tapping his forefinger definitively on the arm of the chair with every word, "I think that in time, the throne of Joymaril will be ours."

Something crackled behind Wolf's eyes, a spark that was as unsettling as the first motion he had made from his prior immobility. He seized the paper and scribbled so furiously that when Cade read the words, he had to squint slightly to read them. Wolf's blue eyes were boring into him as he scanned the page.

I do not want the throne

Cade looked up and again saw the familiar fire. "Tell me," he said. "What is it that you want?"

Wolf stared at him and took the pen and parchment. This time, he wrote slowly, taking as much care with each crossed and looped letter as if it had been an engraving on a religious monument:

Her

He silently handed Cade the page. The prince's gray eyes merely flicked down and took in the word, then he sat back and placed the page beside him on the couch. "We are, it seems, once more working towards the same goal," he said quietly. "But there are steps we must take beforehand. I would like nothing better than to ride straight into Faridor, walk up to her, and visit whatever tortures you and I could devise upon her." His voice was more bitter, more filled with hatred than Cade had anticipated. He had trained himself to keep his feelings hidden. He quickly regained his composure. Such a breach was acceptable in Wolf's presence, but when he had to present a face to the members at court, such a thing could be fatal. "I would like nothing more than that," he repeated, and the tiniest stirring in the man before him gave him Wolf's unspoken assent. "But it would not do. If we do this, we are going to do it right. We must start tomorrow. We will regain our strength. I will begin to gather what information I can." For the first time, Cade allowed himself to smile. "We've been given a second chance, Wolf. We must be sure and convey to Lady Vera that we are not...ungrateful."

Wolf did not smile, but there was another subtle shift in the depths of his eyes. Cade noted it and nodded. It pained him to admit it, but he was more than a little frightened of Wolf. *Well, if he makes me nervous, he'll be a hell of a fright to whoever we might be fighting*, Cade thought grimly, and stood. "Nadia," he called out, hoping that the handmaiden had stayed within earshot in case she was needed. Being the good servant that she was, she walked in quietly a moment later and strode up to Cade, eyes questioning.

"Nadia, I need you to get me a full list of all of those who have been released from the prisons and what they were incarcerated for. Also, compile a list of those you know in the city who are loyal to Laith and Athela and have evaded capture. And get me whatever information you can on the state of affairs in Two Falls. Any of the servants who might have visited there recently, chat them up and see what's going on. Don't call attention to yourself, but I want exact details. Do the Strikers exist? What is their presence in Two Falls? How many Kagaian guards are stationed in the city? Does Cira visit frequently, the strength of the resistance, that sort of thing. And I want a full description of all the action going on around the palace here and in the outer city. What the mood is, the general public feeling. And, most of all, I want you to tell me everything you can about Lady Vera, her habits, her intentions. Where we can apply pressure. Can you do it by tomorrow?"

"I can, my Lord," Nadia said quietly, her eyes half lowered, her hands clasped behind her back in a classic servant's pose. Cade was impressed at how easily she took in what was an enormous task.

"Good," he said, satisfied, and sat back. "Except for the list of the released prisoners, I want none of this written down. The list is innocent enough; Vera probably has a few herself, but we will not make a mistake like last time, leaving papers carelessly out for others to read. That will be all."

Nadia nodded shortly and spun on her heel, vanishing out of the room. Cade waited until her footsteps had faded away, then looked back at Wolf, who had sat motionless throughout the entire exchange. "I have ordered you rooms of your own. Is that acceptable?" he asked. Wolf nodded. "Good. I'm going to be sleeping on the balcony. You are welcome to use yours." He considered. "Also, we must find some way to communicate without the use of paper and pen. It slows us up a good deal, and we would be much more effective using a form of speech no one else could decode." Wolf nodded again. "All right," Cade stretched. "Get some sleep. We begin in the morning."

That night, Cade lay beneath the deepening sky. Though he was exhausted, he stayed awake hour after hour, staring at the stars twinkling brightly above him, welcoming him back to the land of the living. He wrapped his heavy blankets closer around him, glad for their warmth, rejoicing in the cold air nipping at his nose and biting his cheeks. When his eyes finally closed, the constellations above him were imprinted onto his dreams.

Nadia cleared her throat and adjusted the piece of paper held in her hand. She was more than a little proud of herself. She had successfully gathered all the information Cade required, and had headed off one of Lady Vera's tantrums by making sure that her breakfast had been sent back and replaced before Vera was able to taste it and find it unsuitable. She found herself clinging desperately to the thread of newfound hope marked by Cade's return. She longed for her freedom more and more every day.

It was with considerable eagerness that she shifted in her seat beneath Cade's and Wolf's gray and blue stares and began to give them her report. She handed Cade the list, alphabetized and copied out carefully in her own minute script. Cade's eyes flickered over the names, and Wolf watched over his shoulder.

"As you can see, most of the political dissenters were imprisoned because of loyalties to Laith and Athela or the King and Queen," she said quietly after a minute or so. Cade nodded mutely, still perusing the papers. "That could be useful to us, couldn't it?"

"Yes," Cade said shortly, his tone clearly implying that he didn't wish for his thoughts to be disturbed by her questions. Nadia bit her lip and forced her words back. She had a thousand questions for Cade. What was he planning, when did he intend to put his plan into effect? Would he fight? Make peace? It took all of her highly disciplined self-restraint to prevent her from exploding.

"We need good fighters," Cade said finally, as if he were speaking mostly to himself. "There are many on this list, though I suspect that after their imprisonment, more than a few of them are out of shape or tortured completely out of commission. You're to now find out the status of each and every potential warrior on this list," Cade ordered, motioning to a few names. "And if they are healthy enough, test the waters. See where their loyalties lie. Whether they'd be willing to join us."

Nadia took in a deep breath. She much preferred Cade's curt orders to Lady Vera's insipid whinings and entreaties. The extra work was nothing if it was effort put toward her liberation. She steeled her jaw, already calculating which servants she could talk to. She was familiar with almost every name on the list. She would have to start with their family homes, see if the released prisoners had been given into the care of their closest living relatives. Some of the individuals had lost all family in the purge Cira had visited upon the palace four years ago. Where those prisoners would go, Nadia had no idea.

Cade leaned up, glancing quickly at Wolf. "Now, what have you heard about Two Falls?"

The city of Joymaril had been put under complete lockdown; news of Two Falls was hard to come by, but every now and again a scroll had managed to be smuggled in. "Cira is still very much in control there, as far as we know," she said grimly. "More guards are stationed there than at Faridor, or so I'm told, though I'm not sure that I believe it. Cira was always more interested in protecting her own skin."

"Well, that and Faridor is harder to attack than Two Falls," Cade pointed out. "Easier to attack a city than an island which only has a thin bridge linking it to land."

Nadia nodded and continued, "Many of the guards she has appointed are graduates of the Academy. She's been shipping off students for quite some time now, changed the Academy's doctrine so that the students are all basically brainwashed to believe in her uncontested supremacy. But the Academy recruits are being sent to Faridor to protect her, not Two Falls. In Two Falls, many of her troops are just locals stuck with green robes and swords."

"Interesting," Cade murmured thoughtfully, fingers steepled beneath his nose, gray eyes staring out vacantly into the wall, lost in thought. The gesture was so reminiscent of his old mannerisms that

Nadia nearly broke out into a smile. Cade bit his lip and ruffled the white-blond hair behind one ear. "Continue," he said tersely.

"The resistance in Two Falls is thought to be fairly large, considering, though Cira's army severely outnumbers them. The Strikers are at the head of the resistance, both as figureheads and fighters. It's said that they've been based in the mountains, though there are suspicions they have moved back to Two Falls recently."

"They're all still alive, then?" Cade asked curiously.

"Yes," Nadia replied.

"Who are the other Strikers? I remember that there was one Ashan who came back from Two Falls with Laith and Athela...quiet, with melancholy eyes."

"Tarr," Nadia smiled confidently. "Tarr. Then Athela and your brother. There are a few others. The boy, Si, who came here the night of the banquet and led to their arrest. It's said he's the heir of Morthenstar."

"Really?" Cade sat up keenly, looking quite interested. "Why hasn't he just gone up and challenged Cira?"

Nadia shrugged. "I don't know. He's really a bit of a mystery."

Cade slouched back down against the back of the chair. "And Cira, does she visit the city very often?"

"No, especially now that the Strikers are rumored to be operating there. She considers it too much of a personal risk."

"As well she might," Cade murmured.

"But the resistance so far has been just the Strikers rescuing and relocating Ashans and their families whenever possible. We haven't heard yet of any major uprising or any attempt to take the city back." Nadia shrugged helplessly. It had been over a month since any word of Two Falls had managed to make its way to Joymaril. "They have more fighters back in the mountains, but they're kept busy robbing Cira's supply trains. Otherwise, Cira has the city in a headlock."

"I see," Cade said slowly. "Nadia, you've done good work."

Nadia lowered her eyes demurely, but inside, her heart warmed at Cade's compliment. "As for Joymaril, I think it is very much how you would expect it. Those who support Lord Argolaith and Lady Athela escaped death and imprisonment by the skin of their teeth. Those who supported Cira have been rewarded richly in promotions and presents and have grown lazy and contented as a result. But there are few in the city who have gone without the loss of a family member. The wounds around here are covered but aren't healed yet."

"I see," Cade said again, and retreated back into his thoughts for a few moments. Nadia let him think, sitting patiently, straightening out her skirt slightly around her knees. She would have to return to Lady Vera's side within a few minutes, or else she would be missed.

Finally, he stirred. "Well, we will begin with you circulating the information with any potential resistance fighters." He smiled and gave a sharp nod, signaling that the meeting was at a close.

Nadia rose and curtsied and rushed off perhaps slightly quicker than was proper decorum, but Cade smiled indulgently and rose to the window. He stepped out onto the balcony, Wolf following him. The sky was overcast; the gray light accented Cade's brilliant blond shock of hair so that it shone like a beacon. Cade leaned out over the balcony for a moment. Even the few minutes of standing made his legs feel wobbly. He straightened and glanced over his shoulder at his bodyguard.

"Now, what I must begin to do is to get well again. I need to ride. I need to run. I need to practice my swordplay. We must regain our strength for the time to come."

Wolf's gaze slid down to Cade's hands and saw that the prince was gripping the rail so hard that his knuckles were white with the effort of holding himself up. He shifted slightly, walked a short way down the curving stone rail, and leaned over, running one finger over the smooth carved wing of a stone bird outstretched against one side of the balcony. Cade's eyes moved along the trees below to the shimmering slate surface of the lake at the bottom of the cliff, and along the clifftop to the Joymarillian city resting beside the palace. Everything looked still and quiet, as if there wasn't a breath of life left in it. It was so silent that Cade gave an involuntary shudder. He had to get away from the silence of stones.

"Wolf, come on," he said. "Let's take a walk down to the lake. I need to get out of here."

Wolf's expression was dubious as the prince began to make his way through the door. When Cade stumbled, Wolf extended an arm to steady him. Cade accepted silently and then moved away as soon as he had gathered enough strength to walk on his own. For the first time in years, Cade walked freely through the halls of Joymaril, Wolf trailing two or three steps behind.

Nadia's news came back to them in small bursts over the next week. Gradually, though the whispers were few and far between, there began the tiniest flurries of motion, undercurrents of change that spread through the marble halls of the palace.

Cade had, for the most part, attempted to completely avoid Lady Vera and was at first successful. Though he rightly had little respect for her intellectual prowess, he was still determined not to underestimate her, and the easiest way to avoid detection was to simply not be seen. Unlike Cira, whose sharp mind could whirl in a dozen directions at once, sniffing out plots wherever they might be hidden (and even where they weren't), Vera would simply not be aware of anyone she didn't see standing before her.

Cade's endeavor to avoid Vera met its end one afternoon, two weeks after his release. He was on a ride through the forest with Wolf and two others: Dominic, who had served with Laith in the Meadows, and Ostella, a cousin of Ilaina's. Though not of enough royal blood to merit a place at court, she had nevertheless been outspoken enough after her cousin's death to earn her a place in the dungeons when Cira had taken over.

Lady Vera and her entourage were riding through the forest along one of her favorite winter trails, which led down one of the back hills and into a meadow where Vera liked to hold picnics for her courtiers during the summer months. Nadia, as always, rode a few steps behind Vera in case she was needed. The horses were plodding along resignedly, hooves slapping through the sloppy mud and steam blowing steadily out of their nostrils. There was little chatter amongst the group, and the atmosphere was rather gloomy. Most of those in attendance had been involuntarily compelled to attend; the day was too brisk to be a comfortable temperature to ride.

"Nadia," Vera's whine came piercing through the still air. Nadia gritted her teeth, urging her horse forward perhaps a bit harder than necessary. She reined back to fall into step beside Vera. Vera liked to dress as extravagantly as possible whenever she had the slightest chance of being seen by someone outside of the palace, and had chosen a riding outfit so expansive that her skirts were in danger of being stepped on by her horse. She wore a hat tipped to one side with a long feather coming out of it, and every time she turned her head, Nadia had to duck to avoid the feather going up her nose.

"I got a letter from Cira yesterday," Vera said in a loud conspiratorial whisper, clearly hoping that the others in her entourage would overhear her.

Nadia gave a theatrical gasp. "Oh, no! Has she found out what you did with the prisoners?"

Vera giggled slightly. "Someone in the palace wrote to her almost as soon as it happened. She's terribly cross with me. She demands that I immediately return the prisoners to the dungeons, or else she'll come over herself and have me thrown out. She's threatening to put one of my cousins on the throne. Says that at least they'll have the brains to follow her orders."

"You've upset her greatly," Nadia observed.

"I know." Vera paused and looked over to one side. "You don't really think she'll do that? She won't really come over and have me thrown out?"

"Of course not," Nadia said, ducking as the feather flew by overhead. "She has far too much to concern herself with on Faridor and in Two Falls. She still thinks that she has you under her thumb. She thinks that a small threat like that is enough to frighten you into submission."

"I'll show her," Vera said with determination. "My plans are already underway for my coronation celebration. It's going to be the most extravagant party this city has ever seen. I've got fifteen seamstresses working on my gown. *And* I've made the decision that soon after the festival, I will announce our official separation from the government of Faridor! I will be a queen, all in my own right!" She looked at Nadia excitedly, clearly searching for some sort of assent.

Nadia forced a quick grin, which seemed to placate her, but inwardly she was absolutely stunned by the leaps in judgment Vera had taken. "What if Cira decides to attack and reclaim the city?" she asked slowly. Vera was clearly stumped, having obviously given her plan little or no thought.

"Well...we have fighters here in the city," she said dubiously. "*They'll* defend it." Then, after a moment, she exclaimed, "We have the Third! I can order them to protect me."

At this, Nadia had to grudgingly admit that Vera had inadvertently stumbled onto a half-decent idea. The Third was Joymaril's most elite cavalry division, made up entirely of non-gendered soldiers, those who were neither man nor woman, male or female. They were not a force to be trifled with.

"My Lady!" came a call from behind them. Nadia twisted around, ducking as Vera did the same. One of the courtiers was pointing into the woods ahead of them. Nadia turned back around in her saddle, peering between the trees.

"Oh, no," she muttered, able to make out Cade's familiar head of hair even from some distance.

"Who is it?" Vera asked keenly, straightening her hat.

"Lord Cade, I believe, my Lady," Nadia murmured, trying to sound nonchalant.

"Ooh!" Vera said with visible excitement, preening. She pulled her horse to a reluctant halt, tugging her jacket and clasping the reins in one hand, draping the other across her lap. She affixed a haughty expression on her face, which reminded Nadia somewhat of a low-rent Cira with a bad smell under her nose. Beneath her, her horse heaved a weary sigh.

The white speck in the distance slid out and into sight through the tree trunks, drawing close enough that Nadia could make out Cade's face. She watched the dawning realization on his face as he recognized who he had run into. His slate eyes were cold as he rode up, knowing that there was no way to pretend as if he hadn't seen the large train riding through the forest. None of Cade's party made the slightest attempt at a feigned smile as they all stiffly inclined their heads an inch or two.

"I hope my Lady is enjoying this afternoon," Cade said courteously. His eyes slid coldly over to Nadia, who tried to mouth the words "*I'm sorry*" but didn't know whether Cade had read her words correctly. Cade's face was stone.

"I *am* enjoying it," Vera said, her voice slightly higher than usual. "I was afraid this morning that it would snow, but I now see that that is no longer a threat."

"I doubt your Ladyship would allow the snow to spoil one of her charming winter picnics," Cade said demurely, his level tones an almost comical contrast to Vera's twittering.

"Oh, of course not; we make the best of whatever comes our way," Vera said chipperly. "Rain or shine, you know. That sort of thing. Keeps the pleasure coming our way."

"Oh yes, one mustn't let one's life be devoid of pleasure," Cade said quietly.

"You're welcome to join us," she said eagerly, and for a second Nadia almost felt warmly towards her, felt her drop the faux-imperious façade of haughty ruler and transform instantaneously into an embarrassed young girl. "I mean, it must have been so long since you've been out on a picnic...We would love you to join us." Vera looked dubiously past Cade at Wolf, who was, in her opinion, probably the last person in the world who should be invited to a picnic. He was staring at her rather like a vulture eyeing a wounded rabbit, and his look was so intimidating and uncomfortable that Vera shifted in her seat and dropped her eyes to fidget with her soft leather riding gloves.

Cade cleared his throat, breaking the palpable tension. "I am honored by the invitation, but I fear that my friends and I were going to go explore a small series of caves farther down the ridge. So I will not impose upon you today, my Lady, but perhaps another time."

"Yes, you must," Vera echoed, looking up, relieved that she didn't have to be around Wolf any longer than was absolutely necessary. "Good day, then."

"Good day," Cade returned, and Vera moved her horse forward. The animal grunted slightly and walked stiffly forward. In the interim, it had fallen asleep, its right hind leg cocked slightly at the fetlock; Nadia could hear its joints creaking as it began to move. Vera thumped it a few times unceremoniously on the barrel of its belly, her spurs unable to connect through the thick folds of her dress cascading over either side. Cade nodded slightly as Nadia passed, sliding his horse to one side out of the way of the train of riders. Behind him, Wolf watched each of the members of the train, memorizing their faces with his piercing blue eyes. Only one looked back. He was older than them, in his late thirties, and Cade recognized him as being a Lord from the Phelean family. The young lord fearlessly matched Wolf's gaze with his own hazel eyes. Cade silently noted this and leaned back to Ostella.

"What's his name? The one watching Wolf?" he inquired in a low voice.

"Lord Sebastian," Ostella returned, eyes flashing from within the folds of her lilac hood. "House of Phelean."

"He suspects us," Cade murmured, mostly to himself.

"Half of the palace suspects us, My Lord," Dominic pointed out, watching as the last members of the train rode out of sight. "Even if they haven't seen or heard anything, they know that we've been released. And they know who you are. Who your family is. They're not all as daft as Vera."

"But most of them aren't willing to do anything about it. I think this one is," Cade observed, his eyes still on Lord Sebastian's retreating back. Slowly, Wolf, who had been watching the train intently, turned his speckled head around and met Cade's eyes. Cade gave an infinitesimal nod.

Further down the trail, Vera whirled in her saddle, peering after the group of riders they'd passed. She whipped her head back around to Nadia so quickly that she was surprised the hat didn't fly off of Vera's head.

"You know Cade, don't you?" Vera asked Nadia breathlessly as soon as they were out of sight of the prince and his followers.

Oh, great. "Yes, somewhat," Nadia replied carefully.

"He's quite handsome, isn't he? I mean, he's not as handsome as Laith, but who is? He's grown up rather well. I remember, before I came to power and everything, he was just sort of a *boy*, if you know what I mean." This was said importantly, as if Vera was much wiser to the ways of the world than someone like Cade. "But he's Laith's brother. And he's looking more like a real *man* now, isn't he?"

Yes, nearly four years of prison has done wonders for his physique, Nadia thought sarcastically. "I suppose he is, my Lady. It's really not my place to say."

"Oh, come on," Vera whined, as if Nadia were a spoilsport, but before Nadia could try to elaborate, Vera continued on with the force of an ox. "I like his hair best, I think. I love boys with blond hair. And I like how he's quiet. Most of the boys around here never shut up. They're always trying to tell you how *important* they are, how *they* should be the ones in charge of the decoration for all of the royal parties when they've barely even hung a strand of *bunting*." Vera heaved a sigh and shook her head disparagingly, then brightened as a thought occurred to her. "Hey, I'm the Queen, right? I can choose who I marry. I think I should like to marry Cade. The former King and Queen thought it was fit to almost engage me to Lord Argolaith. Why shouldn't I marry his brother?"

More reasons than I care to illustrate, Nadia snapped inwardly, but stared stonily ahead. Vera's new scheme was absolutely ludicrous. There was no way in heaven or earth that Cade would ever agree to such a thing, and he couldn't be forced. Still, though, there was the stirring of a deeper feeling in her chest: one of possession, of jealousy. She realized that she didn't want Vera coming anywhere near to Cade. She was his confidante and had gotten him out of prison, and she'd be damned if she'd let Vera try to blunder her way in. She thought again about what Vera had said about Cade being handsome. It was true, she thought suddenly. The gray eyes and the white-blond hair reminded her of the sea on a cloudy day. He was terse, and he was quiet, but she was surrounded daily by people who talked much and knew little. He was attractive. He was more than attractive.

Vera continued to prattle on, oblivious. "Perhaps I should make the announcement at the festival. That way, Cade won't *possibly* be able to refuse me. Not in front of all those people. And then we could get married in the springtime! I've always wanted to get married then, and I think a spring wedding would be absolutely *divine.* We would look so good together; I think that he's definitely going to have to say yes. Maybe I can get some of the servants to suggest it to him. Would you, Nadia?" Vera asked, twisting around so that her entire body was facing Nadia. Nadia refused to acknowledge the gesture and stared ahead as if her life depended on it. Vera's voice changed into a nasal wheedle, "Nadia, you're my *best* friend; you'd ask him for me, wouldn't you? It'd be so much better if it was *Cade's* idea to propose."

"I couldn't possibly do that, my Lady," Nadia said. "I don't know him nearly well enough. He'd think it an impertinence."

"I'm ordering you to," Vera said sharply, her tone changing abruptly.

Nadia clenched her teeth together and gave a curt nod. "Whatever you wish, my Lady."

"Oh, you're the *best!*" Vera exclaimed, clapping her hands together and grinning happily down the trail in front of them. Nadia closed her eyes briefly. She swallowed hard, her hands tightening on the reins, and urged her horse to walk faster through the thickening trees.

One week later, Lord Sebastian, an avowed supporter of Cira Kagai's rule in Joymaril, turned up dead outside one of the doors of the Academy gymnasium, where he was returning from an afternoon at the baths. There were no witnesses and no suspects.

The news of Lord Sebastian's murder flew around the palace like wildfire, setting aflame the tongues of handmaidens, valets, cooks, lords, ladies, and many of those who lived and worked in the surrounding city. At first, many feared for their own safety; the murderer and his intentions hadn't been discerned. But then came the whispers that Lord Sebastian had been plotting. Who had he been plotting against? Lord Cade. And then tongues began to wag even further. Was Lord Cade making designs on the throne? Such a thing was almost unthinkable. And yet the consensus came to be that if there was anyone in the city who could do it, it was Cade.

The atmosphere of the palace changed almost overnight. When Cade walked through the halls of the palace, the courtiers lounging about gossiping fell silent until he had passed, and then their whispers rose behind him like the sounds of cicadas among the trees in summer. People clustered around, pointing and staring as the distant speck of blond hair, so like Cira's, made its way down the halls. Cade stalked through his surroundings as if he were sleepwalking, completely unaware of the attention that followed him wherever he went.

But he stood up straighter now, walked with a longer stride. Along would come the white beacon of hair, and immediately behind would be Wolf, blue eyes sharper every day, penetrating with all the brilliance and hardness of diamonds. The two would *talk*, but it was unlike anything any of the courtiers or citizens had ever seen; they seemed to have devised their own form of sign language. Cade would make a sharp motion down the length of his arm, and Wolf would nod as if Cade had just given him an explicit order. Sometimes, it seemed that Wolf was the only person Cade communicated with anymore; the prince rarely spoke in public. But speaking was almost unnecessary. When Cade's slate eyes fixed upon someone, the power of the look immediately cowed the receiver.

Though there were those who dearly wished for Cade's demise, while Wolf was with him there was absolutely no way to carry out a simple assassination. Wolf was far too careful, his eyes too quick, ears too fast; Cade was no pushover, either. Their caution bordered on paranoia, much to the chagrin of any would-be assassins. Cade kept his activities varied and his schedule random, so there was no chance of laying a trap for him. His food was made under close supervision and was tested before he ate it.

At first, Lord Sebastian's death had shocked Cade's would-be opponents into a retreat. The suddenness of the assassination, the ruthless calculation and execution, gave Lady Cira's supporters pause. They realized that Sebastian was meant as a warning, not a final blow. It was a statement as well as a challenge. Cade had been overlooked most of his life as Lord Argolaith's younger brother, but no longer. He had been given the name of his house, and he was rising up quickly to fill the role. His enemies recognized this and proceeded with much more caution, aware of the intelligence working against them. Frantic letters began to be sent to Cira on Faridor, but things were progressing and developing at such a frenetic pace that there was little hope that she would receive the messages and muster an army in time to prevent a confrontation—besides, there were rumblings that something had happened in Two Falls, some great sort of upheaval not altogether in Cira's favor.

Surprisingly, these changes in the wind had not gone unnoticed by Lady Vera, though they had been interpreted completely inaccurately thanks to Nadia's careful guidance. Upon hearing of Lord Sebastian's death, Lady Vera immediately assumed that Cira was behind it. Vera stepped up her personal security, as well as the security of her closest courtiers, for she was also convinced that Cira was determined to ruin her picnics by picking off her entourage. In this way, Vera inadvertently provided a small hurdle for Cade to leap over, for while her extra security had been placed for the wrong reasons, it was harder for Wolf and Nadia to get close to and spy upon her remaining supporters, many of whom were suspected to be massing together against Cade. Vera was still blissfully unaware of most of the plotting that had been going on around her; no one had bothered to inform her that she was trapped precariously between Cade and Cira's war for the throne. Had she known the brewing maelstrom into which she had been thrust, Vera would certainly have run for cover. But as it was, she continued her daily routine with as much insipid exuberance as ever.

Mostly, she concerned herself with preparations for the ball that she was throwing for herself, at which all the prisoners she freed would come and swear fealty (and, if she played her cards right, Cade would propose.) Needless to say, this program of events was a very exciting prospect for her, and Vera threw herself into the decorations and preparations with enough fervor to threaten the mental well-being of three teams of creative consultants. This also unfortunately meant that Nadia almost always had to be on hand to console Vera whenever the right color of peach couldn't be found to be made into curtains, or when the cook tried to convince her that strawberries were completely out of season and nearly impossible to come by. Vera kept Nadia from doing all the work that Cade required of her, but on the positive side, Nadia found herself surrounded at all hours by bored servants who liked nothing better than gossiping about those they served. Nadia dutifully relayed all relevant information to the young prince, though for reasons she didn't quite want to pinpoint, she hadn't yet mentioned Vera's desire for Cade to propose to her on the night of the party. Eventually, when almost all time had run out, she decided she had to tell him.

The night before the celebration, Cade called a covert meeting of his supporters, held in his most private apartment chamber. The conversation lasted half an hour or so; Cade outlined the following night's plan in detail. When he was done speaking, he leaned back in his chair, reaching for a goblet of water, taking a slow sip, and watching the faces of those around him. There was a small noise at the door, and Nadia let herself in, nodding to Cade and taking her place standing behind his chair.

Dominic slid forward in his chair and faced Cade. "We will be outnumbered, as I'm sure you're aware, my Lord."

Cade set the goblet back down on the table beside his chair. "Look, I have given you all your very specific instructions. As long as you follow these orders, we shouldn't have any trouble tomorrow. I have left a margin for some amount of error."

"I understand, my Lord." Dominic nodded. He was, after all, a soldier, and it had been ingrained in him that trust should ultimately be placed with the decisions of one's general.

"Good, then," Cade stood, and the others rose with him. "Tomorrow it is." He saw looks of grim satisfaction mirrored in the expressions of the circle of people around him. "Spread the word to the others," he commanded, and turned his back, signaling them that it was time for them to go. "And watch yourselves tonight," he added as they began to file out of the door. "I want to see everyone back here tomorrow."

When the last person had left the room, Wolf went over and shut the door. Taking a deep breath and steeling herself, Nadia cleared her voice.

"My Lord...there is something I have been ordered to ask you," she said quietly. Cade nodded, turning half around to hear her better. Nadia bent down close to his ear. "Lady Vera has grown...enamored of you, and she expects you to ask her to marry you tomorrow night. I have been ordered to give you this idea, since Lady Vera would much prefer it if you were the one who proposed, not her. She is...very *particular* about this." Nadia tried hard to keep the bitterness out of her voice.

"Ah-hah," Cade said, absorbing this information in his usual taciturn way. "And how long ago did she ask you to propose this idea to me?"

"Two weeks," Nadia said grudgingly.

"And it's taken you this long to mention it?" Cade asked quietly, though there was hardly a question in his voice. Nadia had been staring at his shoulder, but at something in his tone she looked up and met his eyes. His face was softer than she had ever seen it, the steel edge gone from his face. *He knows*, she thought frantically, as she felt his eyes go straight through her. She stepped back demurely, unable to be close to him any longer. "I see," Cade said quietly and turned around again, allowing her to let out her breath and attempt to calm her pounding heart. "Well, that certainly is a bit of a surprise to me, but I think that I will be able to use it to my advantage," he mused.

Nadia wanted nothing more than to run from the room. Yet Cade had not mocked her. The look in his eyes was soft. She knew better than to allow hope into her heart, but the relief of not being rejected began to lift her spirits. "Yes," Cade said, "I think that that will do very well. Wolf," he said, and made a few motions. Wolf nodded silently and headed for the door.

Cade stood and faced Nadia. She tensed up, refusing to look at him. "Thank you for your help," he said quietly. "I want you to look after yourself. Our enemies know how close you are to me. Good night," he said and turned away, padding quietly across the room to the balcony where he slept every night. Nadia was shocked. It was the closest Cade had ever come to declaring friendship for her since he'd returned from the dungeons. Nadia couldn't help but smile. If that was all she ever got from him, it would be enough.

Vera's celebration began at sundown the next day. The palace, in particular the Great Hall, had been made over in various nauseating shades of peach and purple, with dyed sprigs of birch poking out of vases. Many in the city had turned up for the party, not because of any particular liking for Lady Vera, but mostly for something to do. The winter months were usually slow; besides, there were rumors that some sort of delicious plot was afoot, and none of the courtiers wished to miss out.

Vera was presiding over everything with a comically self-important air. Her gown was highly detailed, expertly sewn, and overall quite resplendent; Vera had clearly gone to great lengths to look as regal as possible. Her pale, reddish hair had been pulled up at the back of her head with two peach and purple flowers. She flitted about merrily from group to group, chitchatting and inserting herself into private conversations, laughing when nothing was funny, and generally making a nuisance of herself. Nadia had been ordered to remain in Vera's apartments until she was summoned, but she had crept out and was hanging around the back of the room, knowing full well that it would only be a matter of time before Vera found something to upset her and didn't want to waste time running to and from her chambers.

The bevy of guests were intermixed with Cade's supporters and those who had openly declared their fealty to Lady Cira, as well as those who had no affiliation whatsoever. When members of the opposing sides passed within a certain distance of one another, glares were exchanged and insults muttered, but no action was taken. Both parties seemed to be under strict orders not to make the first move until commanded to do so. The atmosphere was primed to explode.

The party had been in full swing for nearly an hour before Cade showed up. He walked through the doors, ignoring the countless heads who turned to gawk at him as he stalked through the room, flanked by Wolf. Cade wore a light shade of gray and a Whitsun ornamental battle sword displayed at his hip. The weapon had belonged to his brother Argolaith, presented to him upon his return from service in the Meadows. Though the sight of the sword caused a few murmurs, it was nothing out of the ordinary; royalty would often display arms at formal gatherings. Cade nodded to a few people and walked over to the wine table, poured himself a goblet, and strode deliberately out of the room to stand on the balcony in the fresh air. As soon as he had vanished, a number of people began to buzz eagerly amongst themselves, knowing looks were passed between the fighters on the two sides. Cade's presence signaled that something was about to happen.

But, to the disappointment of many and the relief of others, the party continued on quite smoothly. Cade remained outdoors, talking with a small group of people, minding his own business and making no hidden signals to any of his supporters. From inside the hall, two of Cira's supporters, Lady Matias and Lord Gaspard, eyed him narrowly.

Out on the balcony, Cade was leaning over the railing, looking to the side. A few girls were making hopeful eyes at him, but he ignored them and instead watched the lights flickering from the apartments below. He glanced over to Wolf, whose keen eyes were searching for any sign of trouble. Suddenly, there was a small tap on his shoulder, and Cade turned around to find Nadia.

"Lady Vera's going to start her announcements in about ten minutes," she whispered shortly and sped away lest she be seen talking with him. Cade turned to Wolf and made three motions with one hand over his arm. Wolf nodded silently and padded off a short distance to stand with Dominic. Dominic felt Wolf's touch and quickly moved off into the main room to circulate among Cade's conspirators. Wolf returned to Cade's side, and the young prince stretched and sloped back into the hall.

The banquet was, by this time, packed with dozens of people. There were dancers in the center of the room, doing their best to hear the music over the loud chatter from the partygoers. Cade walked past them, downed another glass of wine, and kept to the back of the throng. He found that he felt surprisingly calm; perhaps it was the effect of the wine, but his nerves were not nearly as tense as he had predicted they would be. He hoped that Nadia would be able to stay safely out of the fight. He couldn't see her, so she must be somewhere, keeping out of sight. He threaded his way around the crowd, gently nudging Ostella in the back. Ilaina's cousin nodded curtly as he passed and continued her conversation. Cade stopped at the very farthest section of the room, folded his arms, and waited, Wolf like a statue by his side.

Vera, who had been one of the dancers, broke away from the circle, giggling merrily, then made her way up the short flight of stairs to stand before the throne at the head of the room. Some of her hair had fallen loose, and she tucked it back haphazardly, trying to catch her breath and regain her composure for her public address. She dabbed at her face with the back of her sleeve and cleared her throat. Surprisingly, even though they had been talking quite loudly, it seemed that everyone in the room had been keeping an eye on Vera and fell into silence more quickly than Cade had anticipated. Vera seemed quite pleased by this result and milked the silence for dramatic effect for a few moments before she began to speak.

"I would like to thank all of you for coming tonight," she said. "I have held this party not only as a celebration of my reign. There have been quite a few changes this year, not only in the people around me but in myself as well. I have decided that we, as a palace, shall no longer be beholden to Lady Cira and the government of Faridor. The palace of Joymaril has, and always will be, the richest and greatest power in this land, and Lady Cira is not going to change that. From now on, I am the ultimate ruler in this city. To demonstrate my commitment to my people, I decided one month ago to pardon some of those who had opposed Cira's rule. I did this to show that I am not my cousin. I have the capacity for mercy. I have the capacity for kindness." Here, Vera leaned back, clearly expecting to hear hurrahs and shouts of agreement from the crowd. When none immediately came, she began to look slightly agitated. Cade took a deep breath. *Here we go*, he thought to himself.

"My Lady, let me be the first of those you freed to step forward and show my gratitude," he said, and there was a ripple of heads flicking back to look at him. He began to walk through the crowd, slowly but purposefully. The people parted for him, making a path down the center of the room. Vera brightened, clearly expecting that Cade was going to come up, thank her, and immediately propose marriage.

The walk through the center of the room was one of the most interminable moments of Cade's life. All the nerves that had so far been absent fluttered through him, but he masked his fear and forced the hint of a smile to show around the edges of his tightly held mouth. Finally, he drew up to the throne, taking the first three steps up to the dais. Vera was grinning widely, and gazed up at him expectantly. Cade sank to one knee, bowing his head in front of her. The air in the room was so tight that Nadia (who was watching from a small side door) could hardly find room to breathe. Vera stood and knelt down to him, cupping his chin in her hand and raising him up to his full height.

"Is there something you would like to say?" she cooed breathlessly.

"Yes," Cade said smoothly. "I command you to step down."

Vera's face blanched. "What?" she demanded sharply. Nadia was biting her lip so hard that she began to taste blood.

"I said," Cade repeated easily, "that neither Cira nor her puppet has any hold on the people of this city. For the years I and the others spent in prison, you are as guilty as she. And for letting us out, even if only out of spite for Cira and a desire to have your feet licked by your betters, I give you whatever thanks you deserve."

Vera's mouth was opening and closing like a gasping fish. She took a step back, clutching her skirts, eyes wide, searching between Cade's face and looking fearfully back at Wolf's cold expression.

"But now it's time, Lady Vera," Cade said, hand going down to the Whitsun sword hanging low on his hip. His fingers closed around the minutely engraved hilt, and he drew it out, the high-pitched sound of metal as it left the scabbard. Lady Vera stumbled back, hitting the throne on the platform, her hands grasping for some sort of support.

"Cade!" Lord Gaspard bellowed from behind him. Cade slowly smiled to himself and turned around. Wolf mirrored his action, fixing his two blue orbs on the Jelani lord's face. Gaspard's face was red, either with anger or fear. His hand shot down to his hip; he threw back his jacket and revealed that he, too, had come to the party armed. Cade looked to Wolf and gave a tiny nod. Wolf opened his mouth and let out a bloodcurdling, animalistic roar and hurled himself forward towards Gaspard. For a moment, the Lord was frozen by the hideous, inhuman cry but brought up his blade just in time to parry Wolf's blow. Cade himself turned and ran into the crowd, his sword gripped easily in one hand. And all of a sudden, the room surged together. Screaming bystanders fled for the doors, and the fighters threw off robes and jackets, displaying an array of longswords and knives, which immediately sang out of their scabbards and were put to use.

But Cira's supporters discovered very quickly that Cade had not simply instructed his fighters to throw themselves into a massive, confused brawl. Fighters began dropping like flies, for Cade had instructed each of his followers to mark two or three targets close together and stand behind them, waiting for the signal. Then, when the fighting began, they struck before their opponents even had time to reach for their swords. Because of this, after only a minute or so of fighting, the odds were slowly tipping in Cade's favor as the fighters spread out to fill the room. Cade threw himself against Lady Matias, who, though she was not much of a swordswoman, had a great sense of self-preservation that protected her against many of Cade's initial blows. Beside him, Dominic and three other fighters were cleaving a path through their opponents with a beautiful, deadly efficiency strongly reminiscent of Laith himself.

Lord Gaspard barely had time to register what was going on around him, so busy was he trying to fight off Wolf, whose force came on with all the power of his namesake animal. His blows didn't come very fast or with much flourish, but every time Wolf's blade hit his, it was like being struck in the arm with a sledgehammer. Through his parries and thrusts, Gaspard wondered fleetingly how on earth Cade had once more managed to outwit them. He took a step back, allowing Wolf to get the slightest edge forward. The bodyguard's face was truly hideous; lips pulled back over his teeth in an animalistic snarl, the broad shoulders pushing forward, slicing and hacking with such ferocity that if any of the blows managed to connect, Gaspard would easily be losing his limbs one right after the other.

Vera had shrunk back against the throne, clutching at it and hiding between its legs like a child cowering behind a parent. She tried to cover her eyes against the carnage playing out in front of her, felt tears cascading down her cheeks. Whatever the outcome of this fight was, she was no longer going to be in power. And she had seen such hatred in Cade's eyes when he had looked at her; if he managed to win the fight, there was very little doubt in her mind that he would kill her. She whimpered as two fighters came close to her, spattering blood on the long train of her dress, and she shrunk back even further, looking for a place to run.

From the small door to the side of the room, Nadia was watching the fighting with her fingers twisted in a swath of peach curtain. Cade was all right. His hair was easy to pick out in the broad knot of struggling duelers. Their side seemed to be gaining the upper hand, and she realized that Cade had once more been three steps ahead of his opponents, playing them right into his hands like a cat with a wounded bird. She saw him sink his sword into Lady Matias's chest and realized that it was time for her to act. She ran out onto the platform and caught Lady Vera around the arm, tugging at her. At first, Vera screamed, thinking that Nadia was someone coming to attack her, but when she recognized her handmaiden, she let out a shriek of relief and threw herself into Nadia's arms.

"Nadia!" she screamed. "He's going to kill me!"

"Quiet, my Lady!" Nadia told her urgently and pulled one of her arms. "Come with me, I can hide you. Come!" she ordered, and Lady Vera was so frightened that she obeyed without any protest. Nadia pulled her across the platform and out of the small side door, through a series of passageways towards the servants' chambers.

Cade kicked the body of Lady Matias to one side and spun around, streaks of crimson blood in his white hair. Lady Vera was gone, as they had planned. Cade turned around and signaled to Dominic and one of his other fighters, and the three of them broke off and headed off after Lady Vera and Nadia. Cade didn't have time to assess the battle, but while Wolf was still up and fighting, he was certain that they had the upper hand.

Wolf, meanwhile, was clearly enjoying his fight with Gaspard, tiring him out and weakening him until it was time to make the killing blow. Gaspard was hanging on gamely, but he lacked the rage and the ferocity that drove Wolf forward with every step. Finally, Wolf tired of him, ducked a blow and swung his blade cleanly through Gaspard's neck. The Lord's head flew off to one side, landing on the floor, his body collapsing into itself and crumpling onto the white marble floor. Wolf turned around, searching eagerly for someone new to fight, and was only slightly surprised to find that the brawl was already almost over. Cade's plan had worked like a charm, whittling down the best fighters on the opposition early on so that the rest of the battle was just cleaning up the mess.

The bloodlust filled Wolf's blue eyes, and he let out another bellow, his sword out and ready, challenging any standing fighters to come and try their luck with him. The sound invigorated the rest of Cade's fighters; they shouted back in return and pushed forward with even greater intensity. The floor was stained a blood red, littered with the bodies of the slain and the slowly creeping figures of the wounded. Wolf stepped over a few bodies and stabbed a fighter in the back, watching him drop and swiftly whipping around to face any oncomers.

Cade and his two flankers made their way through the short series of passageways along the meticulously detailed route outlined to him by Nadia. Three doorways...last one on the left, Cade stopped in front of it and opened it. He and the others spilled into the small room.

Vera spun around and looked at him, the expression of shock on her face almost comical. Nadia stood a few feet behind her. She immediately lowered her eyes and backed away as Cade entered and strode towards Vera. The former regent's eyes filled with tears, and she turned around to Nadia.

"You said we'd be safe here!" she sobbed accusingly. "You said we'd be safe here until you could find me passage out of the city!"

"Thank you, Nadia," Cade said coolly, and Vera stopped crying, staring disbelievingly at her handmaiden, her eyes wet, makeup running down her cheeks. For the first time, Nadia looked squarely at Vera. *There. Now you know.*

"I serve Queens," Nadia said in a low voice. "I never served you."

Vera's mouth fell open and she turned around to Cade, realizing finally that there was no one left in the room to help her. She fell to her knees and grasped Cade around the legs. Cade waited patiently, looking mildly disinterested as Vera began to sob uncontrollably. Finally, Cade flicked one of his fingers in her direction, and the two fighters behind him walked around him and grabbed her by the elbows.

"Cade, please," she said, clasping her hands together. "Cade, please don't have me killed. I beg you, please."

Nadia looked from Vera to Cade, who frowned slightly, his dark eyebrows coming together. Cade would very much have liked to kill her and stamp out every vestige of Cira's rule within the palace, but on the other hand, it had been Vera who had released him and made his takeover possible.

"Be quiet, you foolish girl," he said sharply. "I'm not going to kill you." At this, Vera looked up, her eyes red and moist, her face hopeful. "In fact, I'm going to be quite a deal kinder to you than you were to me. You'll be placed under house arrest, moved from the Queen's apartments to the servants' quarters. And there you will stay. You will not leave your rooms unless I give the order. Your life now belongs to me."

Vera threw herself forward and clasped Cade's hand in hers, kissing the silver ring on his left middle finger over and over. Cade reached forward, took her hand, and pulled off the royal ring and bracelet, the symbol of a Joymarillian queen's ruling power. He stared at them briefly as they glittered in his palm. With a single deliberate, fluid motion, he slid the jewels over his own hand. The ring had been made for a woman's hand, so he fit it over his little finger. The bracelet's clasp slid into place with a tiny metallic *click*. Vera watched her power be taken away from her in anguished silence. Then Cade moved his head, and the two fighters summarily escorted her out of the room.

"What about the battle?" Nadia asked after the door had closed behind them. Cade was about to respond when there was a sudden yell down the hallway. A few moments later, the door opened and Wolf walked in, followed by some of the other fighters. Wolf's eyes were light with the pleasure of the kill, and his hair was clotted and slicked with dried brown blood. He walked forward and knelt in front of Cade, holding up his sword. A moment later, everyone in the room followed suit. Cade looked around at them.

"We have won?" he inquired, as if he needed to be told.

"We have won, my Lord. You are now King," one of the fighters informed him.

"Good," Cade said nonchalantly, though inwardly, his heart was singing out with victory. "I want you to go and immediately secure the city and the Academy. Throw out whoever is in charge over there; put someone we trust in control. The students will be retaught. Then," he continued, "I want a letter written to Cira. We sever all ties today; Lady Vera was right about that, at least. Once the city is secured, I want everyone to round up all of the pro-Cira supporters. We'll decide what's to be done with them at a later time. Then, I want anyone willing to fight for us to come and report to me at the palace. I will have no overwrought coronations or any ceremony. Things around here are about to change. Rise," he ordered, and everyone straightened to their feet. A few were smiling slowly, the creeping realization of their new reality just beginning to set in. Cade looked around at their faces, allowing himself to grin slowly, as if they were all sharing the same inside joke.

"Come," he said quietly. His fighters began to grin in anticipation of what was to come. "We have much work to do. It will take time. I want no half-measures taken; I want our position in Joymaril to be secure. Put the Third in command," he ordered, stopping in front of Wolf and meeting his piercing eyes. "And then we ride. We have some business to attend to in Two Falls."

The fighters broke out into cheers, waving their swords and

pumping their fists. Nadia even felt herself let out a whoop, so satisfying was their victory. She clapped her hands together, smiling so hard that she felt as though her cheeks would break apart. Cade smiled serenely, his gray eyes flashing, and walked between the fighters, their hands slapping him on the back, touching the ring on his finger. Wolf paused only a moment, letting Cade walk past, marveling at the cheers that surrounded them. He then fell into his usual stride, stalking down the corridor behind the King of Joymaril.

ACKNOWLEDGEMENTS

I owe many people a great deal of thanks for helping this book come to be. Dita, Elli, Rachel, Scott, Sarah, Dad, Keith, Ann...your positive feedback has meant more than I can fully articulate here.

Profound thanks go to Jenna Beacom for her invaluable input and for the important work she does.

I don't know if I'm ever going to write another book series, but Daphne, if I do you will be the first person I send it to for edits. To Kat, for reading and championing my first book even though you had to read it with your eyeballs instead of listening with your ears. Thank you to Alex for remembering and telling me what efflorescence is. Thank you to Tim because I told you I would include you in these acknowledgements for some reason. Adrian, thank you for giving me the idea for the Serpens all those many years ago.

To Piper for being my eternal cheerleader when I needed it most. I wrote so much of this hoping you would love it and it means the world to me that you do.

Last but not least, thank you to my sweet little family: Peter, Theo, and Siena. You gave me the space, encouragement, and inspiration I needed to make my dream of writing this trilogy a reality. I love you so very much.

www.ingramcontent.com/pod-product-compliance
Lightning Source LLC
Chambersburg PA
CBHW051055030726
47504CB00006B/1639